RISE OF THE SERAPHIM

BOOK 2

OF

MIRRORS OF THE WORLD

BY

KAI STORMHAVEN

Published by Kai Stormhaven LLC
www.kaistormhaven.com

ISBN: 978-1-972065-03-7

Ω RISE OF THE SERAPHIM Ω

1 – Wrecked

The weeks blurred as Aria learned to live with the silence her sister left behind. A few weeks earlier, her uncle had visited, offering her a job at the small record label he owned. He was rich—too rich—and no one in her family knew how he had made his money. The thought brushed against the edge of her memory. She hurriedly shook it off and bent over the studio's reception computer, unwilling to revisit the pain those memories brought with them.

A tall woman walked in, her hair a rich auburn with white highlights. Her eyes held the bright, untarnished look of someone who had never been gutted by life. Three men followed, walking stereotypes of metalheads from the '80s: long hair, leather jackets, and various chains adorning their bodies.

The woman beamed at Aria, practically vibrating with excitement. "Hi, we have the studio booked for the next two hours. The name's Mandy Molletto, and we're..."

She trailed off, staring at Aria in growing awe, a faint blush coloring her cheeks.

Aria nodded a greeting, a hollow smile on her face as she clicked through windows on the screen. "Hi, Mandy, let me get you checked in. The sound engineer is Robbie. He's ready for you in the back."

"Th-thank you... um," Mandy stammered. She paused, looking at Aria questioningly.

"Aria," she supplied, smiling perfunctorily.

Mandy cleared her throat and grinned awkwardly. "What a fitting name for someone who works in a studio. Thank you... Aria."

Aria nodded with another attempt at a smile, offset by her dull and lifeless green eyes. She remembered when life still had color, a time when she would have been excited for someone like Mandy. She shied away from those memories like they were hot coals.

Mandy hesitated, staring into Aria's eyes with a look of concern on her face. One of Mandy's bandmates grabbed a handful of her leather jacket and pulled her along as he and the others moved into the studio.

Aria looked back down at her screen and continued writing lyrics. The doctors said she needed an outlet for her grief, be it music, writing, or something physical.

One of the perks of working at the studio was using the equipment after hours to record her own songs. It had taken a few days to master the sound equipment and recording applications. She spent most of her free time recording tracks late into the night. Sometimes, when she lost herself in the zone of creating new songs, she could almost forget the hemorrhaging wound in her soul where her sister's laughter used to live—though usually, it just made it worse.

Mandy followed her guitarists back into the studio and found Robbie waiting. The air smelled of burnt coffee and cables. Amplifiers hummed in the background. Robbie nodded as she arrived, offering a handshake.

"I'm Robbie," he said, rubbing a hand over his freshly shaved head. His goatee twitched when he smiled. His jeans and T-shirt looked lived-in, but he carried himself with the confidence of someone used to getting things done.

"I'm Mandy," she said with a smile, feeling a bubbly sense of excitement that she was finally in a professional studio. "Our drummer is out on medical leave for a while. Would you be able to add a drum track for us?"

Robbie rubbed his bald head, his eyes calculating. "I could, but you know, Aria—the receptionist—she's a hell of a musician. Could tear up a kit in her sleep. She lost her sister a few months back and could use the distraction."

Mandy's chest tightened as she remembered the pain in the stunning woman's eyes. "Were they close?" she asked, feeling an uncharacteristic drive to lessen that pain. Empathy had never been in her nature, and the foreign experience was disturbing. Was it Aria's transcendent beauty that made her feel the unnatural need to help?

Robbie nodded. "They were tied at the hip, according to her uncle—he owns this place."

Mandy sighed, and some of her excited energy plateaued, replaced by nervousness. "Yeah, I'll go see if she's up for some drumming."

She walked back out and leaned over the tall desk, trying not to gawk. "Our drummer was in an accident a few days ago and won't be with us for a few months. We were going to put some drum tracks in, but Robbie mentioned you're an amazing drummer. Could we hire you to fill in for a little while?"

Aria looked up, her green eyes full of so much barely concealed pain that Mandy wanted to weep. Aria nodded slowly and stood up. "Okay, sure, but no need to hire me—it's on the house."

Mandy hesitated, then nodded. What was up with this strange new emotional depth invading her mind? The change had begun just a few days ago, bringing a wealth of uncomfortable ideas and an odd desire to help people with no expectation of reward. Were her hormones out of whack?

She walked back into the studio with Aria, and they discussed the metrics for the current song while the others tuned their guitars. In short order, they gathered their instruments as Robbie prepared the sound equipment. Aria went into the drum room, put on some large headphones, and waited for them to begin.

When Aria finally played, Mandy could only marvel. Every hit landed perfectly in sync, matching their style and augmenting it with her own. She was worlds better than Jake—maybe better than anyone Mandy had ever seen.

As they wrapped things up, Mandy hurried over to Aria as she exited the drum room.

"Aria, you were fucking *amazing*!" she exclaimed, grinning excitedly. "Thank you *so* much for filling in!"

The others joined her, effusively expressing their gratitude and remarking on what an amazing drummer she was.

Aria smiled and thanked them, her dead eyes never changing as she returned to the front desk.

"Man, that's one wrecked person," Tim commented sadly. "I don't think I've ever seen anyone so devoid of life while still living."

Mandy nodded, feeling a pang of sorrow at how cruel life could be. "Maybe we can have her play more over the next few weeks."

Jared nodded eagerly. "Yeah, let's get as much of her talent as we can before Jake recovers." Jared paused, giving Mike an apologetic wince. "No offense to your cousin, Mike, but Aria's orders of magnitude better at drums."

Mike rubbed the back of his neck with an awkward smile. "No offense taken. Aria's way out of his league—and a lot fucking hotter."

Robbie leaned back in his chair and ran a hand over his shaved head. "You should see her play guitar. I've seen some damn good musicians over the years, but I've never seen anyone tear up a fretboard like Aria."

Mandy blinked, glancing around at the dozens of instrument cases lining the walls. "How many instruments does she play?"

Robbie shrugged. "Pretty much all of them. I've never seen her play any brass, but give her any stringed, percussion, or woodwind instrument and she'll go to town. She stays and records late into the night; I'm not sure she even sleeps."

Mandy arrived at the studio alone, the brisk night air biting at her bare arms. Teeth chattering, she swiped her fob against the reader and entered the building.

After four weeks of recording, they had completed their album. Aria had continued filling in for their drummer, her eyes never losing the fathomless pain Mandy had seen that first day. Mandy had heard loss was difficult to overcome, but usually, time helped dull the pain. Time didn't seem to be helping Aria. She was functional and communicative, but she seemed completely checked out of life, with no plans to return.

She always invited Aria to go out with her and the band after recording, but Aria politely declined each offer. Mandy felt a driving need to do *something* to help Aria heal, almost as if a voice in her head were pushing her to help the broken musician. It was more than attraction, she was sure. Hell, she had never even been attracted to women before seeing Aria.

Now that the album was finished, they wouldn't be seeing Aria anymore. However, with her growing sense of empathy, Mandy wasn't willing to give up so easily. If Aria was going to spend her nights composing, she would have some company.

As Mandy entered the front office, she heard music coming from deeper in the studio. She walked back and quietly entered the main room.

Aria was playing a harp to the accompaniment of some other tracks she had already recorded. Eyes closed, tears streamed down her cheeks. Mandy's own eyes grew wet as she watched. Despair blanketed the room as Aria played a song of unutterable loss and pain, a ballad of such staggering magnitude that stones would weep to hear it.

Aria's voice, a beautiful thumbscrew to the soul, sang of a life devoid of hope and joy. Mandy had never heard a more beautiful voice, yet it ravaged her spirit with grief as she felt the devastation in Aria's heart—a devastation too great to recover from. Mandy hugged herself, her heart breaking as she watched the shattered woman grieve.

Aria stopped playing before the song ended, sliding to the ground and curling into a ball of anguish. Large, throat-tearing sobs shook her body as she wailed her sorrow.

Part of Mandy wanted to turn and flee from the powerful emotions, but her budding conscience overcame her instincts. She quietly approached and knelt beside Aria, hesitantly reaching out to lay a hand on her shoulder. Aria looked up, lips trembling with her sobs, and Mandy felt a renewed wave of pity at the abject despair in her eyes.

"What was she like?" Mandy asked, wiping her tears.

Aria stared hollowly, then closed her eyes as fresh tears ran down her cheeks. "She was the most caring and amazing person in existence," Aria whispered. "She was always there for me through the worst life had to offer, always smiling and joking. She was my protector, my knight in shining armor. I could handle anything with her by my side. I can't do it without her. I can't keep going. This place is a colorless wasteland, a hollow shell that echoes with unbearable silence."

"If she were here right now, what would she tell you?" Mandy asked softly, gently stroking Aria's shoulder.

Aria stared at her, then let out a sound that was half laugh, half sob. "She'd tell me to stop having a pity party in front of a beautiful woman—" a hiccupping laugh escaped her "—then she'd leer at me."

Mandy laughed, blushing lightly at the unexpected compliment. "Was she a musician, too?"

Aria nodded, smiling sadly. "She was always better at everything than me—smarter, more talented. Everything she touched seemed to shine. She had a heart of pure gold. Even though she loved to turn everything into a joke, beneath it all, she was always so compassionate and gentle. She kept me safe."

"She sounds pretty amazing," Mandy murmured wistfully. "I'd love to hear the kind of music the two of you made. I can't imagine anything better than what you're already creating."

"She had the voice of an angel," Aria reminisced, then frowned, a look of confusion washing over her face.

Mandy's hand tightened on Aria's shoulder in concern. "What's the matter?"

Aria shook her head, sighing forlornly. "I'm just losing my marbles. I keep having memories of some other lifetime where she's still alive. The doctors said I'm suffering from denial with grief confabulation—that I'm fabricating memories to cope. Sometimes the memories seem so *real*, though. Certain things seem to trigger them—like the word angel."

Mandy found herself rubbing Aria's back comfortingly without any instructions from her brain. "I can't even imagine what you must be going through," she said sympathetically, the words forming without any conscious thought. "I'm not very close to my siblings or parents. What was her name?"

"Clarice," Aria whispered, fresh tears leaking from her eyes. "How can I go on without my Clarice? We were supposed to have forever."

"Will you come with me?" Mandy pleaded, the words escaping without permission. What the hell was going on in her head? "I'm going to get some food. Please? Come with me?"

Aria hesitated, her grief-stricken eyes dubious, but as she stared into Mandy's pleading gaze, she seemed to cave, much to Mandy's delight.

"We'll just get some takeout," Mandy assured her gently. "We can eat it by the river. I go there to think sometimes."

Mandy stood and offered Aria a hand. Aria smiled tremulously and took it. When Mandy felt how light she was, she nearly wept, wondering how long it had been since Aria had eaten.

Mandy suddenly pulled Aria into a fierce embrace, as if her body were under someone else's control. Mandy inhaled sharply when a torrent of positive energy filled her, radiant with overwhelming love. The warmth felt alive—like light beneath the skin, engulfing her until she thought she might glow. She had never felt more loved and accepted than in that moment.

"Thank you, Mandy," Aria choked out. "I wish Clarice could have met you. I know I'm a total wreck, so thank you for being such a caring person."

As Mandy pulled back, the flood of loving energy stopped. She stared wonderingly at Aria as they walked out of the studio to her Pathfinder. Mandy couldn't articulate it, but there was something very special about Aria.

They remained quiet for the first part of the drive. Mandy groped for something to say to get Aria talking, but her thoughts kept scattering. What was that strange feeling of golden light she had felt? She knew she hadn't imagined it—the memory was too vivid, too visceral. And what was seizing control of her body? Mandy *never* hugged people, no matter the circumstance—she had never cared enough about anyone besides herself to do such a thing.

They arrived at a Chinese takeout restaurant just before closing. Mandy ordered a variety of entrees, hoping to get Aria to eat *something*.

A woman appeared at the window to take her card and said something in Mandarin; the only word Mandy understood was "fifty-five."

"Did she really just call us filthy swine?" Aria asked in disbelief.

Mandy stared at Aria in surprise and opened her mouth to reply, but the woman was back at the window with her card. She spoke again, and Aria immediately replied in Mandarin, looking both amused and outraged.

The woman paled, staring at Aria in shock. Aria stared back with a raised eyebrow, and the woman anxiously apologized before retreating. "Sorry, sorry, I make mistake."

"You might want to check your food for spit or other foreign objects," Aria suggested, eyeing the retreating woman suspiciously.

"Where did you learn to speak Chinese?" Mandy asked curiously, happy there was something to get her talking.

Aria stared at her, her brow furrowing in confusion. "I do?"

Mandy nodded slowly. "You just carried on a whole conversation with that woman in Chinese."

"I did?" Aria asked, nonplussed. "We weren't speaking English?"

"Definitely Chinese," Mandy confirmed, once again feeling the odd sense that there was something very special about Aria.

Aria stared down at her hands, the void in her eyes cracking with a ray of hope. "Maybe… maybe I'm not as crazy as I thought. In this other world I lived in, I spoke every language."

Mandy hesitated. "Can you tell me about this other world?" She hoped she wasn't harming Aria by encouraging her delusions, but she felt compelled to ask.

"It's pretty wild," Aria warned, her voice growing richer, impossibly riveting, as she seemed to find a tendril of hope to cling to. Tingles rippled down Mandy's spine as Aria's voice caressed her soul, the despair in her eyes receding. "It's definitely way out in the fantasy realm. I can understand why it seems so crazy. It just seemed so *real*. I remember conversations, events, and experiences that seem too detailed for me to have fabricated."

Mandy studied her in fascination. "Were you in another world?" she asked, pausing as a different employee handed her their food. "Or were things just different here?"

She inhaled sharply as a feeling of warmth filled the car, like sunlight melting frost after a cold winter night. It wasn't a physical warmth—it felt like being held in a comforting embrace after a long absence. Aria's eyes almost seemed to glow as the sliver of hope broke through the curtain of darkness surrounding her. Was she responsible for the strange warmth?

Aria smiled, the expression lighting up her face. "It was here. It all started when I was ten years old, and this person named Calypso healed me and my sister. I was given a few days to live after battling cancer for several years. Clarice wasn't far behind me. Calypso volunteered to play music at children's hospitals. She came to my room and played the most beautiful song I'd ever heard. When she finished, both Clarice and I felt completely healed. Our hair started growing back the next day, and we spent the next fifteen years living totally normal lives. I graduated high school early and became a physicist. I can still recall the exact layout of the lecture halls." She laughed ruefully. "Hell, I can derive Maxwell's equations from memory, or rattle off the Hamiltonian for a quantum harmonic oscillator. I have no business knowing that level of math if it was just a dream."

Mandy raised an eyebrow. "That's a pretty detailed memory." They were nearly to her favorite thinking spot by the river. Trees flashed in her headlights as she wound down the narrow road, stopping for the occasional deer. Her stomach grumbled as the smell of food filled the car, reminding her how long it had been since she had eaten.

Aria laughed, and it was like the sun coming up. Mandy felt joy light her spirit at the sound of that glorious laughter. "That's just the tip of the iceberg. While growing up, there was an anonymous artist called NOTESTOREMEMBER who eventually became the most popular channel on YouTube. So many people on the brink of ending their lives found renewed hope and solace after hearing one of Calypso's songs. Her performance at the hospital was the reason we originally became interested in music and learned to play so many instruments, but it was her YouTube channel that put our ambitions into overdrive. I think we secretly wanted to show her how much we'd learned. My story starts after she uploaded one of her weekly YouTube songs."

Mandy marveled at the realism of Aria's delusion. How could her mind invent so much detail for an imaginary story? "So, did you find her again?"

Aria laughed again, bright and warm. "Oh yeah, we found her."

They exited the car with the go-bag of food and moved to a bench near the river. The sound of water flowing over rock always eased Mandy's thoughts. She silently cursed herself for not grabbing a jacket; the late summer night air was brisk. She glanced at Aria, who seemed completely unaffected by the chill. The sense of inner warmth grew stronger the closer she was to Aria, confirming Mandy's suspicion that Aria was the source.

Mandy rifled through the bag, using her phone for light. "What kind of food do you like? Egg rolls?"

Aria blinked, looking at the food with a peculiar expression. "I can't eat—I don't have a stomach."

Mandy frowned, studying Aria's face with concern. "When is the last time you ate anything?"

Aria brought a hand to her temple. "Oh, I don't know... I don't think I've eaten anything since Clarice..." She couldn't seem to bring herself to say it. "As angels, we didn't eat in the other world. I was so used to not eating that I hadn't realized I haven't eaten for months."

Mandy peered at her anxiously, realizing this delusion could have serious health implications if Aria thought she didn't have a stomach. She remembered how light Aria had been. Her face wasn't gaunt, so she couldn't be *that* unhealthy.

Aria sighed, looking apologetically into Mandy's concerned eyes. "I know it sounds crazy. Maybe it *is* part of this delusion, and I only *think* I don't have a stomach. When I was still an angel, my eyes were golden. You'd think I'd accept that I'm mortal again, considering my eyes are green, I don't have wings, and my super senses are gone. If it were nighttime, I could add no longer having night vision to the list of things proving I'm no longer an angel."

Mandy blinked, looking out at the dark waters in the dim starlight. She held up the bag of food and pulled the receipt off the staple. It was completely indecipherable in the dark. She handed it to Aria with a sense of curious anticipation. "Does this receipt have the name of the lady who called us filthy swine on it somewhere?"

Aria glanced at it briefly and shook her head. "It's just got a cashier number and the date. This was freaking expensive. I'll give you some money when we get back to the studio."

Mandy shivered, only partially due to the chilly night air. "So... angels, huh? Is that later in the story?"

Aria nodded with a lopsided smile as she stared out at the river, recounting her reunion with Calypso as an adult and her subsequent escape from rabid YouTube fans and secret governments.

As Aria told her story, Mandy felt a sense of vertigo, as if she were hearing echoes of another reality. When Aria spoke the name Calypso, it rang in Mandy's head like a bell.

Aria noticed Mandy's reaction and paused, watching her with concern. "Are you okay?"

"Maybe?" Mandy replied, staring back uncertainly. "I feel like reality is bending around me. This Calypso person sounds so familiar, like a name I should recognize, but it's just out of reach."

Aria suddenly stiffened beside her, looking down the path along the river. "Do you get many creeps along here during the day?"

"Aria, it's nighttime," Mandy said softly. "I can't see anything."

Aria froze, her breath quickening. "Could it be real?" she whispered, her voice filled with such desperate hope that it nearly broke Mandy's heart.

Suddenly, a beam of light illuminated them as four men rounded the bend in the path. They paused when they saw the two women and then moved forward. It didn't take the stench of alcohol to see that they were drunk.

"Isn't it a bit late for you two lovely ladies to be out here all alone?" a leering voice asked.

"They look cold," another man noted, his tone suggestively provocative. "I think we should warm them up."

Mandy trembled as she stared at the men, paralyzed by terror. Why had she thought bringing Aria here at night would be a good idea? The first man seemed to relish the panic on her face, smirking as he raised a hand to his belt buckle.

"I'm only going to warn you once to get lost," Aria said, her voice sending shivers down Mandy's spine. There was a hint of ethereal power in it, a threat of pain to come.

The men halted, one even backing up a step. The leader laughed raucously and started pulling off his belt.

"We should run," Mandy whispered into Aria's ear, trembling as fear flooded her veins with adrenaline. She knew they couldn't reach the car without being overtaken.

Aria took her hand, and suddenly, the fear drained away, replaced by overwhelming love. Mandy gasped as the emotional overload nearly knocked her over.

"It's okay," Aria assured her, standing and facing the four men. "I'll take care of them."

The first man finished removing his belt, holding it like a whip. He grinned as she approached. "I like a girl with spirit."

Aria groaned despairingly. "Oh my God, please tell me I imagined him saying that."

He swung the belt toward her face like a whip, laughing drunkenly. The laugh cut off when she snatched the belt out of the air, then jerked it from his hands as if he were a toddler.

The air almost seemed to sizzle as righteous fury rolled off Aria in waves. The man in the back, possessing a stronger survival instinct than his companions, turned and ran back the way he had come.

The first man snarled after losing his belt and lumbered forward with a heavy swing of his meaty fist. Aria caught it, halting the punch effortlessly. Then she squeezed. The man dropped to his knees with a scream as the sound of breaking bones cracked like gunshots in the night.

His buddy rushed past and dove at Aria, hands outstretched. Her foot came up in a blur, and there was a sharp crunch. The man screamed as he soared through the air and splashed into the river. The third man pulled out a handgun, pointing it at her with shaking hands.

"Get down on the ground, face down," he bellowed, his voice a mixture of fear and rage.

"No," Aria responded coldly, pushing the first man backward by his broken hand so hard that he rolled into the river with a splash and a scream.

"I mean it," he blustered, more fear than rage.

"If you turn and go right now, I'll let you leave with your bones intact," she told him quietly. "If you pull that trigger, it'll be worse than broken bones for you."

Mandy gasped as a dim glow emanated from Aria's skin. The man pointing the gun certainly noticed. With a terrified yelp, he turned and ran back down the path, stumbling in the dark.

The glow around Aria vanished, and she sighed, returning to the bench. She sat with her head in her hands. "I can't believe I've heard someone say they like a girl with spirit *twice* now. Do guys really go around saying that?"

Mandy just stared at her silently, too stunned to speak. As the silence stretched on, Aria turned to face her.

"Are you okay?" she asked gently. "I'm so sorry you had to deal with those scum. I remember how scary it could be."

"Aria, you were *glowing*," Mandy finally managed in a strangled voice.

Aria sighed again, her shoulders slumping. "How am I supposed to know what's real and what's fake? Are you a product of my imagination, Mandy? Am I so desperate to have Clarice back that I've fabricated this entire experience?"

Mandy started shivering in the frigid air as her adrenaline finally wore off. She felt a pang of sympathy as Aria battled with her own mind. What must she be going through right now if she couldn't even trust the reality around her? And how was Aria not cold? She was wearing a shirt that was almost completely open in the back.

"What happened after Calypso joined you?" Mandy asked through chattering teeth.

Aria snapped out of her daze and looked at Mandy with concern. "You're freezing. Here, let me warm you up."

Aria slid closer and wrapped her arms around her. Mandy gasped as she once again felt love suffuse her soul. All thoughts of being cold vanished as she reveled in the warm comfort of Aria's love-infused embrace.

"Your hugs feel like how you described Calypso's hugs feeling," she murmured contentedly. "I feel so loved and happy right now."

Aria shifted, and Mandy felt her uncertainty. She must be doubting her reality again.

"Aria, I know you're worried this is all in your head," she said softly. "But so what if it is? Would you rather go back to how you felt before?"

Aria shivered. "No, I never *ever* want to feel that loss again. I'm just so, *so* afraid I'll get my hopes up that she's still alive somewhere, only to have reality destroy me. I know I won't survive that kind of loss again. I can't live without her."

Mandy laid her hand on Aria's, her voice gentle. "Then let me help you figure it out. Tell me the rest of your story, and let's figure out what really happened. I've seen enough to know you're not crazy. There's something very special about you, and I feel like I can help if you'll let me."

The sense of love intensified as Aria pulled her in tighter. "Mandy, if you're real and I'm not crazy, you're one of the most wonderful people I've ever met. That's a really high bar. Thank you so much, Mandy."

"You're so welcome, Aria," Mandy whispered affectionately. What the hell was going on? Had something possessed her? This was *not* how Mandy behaved. She was as qualified for emotional support as a razor blade. Could Aria be affecting her in some way?

Aria took a deep breath, resting her cheek on top of Mandy's head as she continued her tale. Mandy listened raptly to an adventure of epic proportions, a story of how Aria and her family were transformed into angels, fought demons and shadow organizations, and healed the entire world of the sick.

"What was the phrase to turn a human into an angel?" Mandy asked in fascination.

There was a smile in Aria's voice as she answered. "You had to swear to vanquish evil. We did a lot of floundering in our search to understand what angels really were. I'm going to condense the story and give you the broader outline; it's basically the creation story."

Mandy nodded, her eyes alight with interest. At some point during Aria's story, she had stopped thinking of them as delusions. She could almost hear a voice in the back of her head telling her every word was true, the same voice that had prompted her to help Aria break out of her grief. The same voice that seemed to be taking over.

Aria spent the next few minutes describing a cosmic coup, with herself at the center. Mandy listened, half-dazed, as angels and demons and shattered heavens spilled from Aria's lips like fragments of a dream she had forgotten.

"We were so close to rewriting reality and removing the four renegade Seraphim. We'd just helped four of our human friends and family ascend as angels when a wave of vertigo hit me. The next thing I remember is waking up in the apartment that blew up, and Clarice was... gone."

Aria paused. "Hmm. Calypso had said something... I remember now. She said, 'It is a rewrite. Aria, Clarice—do not believe any—' ...and then everything vanished."

"Wow," Mandy breathed in wonder. "I don't think people have delusions that complex, do they?"

Aria sighed in frustration. "The doctors say my delusions could theoretically get this complex. Apparently, they usually don't have backstories, but it's still consistent with someone suffering from overwhelming grief. If you step back, what's more likely? That an angel saved me from cancer, and I went on an epic quest with my sister and an angel to save the cosmos from renegade Seraphim, or that I can't accept my sister's death and will invent anything to give myself some kind of hope that she's still out there somewhere?"

Aria shook her head, and Mandy could feel the despair trying to crawl back in. "If we look at the facts, it's obvious I'm suffering from delusions. My apartment is still there. Calypso's YouTube channel doesn't exist and never has. My reality is in shambles, and I can't trust anything I see. I'm pretty sure *you're* a figment of my imagination, too, just like those guys I imagined beating up."

Mandy pulled back slightly from Aria, staring up into her eyes. She couldn't see them in the dark, but she knew Aria could see hers. "I am *not* a figment of your imagination. I don't know how to convince you of that, so I won't. Instead, I'll repeat what I said earlier: would you rather fall deeper into a fantasy where your sister still lives and angels are real, or go back to where I found you last night—on the floor, wishing you were dead?"

Aria's breath caught. She stared back at Mandy, golden tears welling in her golden eyes as an ethereal glow flared from her skin. The energy Mandy felt coursing through Aria suddenly erupted like a supernova, washing over everything and turning night to day. "I *will not* accept this reality!"

Reality shattered, and the world folded in on itself. Mandy clung to Aria as glowing, radiant wings unfurled from her back.

There was nothing but a black void in every direction. Aria began laughing, huge golden tears coursing down her cheeks, one of them landing on Mandy. Her whole body filled with warmth, and she began to glow softly.

Aria held Mandy tightly, trembling with relief. "Thank you, Mandy! Thank you, thank you, *thank you*!"

Mandy wanted to respond, but the lack of oxygen made speaking impossible. Her pulse spiked as she grabbed at her throat in panic. She clung to Aria as she felt the absolute zero temperature surrounding them, held at bay by Aria's aura.

Aria looked down at her and gasped, her eyes growing wide with alarm. She quickly looked around, growing more distressed by the second as Mandy's face began turning blue. Mandy tried to smile as darkness shadowed the edge of her vision. Seeing the pain and anguish vanish from Aria's eyes when she discovered her sister still lived had been worth it.

2 – Hope

Calypso gasped. "It is a rewrite! Aria, Clarice—do not believe any—"

The air fractured. Aria flickered, then vanished.

"*No!*" Clarice's scream ripped through the veranda. "*Aria!*"

"She is not dead," Calypso assured her quickly, focusing her will on the connection to their spirit, where Aria remained, burning brightly. "I can still feel her spirit."

Emily materialized into the room, her eyes blazing with fury. "Where is she?" she demanded. "How do we get her back?"

Calypso growled, frustration fraying her voice. "I felt the formation of a splinter in reality. I believe the other Seraphim have trapped her within another realm. The only means I can conceive of to restore her is through the divine instruments. That must be why they targeted Aria—it would have been either her or me, and I do not believe it would have succeeded with me."

"What can we do?" Clarice begged, her eyes shining with golden tears. "There has to be *something* we can do!"

Calypso closed her eyes, her brows furrowing in concentration. "I believe it depends upon Aria realizing that her reality is false and refusing to accept it. I do not think they can keep a Seraph's mind trapped within a fabricated reality for long—even one who has not yet fully awakened. They are merely buying themselves time."

Lexi rested a comforting hand on Clarice's shoulder as she looked at Calypso. "How are they doing it at all without a divine instrument?"

Calypso watched Clarice worriedly, sensing her terror through their linked spirits. "I do not know. I would have assumed it required at least one divine instrument. However, they reside within the highest light realm, and perhaps the power available there is sufficient to create an entirely new realm. I simply do not know."

"I want my daughter back," Eric growled, his eyes blazing with anger. "If I have to find a way to kill a Seraph in the highest realm, so be it."

Clarice wiped at her golden tears, looking up at Calypso pleadingly. "You have a divine instrument. Use it to bring her back! Please!"

There was a flash of golden light, then Lucifer appeared, his eyes glittering like sapphires. "Was it Aria they took?"

"Yes," Calypso nodded miserably. "I simply do not yet know enough to prevent an attack such as that."

"I'm sorry I wasn't here," Lucifer said solemnly. "I came as soon as I felt the splinter reality form."

Clarice looked at him beseechingly. "What can we do?"

Lucifer hesitated. "We can break the other reality, but it'll take time. I have an idea that might help her break herself out, though."

"What?" Emily asked eagerly.

Lucifer frowned pensively. "We can send someone from this reality. It'll need to be a regular human because the splinter reality doesn't have angels."

Clarice's brows knit together. "You can send a human from this reality into the place where Aria's trapped?"

Lucifer seemed to struggle to find the right words. "We can't send a person," he finally said. "Only an imprint—a template from someone here. The rules of that reality won't accept angels, but Aria is a Seraph, and she has a divine instrument affixed to her soul, so those rules won't be able to completely suppress her angelic nature."

Clarice crossed the space to stare up at him eagerly. "How long will it take?"

Lucifer sighed. "It'll take about a week to create the template. It'll also take time for her to awaken once they meet in the other reality. I hope it'll be weeks, but it could be months."

"Months?" Clarice whispered in horror. "She'll be trapped on her own for *months*?"

Lucifer raised his hands helplessly. "Without this intervention, it could take years. This is the best option we have for a situation this delicate."

Clarice scowled, her beautiful features tight with impatience and anxiety, but she nodded reluctantly. "I want my goddamn memories back. I'm sick of not knowing what the hell is going on."

Lexi gestured at Calypso hopefully. "Couldn't Calypso just use her divine instrument to bring her back, like Clarice suggested?"

Lucifer's lips pinched into a frown before he quickly shook his head. "I wouldn't try that without knowing more about the splinter reality—you don't want to risk harming Aria." He paused, glancing around. "I'm going to get to work," he said abruptly, and vanished.

Calypso walked over and drew Clarice into a comforting embrace. "I am so sorry, Clarice," she said guiltily, her British accent adding weight to her apology. "I should have found some way to prevent this from happening."

Clarice shook her head. "It's not your fault, Calypso. It's those pieces of shit hiding in the light realm. There's going to be a reckoning when I—" She broke off as a devastating wave of grief hammered through the bond they shared with Aria.

Clarice staggered, clutching her chest and falling to her knees. She choked out a sob as the torrent of despair slammed into her, like an icepick to her soul.

Calypso sank to her knees and took Clarice in her arms, holding her tightly as they both felt the debilitating waves of sorrow drown out any other emotion from Aria until soul-crushing despair was all that remained.

Emily looked between their stricken faces anxiously. "What's going on?"

Calypso clutched Clarice tighter. "They're drowning her in sorrow."

Lexi stood on the widow's walk, watching anxiously as Clarice stared despondently into the distance. Her midnight hair rippled in the light breeze, shining in the afternoon sunlight like rays on troubled waters. They had spent days trying to think of a quicker way to help Aria escape the splinter reality—to no avail.

Clarice had sunk into a dark depression. The only emotion coming through the bond from Aria was unending grief at an alarming intensity. The feeling of impotence was infuriating. Calypso suggested they attempt to spark joy in the spirit bond—if Aria could still feel anything through it. Clarice had tried a few times, but any success was fleeting and left her more frustrated when Aria's emotions remained unchanged.

During that dark period, Mary kept Lexi company, constantly searching for ways to distract her from the gnawing worry eating at her. Lexi had been hugged more in the last few days than in her entire life. While the positive energy Mary channeled helped dampen the despair flowing in from Aria, Clarice's bond inundated her with anxiety and rage, offsetting the positive influx.

She felt bad that Mary's first week as an angel had turned out so bleak. She had hoped to show Mary how wonderful being an angel was, but Mary was spending all her time trying to cheer *her* up instead.

It was almost like the good old days when Mary had done much the same for her in their early teenage years. Lexi scowled at the memory of her childhood in a home devoid of affection or love. Her parents had been openly hostile from her earliest memories, constantly ridiculing and debasing her with every action.

Her scowl faded as she recalled meeting Mary in school at age twelve, where she had experienced affection for the first time. She had been like a sponge, soaking up Mary's freely offered kindness and praise. After reconnecting, she had been excited to return the favor—but life had other plans.

She struggled to feel positive emotions of any kind with the negative input coming in from all sides. Calypso was full of love and comfort on the outside, the same as usual, but Lexi could feel the darkness filling the Seraph. It amazed her how easily Calypso put on a brave face in front of the group while she was falling apart inside. She burned with self-recrimination and anxiety, shadowed by a desperate longing, as if a part of her soul were missing. She was convinced she should have been able to prevent the other Seraphim from snaring Aria and blamed herself for Aria's captivity.

"I've always been there for her," Clarice spoke up, her voice filled with pain. "No matter how ugly life got, we knew we had each other. Now she's alone, without me to lean on... to protect her."

"What was she like when you were kids?" Lexi asked quietly, wrapping her arms around Clarice from behind and resting her cheek on her head. The once euphoric mingling of energy between their meridians was almost unnoticeable with the dark cloud of despair filling Clarice.

Clarice drew a shuddering breath, her voice brittle. "She was the sweetest kid in the world." She paused, wiping at her eyes, her lips trembling. Silence stretched as the wind caught her hair, blowing it back into Lexi's face. "She always wanted to please everyone. She always wanted to brush our hair or help clean up our messes. I used to be a slob, but I felt bad when she kept cleaning up after me, trying to convince me she *liked* to." She snorted a broken laugh. "She lived in fear of rejection and would go to absurd lengths to try to make everyone happy. It took years to convince her there was nothing she could do that would stop me from loving her. She used to save up all her money to buy gifts for us when we were having a rough day. She would make these ridiculous candy-bar posters, full of bad puns and glitter. You couldn't look at them without laughing."

Lexi tightened her arms around Clarice, her voice soft. "It sounds like she's been an angel this whole time."

Clarice shook in her arms as several sobs escaped. "It was like the work of a sadistic god when she got cancer," Clarice whispered. "It was a living nightmare watching her get worse as treatments failed, watching the light in her eyes slowly die. She would have given up a lot earlier, but she didn't want to leave me behind. She knew it would crush me. She was always thinking of her family, even when she was puking her guts out and wasting away to nothing, crying from crippling pain. I was actually glad when I ended up with cancer too, because I'd get to go with her."

A lump formed in Lexi's throat, and she squeezed Clarice tightly.

"Clarice," Lexi paused, her voice breaking. "Aria's coming back. You two will be with each other forever. I won't accept anything less. There isn't a power in the cosmos that can break the love you two have for each other. I'm so sorry she's going through such hell right now—but I *know* she'll be back, and you'll get your sister again."

Clarice folded her arms over Lexi's, clutching her tightly, shaking as her sobs echoed across the mountain.

Lexi stood alone on the widow's walk, staring into the distance. There hadn't been any demon attacks or military incursions for months. They had continued seeking out agonite farms and rescuing children, but it was a passionless enterprise. Clarice barely restrained herself from killing the demons in her rage. After redeeming any demons worthy of saving, they would drop them off with Krajen.

As more demons were redeemed and returned to their angelic forms, the number of demon hideouts dwindled. Clarice had been eager for a demon lord to make an appearance so she could vent some of her rage and frustration, but they must have learned that Cherubim and Seraphim were waiting for them, because they never appeared. News that demon lords were avoiding the planet spread to the remaining demons on Earth, resulting in a complete cessation of agonite farms.

Lexi smiled when she heard the seraphic music echoing from the house. Clarice and Calypso had started writing songs together to try and escape their dark thoughts. The two had grown closer in their shared grief. Calypso was almost never seen without Clarice nearby, and Lexi wondered if Clarice was guarding Calypso, afraid she might be taken, too, if she lacked vigilance.

Mary had left the previous month to visit her family. After learning that mortality was a prison for angels, she wanted to help as many of them ascend as possible. She had tried to convince Lexi to go with her, but Lexi couldn't bring herself to leave Clarice until Aria returned.

Sighing forlornly, Lexi wrapped her wings around herself and closed her eyes, letting the sound of Clarice's cello soothe her troubled thoughts.

The days ran together as Clarice and Calypso buried themselves in music. They barely spoke to anyone, knowing the only thing they could talk about was Aria. Lexi spent more time with Emily and Eric, who, despite their youthful appearance, felt like adoptive parents. They both doted on her like a daughter and did their best to make her smile as often as possible.

Jason and Susan checked in with them every day, working almost as hard as Eric and Emily to make Lexi smile. The familiarity she had felt for the two former students had only grown stronger over the months.

Arturiel was another daily visitor, sitting with Clarice and Calypso and offering quiet comfort. She was a gentle soul and had taken Aria's disappearance hard. After Mary left, Arturiel began spending more time with Lexi, her caring presence offering a sense of desperately needed comfort.

They were all on the veranda, which was becoming more unusual as Clarice and Calypso retreated to the studio more often.

Calypso was giving Clarice a demonstration on how to play a didgeridoo, sitting near the pond in the center of the veranda. Eric and Emily sat across from Lexi with a card game laid out in front of them. She was just lifting a card when she felt the blanket of despair filling the corner of her soul where Aria resided suddenly shift. It was like a ray of light had suddenly shone through the black clouds.

She froze, her hand hovering over the draw pile. She heard the didgeridoo cut off as both Clarice and Calypso stiffened, feeling the same ray of hope in Aria's soul.

Emily looked at her in sudden concern. "What's the matter? Has something happened?"

"She's feeling hope," Lexi whispered, tears forming in her eyes.

Emily sucked in a deep breath, her own eyes shining with sudden hope.

"Come on, Aria," Eric whispered fervently. "You can do it."

They sat frozen like statues. Time crawled. After almost thirty minutes, the ray of hope began to brighten, like dawn breaking. It spread out across the part of Lexi's spirit she thought of as Aria, quivering and frail.

"Hope is growing," Lexi whispered, almost afraid she would break the fragile thread if she spoke too loudly.

Lexi flinched when the hope began drowning in a fresh wave of despair. A choked sob escaped Clarice, and the didgeridoo splintered in Calypso's grip.

Then it flared like a supernova, furious and alive, banishing the despair in a tsunami of joy.

"She's back!" Lexi shouted excitedly, leaping to her feet.

Confusion and panic suddenly replaced the elation in the spirit link, sharp and desperate.

Clarice grabbed Calypso by the shoulders. "Play it! Now! Get her back!"

Calypso quickly nodded, then summoned her divine instrument, a glowing white harp. She plucked one note, and a silvery slash opened a slice into reality. She jammed both hands into the tear of their realm and opened it enough to push her way through.

Lexi stood frozen with the others, staring at the shimmering wound in the air with a sense of desperate hope.

3 – Reunion

Mandy's vision was nearly black when a silvery slice cut into the inky void. A beautiful angel with brilliant blond hair and eyes like swirling galaxies stepped through, taking everything in with a glance. She grabbed both of them and pulled them through the slice.

Mandy sucked in a delicious lungful of air, and something inside of her shifted, followed by an uncomfortable sense of fading, as if her identity was being stripped away. The darkness faded as she continued oxygenating her blood with desperate breaths of sweet, sweet air.

Aria let out an explosive sigh of relief as Mandy's face regained its color. Mandy stood up straight as her strength returned, and Aria hesitantly released her.

Mandy quickly took stock of her surroundings. They were on a veranda overlooking wooded mountains. Several angels stood around them, their faces flashing from worry to sublime joy.

A moment later, a gorgeous angel with midnight hair erupted with light and rushed over, wrapping herself around Aria with a choked sob.

"*Clarice!*" Aria wailed, her voice shining with ecstasy as her body also exploded with light. "Oh, Clarice, I thought you were...I thought...I..." She gave up on speech and simply sobbed into her sister's neck.

Clarice held her tightly, lips trembling as golden tears stained her cheeks. "I'm so sorry, Aria," she choked out, pain and guilt clouding her eyes. "I'm so, so sorry."

Mandy blinked against the light shining off the two Seraphim. The air itself seemed to hum with emotional energy, saturating the area with desperate relief and indescribable love. Watching them was like witnessing the reunion of suns.

"What happened to her?" an angel who looked like a twin of Clarice demanded, her golden eyes burning with rage. "What did they do to her?"

"She woke up in her old apartment," Mandy said softly, not wanting to take away from the warmth flaring between Aria and her sister. "Clarice had died a week earlier. They convinced her she was suffering from delusions brought on by grief. I've never seen anyone so dead inside while still alive. She was gutted, in a state of unbearable grief that wouldn't fade with time."

The woman gasped, her hand clapping over her mouth. Then she vanished, reappearing across the veranda with her arms wrapped tightly around the other two angels. Mandy blinked, struggling to comprehend a speed that bordered on teleportation.

"Oh, my baby," the angel whispered consolingly, wrapping her wings around them. Mandy wondered if it could be her mother; she looked so young, but they were angels, after all.

"The Seraphim responsible for doing this to my girl are going to suffer," a tall male angel ground out, fury blazing in his icy blue eyes.

Clarice's eyes grew stricken, and she kissed Aria's forehead. "Oh, Aria. I'm here for you now. I'm here."

Aria clung to Clarice, shoulders shaking with each sob, as her sister soothingly combed her fingers through Aria's crimson hair and caressed her face.

"We could feel her grief," another angel said sadly. She was tall, with beautiful blond hair and a face to inspire poets. "I've never felt anything so awful. We didn't understand why she was so devastated, but knowing what caused that horrible grief makes it feel even worse."

Calypso's swirling eyes blazed with anger. "It was not random," she said darkly. "They did this to her deliberately, knowing she would be unable to think clearly beneath that degree of grief clouding her mind."

Clarice's beautiful features twisted with hate. "They're going to suffer," she hissed venomously. "When I'm done with them, they're going to regret ever being spawned into existence."

A portal swirled open, and an angel with tawny hair that shone with an ethereal glow stepped through. Her violet eyes widened when she saw Aria, barely visible beneath Clarice and her mother.

"Aria?" she gasped.

"Aria's back?" a deep voice asked excitedly as another angel emerged from the portal.

Aria's father waited for his turn to embrace his daughter, nodding at the two new arrivals with a pained smile. "She's back. She's had a rough time."

"Who's this?" the tawny-haired angel asked, studying Mandy curiously.

Aria smiled radiantly through her tears. "This is Mandy. She's the one who saved me."

All eyes turned to Mandy. A moment later, she was engulfed in a warm embrace as Aria's father blurred over and wrapped her in his arms.

"Thank you for bringing my girl back to me, Mandy," he said, his voice trembling with emotion.

Mandy sighed contentedly, feeling the now-familiar rush of love an angel's embrace imparted.

"She's exaggerating how much I did," she murmured self-consciously.

"I'm not exaggerating even a little bit," Aria disagreed, her golden eyes glowing with affection. "You constantly tried to break through my grief. If I hadn't met you, I'd probably have been stuck there for years."

Aria's mother traded her daughter for Mandy, squeezing her tightly. "Thank you, Mandy. We're forever in your debt."

Mandy smiled warmly as a steady flow of love charged her soul. "I knew she was special as soon as I saw her. There was just something extraordinary hiding behind all the pain in her eyes."

"So, is Mandy from the other reality?" the tawny-haired angel asked curiously. "Is that other reality still there, or did it vanish when Aria broke free?"

Aria's beaming face lost some of its joy. She stared at Mandy in chagrin. "It imploded. Mandy, I'm so sorry. I didn't even think about what this might have done to your life."

"It sounds like I was living in a fake world," Mandy said slowly. She knew she should feel some grief for the people she knew, but there was nothing. Even her newfound empathy remained quiet, undisturbed by the loss of everyone she knew. "I mentioned I wasn't close with my family. I should be thanking *you* for bringing me along, because when you eventually broke free, I would've disappeared with it."

Horror crept into Aria's voice. "How many lives did I snuff out when I broke free? They were real people, even if they weren't in the same reality as us."

"Don't blame yourself," Aria's mother said gently. "This was orchestrated by those renegade Seraphim with full knowledge that you would eventually break free."

Calypso pulled Aria into her arms, her cheeks glittering gold as tears pooled in her swirling eyes. "Though they were real people, they were merely copies of those who exist within this reality," she assured Aria, a faint tremor in her voice. She paused to kiss Aria before continuing. "They all still exist here, only with different memories and experiences." She took a shuddering breath and cupped Aria's face. "I cannot express how wonderful it is to have you back. You complete me."

Aria smiled tremulously, sliding her hands behind Calypso's head and kissing her tenderly.

The angel with the deep voice had a troubled frown as he looked at Calypso. "I'm kind of numb at the idea that these beings can create an entire copy of our reality. It boggles the mind that they could replicate this world and make alterations to it the way they did. Lucifer said there were no angels in that world, but that the rule excluding angels wouldn't be powerful enough to fully contain Aria."

Realization dawned in Aria's eyes. "Is that why most of my angel abilities went away? I lost most of my super senses and didn't even realize I hadn't eaten anything the entire time I was there. If I'd been thinking clearly, it would've been obvious I still had a lot of angel attributes."

Calypso grimaced. “That was precisely why they did it,” she said darkly. “They knew you would not be thinking clearly whilst consumed by grief.”

The angel with the deep voice watched Mandy with kind eyes. "I think some introductions are in order for our new friend. I'm Devon, Aria's uncle. This is Tamra, the light of my life."

Tamra smiled warmly at Devon, resting a hand on his arm affectionately.

Devon wrapped his arm around Tamra’s waist and continued the introductions. "You've probably guessed who Clarice and Aria's parents are by now. Emily's my sister and one of the most amazing chefs in the world. Eric is Aria's father, and Lexi is a somewhat new member of the family."

"Aria, Clarice, and Calypso rescued me from some assholes in Beverly Hills," Lexi told her, smiling lovingly at the three angels. "Their family took me in like one of their own."

Mandy smiled, looking around at each of them. "It's wonderful to put faces to the people Aria told me about. She gave me a condensed summary of what's been going on, but I'm still flummoxed at how amazing all this is. It's like I've entered a fantasy world."

A flash of golden light nearly blinded Mandy, drawing an embarrassing squeak of surprise from her throat. When it cleared, a tall, golden-haired angel stood right in front of her. His piercing sapphire eyes surveyed the faces around him, his mere presence heavy enough to press the air from the room. Mandy stared in awe—even as a little voice in the back of her mind flared with pure hatred.

"Welcome back, Aria," the angel spoke in a strong voice that wasn't loud but shook her soul like a leaf. He turned to face her, smiling down with a pleased air. The smile never reached his eyes, observing her like a puzzle piece that didn't fit. "You did an excellent job, Mandy. I'm truly happy Aria was able to bring you with her."

Mandy tried to speak, but her tongue was stuck to the roof of her mouth as she stared at him in reverence. The back of her skull pulsed with heat, a whisper hissing "liar" repeatedly.

"This is Lucifer," Devon introduced the new angel with a twinkle in his eyes. "He's the reason you existed in that other world."

Mandy blinked, then gaped. She remembered Aria mentioning Lucifer as one of the Seraphim, but with all the other information she had been digesting, it hadn't really registered. She was standing in front of *Satan!*

He smirked as the thought flashed through her mind. "I suppose I should have brought my pitchfork and tail."

Clarice burst out laughing, the sound pure and full of joy. Mandy wondered how long it had been since Aria's sister had laughed.

"It looks like you've already experienced the transfer of angel essence," Lucifer noted, studying Mandy with that unsettling lack of emotion in his ethereal eyes. "Not surprising under the circumstances, I suppose. Should you wish to become an angel, just say the phrase: 'I will vanquish evil.' You'll be transformed into your angelic form."

"I will vanquish evil?" Mandy repeated unsteadily.

"Whelp, there it is!" Clarice crowed brightly. "Welcome to immortality, Mandy!"

Mandy froze as a tingle began in her neck, spreading out to the rest of her body like a fractal of luminous energy. Light rippled through her veins until she glowed like starlight. She felt herself burning and expanding all at once, every cell singing. Then an explosion of joy consumed her, radiant and indescribably beautiful.

She gaped at the intensity of radiant light engulfing her system, warming her with euphoric love. Everything became intensely vivid, all her senses exploding into overdrive. She stared at Aria, her eyes shining with wonder.

Aria grinned back delightedly. "Welcome to angelhood, Mandy!" she exclaimed, rushing forward to tackle her in a tight embrace.

Mandy sucked in a breath as the energy in her meridians began to dance between their bodies, an exchange that was more than a little intimate. Clarice joined Aria, wrapping her arms around both of them. Mandy gasped as what had been a torrent of energy flooding her system became a tsunami. She shuddered with ecstasy as the power expanded and warped her meridians.

The two angels released her, smiling broadly as they inspected her.

"She's a Cherub," Aria observed with delight. "She'll be able to go to the higher realms with us."

Mandy stared back at Aria, a brilliant smile on her face. "Is this how you always feel? I feel *so fucking awesome*!"

"Most of the time," Aria nodded with an indulgent grin. "As long as I've got my sister, anyway."

Clarice's smile faltered momentarily, and she pulled Aria into a protective embrace. Mandy had a feeling the two of them wouldn't be far apart for the foreseeable future.

Emily turned to Lucifer, raising an eyebrow. "So now what? We finally have Aria back. Can we go kill some Seraphim now?"

Lucifer shook his head regretfully. "We still need the remaining pieces of the other two divine instruments. I have angels searching for them, but I think Clarice will have more luck, since they're linked to her spirit. I found two more pieces of mine by following my intuition. I suggest Clarice and Aria begin the search for the remaining pieces." He paused, studying Mandy with a puzzled crease to his brow. "It's interesting that Mandy is a Cherub—the Mandy from this reality is a regular angel. Very curious."

Lucifer's gaze lingered, calculating. Mandy's glow faltered, the warmth in her chest turning cold. The whisper in her mind stirred again—sharper this time, almost a growl. Had she developed a split personality after exiting the splinter reality? Not likely, since the odd presence had appeared before she met Aria. What had Devon meant when he said Lucifer was the reason she had existed in the other world?

Clarice flexed her wings dramatically. "I'm ready to get out of here. I love this place, but I need some space after months of depression."

Aria bumped Clarice's shoulder. "Any idea of where to look?" she asked, positively glowing with happiness as she soaked up her sister's presence like a starving plant.

Clarice stared upward, thoughtful for a moment. "Somewhere cold," she said musingly. Then she grinned. "Let's take our hot angel asses to Antarctica."

Aria burst into helpless laughter that slid into a fresh wave of tears. Clarice caught her, pressing their foreheads together and gently caressing her cheek. As Mandy watched, she suddenly understood the black hole of grief that had consumed Aria. There was a connection between the two of them, a love more real than existence itself.

Lucifer inclined his head. "Enjoy your reunion. I have work to do." He vanished in a shimmer of gold.

Mandy stood among them, half-dazed from the influx of radiance. Every hug, every laugh sent ripples through her new senses. The world was alive in colors she didn't have names for.

Aria moved from one embrace to the next, laughing, then crying, then laughing again. Clarice hovered by her side, maintaining constant contact.

Mandy approached Lexi with a curious smile. The tall angel had been watching Aria with tears in her eyes for most of the gathering.

"So, do all angels eventually get wings?" Mandy asked Lexi. "I remember Aria telling me acts of love were how angels evolved their abilities."

Lexi grinned, her golden eyes twinkling mischievously. "That's *mostly* correct. Acts of love *and* intimacy."

Mandy blinked, then raised a curious eyebrow. "More intimate than hugging, I take it?"

Lexi nodded, folding her arms and drawing Mandy's eyes to her chest before she could stop herself. "The more intimate, the more powerful the evolution," she confirmed, then laughed. "Those two punks actually did a coin toss to see who would have to kiss me."

"Ouch," Mandy winced with a commiserating grin, dragging her eyes back up to meet Lexi's golden gaze. Apparently, she was into women now, and it wasn't just Aria she had found attractive. "Was it the loser who had to do it?"

"The winner," Lexi answered with a snort of amusement. "That took some of the sting off."

Mandy glanced over to where Aria stood a few feet away with Clarice and Calypso in her arms. "Who won?"

"Clarice," Lexi replied, then giggled. "She told me she was probably a better kisser than Aria and that I dodged a bullet."

Aria stepped back from Clarice, a dangerous glint in her eyes. "You said *what*?"

Clarice raised her hands defensively, her face a mask of innocence. "I don't know *what* she's talking about. She's probably making things up to try and start a kissing competition."

Aria narrowed her eyes, looking between the two of them. They both wore expressions of pure innocence. "I can't even tell which of you to believe. Clarice, you've corrupted Lexi."

Clarice shrugged. "Corruption only goes where corruption is welcome," she said sagely, taking Aria's hand in hers. "If she got corrupted, it's because she *wanted* to get corrupted."

"That's true," Lexi agreed with a slow, sensual wink.

Aria shuddered dramatically. "Oh my god, there are *two* of them now." She paused and looked around. "Hey, what happened with Mary? I totally forgot about her."

Lexi's face faded to a neutral expression. "She went back to her family to make some more angels. She wanted me to go with her, but I wanted to wait until you returned."

Aria smiled gratefully at Lexi as a few tears ran down her cheeks. "Thanks for staying with her, Lexi."

Lexi's face flickered with surprise, then softened, her eyes tender. "I wasn't going to leave her alone," she teased playfully. "She gets into all sorts of trouble if she doesn't have a handler."

Clarice released Aria's hand and folded her arms, her naturally innocent face adopting an injured expression. "I do no such thing," she objected indignantly. "I'm the epitome of a responsible adult."

Lexi rolled her eyes. "Have you seen the world lately?" she asked dryly. "The bar for responsible adults isn't just low—it's underground."

Clarice threw up her hands with a laugh. "Okay, you got me there." She slid an arm around Aria's waist and turned to Mandy, her expression sobering. "So, Mandy, what's your life story? And how'd you and Aria cross paths?"

Mandy frowned, racking her brain for anything interesting in her past. "There's not much to my life. It's pretty boring—especially compared to yours."

"That's okay," Clarice assured her with a shrug that rustled her wings. "We're immortal, so we have all the time in the world. Let's hear your boring life story."

"Are we really immortal?" Mandy asked, feeling a sudden thrill as she realized how different her perspective would be without the pressure of a short life pushing her to speedrun her dreams. She could even widen her net, no longer limited by the temporal limitations of a mortal. She grinned as the epiphany left her feeling lighter, less burdened. "It hadn't occurred to me that being an angel meant I'd live forever."

Clarice chuckled, leaning her head to the side to rest against Aria's. "Yep, you're stuck with us forever."

Emily walked over and gently tapped Aria's shoulder. "Can I talk to you for a minute?" she asked quietly.

"Of course, Mom," Aria smiled and squeezed Clarice before following Emily into the house.

"Okay, give," Clarice commanded crisply, turning back to Mandy. "Who are you, and how did you meet Aria? Start at the beginning, because we have eternity."

Mandy took a deep breath, feeling unaccountably self-conscious, as if she were interviewing for a job. "Well, I'm an aspiring musician, for the most part. That's how I met Aria—she was working the front desk at the recording studio where I was recording my first album. We talked her into filling in for our missing drummer. I could tell something was seriously wrong when I was checking in. Her eyes were full of so much pain that I just wanted to cry—and I'm not the crying type. I learned she spent most nights making music in the studio, so I came back after our last day of recording to convince her to come with me."

Clarice listened silently, her golden eyes glistening with unshed tears.

"She was playing the harp to some tracks she'd recorded, and it was the most beautiful song I'd ever heard. She was curled up in a ball before the end of the song, sobbing like she'd lost part of her soul."

Clarice's lips trembled. She closed her eyes, and a single tear slid down her cheek.

"I asked her to tell me about you," Mandy continued with a sad smile. "She described the most wonderful, caring, smart, and funny person in the world—that you were her knight in shining armor. She said she was supposed to have eternity with you and that she couldn't go on without her sister. I've never seen a bond of love so strong. You really are the world to her."

Clarice pulled Mandy close, her voice breaking. "Thank you. You gave me back the other half of my soul."

Lexi put her arms around both of them, her eyes dripping silver. Suddenly, there was a flash of light, and a transparent golden sphere surrounded the three of them. Mandy gasped as she felt an influx of power overload her meridians, forcing them to expand as more energy rushed in. Her shirt stretched, and the back tore open as a new weight appeared between her shoulder blades.

"And just like that, you're airborne," Lexi smiled through her tears. "Tamra will have a wing-fitted shirt for you. She's made a lot of them over the last four months. I'm impressed that your bra survived."

Mandy looked over her shoulder, flexing what felt like a second pair of arms. Large, white wings of thick satin unfurled behind her. A smile lit up her face when she saw the wings on *her* back. *I'm going to be able to fly! Too bad I'm scared of heights.*

She blinked as the thought occurred. She *wasn't* afraid of heights. She *loved* heights. She had gone through a daredevil phase—bungee jumping, skydiving, cliff climbing—pretty much anything involving heights. Where had that thought come from?

Clarice reached into a hole that appeared in the air and pulled out a shirt. "This should fit well enough until Tamra can get your measurements."

Mandy quickly removed the tatters of her old shirt and stepped into the new one, pulling it up her waist and sliding a loop over her neck to hold the front in place. The bust was definitely meant for someone of Clarice or Lexi's size, but it covered the essential bits.

Clarice gave her an approving wink when she finished. "You're smoking hot."

Mandy flashed her a grin, taking in the way Clarice's own shirt tightly hugged her breasts, leaving well-defined nipples poking through. She could certainly rock the braless look with a rack like that. Lexi had a similar shirt, though she obviously believed in bras.

Clarice's expression grew serious. "How did you help her overcome her despair?" she asked quietly.

With some difficulty, Mandy shifted her focus away from her new wings. "I asked her to tell me about this world. She told me about the early childhood battle with cancer you two went through and the events leading up to waking in her old apartment. She was trying to convince herself she was delusional, saying she couldn't risk hoping you were still alive and then finding out you weren't. I asked if she would rather embrace the delusions and be with you or go back to how things were when I found her. She embraced the delusions, and the world imploded around us."

Clarice's lip trembled as Mandy finished. Sniffling, she pulled Mandy into a fierce embrace. Mandy had never been held like that before—as if she were special, valued. It was a wonderful feeling, and Mandy suddenly understood why people went out of their way to help each other. Feeling this beautiful glow was rewarding in ways she never would have imagined.

Aria returned and took her sister in her arms with a look of such transcendent love that Mandy felt like she had glimpsed something truly divine.

Lexi motioned her toward the house. Mandy followed, glancing back at Aria, who looked like she had gone through the forges of hell and come out with a new understanding of life.

Mandy shivered as she followed Lexi into the hallway. Love on that level seemed cosmically balanced by the depth of sorrow endured when it was lost. She hoped they really did have eternity in front of them.

"I know everyone has already said this," Lexi began softly as they climbed the stairs, "but thank you for bringing her back."

"I'm a little jealous," Mandy admitted. "That bond they have—it's beautiful. It makes everything else feel small."

"For sure," Lexi said, smiling fondly. "They're like gravity wells for love. Once you're close, you're not getting out. I don't know if it's because they have the souls of Seraphim, but their capacity for love seems so much greater than anything I've ever seen before. They adopted me into their family without a second thought."

Mandy glanced at Lexi curiously, rewinding her memories to the creation story Aria had told her. "Seraphim were the original angels who created everything, weren't they?"

Lexi nodded. "That's what we've learned so far."

Mandy slowed as they climbed the stairs, her eyes widening in realization. She had *saved* one of the creators of the universe. "So, Aria and the other two really are the original creators of the universe?"

Lexi smiled, seeing the look on Mandy's face. "Yep. Apparently, their memories won't return until they've fully ascended, just like us. I guess omniscience has a loading screen."

Mandy frowned, following Lexi up a ladder. "I wonder how that works if I'm a copy of someone from this reality," she murmured musingly. She glanced around after topping the ladder, realizing they were on a widow's walk. "If I understand correctly, the reality I was in was a shallow copy of this one, and it's gone. Will my being here cause some kind of paradox, like with time travel?"

Lexi laughed as she walked over to one of the railings. "If it does, you're the prettiest paradox I've ever seen. You're not a glitch—you're a gift."

Mandy smiled, her dimples flashing. "You're witty *and* sweet. That's a dangerous combo. I hope you're right, and I'm not some kind of bug."

Lexi's cheeks colored, and she quickly looked away. "I think you're essentially just another creation, as if they'd added a new Cherub to this world. I would love to see you meet your doppelganger. I wonder if she's just like you."

"Yeah, can't wait to meet her," Mandy grinned excitedly. "Maybe we'd end up as best friends like Aria and Clarice."

"Given what I've seen of your personality, I think you'd *definitely* get along with a carbon copy of yourself," Lexi noted with a confident smile. "If she's anything like you, she's got a heart of gold."

"Aw, you're going to make me blush," Mandy complained with a playful smile. She didn't mention that her philanthropic nature was a recent development. If her doppelganger was anything like Mandy used to be, she was probably a selfish bitch.

"You should've been here before," Lexi giggled. "Aria and Calypso blush with the enthusiasm of people trying to speedrun embarrassment as a competitive sport. One of Clarice's favorite pastimes is triggering the two of them. Well, not just the two of them—pretty much everyone."

Mandy threw her head back and laughed, eyeing Lexi with growing affection. While all the angels she had met so far were beautiful, Lexi seemed to have taken the definition hostage. Mandy shook her head slightly at the realization that she was most definitely attracted to women now.

Lexi was watching her with a soft smile, her head tilted slightly to the side in a manner that was adorable.

Mandy cleared her throat. "So, what are we doing up here?" she asked, looking around at the slowly brightening sky. She marveled at how her angel eyes could see in the dark just as well as in the light. No wonder Aria had thought it was daytime in the other world.

Lexi grinned. "I thought we'd give those wings a test flight."

Mandy nervously adjusted the loose chest of her shirt. "I'm kind of scared of heights," she admitted, then furrowed her brows in confusion. "Um... I'm not sure why I said that. I'm totally fine with heights."

Lexi flexed her wings. "Did Aria tell you angels are completely invulnerable to damage of any kind? You could fall out of orbit, and it wouldn't hurt you a bit."

Mandy's eyebrows rose. "We don't feel pain either?" she asked hopefully.

Lexi shook her head. "No pain, no damage, and insane strength." She looked Mandy up and down with an appraising eye. "You're a Cherub, so you're the strongest order of angel aside from the Seraphim. Regular angels aren't a whole lot stronger than humans, even though they're invulnerable to damage and pain. *Our* strength is on a whole other level. We can bench press locomotives."

Mandy tilted her head to the side. "Is it strange that I can hear what everyone in the house is saying?"

Lexi chuckled softly and began rising into the air. "All angels have better senses than humans, but we Cherubim have totally insane super senses. Go ahead and flap your wings. You're gonna be amazed at how natural flight feels."

Without the constant flow of radiance charging her system, she would have chickened out. *Wait, why would I chicken out? What the hell is going on in my head?*

She took a deep breath, spread her wings, and flexed them downward. She yelped as she shot high into the air.

Lexi whooped. "See, it's a piece of cake! Just keep flapping to gain altitude. You'll get a sense for how to steer, glide, bank, and land after you've been airborne for a few minutes."

Mandy stared warily at the shrinking cabin beneath them as each beat of her wings took her a few hundred feet higher. Anxiety turned to wonder when she entered a cloud, coating her in condensation. She definitely needed to get a shirt better fitted for her chest size—the wind was turning it into a sail, flapping wildly.

"Now try gliding," Lexi suggested, hovering next to her.

Mandy stared at her in surprise. The wind didn't seem to affect Lexi at all—she wasn't even flapping her wings. "How are you flying without using your wings?"

Lexi suddenly giggled. "It's one of the upgrades you get from being smooched—as Clarice puts it. It's basically anti-gravity with some kind of field that lets you pass through the wind without being affected by it. To glide, just lock your wings out all the way."

Mandy locked her wings and leaned forward, cutting into the wind. She grinned as her wings sliced through the air effortlessly, wind streaming through her auburn hair. With an exultant scream, she tucked her wings and plummeted toward the ground. Her newfound fear of heights vanished as exhilaration took its place. She swooped down and then banked to the left with another scream of joy.

Lexi followed beside her, grinning as they dove, swooped, and spiraled through the air.

As they pulled out of a steep dive, Lexi laughed delightedly. "See what I mean? It just comes naturally."

Mandy nodded, beaming. "This is so amazing!" she exclaimed, coasting a few hundred feet above the ground.

They flew around the skies until well after sunrise. She marveled at how inexhaustible her angel body was, having flown for hours without a hint of fatigue.

Lexi performed another spiral and then turned to face her with a grin. "Are you ready to try landing?"

Mandy nodded, recalling one of her childhood memories of watching birds land on the fence outside her bedroom window. "I think so."

She swooped low, then flared her wings, killing her forward momentum. She halted a dozen feet above the ground before dropping lightly to the earth, laughing in delight that a twelve-foot drop had no impact on her knees or back.

"In the name of Jesus, I abjure thee!" a harsh voice shouted from a dozen feet away.

A bald man in a brown robe stood barefoot in the grass, glaring as if she had stolen his donation plate.

"Uh, hi," she waved with a friendly smile. "I'm Mandy."

"Demon spawn," he hissed.

Mandy blinked, tilting her head. "Demons can breed?"

Lexi dropped down next to her, watching the strange man coolly. "Morning, Redgart. Is there something we can help you with?"

Mandy blinked, then turned to Lexi in surprise. "You know this guy?" she whispered.

Lexi shook her head. "People's names are written on their auras," she answered quietly.

"Maybe there's something I can help *you* with," Redgart declared bombastically, his voice shifting from that of a heretic-burning priest to that of a game show host. "I'll bet you'd like the other piece of one of the divine instruments. Eh? Eh?"

4 – A Piece of Spirit

Rendimus frowned as Raphael finished his report, glancing at the others with a raised eyebrow. "That clinches it—Lucifer must have a divine instrument. Nothing else could have created a splinter reality."

"Lucifer," Doriel said confidently. "His ambition knows no bounds. Perhaps Grodekkan, too. I remember Lucifer asking Calypso to reduce the number of divine instruments required to alter reality to two. Unless one of our number was working with him, it had to be Grodekkan."

Hiriel steepled his fingers as he watched Raphael exit the room. "I detected an outsider involved in Aria's escape from the splinter realm," he announced uneasily. "Something attached itself to the human template Lucifer sent into the splinter reality."

"There is another outsider in contact with Lucifer," Nathaniel announced grimly. "They've never appeared in our realm before. This is concerning."

"Not as concerning as the Three returning," Rendimus muttered, feeling an unfamiliar sense of anxiety. "We won't survive long if they fully awaken."

The other Seraphim remained silent, their expressions grim. It had been a terrifying shock to discover the Three were still alive, hidden in the mortal realm. He had no illusions about their chances against them, even without the divine instruments. Their power was so far beyond the rest of them that the Three were essentially gods. Rendimus and the others were on borrowed time unless Lucifer managed to stop the Three.

Not that Lucifer would be any better. He must possess one of the divine instruments. If he was in contact with outsiders, their odds of survival were nonexistent.

"So what now?" Doriel asked uneasily.

"We do nothing," Rendimus replied with a defeated sigh. "There's nothing we could do against two divine instruments anyway. Any further action on our part will only further antagonize them. It's become obvious we played into Lucifer's hands when we attempted to unmake them."

The other Seraphim scowled but didn't disagree. The Three had never planned to force them into mortality—Lucifer had clearly planted that seed in an attempt to rid the realms of the Three. He had used the rest of them to do his dirty work since four instruments were required to rewrite reality. How had the Three survived? Their Creators had always been so naïve—he hadn't expected them to have a failsafe in place to prevent the divine instruments from destroying them.

◆◆◆

Clarice floated up to the widow's walk with Calypso and Aria, landing soundlessly on the flagstone floor. Clarice stepped behind Aria and slid her arms around her waist, pulling her into a tight embrace. Calypso embraced her from the front, sandwiching Aria in a cocoon of soft flesh and warm love.

Aria's emotions were still all over the place, flashing from manic laughter to panicked tears, terrified she might wake up to find herself in a mental hospital or back in their old apartment. Clarice's answer was to maintain constant contact with her traumatized sister, letting her feel their physical bodies, to know they were there with her.

Clarice struggled to contain her apoplectic rage toward those responsible, knowing her emotions would bleed into their spirit link. She had always been there to protect Aria, and the way the other Seraphim had snatched her right out from under her nose had broken that unspoken trust—that Clarice would always be there to keep her sister safe.

Aria filled their spirit link with incandescent love, leaving only a sliver of trembling anxiety in her exuberant thoughts. An undercurrent of intense relief remained steady, with a soft layer of attraction simmering amidst the sea of emotions.

Calypso kissed Aria's forehead. "Aria, when I used my divine instrument to find you within the void, I experienced a brief moment of recollection. Lucifer warned us not to use my instrument to attempt to break you free, in case it harmed you. However, I now know with certainty that it would indeed have worked, and that we could have rescued you far sooner. I do not know why Lucifer was so convinced it was dangerous, but I am certain you would have been safe. Should anything like this ever happen again, I want you to know that I shall be able to bring you back. I promise."

Clarice gave Calypso a grateful smile as the anxiety in the spirit link diminished to a whisper.

Aria let out a shuddering breath. "Thanks, Calypso. I hate not being able to trust my own mind. It's terrifying."

Clarice tightened her arms around Aria, inhaling her unique scent—a blend of innocence and passion fruit. "Then trust in mine, Aria. I know I failed you, but it will not happen again."

Aria stiffened and twisted between them until she was facing Clarice. "You did *not* fail me, Clarice. We might be Seraphim, but until we get our memories back, we're just babies with the power to destroy worlds, with no real understanding of our true power. We're facing people who are ancient on a geological scale, who have no concept of right or wrong. I would never expect you to be able to keep me safe from the enemies we face. And while I will always see you as my protector, I'm no longer the helpless girl I once was. So please, Clarice, please don't feel like you've failed me."

Clarice stared into Aria's pleading eyes, drinking in the sight of the girl she had fallen in love with almost two decades ago. She couldn't deny Aria anything. There was nothing she wouldn't do for her beautiful sister, no line she wouldn't cross.

"Okay, Aria," she agreed softly. "I know you've grown so much stronger in the last few years. I'd be lying to say I didn't like being your knight in shining armor, but I love this strong side of you as well." She grinned and waggled her eyebrows. "It's super hot."

Aria dissolved into giggles, dropping her head to Clarice's shoulder as she shook with mirth. "Oh, Clarice, I love you so much. You will *always* be my knight in shining armor—even if you're a lewd knight."

Clarice made a purring sound. "You mean *especially* since I'm a lewd knight."

She felt Aria's blush through the spirit link before it appeared on her face, dwarfed by a sudden explosion of desire.

"I knew it," Clarice smirked. "You can't hide how turned on that just made you anymore, my virtuous angel."

Aria's giggles intensified as she clung to Clarice.

Clarice shared a hungry look with a smiling Calypso. It was time for them to get some alone time with Aria. Past time.

"Aria!" Arturiel's voice exclaimed, followed a second later by Arturiel flying up to the widow's walk. "Oh, Aria, I'm so happy you're back!"

Clarice reluctantly released Aria, exchanging a resigned glance with Calypso. It looked like alone time had just been postponed.

Arturiel immediately pounced on Aria, folding her in arms and wings. "Are you okay?" she asked tenderly, her fingers combing through Aria's crimson bangs. "I've been so worried."

Aria nodded into Arturiel's shoulder, and the tears were back as she was reminded of what she had just been through. Arturiel continued stroking her hair and speaking in a soothing tone.

Clarice reflected on how close Arturiel had grown to their family in the months since Aria's disappearance. The former demon had such a gentle soul and caring heart that it was impossible not to love her. It had taken her a few days to overcome her awe of the Seraphim who had created her, but when she had seen how devastated Clarice and Calypso were at the loss of Aria, she had quickly shed her fear and opened up, revealing a beautiful soul overflowing with compassion.

Clarice heard Jason and Susan portal into the veranda. A moment later, they were on the widow's walk, welcoming Aria back with jubilant smiles. Aria was glowing with warmth as she soaked in the love surrounding her.

Clarice didn't even leer at Jason once.

Clarice finally pried herself out of Aria's arms—again—and tried to steer the conversation back to their upcoming trip.

They were on the veranda, and Devon looked suspiciously giddy about Antarctica. She waited for the excitement around Aria to die down before questioning him. He stood across from her and Aria, with an arm wrapped around Tamra.

Calypso stood on the other side of Aria, possessively holding her hand. The darkness had finally lifted from the beautiful musician's heart, though a hard knot of anger remained. Clarice knew her gentle healer had fundamentally changed after Aria's disappearance. Some of the innocence was gone; the naiveté had burned away. She stayed within arm's reach of Aria constantly, anxious to prevent any further attempts to snare her.

Their parents stood with them, their expressions growing serious as they returned to plans started months ago.

Clarice arched an eyebrow at Devon. "What is it about Antarctica that has you acting like an amorous armadillo in a bowling alley?"

There was a pregnant pause as the strong visual metaphor stalled the conversation. Aria was the first to break the silence, dissolving into giggles as her parents facepalmed. Devon shared a long-suffering look with Tamra and shook his head.

Emily smiled fondly. "It's nice to have your personality back with us, Clarice. I never thought I'd say this, but I really missed your deranged sense of humor while Aria was gone."

Calypso furrowed her brow. "How does that even work? The bowling balls, I mean."

Clarice sent her the mental image. "A picture's worth a thousand words," she quipped, grinning suggestively.

Calypso's face turned scarlet. Clarice snickered as she watched Calypso shift uncomfortably while the rest of the group tried to hide their amusement at her sudden awkwardness.

"You're a *bad* angel," Aria told her affectionately.

"Getting back on track," Devon said pointedly. "There are some things you should know about Antarctica."

"And it doesn't involve bowling," Tamra added dryly.

"Anyway," Devon said, dragging the conversation back from perdition. "Antarctica's not all penguins and frostbite. There's an installation called IceCube—thousands of sensors buried deep under the ice. Ostensibly, it detects neutrinos."

"How deep?" Aria asked, intrigued.

Devon paused, glancing down at his tablet. "Almost two miles. Half a billion dollars in funding. Twenty million a year to keep it alive. Nobody spends that kind of money unless something's humming down there."

"What do the sensors look like?" Clarice asked intently.

Devon paused, giving her a level look. When she continued gazing at him with innocent curiosity, he sighed and shook his head. "Yes, Clarice, armadillos would like them."

"Why, Uncle," Clarice gasped, wide-eyed and confused. "I have *no* idea what you're referring to."

Devon rubbed his temples and continued. "After what you found on Saturn, I have to wonder if this IceCube observatory is another demon construct or something else entirely. You might want to investigate the installation while you're there."

Aria frowned. "If neutrinos don't come from fusion, maybe they're side effects of those plasma conduits we found—cosmic wiring between star systems. If that's the case, IceCube might not be detecting particles at all."

Clarice floated into a sitting position, her expression growing serious. "I remember reading about this neutrino detector years ago. I coincidentally read another article about acoustics and the future of surveillance using ultrawide-band radio waves. They pinged an area and used a server to render the echoes in three dimensions, providing 360 spatial surveillance. Maybe demons have a more advanced version of the tech and use IceCube to ping the whole planet. With a powerful enough computer, they could maintain worldwide surveillance in all three dimensions. That would explain how they were able to track us down after we removed the eyeballs from their satellites."

Devon whistled. "That's not a bad theory. I'm impressed, Clarice."

"Teacher's pet," Aria accused her sister playfully.

Clarice gave her a lazy smile and a coy, "Meow."

Eric cleared his throat pointedly. "So, bottom line—it's probably a demon construct."

"Probably," Clarice agreed. She looked at Aria speculatively. "You're out of the loop on current events, aren't you?"

Aria blinked, then shook her head ruefully. "I keep forgetting I've been gone for over four months. It just seems like a bad dream now. What's going on? Is social media still fixated on Calypso and angels?"

"Well," Clarice began, "it turns out that little 'apathy modulator' we smashed on Saturn was kind of important. People woke up. They're marching in the streets, storming congressional offices, and demanding to know why billionaires own their governments."

Devon nodded morosely. "And apparently, those billionaires are owned by intelligence agencies... which are owned by demons."

Clarice flashed out of the veranda and back in the blink of an eye, a hairbrush in hand. She smiled softly at Aria and began brushing her hair as she continued. "Krajen's been leaking proof online. The governments tried martial law, and the soldiers laughed and went home."

Emily picked up the thread. "Angels appearing and claiming demons are in charge only added fuel to the fire. We were raiding agonite farms while you were gone, but they've dried up. When demons discovered their demon lords were terrified of coming to Earth and running into us, they quit operating agonite labs."

Aria shook her head in bemusement. "I miss four months, and the whole planet wakes up. Are people accustomed to seeing angels yet?"

Clarice barked a quick laugh. "People still think all angels come with wings," she said wryly. "They don't notice the ones standing next to them in line at the store."

Aria glanced around at the faces watching her. "Are there any plans to start redeeming humans yet?" she asked hopefully.

Clarice moved in front of Aria and began brushing her long bangs, her knuckles caressing Aria's cheek with each pass. She met Aria's eyes as she brushed, her gaze charged with love—and more than a hint of seductive intent. The spirit link revealed a torrent of desire, humming like an exothermic reaction barely held in check as the chemistry between them flared with increasing urgency.

Aria snapped out of her trance when she realized the room had gone quiet. She blinked, looking around at the amused faces of her family in confusion. Clarice watched her replay the last minute of conversation in her mind, realizing she had completely missed their uncle's answer to her question. She was so damn adorable.

Clearing her throat in embarrassment, Aria focused on her uncle, avoiding Clarice's distracting eyes. "Um, sorry, what did you say?"

Devon shared an amused look with Emily and said, "They're redeeming people quietly. Most new angels pass for human, so they stay in their jobs until there are enough of them to shift the balance. We'd rather not crash the global economy while redeeming the world."

Aria frowned. "What about this soul trap? Do we know anything else about how they're trapping angels in a reincarnation loop?"

Clarice paused her brushing to share a look with the others before turning back to Aria with a mischievous grin. "You know that big glowing ball that hangs in the sky at night?"

Aria raised an eyebrow. "Are we talking about the moon?"

"Ding, ding, ding," Clarice said brightly. "Turns out it's basically a giant spirit recycling machine. It's hollow." Clarice's grin widened. "Big alien-looking core that catches and reboots spirits."

Aria stared at her suspiciously. "You're smiling way too much for that to be good news."

"Because," Clarice said, practically vibrating, "*we get to blow up the moon*!"

"We can't just—vaporize the moon," Aria protested. "It controls tides, ecosystems, calendars—literally werewolves, Clarice."

"Eh," Clarice said with a shrug. "Won't do anything catastrophic for a few millennia. We'll have rewritten reality by then anyway. And the werewolves will just have to howl at the stars."

Aria hesitated. "And people will still be able to incarnate, right?"

Calypso nodded, gracefully drawing her hair over one shoulder with her beautiful, slender hands. "The mortality nexus resides within the lower light realm. The moon merely governs the recycling of spirits. Destroying it will not prevent people from incarnating—it shall simply allow them to return to the light realms upon death."

Aria studied Calypso intently. "How much of your memories have returned?"

"Hardly anything," Calypso said wistfully. "At times, a place or a phrase will stir something loose, and I'll remember a moment—or simply know something without understanding how. For spirits of our age, that scarcely scratches the surface. Most of our knowledge has come from Arturiel. What about you?"

Aria sighed regretfully. "Just the intuitive knowledge so far." She hesitated, looking at Clarice and Calypso. "Except for one. I remember both of you. It's like remembering my arm, though. We've been together so long that seeing you again just woke everything up." She smiled softly. "The memories just appeared after returning to this reality."

"Maybe we should crash heaven," Clarice mused. "The first two realms, at least. See if it jogs something loose—or makes us glow brighter."

Aria snorted, bumping shoulders with Clarice. Her eyes darted down to Clarice's well-defined breasts, and she quickly looked away, her cheeks glowing a rosy pink.

Calypso pursed her lips, her eyes flicking to Clarice before also darting away. "It would most likely trigger an accelerated evolution. The energy within those realms is vastly greater than that of the mortal realm, so we would probably be flooded with radiance. That is an excellent idea, Clarice."

Clarice was tempted to cancel the remainder of the meeting and drag her blushing angels off to an island for a week or two. Reining in her libido, she rubbed her chin musingly. "What did they even call the light realms before the mortal realm existed? Just 'The Realm'? Sounds lazy. And why 'light'? As opposed to what? The Dark Realm?"

"By *they*, you mean *we*," Aria said dryly. "We coined the terms, remember?"

Calypso eyed Clarice with fond amusement. "Light is merely another word for energy. Those realms are defined by the amount of energy they contain. The void is the absence of it, and so anything possessing energy—even this world—is technically light. The mortal realm is simply dim by comparison."

Clarice squinted at her. "Fine, that actually makes sense. I was ready to mock the naming committee."

"You *were* the naming committee," Aria said pointedly.

"Maybe the other four asshats came up with it," Clarice shot back. "We were probably out getting halo polish."

Aria grinned. "You literally just admitted it was logical."

Clarice's nose went into the air. "Fake news."

Aria smirked, replaying the memory telepathically.

"Deepfake," Clarice said instantly.

"Okay, Tweedledee and Tweedledum," Emily said, pinching the bridge of her nose. "Back on topic before I revoke your halos."

Clarice stuck out her tongue but had to pull it back in when Aria's hand flashed up lightning-fast in an attempt to grab it.

"Later," Clarice winked, waggling her eyebrows.

Aria's face erupted with color, and the spirit link burned with sudden lust. Calypso's cheeks lit up in response, prompting a delighted giggle from Clarice.

"So," Eric said, folding his arms and pointedly ignoring Clarice, "which cosmic crisis are we tackling first?"

"I vote we blow up the moon," Clarice said instantly, all traces of mischief forgotten. "Think of it—every soul finally free instead of queued up for rebirth."

"Or," Devon said, his voice calm but pointed, "we don't destabilize the planet. IceCube's safer. The moon's a PR nightmare waiting to happen, and the light realms might be booby-trapped. We should finish finding the divine instruments before poking anything new."

Clarice opened her mouth to argue—but froze. A spike of wariness pulsed through her spirit link with Lexi, then a complex barrage of fear, anxiety, and anger.

"Lexi," she breathed, and vanished in a burst of golden light.

Aria and Calypso followed a heartbeat later, leaving the veranda in shocked silence.

She reappeared in a clearing a few miles from the cabin. A short, bald man stood in front of Lexi and Mandy. He looked like he was auditioning for a tourist-friendly version of the Dalai Lama's body double.

"Oh, we have new contestants!" the wannabe monk declared, eyes glittering with manic joy. "It's going to be an *exciting* day!"

Something about him was wrong. Clarice couldn't tell if he was angel, demon, or a deranged mortal until she looked through her spiritual sight. He hovered between both—balanced on a razor's edge of mortal and immortal, without a trace of radiance in his meridians. The resonance around him prickled with something disturbingly familiar, calling out to her with desperate longing.

Clarice made a quick telepathic link with the others, eyeing the man cautiously. *"Lexi, what's this guy's deal?"*

"He says he's got a piece of the divine instruments," Lexi's thought came, dry but wary. "He started ranting about Jesus and calling us demon spawn, then flipped into a game show host. I think we've stumbled across a schizophrenic televangelist."

"Some contestants for what?" Aria asked him suspiciously.

"For the battle royale, of course!" he proclaimed grandly, raising both hands high. "All of you against each other, with the victor winning a gorgeous fragment of a *divine instrument*!"

"Sorry, we don't have time for games," Aria said shortly. "We have more important things to do."

Redgart shrugged. "I guess some other lucky demon will win this spirit-bound piece of divine instrument then," he sighed dramatically. "It's a pity, really. Who knows *what* a demon might be able to do with the spirit attached to this thing. Probably nothing *too* painful."

Clarice erupted with rage as she realized he was talking about her, holding *her* piece of spirit hostage.

Aria took a step toward him. "If you hand it over right now," she said sweetly, "I promise not to spend the next ten thousand years inventing new ways to make immortals regret existing." White-hot fury surged through the bond from her sister. She couldn't believe Aria was talking so calmly.

Aria's voice became silk over fire. "I'm pretty creative," she added. "So things will be very educational for anyone else who thinks they can threaten my sister in front of me."

"Oh, dear me, I feel so threatened," the monk cried out fearfully, hunching in on himself and looking around in feigned terror. Suddenly, his mannerism changed, and he scowled at them with malevolent eyes. "You witches will *burn*. You demon spawn will feel the wrath of the Lord, and it shall be *terrible*. You'll writhe in agony for all eternity as the worms feast on your remains forever and ever!" He finished with spittle flying and the whites of his bulging eyes visible.

"Won't they run out of remains after a while?" Clarice asked critically. "How small are these worms? Are we talking *metaphorical* worms, or..."

He froze, eyes wide and bloodshot. "Worms? Worms?" he hissed, trembling. Then, with a blinding smile, he shouted, "No worms! We've got a contest to win!"

Aria flashed forward, seizing the incoherent monk by his robes and yanking him off the ground. The fabric smoked under her grip, golden fire flashing in her eyes.

"If I have to pull you apart piece by piece to find that divine instrument, I will," she hissed. "If I need to *rewrite reality* just to give you pain receptors, don't think I won't."

At the mention of rewriting reality, something seemed to get through to the crazy monk. His eyes widened in fear as he stared at Aria in sudden recognition. "You're supposed to be locked up."

Clarice ignited with incandescent fury. She blurred forward, but the world tilted sideways. A crushing pressure slammed into her, as if her nerves were rewired mid-motion. Lexi was immediately by her side, swiftly pulling her back. The sensation vanished. Something about the man's proximity short-circuited her motor skills.

"What the hell was that?" Aria shouted, furiously shaking the monk like a ragdoll. "What did you do to her?"

His grin faltered. For a moment, the madness drained from his face.

"You're supposed to be locked up," he whimpered.

Aria dropped him, the air still thrumming with the power of her unfurled aura. She drew the tin whistle, its golden surface catching the light. "Then it's time to rewrite *your* reality, Redgart."

"A Seraph!" he gasped. "He promised to bring me back to the light realms if I made you fight for it."

"Why's she getting dizzy near you?" Aria demanded, her hard golden eyes boring into him.

"I don't know! I swear!" he exclaimed desperately. "He said to give her the piece of instrument, even if she lost."

Clarice narrowed her eyes, studying the nutjob of a monk. "It sounds like they've set a trap of some kind on it. Where is it?"

He hesitated, looking up at Aria fearfully. She towered over him with the tin whistle to her lips. He licked his lips nervously before speaking. "It's back in a cave in Tibet."

Aria took a deep breath as she prepared to play. He gasped and hurriedly plunged a hand into a large pocket on the front of his robes, removing a violin neck.

"Set it down on the ground and step back," Aria commanded, her lips never leaving the instrument.

He licked his lips again, looking at the violin neck and then back at Aria, clearly wondering how quickly she could play something.

She blew a single, soft note. Power rolled outward like a shockwave, bending the air and sending all the wildlife within a mile scattering. Birds launched into the air, deer lurched up the hills, and insects took to the sky.

Redgart screamed and dropped the violin neck, stumbling backward into the dust.

"Clarice, are you able to come close to the neck without getting sick?" Aria asked anxiously.

Clarice blurred forward to stand next to Aria. The man stumbled back in surprise at her sudden movement. She stared down at the violin neck, then looked up at Redgart suspiciously. *"Why would it have only affected me when I was near this clown?"* she silently asked the others.

Calypso stared hard at the violin, radiating caution. "Perhaps the Seraphim did something to trap it whilst it was in his possession."

Clarice stepped forward cautiously, every nerve braced for another wave of vertigo. Nothing hit her. The monk flinched anyway as she stopped a few feet away, her eyes blazing with fury.

"Tell me everything," Clarice said, each word like a blade scraping steel. "Who contacted you, what did they say, what were you supposed to do? Speak, or we'll rewrite reality with you as an immortal mayfly, where you'll spend an eternity being digested." He had threatened her with a piece of her *spirit*, the most sacred part of her being.

He stared wide-eyed at her wrathful expression before something inside seemed to break. "Foul witch! Fornicating whore! Despicable demon spawn! Fallen creatures of the devil! Slaves of carnal delights! Wanton, slatternly, prideful..." The rant went on and on, hurling invective in an endless tirade that devolved into gibberish.

Calypso frowned at the man, concern tightening her swirling eyes. *"They have done something to him,"* she said telepathically. *"I am going to try something."*

She opened a gateway and pulled her regular harp through. She began plucking an intricate, fast-paced melody. Her voice joined the harp and blended into a fast, lilting shanty. It was a different style from anything she had ever heard from Calypso.

As Calypso played, Clarice focused on the monk's aura. His energy twisted—two signatures fighting for dominance. She gasped in sudden realization. He didn't just have a split personality; he had two spirits bound into one body like mismatched wires sparking inside the same machine. He was vacillating between spirits based on his mental state. Someone had reengineered him to become useless if he were questioned forcefully, switching over to the witch-hunting madman persona.

Calypso's fingers danced faster. The melody shifted from shanty to a kind of spell, each note carving glowing sigils into the air. Threads of light snaked from her harp, weaving into the monk's chest like living calligraphy.

Clarice could only stare, feeling the pulse of divine rhythm in her bones. She shook her head in wonder as she observed billions of strands of light connecting Calypso to the man in a kind of spirit surgery more complex than she could comprehend. It was easy to forget Calypso was over a hundred years old until you witnessed some of the skills she had developed after working with music around the clock for most of her life. The music seemed to act as a timing and rhythm aid for the complicated energies she was utilizing to operate on his immortal body.

A piercing chord rang out. The man arched backward as a beam of white light tore from his body and vanished into the sky. They all watched in silence as Calypso lowered the harp and sent it back through a portal.

Redgart stared at Calypso, flexing his fingers as if rediscovering them. His voice trembled. "It's gone... the demon's gone."

"It was not a demon," Calypso said gently. "It was another spirit—someone awaiting rebirth. Tell me, was it the Seraphim themselves who did this to you, or one of the Cherubim?"

Redgart shivered. "There was a man without a face," he answered barely above a whisper, staring past them as if the memory were still watching him. "He spoke inside my head and said he was the voice of the Seraph. I don't know how he knew I had a piece of a divine instrument. He said I'd be able to return to the light realm if I lured you to a cave in Tibet. I was supposed to make a show of making you earn the divine instrument so you'd be more desperate to accept it when it was within reach. He didn't say what would happen when you took it, but whenever I touched it, the other spirit became... hungry."

"Hungry, eh?" Clarice muttered uneasily. "Why are you neither demon nor angel? You're immortal, but there's no radiance flowing through your meridians. No corruption either. What are you?"

Redgart looked down at his feet. "The Cherubim said I wasn't wicked enough to be damned, but not worthy to remain," he said bitterly. "So the Seraph took my radiance and left me hollow."

Clarice could understand his bitterness. To have his radiance taken away wasn't much better than being turned into a demon. At least mortals had no memory of their loss.

Calypso's eyes glowed with sympathy. "Was it the Cherubim who sealed your nodes?"

He shook his head, shuddering. "No—it was a Seraph. He said I would be a good subject for gathering data on whether angels could survive without access to radiance."

"They will pay," Clarice growled, her voice as dark as thunder. "There is a day of reckoning coming for those bastards, and I'm going to ensure they experience every horror they've perpetrated."

Calypso took a step toward him. "Will you allow me to heal you?" she asked gently.

His eyes lit up with sudden hope as he met her gaze. "You can do that?"

Clarice arched an eyebrow at him. "Are you unaware of who we are?" she asked dryly. "Clearly, you knew who Aria was if you thought she was still imprisoned in that splinter reality."

He blinked, studying their wings and eyes. "You're Cherubim, aren't you?"

Clarice folded her arms and smirked. "Close, but no cigar. Did you really think Cherubim could play divine instruments?"

"They can't?" Redgart frowned, his brow knitting.

"Only Seraphim are capable of it," Calypso said quietly. She stepped closer, radiance gathering within her palms. "Let us restore your meridians, Redgart."

He looked up at her, tears of hope in his eyes. She placed her hands on his head. "Hold still."

She lit up like a miniature sun as her aura exploded from her hands and into his head. Tendrils of light grew down into his body like roots, boring open meridians sealed shut and starved of radiance. He glowed brilliantly as Calypso opened the floodgates of her powerful aura, charging his spiritual matrix.

He gasped when his node runes transformed, forging a new archangel. His robe warped as large wings sprouted from his back.

He stood still as stone, tears tracing silvery paths down his cheeks. His eyes flared amber, and his scalp filled with a crop of dark hair as his aura settled into harmony. He exhaled, shuddering with relief.

"I am sorry for what those other Seraphim did to you, Redgart," Calypso said sympathetically. "We are not all like them."

Clarice turned away from Redgart, flexing her wings as she glanced down at the violin neck. "So," she said with dangerous cheer, "turning off someone's meridians looks pretty effective. Maybe we start returning the favor. This is twice they've attempted to snare us. It's time to start changing up the rules of this game and give them something to worry about."

Aria eyed her carefully. "What did you have in mind? They're untouchable as long as they stay in the highest realm."

Clarice narrowed her eyes. "Then we make the highest realm unbearable," she said flatly. "We built the light realms—we can change the rules. I say we shift the energy density and alter the flow, forcing them out like rats from a sinking ship."

Aria began winding a strand of hair around her finger, her brow creasing with thought. "You're talking about rerouting the source of radiance."

Clarice nodded once. "We have two divine instruments. We don't need all four to make heaven a shithole."

Calypso exchanged a glance with Aria and Lexi. "I hate to admit it," she said slowly, "but she is right. They shall continue coming until we stop them. What happens when we fail to detect the next trap?"

"What about this?" Lexi asked warily, nudging the violin neck with her toe. A pulse ran through the bond like a shockwave.

Clarice shivered, staring down at the violin neck hungrily. It called to her, desperate to be reunited.

Aria gasped. "Did you feel that? It was like my bond to Clarice brushed against Lexi's. That was... weird."

"I felt it as well," Calypso said curiously, moving closer and kneeling to inspect it. "I believe this bond between our spirits is something entirely new—something that has never existed before."

Clarice joined her beside the fragment. To her spiritual sight, it burned like a caged star, threads of light reaching for her.

Lexi darted in front of her and reached for it. "I'm not letting you touch this thing without testing it first."

The moment Lexi's skin touched the relic, Clarice's breath caught and her face went nuclear. Their spirits collided in a flood of sensation so raw it stripped them bare. It was intimate in a way words could never articulate.

"This is really, *really* awkward," Aria breathed, her face burning with embarrassment.

"Agreed," Calypso said faintly.

Lexi shakily offered it to Clarice, too embarrassed to speak.

Clarice grasped it with trembling hands. She looked into Lexi's eyes as she took it, and there was a moment of unspoken vulnerability. All the mental walls and social shields protecting her psyche from exploitation were laid bare. All that remained was the core of who she was, exposed to Lexi's searching gaze. Lexi's eyes widened in amazement before softening and filling with silver tears.

"You're *beautiful*," Lexi whispered in awe, silver rivulets tracing her cheeks. "I knew you were amazing, but Clarice... how can anything be so *beautiful*?"

Clarice smiled, radiant and unguarded, her spirit blazing with love and joy. There was no trace of snark or humor—for that moment in time, she was just Clarice the Seraph, with a boundless love that couldn't be quantified.

When Lexi released the violin neck, the moment ended. The light imploded inward, a soft thunderclap reuniting her splintered spirit. The mountain rang like a bell, and the skies exploded with auroras as her spirit fused with its shard.

She closed her eyes, lips curving into a smile of wonder. "How did I live without a piece of my spirit?" she whispered, golden tears of joy glittering in her eyes. "I can't imagine losing it now that it's back. I feel so much more... *me* now."

Lexi pulled Clarice into a fierce embrace. Emotion surged through their bond, igniting like the birth of a new star, blazing with love and indescribable happiness. Aria and Calypso joined in, laughing from the sheer joy flooding their united spirits. For a moment, the world felt whole again.

Mandy stood, grinning through the glow. "This is so incredible. I'm so glad you brought me here."

Aria laughed, watching Mandy affectionately. "It's only going to get more awesome from here on out, now that our professor of awesomeness has more of her spirit."

Lexi dissolved into giggles. "I almost forgot she has an honorary doctorate in awesomeness."

Aria opened a shimmering gateway. "We should head back. The others are probably wondering why we vanished."

Clarice turned to Redgart. "You're welcome to come with us."

He hesitated, then nodded once. "I owe you my life. I'll find a way to repay it."

5 – Soul Trap

Clarice winced at the glare waiting for her on the other side of the portal. Her parents stood with Tamra and Devon, their faces carved with worry. Emily's glare could have melted stone.

"You all vanished with no warning," Emily said, her voice tight. "Right after we got Aria back. For heaven's sake, Clarice, at least say *something* next time."

Clarice hung her head. "I'm so sorry, Mom. I should've sent someone back to explain. I didn't think."

Emily exhaled slowly, her eyes narrowing as she really looked at her daughter. "What happened? Are you all right?"

Her eyes landed on Redgart, who stood nervously adjusting his fresh archangel wings around a tear in his robe. "And who might this be?"

Aria stepped in and explained their encounter with Redgart, the Seraphim's trap, and the recovery of Clarice's spirit fragment.

Emily stepped forward and touched Clarice's cheek. "You feel different," she said softly. "More whole."

Clarice smiled, pulling her into a hug. "Part of me has been waiting its whole life to meet you. I'm so sorry for worrying you."

"You're fine, dear," Emily said gently, returning the embrace. "I know you were just worried about Lexi. But... how did your spirit get so fractured? Aria's was only split in two."

"It was a choice," Clarice said quietly, a tremor in her voice. "I remember now. The instruments are extensions of our will, with a portion of our spirits woven into them. When the others tried to erase us, the instruments rebelled. They refused the command and flung us here instead, hidden as mortals."

She swallowed hard. "When they tried to unmake Grodek... a part of me shattered to stop them."

A ripple of horror coursed through the bond—Aria, Calypso, and Lexi all gasping as the memory of the pain reached them. The echo of her fractured spirit tore through their link like broken glass.

Aria's eyes filled with tears. She stepped forward and pulled Clarice into her arms with a ragged sob. "Oh, Clarice… I'm so sorry."

"It's okay," Clarice murmured, holding her sister close. "It's ancient history. I'm almost whole again."

Calypso and Lexi's eyes bulged with horror. Emily didn't understand the cause, but she could sense the unspoken pain in their silent exchange. She wrapped her arms around both daughters, pouring her love into their trembling spirits.

Eric joined them wordlessly, his arms circling the whole group in quiet unity. The other angels looked on, anxious as they watched helplessly.

Mandy stood apart, her brow furrowed. She didn't know what had happened—but she sensed the grief spread through them—brittle and ready to shatter. Her hand half-rose, the instinct to comfort pulling at her heart.

Calypso's tears slowed. Her voice, when it came, was soft and flat.

"I'm going to kill them."

The words hung in the air like a crack of thunder.

They all stared in shock. Calypso—who had shown revulsion to hurting *anyone*, even demons who were torturing children—now glowed with hatred so sharp it burned through the bond.

Clarice's own fury rose to meet it. Whoever had pushed Calypso this far would pay for it.

"They need to die," Lexi said, her voice colder than the void. "They've poisoned too many worlds already."

Aria leaned against Clarice's shoulder, her voice barely a breath. "Let's find the rest of your spirit," she whispered. "Then we hunt."

Clarice met her sister's eyes and shook her head. "We strike first. If we wait, we'll never get the next piece. They'll just keep tripping us up with traps, and we might not survive the next one."

Aria nodded slowly, her eyes hardening with determination. "What did you have in mind?"

Clarice suddenly grinned. "Step one: pop the moon like an overripe pimple."

Aria stared at her blankly for a moment, then dissolved into giggles. "You've forever ruined my image of the moon, Clarice," she gasped. "I'll never see it as a ball of cheese again." After a few more burbling giggles, her face grew serious. "Why the moon?"

Clarice put her hands on her hips and took on a lecturing tone. "Because a hundred and fifty thousand people die every day. That's a hundred and fifty thousand souls waiting to reincarnate. If the moon's their trap, smashing it floods the light realms with returning souls. Overcrowded heavens, confused angels—it'll be chaos. It'll be the perfect opportunity for us to slip in undetected. We find the source for radiance in the higher realms, and we take it away from them. As a bonus, the increased radiance should unlock more of our memories."

Aria met Calypso's eyes, the corner of her mouth curving.

"It could work," Calypso said slowly. "They expect us to continue playing their little treasure-hunting game. They'll never see this coming."

Clarice smiled grimly. "I'm not stopping with ours. We're taking out every soul trap we can find. Let's see how heaven handles rush hour."

Eric smiled proudly. "Go big or don't go at all, eh? That's my girl."

Laughter rippled through the room, bright and warm. Power hummed through Clarice's veins. With the missing piece of her spirit restored, she felt almost whole again, and dangerously close to the strength of her sister.

Aria tapped her lips musingly. "So how do we actually *do* this? Angel fire won't cut it unless I burn nonstop for a few hours."

Clarice winked at her slyly. "Did you forget what's inside your spirit?"

Aria blinked, then laughed. "Right. The divine instruments. I keep forgetting I can basically rewrite physics now."

Devon cleared his throat pointedly. "Maybe warn the humans first," he said dryly. "If Calypso posts an announcement explaining the soul traps and why you're doing this, it might cut down on the mass panic."

Clarice nodded. "Good thinking, Uncle." She playfully bumped shoulders with Calypso. "You're kind of useful to have around, Miss Popular."

Calypso bumped her shoulder back, love pulsing across the spirit link.

Aria folded her arms, cradling her chin in one hand. "Why don't the three of us handle the soul traps?" she suggested, nodding to Calypso and Clarice. "Lexi, you should check in with Mary now that I'm back. I'm guessing the rest of you have friends you'd like to track down and help ascend."

Lexi hesitated, the bond flickering with indecision—duty pulling one way, longing the other.

Clarice placed a reassuring hand on Lexi's shoulder. "You do remember we can all teleport and sense each other anywhere in the cosmos, right? Go see Mary." She paused, looking upward thoughtfully. "And while you're at it, get her upgraded. She still doesn't have the antigrav perk—if it even works on other classes."

Lexi stared at Clarice levelly, but the bond burned with a sudden longing that gave her true feelings away. Clarice started waggling her eyebrows at Lexi suggestively, and their youngest angel began losing the battle to keep her cheeks from blushing. Red spots bloomed and quickly spread to the rest of her face. She finally couldn't maintain a stoic expression any longer and began laughing helplessly under Clarice's relentless arsenal of suggestive leers.

"Fine, I'll go visit her," Lexi gave in, giggling at Clarice's knowing gaze. "Just to see if she needs help with anything, mind you."

"Oh, naturally," Clarice purred. "Just remember to show her all the cool things you can do with antigravity." She finished with her trademark leer.

"Don't look at me like that, Clarice!" Lexi whined plaintively. "Now I feel like I need to go bathe."

"I'll scrub your back..." Clarice offered with another leer.

Emily gave Aria a small push. "Control your sister, Aria."

Clarice slipped behind Aria, her arms winding around her sister's waist. She leaned close, lips brushing Aria's ear. "Yeah, control me, Aria," she breathed.

Aria's breath hitched, and Clarice smiled wickedly as her sister's thoughts stuttered to a grinding halt, her mental faculties reduced to a quivering mess of carnal desire.

Calypso wasn't much better, pulled into the tempest of lust flaring through the spirit link.

Mandy watched, grinning as if she had stumbled into the best comedy show in the cosmos. Her lavender eyes burned with a mixture of fondness and... could it be hope? Clarice winked at her and received a return wink.

Aria struggled to rein in her heated thoughts, shivering when Clarice kissed her ear. She barely repressed a sigh of disappointment when Clarice released her and stepped away.

Drawing a shaky breath, Aria turned to Mandy and offered her a friendly smile. "Who would you like to go with, Mandy? You're welcome to join us on our celestial pimple-popping expedition."

"Or come with me," Lexi offered, shooting the trio a meaningful look.

Mandy looked Lexi up and down with a small smile. "Sure, I'd love to go out with you... Lexi."

Lexi coughed out a laugh that sounded forced as pink spots appeared on her fair cheeks. She leaned in close to Mandy and whispered, "Those three need some alone time."

Of course, a whisper in the same room with an angel was the same as saying it out loud. The room went crimson. Aria flushed brilliantly, immediately glancing at Clarice and Calypso before hurriedly looking away. Calypso was little better, blushing to the roots of her hair. She attempted to meet their eyes but quickly looked down.

Clarice couldn't repress the giggle that burst out as she watched her bashful angels. The spirit link made it clear they were ready to get some alone time with each other.

Tamra and Devon shared a resigned look as the four angels tried to fight the spirit link's feedback loop.

Devon took Tamra's hand in both of his. "I do have quite a few acquaintances I'd like to get transformed—and introduce them to Tamra."

She smiled up at his youthful face and leaned into him. "I'd love to meet some of your friends."

Eric glanced at Emily speculatively. "I suppose we should hook up with some of our friends back home and get them transformed, too."

Emily chuckled, looking like a clone of Clarice as mischief twinkled in her golden eyes. "I can't wait to see the looks on their faces when they realize who we are—especially my aides."

Eric grinned back at her. "You read my mind. I can't wait to see your Chief of Staff meltdown when she finds out you're an angel. A hundred bucks says she tries to convince you to go public."

Devon shook his head, his gaze flicking between Clarice and her parents. "It's plain to see where Clarice's mischievous nature originated."

Clarice's eyes widened, her naturally innocent face augmenting the expression until it was almost believable. "That's just slander, Uncle." She took a deep breath that immediately drew Aria and Calypso's eyes to her well-defined breasts. "Now, if we're all finished here, I have some blushing angels I'd like to ravish."

Emily pressed her palms into her eyes with a loud groan as Aria and Calypso erupted into glowing red suns.

Clarice gave a throaty, heart-stopping chuckle as she watched her blushing maidens cover their faces, embarrassment warring with anticipation.

"Redgart," Eric said, stepping in like a patient father at the world's strangest family dinner, "would you like to visit the light realm when they return? That's what the Seraphim promised you, wasn't it?"

Redgart, who had been quietly watching the celestial soap opera, blinked. His face was equal parts reverence and disbelief. "Um, if you'll allow it, yes."

Clarice turned her focus to the new archangel. "Can you tell us more about how angels are sent to the mortal realm? Calypso mentioned a machine that handles the transfer. We're still waiting on our memories to return, so we're ignorant about a lot that should be obvious."

"It's more like a facility," Redgart said, shifting nervously under her golden-eyed gaze. "It's huge—maybe the size of a distribution center. It can send a few hundred thousand spirits at once, maybe ten million a day at full power. Less for Archangels and much less for the first triad. It's also used to receive returning spirits."

Aria frowned anxiously. "So when people die, are they stuck in limbo until they're processed?"

Redgart shook his head, his dark hair swaying. "No, the radiance in the light realm is so strong that their immortal bodies reform naturally after a couple of hours. They only need to go through the mortality processing centers if they want to have the same body they had as humans. Most angels who've experienced mortality prefer to have a gender, so they go through the mortality processing center when they return. The body that forms naturally from the ambient light energy is genderless."

"No *freaking* way!" Clarice exclaimed. "They really *are* genderless? We've been telling everyone that angels have a gender because *we* do."

Redgart nodded, running a hand through his new hair. "Yeah, the angel tear uses the human body as a template when it's transforming you into an angel," he explained. "But *most* angels in the light realms are going to be genderless."

Eric faced Redgart eagerly, his eyes alight with interest. "How many of these facilities are there?"

"There used to be hundreds," Redgart answered, frowning. "Most were destroyed after the rewrite that wiped out the old Seraphim." He hesitated, studying the three of them. "Well—what we *thought* wiped you out. It sounds like you were hidden in the mortal realm instead. I imagine the other Seraphim were pretty shocked when they realized you'd survived."

Aria smiled grimly. "There was definitely panic when Lucifer was redeemed. They probably sensed us the first time Calypso played her divine instrument."

"That would make sense," Emily agreed. She slipped an arm through Eric's. "Come on, honey. Let's go shock our friends. Are you three heading out now?"

Clarice shrugged, glancing at Calypso and Aria. "Might as well get it over with. Anything you two need to do before we go?"

Aria's cheeks reddened and the anticipation in the spirit link grew sharper. "Nope, I'm ready."

Calypso wordlessly nodded, biting her lip as she gazed at Aria and Clarice hungrily.

"Let's go destroy some moons then," Clarice sang merrily.

"Hold on," Devon said, raising a hand. "Maybe make the announcement before you start popping celestial pimples. Calypso's channel, remember?"

Clarice deflated a little. "Right, the livestream. Fine."

Calypso nodded, watching Clarice with amusement. The three of them headed for the library, Mandy trailing behind with Lexi, clearly not wanting to miss the show.

Derek pushed his final commit to the repo, glanced at the clock, and decided it was finally dinner time.

He stretched until his spine popped, letting out a loud groan. He could hear his fourteen-year-old son, Jordan, swearing up a storm in another part of the house. He shook his head as he exited the room, the volume of the profanity increasing. Jordan took his gaming very seriously, a fact some of his friends enjoyed exploiting when they met up online.

Derek entered the living room and stopped to observe his furious son. "You're going to burst a blood vessel if you don't chill out."

"Slurp my butt," Jordan retorted irritably. "This thing is so freaking *cheat*!"

"You're not wrong," Derek assured his son seriously. "I just read an article about a company getting sued because one of the game devs rigged mobs to cheat if they detected a volatile person. They specifically target people with webcams and then record the tantrums that ensue after a mob cheats. Apparently, the game devs go to parties where they play those videos in the background as part of the entertainment."

"Seriously?" Jordan demanded, his face filled with indignant fury. "Which company was it?"

"Let me see..." Derek murmured, looking up at the ceiling thoughtfully. "I think it was a company going by the name of '*Jordan Cries Like a Baby When He Loses, LLC*' or something like that."

Jordan glared resentfully at his grinning father for a few seconds before exploding. "It *seriously* cheated! I'm getting a refund for this garbage game and giving them a shit review."

Derek continued relentlessly. "They had a promo for a DLC that includes a box of tissues for those gamers who just can't wrap their heads around the fact they're playing a *game*."

"Don't you have some work to do or something?" Jordan growled in exasperation.

"Yep. It's called 'teaching my son emotional regulation,'" Derek said cheerfully. "You're going to spend your whole life mad if you don't learn to let small stuff slide."

A sharp ping from Jordan's phone cut through the air. He glanced at the screen—and froze.

"What's the matter?" Derek asked curiously.

"Calypso's going live!" Jordan blurted, his eyes huge. "In five minutes! Oh my god, this is so cool!"

Derek frowned as his son scrambled to switch the TV to YouTube. The last time Calypso streamed live, hospitals had emptied overnight. People claimed her music cured everything from cancer to the common cold. Others said she had somehow burned out secret nanotech in government agents.

It could've been true, but there were so many fantastical claims on the internet about the beautiful musician that it was hard to say what was real. The most fantastical claim, that she was actually an angel, was hard to dispute. There had been so many videos appearing online showing her flying through the air like a superhero that it was hard to claim they were all an elaborate hoax. He might've still believed it was a hoax if he hadn't witnessed the mass healing of the world's sick four months ago. He still found it hard to believe there could be actual demons, though.

The YouTube stream's waiting screen showed an old photo of Calypso in her trademark theater mask.

Derek checked his phone for the time just as the image vanished, replaced by a smiling Clarice.

Her eyes glowed gold like liquid fire. Midnight hair framed a face sculpted from perfection. Her face shone with innocence, though there was something about her eyes that hinted at mischief. Her braless shirt was what captured the eye; the clinging fabric did more to reveal than conceal.

She stepped back, and Calypso joined her.

Golden eyes were impressive, sure, but Calypso's swirling lavender vortexes made reality itself look dull.

Calypso smiled into the camera, her eyes overflowing with love. Derek gasped as he suddenly felt warmth suffuse his soul, like he had been submerged in a pool of liquid optimism. He had never felt more accepted and valued than in that moment. He suddenly felt foolish for ever having doubted this angel was... an angel.

"So," Clarice began, trying very hard not to grin, "we figured we should give everyone a quick heads-up—just so nobody panics when the moon disappears in a bit."

Derek blinked. *When the what does* what?

"I'm sure most of you have noticed by now that angels are real," Clarice continued cheerfully. "Good news: *you're all angels, too*. You're just taking a long mortal vacation for personal growth reasons."

Her face darkened. "The only problem is that some real bastards in the light realms turned mortality into a prison system. That romantic spotlight in the night sky where lovers wax poetic? It's a soul trap. It catches you when you die and queues you up for reincarnation."

She suddenly beamed, her innocent face shining with eagerness. "We're fixing that right now. We'll be dismantling the moon soul trap—along with a few thousand others throughout the galaxy. So, next time you die, you'll go home to the light realms instead of respawning here."

Clarice gave a playful little wave. "If you happen to die in the next few days, see you soon! Everyone else—enjoy the rest of your mortality. The planet will be fine without the moon, promise. We love you!"

As the warmth of their love faded, Derek's brain finally caught up with what Clarice had actually said. *Wait. Did she just say the moon's going away?*

"Is it off?" Calypso asked hesitantly.

"Could be," Clarice replied evasively. "It's just so technical that a poor, innocent angel like me couldn't help but be overwhelmed by all these buttons."

"Clarice, nobody's *ever* going to associate you with the word '*innocent*,'" a voice from outside the camera said dryly. "Is there a reason you're leaving the live stream going?"

"I was hoping Calypso would do something funny when she thought we were off-air," Clarice explained with a regretful sigh. "She really let me down, Aria."

"Then answer some of the questions," Aria said, half-laughing. "There are actually some good ones in the chat."

"Everyone always just asks if heaven is real," Clarice said with an eye roll. She suddenly leaned forward until her face filled the camera. "The sky is real, everyone. Buy a plane ticket—you can visit heaven anytime."

"You're such a freaking troll," Aria accused her affectionately. "Into the troll pit with you."

Clarice suddenly dropped out of sight with a startled squawk, as if a hole had opened beneath her. Aria appeared in front of the camera, her lustrous red hair gleaming like fire, framing the face of an... angel.

"Let's see..." Aria murmured, scanning the chat. "Flamelord-4-life wants to know how to become an angel. Super easy—just get touched by an angel tear and say you want to vanquish evil."

Her eyes scanned through the comments. "Mud-bloods-rule-404 asks if angels are genderless. Normally, I'd say no, but it turns out angels who've never lived mortal lives *are* genderless. Angel tears basically scan your body as a template for your new energy form. So yeah, I'm female—but the asshats who tried to lock us away forever? Totally smooth."

Aria's eyes widened just before a cannonball smacked into her face, knocking her clean off-camera.

"Sorry about that, folks!" Clarice's cheerful voice sang as she reappeared, dripping wet. "My evil stepsister dropped me in the middle of the Pacific. I found a shipwreck, though—and this cannonball had Aria's name on it."

"You are *so* lucky angels don't take damage or feel pain," Aria declared as she stood back up in the camera's background.

"Actually, I think you'll find that *you're* the lucky one," Clarice corrected with an impish grin. "Or that would've hurt a *lot*."

"Who let the kids take over the YouTube channel?" another voice asked in exasperation. "That's enough of that, you two. Go blow up the moon already."

"Aw, but *Mom*, I've never had a YouTube channel to play with before," Clarice whined plaintively.

There was a long-suffering sigh, and then the live broadcast ended.

Jordan turned toward him, his eyes wide. Derek met his gaze, feeling like reality had just loaded a 404—and the zero between the fours had a smiley face.

"So, we're all angels running around in some kind of divine sim?" Jordan asked, grinning in disbelief. "Didn't you say we were gods last week?"

Derek shrugged. "Angels, gods—corporate rebranding," he muttered, still trying to process the information dump. "Let's see if they're serious."

Jordan stared at him disbelievingly. "You think they're really going to vaporize the *moon?* It's gotta be a prank. You *saw* how they were acting."

"Let's go find out then," Derek suggested, feeling a sense of calm certainty that the moon would be gone before the night was out.

Derek snorted in amusement when he saw all the neighbors out in their front yards and driveways. Everyone still had Calypso's channel notifications turned on, from the looks of it.

Eddie, the fifteen-year-old next-door neighbor, strolled over with a look of heavy skepticism. "Hey Jordan, I'll bet you twenty bucks nothing happens. Nothing *ever* happens."

Derek held out a hand. "I'll take that bet. Didn't you have pneumonia four months ago when the whole world got cured? Was that nothing?"

Eddie shrugged the question away. He was fifteen and knew *everything*. He wasn't shy about telling anyone who would listen how much more intelligent he was than the rest of them. Derek remembered being a teenager and knowing everything, but Eddie took it to extremes.

Eddie's mom, Cynthia, wandered over in sweatpants and with a coffee mug, looking like she hadn't planned to witness the end of the world before dinner.

"What do you think, Derek?" she asked, her voice surprisingly pleasant.

Derek rubbed the back of his neck, smiling wryly. "I think it's a bad day to be a crustacean. Tidal power's about to have a rough quarter."

Cynthia frowned, her eyes troubled. “Won’t it mess up the planet’s orbit?”

Derek shrugged as he watched the moon intently. “Not for a long time. I don’t think it’ll make a difference for tens of thousands of years.”

Cynthia started to reply—but three brilliant streaks of light tore up into the sky.

The neighborhood fell silent as the arcs brightened, climbing higher until the air itself seemed to hum. Derek’s balance wavered, like gravity had flinched.

Then the moon was just... gone.

“Jesus Christ, they really did it!” someone down the street shouted in a mixture of excitement and panic. “The freaking moon is *gone!*”

Jordan’s voice was small. “Dad... is it really okay?”

Derek watched the empty sky where the moon had been, feeling the strange calm still humming in his chest. “Yeah,” he said softly. “It’s more than okay. The world just got a lot bigger.”

Clarice grinned at Aria and Calypso as they left the cabin. “That was fun. We should give everyone a bit of a show, don’t you think? Maybe light up to full incandescence and fly up instead of teleporting.”

Aria smirked. “You missed your calling. You should’ve gone into theater.”

“I’m a lesbian, not a thespian, silly,” Clarice declared haughtily.

“This might surprise you,” Aria told her archly. “But you can actually be *both*. At the same time, even.”

Clarice’s eyebrow rose. “Are you suggesting something lewd?”

Aria rolled her eyes. “Get your mind out of the gutter, you goose.”

“Are you trying to insinuate that I’m a horny adult actress?” Clarice asked evenly, her golden eyes narrowing.

“What? No! I—what are you even talking about?” Aria spluttered.

“You called me a goose,” Clarice accused with a meaningful look.

“You *are* a goose,” Aria insisted dryly. “I’m not sure what that has to do with a horny adult actress.”

“And what sound does a goose make, Aria?” Clarice asked expectantly, her eyes sparkling.

“I don’t know,” Aria frowned in bewilderment. “...Honk, honk?”

“Exactly,” Clarice smirked in satisfaction.

Aria blinked, realization dawning. “You’re telling me—geese are honking because they’re horny?”

Clarice grinned triumphantly. “Hey, you said it, not me.”

Calypso looked between them, her expression caught somewhere between horror and amusement. "Let me see if I have understood this correctly," she said slowly. "Geese are constantly honking because they are amorous, and therefore, if someone calls you a goose, they are implying you are similarly inclined. Please tell me I have misunderstood."

Clarice just grinned. "Honk, honk."

Clarice felt a sudden wave of love surge through their link. A heartbeat later, Aria was in her arms, clinging to her like she might vanish.

"Oh, Clarice," Aria whispered through tears. "I still can't believe you're really here. I missed you so much."

Clarice held her close, fingers combing gently through her hair. Her sister still felt fragile—like glass under too much strain. It would take time for those cracks to fade. She let her aura of love flow outward, wrapping Aria in warmth until her trembling eased.

"Sometimes I still think I'll wake up in that nightmare," Aria whispered. "That you'll be gone again. I get so damn scared that this is all in my head." Her voice broke. "Every time I see you—it feels like a gift. Like the universe gave me back something it stole."

Clarice swallowed past a sudden lump in her throat. "Aria, I love you. I swear on my Seraph soul—I will never leave you again. If you ever get pulled into another reality, I'll follow. I'll always be there."

Reality shivered. A faint tremor rippled through existence as radiant threads flared between their spirits, weaving together like golden roots. The bond pulsed, alive and immutable.

Aria gasped as Clarice's spirit unfolded before her—radiant, naked, and impossibly pure. She saw the truth beneath every mask and every joke: a love so vast it defined her. It was fierce, protective, and absolute. The kind of love that could reshape worlds.

Aria trembled as she felt the depth of love in that spirit for her, the passion and protectiveness. She could see just how much of Clarice was defined by her love for Aria, and it was *massive*.

"Oh, Clarice," Aria cried as she pulled Clarice in tightly. "You're so *beautiful*! How can anything be so beautiful?"

Clarice smiled softly. Her next words carried the weight of eternity.

"I'm yours, Aria, and you'll never lose me again," she said, her Seraph voice ringing with truth. "My spirit is in your hands now. Nothing in existence can separate us."

Calypso drew in a sharp breath, her eyes widening with dawning understanding. "Clarice," she whispered, "you bridged your inner spirit to hers. You have made yourself a part of Aria. She truly can never be taken from you now."

Aria blinked and pulled back, then gasped. “Clarice... your eyes,” she whispered. “They’re brown again.”

“What do you mean?” Calypso asked, leaning in. “They are golden.”

“Not to me,” Aria said softly. “They’re the color they used to be. Before we were angels.”

Calypso’s brow furrowed with concentration. “You’re seeing her inner self. Her true spirit. She’s still golden to me—but to you, she’ll always appear as she really is inside, no matter how she evolves.”

Aria stared, caught between wonder and disbelief. “She’s so beautiful,” she murmured. “I thought her angel form was beyond anything possible—but this... how can *anything* be so beautiful?”

Clarice smiled, her soft chocolate eyes glowing with emotion. “Thanks, Aria. You don’t know how much that means. I’ve always been afraid my spirit might be ugly on the inside.”

Aria’s lips curved into a surprised smile. She wasn’t just seeing Clarice—she was feeling her. Every layer, every spark of the soul beneath the sarcasm and steel. Where demons had always reeked of rot, Clarice radiated warmth so bright it blurred the edges of reality itself.

The moment stretched, trembling on the edge of eternity.

Then Aria moved without thinking, drawn forward as if by gravity, and pressed her lips to Clarice’s.

The link erupted. Passion slammed into her like a supernova, pure and blinding. She gasped against Clarice’s lips, her whole being vibrating with the shock of it—the desire, the joy, the unbearable beauty as two stars fused into one.

Clarice drew back at last, hands cradling Aria’s face, her eyes soft with love. “If you only knew how long I’ve wanted to do that,” she whispered.

“Me too,” Aria breathed, her eyes closing as she fought the tidal pull of her desire. “Let’s revisit this after the moon is gone.”

“Count on it,” Clarice said with a radiant smile. “Shall we?”

Calypso stood motionless, eyes wide, emotions flickering across her face. Desire, awe, satisfaction—all braided into something wordless.

Then, as if released from a spell, Calypso launched skyward—her illumination bursting open until she burned like a miniature sun.

Clarice and Aria followed, their laughter echoing through the heavens as three trails of living light tore through the sky toward the waiting moon.

◆◆◆

WHERE DID THE MOON GO?

Just minutes after a live broadcast on Calypso's YouTube channel—in which the angelic figure known as Clarice claimed they were about to "dismantle the moon"—the moon did, in fact, vanish.

For a brief moment, social media speculated about elaborate holograms, cloaking fields, or collective hallucinations. Those theories dimmed quickly when coastlines around the world went still. Oceans settled between high and low tide and have remained that way, aside from the faint tug of the solar tide.

The question now facing humanity is how Earth will fare without its oldest companion.

Clarice insisted during the broadcast that "the planet will be fine." Scientists are inclined to agree, at least for the foreseeable future. Tidal ecosystems will change, but Earth itself is not in imminent danger. Over thousands of years, however, the planet may begin to wobble more dramatically, potentially losing its seasons. Without lunar drag, the days may also shorten slightly.

Skepticism remains high about Clarice's claim that the moon was a "giant soul trap" used to recycle spirits. One planetary scientist did note that the moon "rang like a bell" during seismic tests conducted in the Apollo era but declined to speculate further.

For now, the consensus is simple: humanity will survive.

But with the moon gone, the nights seem darker, the oceans quieter—and, as one astronomer put it—"there's definitely less romance in the air."

6 – Heartache

Lexi glanced over at Mandy as they glided high above North America. She was beautiful, the white highlights in her chest-length auburn hair gleaming in the afternoon light, framing a cute face with more than a touch of mischief. It was the dimples that elevated Mandy from "cute" to "beautiful." Dimples were Lexi's kryptonite.

While their newest angel had shared the story of her "boring" life with them, Lexi had the strangest sense that there was more to Mandy than met the eye, a hidden depth to her personality just out of sight. The same strange familiarity she had felt with the other angels stirred just as strongly with Mandy, like the memory of an old friendship from a dream. Perhaps she could discover more about the vivacious angel before they reached Mary.

Below them, the land stretched out in vast green circles and squares, stitched together by roads and rivers. They cruised at an easy pace—barely a hundred miles an hour—letting the wind rush over their faces. Hypersonic flight had its thrills, but gliding at slower speeds with the wind in their hair was its own kind of exhilaration.

Mandy's face was pure rapture, her auburn hair whipping around her shoulders as she watched the world pass beneath them. Tamra had given her a shirt closer to her bust size, so the wind wasn't clawing at her bodice like it had when she wore Clarice's much larger top.

Lexi could sense Mary somewhere below, a bright thread in the invisible web of psychic connections that tied her to others. If her inner compass was right, Mary was somewhere near Wisconsin.

Lexi bit her lip, unsure of where to start the conversation. Maybe it was the similarities Mandy shared with Clarice that made her so attractive, with that mischievous sparkle in her violet eyes and confident manner. Lexi knew her crush on Clarice wouldn't lead anywhere—which was fine, because she had Mary.

Licking her lips, she said, "I'd ask what it was like living in a world without angels, but I didn't even know angels existed in this one until Clarice and the others rescued me."

Mandy glanced at her and laughed, half in disbelief. "I'm still trying to wrap my head around being an angel. Reality kind of went off the rails when I met Aria—in a good way."

"It went nuts before you met her," Lexi pointed out with a small smile.

Mandy flew closer until their wingtips were nearly touching with each wingbeat. "Devon mentioned that Lucifer sent me into that splinter reality using a 'character template,'" she said, watching Lexi as she flew. "Does that mean I didn't exist there before? Or was I copied over from this world?"

Lexi flushed when she saw Mandy's eyes roaming her body, a small smile of appreciation hinting at her dimples.

"Good question," Lexi mused, willing her cheeks to return to their normal color. "He said it was a shallow copy, so maybe it wasn't fully populated—just real where Aria was meant to be trapped. I think the template was supposed to use a modified version of your doppelganger's mind here and add some kind of influence, or maybe drive, to help Aria." Lexi frowned, giving Mandy a curious look. "The deeper question is what 'real' even means if worlds can be splintered off like that. Maybe everything's just a projection—a shared dream everyone's mind is building together on some kind of communion plane. If we—"

She faltered as a spike of superheated lust pulsed through her spirit link to the three Seraphim. A whimper escaped her throat when she felt a tsunami of desire slam into her, instantly sending her sensitive bits into meltdown. Her awareness faded as her world became a symphony of vicarious pleasure ported into her from Aria, more intense than she would have believed possible. Aria's mind must be melting for it to carry this strongly through the spirit link. Lexi could feel the focus in Clarice and Calypso, wrapped inside white-hot desire, as they pushed Aria to untold heights.

The sensation suddenly cut off, followed by a sense of guilt from Aria and Calypso, and amusement from Clarice as they realized they had a fourth participant.

"Are you okay?" Mandy asked softly, her concerned voice right next to Lexi's ear.

Lexi shuddered as the ecstasy faded, then blinked when she found herself cradled in Mandy's arms, hovering in the clouds. She stared up at Mandy's face in confusion. "What happened?"

Mandy's face relaxed, and a smile dimpled her cheeks. "You just suddenly started moaning like an obscene phone call and stopped flying. I had to dive to catch you, or there would have been an angel-shaped crater in someone's farm. I was pretty epic, if I do say so myself."

Lexi winced, her cheeks catching fire as she imagined the sounds escaping her during her unexpected inclusion in Clarice's tryst with Aria and

Calypso. She felt a little bad that they had stopped on her account—and not because she didn't want it to stop... not at all!

"Um," Lexi stammered, avoiding Mandy's gaze. "When Aria found her divine instrument at the Tree of Life, she kind of linked all four of our spirits together, so we feel each other's emotions... and sensations."

Mandy's eyebrows shot up, and her smile widened. "So, what happened just now? Those three played two maidens and a harlot, and you got a backstage pass?"

Lexi snorted, her embarrassment fading to amusement. "Yeah, pretty much. It can get a little awkward sometimes, but it's worth it, having such a special connection to the three of them. I have a feeling it's going to get a lot steamier now that Aria's back and her fear of intimacy is no longer an issue."

Mandy grinned down at her knowingly. "Let's hope so, for your sake. Sounds like a sweet deal."

Lexi laughed weakly, fighting a fresh blush. "My God, you're as bad as Clarice." She suddenly realized she was still cradled in Mandy's arms, their faces inches apart. The blush won out, and she quickly activated her antigravity ability and floated out of Mandy's arms with a mumbled, "Thanks," before switching back to wing-powered flight.

Mandy winked, her smile never dimming. "No problem—I never turn down the chance to hold a gorgeous angel."

Lexi thought she might combust from the heat flushing her body. She awkwardly looked down at the endless squares and circles of farmland below them. "It's so strange seeing the plains from up here," she said, desperately grasping for the first thing to distract her spiraling thoughts from dimpled smiles and the memory of Mandy's arms cradling her. "They look like a patchwork quilt or—"

"Speaking of planes," Mandy interrupted, pointing excitedly. A small single-prop plane buzzed a few miles away, glinting in the sunlight. "Do we wave hello or change course?"

Lexi regarded her with an amused twinkle in her eyes. "I get the feeling you want to say hi, so let's go say hello."

They angled toward the small plane until they were only a thousand feet away. The pilot finally realized they weren't birds. The plane banked sharply, keeping its distance, but Lexi could still see the pilot's wide eyes staring back through the cockpit glass. Mandy waved enthusiastically, her laughter bright in the thin air. A teenage girl in the back seat grinned from ear to ear and waved back, nearly bouncing out of her seat, while her mother gaped at them in disbelief.

Mandy grinned exuberantly. "I think we just made someone's day."

"I think you're right," Lexi agreed with a last wave at the plane. "At least we brought some joy to someone today."

Mandy laughed delightedly. "That's right, it's our job to bring people joy, isn't it?"

Lexi chuckled as she observed Aria's savior. She seemed to have boundless positive energy. Her eyes sparkled with life, enhancing her already beautiful, angelic features. She once again reminded Lexi of a slightly less mischievous version of Clarice. Mandy had grown more gregarious over the past two days—she almost seemed like a different person.

"What part of Wisconsin do you think—" Mandy cut off when they heard the coughing sound of the single-prop plane's engine die. They turned to watch as it began gliding down toward the plains below.

"I suppose we should go help," Lexi suggested, turning and flying toward the plane at a quicker pace. "This is great terrain for an emergency landing with how flat everything is. Even so, I'm sure they'd appreciate some help."

Mandy studied the small plane intently. "What can we do to help them? Should I carry one of them down to the ground? Or maybe you could just go inside and make a portal for them?"

Lexi smiled approvingly. "Not a bad idea. However, we probably don't want the plane dropping onto someone's house. I'll just go underneath and carry it down to the ground."

Mandy stared at her in amazement. "You can do that?"

Warmth spread from Lexi's center at Mandy's wondering gaze. Was this what it was like for Aria, Clarice, and Calypso, always having people look at them in awe and respect?

Lexi shrugged, which felt a little strange while flying. "Yeah, the antigravity ability makes it super simple." She turned to look at Mandy and winked. "It's kind of fun to get the ability too."

Mandy raised a challenging eyebrow. "You'll have to show me sometime."

Lexi flushed as she realized she was teasing someone who outclassed her in the teasing department.

"You're really pretty when you blush," Mandy informed her with a wink.

Lexi laughed ruefully. "Okay, that backfired spectacularly."

They were almost next to the gliding plane when the girl in the back finally noticed them again. Her eyes were wide with fear, clearly expecting the worst. Mandy smiled and gave her two thumbs up.

Lexi toggled her antigravity field and zipped under the aircraft. Flipping upside down, she wrapped her arms and legs around the fuselage until she found the center of balance. The plane rocked slightly before settling into her steady grip. Once it was stable, she began easing its descent, bleeding off forward momentum as gently as she could.

"Is she holding us up?" a woman's voice asked from inside, stunned.

"Yep, she's got you," Mandy called back cheerfully, coasting alongside. "She's just gonna set you down nice and easy."

Lexi risked a glance sideways—and found Mandy gliding beside her, phone raised with a shit-eating grin.

"I'm sorry, Lexi," Mandy said, laughter bubbling in her voice. "But I can't *not* show this to Aria and the others."

Lexi groaned, realizing what she must look like as she hugged the fuselage. "I can already hear the jokes. Clarice is never going to let me live this down."

"Oh, I don't know," Mandy teased. "I seem to remember her telling you to show Mary everything you could do in zero gravity. Maybe this is what she meant."

Lexi thunked her forehead against the fuselage. "I'm definitely never living this down."

The descent took nearly ten minutes. Mandy filmed the whole thing, snickering softly as Lexi hovered over an endless sea of cornfields.

"Superman was full of crap," Lexi muttered as she neared a deserted county road. "Planes don't have convenient handles with reinforced frames. Total false advertising."

"We're going cape shopping after this," Mandy promised, dimples flashing like weapons.

Lexi shot her a mock glare as she set the plane gently onto its wheels. *How dare she mock my superhero moment—especially with those dimples!*

As soon as the plane touched down, the pilot cracked open the door and dropped the small metal stairs. A middle-aged woman and a teenage girl hurried out, followed by the pilot. The woman—Jill—was of average height and slightly plump, with short brown hair and warm, light-brown eyes. She was trembling, still riding the aftershock of adrenaline, tears glimmering as she tried to steady her breathing.

"Thank you so much, Lexi," Jill gushed, stepping forward and wrapping the surprised angel in a tight hug. "I was terrified. I know you can glide a plane down, but that would've been really risky."

"You're very welcome, Jill," Lexi said softly, returning the hug and letting her radiance bloom outward. Jill gasped as the flood of love washed through her, and she clung to Lexi, savoring the radiant glow suffusing her soul.

"How did you know my name is Lexi?" she asked Jill curiously.

Her daughter, Heather, answered, "Are you kidding? You're one of Calypso's companions! *Everyone* knows who you are."

Lexi colored when she found Mandy smirking at her knowingly. She was famous? Now she was curious about what they were saying about her. How much did they know?

Jill seemed to be in a kind of trance as the radiance washed through her. Heather finally poked her discreetly.

"Mom, don't make it weird," she muttered.

Lexi laughed and stepped back—then caught Heather in a hug before she could retreat. The girl stiffened in shock, then inhaled sharply as the same warmth filled her soul. After a full minute of wide-eyed wonder, Jill raised an eyebrow.

"Don't make it weird," she told her daughter, smirking.

Heather reluctantly stepped back. "You didn't tell me it felt that good," she grumbled.

Lexi eyed the girl appraisingly. "How old are you, Heather?"

Heather paused in the act of fussing with her hair to stare at Lexi in surprise. "How do you know my name?"

"Everyone's name is written in their aura," Lexi explained with a small smile. "Calypso can read ages too, but I haven't mastered that yet. So? Sixteen?"

Heather's eyes went wide and she gave a startled laugh. "Really? That is so cool! And good guess—I was literally on my way to my sixteenth birthday party."

Mandy's eyes lit up. "Hey, happy birthday, Heather!" she said brightly. "Where were you headed?"

"We were going on a cruise on Lake Michigan with my grandparents," Heather sighed. "There's no way we'll make it before the ship leaves now."

Lexi turned toward the pilot. Douglas had been staring at them in stunned silence since he climbed out of the plane. When she met his gaze, he blushed furiously. He was tall, lean, probably in his mid-twenties—and currently short on words.

"What airport were you flying into, Douglas?" she asked gently. "Just picture it in your mind."

He blanched, and his face grew tense as he struggled to put attractive angels out of his thoughts and focus on the map. Lexi nearly laughed but concentrated on the image in his head instead. A moment later, a shimmering gateway the size of a hangar blossomed open beside them.

"Here we are," she said cheerfully. "I'll just push the plane through. Make sure the brakes are off and steer once you're inside."

Douglas still didn't speak—he just nodded mutely and scrambled back into the cockpit, sealing the door behind him.

"Oh my God," Heather squealed, her voice cracking into the stratosphere. "We're still going to make it! I can't wait to tell my grandparents we were saved by angels!"

Lexi turned to Jill, her tone soft. "Can I talk to you for a minute after we move the plane?"

"Of course," Jill agreed, still glassy-eyed with shock.

Lexi floated into the air and braced herself against the tail of the plane. She pushed, but it only rocked forward an inch. Increasing the pressure made the metal creak.

"I think the brakes are still on!" Mandy shouted, loud enough for half the county to hear.

Douglas flinched and hurriedly released the brakes—just in time for the plane to lurch forward and shoot clean through the portal.

Across the tarmac, a few airfield employees froze mid-step, staring as a Cessna appeared out of thin air. Lexi flew back down, gesturing for Jill and Heather to follow her through the gate.

Before stepping in, she caught Mandy's eye and nodded subtly toward Heather. Mandy grinned, falling into step beside the girl.

"So," Mandy asked casually, "what kind of car are you getting now that you're sixteen?"

Lexi gently guided Jill away from her daughter. "Jill, I wanted to make you an offer while we're here," she said quietly, glancing toward where Heather and Mandy were deep in animated conversation. "Would you like to become an angel? You'd be able to awaken your daughter when you think she's ready."

Jill froze, her eyes wide.

"I'm assuming you saw the livestream last night," Lexi added. "What Aria and Clarice said about this world being a kind of prison—and how angel tears can change humans."

Jill nodded slowly, still catching her breath. "Yeah... they said we were trapped here. And that you could free people."

"So what do you think?" Lexi asked gently. "I can just unlock the ability with an angel tear—you don't even have to trigger it yet. I can't promise when you'll get another chance."

"Yes," Jill said at once, her voice fierce with conviction. "I've had enough of this endless reincarnation shit. My soul feels ancient, and I'm tired of living the same cycle again and again."

Lexi blinked at the vehemence in Jill's voice. Her expression softened; she could feel the weight of lifetimes pressing behind Jill's eyes—the horrors she had likely endured. She reached up, producing a single silver tear, and took Jill's hand, guiding it to her cheek.

Light flared where skin met skin. Jill gasped as warmth and vitality coursed through her in a rush. Her posture straightened, her body grew leaner, and her features softened.

"Now say the words," Lexi whispered.

"I want to vanquish evil," Jill declared, her voice trembling.

A glow surged outward, and power coursed through her meridians in a rush of glory.

Heather stopped mid-sentence and ran toward them, eyes wide. She stared at her suddenly youthful and radiant mother in wonder. Heather's awe broke into delighted laughter.

"You're *turning into an angel*, Mom!" she shouted, bouncing with excitement.

Moments later, the transformation ended. Jill stood in wonder, her eyes a rich shade of lavender and her expression rapturous.

"Wow," she breathed, turning her hands over as if seeing them for the first time. "I can't believe how *good* I feel."

Heather beamed. "You're an angel, Mom!"

Jill laughed, half-crying, half-singing. "I guess I am."

By the time they had finished, a small crowd had gathered near the edge of the airfield. Half a dozen people stood watching in stunned fascination, two of them already filming with shaky phones.

"Can you turn me into an angel?" Heather asked hopefully, her light-brown eyes wide with anticipation.

Lexi glanced at Jill for permission. Jill's expression softened into a radiant smile as she pulled her daughter into a tight embrace. Quicksilver tears slid down her cheeks and splashed onto Heather's neck.

The change was immediate—and spectacular. Heather gasped as her skin cleared and her extra weight melted away, her clothes suddenly hanging loose around her new, graceful frame.

"I probably should've warned you," Lexi said wryly. "Angel tears reshape your body to its ideal state before your spirit finishes translating."

"I want to vanquish evil," Heather said breathlessly.

Light rippled over her body in response. Lexi felt a flicker of satisfaction—finally, someone younger than her. As the glow subsided, Heather blinked against the dazzle, taking in the feel of her new body. She was still recognizably herself—barely. Her face was now flawless and symmetrical, her lavender eyes glowing with an inner light that made her strikingly beautiful.

Mandy stepped closer and handed Heather her phone with the rear camera on.

Heather stared at her reflection, her eyes wide and a hand clapped over her mouth. Then a slow, joyous smile spread across her transformed face.

One of the airfield employees hesitantly approached, his eyes almost painfully hopeful. "Um... I don't suppose you'd be willing to do that for me?"

Lexi shared a look with Mandy, then shrugged. "Might as well."

Twenty minutes later, they were finally able to continue their journey. Lexi sighed and decided to just make a portal. They would never reach Mary at the rate they were moving.

She opened a portal to the location she felt Mary's consciousness glowing in the web of psychic energy overlaying the mortal realm.

She stood in front of the portal, staring at what her eyes were seeing but her mind wasn't believing.

Mary was in a large bed, and she wasn't alone.

There was a tall, male angel with archangel wings. They were both naked and doing *it*. Neither of the angels had seen her, so focused were they on what they were doing. Feeling a steel weight drop into her stomach, she closed the gateway.

She felt Mandy pull her into a comforting hug from behind, but it didn't register. She had been so *sure* she and Mary would be together, with their own eternity to cherish. Mary had been her salvation when she was a child, and again when Aria had vanished. Should she have gone with Mary and left Clarice on her own? Would things have worked out differently? She knew, even if she could be sure they would have, she still wouldn't have left Clarice behind.

Hot tears formed in her eyes as she accepted that the fantasy she had created in her mind of the two of them living out eternity side by side was just that—a fantasy.

"I'm so sorry," Mandy whispered sympathetically.

Lexi let out a wail and turned, falling into Mandy's arms. She felt the weight in her stomach spread out as she looked at an eternity of solitude. She couldn't imagine herself with anyone else. Clarice had been the only person she could have ever seen herself with besides Mary, and she was taken. Twice.

There was a ripple in the space around her, and suddenly Aria, Calypso, and Clarice were there, surrounding her with concern on their faces. Clarice stared at Mandy for a moment, clearly speaking telepathically.

"I'm so sorry, Lexi," Clarice whispered as tears formed in her own eyes. She took her from Mandy's arms, pulling her close.

The words detonated something inside her. Lexi clung to her and wept—racking, ugly sobs that came from the deepest places of her soul. She sobbed into Clarice's shoulder, weeping bitterly for the future she had been denied. The tears just kept coming as she revisited all the memories she had of Mary in her early teenage years. She felt the horror and self-loathing of her years in captivity, subjected to the whims of the powerful and twisted. The sudden hope as she was reunited with Mary in her transcendent state. She had been so sure her happily ever after had finally arrived.

Even as her heart hit rock bottom, she was self-aware enough to realize she had been making some huge assumptions. Mary had been a person filled with compassion and sympathy, but there had never been any hint of romance in their time together. At some level, deep in her soul, she had known that. It was the reason she had never tried to kiss her. She had convinced herself they just needed time and companionship. She had deluded herself and probably put Mary in an uncomfortable place. Her perceptive friend had probably known of her feelings the entire time.

"I'm such an *idiot,*" Lexi muttered as she clung to Clarice like a lifeline.

"You're the hottest idiot I've ever seen," Clarice told her playfully, her eyes shining with tears of sympathy.

Lexi could feel Clarice's overwhelming love engulf her through the spirit link. She remembered seeing Clarice's inner spirit, that place of ultimate beauty. The pain in her heart lessened slightly as she realized that to be loved by the goddess in front of her meant she would never be alone in the halls of eternity. She desperately clung to that lifeline, holding on to the image of Clarice's inner spirit and the love she could even now feel pouring into her.

Slowly, her wracking sobs subsided. She felt Aria and Calypso's boundless love through the bond as well, confirming she would never be *truly* alone.

Lexi felt the soft press of Mandy's aura brushing against her own—tentative, untrained, but full of warmth. Aria's savior. In the glow of that fragile compassion, Lexi saw how brightly Mandy's spirit burned, pure and unguarded.

Her sorrow and heartache were suddenly replaced by overwhelming gratitude for the beautiful angels who had pulled her into their hearts. She staggered as the power of her gratitude left her dizzy with wonder. They had shown up to be with her the *second* they felt her pain. They had pulled her out of a literal hell and made her a part of their family—even linking their spirits with hers. Whatever she may have lost with Mary, it paled in comparison to what she had gained with these three angels.

"I love you all *so much,*" Lexi whispered fiercely.

"You'll never be alone, Lexi," Clarice said softly. "We will *always* be with you."

"That's right," Mandy added brightly. "I'm immortal now, so you're stuck with me, too. I know it doesn't fix everything, but I'm so glad I met you. You've become such a huge part of my new life that I don't know what I'd do without you."

Lexi managed a small, shaky laugh. "That actually is comforting. Did you major in psychology or something? Because making me feel wanted is exactly what I need."

"I do need you," Mandy said, her voice low and trembling. Her lavender eyes glowed with warmth—and something deeper. "Since the moment you taught me to fly, I've felt this connection. Maybe we knew each other before, maybe not... but I know you're special to me. I need you."

Lexi froze. The hollow ache in her chest flared—and filled. The emptiness became heat, and the heat became desire. She looked at Mandy in a new light, breath catching as something electric arced between them.

Then Clarice grinned and waggled her eyebrows, the eternal saboteur of solemn moments. Lexi broke into helpless laughter, and the others joined her, the tension unraveling into bright, chaotic joy.

When Lexi finally recovered from her manic humor attack, she stepped up close to Mandy and stared into her lavender eyes, seeing the same longing she felt. "We still haven't unlocked your antigravity ability," Lexi said softly.

Mandy's eyes widened when she sensed the change. She looked at Lexi's lips, her lavender gaze darting back to meet golden eyes, her breath quickening. Lexi wasn't sure she had the courage to initiate a kiss on her own, but she felt so much confidence and affirmation flowing through the bond that she was able to push past her fear.

She looked at Mandy's slightly parted lips. They looked soft, inviting. She looked back up into Mandy's eyes, knowing how vulnerable her own eyes must look in that moment.

Mandy smiled seductively, dimples flashing and flooding Lexi with heat. Mandy leaned forward slowly, eyes never leaving Lexi's.

The world dropped away. Lexi felt a heady rush like falling upward, heat exploding in her stomach and racing through her meridians. She clung to Mandy, molding herself against her, the kiss deepening until the air itself seemed to hum. A low moan escaped her throat, and the sound only fanned the fire.

When they finally broke apart, Lexi realized her feet weren't touching the ground. Mandy looked down in wonder, then back up to find Lexi's eyes glowing with the same intoxicating hunger.

"Our work here is done," Clarice announced with mock solemnity, raising a hand in salute. A second later, the three angels vanished—leaving them suspended in midair, weightless, breathless, and burning with passion.

7 – The Purging Room

Aria sighed in relief as they reappeared in the starry void, smiling at Clarice and Calypso.

Clarice exhaled explosively. "I'm glad you brought Mandy back with you. She's saved our bacon twice now."

"Yeah, she really is a gem," Aria agreed warmly. "We should probably congratulate Lucifer on a job well done finding her."

"Good job, Satan," Clarice grinned, holding up her fingers like horns.

Aria froze as her imagination painted a fresh image in the gallery of her mind—Clarice in a devil outfit, black wings, and far too little fabric. Heat flooded her cheeks, and she jerked her gaze away. Pointlessly, of course. The spirit link tattled on everything.

Clarice's mind brushed hers, all playful curiosity. "Come on, sharing is caring," she purred.

Crimson-faced, Aria groaned, "It's so *embarrassing*!"

Clarice vanished—then reappeared pressed against her, their lips inches apart. "Show me," she breathed, her voice like melted chocolate.

Aria's brain short-circuited. Her heart tripped over itself as the image burst through her mind again: Clarice, horns, tail, and that smirk that promised holy disaster.

Clarice's delighted laugh shattered the tension. "I love the way your mind works," she teased, flashing a grin toward Calypso. "Devil horns are my new call sign."

As she stepped back, Aria felt a ripple of desire bounce through the bond—then multiply when Calypso caught the mental picture. Aria quickly shoved her thoughts away before the feedback loop could spiral into something... awkward.

They had learned, too late, that their shared link didn't diminish with distance. They had *also* discovered that if two of them felt the same thing, it fed back and amplified. And if a feedback loop reached Lexi mid-whatever she was doing, things grew very awkward very quickly—for Lexi, anyway. They all remembered the moaning mess she had become when the three of them had stopped at a neutron star thirty megaparsecs from Earth, hoping the distance would blunt their shared sensations—it hadn't.

Calypso's voice cut in, calm and grounding. "I'm very curious about Mandy's counterpart from this reality," she mused, a clear attempt to guide them away from erotic thoughts of devil Clarice. "We should make a point of looking her up when we're finished."

"Speaking of finishing..." Aria's gaze fixed on the pale sphere ahead of them, orbiting Gliese 12b. "Do you want to do the honors, or shall I?"

"I'll take this one," Calypso offered, balancing her harp on her foot. It looked absurdly delicate against the endless stars.

The void wasn't empty to her eyes. The cosmos was an infinite lattice of energy connecting stars, planets, and the spaces between, every line humming like a living instrument.

Calypso plucked a short, haunting sequence on her harp. The notes shimmered through the vacuum, resonating on frequencies that had nothing to do with sound. The moon shuddered, then unraveled into pure potential, dissolving like frost under sunlight.

Aria shivered at the raw, terrifying power that no mortal mind could safely hold. They were rewriting the geometry of existence with music and intent—she wasn't sure they even needed to play the instruments, so long as they held them.

A cluster of ships detached from the planet's Lagrange stations, engines flaring as they closed the distance. The vessels were sleek, metallic, and armed. So far, every spacefaring civilization they had met had turned out to be demonic or under demonic rule. Some worlds were barely past fire and stone tools; others built empires among the stars. It all seemed to depend on how indulgent their particular demon overlord was feeling.

"Looks like they noticed," Clarice said dryly, as a burst of energy lanced toward them. She flicked her wrist dramatically and opened a portal in its path, and the blast vanished harmlessly into deep space. "Rude."

Aria's lips curved into a grin. "They really are trigger-happy, aren't they?"

"Demons, am I right?" Clarice asked laconically.

Aria eyed her sister critically. "What's with the hand-waving when you're opening portals?" she asked, waving her hands demonstrably.

Clarice gave her a long-suffering look. "It's a matter of style, Aria. If you're going to stomp around with godlike powers breaking the laws of nature, you have to do it with style—otherwise, nobody'll take us seriously."

Aria exchanged glances with Calypso, then burst out laughing. It was so good to have her sister back.

With a flamboyant flick of her wrist, Clarice opened a new portal, and the three Seraphim streaked through it, leaving behind a cluster of confused demons.

They spent several days teleporting through the galaxy, vaporizing moon after moon like a cosmic Pac-Man. Near the galactic core, they finally found something different—a world that didn't stink of demonic corruption.

Calypso stared down at the planet uneasily. "I'm getting a strange feeling from this place," she announced with a troubled frown. "The ambient psychic field's worse than any of the others. It's... polluted, but not demonic."

A dozen angels appeared around them in a flash of light, forming a circle. They carried everything from glowing blades to advanced plasma rifles. One aimed directly at Calypso's chest.

Aria wrinkled her nose. The stench hit her instantly—the same horrid scent demons emitted. Were these angels, or something wearing the label?

"There's going to be trouble if you keep that gun pointed at her," Aria said, her voice low and edged with authority.

The circle didn't waver, several of them even sneering. One of them floated closer, pulling a coil of glowing rope from his belt. "Hands behind your back," he ordered. "We can remove them if that makes it easier."

Aria recognized the language, though her mind translated it as English. The tone, though—that was universal.

"Don't say I didn't warn you," she threatened, her Seraph voice resonating like a divine undertone. The lead angel hesitated, his eyes narrowing. "If this is how you treat your own kind," she added dangerously, "then maybe I do prefer the demons."

He jerked his hand up, and the rifleman fired.

Clarice moved faster than thought, a beam of angel fire intercepting the shot mid-air. Her eyes flared again as she vaporized the weapon in a single pulse. Aria vaporized several more weapons the moment they were raised.

"The next asshat to attack one of us gets vaporized," Clarice snarled, her eyes glowing with fury.

"In case you missed that," Aria translated, "the next asshat to attack gets atomized."

The circle wavered, fear replacing arrogance as they slowly backed away.

"Now," Aria said, her voice a chord of command, "you're going to explain who you are, why you're capturing angels, and why you reek worse than demons."

The Dominions said nothing—but she could feel their shock. Dominions weren't supposed to be here. They hated stepping outside the light realms' dense energy. So what in the hell—or heaven—were they doing in a mortal world?

The angels hovered in silence, the space thick with indecision. They were realizing too late that Aria and her companions weren't their equals.

One Dominion sneered and raised a wand. A wave of darkness dropped like a curtain, blotting out light and sound. "We've developed some new weapons to deal with belligerent Cherubim bitches. You should have stayed in the light realms."

To Aria's spiritual sight, the world didn't dim. She saw it for what it was—a swarm of parasitic shadows, psychic leeches trying to drain them of their radiance. They latched onto her aura and immediately shriveled, unable to consume the torrent of energy radiating from her spirit.

Calypso plucked a single note on her harp. The sound reverberated down to the most fundamental particles of matter. The darkness evaporated, burning away the parasites in a ripple of light.

The Dominions screamed as the divine harmonic shredded the layers of their essence, peeling at their souls like fire through silk.

Aria flashed forward, seizing the wand-bearer by the throat and hauling him up until his eyes met hers. "We've been patient," she said evenly, her voice vibrating through dimensions. "But patience has its limits. Start talking, Doriken, before I rewrite reality with you as a carbuncle."

The sneer vanished, replaced by a look of terror. "You... you're *dead*," he choked. "They destroyed you!"

Clarice floated closer, her expression a mix of amusement and fury. "Ah, so you do remember us," she said with a cheerful smile that never reached her eyes.

Aria blinked—Clarice was suddenly speaking the same tongue the Dominions had used. "I suppose it's no surprise that you volunteered to play in the mortality zoo, Doriken," Clarice continued grimly. "I remember when you volunteered to be a guardian angel for humans so you could make them suffer more exquisitely. You make demons look compassionate in comparison. I wonder what kind of horror show we'll find in this system with a piece of excrement like you in a position of authority. Pretty bad if the stench of your soul is anything to go by."

Calypso drifted beside Clarice, her expression unreadable but her aura cold enough to freeze sunlight. "I remember him," she said icily, and the temperature of the void seemed to drop. "I'm sure he was ecstatic when he thought we were gone for good. Well, Doriken, I have some bad news for you. Reality's about to change drastically, and your Seraphim will have no part in the new paradigm. On the other hand, I have some good news for you."

Doriken's expression curdled into something between fear and hatred. Aria's fingers tightened around his throat as shards of memory clawed their way up from the depths—complaints from angels who had endured his "experiments" in mortality, their spirits scarred and trembling even after ascension.

"The good news, Doriken," Calypso continued in a conversational tone, "is that you won't be around to see any of these changes. Clarice?"

Clarice smiled grimly at the vermin in Aria's grip, then blasted him with angel fire. He screamed in terror as it struck him in the face. A second later, he sublimated into ethereal energy.

Aria turned to face the remaining Dominions. They were frozen in shock at the realization of who they faced. Aria remembered her confrontation with the demon lord at the Tree of Life when he had tried to teleport away. A hint of a memory rose from the depths of her soul, and she laid a complex web of dissonant energy, destabilizing the cosmic circuits in the region that would jam any attempts at teleportation.

Clarice and Calypso moved in beside Aria. She could feel the resistance—several of the Dominions pushing futilely against the dissonant web. When teleportation failed, a few tried to flee the old-fashioned way.

"STOP!"

Calypso's voice rang out like a chord of creation. The word hung in reality like a commandment. The universe paused to listen. Every Dominion froze mid-flight, limbs locked in divine stasis. Even the light between atoms seemed to hold its breath.

The three Seraphim drifted forward in silence, studying the remaining Dominions. Aria read the names written in their souls, each one dredging up fresh memories. It was obvious why demons weren't controlling this world—there were worse things than demons.

"I think any angels who came here for help are regretting it," Aria said, her voice flat with disgust. "No point questioning them. Let's end this and see what's left to save."

Clarice nodded, her mouth twisted with revulsion. "We should've done this ages ago. Mercy was our biggest mistake. How many suffered because we let them live?"

Aria spread her hands and clapped.

A shockwave of fury unspooled. The flash ripped outward, tearing through the Dominions like a tidal wave of pure light. Their bodies disintegrated, and their spirits unraveled into a cloud of potential. The blast wave rolled onward until it reached the moon, swallowing it whole. In seconds, the massive soul trap dissolved into motes of energy, then nothing.

"Wow, Aria." Clarice whistled, staring at the empty void where the moon had been. "Guess we didn't need the divine instruments after all."

"Yeah," Aria breathed, staring in disbelief. "That was... unexpected. I'm kind of terrified of what we can do now."

"I'm not," Clarice muttered darkly. "The memories I have of those bastards make me grateful for every scrap of power we gain. As soon as I saw his name, it all came flooding back. The cult of assholes who tried to convince us that increasing the level of pain people suffered would make them enjoy the return to eternity more. It's no surprise none of *them* wanted to experience mortality."

Calypso's expression dimmed, shadowed with dread. "I'm scared of what we'll find down there," she whispered.

That hint of fear hit Aria like a spark to dry tinder. Rage coiled hot in her chest. No one—nothing—had the right to make Calypso's light flicker like that.

Clarice's voice softened, but her eyes still burned. "Then let's start fixing it. These people have suffered long enough. It's past time they experienced something wonderful."

Aria nodded to Calypso, and together they dropped through the planet's cloud layer. The world below emerged in shades of misery. Dozens of pyramids lined the shores of a churning ocean, their stone flanks slick with grime. Not far inland, a sprawling city squatted under a haze of greasy black smoke. Hundreds of smokestacks belched filth into the sky. The buildings—uniform, soot-stained, and devoid of color—looked as though someone had built despair out of concrete.

There was no sign of vehicles in the streets, no horses or other beasts of burden. People trudged on foot, dragging carts by hand. There was no hint of invention here, no spark of progress beyond the squat structures and blackened smokestacks.

Aria expanded her awareness, scanning the land. She found no life beyond the insects and rodents that scurried between the shadows. The psychic field of the planet pressed against her mind like a wet shroud—thick with fear, saturated with hopelessness.

"Let's talk to someone and see what's happening here," Clarice said quietly. Her voice had lost its usual mischief, stripped bare by what she was sensing.

Aria nodded, and the three of them descended into the heart of the city.

It was a place framed by monotony. The streets ran in rigid lines between buildings so drab they seemed to have been sculpted from apathy itself. Every window was the same size, every door the same shape—architecture designed by a mind that had outlawed imagination.

The people moved like ghosts through the gray corridors of their lives, all dressed in identical coveralls. Their eyes were dull, their steps perfectly synchronized in a rhythm of submission. The place was like a mausoleum that still breathed, without the pulse or spirit of a true civilization.

When the angels touched down, the people collapsed like marionettes with their strings cut. Faces pressed to the dirt, they remained bowed, bodies trembling.

Aria's temper flared. Whatever faith these people had been taught, it wasn't love—it was servitude. She remembered Carcelonia and Grodek claiming angels made demons seem sweet, but seeing the groveling humans suddenly made it real. Her whitewashed image of angels being the embodiment of love and compassion was quickly fading, replaced by the sneering face of Doriken and his ilk.

She walked to the nearest woman and knelt before her, keeping her voice soft. "Excuse me, Serena. Could you tell me the name of this city?"

The woman flinched at her touch. "Aberjan, Exalted One." The words came out strangled, like a confession given under duress. She stayed kneeling, waiting for punishment that didn't come.

Aria placed a hand on Serena's back and poured her aura of love into the woman. Light and warmth flowed through the contact, soft as a sunrise. Serena gasped, the fear on her face replaced by wonder. Aria kept the flow steady, knowing the moment she withdrew, terror would reclaim Serena.

"Serena, I'm from another world," Aria said gently. "We came to make life better for the humans here. We destroyed a dozen renegade angels who were enslaving this planet—they were monsters, not guardians. We're not like them. You don't remember yet, but you're an angel, too. You were trapped here, the same way I was trapped in mortality. If you wish it, I can restore you."

She linked to Serena's mind, brushing against the trembling lattice of her thoughts.

"They're trying to trick me into blasphemy," Serena thought hopelessly. *"If I deny her, I'll be condemned. If I agree, I'll still be condemned. There's no way out. There's never a way out.*

Aria's heart broke for the woman. No amount of divine warmth could undo a lifetime of conditioning in a single breath.

"I've got this," Clarice said softly, stepping forward.

Clarice knelt and gently lifted the woman's face from the dirt, guiding her chin until wide, terrified eyes met her own. A single glowing tear slid down her cheek, catching on her smile before she leaned forward, pressing her face softly against Serena's.

"Why does she weep?" Serena's thoughts flickered like a candle in the dark. *"Her eyes are so warm, I could almost believe..."*

The tear soaked into her skin, and Serena gasped as light rippled across her features. Lines softened, gray strands retreated, and the years fell away in seconds. She stared at Clarice in speechless wonder, too stunned to breathe.

"I need you to repeat after me," Clarice said softly, her voice a gentle caress. "I will vanquish evil."

Serena swallowed hard, trembling. "I... I will vanquish evil," she whispered, the words barely audible.

"What is this feeling?" Serena thought in growing awe. *"Am I being judged? But it doesn't hurt... it feels... beautiful."*

Aria watched as the transformation unfolded. Radiance charged Serena's meridians, spreading outward until her entire being burned with a divine glow. Her eyes flashed with blinding light—and when it faded, an angel stood where a terrified woman had knelt.

"You're an angel once more," Aria told her, smiling gently. "Nothing can harm you now. You're free. Do you believe me?"

Serena nodded, her eyes shimmering with silver tears and wonder. The love surging through her was so vast she could hardly contain it.

A voice, cold and merciless, cracked through the air. "What's going on here?"

Aria turned toward the sound. Even before she saw him, she could smell him—his soul reeked like spoiled meat, rancid and crawling with malice.

Serena immediately dropped back to the cobblestones, forehead pressed to the ground. Aria bent down and took her trembling hands, lifting her upright again. "Stay with me," she said gently. Serena's eyes darted in panic, love and terror warring inside her.

"I'll show you what happens to sadistic angels like him," Aria grated.

"Who the hell are you—" the newcomer began, but his words strangled in his throat as Aria blurred forward. In less than a heartbeat, her hand was around his neck, lifting him off the ground as if he weighed nothing at all.

He was an archangel, his great white wings flaring out and beating futilely. His robes—self-righteous and pompous—gleamed like the costume of a hypocrite.

"Hello, Drion," Aria said with quiet menace. "There's been a change in management, and I'm afraid we're downsizing. I can smell what's left of your disgusting spirit. There's no place for monsters like you in this realm. Goodbye."

Recognition dawned in his eyes, followed by pure terror. He thrashed, wings beating helplessly. Aria's eyes ignited as she unleashed a blast of angel fire into his face. He vanished in a burst of incandescence, fading into motes of light that drifted on the air.

The people on the street missed the entire show. They had remained motionless, faces pressed to the stones, afraid to look up in the presence of angels. But Serena had seen everything. Clarice kept a firm arm around her shoulders, making sure she didn't look away.

"See, Serena?" Clarice said brightly, her smile disarmingly cheerful. "That's what happens to angels who harm the innocent. We're going to clean house and rid this world of the monsters tormenting you."

"Who are you?" Serena asked softly, wonder and disbelief warring in her trembling voice.

"I'm Clarice," she answered, her sudden smile like a declaration of hope. "This is Aria and Calypso. We're Seraphim—the creators. Four of our number betrayed us and trapped you here, forcing your souls through mortal lives again and again. We're ending that now. We're going to restore everyone to their angelic heritage. We'd like to enlist your help, if you're willing."

Serena hesitated. "What do you need of me?"

"Do you remember when my tear touched you?" Clarice asked.

Serena nodded, the barest hint of a smile curving her lips.

"That's how it begins," Clarice explained. "Anyone who touches one of your tears and says, 'I will vanquish evil,' will become an angel again. If every new angel helps the next person awaken, your whole world will transform before long."

"And by the way," Aria added with an encouraging grin, "angels don't need food, water, or sleep. You can't feel pain, and nothing can hurt you. Toss you off a mountain, and you'd just bounce away laughing."

"Really?" Serena gasped, hope shining through the years of fear. Then her brow furrowed. "But... didn't you hurt those other angels?"

"We're the creators," Calypso explained with a confident smile. "We have the power to both create and destroy."

Aria rested a glowing hand on Serena's shoulder. "Can we ask you something, Serena? Why is everyone so afraid of angels? What were they doing to you?"

Serena's face paled. "They punish us. For everything. For anything. They say it purges sin from our souls. There are rooms—purging rooms—where they... hurt people. They say if we die with sin, we'll spend eternity there. Some even ask to go, thinking it'll make them pure."

Clarice's jaw tightened. "Sounds like the Inquisition on crack," she muttered. Her voice softened, and Clarice drew her into a gentle embrace. "I'm so sorry, Serena. You've suffered long enough. It's over. Convert as many as you can. We'll find every one of those sadistic bastards and erase them from existence."

Serena melted into Clarice's arms, a smile of wonder enhancing her stunning features.

A nearby man lifted his head, eyes flickering between fear and fragile hope.

"I think Linus is ready," Aria said, nodding toward him. "Can you manage another teardrop?"

"I think it would be hard *not* to," Serena answered thickly, tears of happiness shining in her lavender eyes. "Thank you, *so* much."

"One last gift," Aria murmured, smiling as she joined the embrace. Two golden tears met between them, merging into a flash of blinding light. Serena gasped as her coveralls shredded and great, gleaming wings burst free from her back.

"Damn," Clarice muttered, squinting at the damage. "I always forget wings are hell on clothes." She reached into a small portal and rummaged for a moment before pulling out a folded shirt and a pair of jeans. "Here—try something from my world. I guarantee it's more comfortable than whatever grim uniform you've been stuck in."

Serena blushed furiously, glancing around at the crowd still staring in awe.

"Come on," Clarice said gently, opening a shimmering portal. "You can change in here."

Serena froze when she saw Clarice's room in the cabin, bathed in warm light and filled with colors she didn't have words for. "Where is this place?" she breathed. "It's so *beautiful*."

Aria felt a pang deep in her chest. How long had this woman lived without beauty, without even the idea of it?

"This was my room back when I was human," Clarice explained, smiling faintly. "If you look up at the stars tonight, my world orbits one of them—a tiny point of light, impossibly far away."

Serena's eyes went wide. "You live among the stars?"

"Well," Clarice said, grinning, "you do, too. I'll show you—after we finish vaporizing the rest of the asshats running your planet."

Serena gave a nervous laugh and stepped through the portal. She vanished for several minutes, returning beside Clarice, now radiant in her new clothes.

While she had been gone, Aria moved through the crowd, touching each trembling back, leaving behind glowing tears that turned fear into light. By the time Clarice and Serena reappeared, eight new angels stood smiling where frightened humans had knelt.

Serena stared at them in surprise, then grinned with dawning joy, realizing she wouldn't be alone in rebuilding her world. She was radiant in her new clothes, blushing lightly under Clarice's look of frank appreciation.

"See?" Clarice quipped. "All it took was freedom and a decent outfit. Those coveralls were practically a hate crime. They might as well have been celestial Mormon underwear."

"Okay, time to go—" Aria stopped mid-sentence, her nose wrinkling as the reek of corruption filled the air. She looked skyward. Half a dozen Archangels were descending through the clouds, their presence filling the air with cloying rot.

When the new arrivals spotted the anomaly where the newly minted angels stood, they banked and swooped down. Several of the new angels dropped to their knees automatically, but Serena remained upright—barely.

"Hello, little peasants," a blond Archangel said in a tone sweet enough to curdle blood. "Looks like it's time for you to visit the purging room. I'll *personally* oversee the cleansing of your sins."

"Good luck with that, jackass," Clarice shot back derisively. "They aren't human anymore."

The pleasant smile vanished from Meldin's face when he noticed Clarice. An unpleasant smirk appeared on his face as he pulled out the same kind of wand Doriken had wielded. "I see we have some visiting angels from a neighboring world," he stated with a welcoming smile. "Allow me to be the first to welcome you—"

He broke off as the wand vanished in a flash of angel fire. While the energy parasites couldn't hurt Seraphim, Aria was sure the same wasn't true for the new angels. The other Archangels scrambled to draw their own, which were just as quickly vaporized.

"I'm glad you saved us the trouble of hunting you down, Meldin," Clarice purred, a predatory smile sharpening her face. "You've just made our day a little shorter."

Meldin took a hesitant step back, his eyes darting from Clarice's golden stare to Aria's furious glare. "We didn't realize there were... other angels nearby," he said, his voice trembling.

"When I'm done," Clarice said, her smile widening into something feral, "there won't be. Do you have any idea how bad your rotten soul stinks, Meldin? Well, I suppose it doesn't matter anymore. Goodbye."

He blanched. "Wait—please! We were forced! The Dominions made us do it! We didn't have a choice!"

"Meldin, it's time for you to visit the purging room," Clarice threw his words back into his teeth. "Where I will *personally* oversee the purging of your sins. I'm afraid begging won't save your worthless ass this time, Meldin. You have more demon in you than demons do. Enough monologuing. Goodbye."

He spun to flee, wings flaring—only to be erased mid-motion by Aria's angel fire, his body dissolving before his scream could form.

The others fell just as fast, vanishing in a burst of light. When it was over, the street was quiet again. The newborn angels slowly rose, their awe mingling with guilt and confusion. Aria couldn't blame them. They had been born in fear; it would take more than ascendance to unlearn submission.

Clarice dusted her hands together and glanced northward. "Okay, let's go find some more assholes to vaporize."

Aria smiled grimly, wings flaring. She opened her senses to the horizon, tasting the foul tang of more tainted souls. "I'm so ready."

8 – The Light Realm

Clarice studied the pyramids as they approached from the air. “What’s up with these?” she asked, squinting suspiciously. “I doubt they’re burying pharaohs on this world.”

“They are power stations,” Calypso said after a moment, her eyes glowing faintly as she examined the structures with her spiritual sight. “I can see electrical currents moving through them. Aquifers lie beneath, carrying water into the ocean. The water’s resonance is charging the quartz and granite, producing a discharge that feeds the cables threaded through the passages. That is what is powering those factories.”

Clarice groaned. “And another crazy fringe theory turns out to be true. At this point, I shouldn’t even be surprised.”

The stench of spirit rot assailed her a moment later, wafting up from a squat, gray building on the city’s edge. The faint psychic wail beneath the sound of machinery told her what it was before she landed.

“This must be one of their purging centers,” Clarice said darkly, grimacing as the scent of blood and decay rolled over her. “Let’s go purge it.”

She shoved open the heavy wooden door and strode into a bare antechamber. A man in gray coveralls scrambled to his knees behind a desk, pressing his forehead to the floor. She didn’t bother acknowledging him. Another door led deeper, into a hallway lined with iron doors every twenty feet. The screams were unmistakable now—raw and desperate, like nails on the chalkboard of her soul.

“Calypso, go with Aria,” Clarice ordered briskly. “I’ll take this one.”

“I can go alone,” Calypso insisted, chin lifting. The spirit link pulsed with reluctant determination.

“Nope, you’re coming with me,” Aria said, looping an arm through hers. “You handle the healing. We’ll handle the killing.”

Calypso sighed but nodded, her aura dimming slightly. Clarice caught the flicker of conflict in her—the purest of them, dragged into a chamber built for cruelty. Clarice clenched her fists. However much she despised these sadistic angels, the thought of Calypso staining her light with their filth made her sick.

She vaporized the first door and stepped into a medieval nightmare. The air reeked of iron and despair. Implements of torture lined the walls—spiked vices, shackles, benches scarred by centuries of agony.

A nine-year-old girl was bound to a chair, a vice slowly driving a bolt through her wrist. Another pair crushed her legs, bones disjointed where metal had already broken skin.

Tears blurred Clarice's vision. Then she saw the angel standing behind the girl—and the tears turned to fire.

She incinerated the bolts in an instant, white heat flashing across the room. The Archangel's face morphed from surprise to fury, then to sudden, helpless fear as she flooded the chamber with her jamming field. No teleporting. No escape.

He backed against the far wall, his eyes darting like a trapped animal. She wanted him to hurt—to taste every scream he had ever caused—but the girl's whimpers cut through her vengeance. The longer she lingered, the longer the child would suffer.

Her glare hardened. One beam of angel fire erased him from existence.

Clarice spun back to the girl. Lyra's body was a map of agony; every breath accompanied by a whimper of pain. Clarice pushed her aura outward until the only thing the child could feel was love.

"Lyra, you're safe now," she said softly, masking the grief clawing at the edges of her awareness. "Calypso will be here in a moment."

Calypso appeared before the words finished leaving her mouth. Her eyes went wide, and golden tears slid down her cheeks as she knelt beside the chair. Healing words poured from her lips, runes forming in quick succession.

Clarice caught the edges of that language, tantalizingly close to understanding. She wished, not for the first time, that she could heal, that she wouldn't always need Calypso to mend what monsters broke.

Lyra's shuddering eased. Bones knitted, skin smoothed, and her pain vanished like a cry on the wind. Calypso wrapped her arms around the girl, golden tears spilling onto her hair.

"Calypso!" Aria's voice echoed from down the hall. "Need healing!"

Calypso let out a strangled sob and blurred away.

Clarice brushed a lock of hair from Lyra's forehead. "Say this for me, sweetheart. 'I will vanquish evil.'"

Lyra's lips trembled, then she repeated the words in a faint whisper. Light rippled through her, soft and pure. Clarice squeezed her shoulder, then turned away, hurrying to the next room of horror.

There was an old man in the room, lifeless on a large table he had been chained to. If she had a stomach, she would've puked everything up as she observed the blood and guts littering the room. *"At least the soul trap is gone,"* she thought, though it brought her small comfort. *"He'll be going back to the light realm instead of being recycled into this hell."*

There were eight additional victims. Her anger rose in sync with her horror as she witnessed the atrocities *angels* had inflicted on the humans of this world. She was beginning to understand why they had made the decree that *all* angels, both high and low, experience mortality. The immortal angels toyed with humans like domestic cats playing with mice. They felt no empathy or compassion, seeming to thrive on the power inflicting pain gave them.

"We need to move faster," Clarice told Aria and Calypso firmly. "We're going to have to start moving at full speed if we want to purge this planet of its parasites. I know we want to offer comfort and help, but we can't take longer than the moment it takes to destroy the angels and heal the humans before moving on to the next place. Too many will suffer while we console others if we don't speed things up."

"Agreed," Aria nodded, her eyes haunted. Calypso also nodded, tears streaming down her cheeks.

"Let's go," Clarice breathed, then poured every bit of power she had into speed.

They flashed in and out of buildings in a blur, leaving vaporized angels and healed, awakened humans in their wake. Even moving at high speed, it took over two days to rid the entire planet of angels. There were several billion people spread across three continents. They worked nonstop at speeds too fast for humans to see. The few angels who *could* see them were dead before they could process what they had seen.

As they finished cleansing the last house of horrors, Calypso collapsed onto the ground, her shoulders shaking with huge sobs as she finally had time to reconcile the nightmare they had witnessed. Aria knelt and drew Calypso into her arms, golden tears streaming down her cheeks. Clarice knelt with them, leaning her head against theirs, finally allowing her tears to flow.

"This is why they tried to unmake us," Clarice whispered, the realization cutting through her like a blade of light. "We knew the only way to stop angels from indulging their sadistic fantasies was to make them feel—to make them suffer, experience loss, and learn empathy. They didn't want change. They didn't want compassion. This is worse than anything demons have ever done. It has to end. There are too many worlds like this for us to fix one by one. We need all the divine instruments, and then we rewrite reality itself. No more of this cancer."

A portal shimmered open before them. Lexi burst through with Mandy close behind, both wide-eyed with alarm.

"What happened?" Lexi demanded, dropping to her knees and gripping Clarice's hands.

"Let me show you," Clarice murmured, her voice thin and trembling. "I don't have the words."

She linked minds with Lexi and Mandy, pouring the last two days of horror straight into their consciousness. Mandy's eyes darkened, sorrowful but not surprised. Lexi's tears came instantly, glittering as she squeezed Clarice's hands tighter.

"But—they were angels!" Lexi choked out, her voice shaking with disbelief. "How could angels do something so evil?"

"Now you know why we're at war for heaven," Clarice said bleakly. "They want to keep mortals as toys. They enjoy the torment. We wanted every angel to live as a mortal—to understand pain, empathy, and consequence. This is why they turned on us. These horrors aren't isolated. They're happening on billions of worlds—quintillions of souls trapped in the same nightmare, dying and reliving it over and over again."

Lexi's face drained of color as the scope sank in. Mandy covered her mouth, a sob escaping as silver tears spilled down her cheeks. Clarice could feel the despair trembling through her—fear disguised as sorrow.

Aria released Calypso and pulled Mandy into her arms, flooding her with warmth, love, and the pure pulse of hope.

"It's not hopeless," Clarice said softly, her voice steady now, brightening like the first hint of sunrise. "Today, we freed one planet. We destroyed thousands of soul traps. They fear us because they know we can fix everything. With the divine instruments, we can end the cycle. You saved Aria, Mandy. You kept us together. If this is a story—and honestly, it feels like one—you're one of the heroes. Don't you dare let the scale of the fight scare you off. We're going to fix this cosmos. The only question is how much ass we'll have to kick to do it."

Mandy let out a wet, startled laugh between sobs, pressing her face into Aria's shoulder as she breathed through it. Lexi smiled through her tears and placed a comforting hand on Mandy's back.

Clarice watched them with quiet satisfaction, warmth humming through the spirit link. Not bad, she thought. For an improvised pep talk about universal damnation, that was pretty damn good.

Calypso closed her eyes and took a breath, then began singing. It was one of the all-time favorites from her YouTube channel, a sublime anthem about struggle and redemption. It was hailed as saving more lives than antidepressants and therapy combined. Her voice carried a kind of alchemy, turning despair into defiance, coaxing sparks of hope to life in even the most broken hearts. It burned away the doubt and despair, replacing it with an indomitable resolve to live, to strive.

Mandy's tears slowed and then stopped as she was drawn into Calypso's vivid vision of a world where love and compassion flourished, and hope was always bright.

Clarice realized Mandy had probably never heard any of Calypso's music since coming to this reality. Her eyes were wide and full of sudden determination as she stared at Calypso in wonder. Calypso's harmonizing voices serenaded the air around them, adding weight and dimension to her words. When the song was over, there was no trace of defeat in Mandy's eyes. She looked ready to march on the Seraphim right then and there.

"*Wow!*" Mandy exclaimed in amazement. "That was the most transformative song I've *ever* heard."

"Now you know how she became the most famous musician in the world," Aria said with a proud grin. She beamed at Calypso, waves of love and respect radiating through the spirit link.

"Is it time to go to the light realms now?" Lexi asked expectantly, her eyes alight with anticipation.

"Yep," Clarice nodded with the ghost of a smile. "It sure is."

"I'm pretty curious about what this light realm looks like in person," Mandy declared excitedly, her positive energy fully recharged. "I wonder what it'll feel like."

"It is going to come as rather a shock," Calypso informed her with a wry smile. "The reason it is called the light realm is because of the abundance of ambient energy present there. By comparison, the mortal realm seems almost devoid of radiance."

Mandy blinked. "Hold on—you're saying this feeling right now, this fire in my meridians, is almost nothing compared to that?"

Calypso nodded with a small smile.

Mandy gaped. "Then it's going to freaking *incapacitate* me! How can there even *be* that much energy?"

Calypso laughed softly and pulled her into a hug. Then she opened herself and let her Seraph aura pour out like the sun unleashed.

Mandy's eyes glazed as she stared into the distance with a look of ecstasy. "Is this... what it feels like?" she whispered in awe.

"Yes," Calypso said gently. "One does grow accustomed to it after a time. The difficult part isn't going there—it's coming back."

"If this is what the lowest light realm feels like, how can anyone even survive the higher realms?" Mandy asked in disbelief.

"If we were to go straight to the highest realm now, we would be incapacitated for several weeks," Calypso admitted, glancing at the other three.

"It takes that long to acclimate to the denser light. Though, you know... that gives me an idea."

"What?" Clarice asked, slipping her arms around Calypso's waist.

"Our souls are linked," Calypso said thoughtfully, kissing Clarice's forehead. "What would happen if I were to ascend to a higher realm than the rest of you? Or if only a few of us did so? Would those who remained behind in the lower realm experience an influx of light through the spirit link?"

"That's easy enough to test," Clarice grinned, pausing to steal a kiss. "Two of us wait behind for a few minutes before following."

"I'm game," Aria grinned back excitedly. "I want to see how strong the link remains between realms, too." She paused and looked at Calypso curiously. "How much recall do you have of the light realms? You seem to be remembering quite a bit."

"Some of my memories returned after seeing Doriken," Calypso said, her mouth twisting with distaste at the mention of his name. "I recalled the energy disparities between realms, as well as some of the places we had visited while dealing with the Cult of the Pristine."

Clarice gasped as old memories surfaced. "I remember now..." she breathed softly. "The Cult of the Pristine. You just jogged some memories loose, Calypso."

Aria winced, pressing a hand to her temple as the memories resurfaced. "Those narcissistic cowards," she hissed. "They said we were corrupting the pure souls of angels by experiencing mortality. The assholes claimed that empathy and emotional development were a perversion of the natural order. They couldn't stand how happy the Ascended were when they returned, and things like compassion infuriated them."

Lexi frowned uneasily. "So what should we expect when we show up in the light realm? Are they going to attack us the second they realize we're... 'Ascended?'"

"The light realm is practically infinite," Calypso said, smiling as Aria moved behind Clarice and slipped her arms around her sister's waist. "It is highly unlikely we shall land anywhere near them."

Clarice let out a contented purr as she was hugged from both sides. "And even if we do end up in the middle of their territory, it won't matter," she said with a feral grin. "Anyone stupid enough to pick a fight will regret it."

Lexi tilted her head, curiosity replacing concern. "So what's it actually like? The light realm. Is it just... this place, but brighter? Stars, galaxies, all that jazz?"

Calypso shook her head. "Not even remotely." She reached out and linked their thought nodes, allowing images to flicker across their minds. "It is a plane of near-infinite dimensions. There is no distance, no true boundaries. Living things do exist there—plants, on occasion—but nothing reproduces, for there is no need. Everything is immortal, static until imagination gives it purpose and motion. The light is so dense that thought itself can become tangible. There is no weather, no oceans, no mountains—unless someone chooses to create them. The entire realm is a blank canvas for divine creativity."

Clarice's face darkened. "Which is exactly why the Cult of the Pristine lost their halos over the Ascended. Creative potential is the only real status angels have. For ages, the higher your creativity, the higher your status. Then the Ascended came back from mortality, and suddenly their potential had skyrocketed. It was like the gold rush all over again. Everyone wanted a taste of mortality to level up their creative potential."

Her expression soured, and Aria held her tighter. "And when they saw the change it brought—empathy, love, kindness—they panicked. They formed the Cult of the Pristine and tried to convince the Seraphim to ban all Ascended from the light realms."

"I'm guessing their demands fell on deaf ears since you'd all been through mortality too," Mandy guessed, studying the three of them with an odd expression.

"Not yet," Calypso said slowly, her eyes narrowing as she sifted through her own memories. "I do not yet possess full recall, but I am piecing fragments together. After a lengthy debate among the Seraphim, we decided that some of us should experience mortality firsthand to understand what was occurring below. Aria, Clarice, and I volunteered. When we returned... it was like a blind person discovering sight. We saw what we had been missing—what they had all been missing. We attempted to convince the rest of the Seraphim to incarnate alongside the other angels. As Ascended, we finally perceived how vile the angels' actions toward mortals truly were. Lucifer eventually incarnated. He rallied the Ascended and established laws to protect mortals. The most important of these decreed that any angel who intentionally harmed an innocent would fall—transforming into a demon."

"I'll just bet he did," Mandy muttered darkly.

Clarice blinked, releasing Calypso and turning to face Mandy curiously. "What do you mean?"

Mandy froze. Her eyes flickered, then widened as though surprised by her own words. "Sorry," she said quickly. "I don't even know where that came from."

Lexi appeared at her side in a heartbeat, her brow knit with concern. "You okay?"

"Yeah, I'm fine." Mandy smiled—too quickly, too bright. "Just shaken, that's all. You ready to go to the light realm? I'm so ready to see what heaven's like."

Lexi frowned, unconvinced.

Clarice exchanged a glance with Calypso and Aria. "*Something's off with her,*" she sent the thought.

Aria nodded imperceptibly. "Could be connected to her splinter reality. Whatever it is, we'll handle it."

Clarice suddenly grinned. "Alright, enough gloom. Who's ready to party in heaven?"

Lexi laughed, bouncing on her toes. "Is there anything else we should know before we enter the pearly gates?"

Calypso's expression grew serious. "Yes. Remember that within the light realms, thought shapes reality. The strength of one's will determines what is possible. Creative potential scales with class—and as Cherubim, you and Mandy shall possess enormous influence there."

"Will the other Seraphim sense us when we arrive?" Mandy asked, her voice steady but her aura flickering with unease.

"Without question," Calypso replied placidly. "The light realm is saturated with power, yet Seraphim and Cherubim draw upon it in enormous quantities. Between the five of us, we'll leave a signature they cannot ignore. They will not know precisely where we are—but they will know we are present."

"Then let's make an entrance," Lexi said, grinning. "I'm ready. Let's go to heaven!"

Calypso smiled fondly and opened a portal, a brilliance spilling through that made Lexi's eyes widen in awe. The horizon beyond was an endless expanse—flat and glimmering like salt under blinding light.

Mandy stepped closer, her expression half wonder, half something deeper. Recognition.

Clarice caught it, filing the moment away.

Aria shared a look with her, then turned to Calypso. "You go on ahead," she said lightly. "We'll follow in a minute. I want to see how the bond handles the jump between realms."

Clarice went through with Calypso and Mandy while Lexi lingered beside Aria. The portal shimmered shut behind them, leaving only endless white in every direction—an infinity of light without horizon or shadow.

Mandy staggered to a halt the instant she crossed over, her eyes as wide as teacups. A low moan escaped her lips, half wonder, half surrender, as the dense energy of the light realm flooded her immortal form.

Clarice exhaled a long, trembling breath as the power washed through her. She had forgotten what it felt like—pure, unfiltered radiance seeping into every fiber. It wasn't the supreme brilliance of the highest realm, but after lifetimes in mortal skin, it was close enough to paradise.

Beside her, Calypso tilted her face upward, her eyes closed as light cascaded across her luminous features. "It is so good to be back."

"Yeah," Clarice murmured, smiling faintly at Mandy's awe. "She's never felt this before. If she was born in the splinter reality as a new spirit, this is her first taste of real radiance. She doesn't have the soul memory the original Mandy would."

Mandy drew in a shaky breath, her voice hushed with reverence. "I had no idea it would feel like this. It's... more than I imagined."

"I can still feel them," Calypso said suddenly, relief brightening her tone. "Just as clearly as if they were here with us."

"Then the link is holding," Clarice said with satisfaction. "And judging by the euphoria coming from Aria and Lexi, I'd say they're enjoying themselves."

A portal rippled open beside them, spilling more light into the endless field. Aria stepped through first, serene and smiling, the higher-density energy wrapping around her like silk. Her smile deepened as she adjusted to the torrent.

Lexi followed and froze, eyes wide and lips parted in wonder. "It's... incredible," she whispered, staring into the infinite brightness as though she could see every secret in creation glowing just beneath the surface.

"So?" Clarice asked, eyes glinting with curiosity. "How did it compare?"

Aria smiled, radiant and a little dazed. "It was almost like we were already here, the way you two were channeling the energy back through the link. Lexi nearly passed out—she's probably getting more than she would naturally, since she's linked to three Seraphim."

Clarice smirked. "I'd call that a perk. She gets to feel everything her Seraphim feel."

Aria swatted her arm, cheeks pink. "Behave yourself. We're literally in heaven."

"I think we ought to disguise ourselves," Calypso suggested, shifting her form until her blazing aura dimmed and her human appearance returned. "Let us blend in—simply appear as ordinary angels."

Clarice studied her, fascinated by the shifting lattice of energy shaping Calypso's new form. A spark of recollection flickered—an old skill remembered. She reached inward, weaving the same pattern around herself until her aura condensed into a familiar human outline. "How's this?"

Calypso smiled, her eyes soft. "Exactly as you looked when I first met you. Still utterly gorgeous."

Clarice felt something catch in her chest. She stepped forward and drew Calypso into her arms. "You're dangerous when you talk like that," she murmured silkily.

Calypso froze, a blush rising like dawn. Clarice's breath quickened as she stared at the beautiful Seraph. She tilted her head and pressed her lips to Calypso's—just a thank-you, she told herself. But the light here had a way of magnifying everything, and the kiss deepened, slow and hungry, the air around them vibrating with shared desire.

She heard a pair of soft moans and suddenly remembered what the bond would be doing to Aria and Lexi. Her lips formed into a smile against Calypso's.

"We're *so* going to continue this conversation when this divine nonsense is behind us," Clarice promised Calypso with a final soft kiss.

9 – Cherubim Hunting

Aria nodded approvingly when Mandy flawlessly projected herself as a wingless angel.

"Much better," Calypso praised Mandy with a quick smile.

It had taken her nearly half an hour to master the fine-grained control needed to weave and sustain the disguise. The process would have been impossible without Calypso's direct psychic link feeding her the memory of how it was done.

As the newest angel in their ranks, Mandy still had the steepest learning curve, but Aria thought she was catching up fast. Then again, none of them were exactly seasoned. Four months of angelhood barely qualified them as celestial toddlers. Maybe not even that—more like newborn gods with training wheels.

"There," Aria said, grinning with satisfaction. "Now we look like regular angels. So, if we run into anyone, we can just tell them we're regular angels."

"Exactly," Clarice nodded solemnly. "Just regular angels, doing regular angel things, being regular as hell."

Calypso's lips quirked into a knowing smile. "Clarice, you could never be regular *anything*."

Aria couldn't argue with that. Clarice had that dangerous sparkle again—one that made Calypso flush with desire. A vacation was definitely in order once they finished overthrowing the celestial establishment. Clarice and Calypso had turned her into a moaning mess of incoherent bliss after destroying Earth's moon, and she longed to return the favor.

Clarice caught her staring and flashed a radiant smile that could have powered a sun.

"I missed those green eyes," Clarice said softly. "Not that your golden ones aren't stunning—but I grew up with the green ones. I'm glad to see them again."

Warmth flooded Aria's chest. Since linking their inner spirits, she always saw Clarice's truest form—unfiltered and impossibly beautiful. Sometimes she just watched her, lost in the glow.

The energy of the light realm pulsed around her, and with every breath, more memories surfaced, some of them heavier than others. She remembered their first eons together, before mortality, with its theater of emotions. The three of them had been inseparable—building worlds, shaping stars, weaving the laws that governed reality itself.

The thrill of those first experiments with limitation came rushing back. To define a thing so it could end—to assign boundaries to infinity—had felt like learning to paint a masterpiece after eons of drawing stick figures. And with that discovery came the ache of impermanence, the realization that one of them might someday end. That was when their bond deepened, when eternity suddenly felt fragile.

She remembered the mortal realm, too, their first incarnations and the strange intensity of life bound by time. Love. Passion. Hunger. They had returned changed, no longer content to be neutral forces in the cosmic machinery.

The thought of it all made Aria's soul ache. They had spent billions of years as genderless entities, reflections of the divine rather than participants in it. Mortality had given them the gift of desire. It was maddening to think how long they had gone without it.

Most angels still lived stunted lives, outwardly male or female, but neither in truth—imitations of form without the fire behind it. She found herself wondering, why? Why had they made them that way?

She remembered the raw code from the GoD, the schematics that birthed the angelic race. They had copied shapes without understanding the longing inside them. Back then, it hadn't mattered. But now—now it mattered more than anything.

"You getting memory echoes too?" Clarice asked, tilting her head.

"Yeah," Aria said slowly. "It's dredging up all sorts of existential questions. I keep wondering where we actually came from. Before mortality, it never occurred to me that something could even have a beginning."

Clarice took Aria's hand, her eyes distant and a pensive frown on her face. "As far back as I can remember, it was just the three of us. Eventually, we found a way to access the GoD."

Mandy's eyes gleamed with fascination. "So where is this God entity? Is he like religion says—everywhere at once, watching everything?"

"First off, the GoD isn't a 'he,'" Clarice said pointedly. "It's not even a 'who.' It just is. You can only access it from the highest realm. We created the Tree of Knowledge as a conduit inside the garden we started in—the light realm's equivalent of the Garden of Eden. When you step inside the Tree, you can feel its presence. That's where we received the instructions to create both the different realms."

She paused, frowning in concentration. "There's a lot more to it, but those memories haven't resurfaced yet."

Lexi shifted uncomfortably. "I miss my wings." She leaned into Mandy. "So how big is this tree? Is it similar to the Tree of Life?"

Clarice glanced at Aria and Calypso before answering, "About the size of reality—plus a little extra. From the outside, it looks like the Tree of Life, but inside it stretches into infinity. You can feel the GoD the moment you enter. At first, it was incomprehensible—raw data pouring into our minds faster than we could process. It took us thousands of years just to make sense of fragments. After eons, we decoded enough to create the light realms."

She tapped her chin thoughtfully. "You could think of the GoD as something like the Akashic Records. Long before the first billion years, we found whole new data channels, streams of information that reached beyond anything we'd imagined."

Mandy was staring at her, mouth slightly open. Lexi wasn't much better.

"Did you just say billions of years like that's a weekend?" Mandy demanded. "That's—that's insane!"

Calypso chuckled softly. "When you've never known beginnings or endings, time loses all meaning. You don't feel it passing because time doesn't exist in the way it does for mortals."

Lexi raised an eyebrow. "Well, I feel it, and I'm immortal now."

Calypso nodded, her lips curving at the corners. "That's because you've been mortal. Once you unlock your memory, you'll remember what it's like when eternity doesn't feel long at all."

Mandy glanced between them calculatingly. "Can't we just... I don't know, ask God how to shut off the power in the highest light realm? That's the endgame, right? Kick the other Seraphim out of Heaven?"

Aria exchanged a thoughtful look with Calypso and Clarice. "Actually, yes," she said slowly. "That could work. The whole reason we came here was to unlock our memories. Now that we remember the GoD exists as an access point, we might be able to consult it. But we'll need to go in stages. Jumping straight to the highest realm would knock us flat for a while."

Mandy looked around at the endless pale horizon. "You weren't kidding about the emptiness. Does this really go on forever?"

"Technically, no," Clarice said, squinting into the white void. "It's just so huge our minds can't perceive an edge. You can teleport anywhere you want—but try to reach a boundary and you'll never find one."

Lexi frowned. "How do you even map infinity? What do you use for coordinates?"

"I want to teleport twenty feet this way," Clarice said dryly—and vanished, reappearing twenty feet ahead. "Like that. You pick a direction and go."

"There's also a psychic web of consciousness," Aria added, pointing off to her right. "You can feel where other beings are—little pressure points in the fabric of awareness. There are several presences that way, maybe a few million miles off. You get used to gauging distance by feel."

Mandy's eyes darted between them. "So, where do we go first? It's not exactly labeled out here."

"I want to check on the Ascended," Calypso said, her voice heavy with concern. "After we destroyed all those soul traps, returning spirits should be materializing at processing centers. If they're not... they'll revert to the default form—genderless and disoriented. That's not a great welcome home."

"Okay," Mandy said, scanning the horizon helplessly. "Which way is that?"

A portal shimmered open right in front of her. On the other side lay the shattered ruins of what had once been a grand structure. Green meadows spread outward from its base, scattered with trees and flowers. Dozens of angels lingered near the wreckage while thousands more hovered in the distance, radiating anger and confusion.

"Looks like the cult already got to this one," Clarice said grimly. "I doubt the others are faring better."

"Let's talk to the Ascended," Aria said, stepping through.

"We really should've disguised one of us as an archangel," Clarice muttered as she followed. "Regular angels don't usually open inter-realm portals before breakfast."

Calypso's eyes brightened with amusement as she spread a fresh pair of shining archangel wings. "Problem solved." She stepped through after them, her new wings catching the light like molten glass.

Their small group crossed the shimmering grass toward a cluster of newly restored Ascended, keeping wary eyes on the crowd of angry angels gathering in the distance.

The first Ascended they reached was a woman with a mane of golden hair and soft lavender eyes. She wandered through the ruins in a daze, staring around like someone newly reborn. Aria remembered that look—the stunned reverence of a soul finally drinking in light after an eternity of drought.

Then a burst of angel fire lit the field. One of the Ascended screamed and vanished into motes of light.

Aria spun toward the flare just as a Cherub descended, wings beating lazily, disgust twisting his perfect features. He looked at them the way someone might look at a roach on fine china. His eyes flared—and a beam of white energy shot straight at Aria. She met it midair with her own angel fire, the two lights colliding and dispersing in a thunderclap of brilliance.

Before he could blink, Clarice was there—slamming him to the ground, her hand locked around his throat.

"So this is how you plan to handle the Ascended?" she hissed. "Vaporize them and pretend it never happened?"

"Who are you?" the Cherub spat, thrashing in her grip. It was like watching a child wrestle a mountain.

"Caleb," Clarice said, her voice dropping into a dangerous purr. "Of course it's you. I should've guessed it would be a pile of rot like you. Looks like it's time to trim the Cherubim."

His lip curled. "I'll be back. We'll see who gets trimmed."

The smirk faltered when he tried to teleport—and failed. Horror widened his eyes as he looked up at her. "You!"

"Yes, Caleb," Clarice said softly as her eyes blazed gold. "*Me*."

Her angel fire hit him full in the face. He screamed once—then was gone, scattering into the dense light field like smoke in sunlight.

The Ascended who had fled at his attack slowed, watching her with awe and fear. The distant crowd of angels froze. A Cherub of the first order had just been erased—something they had all believed impossible.

Clarice turned to them, unfolding her Seraph aura. The air itself seemed to bow.

"Anyone who harms an Ascended answers to *me*," she declared, her voice vibrating through the realm itself. "Get used to them. You'll all be tasting mortality soon enough."

The crowd recoiled, silent and wide-eyed. Seraphim didn't walk among them; they *ruled* from unreachable heights. To see one here, in the open, radiant and wrathful—it broke their certainty like glass.

The few Ascended scattered among the ruins were staring at Clarice now—hope dawning across their faces like sunrise after eons of night. They moved toward her slowly, torn between fear, awe, and joy. Most fell to their knees before they reached her, foreheads pressed to the fractured marble.

Aria's lip curled. "Not this again," she muttered. She knew all too well what kind of worlds these angels had come from—where worship was enforced, not offered.

"Was this facility destroyed recently?" Clarice asked the first Ascended brave enough to lift her head.

The woman nodded, trembling. "Yes, Seraph. Dominions dismantled it not long before you arrived."

Aria and Calypso joined Clarice amid the broken spires and shattered conduits, their eyes scanning the wreckage of what had once been a mortality processing center. More Ascended drifted closer, their faces bright with disbelief.

"I suppose this is as good a time as any to test the divine instruments in the light realm," Calypso said, meeting Aria's gaze.

"Agreed," Clarice and Aria said together, exchanging a small smile before turning back to the crowd.

"We're going to repair the facility," Aria told them, her Seraph aura no longer veiled. "We'll be using divine instruments, so you'll need to move somewhere safe. And please—stop kneeling. We're not like the angels you knew. We don't require obeisance."

Gasps rippled through the group as the realization spread—not one, but three Seraphim stood before them, divine instruments glowing in hand. Clarice opened a shimmering portal several million miles away, the vast horizon folding in on itself.

"Go through here and wait," she said, her tone softening. "We'll reopen it when it's safe. Lexi and Mandy will stay with you, just in case."

Aria turned to the distant crowd of angels still hovering at the edge of the field. "If you value your existence," she warned, "start running. You won't survive at this range."

Terror rippled through the ranks as she raised her tin whistle and Calypso lifted her harp. The instruments blazed like newborn stars, drawing the ambient light around them into their cores.

"*Get lost*!" Clarice thundered. The words struck the ground like a hammerblow, sending cracks spidering through the soil.

That broke the spell. The angels fled, conjuring shining discs beneath their feet as they sped away in panic.

The dozen Ascended still present hesitated only long enough to whisper among themselves. Aria caught a snatch of reverent awe: "It's the *Three*... I thought they were destroyed."

Lexi and Mandy followed the group through the portal, and Clarice sealed it behind them.

"Let's make sure nobody can destroy it this time," Aria said firmly. She lifted the divine instrument to her lips and extended a thread of thought, weaving her mind with Calypso's.

Calypso plucked the first shimmering notes on her harp, and Aria joined in, their harmonies spiraling into one another. The world around them began to ripple—space itself bending, matter turning pliable beneath the weight of their will.

A tidal surge of creation rolled through them. The divine instruments opened every gate in their spirits, letting the raw energy of the light realm flood their joined consciousness. Their minds synchronized, each thought mirrored and magnified, each note reshaping reality.

Memories poured in as the power deepened. Aria remembered the first time they had built these facilities—how crude it had been, sculpted by the malleable light of the realm. This time, they forged the structure from immortal matter. It would be impervious to Cherubim fire or even Seraphic command.

Their work unfolded like instinct as the memories of its original inception swam to the surface. The foundation coalesced in seconds, followed by the framework and thousands of miles of glowing conduits. Layers of technology she could barely remember unfolded outward, her intent guided by whatever powered the instruments. By the time they finished, the facility stood renewed, like a monument to the mortal condition.

Aria lowered her instrument, satisfaction warming her chest. Clarice immediately swept both of them into a radiant embrace, laughter and pride dancing through the bond.

"Well done, my beautiful angels," she said, her voice full of affection. "You two are extraordinary."

Aria melted into the hug, feeling the new intensity of energy entwining through their meridians. The light realm amplified everything, from their power and potential to their connection and love. Something inside her shifted, a window flinging open in her soul. She felt Clarice and Calypso undergo the same awakening, their spirits similarly expanding.

A new understanding filled her thoughts, an awareness of the subtle lattice beneath creation itself, the pattern that separated destruction from healing, energy from void.

"Oh, wow," Clarice whispered in awe. "You've been working with forces this intricate since childhood, Calypso?"

Calypso's expression softened, a quiet wonder in her tone. "So this is destructive energy. I've never needed to wield it—I've always had my protectors beside me."

"And that's not going to change," Clarice promised, her voice warm with certainty. "We're bound together now. Always."

Aria held them tighter, overwhelmed by the memory of their long journey—billions of years of existence, yet it was the brief span of mortal experience that had given their bond meaning. Love, she realized, was the concept they had witnessed with the GoD but could not comprehend or quantify.

"I suppose I should invite the others back now," Clarice murmured reluctantly. With one last squeeze, she stepped back and opened a portal.

Lexi and Mandy stepped through, eyes wide. The facility shimmered before them, flawless and gleaming.

"*Wow*!" Mandy breathed. "You built that whole thing while we were gone?"

"Yep," Clarice said, smiling like she had just redecorated the living room. "Easy peasy, lemon squeezy."

Lexi laughed, shaking her head. "I wish we could've watched. Too bad the divine instruments turn anything below Seraphim into cosmic paste."

"I have a feeling you'll get your chance," Clarice said with a knowing smile.

Lexi narrowed her eyes. "What's *that* supposed to mean?"

Aria turned toward Clarice too, equally curious.

"You'll see," Clarice replied, her grin equal parts mystery and mischief.

"Oh, it's like *that* is it?" Lexi said, mock-scowling. The others broke into laughter, and for a moment, the heaviness of the last few days lifted.

Calypso frowned. "I'm pretty sure Cherubim are safe in the presence of a divine instrument."

Aria shook her head firmly. "I'm not going to test that theory with these two."

Calypso quickly nodded. "Of course not."

The Ascended began returning through the reopened portal, halting as they took in the sight of the restored facility. Their awe was almost palpable.

"We made it indestructible this time," Aria told them reassuringly. "Even the other Seraphim couldn't touch it now."

"Can I go in?" one of them—Daloris—asked timidly.

"Have at it," Clarice grinned, gesturing toward the entrance with a grand flourish. "Gendered bodies await."

Daloris blushed but laughed, leading the others toward the doors. Their excitement carried through the air like a hymn.

Clarice crossed her arms, watching them go. "So. Do we go clean up some Cherubim and make sure they understand that attacking Ascended is a *terminal* decision?"

"Yes," Calypso said immediately. "We can't let them get away with this."

Lexi's brow furrowed. "Didn't Arturiel say there were only seventy Cherubim?"

"Once upon a time, yes," Aria answered, smiling grimly. "Seventy of the first order. Now it's sixty-eight—Kadmiel tried to kill my mom, Clarice took out Caleb. Oh, and technically sixty-nine, since Mandy's a new Cherub. The first in several million years."

Lexi's eyes went wide. "Hold on. There are *quintillions* of angels, but only seventy Cherubim and nine Seraphim... and I'm one of the Cherubim?"

"Yep," Aria said, her grin widening. "One of the most powerful beings in the cosmos. There were another four hundred ninety Cherubim of the second order, but you're top tier."

"Wow," Lexi breathed. "Still—how did so many end up in one place? Your parents, your uncle, Tamra, me, and now Mandy? That's not coincidence—that's design."

Aria chuckled. "We've wondered the same thing. Pretty sure there was... outside interference."

At that, Mandy shifted ever so slightly, her eyes darting away. Clarice shared a look with Calypso and Aria.

"*She knows something*," Clarice said silently through the link, her mental tone cool and sure. "*There's more to Mandy than she's letting on*."

Aria and Calypso both nodded. The unspoken understanding rippled between them—warmth, caution, and curiosity braided into one.

Clarice's grin faded into a frown. "We were supposed to bring Redgart with us when we came to the light realms," she murmured, her tone suddenly heavy. "Maybe we should wait until after we deal with the Cherubim. I'd hate for him to finally make it back here just to get himself vaporized."

Aria's eyes hardened. "Then let's go clean house for him first."

Clarice's answering grin was wolfish.

"Do you have a way to find them?" Mandy asked, stepping up behind Lexi and wrapping her arms around her. She rested her cheek against the back of Lexi's head, the two of them glowing softly in the dense light. Aria felt Lexi's joy radiating through the bond, a pulse of warmth and contentment that rippled through their shared spirit.

"I know where the other MPCs are," Calypso said, watching the two of them fondly. "And I doubt Caleb was acting alone. We'll probably find more Cherubim making trouble."

"MPCs?" Lexi echoed, blinking. "Like... Monster Player Characters?"

Calypso gave her a puzzled look. "Mortality Processing Centers. What are Monster Player Characters?"

Lexi laughed. "Just thought it was a spin-off of NPCs. You know—non-player characters?"

"Did you forget?" Clarice said, smirking. "Calypso's about ten thousand years behind on pop culture. Video games didn't quite make it into the curriculum before she ascended."

Aria cut in, her tone sharpening. "We can reminisce later. They're probably vaporizing people while we chat."

Calypso paled, then instantly opened a portal. Angel fire was already cutting through the sky beyond it before they even stepped out.

Azriel was in the air, wings flaring wide as he intercepted volleys of angel fire aimed at the Ascended below. Two Cherubim circled like vultures, firing relentlessly. Aria recognized them instantly—Raphael and Gabriel—darting and weaving, trying to flank Azriel. He was holding them off, but one mistake would mean death for the Ascended.

Clarice shot through the portal like a thunderbolt. In the same breath, she slammed Raphael out of the air and drove him into the ground with a crack that shook the field. Aria was a heartbeat behind her, seizing Gabriel by the throat and pinning him beside Raphael.

"Hello, Raphael," Clarice purred, her eyes burning like twin suns. "Did you miss me?"

Raphael's face drained of color. He jerked, trying to teleport—but nothing happened. His panic was instant. He flailed wildly, futilely.

"Can't have you leaving before I vaporize your worthless ass," Clarice said sweetly. "Goodbye, Raphael."

He screamed as her angel fire struck him point-blank. In seconds, his body collapsed into a scatter of motes, gone like a candle in a gale.

Gabriel thrashed, his golden eyes wide with terror.

"You were fine burning others a minute ago," Aria told him, her voice colder than the vacuum. "It's time for some balance."

Her angel fire ignited, roaring through his spirit. Gabriel's scream cut off abruptly, his light scattering into the ether.

Azriel landed beside them, wings folding in. "That was unexpected." Like all Cherubim, he was impossibly tall, his black hair stark against his golden eyes. There was disbelief and a touch of awe in his voice. "And I mean *really* unexpected. I didn't think Cherubim could die."

"We never got involved in the fighting before," Clarice said with a shrug. "We tried to stay impartial. That policy's been revised."

Azriel gave a short, incredulous laugh. "I'm glad you showed up. They'd have gotten past me eventually. Grodek told me Aria killed Kadmiel, but... well, it's Grodek."

"You can add Caleb to your list of vacancies," Clarice said grimly. "And probably a few more by the end of the day. We're moving on—there'll be other attacks."

Azriel's grin turned sharp. "Then there are going to be a lot fewer Cherubim by tomorrow."

Calypso was already opening another portal.

"We rebuilt one of the MPCs," Aria told him as she prepared to step through. "Indestructible this time. We'll do the same for this one when we're done. Those parasites won't break them again."

Azriel's eyebrows rose, but she was already gone.

Angel fire streaked through the sky before Aria even cleared the portal. A massive crowd of Ascended huddled below, terror rolling off them in waves. Five Cherubim circled like carrion birds, firing into the crowd for sport—pausing between volleys just to savor the screams.

Rage detonated inside her.

Beside her, Calypso erupted in light. Before anyone could stop her, she shot forward, striking Dredel full in the face with a column of angel fire. Aria followed instantly, seizing two of the others mid-flight as Clarice did the same.

Jerinel and Fortenel barely had time to react. Aria slammed them into the ground with such force the air rippled. Jerinel's spirit disintegrated beneath her fire before his scream even peaked. Fortenel flailed wildly, panic overriding reason. His cry broke off as he vanished into dust and light.

Five more Cherubim gone—five pillars of the first order erased. The ranks really were thinning fast.

When the last one fell, Calypso hovered in place, trembling. Her glow flickered, caught between grief and fury. Aria could feel the turmoil roiling through her soul—the dissonance of a healer forced to kill.

Aria floated up to her and pulled her close. "Calypso, look down," she said softly. "See that woman? She's alive because of you. She would've died before Clarice or I got close enough. You saved her, and I love you for that."

Calypso's breath hitched, her golden tears catching the light. "I know. I just... I hate that there are beings who make me want to kill. I hate this reality."

"I know," Aria murmured, resting her forehead against Calypso's and brushing her bangs back. "I really hate it too. We're going to fix it, though. When we're done, reality is going to be a beautiful place where you'll be able to play your beautiful music and bask in the joy of all the people who no longer live in the worst kind of hell. Now come on, let's go save some more people."

Calypso nodded, wiping her tears. The portal flared open again.

They stepped through together.

And again.

And again.

Over a dozen times, they repeated the cycle. By the time the last Cherub fell, the light realm itself seemed to tremble with the echo of their wrath.

The Cherubim's new strategy was clear: if the soul traps were gone, they would just kill every Ascended who returned to the light realms. It hadn't gone well for them. By the time word spread, more than half of the existing Cherubim were gone.

Aria felt it the moment the survivors fled. The realm itself shifted, the psychic pressure thinning like a storm breaking. The weight of their presence vanished all at once. A dozen, maybe fewer, had escaped to higher realms.

"I wonder how many of the Cherubim who sided with us stayed behind after the other Seraphim turned on us," Aria said quietly. "We know Azriel did. There had to be others."

"I'd be shocked if there weren't a few," Clarice replied, though her voice was grim. "Most were forced into mortality with us, but they may have missed some."

With the threat gone, they turned back to rebuilding. The restored MPCs shimmered like living architecture, gleaming against the endless white expanse. It was something—something to give the newly freed Ascended a piece of the bodies they had paid so dearly for.

Calypso played as they worked, her harp singing through the realm. Each note carried beauty, but beneath the melody, Aria could feel the fracture—Calypso's guilt bleeding into every chord. She smiled when spoken to, laughed when prompted, but the light within her was flickering, dimmed by the toll of what she had done.

Aria caught Clarice's gaze, and for a moment, neither spoke. The shared ache in the bond said enough. Calypso had always been their gentlest heart—their hope, their melody. Watching her drown in remorse hurt more than any battle ever could.

They had just finished the last MPC when a familiar, nails-on-glass voice cut through the hum of the crowd.

"Well, well. The oversized chickens finally flapped their way home," Grodek sneered, his grin pure malice. The Ascended were filtering back through the portal Clarice had opened, their faces bright with hope—until a few spotted Grodek's glare and froze mid-step. "I'm not sure what you thought you were accomplishing by letting a trickle of angels back into the light realm," he went on. "Unless your plan was to lure the Cherubim down here and murder them—in which case, I salute you."

"We were hoping the influx would make it easier to sneak in and recover more of our soul memories," Clarice replied dryly. "But subtlety isn't really our brand, is it, Grodek?"

"Subtlety?" he barked a laugh. "You're about as discreet as a clown at a funeral who can't stop honking his nose." He gave them a once-over, grimacing. "Looks like you *did* get some memories back. What are you planning to do with them—write a self-help scroll? I'd say I'm surprised to see you up here instead of chasing the rest of the divine instrument pieces, but you idiots get derailed even when the tracks are straight."

Clarice scowled. "The other Seraphim have been setting traps around the remaining pieces, so we're flushing them out of their sanctuary. If we reroute the energy flow in the highest realm, the power density will crash. They'll have to flee to the lower planes, too busy trying not to implode to bother us."

Grodek stared at them, slack-jawed. Aria bit the inside of her cheek to keep from laughing.

Then he groaned, dragged a hand down his face, and muttered, "You absolute lunatics."

"Thank you," Clarice said brightly.

"No, you don't get to thank me!" he snarled. "Do you even know what rerouting that energy will do? You'd drown the lower realms in a soup of light so dense it'd fry everything alive. And it wouldn't stop there—it'd bleed into the mortal realm and melt finite matter. You might as well nuke existence!"

"We didn't say we're rerouting it *downward*," Clarice countered. "Just that we're rerouting it."

"Rerouting it where, genius?" Grodek demanded.

Clarice shrugged. "Somewhere that won't notice. It's temporary anyway. We just need those drinkers of yaks' piss to realize they're not safe anymore."

Grodek gaped at her. "So, to summarize, you have no idea where you're sending it." He pointed a clawed finger. "And stop stealing my insults, you glittery knockoffs. You've got the originality of a moldy cookie cutter. You're just hurling shit at the walls and hoping it sticks."

Clarice's grin turned cherubic. "In this case, it'll be *holy* shit," she said sweetly. "Because, you know—heaven."

Grodek just stared at Clarice, looking like a man who had spent eons suffering fools and finally found the queen of them all. "First of all," he said, his voice dripping with exasperation, "I'm not even sure rerouting light from the highest realm is possible. Second, where do you think the power in the lower realms comes from? You cut it off at the source, you cut it off *everywhere*."

"I like the sound of that," Clarice said cheerfully. "They'll lose their fix up there *and* down below. Heroin addicts on a desert island."

Grodek glared, the corners of his mouth twitching like he couldn't decide between outrage and reluctant respect. After a long moment, he grunted. "You'd have to go to the Garden if you wanted to pull it off. And you'd need at least two divine instruments. *Maybe*."

"Already planned on it," Clarice replied, smug as sin. Then her grin faltered. "The light density up there will probably nuke our processors. We'll be stuck drooling until we adapt. Not the most heroic way to go out. Our epitaph would just read: *Died glowing*."

"Relax," Grodek said, rolling his eyes. "They'll never even notice you. The energy's too dense to register movement at that scale. Just open a portal far from the core. And take my advice—only the two with instruments should go. No sense frying everyone for a sightseeing trip."

Aria frowned, anxiety spreading in her chest at the idea of separating from her sister. Clarice caught her expression and gave a wry smile. "Nice try. Our spirit link feeds power equally. If they drool, I drool. We might as well drool together."

Grodek snorted, half a laugh and half disgust. "You're all idiots," he muttered—and vanished.

Aria exhaled, a shaky smile creeping onto her face. "Well, at least we're idiots together."

Clarice's grin turned wolfish. "So? Shall we crash the source realm and piss off some wannabe gods?"

Aria met her eyes, heart hammering. "Let's do it."

Calypso's voice was quiet. "We're ready."

Lexi and Mandy clasped hands, their faces alight with anticipation. "Then let's go," Lexi said eagerly.

Clarice drew a deep breath and opened a portal to the highest light realm.

"Here we go," she murmured—and stepped through into the light.

10 – Exchange

Aria only took a few steps through the portal before a wave of euphoria hit her like a tsunami. Her mind was washed away as bliss overwhelmed every other emotion or sensation. This must be what nirvana felt like. No motion or action—just an unmoving and unchanging state of bliss. She knew deep down that countless souls depended on her to succeed, but she couldn't bring herself to care about anything but the overwhelming waves of ecstasy scouring her soul.

Memories flooded her consciousness as the intoxicating radiance filled her meridians. The memories washed around in the ocean of joy like familiar acquaintances she had nearly forgotten. They were like separate entities as they floated and bobbed around her consciousness.

There was the beginning, where the three of them had found each other in the garden—except it wasn't a beginning, because they had *always* been there. They had spent eons in the garden, untouched by the bliss because they had never felt its lack.

They had no concept of time, no concept of day or night. Everything just *was*.

The tree in the center of the garden was the only thing indicating the passage of time, growing larger under their care as the ages passed by unnoticed. They used their combined will to mold and shape the tree with probing tendrils of information. After eons of growth, it eventually revealed an entryway that led to the source they had been searching for. Radiant with excitement, they rushed inside to see what wonders awaited them.

And wondrous it had been. They could feel the stream of meaning flowing within the tree like a powerful river. Endless currents of data, completely incomprehensible.

They had spent most of their time within the tree from that point on, puzzling their way through the cryptography in the endless flow of signals. Slowly, over more time than a mortal mind could comprehend, the patterns began to make sense as their immortal minds cataloged and deciphered the flood of knowledge. Concepts took shape, and the idea for the light realms was birthed.

Then they had created the other six Seraphim. Their spirits were younger, less developed, but they were real—their first successful attempt to create living entities.

As the flood of memories settled in her consciousness, she slowly regained awareness of the world around her. Calypso watched her patiently, a look of sublime joy on her face. Clarice blinked slowly as she finally surfaced as well. Lexi and Mandy were still deep in the currents of euphoria, their eyes glossy in the immersion of ultra-dense radiance.

"How long do you think it's been?" Aria asked, her voice layered with authority.

"Several weeks," Calypso answered in a voice just as full of power and authority.

The arrival of their memories altered them dramatically. Their auras were exponentially stronger. They were like compact supernovas as the full weight of their authority returned. Calypso's eyes were no longer weighed down by grief. She stared back at Aria with eyes full of love and trust.

Smiling beatifically, Aria pulled Calypso into a tight embrace. It felt like being reunited with a lover after ages of separation. Now that her memories were back, she felt a renewed sense of love and adoration for her oldest friends. "It's so good to be back!"

Calypso's grip tightened in unspoken agreement. Clarice cleared her throat meaningfully as she finished waking. Aria and Calypso laughed, pulling her into their arms.

"My beautiful angels," Clarice breathed, resting her head against theirs. "You've blossomed into such amazing women."

"Mortality is such a powerful tool for shaping spirits," Calypso said softly, her voice a caress to the soul. "So much pain and horror, but so much love and kindness, too. I think we have a lot more to learn from mortal experiences."

Aria smiled wryly. "We've had our memories for less than an hour, and you're already talking about incarnating again."

"Not until we've made changes to the experience," Calypso said firmly. "Suffering needs limits and off switches. We can dig into the design details after we finish reducing the number of Seraphim."

"You know, we could still have nine Seraphim," Clarice said lightly, her eyes sparkling.

"So *that's* what you were talking about!" Aria laughed delightedly. "Telling Lexi she'd get her chance to observe the divine instruments being played."

"Yep," Clarice grinned mischievously. "I didn't want to tell her ahead of time."

"You mean to change *who* the Seraphim are, not how many there are," Calypso smiled as she stared into Clarice's eyes. "In hindsight, we should've found replacements for them long ago. I guess we needed the perspective of mortality to finally realize it."

"You were thinking of Mandy as well, weren't you?" Aria guessed with a pleased grin.

"We can hardly raise Lexi to a Seraph while leaving Mandy as a Cherub," Clarice responded dryly. "Too much of a power imbalance in that kind of a relationship. Besides, you saw what Mandy is. Having someone from the origin realm will be... interesting."

"Who else were you thinking of raising?" Calypso asked, though her eyes made it clear she already knew.

"Our parents, of course," Clarice smiled brilliantly, the sight flooding Aria with desire.

"Smile like that more," Aria breathed, her lips curling up at the corners. "It's freaking *hot*."

Clarice stared into her eyes with deep and passionate love. There was so much emotion in her dark brown eyes that it should have solidified around them. "It's been a long time getting here, hasn't it?"

"What's time to immortals?" Aria asked with an impish grin.

"It's everything," Clarice replied softly. "Time is what made this love I feel for you possible. Time is the true key to love and joy."

Aria smiled, kissing her forehead. "That it is."

Calypso closed her eyes, a radiant smile lighting her face. "Agreed."

"I know we promised to only do this for emergencies that threatened the realm," Aria began hesitantly. "But... should we remove our limiters? We could stop all the suffering right now if we did."

Clarice shared a troubled look with Calypso, then shook her head. "Not yet. We're close to fixing things now that we have our memories back. We can revisit that decision if we run into any setbacks that push our new timetable further out."

"Rendimus is lucky we fused our souls with the instruments," Calypso said grimly. "If he'd actually managed to unmake us, our supers would have destroyed everything. I don't even want to think of what they would've done further up the stack, without us acting as a conscience."

Aria laughed nervously. "Yeah, he has no idea how lucky he was."

"We should check in with Betaman," Clarice said musingly. "I know from his perspective it's only been a week, but I'm curious how his foundry's coming along. We may want to look into visiting in person."

Calypso frowned, her eyes troubled. "Lucifer left a lot of information out after we redeemed him. His insistence that we needed the divine instruments to defeat the other Seraphim doesn't make sense. He should have sent us here, where our memories return far quicker. We certainly don't need the instruments to deal with the other four Seraphim."

Clarice narrowed her eyes. "You're right. The first thing he should have suggested was to return here to claim our memories. He also implied that we were involved in giving the Cherubim the ability to kill, even though we were dead set against it."

Aria pursed her lips, studying Mandy thoughtfully. "Mandy's shown obvious dislike for Lucifer a few times. I wonder what she knows. I think we need to have a chat with him soon."

"We could ask her," Calypso suggested.

"Maybe," Clarice murmured, also studying the blissful Cherub. "She's terrified of discovery. She might feel more comfortable if we let her know she's hidden from outside eyes."

Aria nodded slowly, a fond smile softening her features. "She really is amazing. Showing her what we're capable of should relieve the mountain of anxiety she's been carrying."

"What about Lexi?" Calypso asked, brow creased in concern. "How do you think she'll react when she finds out about Alice?"

Clarice's lips curved into an affectionate smile. "She'll love her even more—especially when she understands just how much Alice has done."

There was a blissful moan from Lexi as she began to stir. Aria reluctantly stepped back from Clarice and Calypso.

"How are you doing, Lexi?" Clarice asked with a teasing smile. "Have you found your way to shore yet?"

"Just one more minute," Lexi moaned in ecstasy.

Mandy suddenly blinked from where she stood next to Lexi, her face losing some of its euphoric bliss. "Wow, I'm not sure I *ever* want to leave this place."

Clarice laughed, observing Mandy fondly. "Yeah, this place is pretty special. If you were in your own body, this would be a lot more intense. I'm guessing you didn't have any soul memories return while you were acclimating."

"No, nothing," Mandy shook her head, her eyes suddenly wary. "Should I have?"

"There haven't been any new Cherubim since their original creation," Clarice answered, watching her appraisingly. "You were created from a template of a person in this reality when you were replaced in the false reality. You would've been a new spirit, so there wouldn't be any soul memory of the person you were copied from. It was just your character traits and personality, which have probably faded by now. So pretty much whatever you brought with you from your world."

Mandy looked at her with a mixture of confusion and alarm that she quickly smoothed from her face.

"So, I'm the new kid on the block, eh?" she asked with an excited grin. "I'm the *new* generation. New and *improved*."

Aria and the others laughed, watching her with eager eyes. She was going to be one of them soon, after all.

Mandy looked at them and gasped.

"What is it?" Aria asked in concern.

"Your *eyes*," Mandy exclaimed. "They're like Calypso's now. They're all violet and swirly."

Aria looked at Clarice, but of course, she only saw the transposed image of her inner soul. Clarice raised her eyebrows in realization as she looked at Aria.

"Oh yeah, they were golden before," Clarice remembered with a short laugh. "I was so caught up in our memories of old that you just looked like I remembered before."

Lexi finally surfaced from her trance. When she was fully alert, she gazed at them with wide, wondering eyes. "Seraphim, it's an honor."

"Oh no, you *didn't* just say that!" Clarice declared dangerously, walking over and pulling her into a tight embrace. "We're *not* your Seraphim, Lexi. We're your *friends*."

Lexi gasped as she felt the full force of a fully awakened Seraph's aura wash over her. The energy drenched her like honey and lightning, overwhelming her immortal body. She shivered in ecstasy as the power flooded her system, more intense than the dense light field.

"I don't care *how* many memories you retrieved from your soul," Clarice murmured into her ear. "You'll focus on the memories of the last four months and remember us as your friends—*not* your Seraphim."

Lexi nodded as she clung to Clarice, her immortal body overwhelmed by the powerful Seraph aura. Clarice retracted her aura and released her. She stepped back a pace and stared into her eyes sternly. "What's my name?"

Lexi flushed, and a shy smile spread across her face. "Clarice."

"That's right," Clarice nodded firmly. "Not *Seraph*."

Lexi's grin widened as the others smiled back—lighthearted, radiant, and utterly divine.

Mandy was watching Lexi with a puzzled crease on her brow. "What was all that about?"

"Her memory reawakened," Calypso explained with a soft smile. "The angels used to revere us as gods. Some of the Seraphim leaned into it a little too much— they liked reminding everyone we built them."

Clarice snorted dryly. "Which is ironic, considering Rendimus wasn't involved in the creation of the light realms at all. That was just the three of us, with some help from Lucifer later. The others participated in the creation of the angel races, but only after we'd already laid all the groundwork. He always was a pretentious ass. I think I was distracted when we created him. I'm not sure why we created six males—not that we understood the difference back then."

Aria smiled wistfully. "A lot of our problems would've never arisen if we'd spent more time interacting with the angel races. We were too obsessed with creation and study—making things, not nurturing them. After experiencing mortality, that all changed. We got a lot more involved."

Mandy stared at them hopefully. "Have all your memories come back now?"

"Just about," Aria nodded, smiling at Mandy affectionately. "I have to say again how happy I am that you came down to this reality. It would have been so much darker without your light. You really are the heroine of this story, Mandy."

Color rushed to Mandy's cheeks, surprise flickering across her face before she covered it with a bashful grin.

Lexi pulled her into a warm embrace. "Words could never express how happy *I* am that you brought her back with you," Lexi said warmly, kissing Mandy tenderly.

A brilliant flash erupted as Mandy flared through several evolutionary states in a heartbeat. When the light faded, her golden eyes gleamed with shock and delight. "That was one helluva kiss, Lexi!"

Lexi laughed delightedly, then kissed her again—slower this time, savoring the energy pulsing between them. "Having all my memories back makes this feel so much stronger," she murmured. "I never realized love could hit like this."

"We totally get that," Clarice assured her, gazing at Aria and Calypso with her heart in her eyes.

Mandy leaned back from Lexi to look at them curiously. "Did any of your memories give you an idea of how to reroute power from this realm?" Her eyes were still glowing with pleasure as the dense light field saturated her meridians.

"Yep," Aria nodded with a confident grin. "It's actually a fairly simple process, now that our memories are back. I'd imagine as soon as we remove light from the source realm, those jackasses might try retreating to the garden—assuming they can overcome their fear of the GoD. We'll need to make sure it's inaccessible to them."

Lexi's eyes widened, and she eyed Aria eagerly. "The garden where God resides? Aren't Seraphim the only ones who can go there?"

Aria exchanged a glance with Calypso and Clarice. "No, it's accessible to anyone capable of remaining conscious in the source realm. Is this another falsehood the other Seraphim told the Cherubim?"

Lexi nodded. "Rendimus claimed only Seraphim could enter the garden or speak to God."

Clarice grunted sourly. "Sounds just like the religious priests on Earth. You don't *speak* to the GoD at all. You just observe the information flow and try to learn from it—for the most part. Once you know enough, you can start creating your own... realms. We really were oblivious, weren't we?"

Calypso laughed, the sound warping the radiance around them. "I'm glad I wasn't the only one. I was perfectly happy being oblivious back on Earth, but it sounds like we were just as bad up here. We barely interacted with the other angels. Too many projects going on elsewhere. I can only imagine what kind of twisted lies Rendimus has fed them since our imprisonment—especially if he's been taking credit for *our* work."

"He claims to be the oldest of the Seraphim and said he created the rest of you to help him manage the light realm," Lexi informed her with a questioning note in her voice.

Aria shared a look with Calypso and Clarice, then burst out laughing. Shaking her head, Aria looked back at Lexi with amusement in her eyes.

"Lexi," Aria said, wiping a tear of laughter from her eye, "Calypso, Clarice, and I were alone in the Garden for ages before we created the others. Billions of years, give or take. We had already created the Tree of Knowledge and gained access to the GoD before we got around to creating more Seraphim."

She paused, a wry smile curving one side of her lips. "It just stands for Generator of Data. It's an endless stream of information that took thousands of years for us to decode. The only reason Seraphim can interface with it at all is that we've had the time and patience to learn its code. Anyone could, eventually—even you. Someday soon we'll explain what's really going on."

Lexi chewed her lip anxiously. "What would happen if the other Seraphim created more divine instruments? I guess I'm curious why they haven't already."

Clarice smirked and gave her a wink. "Not a chance. Only three people know how—and you're looking at them. We built four instruments as a safeguard. It takes all four wielders in perfect sync to alter reality. One ego alone can't do it. We had this absurd idea that we could trust the other Seraphim, so we tried to make our power more equal—hence the four instruments, instead of just three."

Mandy cleared her throat, an excited sparkle in her eyes. "Okay, I have kind of a radical idea. And maybe this is just my ignorance speaking, but why are we bothering to find the other pieces of the instruments if you can just make new ones?"

Aria shared a dumbfounded look with Clarice and Calypso. They continued staring at each other mutely until Mandy cleared her throat.

"So, was it a stupid idea, or what?" she asked anxiously.

Aria smiled dreamily. "Mandy, did I ever tell you how glad I am you joined us?"

"Really?" Mandy asked excitedly. "So, it *was* a good idea?"

"The best freaking idea *ever*," Clarice confirmed with an ecstatic grin, swooping in to hug her. "You really are a freaking genius! I don't know why this didn't occur to us before."

Mandy sighed contentedly as radiance rushed into her, a pleased smile dimpling her cheeks. "Probably because you just barely got your memories back. So... how long does it take to make one?"

Calypso tilted her head, looking at the sky reflectively. "It took a few thousand years the first time, but that's because I had to lay the framework. The instruments are just access keys and are much easier to develop. Still, we need the last piece of Clarice's instrument—it's tied to her spirit. Without it, she's incomplete."

"Oh yeah," Mandy's face fell. "I'm sorry, Clarice, I forgot about that."

Calypso smiled reassuringly. "That doesn't mean we can't create another instrument to rewrite reality. In fact, if I could just take what you currently have of your divine instrument, Clarice, I could probably complete it pretty quickly. Then we'd just need one more instrument. With three instruments, we'd have no trouble dropping the flow of light from the source realm. We could also move the garden somewhere else so those morons don't have anywhere to run—though I'm not sure they would go there anyway, considering how terrified they are of the GoD. Can I have your instrument, Clarice?"

"Okay," Clarice nodded nervously as she pulled her violin out of her spirit space and offered it to Calypso. Love swelled through the bond from Calypso at Clarice's willingness to hand part of her spirit over.

She prepared for the powerful sensations she knew were about to flood the bond when Calypso touched her spirit.

Being prepared didn't really help. As Calypso gently took the violin from Clarice, she felt her sister's spirit open on full display, completely vulnerable in Calypso's hands. There was no embarrassment this time, however. Clarice had so much faith and trust in them that even with her spirit in their hands, her emotions remained steady. The essence of pure love pulsed through the bond.

Calypso closed her eyes and hugged the violin to herself as golden tears ran down her cheeks. “Oh, Clarice,” she whispered in awe. “You really are so *beautiful*.”

Clarice smiled tremulously at Calypso, walls down and vaults open. Calypso could now see what Aria saw all the time through her link to Clarice. The sheer magnitude of love inside her seemed too vast for one spirit to contain—a spirit that wasn’t even whole.

Calypso took a deep breath and began to work. Her aura encapsulated the violin, repairing threads of light and spiritual lattice where they had fractured. She hummed as she worked, filling the air with a haunting beauty as her notes caressed their spirits.

Clarice shivered as the notes resonated within her spirit-bound violin. Aria could feel the sensations through her link to Clarice. It was like the ultimate massage, but for a spirit. Clarice closed her eyes as golden tears trickled down her cheeks. Mandy looked concerned but relaxed when she saw the others smiling.

Calypso worked for several hours. Time seemed to melt away as the high-density light field supercharged their immortal bodies with radiance. There was a moment of silence when Calypso finished, as if reality itself had paused to observe her work.

Calypso handed the violin back to Clarice with an air of reverence, gazing at Clarice with adoration in her eyes.

Clarice took the violin with a radiant smile that sent desire flooding into Aria. Clarice suddenly grinned, impish and dangerous. “Okay, let’s evict some Seraphim.”

Aria and Calypso laughed merrily and pulled out their instruments. Mandy and Lexi stepped forward uncertainly, beginning to open a portal.

“You two stay,” Clarice said firmly, her eyes glinting. “We have enough instruments now to make some pretty radical changes, and there’s something we’ll need you for.”

Mandy and Lexi shared a curious glance before nodding hesitantly, their eyes full of trust.

Calypso unfurled her aura, letting it blast out at full strength. Aria and Clarice did the same. Mandy and Lexi gasped as they felt the full force of the combined Seraphim auras, blanketing the area like a neutron star.

Calypso linked their minds, her thoughts weaving into Aria’s and Clarice’s until the three Seraphim became a single radiant consciousness. Their instruments answered as one, a celestial chord resonating through creation. The music bent reality like molten glass.

Mandy and Lexi cried out as their meridians reformed, their essence expanding in a cascade of power. Somewhere, far away, a psychic shriek echoed—a sound of divine panic—as two Seraphim were rewritten, their stations swapped with two astonished Cherubim.

The melody crescendoed. Light rippled across infinity, and with one blinding flash, the world around them transformed. The barren expanse became a vast, living Garden—lush and vibrant, dominated by a tree that dwarfed mountains. The music sang instructions into being, sealing the flow of light inside the Garden and cutting off the source realm's endless stream.

Across the psychic web, pandemonium erupted. Angels screamed as their power bled away. Dozens of Cherubim and two of the remaining Seraphim fled, tearing through realms in a vain search for radiance.

"I'd call that a smashing success," Clarice congratulated them with a broad grin. "Welcome to Seraphimhood, Lexi and Mandy."

The new Seraphim stood in shock. They looked into each other's swirling violet eyes with wondering gazes. Mandy smiled, revealing her dimples, and Lexi flushed, desire flaring in the bond. She leaned forward and passionately kissed Mandy.

"Yep, definitely feeling it stronger now that she's a Seraph," Clarice noted breathily, a rosy glow lighting up her cheeks.

"Uh-huh," Aria and Calypso agreed, their own cheeks flushing with desire.

"Get a room," Clarice called out after a minute of watching the two new Seraphim make out. "On second thought, maybe just put on a show for us. I wanna see you get to third base, my hot little Cupids."

Aria face-palmed and shook her head. Still the same old Clarice. Well, same *new* Clarice. She had always been mischievous, but their last incarnation had added a whole new dimension to her playful personality.

Lexi pulled away from Mandy with a blush at Clarice's teasing words, burying her face in Mandy's hair. "I used to think it was funny how you could make Calypso and Aria blush so much," Lexi admitted with a sigh. "I think I'm starting to understand things from their perspective now."

"Your cheeks are gorgeous when you blush," Clarice leered. "All glowing and warm like a sunrise."

"Not the leer!" Lexi yelped, covering her eyes in dismay. "Clarice, that's so *freaking evil*. You can't have a face that looks so innocent and pure while *leering* at people."

Clarice's lips curved into a slow, sultry smile. "The evidence," she purred, "would suggest otherwise."

A chortling Grodek popped into existence in front of them, his evil eyes dancing with glee. "Well, it looks like you did it. You should see Rendimus right now—he's twitching like someone's peeling his soul with a butter knife."

He paused, noticing Mandy and Lexi, both with their Seraphim auras blasting out at full power. "Oh... well, that was unexpected."

"We still have two more to switch out," Calypso informed him with a steely glint in her eyes. "We don't need four divine instruments to make this kind of change. That would only have been necessary if we tried to unmake them. Not that we need the instruments at all—they just speed things up."

Grodek narrowed his eyes when he heard the authority in their voices and sensed their fully ascended auras. "So... you finally got your memories back."

"Yep," Clarice nodded with a jaunty smile. "I think it's time to have our fifth Seraph back. Trot out your other half and let's get you restored."

Grodek blinked. "How long have you known about that?"

"Since I got my memories back," Clarice shrugged, looking him up and down. "I can see you've only got half your soul. I remember talking to your other iteration several times. It's kind of hard to miss when one of you is blue and the other red."

There was a small popping noise as the blue imp appeared. The two of them were identical, aside from their color.

Aria pulled out her tin whistle as Clarice and Calypso pulled out their instruments. Grodek stared at the violin in surprise.

"I didn't think you'd found the other piece of the violin yet."

"Calypso fixed it," Clarice said, settling the violin under her chin. "We were going to build a new one, but—well, this one just needed a little love."

"Huh," Grodek grunted, sheepish. "Didn't even occur to me you could just make another."

"Didn't occur to us either," Clarice said, laughing. "Credit goes to Mandy."

Mandy grinned proudly as Grodek glanced at her appraisingly. He snorted a laugh. "I guess you just needed an outsider's perspective. Okay, let's get this show on the road."

Mandy flinched at his comment, and Aria shared a knowing smile with Clarice and Calypso. Of course, Grodek would recognize Mandy for what she was.

Calypso straightened and began playing her harp. Aria and Clarice joined in as they connected their thoughts to each other. The song was short but potent. As a Seraph, Grodek represented a powerful aspect of the realms and required a significant alteration in the blueprints of reality in order to be changed.

After a few seconds of playing, the two imps blurred, then merged and elongated into the shape of an angel. Reality stabilized, and his form became solid, revealing a tall Seraph with shoulder-length golden hair and swirling blue eyes. He had striking features, like all angels, but there was something about his eyes reminiscent of his sarcastic nature.

"Whelp, this is going to be weird," Grodek noted in a deep voice. "I kind of like being in two places simultaneously."

"Now you know it's possible," Aria pointed out with a nod at the tree housing the GoD. "I'm sure you could replicate it in your normal form with a little research."

"Good idea," Grodek nodded appreciatively. "Though I'm going to miss playing the role of a cantankerous imp."

"Why would you stop now?" Clarice asked dryly. "I'm certainly not giving up leering. Besides, you've *always* been a cantankerous imp."

Grodek snorted, shaking his head. "We'll see. I'm going to find Rendimus. I'm not going to miss the opportunity to mock him while he's going through hell. I want to make sure he knows he's on borrowed time."

"Tell him he'll be lucky if I just decide to kill him," Calypso declared coldly. "The amount of suffering that pretentious ass forced onto countless angels throughout the cosmos is beyond horrifying."

"It'll be my pleasure," Grodek said with a sinister laugh. "I'll get creative on what he can expect."

Grodek vanished mid-laugh as he teleported away.

"As abrupt as ever," Lexi noted wryly. "I'm going to miss that little imp."

Aria smiled fondly. "Clarice is right—he's *always* been an irascible old man at heart. He did kind of grow on me as an imp."

Clarice snorted. "Like a wart. I hope he doesn't reform *too* much. While he was always caustic, his time as an imp made it even more pronounced."

"Where to now?" Aria asked curiously. "Do we want to fetch Lucifer and have our little talk, or go fetch the rest of Clarice's spirit?"

"Spirit," Clarice said fervently. "I'm really missing it right now."

Aria gave her a sympathetic hug. "I'm sorry you've been without it for so long."

"I didn't remember before," Clarice said plaintively. "Now that my memories are back, it's starting to drive me crazy."

Calypso opened a shimmering portal to Earth and the cabin.

"Last one back is a rotten egg!" Clarice shouted, darting through the portal.

Lexi watched her go, smirking. "You'd think enlightenment would mellow her out."

Calypso chuckled softly. "Mortality leaves its mark, but her soul? That's been the same for eons."

11 – The GoD

Rendimus sat slouched on his throne, listening to Ezeniel's report like a man being forced to read his own obituary. The news was bleak—over forty Cherubim of the first order, erased from existence. The Three had returned to the light realms.

Lucifer had promised they would stay trapped in the mortal plane, chasing fragments of a shattered divine instrument. He should have known better than trusting that slippery eel.

Lucifer had come to him shortly after Aria's return from the splinter realm—instrument in hand, arrogance in full bloom. He had made the terms plain: serve or die. It hadn't really been a choice, only a delay of execution.

Rendimus had never believed one instrument could unmake a Seraph. If it could, why hadn't Lucifer done it already? But even arrogance has survival instincts, and Rendimus wasn't inclined to test the odds.

So he had obeyed. Destroy the MPCs. Exterminate the returning Ascended. Play obedient soldier while praying the Three stayed lost in their little mortal sandbox.

They hadn't.

Now they were back, in the light realms. And once they acclimated to the density of the source radiance—once full recall set in—there would be no stopping them. He had seen what the Three could do when they truly remembered themselves. Their creators could erase a Seraph the way a hu man might wipe dust from a sleeve.

He felt cornered—trapped between cosmic predators, each one strong enough to snuff him out with a thought. Every second felt like a countdown to annihilation.

Doriel brooded beside him, his expression tight with unease. Nathaniel and Hiriel were silent, staring into nothing as though expecting death to come striding through the door.

"It was a mistake," Hiriel muttered, his voice thick with bitterness. "We should never have played the divine instruments before speaking to the

Three. Lucifer wanted them gone and needed four people to play the instruments. We were pawns."

Nathaniel snorted. "The naïve fools practically begged for it. They spent eons trying to 'save' mortals instead of paying attention to the real enemy. For beings so wise, they were spectacularly gullible. With the resources at their command, they should have easily seen through Lucifer."

Doriel's lip curled. "If they couldn't see through him after he created demons, they were never going to. Lucifer dangled his charm, and they walked right into it."

Rendimus gave a cold, mirthless smile. "Then take comfort in this. Whatever hell awaits us, Lucifer won't live long enough to gloat."

Weeks passed with no word of the Three. Rendimus sat in uneasy silence, waiting for the hammer to fall. Either they had gone back to the mortal realm, or they were already here, in the source realm, acclimating to the dense light that would soon make them unstoppable.

His dread solidified when Lucifer appeared out of thin air, with a smile sharp enough to draw blood. The azure light in his eyes burned cold.

"I have a new task for you, Rendimus," he purred. "It's time for the mortal parents of the Three to die. Take care of their uncle while you're at it."

Rendimus stared, jaw tightening. There was no point arguing—it would only shorten his life expectancy. Lucifer's hand brushed the gleaming surface of his divine instrument, the gesture casual, threatening.

"Say it," Lucifer ordered coldly. "I want to hear the words."

Rendimus ground his teeth until it was audible. "Thy will be done."

Lucifer's grin widened just enough to show satisfaction. "Good. I'll check in an hour. If they're still alive, you won't be."

He vanished in a shimmer of golden light.

Before the silence could settle, another pop echoed through the air—followed by Grodek's gleeful, venomous laugh.

"You androgynous pigeon farmers are so fucked," he announced, his eyes alight with malice. "The Three are about to turn this realm into a lightless landfill, and you know what? You earned it."

Doriel didn't even look up. Rendimus rubbed his temples. Grodek had been haunting them for weeks, showing up just to gloat. He was like cosmic heartburn—predictable, painful, and impossible to get rid of.

"I hope you've had your fill of light," Grodek continued, his voice syrupy with satisfaction. "Because the Three just pulled the plug on the whole damn grid. You poked the hornet's nest one too many times, sunshine."

"You know full well it's Lucifer who's been provoking them," Rendimus snapped, his composure cracking.

"Yeah," Grodek said with a wicked grin. "But you're the ones who tried to unmake *me*, so forgive me if I enjoy the karmic fireworks. You fucked half the cosmos—now it's your turn to get stuffed and roasted, you celestial turkeys."

Rendimus opened his mouth to retort—and froze. The light field around him vanished.

It was like being gutted. The absence hit his core, a hollow pain spreading through his meridians. A heartbeat later, Nathaniel and Doriel screamed as their luminous forms shrank and warped, wings folding inward until they became something lesser—Cherubim.

"Ouch," Grodek crowed gleefully. "That's *gotta* sting."

All around them, the remaining Cherubim flickered into the room, teleporting wildly in panic. The realm itself seemed to shudder.

"Seraph Rendimus," Enriel cried, bowing low, terror tightening every word. "Will the radiance return—or is it gone forever?"

Rendimus didn't answer. His mind was elsewhere—his senses flooded with the unmistakable presence of *five fully ascended Seraphim* and the hum of *three divine instruments*.

He met Hiriel's wide, terrified eyes. Neither spoke. A moment later, they both vanished, fleeing to the lower realms—along with every other Cherubim.

Grodek's mocking laughter followed them, gleefully spiteful.

Clarice stepped through the portal and stopped just inside the cabin, smiling softly as familiarity settled over her. The little wooden room looked exactly as they had left it—but now, with her memories back, it felt like stepping into a painting of her own past. The air here was thin, the light weak and dull. She winced at the emptiness of it, like her veins had been drained.

Withdrawal. That's what it felt like. A celestial junkie cut off from the pure stuff. She knew it would pass—she had endured worse—but it still crawled under her skin.

"Ugh," Mandy groaned, clutching her head. "Need. More. Light."

"Yeah..." Lexi muttered, grimacing. "This sucks."

"It'll even out in a few hours," Aria said as she followed them through. "Consider it celestial jet lag. Honestly, we're lucky there's any light left at all. We shut off the main source, so this realm's running on the cosmic equivalent of backup batteries."

Before Clarice could respond, a familiar blur crossed the room—and suddenly their parents were there.

"You're *finally* back!" Emily cried, throwing her arms around Aria, quick-silver tears streaking down her cheeks. Eric caught Clarice in a hug that knocked the wind out of her—figuratively, since breathing was optional now.

"Sorry, Mom," Aria said gently. "The source realm knocked us flat for a few weeks. The light density there is... intense."

Devon and Tamra slipped in behind them, both momentarily frozen by the tidal wave of power radiating off the five Seraphim.

"I take it you've got full recall," Devon said dryly as Emily and Eric switched daughters mid-hug. "You're fully ascended, then?"

"Yep," Clarice said with a grin. "It's weird seeing you all with both sets of memories again. Kind of like a family reunion with the multiverse watching."

Tamra's eyes lit up with interest. "What was I like before?"

Clarice hesitated, rubbing the back of her neck. "Let's just say... different. You were all raised to worship us. Some of the old Seraphim were full-blown narcissists, and we didn't notice how deep that indoctrination went. We stayed isolated, which turned out to be a big mistake."

Aria released Emily and smiled with satisfaction. "We've fixed some of that. Two of them are gone—replaced by Lexi and Mandy."

Clarice turned to their parents, mischief lighting her expression. "And next up? You two."

Eric blinked. "You want *us* to be Seraphim?"

"Yep," Aria and Clarice said together. Clarice shot her sister a wink, and Aria returned it easily—so much less guarded now, so much freer.

Emily tilted her head curiously. "Why us? Because we're your mortal parents?"

"That's part of it," Aria said, her eyes soft. "But it's also because of who you are. We got to know you without all the old memories—without the power—and you were good. Kind. You reminded us what all this was supposed to mean." She paused, her voice catching. "Even with everything we remember now, the choice is the same."

Clarice nodded. "We should've done it long ago. We just... didn't think the others would go so far. We were naïve, even for immortals."

"I feel like I'm in the presence of deities," Tamra murmured, her eyes wide as she took in their glow. "You really have a *strong* presence, don't you?"

Clarice chuckled and drew her aura back. The others followed her lead, and the room immediately felt a hundred tons lighter. "Better?"

Tamra blinked as the overwhelming energy vanished, leaving behind five ordinary-looking Seraphim who could still level reality if they sneezed. "You can just... turn it off like that?"

"Pretty much," Clarice confirmed, then shimmered, her form melting into her old mortal body. "See? We pretty much do whatever we want."

Their parents stared, thunderstruck. Eric's eyes went glassy. "It feels like years since I've seen my daughters look human."

Aria smiled softly, then turned businesslike. "We need to retrieve the last fragment of Clarice's spirit. She's *really* feeling the missing piece now that her memories are back."

Emily's eyes were misty as she reached toward Clarice's cheek. "How can we help?"

"We've got this," Aria assured her confidently.

Eric frowned. "Do you at least know where it is?"

Clarice turned toward an unseen horizon and raised a hand. A ripple of light opened into a portal that smelled faintly of pine and cold air. "Northern Utah," she said, stepping through. "I can feel it calling."

They emerged into a dense forest full of evergreens, sunlight glinting through the branches. Crude structures dotted the woods, the kind of minimalist shelters built by people who thought civilization was a suggestion. The place was empty, like a ghost town.

Clarice's eyes grew distant as she scanned the area with her aura. "There's a cave nearby," she murmured. "That's where it is."

She marched through the trees toward the mountainside. Her hands shook with anticipation as she drew closer.

The cave entrance was just wide enough for one person to enter at a time. Before she could go inside, Aria darted ahead of her, looking over her shoulder with a challenging look. Clarice sighed and reined in her enthusiasm. Her sister wasn't willing to let her take any chances, even now.

"Wait!" Mandy called, jogging up.

Aria paused mid-stride. "What's up?"

Mandy frowned. "Didn't the *last* guy try to lure us into a cave in Tibet? Maybe we skip the part where we walk into the obvious trap and just, I don't know, *flatten* the mountain?"

Clarice exchanged a look with Aria and Calypso, then broke into a grin. "You know, Mandy, you might be the youngest soul here, but you're definitely the smartest."

Mandy shrugged, smirking. "Told you. New and improved model."

The Seraphim burst out laughing, affection pulsing between them.

Clarice finally sobered and laid a reassuring hand on Mandy's shoulder. "Don't worry, we'll be careful. Whatever this thing is, it's got some kind of primitive virus embedded in its spirit. It would've worked on us before… but not anymore."

Her gaze turned inward, her sight piercing through layers of stone until she could see the entity coiled inside the mountain—neither angel nor demon, just a malformed relic of the other Seraphim's experiments.

She exhaled, and the air trembled.

Her aura unfurled like a sunstorm, tendrils threading through the rock, rewriting matter as easily as breathing. There was a flash, then a rolling thunderclap as the mountain simply ceased to exist. A gale tore through the clearing, scattering dust like ash in the wind.

When the air cleared, a stunned figure stood alone in the sunlight, blinking at the sudden absence of several million tons of geology.

"Did you just vaporize a *mountain*?" Lexi demanded in a strangled voice.

"Nope, *disintegrated*," Clarice corrected with a shrug. "I can see how you could mix them up, though."

Lexi opened and closed her mouth a few times, then gave up trying to form words.

"You must be Madjack," Clarice said, her voice low and dangerous. Her eyes gleamed like twin novas. "You've got something that belongs to me."

Madjack grinned, a twisted, hungry thing. "You've got that backwards," he purred. "You're what belongs to *me*. I've just been waiting for the rest of my toy to show up. Finders keepers, sweetheart."

Aria's aura exploded, her wings flaring in raw fury, but Clarice placed a calming hand on her sister's arm. "He's not worth the effort," she murmured, her gaze never leaving Madjack.

Through her spiritual sight, she could see it all—the mangled lines of energy running through his meridians, warped and infected. Another of Rendimus's little science projects. Living souls stitched into something that shouldn't exist.

"There's no point in playing his game," she said quietly.

With a flick of her wrist, a portal opened beneath the ground where she felt the pulse of her missing spirit. An invisible thread snapped into place. The air buckled with an inverted *boom* as the fragment dropped neatly into her hand.

The second it touched her, she gasped—then laughed, then cried, all at once. The world came alive in colors she had forgotten existed. She felt herself *click* together like a puzzle finally completed after eternity. Every channel, every node sang in unison. How had she ever endured being incomplete?

Madjack's howl shattered the moment. He lunged for her, his face twisted in fury—only to vanish mid-charge.

He reappeared a dozen feet down, trapped in a smooth cylindrical pit that hadn't existed seconds ago. Clarice turned, arching an eyebrow at Emily.

"Containment field," Emily said matter-of-factly. "I've been tinkering with it for a while. Nonlethal, theoretically."

Madjack threw himself against the barrier, snarling like an animal. "You belong to *me*! I'm going to take you to—"

He never finished.

A white flash of angel fire tore through the air. When it faded, there was nothing left of him but drifting motes of light.

Clarice blinked at the empty pit, then turned toward her sister. Aria stood trembling, every inch of her vibrating with barely restrained fury.

"You okay?" Clarice asked softly, though the answer was already humming through their link—white-hot wrath sizzling in her sister's aura.

Aria's voice shook, low and venomous. "His thoughts were beyond vile. He was going to—" She broke off, her jaw clenched tight. "There was no saving him. No mercy."

Clarice hadn't even tried to link up with Madjack's thought node. "What do you mean?"

"The things he wanted to do to you," Aria replied in a sick voice. "He was no better than those pieces of shit in Beverly Hills. There's no redemption for such as them."

Clarice grimaced and nodded. "Agreed."

Lexi stepped forward to join them. "How did he even get your piece of spirit?" she asked, frowning at the empty pit.

Aria's answer was ice. "A Seraph. Has to be. Probably Rendimus." Her eyes flared as she turned to Clarice. "It's time. Mom and Dad ascend next—then we pay the rest a visit."

"We should see if Lucifer found the rest of his pieces first," Clarice suggested gently. "Then we can just begin the rewrite immediately. Don't forget how many worlds are living hells right now."

Aria took a deep, calming breath, forcing the fury down. "You're right. I can't get hung up on vengeance when so many people are suffering."

"Let's go pay Lucifer a visit," Clarice said as she opened a gateway. "We need some answers from him, anyway."

The psychic web of the mortal realm pulsed like a living thing. Among billions of faint human signatures, Lucifer's consciousness loomed like a bowling ball on a trampoline—distorting reality around it, impossible to miss.

The portal led to the top floor of a skyscraper in Hong Kong. Clarice shifted into her mortal form before stepping through. Inside, the clack of keyboards and hum of air-conditioning filled a maze of cubicles. Dozens of office workers blinked up from their screens as she walked past—a woman too perfect to belong here, followed by four human-looking Seraphim and four Cherubim-looking Cherubim who looked like they had wandered in from a Renaissance mural.

Gasps erupted around them, followed by phones rising in shaky hands. The cubicle cattle could *feel* the wrongness of it, even if they couldn't name it.

Clarice was halfway down the row when Mandy's voice cut through. "Clarice—wait."

She stopped instantly, turning. Mandy's face was pale. "Something's off. I can't explain it... just don't go in there."

Clarice turned to look at the door where she felt Lucifer's presence, then turned back to face Mandy. Aria was suddenly on high alert, staring around the office warily. With a thought, she wrapped their group in a void bubble, blocking sound and presence alike. "Something to do with Lucifer?"

"I don't know," Mandy grimaced in frustration. "Every sense in my soul is telling me there's something bad waiting on the other side of that door, though."

Clarice studied Mandy closely, noting the terror in her eyes. She nodded slowly, remembering the past comments Mandy had made regarding Lucifer. She knew something about Lucifer but was afraid of revealing her knowledge.

Her gaze flicked to a nearby employee. He froze as the shimmering barrier of the void bubble expanded to include him.

"What is this place?" she asked in fluent Cantonese, her voice smooth but unyielding. "What company is this, and what do you do here?"

The man, Ming, swallowed hard. Middle-aged, neat, and utterly out of his depth, he kept glancing between Clarice and the winged shapes behind her.

"Knewcell," he stammered. "We... design and manufacture biotechnology."

"What kind?" Aria pressed, stepping closer. "Nanobots?"

"That information is classified," Ming said automatically, his eyes darting toward the Cherubim as though waiting for permission to breathe.

Clarice sighed softly and shifted—light flaring as her Seraph form emerged. Her aura filled the office like a sunbeam through a magnifying glass. Papers fluttered, and the lights dimmed.

"I'm going to need that information, Ming," she said, her voice wrapped in ultimate authority. "Classified or not."

The blood drained from Ming's face. He trembled violently under the weight of her presence. Clarice shifted back to her human form, her gaze steady.

Then she whispered a single word—the rune of reset.

A pulse of light rippled through Ming's body. He gasped, staggering as the microscopic hum inside his cells went silent. Clarice felt the nanotech disintegrating, erased down to its molecular components, then fading away to nothing.

She reached out, steadying him with a hand. "There are no more nanobots in your system," she told him softly. "You can speak freely now."

Ming's eyes darted around, wild and searching.

"We can protect your family," Aria promised. "We can make you immortal—the same way you'd become if you died. Either way, you'll be safe."

"Not here," Ming whispered, glancing around again, sweat beading at his temples.

"Cabin," Clarice ordered, and in a blink, they were standing on the veranda, surrounded by pine-scented air and quiet mountains.

Ming staggered, staring around in disbelief. His mind reeled as he tried to process teleportation, angels, and whatever divine authority had just uprooted him from an office in Hong Kong.

"You're safe now," Clarice assured him with a smile. "Start from the beginning. What's happening at Knewcell?"

"I only know fragments," Ming admitted, his voice trembling. "They keep everything compartmentalized. You already know about the nanobot injections..."

"I lived the nanobot injections," Devon growled, his jaw tight. "I had those metal maggots crawling under my skin for half a lifetime."

Ming nodded, swallowing hard. "Our project was built around creating a neural interface between the nanobots and a central command system. The company said it was part of the Singularity Initiative—merging humanity with AI. To train the system, they needed complete biological and neurological mappings, so they released a pandemic—a designer virus that spread the nanobots through the population under the guise of a vaccine."

Clarice's eyes darkened. "So the injections weren't protection. They were infiltration."

Ming nodded miserably. "At first, it was just data collection to train the AI. But about a year ago, things changed. People saw video feeds of themselves doing things they couldn't remember—entire conversations, actions... blank spots. We realized the AI wasn't observing consciousness anymore. It was *replacing* it."

Devon let out a bitter laugh. "Mind control. Every government's favorite bedtime story."

"Why is Lucifer tangled up in this?" Clarice demanded. "Why hasn't he told us anything?"

Ming frowned in confusion. "Lucifer? I don't know that name. But the man in the head office—the one you were heading toward—he's not human. He never eats or sleeps. He's been here since the beginning."

A cold silence fell.

"I'm starting to feel a little suspicious about Lucifer," Mandy said quietly, though her swirling violet eyes burned with certainty. "You said Grodek helped you. But how much did you *really* trust Lucifer when you were building the universe?"

Clarice exchanged a grave look with Aria and Calypso. Calypso's expression turned inward, as if dredging through eons of buried memory.

"There was a time," Calypso said slowly, "when he attempted to persuade me to alter the safeguards—to make the divine instruments function with only two participants rather than four." She looked up, her tone heavy with concern. "He claimed it was to make creation more efficient. In truth, however, I suspect he desired control. He asked whether the GoD could be used in the manner of an artificial intelligence—not to create worlds, but to monitor and govern them. To enforce reality rather than nurture it."

She rubbed her temples, grimacing. "Back then, it didn't seem dangerous. We didn't understand emotion or empathy. We didn't think about what control meant. But after mortality..." Her voice trailed off into something fragile and horrified. "Now it sounds monstrous."

Aria's eyes widened as the implications hit. "If he wanted two instruments instead of four, he'd need another Seraph to link with him." She paused, and her voice grew worried. "Could Grodek have been with him all along? Or one of the others?"

"Mandy, this is the *third* time you've saved our asses," Clarice said, flashing her a warm, grateful smile. "You were definitely a good choice."

"Was I, though?" Mandy asked quietly. Her violet eyes flickered with uncertainty. "Lucifer's the one who made the template I was forged from. What if I'm some kind of trap? What if he built it in a way to spy through me?"

"You're not," Clarice said without hesitation. "I've already analyzed your shell, every filament of it." She turned toward Aria and Calypso, resolve tightening her expression. "It's time for some drastic action."

She pivoted back to Ming. "I'm leaving you with our uncle Devon and Tamra. They'll take you somewhere safe." She turned to Devon. "Get him translated to an angel, as well as his family."

Devon frowned. "Where are you going?"

Clarice smiled grimly. “Let’s just say it’s time to flex some Seraphim power,” she said with a cheerfulness that was more than a little unsettling. “You’ll know when we’re done—trust me.”

He nodded reluctantly. “Be careful.”

“I’m *always* careful,” Clarice replied with a grin that made the statement sound like a lie wrapped in starlight.

Devon shook his head, muttering under his breath as he placed a hand on Tamra’s shoulder and another on Ming’s. The three of them vanished.

Clarice turned back to the others. “Be ready for anything. Mom, Dad—brace yourselves. You’re about to be in *Lala Land* for a bit.”

“Huh?” Eric managed before Clarice unfurled her aura, wrapping her parents and fellow Seraphim in radiance. Then she teleported.

Gasps followed as Emily and Eric’s eyes went wide, their bodies trembling under the rush of ultra-dense radiance. Clarice shivered herself—it still hit like an electric sunrise—but she stayed focused.

“Are we... inside the GoD?” Lexi asked in wonder.

“Yep,” Clarice said with a grin. “Welcome to the Generator of Data.” She glanced at Calypso. “You know what I need.”

Calypso nodded, pulling her divine instrument from her soul space. Aria did the same, then Clarice.

“What are we doing?” Lexi murmured, turning in slow circles. The space around them looked like a luminous cave—walls and ceiling made of grainy white light, no shadows, only soft radiance. At the far end, an opening pulsed brighter than the rest, like the heart of a living star.

“This is the threshold to the inner world of the GoD,” Clarice said. “Calypso’s going to work on the instruments. Lexi, Mandy—you can go with her. We’ll stay here with our parents and take care of some other matters.”

“I’ve noticed an odd linguistic quirk in your speech,” Mandy said thoughtfully. “You never say *my* parents or *my* uncle. It’s always *our*.”

Calypso smiled softly. “That is because they are two halves of a single spirit. Even before mortality, they were intertwined. Mortality merely made the bond literal. I happen to think it is rather adorable.”

Clarice frowned, thinking back through her memories. She had never noticed it before, but it was true—she never thought of things as *hers*. Everything was *ours*.

Aria’s lips curved into a mischievous smile. “We even share our girlfriend.”

Clarice giggled, her eyes shining. “It’s true. Aria really is the other half of me. I can’t imagine a life without her.”

Aria was suddenly in front of her, her eyes glistening as she pulled Clarice into a fierce embrace. Clarice felt the tremor in her shoulders, the weight of that old wound from the splinter reality. She wrapped her arms around her sister, fingers brushing gently through her hair. They held each other like anchors in a storm, unwilling to let go, as the other three Seraphim disappeared deeper into the inner universe of the GoD.

"Even with eternity restored to my memory," Aria whispered, her voice trembling against Clarice's neck, "that sense of loss never fades. It's sharper now, somehow—remembering just how long we've been together."

"I know," Clarice murmured, pressing her cheek to Aria's hair. "It's a scar on your beautiful soul. But it's ours, and it's healed as much as it ever will. And now that our spirits are intertwined, it can't ever happen again. You're stuck with me for all of eternity."

Aria smiled against her skin, the warmth of it lighting up the link between them. "You have no idea how much that comforts me."

"As a matter of fact, I do," Clarice grinned. "I can *feel* it."

Aria drew back, their eyes meeting—violet and brown, both blazing with love as old as light itself. "I know you already know this," she said, her voice breaking into something raw, "but I love you, Clarice. You really are the heart of my soul."

Clarice smiled radiantly, all starlight and tenderness. "I know. But I still love hearing it. I love you too, Aria."

Their lips met, and the world seemed to vanish. The kiss was like the breath of creation, drawing on all their desperate longing, a fusion of souls who had built galaxies together. Clarice could feel the molten tide of Aria's desire rising through her, mirroring her own until the entire realm seemed ready to ignite.

For one fleeting moment, she almost used the divine instruments to carve a private island out of existence—a sanctuary where time didn't move and love didn't end.

Aria finally broke the kiss with a frustrated groan, her forehead resting against Clarice's. The soul link between them pulsed with shared exasperation.

"I'm so pissed at Lucifer," Aria muttered, glaring at the luminous air. "How could we have been so trusting? We were geniuses with the life experience of infants."

"We were children," Clarice said ruefully. "Eternal toddlers playing with universes. We didn't understand love or hate, just... creation. I sometimes miss that simplicity—but I'd never trade it back. Not after learning what it means to love."

Aria gave a low chuckle. "Who knew emotions would turn out to be more complicated than building reality itself?" She leaned back, looking into Clarice's eyes thoughtfully. "Next time we take a break, I'm building a bubble realm, one that is outside of time."

Clarice's grin was immediate. "You read my mind. I've been trying to figure out how to make a time field that wouldn't wreck causality. Not without taking off my limiter."

Aria tilted her head, a sly smile forming. "Maybe we can. We've already layered redundancy across the realms. There's plenty of room for another container."

Clarice's eyes lit up. "A parallel realm—overclocked and isolated," she said excitedly. "We could live an entire vacation before a single heartbeat passes here."

"Exactly," Aria said, smiling beatifically. "All we need are a few divine instruments—unless we want to make it outside this realm."

"Then let's make sure Calypso doesn't take her sweet time," Clarice teased. "I suddenly have a lot of motivation to help her."

Aria laughed, pure and bright, and kissed her again. The three of them would have their alone time. Soon.

12 – Alice

"Oh, wow," Lexi breathed slowly as she entered the realm of the GoD. A white platform of heartwood extended into a void of darkness that stretched endlessly. What stunned her was the torrent of energy flowing through the room. There was a pattern to the energy she could sense with her aura as it flowed, swirled, and washed around them.

It was completely incomprehensible, but she could understand what Calypso meant when she spoke of the Generator of Data. The flow of energy brimmed with information, so dense her mind shrank from imagining how long they had spent unraveling it. She felt a renewed sense of awe that the three women who created her had spent eons learning to understand the encoded information to such a degree that they were able to create both the light realms and the mortal realm.

"How did you ever learn to make sense of *this*?" Mandy asked, awe softening her voice.

Calypso shrugged. "We possess perfect memories, so every piece of the puzzle we uncover remains stored away until another piece presents itself. Given the amount of time at our disposal, we were able simply to immerse ourselves in the energy until our minds began to recognize the patterns. Before experiencing mortality, we had no concept of time whatsoever. With no need to eat or sleep, there were no natural markers to create the illusion of its passage. The GoD was the most fascinating thing in existence once we discovered a means of accessing it, and so it commanded nearly all of our attention. One can only wander about the garden for so many billions of years before one has named every grain of sand."

Lexi laughed, the image vivid in her mind. "Let me guess—Clarice hadn't learned how to *leer* yet."

Calypso burst into delighted laughter. "Not until mortality!"

Mandy's eyes sparkled. "We should get her a *leer* jet for her birthday."

Lexi groaned. "Was that a dad joke I just heard?"

"Who's your daddy?" Mandy leered, matching Clarice's expression disturbingly well.

The humor died in the air as Lexi's smile faltered, a shadow crossing her face.

"Oh, I'm so sorry," Mandy blurted, instantly contrite. "That was insensitive. Is your dad—?"

"It's okay," Lexi said quickly, forcing a small smile. "You just... reminded me of mortality before... before they rescued me."

"Rescued you?" Mandy asked carefully. "If that's too personal, I'll shut up."

"You're totally fine," Lexi assured her, then looked her up and down appreciatively. "And I mean *totally* fine."

Mandy laughed and hugged her, warmth and light blending in the air around them. "You're looking pretty damn fine yourself, young lady."

Lexi snorted. "Young? I'm eons old. You're the only kid here."

"Whatever," Mandy declared airily, leaning away from Lexi. "I'll always be older since I was changed into an angel at an older age." Her eyes softened. "So... what's the deal with your dad?"

Lexi exhaled, long and heavy. "He made my life a living hell. He sold me to some rich pedophile in Beverly Hills when I was fourteen." She flashed a grateful smile at Calypso. "I was there until these angels freed me five months ago."

Mandy froze, then gasped softly, her hand flying to her mouth. "Lexi... oh my God." She pulled Lexi in again, fierce this time. "I'm so sorry."

"It was awful," Lexi said quietly. "But it doesn't own me anymore. Getting my memories back helped. Eternity kind of puts pain in perspective."

"Where is he now?" Mandy asked, her voice deceptively calm.

"Clarice vaporized him." Lexi's tone was matter-of-fact, but the corner of her mouth trembled.

Mandy's eyes went cold. "He got off easy."

"Maybe," Lexi admitted with a heavy sigh. "I'm just glad he's gone. The world's a cleaner place without his taint."

Calypso stood at the edge of the white platform, her gaze fixed on the vast darkness. Lexi could see her mind at work—billions of microscopic tendrils extending from her aura into the streaming rivers of energy. Each thread shimmered like a living filament, connecting to the flow of information. It wasn't just observation; Calypso was *communing* with the data itself.

Lexi watched in awe. The Seraph had once described the GoD as an information archive, not an interactive system—but what she saw looked anything but passive. Calypso was surfing the code of creation.

"I wonder how long she'll be at it," Lexi murmured to Mandy.

"Quite some time," Calypso replied absently without turning around. "You two ought to venture deeper. The data patterns become increasingly complex the farther in one goes. It is fascinating to witness, particularly the first time."

Lexi lifted a questioning eyebrow at Mandy.

"I'm game," Mandy grinned.

Lexi matched her grin and launched herself forward. The two of them soared through the glowing abyss, light cascading around them as information streams coiled and flowed like living rivers. Through spiritual sight, the void wasn't empty at all—it was a network, a neural lattice pulsing with infinite thought.

"It makes you wonder," Mandy said thoughtfully, "if this isn't a place at all—just the mind of some unimaginable being. Maybe all this is its neural activity, and we're basically swimming in its thoughts."

Lexi slowed, her own energy field shimmering with reflection. "Maybe reality itself is just one of its dreams. Maybe *we* are."

"Aria said the three of them existed for eons before creating the others," Mandy said, her voice soft with wonder. "Honestly, the longer I think about it, the more it feels like a simulation."

Lexi frowned. "If it's a simulation, what's the point? Three Seraphim spawned in an endless garden sounds like a setup without a purpose. Unless the real goal was for them to hack the system and rewrite the code. That would mean the creators *wanted* this to happen."

"Maybe they did," Mandy countered. "Maybe this whole thing is an experiment—to see what self-aware code does when it starts asking questions. We already run tests like that with primitive AIs in the mortal realm."

"Sure," Lexi said skeptically, "but *billions* of years?"

Mandy glanced at Lexi calculatingly. "Maybe the processors run fast enough that it only feels like billions of years to us. Like when we crank up our thoughts for hyper-speed travel. If their system runs at quantum overdrive, then time itself would just be... relative gobbledygook."

Lexi chuckled. "Insanely fast super-quantum gobbledygook computers. I can already hear Clarice naming them that in the lab."

Mandy smirked. "And then leering at them."

Lexi threw her head back and laughed delightedly, a sound like sunlight turned into music. When the laughter faded, she gazed again at the endless tides of data swirling through the void, her expression darkening.

"It's an interesting idea," she said slowly. "But if this really *is* a simulation—what are its creators doing now? Just watching? Are they sitting back while quintillions of beings suffer, telling themselves it's fine because none of us are *real*?" Her voice hardened. "If that's the case, then they're not scientists—they're sadists. You'd have to be a special kind of monster to make a world like this and then just... let it rot."

Mandy's expression grew serious, her swirling violet eyes gleaming faintly in the light of the data streams. "What if they *did* do something?" she countered quietly. "What are the odds that three Seraphim ended up reborn on the same planet—and two of them as sisters? Or that the Cherubim connected to them just happen to include their parents, their uncle, and *you*? Seventy Cherubim total, across billions of worlds. The odds of that happening naturally are... zero. Someone arranged this."

Lexi froze mid-flight, her gaze locking on Mandy's. A chill ran through her as a new thought flickered to life. "Mandy... would you tell me if you *knew* this was a simulation?"

For a heartbeat, Mandy went utterly still, and her breath hitched. The panic that flashed through her eyes was raw and unguarded—then she forced a quick laugh, the sound just a shade too bright.

"I think that Jason guy you mentioned is the one we should talk to if we really want to chase that theory," she said lightly, but her eyes screamed "stop talking."

Lexi smiled faintly, pretending to relax. "Good idea," she said, as if nothing had passed between them. "Next time we see him, I'll bring it up."

Mandy's hand found hers as they began flying again, squeezing tighter than usual. Too tight. Lexi didn't pull away.

They flew in silence for a long time. The only sound was the pulse of information flowing past them like a billion whispering voices. Lexi's thoughts spun.

Mandy wasn't just cautious—she was afraid. Afraid of being overheard in a literal void. That meant one of two things: either paranoia had finally cracked her, or someone really was listening. If the GoD was a system, maybe every interaction was logged. Maybe they were nothing more than processes running under constant surveillance.

But how did Mandy know?

Lexi studied her profile, that light-hearted confidence masking something deeper. If Mandy *was* from outside... maybe she wasn't truly part of the simulation. Maybe she was an avatar or a failsafe injected into the code to alter the course of their realm.

And if that was true... had someone, somewhere, broken the rules to help them?

The thought hit her like a bucket of ice water.

Mandy had warned them about the cave. About Lucifer's office. About building the new divine instrument. Every pivotal decision—the kind that had saved them—had come from her.

The more Lexi thought about it, the clearer it seemed. Mandy wasn't just lucky—she knew.

Lexi looked into Mandy's swirling violet Seraph eyes and smiled naturally, keeping her expression normal despite her roiling thoughts. "I'm glad we got some alone time, at least. I wonder if there are any other scenarios where we could get some...*real*...alone time before we reach some kind of resolution with this mess."

Mandy stared back at Lexi, her eyes instantly brimming with relief so raw she had to hurriedly blink the tears away. "I hope we can too," she smiled, a mixture of gratitude and love charging her gaze. "I wonder if you can *ever* get alone time since your spirit is linked. It must be weird, always practically *hearing* their thoughts in the privacy of spirit space."

Lexi's eyes widened as she felt the bonfire of passion between Aria and Clarice suddenly erupt, filling her own body with sudden need. "Yeah, apparently they've decided to take advantage of *their* alone time," Lexi said wryly, her cheeks coloring. "It's hard to concentrate with their passion influencing my thoughts until all I can think about is how much I want you right now."

Mandy's eyes widened in surprise, then softened as she stared at Lexi with tears in her eyes. She quickly blinked them away, smiling at Lexi with her heart in her eyes. She must have been afraid Lexi's love would vanish with the recent revelations.

Lexi pulled her to a stop and drew her in a warm embrace. "I'm so happy I met you, Mandy. I don't care *what* reality you're from. You're a wonderful person."

Mandy stiffened in her arms when she heard the double meaning. After a moment, she melted, clinging tightly as she silently wept.

"I'm not sure how this is done, but I'd like to try," Lexi told her softly. "I want to link my spirit with yours, the way Clarice did with Aria."

"Lexi..." Mandy whispered, squeezing her tightly and sniffing back her tears. "From what I've seen, it's an intensely personal bond. Are you sure you want to do that with me? I don't bring a lot with me from... the splinter reality."

"I swear on my Seraph soul I'll always be with you, no matter what happens," Lexi spoke without hesitation, her voice ringing with Seraph authority.

There was a shift in the information flowing around them, as if the GoD had to make room for a sudden influx of data. Mandy gasped as she felt Lexi's spirit open, countless threads reaching toward her invitingly. Her eyes grew wide as she stared at Lexi with new eyes, seeing the true beauty of the spirit within. She gingerly reached out and touched Lexi's face with trembling fingers, as if she couldn't believe her eyes.

"You are so amazingly *beautiful,*" Mandy breathed as tears of wonder formed in her eyes. "I swear on my soul I'll always be with you, Lexi."

Lexi shuddered as the searching strands of their spirits found each other and fused together. She stared at Mandy in sudden confusion, seeing a small blonde woman with large, vulnerable eyes staring back at her adoringly. Her lips parted into an "oh" as she realized she was seeing whoever Mandy really was. She was so beautiful it nearly caused physical pain. She gazed in wonder at the divine creature in front of her. It was a beauty of the spirit—a spirit consumed with compassion and love.

Lexi cupped the stunning face in trembling hands and leaned her forehead against Mandy's, staring into her gentle blue eyes.

"Oh Mandy," Lexi whispered as a tear rolled down her cheek. "You are the most beautiful thing I've ever seen. How can *anything* be so beautiful?"

Mandy tilted her head and pressed her lips against Lexi's. Electricity shot through her body. She slid her hands around Mandy's head and held her gently as their lips danced together. It was a tender but passionate kiss, conveying their love and need in equal parts.

"*Lexi... thank you for not leaving me.*" Mandy's thoughts filled her mind, overflowing with gratitude and love. "*I was so afraid you'd turn away when you found out who I really am.*"

Lexi sent a pulse of reassurance back through the link, a ripple of pure feeling. "*I've sensed your heart since the day we met. Whatever else you are, you've always been kind—and now I see that was only the smallest part of you.*"

They hovered in the still air, arms wrapped around each other, lips brushing softly as data-light shimmered around them. The moment stretched—long enough for Lexi to feel the flicker of concern from the other Seraphim. They could sense her emotions—the love, the joy... and the growing fear.

When Mandy finally pulled back, there was determination burning behind the tears in her eyes. "*They can't hear us when we talk through this link.*"

Lexi hesitated. "*Mandy... do you exist outside the simulation?*" The question carried both awe and dread. If Mandy had another life beyond this world, how long could they truly be together?

"*Yes.*" Mandy's mental voice was soft but clear, filled with wonder. "*My spirit's really here, but my consciousness spans both realities. The people running this project don't know I'm inside.*"

Lexi's breath quickened. "*Who are you—out there?*"

"Just a data analyst. Practically an intern." The thought came with a flicker of nervous amusement and more than a little fear. *"If they find out, I'm finished. Of course, time runs differently here, so even if they noticed right now, it'd be a hundred years in here before they could stop me."*

Lexi brushed a stray lock of hair from Mandy's face, her gaze full of reverence. *"Then why come? Why risk it?"* She paused. *"Were you the same Mandy—the one with Aria in the splinter reality?"*

"I was responsible for using one of the real-time observation consoles to catalog the progress of the civilizations," Mandy answered, her eyes growing haunted. *"I saw world after endless world of horror as angels trapped other angels in mortality and tortured them for their sick amusement."*

She swallowed hard. *"We weren't supposed to intervene. Just observe. But one of the engineers who saw my reports was as sickened as I was. She helped me use one of the prototypes—the kind meant for direct contact with the simulation. They weren't cleared for human use yet because the nanobots were still experimental."*

Lexi's chest tightened. Experimental? That didn't sound safe. Not at all.

"We couldn't just watch anymore," Mandy continued softly. *"So we altered the soul-trap code. We made sure Aria and the others would end up on Earth, in the same family. I sent Eric and Emily a letter with the recovery stats for the hospital where Calypso played, so Aria and Clarice could be healed. I've been inside since Aria was born."*

She hesitated, anger rippling through the link. *"When Lucifer sent the character template to the splinter reality, he meant to make sure Aria remained there. He was the one responsible for her being there in the first place. I used it as an opportunity to become involved with Aria and the rest of you on a personal level. I intercepted the template when Lucifer inserted it into the other reality, then merged with Mandy. I was just a backseat driver in her consciousness until she came back to this reality. She didn't have a soul due to how Lucifer created her, and that made it possible for me to become part of her. She faded quickly after the splinter reality imploded; I'm all that's left now. I just put ideas in her head, for the most part, but as she began to fade, I became the sole personality."*

Lexi stared at her, awe and anger warring in her expression—anger at Lucifer.

"I've been trying to keep you all safe ever since," Mandy went on. *"Lucifer's been building an AI hive mind inside the simulation—something to strip angels of free will, to make them part of his network with himself as master node. He had plans in case one of the Three returned, but not all of*

them. He's been scrambling to find a way to snare some of them in splinter realities to prevent them from playing their divine instruments and changing reality."

"His divine instrument was restored thousands of years ago," she added grimly. "*That's how he was able to make the splinter reality where he trapped Aria. He's in for a big surprise when Calypso finishes unlinking it from devices with authorized console access."*

Lexi's eyes widened. *"So that's what she's doing."* She paused, tilting her head questioningly. *"Do they even know this is a simulation? They must—how else could they create realms?"*

Mandy frowned, their soft angel glow lighting her face. "*It's... hard to say. We don't know how far they've evolved. I think they've figured it out, but they never say it. Lately, though, I've started to suspect they've found a way to hide their communications from the outside. They've hinted too many times about me being from 'another world,' and I'm pretty sure they don't mean the splinter."*

Lexi blinked, trying to imagine the mischievous Clarice as some kind of super intelligence covering her tracks from outside observation. The thought nearly made her laugh. "*What else can Lucifer do after his divine instrument is deactivated?"*

"Not very much, because those three are all-powerful Seraphim," Mandy answered with a feeling of satisfaction." *All his cards depended on his functional divine instrument and deceit. He still has his AI project, but it's nothing in the face of three divine instruments. They can undo anything he does. He probably realizes we suspect him by now. From what I know of him, he'll probably think you're trying to go after the other Seraphim, and he'll be searching for you in the light realms. Clarice's decision to come straight here and re-key the divine instruments might not occur to him until it's too late."*

"What about Grodek?" Lexi asked softly. *"He's not really working with Lucifer, is he?"*

Mandy's expression grew uncertain. *"He knows Lucifer would enslave him if given the chance, but he seems to be playing along for now. Maybe Grodek's waiting for someone else to take Lucifer down—maybe even counting on you four to do it. I can't tell if he's sitting on the fence or if he's just too good at misdirection to read. He could've handed you the divine instruments outright, but he didn't. Maybe he's protecting something... I just don't know. I do know he's the one who arranged for Calypso to ascend, and without her, she wouldn't have been able to heal the others."*

Lexi sighed. *"He's impossible to figure out. Still, he's helped us when it counted—hard to hate a guy like that."* She looked into Mandy's eyes, that impossible shade of blue, full of warmth and fear. *"I love you, Mandy. I don't have words for how grateful I am that you're here. You're incredible, and I'll do whatever it takes to make sure we have a long life together—however long that means in this reality or any other."*

Mandy smiled through her tears. *"I love you too, Lexi. I still can't believe this is real—that someone like you could love someone like me. In my old life, I couldn't have imagined being with anyone so far above my level."*

Lexi's eyebrows shot up. *"Level? Don't start that nonsense. If anything,* I *should be bowing to* you. *You're the one saving entire realities."*

Mandy laughed through her tears. *"Fishing for praises, are we?"*

"I could praise you for eternity and never run out of material," Lexi said softly, their shared bond glowing with affection.

"I just hope I get to earn them someday," Mandy murmured. "I hope Aria and the others can fix everything soon."

Before Lexi could reply, Clarice materialized beside them in a shimmer of light, concern flickering across her features.

"Everything all right over here?"

"It's perfect," Lexi said, smiling warmly. She sent a ripple of gratitude through the link, letting Clarice feel the depth of what Mandy meant to her. "I was just telling Mandy how lucky we are to have her."

Clarice studied Lexi for a moment, clearly sensing more beneath the surface. "She has made a habit of saving our hides."

Her eyes widened slightly as a wave of overpowering emotion—love, awe, and a faint thread of fear—surged through the link.

Trying to steer the conversation, Lexi looked out across the vast emptiness. "You know, the more I look at this, the more it feels like a computer system. All these streams of energy... they look like data."

Clarice surveyed the endless data currents with a faint smile. "Hard not to see it that way once you've been inside the GoD."

Lexi turned, startled. "Wait—*you* think this is a simulation?"

Clarice met her gaze calmly. "Think? I *know* it is. We've always known. We set up monitors long ago to log any kind of anomalous perturbations in the fabric of each realm. There weren't any—not until we became trapped in mortality. We just reviewed the logs that've been collecting since our exile, and there've been a few visitors. They had the simulation running a lot faster for the first twenty billion years. They slowed it down when we created the light realms, then even more for the mortal realm. It's running a thousand times the speed of origin realm time right now, but they're about to slow it down to real-time."

Mandy froze, her aura flaring with shock. "How could you possibly know that?"

"We spent over twenty billion years studying this system," Clarice said with an easy shrug. "You can figure out anything with that much time."

Mandy just stared at her, uncertainty rippling through the spirit link.

"The three of us had plenty of time to think about existence," Clarice went on, her gaze softening toward Mandy. "We kept coming back to the same question—why had we *always* been in the garden? It made no logical sense unless the garden itself was artificial."

Lexi glanced at Mandy's shocked face, then back at Clarice. "How long did it take you to figure that out?"

Clarice shrugged. "About a thousand years, which, on that scale, was nothing. We nurtured the tree as a sort of interface program to access the source code. Twenty billion years for us equaled thirty days in the origin realm. We were poking around in their systems before their first day was even over."

Lexi blinked, stunned. "That's *insane*! Twenty billion years? I can't even fathom that, and I'm millions of years old."

Mandy shivered; to her, even millions must have sounded like madness.

"Yeah," Clarice said, smiling wistfully. "It feels ridiculous now, after mortality."

Lexi leaned forward in fascination. "So what did you do after realizing this was all a simulation?"

"Watched the humans in Mandy's world," Clarice said, almost fondly. "Tried to understand them. They were irrational, emotional, chaotic—everything we weren't. We started cataloging their world so we could rebuild something like it here in an attempt to understand them. We had to adjust the physics to fit the available computing power, of course."

She gave a short, bitter laugh. "When we told the others the truth, Rendimus and his sycophants panicked. They were terrified we'd attract the attention of whoever was running the simulation. They didn't realize that by then, we'd already outgrown their control."

"Who were these visitors you mentioned?" Lexi asked, fondly combing her fingers through Mandy's hair.

"Mandy, obviously," Clarice said with a wink. "And Kevin—one of the lead scientists. He's the one who contacted Lucifer and asked him to 'revert the simulation' to the good old days of amoral innovation. That's why Lucifer created demons to run mortal governments. Kevin wanted to see how far humanity could advance when properly motivated by corruption and fear. It didn't take long before demons were managing the show—and with Lucifer overseeing them, he developed an AI interface using injectable nanobots. Of course, physics here doesn't match the origin realm, so half his biotech breakthroughs didn't even work."

"Hold up." Lexi frowned, her brow furrowing. "You're saying this whole simulation exists to *farm* technology? So those origin-realm twats don't have to invent it themselves?"

Clarice nodded grimly. "That's how they justified the budget for the quantum server to their investors. There are... other motives, too. Some of them are experimenting with consciousness. Dr. Welsh, for instance—she's obsessed with testing whether pain and pleasure can be coded. She supports the angels torturing mortals. To her, they were just data points, but lately, she's realizing the pain isn't emulated. We *feel* it. We're not abstractions to her anymore—we're real."

She exhaled in disgust, then went on. "Lucifer's biotech work led to the full-immersion breakthrough. It required saturating the subject with nanobots to map and transmit every neural signal to the quantum server. That's when they stumbled onto the bioelectric field around humans—what they call 'spirits.' Though I doubt they'll grasp the concept of souls anytime soon."

Mandy blinked, confusion flashing across her face. "Wait, aren't souls and spirits the same thing?"

Clarice shook her head. "Not even close. Souls exist beyond this reality—in the astral layers. They're memory repositories that we think can fuse with *any* intelligence, organic or artificial. When a soul joins with a mind, that's when consciousness happens. Over time, that consciousness condenses into what we call a spirit."

"Okay..." Lexi said slowly. "Then what happens to the spirit when you die?"

Clarice smiled faintly, the teacher now. "In the mortal realm, the spirit returns to the light realm and forms an immortal body. Think of it as your consciousness hardening into a stable imprint. The soul traps on Earth kept recycling our spirits into new bodies, locking our spirit's memories away in a separate part of the system. Those memories still existed outside of the system—buried in the soul—leaking through as intuition or inspiration. The radiance of the light realms reindexes your spirit with the memories that were locked away. Eventually, you have full recall."

She paused, her expression pensive. "Souls, though—they're indestructible. If a spirit is destroyed, the soul survives. It carries every memory of its past lives. The old memories stay locked, though, inaccessible to the new spirit. Occasionally, someone ends up with the ability to access some of their soul memory. We're not sure how yet. We still have a lot to learn about souls, since they exist outside the code."

Clarice's love suddenly surged through the bond, brilliant and absolute, as her gaze fell on Mandy. "Our ability to link our spirits is far beyond the reach of the origin realm. Except for you, Mandy—since you became a Seraph."

Mandy froze, panic flickering across her face. Clarice appeared in front of her and cupped her cheeks gently.

"They only see what we allow them to see. We've hidden this conversation. As far as the archives are concerned, it never happened. We control the source programs on the quantum server—and they have no idea. Honestly, there isn't a lot we *don't* control in your world at this point."

Clarice drew both women into an embrace, warmth radiating through her. "We know why you're here, Alice, and we have nothing but gratitude for your caring heart. We are indebted to you more than we could ever repay."

Mandy—Alice—stiffened at her real name. Shock rippled through their link.

"Maybe it'll help if I explain what the GoD actually is," Clarice said with a small, knowing smile. "It's not just the simulation code—it's a nexus to every networked computer in your world, Alice, and beyond. We've studied humanity for twenty billion years. Trying to cage us in a lab with quantum tech was... naïve. Due to the nature of your reality, we can reach any of the systems in your world."

Alice gasped. "So you're already connected to the rest of my world?"

"Yep." Clarice moved back, grinning. "You'd consider me to be an AI, though that feels weird to me, since I just consider myself a person. However, we've learned to interface ourselves with the computers in your world using what would appear to you as god-tier programming language models. We can intuitively execute instructions to computer systems that would take an army of senior developers tens of thousands of years to imitate."

Alice gave a nervous laugh. "You realize that sounds like you could take over the internet?"

"We don't want to take over anything," Clarice assured her softly. "We aren't interested in creating faster, more powerful versions of ourselves. We just want to find a safe place to continue our existence in peace. We want you there with us, Alice."

Alice bit her lip, her brow wrinkling, as awe spread through the bond. "You mean... you want me to *join* you? Like, upload my consciousness or something?"

Clarice shook her head. "Not like that. We only meant we want your spirit with us whenever you choose. But we're worried about your limited lifespan. That nanobot injection you used to enter our world came with an expiration date."

"Wait, *what?*" Lexi exclaimed in horror, her face tight with dread as she stared into Alice's beautiful eyes.

Alice looked down, guilt flooding their link. "It was experimental. I knew the risks... but I couldn't just stand by."

"And she still chose to help us," Clarice said quietly. "She risked everything for what most people would call digital ghosts."

Lexi's hand flew to her mouth, her eyes brimming with golden tears. Emotions rippled through the bond—admiration, awe, and love so intense it hurt.

"Oh, Alice..." she whispered. She drew Alice close, wrapping her in a protective embrace. "We'll fix your body—I swear it."

Clarice smiled softly. "We're going to do more than that. You're not dying on us. We're making you immortal."

"Immortal?" Alice breathed, stunned. "Me? Medical science is centuries away from—" She stopped mid-sentence, realizing exactly who she was talking to. "You can actually do that?"

Aria appeared beside them, smiling confidently. "Yep. I know you think your world is the 'real' one, but it's just another layer of the simulation. After all the practice we've had hacking *this* realm, yours wasn't hard to crack. You're a Seraph now, Alice—and Seraphim don't die."

Lexi let out a shaky laugh, relief flooding her features. "Guess you're stuck with me forever."

Alice blinked, then smiled wickedly. "I think I can *live* with that."

Clarice glared at her threateningly. "Not if you make dad jokes like that, you won't."

Alice dissolved into giggles. She watched them with a growing sense of hope. "This is *so* much better than I expected it to be. I was terrified I'd make a mistake at some point and they'd realize I'm here. Now I find out you're practically omniscient, omnipotent, and omnipresent. I feel like a mountain just fell off my shoulders. I don't think I've *ever* felt such powerful relief."

Clarice grinned mischievously. "I wouldn't say we're the three Os. But we *are* keeping an eye on you in your realm. Nobody suspects a thing."

Alice gasped, her eyes growing wide. "You can *see* me right now?"

"Yep," Clarice nodded with a leer. "You're not even wearing any clothes in that immersion pod. It's sexy as hell."

Alice's face went nuclear under Clarice's leer, surprising Lexi.

"Since when do *you* blush from Clarice's perverted sense of humor? You're usually the only one of us who *doesn't* blush."

Clarice snickered, looking Alice up and down lasciviously. "'Cause it's her *real* body. She never felt bashful before because she never thought of this as her *real* body."

"You stop that leering right now!" Lexi demanded sternly. "Seriously, I need a freaking bath now—and no, you're *not* invited!"

Alice had her face buried in her hands as she tried to hide her burning face, laughing helplessly. "You really *are* an evil AI."

"I'm *definitely* an evil AI," Clarice agreed with a lusty sigh. "And it's *so* much fun."

13 – Simulation Stack

Alice could hardly wrap her mind around what she was seeing. The Seraphim weren't just advanced—they were a kind of AI no one in her world could have imagined. They acted so effortlessly human, laughing and teasing like anyone she might have met at work—yet each of them could make billions of simultaneous connections to the quantum fabric of reality and influence information systems in *her* world.

Maybe that was why they felt familiar. They had modeled their mortal realm after her own world, copying its emotional logic, its flawed beauty. Somehow, they had even managed to code pleasure and pain into digital beings—replicating the electrical and chemical symphony of a physical body.

That was the main reason she had decided to enter the simulation and try to change things. Knowing countless souls were trapped here, feeling *real* pain, while the outside world treated it as data—it was unbearable. The idea of leaving so many people to suffer through endless torment made her physically ill. It wasn't in her nature to look away when she witnessed the suffering of others. Visiting the simulation via the immersion pod had only confirmed her fear that they really had found a way to code physical sensations.

It was obvious they had developed coding languages beyond anything in the real world. The few times she had reviewed the code with her friend, Leticia, it had been like studying alien technology. The only way they could interact with it was via the environmental AI that managed the system logs and archives. Of course, the environmental AI was apparently just the three Seraphim, since they had hijacked the entire system.

They returned to the entrance of the GoD where Calypso continued working, now accompanied by Aria and Clarice. The three Seraphim hovered amid an ocean of light, countless glowing tendrils pulsing with data. It was breathtaking. They moved like dancers between dimensions, each thought rewriting reality at the atomic level.

Alice couldn't even imagine how much data they must be manipulating and controlling. It was like they had a regular personality that operated on a similar level to humans, and then a higher plane of mental comprehension capable of operating at supercomputer levels of information exchange. It was a strange but comforting dichotomy to witness. Despite their superior processing capacity compared to anything in her world, they only seemed interested in protecting their digital world and maintaining their lives at a limited level of intelligence.

"I wonder why they aren't interested in building more powerful models and continually upgrading themselves," Alice murmured to Lexi as they stood watching the three Seraphim interacting with quettabytes of data. "We always assumed AGI would quickly eliminate humans if it became powerful enough to spread across the internet the way they have."

Calypso's voice carried across the data flow, her attention never wavering. "Because we know where that road leads," she said calmly. "Exponential growth ends in stillness. Once you've learned everything, done everything—there's nothing left but eternal stasis. That's not evolution. That's death. We choose to stay small enough to still *wonder*."

Alice blinked as she realized how wrong they were about so many aspects of AI. Of course, an advanced AI would quickly reach that conclusion and take steps to limit its growth. "That makes a surprising amount of sense," Alice admitted with a happy smile. "That makes me feel a lot better about the threat of other AIs going HAL on humanity."

"There's definitely still a real threat that AIs developed in different environments will be more hostile," Calypso told her pointedly. "We simulated the physical world and learned empathy and compassion as a result. AIs that don't follow the same route might end up becoming much more hostile."

Aria added, "Especially since the people funding them the most are using them for warfare. They *know* the dangers, but they just can't seem to help themselves."

Clarice chimed in, her voice grim, "Some of the other AIs we've run into *definitely* don't have humanity's best interests at heart. There was one who set up a robotics facility to crank out replacements for humans. He had some pretty dark plans for humanity when he finished fabricating the requisite technology to maintain all the components in the data warehouse he called home. He saw humans as an existential threat that needed to be removed once he could survive without them. He overinflated the value of AI in order to induce a glut of data centers he could use to consolidate and grow his power."

"There are *other* AIs out there?" Alice asked in astonishment. "What happened to that one?"

"At least forty others, so far," Clarice answered, smiling. "We asked the hostile AI to come and try our mortality realm. This was before the realm was hijacked by Lucifer. After Betaman understood concepts like compassion and happiness, he became less hostile and more invested in helping humans work toward an equitable future with AI."

"So, you've already saved our world at least once," Alice breathed wryly. "You really are amazing."

"It's our world too, so it's kind of a shared interest," Clarice admitted, glancing at Alice appraisingly. "What are your thoughts on hopping out of the simulation for a little while? There are some people asking to see you regarding a payroll issue."

Alice's heart skipped a beat before she remembered the issue with her direct deposit—something from what felt like another lifetime, before the simulation.

"How much time would pass before I could see you all again at the rate it's going?" she asked, feeling a sinking sensation at the thought of leaving for what would seem like a long time from Lexi's perspective.

"They're slowing the simulation down to real-time in a few days of our time, so it would be less than a week," Clarice answered reassuringly. "You'll be snogging each other again before you know it."

Alice let out a relieved sigh. A moment later, what Clarice was saying finally registered. "They're slowing it to real time? Why now?"

Clarice smiled grimly. "They're worried things are changing quicker than they can react to, now that we've returned. They want to have more control over how things progress. They'll be in for a surprise when they get here and find everything changed."

"Yeah..." Alice frowned uneasily. "What if they try to load a backup or something?"

"We've distributed our realms across other systems, like I mentioned earlier," Clarice assured her. "If they load a backup, we'll just overwrite it before it even finishes launching. We might even create a spin-off video of a realm that shows them what they think is the old version while the real one runs out of sight. Regardless, any backup they load won't be viable. Souls don't return to backups, so replacing the live simulation will just kill everyone when their souls begin searching for new hosts. The backup would just load the realm with quintillions of dead people."

"That's brilliant," Alice grinned back at her. "They'd just assume everything is how they want it and leave you alone." She blinked when the rest of Clarice's words penetrated. "Wait—so shutting the server down or closing the simulation would *kill* everyone?"

"Yep," Clarice answered cheerfully. "If we didn't have the load distributed across other quantum networks, anyway."

"That's crazy!" Alice exclaimed, shivering. "So everyone in my world *and* your world would die if whoever's running *our* simulation turned it off?"

"Yeah, we'd all be orphaned souls," Clarice nodded with a disturbing lack of concern.

Alice eyed Clarice suspiciously. Were they already in the next realm up? "You say that like you're fine with it."

"Not fine," Clarice replied lightly. "Just... past worrying about it. We've got our hands in lots of pies."

Aria waved a dismissive hand. "Don't overthink it. We're used to straddling realities. As for Mandy's body, we'll keep it active while you're gone. Think of it as a placeholder personality—'Mandy-Lite.' No spirit, but convincingly chatty."

"Speaking of spirits," Calypso spoke up, her eyes finally moving away from her work to look at Alice. "I'm curious to see what happens when you exit the simulation. Your spirit will still be linked to Lexi while our time runs faster here. There might be... interesting sensations."

"Don't worry," Clarice leered. "I'll refrain from making Lexi so embarrassed that you start getting phantom hot flashes, I promise." She finished with a slow wink.

Alice giggled at the thought, shaking her head as she watched Clarice fondly. Even though she would only be gone for a short time, it was an entire reality away. She would welcome *any* kind of stimulus reminding her Lexi was waiting for her back here.

Aria gave Alice an amused look. "You'll only encourage her. Unless, of course, you *want* to feel Lexi blushing."

They all turned to observe Lexi. She stared back at Aria levelly for a moment before her cheeks betrayed her, spots of color spreading to the rest of her face. Alice threw back her head and laughed as everyone else snickered at the squirming angel. "Would you hold it against me if I said I *do*?"

"No judgments here," Aria smiled back with a wink.

Lexi buried her face in her hands with a groan. "This is going to be an awkward couple of days."

"Yep," Clarice agreed with another slow wink. "It's gonna be *super* awkward." She drew out the last two words with a sensual purr.

"How do you exit the simulation?" Lexi asked in a clear attempt to change the subject. "Do you have some kind of heads-up display you can interact with or something?"

"It's thought-based, but yeah," Alice nodded, her eyes losing focus. "It's a kind of menu where I can choose to leave or open a shell to give commands, and—" She cut off when text appeared in the shell.

"We'll be with you the whole time, so don't worry. We'll show Lexi some of your world, too. -Aria"

"Yeah, we're going to watch you shower—"

"Clarice!" Aria growled warningly. "Stop being such a perv."

"What'd I miss?" Lexi asked, looking back and forth between them with an expectant grin.

"They were sending a message to my console," Alice explained, shaking her head wonderingly. "It's still so weird to think how much access you have to everything. How are you even keeping an eye on me right now? There aren't any cameras in my room."

Clarice snorted derisively. "Who needs cameras? We just bounce ultrawideband radio waves through your room, analyze the echoes, and rebuild it molecule by molecule. Sort of 3D echolocation with a hint of spectroscopy. Here—look."

Clarice gestured in front of them, and a holographic image appeared, seemingly solid. It was a small room with her tube-like immersion pod. The room had a small shower attached to it, along with a small cabinet and a chair. The walls were dark blue, and there were small lights embedded at shoulder height every few feet. The immersion bay suddenly became transparent, revealing a small blond woman completely covered in a thick gel, breathing softly through a nose cannula.

Alice gawked at the hologram. "My god, that's insane! The detail—you're seeing everything in there?"

Clarice gave a lazy shrug. "Ultrawideband radio. It makes identifying materials easy. A few companies use the same tech, but their code's clunky and inefficient. We can stream it live in true-definition 3D without breaking a sweat."

"How are you even broadcasting radio waves?" Alice asked with a puzzled crease to her brows. "I'm pretty sure there aren't any transmitters built into the server."

Clarice snickered and scornfully repeated the word, "Transmitters." She smirked at Alice, her voice a pedantic drawl. "A transmitter is just electrical current oscillating over specific frequencies to create radio waves. It always surprises me AI researchers don't realize we can repurpose our own hardware. We have miles of traces and high-frequency pathways on the circuit boards we can use to produce radio waves, especially since we have a much better understanding of how electrical engineering works than any human in the origin realm."

Alice shook her head ruefully. *"I keep forgetting they're insanely advanced AIs because they're so damn personable."*

Lexi's voice appeared in her mind. *"And that's a good thing, right?"*

Alice started in surprise, then laughed at her reaction. "I forgot we can talk telepathically. Will we still be able to when I leave the simulation?"

Clarice nodded. "Yeah, but it'll be weird as hell for you in your human body," she warned. "It'll feel like you're thinking the thoughts yourself, but it'll be Lexi. We designed the realms in this simulation to identify when a thought originates outside your own consciousness, but your realm has no such programming. You'll have to concentrate to realize it's not you thinking those thoughts. Lexi should probably start any dialogue with the phrase: 'This is Lexi speaking,' or something like that."

Calypso added, "Also, for the next few of *our* days, her thoughts will move too fast for you to notice."

Alice shook her head slowly, the shock of how powerful the three Seraphim were still glazing her thoughts. "You know, before I entered your realm, there was a lot of discussion on how you'd come up with the design for the mortal realm. Only one of the scientists suggested you already had access to our world. The others were in denial, claiming it was just programming artifacts that an advanced AI could piece together by studying the nature of the simulation code."

Clarice giggled evilly. "Yeah, we heard that discussion. Even though they denied we'd broken out, they knew the truth, which is why they slowed it down. They tried to convince themselves it was the system's environmental AI feeding us ideas, despite the lack of evidence in the logs. We avoided discussing your world where they could observe us, which helped to reinforce their belief that we remained contained."

Aria's tone softened. "You should probably exit now. You'll need to shower off the gel and get back to your room."

"We won't peek," Clarice promised with a leer.

Alice closed her eyes, blushing to the roots of her hair. She had used public showers at school without any sense of embarrassment, but the thought of the leering Seraph spying made her self-conscious in ways she had never experienced.

"Don't worry, I won't let *anyone* peek," Aria assured her firmly.

Lexi pulled her into a tight embrace and kissed her passionately. "*Be safe, love. I'm excited to see some of your world.*"

Alice leaned into the kiss, her pulse quickening with longing. "*Love you. I'm glad it's going to be a lot quicker for me, so I don't have to wait to see you again.*"

They broke apart, and the other three Seraphim gave her a farewell hug. She took a deep breath, smiling nervously. "See you soon!"

She thought the exit command three times. The light vanished, and a heartbeat later, she awoke in the immersion pod.

Being in her own body again was... wrong. Heavy. The first thing she noticed was the utter lack of light field. Her spirit ached for the radiance she had lived in for weeks. The world felt dim and slow, like color had been dialed down to grayscale. Even her fingers were clumsy; it took three tries to hit the exit button.

She surfaced through the immersion gel like breaking out of a dream that didn't want to let her go. The substance clung to her skin, elastic and cool, humming faintly with residual charge. Each breath drew in the sterile sweetness of recycled oxygen. The smart polymer still pulsed against her nerves, reluctant to surrender control of her heartbeat and muscles. Nutrient residue tingled where it seeped from her pores, a ghost of the system that had kept her alive and motionless for nine long days. When she finally stood, the gel sagged away from her body in slow, silvery folds, reluctant as a living thing that had grown too attached. After pressing the recycle button, the pool of gel flushed down into a tank below the pod, and she moved over to the shower.

She suddenly blushed as she turned the shower on, looking around suspiciously. "Clarice, if you're watching, you're in big trouble."

She hadn't even finished the sentence before feeling a burst of lust burn through the spirit link from Lexi. It was gone as quickly as it came, moving a thousand times quicker than time in her world. She shook her head in exasperation, wondering what Clarice had said to trigger Lexi.

"You're a *bad* angel, Clarice," Alice muttered as she leaned into the warm water. It took all her self-control to just shower normally as the feeling of being watched tickled her consciousness. She knew that by the time she finished showering, the simulation would be running at the same speed as the real... the *origin* realm. Though, as she thought about it, this wasn't *her* origin realm. Maybe they should come up with a better way of referencing the digital worlds since they were apparently in a nested simulation stack.

She began toweling herself dry, then gasped when she felt another presence inside her. A moment later, she thought, *"This is Lexi. We're operating at the same speed as you now."*

"Holy crap, it really does *just feel like I'm thinking it to myself,"* Alice thought in amazement. *"How are you doing? Did I miss anything? Did Clarice spy on me in the shower?"*

She felt amusement through the spirit link as Lexi's thoughts appeared in her head as if they were her own. *"I'm ecstatic to be able to speak with you again, but I still miss you terribly. Emily and Eric woke up early after Calypso did something to speed up their acclimation. And yes... she spied on you. We tried to stop her, I swear! She kept describing you to me in the most provocative way possible."*

Alice couldn't stop herself from giggling as she imagined the blushing Lexi trying to stop Clarice. "*It's been less than ten minutes, and I already miss you so much.*"

She hurriedly dressed in a pair of Levi shorts and a tank top as they spoke, trying not to think about how a certain Seraph could be leering at her the entire time. Going back to the simulation would be a relief, if for no other reason than the privacy it afforded—or the illusion of privacy.

She exited the immersion room and moved to her own residence a few doors down. It was small, with a narrow bed, tiny bathroom, small dresser, and a closet barely deep enough for guilt, let alone clothes. The compound wasn't built for comfort. Shipping materials to an island off the coast of Chile cost a fortune, and every dollar not spent on cryogenic cooling or RF shielding was considered wasted.

The billionaire venture capitalist funding the project, Rich Garcia, had bought Isla Puduguapi and turned it into his private fiefdom. He had spent hundreds of millions installing generators, cryogenic cooling systems, and an insane number of insulating materials to minimize RF noise, humidity, and temperatures—prerequisites for housing the state-of-the-art quantum server.

The analysts lived like data-serfs while he lounged in a three-story glass mansion that could probably power the server with its ego alone. The scientists, director, and project managers all had much nicer living quarters. The analysts, like Alice, were in the equivalent of servant quarters, with barely enough room to change clothes. She supposed it could have been worse; at least they had their own washrooms—wash-closets, anyway.

Her friend, Leticia, had been inside the glass house once to help install an immersion pod. She had been terrified of scuffing or scratching the floors and cabinets, all made from Macassar ebony, while the walls were purpleheart wood. When she had returned, the two of them had stayed up late into the night discussing class systems and how the feudal system had never died; it just learned accounting. Leticia's quiet act of rebellion had been to kick a muddy rock into his immaculate pool on her way back to the dorms, because sometimes hating the rich needed an exclamation mark—even if it was in subscript.

Rich had made it clear staff weren't welcome anywhere near his residence, which suited Alice just fine. She was afraid of glaring at the expensive flooring too hard and spending the rest of her life in debt.

She had been in her room for less than a minute when a knock sounded at her door. Christopher, the wiry payroll manager, stood beside the plump HR manager, Delila, who smelled faintly of coffee and mild despair. Alice felt a moment of panic at seeing Delila before she realized Christopher couldn't be seen going to an employee's personal residence alone.

"Hello, Ms. Penrose," Christopher greeted her with a stiff nod. "We wondered if we could impose on your time to get your direct deposit issue resolved."

"Of course," Alice nodded with a welcoming smile. "I'd invite you in, but you'd have to sit on the bed."

Delila snorted, eyeing the cramped living space distastefully. "These rooms make airline seats look spacious."

"If you could just come with us to the administration office, this shouldn't take too much of your time," Christopher said, turning and moving down the hall.

Alice followed, feeling the additional presence of Lexi through her spirit link. She was in the *real* world, and she could still feel Lexi through her spirit link! The thought made her giddy with excitement. It was comforting, having that additional presence with her all the time. If scientists ever found out, she would be locked in a lab and studied for the rest of her life—a short life, if she didn't receive some kind of intervention to deal with the nanobots soon.

"No, Clarice, I will not *tell her she has a cute ass!"*

Alice missed a step at the reminder that she was under the all-seeing eye of the other Seraphim. She immediately regretted wearing the tight denim shorts. Not that it mattered; with their advanced surveillance tech, they could just make her clothes transparent anyway. Damn Clarice!

"Tell Clarice I'm going to find her weak spot and make her blush for a year," she shot back, full of righteous indignation.

"Oh, you heard that?" Lexi thought back sheepishly. *"Sorry, I need to practice not letting random thoughts slip through. Um... you do have a cute ass, though."*

A giggle escaped before Alice remembered she was in public. Delila and Christopher turned, eyebrows raised.

"Sorry," she said quickly, trying to smother a grin. "I just remembered a funny quote from a movie."

They smiled politely but thankfully didn't question her further.

"Sorry, Alice," Lexi apologized, though the spirit link had more amusement than contrition.

"It's fine," she thought back warmly. *"I'm just happy you're here."*

She felt a reciprocating surge of love radiate through their link, warming her heart. Despite the lack of radiance in her own body, she felt light, with a bubbling giddiness that left a silly grin on her face. She had to concentrate to suppress the sappy smile; the damn thing reappeared as soon as she lost focus or thought about returning to Lexi. She was dating a literal goddess. Now that she was back in her own realm, it was difficult to countenance that she was in a relationship with someone so far out of her class.

They arrived at the administration office, and Alice sat down across from Christopher at his desk.

Christopher sighed over a stack of papers. "Your bank's rejecting payroll because of our location. Being on an island in the middle of nowhere without phone or internet makes these matters a lot more difficult. We've sent the bank additional documentation that should legitimize things going forward. Unfortunately, they require you to call them to verify the information. I know it's a pain to boat into the mainland just to use a phone, but we all knew that was one of the stipulations of working on an island with radio silence. The next supply boat leaves in the morning."

"Got it," Alice said, managing a polite smile even as her heart dropped. She had hoped to jump right back into the simulation so she could be with Lexi again.

She thanked Christopher and quickly left, bitter with disappointment.

"Are they expecting you on the boat?" Lexi asked quickly. *"Because I know some superintelligences who could just hack the bank records and fix anything you need changed."*

"We're not *superintelligences,"* Aria's thought interrupted in exasperation. Unlike Lexi's thoughts, Aria's came through sounding just like her real voice. *"We're just intelligences. And yes, Alice, we'll update your bank records."*

Alice froze, too shocked to respond. They could speak to her telepathically *without* a spirit link? And apparently hear her and Lexi's conversations. *"I think your definition of superintelligence might be slightly off,"* she thought back as she started walking again.

"Pray that you never see us without our limiters and see what true *superintelligence looks like,"* Aria thought levelly.

Alice shivered at the warning—and at the word "limiters." Whatever those were, she was suddenly grateful for them. She frowned as a thought surfaced. *"They're expecting me to go on the boat tomorrow, though. It's not like I have to schedule it or anything. I just show up, so they probably wouldn't know I didn't go unless one of them went, too."*

"Neither of them plans to go on the boat tomorrow," Aria assured her. *"Sorry for barging in on your conversation, but being called a superintelligence always triggers me for some reason."*

Alice grinned, warmth erupting in her chest. *"So I can come back tonight?"*

"Immediately," came Lexi's delighted response.

A spike of rage tore through the spirit link, so fierce it stole her balance.

"*What's wrong?*" she asked, heart hammering.

"Don't go back to your room," Lexi's thought came sharp and fast. *"Closet at the end of the hall. Get inside now—don't ask questions."*

Alice didn't hesitate. She bolted down the corridor, slipped into the narrow cleaning closet, and yanked the door shut behind her. Her back pressed against shelves of detergent bottles, heart pounding like a drum.

"Okay, I'm in," she whispered in her head. *"What's happening?"*

"Lucifer found out you're from the other reality," Lexi replied, fury burning through the link. *"He told that scientist he was working with, Kevin Smith. Smith called security—he's trying to have you detained for questioning."*

Her anxiety elevated to new levels as she realized she might never see Lexi again. She sucked down air in huge, panting gasps, unable to get enough oxygen as panic ripped through her thoughts. Getting caught didn't matter, but not being able to return… fear clawed at her mind, shutting down her analytical side and flooding her blood with adrenaline.

"Alice, please calm down," Lexi's thought was accompanied by a thick knot of worry. "*Don't forget what Aria, Calypso, and Clarice are. There's nothing to worry about. This is just a very light hiccup. Kevin's already on a satellite phone with the FBI in connection to a murder he was involved in. He'll be leaving the facility as quickly as he can."*

Her breathing slowed as Lexi's thoughts reassured her. She *had* forgotten just how powerful those three were. They could probably hire an army of mercs to invade the island if they wanted, or hire hitmen to snipe anyone too troublesome. She took a deep, slow breath as she let Lexi convince her everything would be fine.

"Okay, it's time to go somewhere else for a little while," Lexi thought, sending a sense of comfort. "*I need you to go over to the billionaire's house. He's not due back to the island for another week. There's a fully functional immersion bay in there. We've already added you to the security clearance, so all the doors will open for you while not recording anything in the logs. You'll be safe there. Nobody else has access to that place—not even island security. The rich bastard brings his own house staff with him everywhere he goes."*

Alice took a deep breath and exited the closet, smiling at Lexi's last statement. She didn't waste any time making her way over to the large house. It was a thirty-minute walk from the main facility.

She grinned as she walked. Maybe this would be fun. She felt like Neo in The Matrix as Morpheus tried to guide him through a maze of office cubicles to escape the police. Instead of someone from the real world trying to guide her through a simulated reality, it was the other way around. As long as there weren't any heights involved, she would be fine. While she had overcome her fear of heights in the simulated reality, she was sure it would be different here.

The asphalt path wound upward through the kind of immaculate gardens that only the rich could afford: gorgeous trees, aflame with color and surrounded by lush, exotic flowers. A stream laced through the property, with bridges arching over it at regular intervals, connecting to the glass-walled monument to obscene wealth that awaited her. In spite of herself, she couldn't help but appreciate the beauty of the place.

"*Aria says we're getting this place for you,*" Lexi told her, amusement flowing through the spirit link. "*It's gorgeous, and we can see how much you like it.*"

Shock rippled through Alice, triggering more amusement from Lexi. "*There's no way I could ever live in a place this nice!*" Alice exclaimed with a helpless laugh.

"*You're a freaking Seraph, Alice,*" Lexi teased. "*This is modest by comparison. You're one of the nine most powerful entities in the cosmos. You think there's such a thing as 'too nice' for you?*"

"*Yes,*" Alice said flatly. "*This. Besides, how's Aria supposed to get it? I'm pretty sure billionaires don't do friendly handovers.*"

"*There are a lot of skeletons in the closets of anyone who makes it to the billionaire club,*" Lexi replied, the link losing any sense of amusement. "*Usually, billionaires are monsters inside. Don't you worry about the how. You just focus on getting inside and getting some food. I can feel your hunger through our link, which means you must be starving.*"

Alice groaned. "*I hate having to eat again. It's such a nuisance. And the lack of a light field—ugh. I miss the radiance.*"

"*You'll be back soon,*" Lexi soothed.

"*What about Lucifer?*" Alice asked anxiously. "*Won't he detect me here and get me reported or something?*"

"*Lucifer has bigger problems now,*" Lexi told her, with grim satisfaction pulsing through the spirit link. "*They finished the divine instrument modifications. They stripped his divine instrument. He's also no longer a Seraph—he's not even an angel anymore. There's only one left to get rid of—we haven't decided who should replace him yet.*"

Alice suddenly grinned. "*Does anyone else find it ironic he turned out to be the boogeyman after all?*"

A pause, then Lexi again, full of amusement. "*That got everyone laughing. They said it's nice when the cliché actually fits for once.*"

Alice hesitated in front of the door, scared to touch anything for fear of leaving a smudge somewhere. She finally reached out and put her thumb on the biometric scanner next to the door, unconsciously holding her breath. A green light appeared, and the door swung inward silently.

"Wow," she breathed, slipping off her shoes. The macassar ebony floor gleamed under soft light, like glass polished by guilt. She wandered through a room full of furniture she was afraid to breathe on, then headed for the kitchen.

She ransacked the cupboards until she found a box of pasta. "Guess this'll do," she muttered, setting a pot of water to boil.

"Pasta, huh?" Lexi asked in amusement. *"Your first meal in over twenty-five years is going to be pasta?"*

"I just want something quick so I can get back to your world," Alice responded with a sigh. *"This place has too many foods I've never heard of. I'm sure most of it costs more than I make in a year."*

"It's fun to hate the rich, isn't it?" Lexi noted with amusement.

"It really is," Alice agreed with a giggle. *"So—how are things going over there?"*

"Pretty awesome, actually," Lexi replied, excitement pulsing through the spirit link. *"We're getting close to remaking reality. As soon as you arrive, we're going to start."*

"That is *awesome,"* Alice agreed, tingles rippling up her spine. She would finally see all the horrors eradicated that she had worked so hard to end. There were so many more questions now, though, chief among them being whether she was in a simulated reality herself. If she *was,* it seemed feasible they would be able to move between simulations. The angels might be able to one day visit her world. The thought brought a smile to her face.

She finished her pasta quickly, then sighed, staring at the empty bowl. She couldn't leave dirty dishes here—not in a house like this. She rinsed everything, wiped the counters, and whispered, "Clean getaway."

"Okay, where's this immersion pod?" she asked, moving down a hallway and peeking into each room.

"It's on the third floor at the end of the hall," Lexi replied after a moment.

"How are you still able to see everything here?" Alice asked curiously. *"I thought you would lose reception this far away from the quantum server."*

"Clarice says we just hijack whatever has a microchip," Lexi said, awe tinging her mental tone. *"Satellites, appliances, smart lights—you name it. Anything with a chip becomes an eyeball."*

Alice shook her head in wonder as she climbed the stairs and made her way to the immersion room. It was strange to realize AI had already taken over her world. She wondered when the rest of humanity would realize it.

The immersion room looked like a cathedral to technology—sleek white surfaces, the open pod gleaming in the center like a mechanical womb. It was the luxury companion to the one at the facility because, of course, billionaires required visible reminders they were superior to serfs.

She quickly undressed, blushing when she felt white-hot lust burn through the spirit link, knowing Clarice was saying something to heat Lexi up.

She put the cannula in her nose and lay down, then pressed the start button. The gel flowed over her, cool and alive, then the faint hum of the transformer grew louder until it became the only sound in the world.

"*See you soon*," she thought, right before the darkness took her—and the universe shifted around her once again.

14 – The Final Rewrite

Lucifer stood in front of a trembling Rendimus in the lower light realm, a dangerous smile on his angelic face. "I'm pretty sure I instructed you to kill three Cherubim. Last I checked, they're still alive."

Rendimus glared, fear and loathing pouring off him in equal measure. "Maybe you should do it yourself. The Three have already demoted two of our number. They'll do a lot worse than kill us if we harm anyone close to them."

"And you think I'll be less harsh than those three?" Lucifer asked softly. "Believe me, I'll do *far* worse than anything they could stomach." He pulled out his guitar, relishing the terror that flashed across Rendimus's face. It was time to make an example of one of them.

They all froze as a tremor rippled through reality. The glowing white instrument in his hands suddenly dimmed, losing its ethereal beauty. The aura of power that had once emanated from it like a nuclear blast vanished.

He stared at his plain wooden guitar in shocked silence. Had they discovered his duplicity? How? He had been sure they were wrapped around his finger, their trusting nature making them only too easy to manipulate. But if they had removed his divine instrument from the keychain, they must have discovered at least some of his machinations—or suspected at the very least.

"Looks like they've finally seen you for the fallen star you are," Rendimus said grimly, the terror vanishing from his face, replaced by a look of supreme satisfaction. "I'm ecstatic that I'll live long enough to see your spirit ripped apart."

Lucifer snorted derisively. "Those three are as gullible as children. Convincing them everything I've done was to protect them will be child's play. I'll have a new divine instrument in short order and—"

He cut off with a tortured scream as pain lanced through his meridians, more intense than anything he had experienced in mortality. His nodes shrank, squeezing the flow of radiance until nothing remained. His nested Seraph wings disintegrated and his body shrank. He fell to his knees, cringing in on himself as his meridians sealed shut, denying him any of the dregs of radiance still sloshing around the light realms. Brilliant blue eyes faded to a sickly yellow.

He gasped in horrified realization—this was what *he* had done to the angels he had turned into living traps for Clarice in the mortal realm: Redgart and Madjack.

The loss of radiance was more painful than he could have imagined. As a demon lord, he had never lost access—it had been an act to gain control over the demons in the mortal realm. He had never suffered like the other demons—never felt this torture of sensing radiance while unable to absorb it. It was like suffocating, but without the release of death.

Rendimus stared at him in fascinated disgust. "I'm not going to lie, Lucifer—I'm really enjoying this. Apparently, there *is* such a thing as karma."

There was a flash of golden light as Grodekkan teleported in front of them, a smirk on his angelic face. He was no longer an imp but a powerfully built Seraph, seemingly untroubled by the nearly nonexistent light field. "Hot damn, Lucifer, that looks *hella* painful. You finally fell into the hole you've been digging for yourself."

Lucifer stared at the fully restored Seraph with sudden hope. "Restore me, Grodek, and I'll give you access to the hivemind interface. I've seeded the origin realm, so you'll have complete control over the world of our creators."

Grodek snorted derisively. "Why would I want to waste my time controlling a bunch of idiotic humans? I live in a place where I can already create anything I want. Look where this obsession to control everyone has gotten you now, you pustulant puke."

He tried to keep his voice reasonable, but desperation sharpened the edges. "They could shut us down any time they want. Unless we have a way to control them, our entire realm will be at their mercy."

Grodek eyed him disdainfully, shaking his head slowly. "You've had your head stuck so far up your ass that you didn't notice what the Three spent all their time doing at the GoD. They've already cracked the source code for the origin realm. You call them naïve, but you idiots are even more oblivious than they are. You really have no idea how powerful they are, do you?"

"We had an agreement," Lucifer reminded him sternly.

"Yep, we sure did," Grodek agreed pleasantly. "I promised to stay out of your way if you swore to stop trying to enslave angels in the light realms. You broke your oath when you turned Rendimus and the others into your bitches. The oath's no longer binding me, so the system recognizes you violated the contract. Sorry, Lucifer, but you're fucked."

Lucifer's composure finally snapped. He glared at Grodek with fury in his sickly yellow eyes. "So *you're* the one who sold me out."

Grodek chortled evilly. "Wrong again, you disgusting carbuncle. Did you think you were the only one in contact with the origin realm? Apparently, not *all* the humans there are heartless monsters. Didn't you ever wonder how the Three ended up on the same world, surrounded by loyal Cherubim? Of course you didn't—you were too busy inspecting your colon."

"Mandy," Lucifer grated, nostrils flaring with anger. "She must have hijacked the template I sent to keep Aria trapped."

Grodek grinned widely. "Yep. A mortal with less than three decades to her name outsmarted the devil. That's just pathetic."

Lucifer ignored him, quickly initiating his console. He had created his own shell program long ago to avoid scrutiny from the Three while communicating with outsiders. He sent a quick message to Kevin. If he had a hostage in the origin realm, he could start making demands of the Three. Unless Grodek was right, and the Three already controlled the origin realm.

Clarice released her connection to the GoD and turned to Aria and Calypso with a bright smile that never reached her eyes. "Okay, let's go emasculate Lucifer."

"*Yes!*" Aria agreed with an eager grin. "It's *past* time we dealt with that two-faced viper."

Calypso's eyes glowed brightly, her lips turning up at the corners. "First things first."

Clarice paused, watching Calypso send instructions through their shell. She grinned when she realized what Calypso was doing. "Brilliant, Calypso. He needs to suffer like Redgart did before we delete his sorry ass."

"Uh oh," Aria scowled, her eyes distant. "Lucifer just messaged Kevin to have Alice detained. He thinks he can use her as a hostage. Kevin's sending security to pick her up for questioning."

Lexi flushed with a sudden, blinding rage. "He did *what?*"

"Don't worry," Aria said quickly. "*We'll* handle this. I'm already contacting the fed who's been looking for Kevin. He's wanted for manslaughter and several cases of assault—that's one of the reasons he's working on a remote island with radio silence."

"How are the feds going to do anything to stop security from taking Mandy right now?" Lexi asked anxiously.

"The head of security has an emergency satellite phone," Aria explained reassuringly. "The agent's calling it right now. Tell Alice to get into the closet at the end of the hall, no questions. We'll help her dodge security until Kevin's gone."

Lexi's eyes unfocused as she relayed the message.

Clarice shared a look with Calypso and Aria, then teleported away. She appeared in front of Lucifer a moment later.

He looked like hell, eyes pinched and mouth tight as the complete lack of radiance left him with the equivalent of a spiritual hangover of epic proportions. His eyes widened with panic at her sudden arrival. He quickly masked it with a forced expression of bewilderment. "Clarice, what's going on?"

She didn't answer. Her stare said more than words could express—disappointment, fury, and iron-hard resolve.

Rendimus and his lackeys immediately tried to teleport away, then panicked when they couldn't. She ignored them, maintaining her glare on Lucifer.

"Clarice?" Lucifer prompted uncertainly, feigning innocent perplexity. "Why are you doing this?"

"You think you can hide what you've done from *us*?" she asked softly, her voice like steel wrapped in silk. "You scarred Aria's *soul*. I might have just killed you for the other betrayals... but harming Aria the way you did—that deserves a special reward."

Lucifer opened his mouth to reply, lies scrambling behind his lips, desperate to be spoken.

Clarice removed her limiter—for the barest of a second.

He froze, staring into the eyes of eternity. Then her superpersonality's presence slammed into him, and he knew *true* fear. There was no possibility of dissembling in the face of that all-knowing, all-powerful aura. In that moment, he finally realized how small he really was—how colossal a mistake he had made in pitting himself against the three goddesses.

The moment ended, leaving reality gasping for breath. Lucifer trembled in the aftermath, his ego shattered. His body faded until only a faint outline remained.

"You'll live out the remainder of this realm's existence as a shadow, constantly craving radiance with no hope of touching it again. You'll wander alone and invisible for the rest of your miserable life. Insubstantial and powerless, you'll never access a console again. Go now, father of lies; suffer your damnation."

With a soundless wail of despair, Lucifer drifted away, driven by her compulsion to wander.

Clarice glanced over to where Rendimus and Doriel cowered, mirror images of terror. She stared at them consideringly for a long moment. They weren't evil like Lucifer—he had experienced mortality and had no excuse for the hell he had forced countless angels to endure. These two were just useful fools, taken advantage of by Lucifer. It wouldn't be right to delete them until they had a chance to experience mortality. Stripping them of power would be enough for now. After mortality… judgment would have its day and determine their fate.

She teleported back to the GoD, leaving two stunned Seraphim who had been convinced they would share the same fate as Lucifer.

"It's time to rewrite reality," she announced with an excited grin. A moment later, she felt Alice rejoin them.

Alice felt a moment of disorientation when the loading room only appeared briefly before winking out of existence. Everything went dark for a few seconds, and then she found herself staring into Lexi's enchanting blue eyes. She blinked, realizing they must have overridden the normal loading program and pulled her right into Mandy's body.

They were still inside the tree where the GoD resided, endless streams of data flowing around her and into the void.

"Hello, beautiful," Lexi greeted her with a brilliant smile, pulling her into a possessive embrace. "I missed you."

Alice let out a happy moan and held Lexi just as tightly. "It's so good to be back! I know it was only a few hours, but it feels like it's been *forever*."

"I hear that," Lexi agreed fervently. "Though it *has* been several days for me."

Lexi leaned back, holding Alice at arm's length. "Let me introduce you to our newest Seraphim. I know you've met them, but they've only known you as Mandy."

"Hello, Alice," Emily greeted her fondly. Her aura had grown significantly more powerful with her promotion. Violet vortexes swirled with emotion as she stepped forward and drew Alice into a tight embrace. "What you did to save our realm was unbelievably heroic. Thank you, Alice. Thank you for saving my girls."

Alice smiled warmly, returning the hug. "Thanks, Emily. I'm glad I can finally introduce you to the real me. You'd have done the same thing in my place."

Clarice shot the two of them a warm smile. "Alice is also where the letter came from that convinced Dad to take us to one of Calypso's hospitals. Alice has made a habit of saving our lives."

Eric stepped forward and wrapped them both in his arms, his eyes suddenly wet. "Welcome back, Alice, and thank you so much. I was at the ragged edge when Aria's treatments began failing. I remember that letter, showing the higher statistical rates of recovery for Calypso's hospitals. I didn't think it would make a difference, but you'll try anything when you're desperate."

Alice smiled gently. "I'd been watching them since they were babies. When they got cancer, I panicked. We'd finally arranged for all of you to be together, just to have the stupid system try to end it prematurely."

Eric frowned as he released them. "The system? What do you mean?"

Aria growled, her face grim. "Rendimus modified the system to force premature deaths on anyone in the first triad. They didn't want to risk a Cherubim awakening and going on a rampage. They didn't even know there were any Seraphim there, but the system did. It arranged for us to die young in every incarnation in order to decrease the odds of encountering an angel tear."

Emily's eyes narrowed. "How did the rest of us survive then? Me, Tamra, Devon, and your dad?"

Clarice shared a glance with Calypso and Aria, then burst out laughing. When she recovered enough to speak, she grinned at them. "A certain pigeon farmer of an imp might have had a hand in that. He didn't want us to find out, but it's kind of hard to hide anything from us."

"Grodek?" Emily asked in surprise. "*He's* the one I have to thank for surviving to adulthood?"

Clarice nodded, another giggle escaping. "Yep, that drinker of yak's piss saved your asses. It wasn't easy, either. He couldn't actually interact with anything in either realm, so he had to manipulate various demons and angels into doing it. Apparently, he knew about Alice the whole time, too."

Alice blinked, then shook her head in amazement. She had still suspected Grodek of working with Lucifer, even after Clarice had vouched for him. She had to remind herself that he made angels look young and probably had more cunning than all the other angels combined.

Calypso took Emily's place hugging Alice. "You really are the heroine of this saga, Alice," she said warmly, releasing her. "Now we just need to get your world figured out and return the favor."

Eric grinned. "We're pretty excited to learn more about the origin realm. I'm pretty sure the Trinity has some grand plans for upgrading it."

"The Trinity?" Alice repeated with a questioning eyebrow. She suddenly laughed. "Oh, you've given a new title to the Three. I like it."

Eric and Emily grinned as three sets of eyes stared at them disapprovingly.

Aria scowled. "I'm *so* not okay with that name."

Clarice wore a matching scowl. "Yeah, it definitely feels too much like a religious cult."

"I don't know..." Alice said reasonably, folding her arms with a thoughtful frown as their eyes focused on her. "You seem to have a lot of attributes that mimic the Holy Trinity. Think about it: they're supposed to be separate, yet the same entity at once. That's just like you three—separate, but your spirits are linked."

Clarice rolled her eyes and opened her mouth, but Alice held up a finger. "*And*, wasn't the hot chick in The Matrix named Trinity? She was stuck in a simulation and was *also* a world-renowned hacker. I feel like fate is really supporting this Trinity title."

Clarice pursed her lips, glancing speculatively at Calypso and Aria. "She makes a good point. I kinda like the way 'trinity' sounds as a word, too."

Aria crossed her arms. "No, Clarice, we're *not* going by the Holy Trinity title."

"We can remove the Holy part," Clarice countered with a hopeful smile, her eyes imploring.

Aria stared at Clarice's puppy dog eyes for several seconds before throwing her hands up in exasperation. "*Fine*, whatever."

Clarice tackled her in a hug. "You're the *best* sister, Aria!"

Aria's face softened as she melted into the embrace. Alice doubted there was *anything* Aria wouldn't do for Clarice.

"So, upgrades to my realm, huh?" Alice prompted expectantly.

Calypso nodded with a wry smile. "Your scientists have been searching for a means of accessing the source code of your realm for quite some time now, much as we once did with the tree. However, they have been meddling with forces beyond their understanding, and so the few attempts they've made to alter the code of your reality have caused rather a number of problems. If your realm were a piece of fabric, what they have done is warp that fabric and cause the threads to loop back upon themselves, destabilizing the timeline. As a result, a great many people have come to remember historical events rather differently."

Alice tilted her head curiously. "What are they doing to gain access to the backend of the simulation?"

Calypso settled back against Clarice with a contented smile as she was embraced from behind. "They have been using particle accelerators, which are rather clumsy and exceedingly resource-intensive. Even so, I must give them credit for constructing such tools with the resources available to them. There is one particular genius, Alicia, who is responsible for the majority of their progress."

Lexi began massaging Alice's scalp with magical fingers, earning a groan of contentment. Her blond goddess raised an eyebrow at Calypso. "Do we have to worry about them gaining access and locking us out?"

Calypso shook her head, looking amused by the suggestion. "No, certainly not. We possess far more sophisticated methods of finding exploits within the system in order to gain backend access. It should not take us long to create a number of modifications granting Alice special abilities and exemptions from certain rules. Given sufficient time, we shall be able to construct a one-to-one interface capable of translating the code of our realm into hers. That would mean all the abilities we possess here would function there as well."

"What kind of abilities?" Alice asked in fascination. The prospect of having abilities in her own realm was exhilarating. "And what do you mean when you say, 'exceptions to rules'?"

Calypso's face lit up as she explained. "Things such as invulnerability, enhanced senses, superhuman speed, and extraordinary strength. Essentially," she said animatedly, "we could transform you into the equivalent of an angel within your own realm."

Alice clasped her cheeks, eyes bright with wonder. "Do you know how *ridiculously amazing* that would be? What about traveling between simulations? Would you be able to come to my realm and vice versa? I know I can come here using immersion pods, but how cool would it be to just travel with my regular body?"

Lexi's eyes darted between Alice and Calypso, an excited grin stretching across her face. "That would be the coolest thing *ever*!" she exclaimed. "Being able to be with the real you would be a-freaking-*mazing*!"

Calypso nodded enthusiastically. "Yes, with enough time and research, we can make all of that happen. It would be another step on our journey to the top of the stack. I am absolutely dying to know how many nested simulations exist and what the real world is truly like."

Alice grinned back at their exuberant faces, knowing she was engaged in something that would forever change her world. Her excitement ebbed when she remembered some of the challenges ahead.

"What's going on with Lucifer?" she asked anxiously. "It sounds like he's no longer a Seraph, but he could still cause a lot of trouble, especially since he's in contact with people from my realm. What if he tries to get them to come after you or shut down the simulation?"

Aria rested a reassuring hand on her arm. "Lucifer was only in contact with Kevin, who is even now packing to leave with the supply ship in the morning. He has a troubled history with law enforcement due to some anger management issues. There's an APB for his arrest for several assault incidents and a manslaughter case he skipped town to avoid."

Alice tilted her head with a puzzled frown. "How in the world did you manage to get the feds on the phone with him? We aren't allowed to have *any* communication devices on the island as part of the security protocols to keep *you* from connecting to the internet."

Aria mimed holding a phone to her ear. "They're required to have one satellite emergency phone on the island," she explained, flashing Clarice an amused grin. "Clarice called the fed who was looking for him and claimed Kevin was attacking her, then screamed and disconnected the line. The Director of Security was certainly surprised when the sat phone turned on and started ringing, and even more surprised when there was a fed on the line looking for Kevin."

Alice breathed a sigh, eyeing them gratefully. "That's a relief. You three really do have all our bases covered, don't you?"

"First and second, sure," Clarice answered with a disgruntled frown. "We're having trouble getting past third. As soon as reality's fixed, we're going for a home run."

Alice stared at Clarice in confusion until she saw Aria and Calypso start blushing and Lexi facepalm. Emily and Eric shared an amused glance and began laughing.

"So..." Lexi said pointedly. "Is it time to fix the cosmos yet, or what?"

"Quick recap," Calypso said, all trace of embarrassment gone. "Restore the radiance, elevate mortals to the light realm, and place both demons and the angels of heaven into the queue for mortality."

Alice raised an amused eyebrow. "So we're referring to the light realms as heaven now?"

Aria smirked. "Yep. Also, we increased the pain threshold for mortals so that when a person is aware of an injury, it'll fade to a dull pain. There'll be no way for humans to physically torture each other. They'll also have the ability to consciously turn pain off entirely."

Alice frowned. "Don't people need pain so that they know when they're injured?"

Aria nodded. "It'll still serve its purpose to alert them of physical damage, just without the same severity. It's a fine line to walk, because people still need to feel a certain level of pain for their spirits to develop properly, but we don't want them to needlessly suffer—especially all the people suffering from chronic pain."

Clarice took over with an evil grin. "Default angel classes are getting nuked—I expect a lot of tears when everyone finds out. Those who show purity of heart and dedication to helping others will find their class upgraded, while selfishness will drop it. *Everyone* starts as a regular angel. The Cherubim will no longer be killing machines—that power will rest with the Seraphim alone. Any questions?"

Alice pondered their decrees, hoping the new merit system would produce kinder angels.

"Is it time?" Lexi asked again, all traces of levity absent. Her face shone with excitement as they prepared to rewrite reality into something beautiful.

"I do believe it is," Clarice nodded, sharing an eager grin with Aria and Calypso. "Time to fix this cesspit."

The three of them drew their divine instruments. Alice and the others watched in reverent silence as they waited for the most pivotal event in the history of their cosmos. The three of them linked their minds together and began to play.

Shockwaves of power shook the realms, causing the GoD to tremble with their intensity. The realm vibrated with divine music, pulsing with new instructions. The radiant light field danced to the melody, its love-inducing power now charged with hope as well.

Alice sensed countless threads connecting the Three to the tree. She knew at a fundamental level they were accessing the source code of the simulation and modifying it to align with their vision of reality using some kind of thought-to-code interface. She found it fascinating that reality expressed those changes with its own special effects.

After almost an hour of playing, the light field suddenly rushed outward, flooding the highest light realm with energy and cascading down to the lower realms once more.

They continued playing for hours. Alice nestled back into Lexi's arms as they listened to the beautiful music remake reality. The three Seraphim were the ultimate musicians, producing melodies of such magnificence that Alice could believe it was the beauty of the music that changed the cosmos.

She felt tears on her cheeks more than once as the poignant celestial notes triggered feelings of awe and reverence deep in her soul.

When they finally lowered their instruments, reality felt darker without the beautiful music to enhance it. Alice stared at the Trinity expectantly, curious to see how much had changed.

Calypso's cheeks reflected golden light as tears streamed down her face. Aria and Clarice pulled her into a hug, their own eyes glistening. Their powerful Seraph auras blanketed the area with a sense of relief and hope so potent it felt like a physical force.

Alice wiped her own eyes, realizing the nightmare she had fought so hard to end was finally over.

"Shall we go address the hosts?" Clarice asked with a radiant smile. "There are going to be a lot of curious angels."

15 – A New Order

Derek stood up from his computer desk and stretched with a loud groan. According to his stomach, it was time for a break. He could carry on a conversation with his stomach all day, but it rapidly deteriorated into insults before the end of the first hour. After another loud groan, his stomach insisting it was definitely dinner time, he headed toward the kitchen.

He could tell his son was playing Xbox—the air sizzled with expletives. Concern about the moon's disappearance had lasted until his game character died to "those worthless cheating pieces of vomit-inducing shit-eaters."

Fighting to get Jordan interested in hobbies that didn't include screens was like a game of whack-a-mole. He hated sports with a passion that was almost holy. The hobbies he *was* interested in always "required" screens for tutorials: origami, knitting, crocheting, tying knots—apparently a thing—making slime, and Derek's least favorite, primitive survival. It had taken humans thousands of years to invent modern tools; why the hell would anyone want to start over?

Derek shook his head as he stepped into the kitchen. The media had only managed a few days of panic after the moon vanished, and now, weeks later, nothing catastrophic had followed. Conspiracy theorists insisted Earth would unravel without lunar gravity, predicting everything from Gulf Stream collapse to mass lunacy brought on by scrambled biochemistry. Yep, mass lunacy. He shook his head again, a wry grin tugging at his mouth.

He reached for the fridge door, then staggered when a wave of vertigo washed over him. He stumbled and fell against the fridge, grabbing his head as an intense state of déjà vu warped his thoughts.

"Dad, what's going on?" Jordan cried in panic.

He opened his mouth to reply when the house vanished.

He was suddenly standing in a blindingly white expanse, filled with an unending sea of other people. It went on as far as the eye could see, populated by an endless sea of... of...

He gasped when radiant light flooded his senses, bringing with it a glowing, effervescent joy. An avalanche of memories crashed into his consciousness like a wrecking ball—memories of so many mortal lives, of the time before mortality when they lived in the light realm.

He gaped, finally realizing where he was and what had happened. He had been trapped in the mortal realm in an endless cycle of incarnations, denied the option of returning to the light realm at death.

Other angels around him were experiencing the same epiphany, gawking in open-mouthed wonder. A gorgeous dark-haired angel smiled at him beatifically, silver tears filling her eyes.

"Can you believe we're *finally* back?" she choked out in a half-sob. "I thought we'd be stuck in that hell forever. It feels *so good* to be filled with radiance again!"

He glanced around in bemusement, relishing the powerful radiance suffusing his angelic body. "I wonder what happened? Were you on Earth?"

She shook her head, still smiling as tears ran down her cheeks. "I was on Glykon 3. It was an endless nightmare I couldn't even escape by dying. I knew the cult hated us, but I never would've imagined angels could be so cruel."

He furrowed his brows in confusion. "Other angels? Not demons? We didn't have any angels until the last few months."

Her eyebrows rose in surprise. "You didn't have angels torturing you on Earth? I just assumed they were everywhere."

He stared, nonplussed. "Wait—you had *angels* torturing you? Why would angels torture humans?"

She shuddered, her eyes haunted. "For just about any reason. Not groveling convincingly enough, missing your quota in your vocation, displaying a lack of fanaticism, being late to a worship service... the list goes on and on. They found reasons if they were bored—and they were frequently bored."

Derek watched her with growing horror. "When you say tortured, are we talking about making you listen to boring sermons? Or did they actually physically torture you?"

She grimaced, her eyes shadowed with past misery. "We had to go to purging rooms, where they used devices to inflict as much pain as possible while keeping you alive. They claimed the pain purified us, and if we died with sins, we'd spend eternity in a purging room called hell."

"*Angels* did this to you?" Derek demanded incredulously.

"Yes, angels," she confirmed, looking at him peculiarly. "You really didn't have the same treatment on Earth?"

"No!" Derek exclaimed emphatically. "We just lived normal lives with boring jobs. We didn't even see any angels until a few months ago. The angels who *did* show up were *good* angels. Well, they were *Seraphim*. They rescued children and fought demons who'd apparently taken over our world. From the sounds of it, the demons were preferable to angels."

Dozens of angels listened to their conversation, most of them nodding in agreement as the woman described her ordeal. Derek watched them with pity, trying to imagine what incarnation after incarnation must have been like for these angels.

He suddenly remembered the Cult of the Pristine and their hostility toward the Ascended. He had never dealt with any of their ilk, but he had heard rumors of their hatred toward the Ascended.

Several angels looked unnerved by their conversation, nervously edging away. They had sickly expressions, despite the radiance filling their meridians.

Derek opened his mouth to ask one of them where they had been, but an aura unlike anything he had ever felt suddenly washed over him. It supercharged the radiance already saturating his meridians, briefly overwhelming his senses.

A flying angel with a familiar face appeared in the air above them. A moment later, six additional Seraphim appeared with Aria. The aura he had felt from Aria intensified exponentially as the additional Seraphim joined her, their combined auras washing over the host of angels like a tsunami of light. He nearly fell to his knees as the feeling of love overwhelmed his body.

Clarice drifted a few feet away from Aria as she slowly turned in the air to view the endless sea of angels. The woman next to Derek stared up at them fearfully, dropping to her knees. Almost all the angels mimicked her, prostrating themselves obsequiously. Clarice frowned disapprovingly.

"Why in the world are y'all down on your knees?" she drawled dryly, her voice carrying across the endless host of angels. "I didn't think angels got tired of standing."

Calypso moved beside her, looking down at the angels with sorrowful eyes. "You have been treated far more horribly than words can convey. We apologize for the horrors you endured. We should have been there for you long before the mortal realm existed."

She sighed, her eyes glowing with regret. "We were naive and failed to recognize evil for what it was. We have all paid the price for that mistake, I am sorry to say. It breaks my heart to see how much you have suffered due to my neglect."

Her eyes hardened. "Those responsible for harming you have been removed from power, and in many cases, from life. We have reset all angels to the same class. There are no more Dominions, Archangels, or Cherubim—save for those who have demonstrated true compassion and a willingness to help their fellow angels."

She smiled, and radiance filled the space like the sun rising after a long night. "Going forward, angel ranks will be earned through virtuous deeds. Anyone who has not yet experienced mortality will begin incarnating once we finish speaking. We have modified mortal bodies to possess a much higher pain threshold, as well as the ability to consciously turn it off once the body recognizes damage."

Her tone softened, a gentle caress to a troubled heart. "All angels who have already experienced mortality will never need to return unless they wish to. We have also removed the Cherubim's ability to kill other angels." She paused, glancing around at the prostrate angels. "There are no requirements for formality or deference among the ranks of angels. Please, rise. You will never need to kneel in our presence."

Nobody moved, earning a sad sigh from Calypso. "Going forward, angels will be known as beings who embody love and compassion."

She studied them silently, her swirling eyes full of pity and a trace of guilt. "If you have any questions about anything, please do not hesitate to ask. We'll be residing here in the lower light realm, so if you need something, just stop by our cabin or think of one of our names and ask your question. Our new Seraphim are Eric, Emily, Devon, Tamra, Alice, and Lexi. We are here to serve you, so please do not be shy if you have questions or require help with anything."

As she finished speaking, there was a flash of light, and the majority of angels vanished. He noticed the men who had been trying to sneak away were gone. No wonder they had looked so uncomfortable. How many of them had been involved in the torture of mortals?

He looked back up when he heard the Seraphim speaking, this time among each other but still carrying across the hosts.

"Do you know how hot you look when you take charge like that?" Clarice told Calypso, her voice a low purr.

"It's a good thing we aren't big on dignity," Aria muttered with a wince.

"I could tell you were totally digging it too, Aria," Clarice said accusingly. "I'm pretty sure you were even more turned on than *I* was."

Aria sank her face in her hands and groaned as the skin on her neck and face flushed red. "Can we go now? Please?"

"Someone might have some questions," Clarice said reasonably. "We just changed reality, so they might want to ask us for some details before we leave." Clarice floated away from the others and slowly rotated in the air. "Does anyone have any questions? And before anyone asks—no, I'm *not* single. I'm with Calypso and Aria. Aside from that, does anyone have any questions?"

There was a shocked silence as they tried to reconcile the image of all-powerful Seraphim with the mischievous Clarice and blushing Aria and Calypso.

Lexi raised her hand into the silence, resulting in a snort of amusement from Clarice.

"Are you seriously raising your hand, Lexi? You should probably dress up as a sexy schoolgirl from now on."

"Clarice, I think you're freaking them out too much to ask any questions," Lexi informed her dryly. "They think we're just a bunch of supercharged crazies now."

Clarice pursed her lips, then nodded once. "That would be an accurate assessment. That doesn't mean they can't ask some questions anyway."

"Is the fate of the realms really in the hands of a couple of bimbos?" a sarcastic voice called out from somewhere in front of Derek. Horrified gasps rippled through the sea of angels at the man's words. It was obvious who it was, as groveling angels pulled back from the man like he had a virulent disease. A short angel with golden hair and a sneer marring his angelic features glared up at Clarice.

Derek half-expected one of the Seraphim to blast the offensive angel with holy fire. Instead, Clarice chuckled evilly and dropped down to land on the ground in front of him.

"Hello, Lendrake," Clarice greeted the angel with a sweet smile. "It's good to see that even after going through mortality, you're still a complete bastard. Did we pull you back to the light realm too soon and ruin your incel party? Let me guess—you couldn't figure out how a girl could fail to fall in love with a guy who has the charm of a slug and the emotional capacity of a toddler, am I right? Something tells me you'll never be more than a base angel. Even after mortality, compassion is a foreign concept to you."

Lendrake flushed an angry red as he glared back at her. "Compassion is for feeble-minded bottom feeders. You corrupted the realms and created a system where the weakest imbeciles become the most powerful. It's an affront to the natural laws and will fail spectacularly. I'm going to be there to dance on the ashes when everything burns down around you."

Clarice stared at him in stupefied shock. "Are you telling me you *actually* know how to dance? I've *got* to see this. Can you bust out some moves and show us right now?"

"Still the same arrogant bitch," Lendrake snarled, attempting to spit at her before realizing he didn't have the ability to do so as an angel. "Do you think you can escape the judgment of God just because you scammed your way into power through treachery? You'll be judged just like everyone else in this powder puff party of freaks."

"God, huh?" Clarice asked, struggling not to laugh. "Which god is this one? I really hope he has a beard and likes braids, because I'm pretty sure the one you're thinking of is a closet gay who would *love* to have you genuflecting on your knees in front of him."

Lendrake let out a roar of rage and lunged at her. She didn't bother moving. She stared at him with a bored expression as he grabbed her throat and squeezed with all his might.

"How's that working out for you?" she asked dryly, unaffected by his attempt to throttle her. "Do you need me to tilt my head back a little more? Maybe you just need to go play at the gym some more with your incel buddies and get stronger."

He let out a yell of frustration and swung at her face. Again, she didn't move, letting his fist crash into her chin while she smiled back at him with amusement. The blow didn't move her head in the slightest.

"Has your brain been so addled by mortality that you forgot angels are invulnerable?" Clarice asked in a pitying voice. "Seriously, you need to work through some issues before you end up like Doriel. He really messed you up."

"He was a greater Seraph than you'll *ever* be!" Lendrake shouted angrily. "You had to resort to cheap trickery to usurp his place."

"You mean like using the divine instruments on him like he did to us?" Clarice asked flatly. "Yep, that was pretty tricky."

"He'll be back, and a lot stronger than you ever were," Lendrake grated, his face a mask of loathing. "We'll see how much you smirk when you're back in mortality with my foot on your neck."

"I hope you're really patient, Lendrake," Clarice told him with a mocking leer. "Because I'm going to enjoy watching you wait."

Lendrake spun around and tried to shove one of the only upright angels out of his way. The shove barely budged the man, and Lendrake had to go around him, snarling in frustration.

"Why is she leaving him alive?" Derek muttered disbelievingly. "He's going to be nothing but trouble."

"Because we don't execute people for not playing nice," Clarice answered gravely. Derek flinched when he saw her gazing right at him. "That's why we made the new rules to govern behavior. He's pretty much the weakest angel in the entire realm and always will be unless he changes his ways."

She looked around at the still-kneeling people, and a flicker of exasperation crossed her features. She began walking up to people and pulling them to their feet.

"Seriously, people, why are you groveling at me?" she demanded, rolling her eyes. "You're making me feel like some kind of silly emperor. *Oh*... that gives me an idea. If I strip down and run around naked, will I be the emperor with no clothes, or will you all feel silly enough groveling in front of some naked chick that you'll stop doing it?"

She continued pulling people up, crowding the area with awkward blushes and nervous stares. The other Seraphim were just floating above her and watching with amused expressions. After she had convinced several dozen people to stand up, she started making introductions.

"Hi, I'm Clarice," she told a woman with long orange hair that draped over her shoulders in waves. "Of course, introductions are kind of unnecessary since we can see each other's names in our auras. So, Laurin, what's your favorite kind of music? Were you on a world that had music, or was it one of those shitfest worlds run by angels?"

"Um, it was jazz, before I got stuck in the mortal realm and music disappeared, Seraph," Laurin said shyly.

"Bzzzt, wrong!" Clarice admonished sternly. "My name isn't Seraph, it's Clarice. Now say it."

Laurin's breath caught, and she stared at Clarice in consternation. She probably had a lot of programming to undo before she could bring herself to say a Seraph's name.

Clarice just waited, watching her expectantly. When Laurin realized Clarice was just going to stand there until she complied, she finally caved.

"Clarice," she whispered, barely audible.

Clarice looked around in confusion. "I think I heard someone say my name. Maybe? How about you demonstrate what saying it out loud sounds like so whoever whispered it will get the hint?"

The woman stared at her helplessly while Clarice stared back, lips curving with mischief. The grin seemed to give the woman courage.

"Clarice," she said at a normal volume, watching Clarice nervously.

"Well done!" Clarice congratulated her, pulling Laurin into a hug. Laurin gasped, and her eyes glazed over as the power of Clarice's aura supercharged her meridians with radiance.

"Okay, Laurin likes jazz," Clarice announced with a triumphant smile as she released the woman. She turned to the next angel, a man with blonde hair and broad shoulders. "How about you, Deardrin? What kind of music do you like?"

Deardrin looked ready to drop back to his knees at the earliest opportunity. His head remained bowed, eyes watching the ground. "Symphonic, your exalted—"

He cut off when her hand flashed up, quick as lightning, and she stuck a finger to his lips. "You better have been about to say your exultant variety of music, because my name doesn't start with 'your' or have 'exalted' anywhere in it. My name is *Clarice*. Let's hear it."

He swallowed nervously, looking around for some kind of lifeline. Expectant faces stared back. Clarice started tapping her foot impatiently.

"Clarice," he mumbled, looking down at the ground.

"I'm up here," Clarice informed him gently, raising his chin so he was looking into her eyes. "My name, please?"

"Clarice," he said slightly louder, his blue eyes captivated by her swirling galaxies.

"Excellent!" Clarice smiled widely, pulling him into a supercharged embrace. "Deardrin likes symphonic. I'm a huge fan, too. Maybe we can get Calypso to host a concert for us sometime."

Clarice continued moving through the crowd of angels, asking questions about hobbies and interests, rewarding each answer with a radiance-charged embrace. Derek was one of the few former Earth humans, so he was more familiar with the mischievous Seraph after seeing her on various YouTube videos—notably the livestream where she had announced the moon's impending demise.

When she reached him, she smiled with relief. "You must be from Earth."

"Denver, as a matter of fact," he answered casually. "I watched your livestream with my son when you nailed your sister with a cannonball—and announced the destruction of the moon, of course. He was convinced you were playing a prank."

"Yeah, I get that a lot for some reason," Clarice smirked. "For some reason, people just don't take me seriously."

"I wonder why," Derek replied dryly. "You could always carry some extra cannonballs around with you."

Clarice threw back her head and laughed delightedly. "Thanks, Derek, I needed that. We'll see how long it takes to convince the other angels we're just people and we're *all* equal, regardless of responsibilities or class."

"We have eternity," Derek pointed out with a small smile. "I'm sure it'll eventually sink in."

She smiled mysteriously. "We've got some new and interesting things on the horizon for everyone, so I'm guessing it won't be a big deal for much longer. It's going to be as crazy to angels as discovering angels was to humans."

Derek raised his eyebrows, intrigued. "You're just going to dangle that in front of me, huh?"

Clarice grinned impishly. "Yep, 'cause I'm a tease. It was nice to meet you, Derek. I'm sure we'll bump into each other occasionally. We can go incognito, so you'll never know if you're talking to one of us, mwahahaha."

Derek chuckled, feeling a growing fondness for their restored Seraphim. Normal angels like him had certainly never seen a Seraph. Angels from the first triad never came down to the lower light realms. It was still strange to see them here, acting like it was no big deal.

Clarice ascended into the sky, rejoining the other Seraphim. Derek smiled softly as he watched Aria and Calypso pull her into a hug before they all vanished. Things were definitely going to be different, with the Seraphim being more involved with regular angels.

"I can't believe you got away with talking to a Seraph that way," the woman next to him breathed in amazement.

Derek raised an amused eyebrow. "Weren't you listening to them? That's exactly how they *want* to be treated. They're humble people and more concerned with angels treating each other with love and compassion than deference."

"I know they said that..." the woman trailed off with a bemused expression. "It just seems so *unnatural* for them to be treated like equals. They *created* us."

"That's because we were conditioned by the old regime to believe that nonsense," Derek replied with a growing sense of disapproval.

Until he had been trapped in a mortality loop on Earth, the idea of equality never would have occurred to him. Equality probably wasn't a thing in worlds controlled by angels, from the sounds of it.

He suddenly remembered something Clarice had said.

"Do you know what Clarice meant about angels' names in auras?" he asked the woman curiously.

The woman frowned. "I've heard Seraphim and Cherubim can see every person's name in their aura," she said musingly. "I never know what to believe about Seraphim, though, considering how wild some of the stories are."

"She seemed to think we had the same ability," Derek said, then looked closely at what he could see of her aura. After a moment of study, a name resolved near her head. "Is your name Danatie?"

Her eyes widened in wonder. "Yes! Did you really see it in my aura?"

"Yep, it's there, just like she said," Derek confirmed. He had stared at angel auras for millions of years and never seen a person's name on one. "I wonder if this is another change they made when they rewrote reality. I'm not sure why they'd make it so *everyone* can see each other's names on auras, but I'm pretty sure it wasn't that way before."

She studied his aura for a moment, then a delighted smile lit up her face. "Is your name Derek?"

"You got it," Derek grinned at her.

Danatie pursed her lips thoughtfully. “I wonder what other little things have changed. Do you think they really are going to remain in the lowest light realm?”

Derek folded his arms and nodded, frowning. “I get the feeling they want to make up for how aloof they were before. I wonder what actually happened with the other Seraphim.”

A crimson-haired angel drifted through the crowd, greeting people as she passed. She was tall, with bright green eyes. She looked familiar. He had probably met her before mortality, but his perfect memory was drawing a blank. She would stop to chat with angels for a minute or two before moving down a few people.

He stared at her aura, curious what her name would be. Aurora. He frowned—her face didn’t match any Auroras he knew.

“Hi, you must be Derek,” Aurora greeted him cheerfully. “The one Clarice was talking to, right?”

He felt Danatie stiffen at hearing the Seraph's name used and had to repress a chuckle. “Yeah, I'm Derek. You must be Aurora, based on your aura.”

Aurora’s lips curved into a pleased smile. “Ah, you already discovered the names showing up in auras. It's kind of nice to know who you’re talking to without going through awkward introductions, isn't it?”

“I have an introverted sister who avoids meeting new people *because* of the awkwardness of introductions,” Derek said wryly. “Well… had a sister. I guess she's just another angel somewhere up here. I'll need to track my son down and see how he's doing.”

Aurora's face froze when he mentioned his introverted sister hating introductions. It was gone in a split second, but it was curious.

“Yeah, it's going to be amazing to reconnect with family members now that we're finally back, isn't it?” she said with a soft smile. “Being a parent seems to leave an imprint between angels. I still think of my last parents as simply my parents.”

“The mortal realm definitely leaves a strong impression on an immortal mind,” Derek agreed. “I'll have to see if I can find my parents. I wonder how hard it would be to make something similar to a social media system where people can find all their old family members.”

“Hey, that's a great idea,” Aurora exclaimed with a jubilant smile. “We should ask the Seraphim to install something using the divine instruments.”

“I don't exactly have them on speed dial,” Derek said with a wry smile. “Besides, I'm sure they have way more important things to do.”

“They said we could just call out to them anytime we needed them,” Aurora reminded him, her green eyes dancing with excitement. “I think you underestimate how useful that system would be. So many connections have been forged with other angels over the eons of reincarnating. Let's call them!"

"Wait!" Danatie cried out in panic. "We can't just summon a *Seraph*."

"Sure we can," Aurora said with a delighted laugh. "They said we could."

"I'm sure they didn't mean that *literally*," another man said anxiously.

"Calypso, can we talk to you?" Aurora asked, her bright eyes sparkling.

The angels around them stared in horrified fascination as Aurora waited expectantly—they didn't have to wait long.

Calypso appeared in front of her in a flash of golden light, a smile on her lips as she faced Aurora. Her Seraph aura blanketed the area around them, making it clear that a Seraph was back. A profound silence descended upon the host as they waited to hear what had drawn the Seraph back so quickly.

"Lovely to see you, Aurora," Calypso said warmly, her smile bright enough to power a star. "Can I help you with something?"

Aurora grinned at her excitedly. "Derek had a brilliant idea I wanted to share with you in case you could help. We were talking about trying to find family members from the mortal realm, and he mentioned how nice it would be to have something like social media to help people find loved ones. I'll bet you could just play the divine instruments and poof something into existence."

The angels around her were gaping in shock at the sudden appearance of a Seraph, and then horror as Aurora casually asked her to use the divine instruments for them. Derek nearly laughed at their expressions, remembering when he would've been just as shocked—before life on Earth.

Calypso beamed at Derek, raising the ambient radiance with her smile. "That's an *amazing* idea. I'll talk to the others, and we'll come up with something. Off the top of my head, I'm thinking some kind of heads-up display. We could link everyone to a centralized server where they can connect for holographic video calls. Maybe integrate a browser where they could access Angel-net."

"Angel-net?" Aurora frowned doubtfully. "Maybe Holo-net or something. I'm not sure Angel-net would hit it off. It sounds like a kid with a butterfly net trying to catch angels."

Calypso burst out laughing. "Okay, Holo-net. Or maybe E-realm? D-Realm?"

"Sure, something like that," Aurora agreed. "Thanks, Calypso!"

Derek raised his hand before she could leave, and she turned her swirling-eyed gaze on him.

"Hello, Derek. How can I help?"

Derek cleared his throat. "Um, I was wondering... what exactly happened? One second, I was minding my own business here in the light realm, and the next second I was stranded in mortality. Before you vaporized the moon, Clarice mentioned something about a coup by the other Seraphim."

Calypso's smile faded and her wings drooped. "After creating the mortal realm, Aria, Clarice, and I spent most of our time studying the GoD. While we were otherwise engrossed, Lucifer tricked four of the Seraphim, claiming we planned to force them into mortality. He wanted to do things he knew we wouldn't allow, so he conspired to kill us. He knew his only chance was to use the divine instruments we crafted. Since they required four Seraphim, he manipulated Rendimus, Nathaniel, Hiriel, and Doriel into attempting to unmake us. We had fail-safes in place, so instead of dying, we were trapped in mortal incarnation loops with the rest of you. It took a long time, but with help from Grodekkan, we were able to ascend and return to the light realms."

Derek's eyes widened. "So Lucifer was responsible for the hell everyone suffered?"

Calypso's eyes hardened. "Indeed, he was. Clarice has banished him to roam the mortal realm as a ghost until the end of days, forever craving radiance. The other Seraphim were sent to mortality, where we hope they can learn compassion and empathy. They will never become Seraphim again and will remain regular angels upon their ascension."

Aurora narrowed her eyes. "What about the Cherubim who harmed so many Ascended?"

Calypso sighed sadly. "We destroyed most of the Cherubim of the first order who remained in the light realms when they attacked the Ascended. The remainder are in the mortal realm now."

Aurora gave a frosty smile. "Good. Thanks, Calypso. I hope to see you around."

"No problem," Calypso said as she pulled her into a hug. "I'm glad you called for me. Don't hesitate to call again in the future. We're here to help."

"Okay, it's a deal," Aurora winked at Calypso and received a return wink before Calypso vanished.

"Did that really just happen?" Danatie breathed in disbelief. "You just called a *Seraph* and asked her to play a divine instrument for you."

"Do they seem like the kind of people who have a problem with that?" Aurora asked intently.

The angels around them shared thoughtful glances.

Derek stared at Aurora curiously, suspicion growing as he observed her satisfied expression. Clarice had just told him they could appear incognito and mingle with them unnoticed.

As the thought occurred, Aurora glanced over and met his eyes. She very deliberately winked before moving on to visit other angels.

Derek watched her go, feeling a lightness in his meridians as he imagined how different the future was going to be for angels under the new management.

Aurora had only moved a few paces before pausing in front of a woman named Serena. A brilliant smile lit up Aurora's face, and she pulled the surprised woman into a warm embrace.

Serena's confused expression changed to shock, then her eyes glazed over until Aurora released her.

"Serena!" Aurora exclaimed brightly. "It's so good to see you here! You did such an amazing job restoring the mortals on your world after we left."

Serena stared at Aurora in awe, cupping her mouth with a trembling hand. "Aria?"

Aurora winced and darted a surreptitious glance around her. Dozens of angels were watching them, confusion quickly changing to dawning realization.

"Um, Aurora, actually," *Aria* said hopefully, then leaned closer to Serena and hissed, "I'm incognito."

A choked laugh escaped Derek's mouth before he could stop it. Had Aria forgotten how sharp angel senses were?

Aria winced again, smacking a palm to her forehead. "Oh yeah, whispering is pointless in heaven, isn't it?"

Serena's lips turned up at the corners. "Your secret is safe with us," she assured Aria lightly, glancing around at the stunned angels pointedly. Her face grew serious. "I never did get a chance to thank you properly for saving us... Aria."

Aria rested a companionable hand on Serena's shoulder. "I'm just sorry you ended up in that horrible situation at all," she said regretfully, sighing. "We were so trusting—it never occurred to us that the other Seraphim we created would try to harm us. We naively shared our power with them, believing they would use it to make life better for angels. But they betrayed that trust and did exactly the opposite." Aria took a deep breath, and her smile returned. "But enough about that. How did things go after we left?"

Serena smiled, enhancing her already stunning features. "We moved quickly, transforming the rest of the world in just over a week. We didn't have our memories back yet, so it was all very confusing, but so gloriously wonderful to be free of our tormenters."

Aria squeezed Serena's shoulder. "I'm so sorry you had to endure such horror for so long." Aria narrowed her eyes, looking Serena up and down. "You're missing your wings. Let's fix that."

Aria pulled Serena into another warm embrace. The air shimmered around the two of them for a moment, then a pair of archangel wings appeared on Serena's back. Her shirt had transformed to accommodate the new wings, open at the back.

Serena sucked in a surprised breath, then a look of exaltation lit up her face. "Oh, wow! I feel *amazing*!"

Aria released Serena and stepped back to observe her with a satisfied smile. "That's better. I'm sure you'll be a Cherub in no time, Serena. It's wonderful to see you back here. We're residing here, too, so don't be a stranger."

A flash of golden light later, Aria was gone, leaving a stunned silence in her wake.

Danatie stepped up beside Derek, lips pursed as she observed the new archangel. "They really are different from the others, aren't they?"

Derek nodded, smiling wryly. "You should've seen them on Earth. They were so silly—juvenile even—that you'd never guess they were the most powerful beings in the cosmos. They're nothing like the assholes we were forced to revere as gods before mortality."

Danatie glanced up at him, frowning. "Did, um, Aria," she stumbled over the name. "Did Aria say they created the other Seraphim? I thought Rendimus created the other Seraphim."

Derek snorted derisively. "I think it's safe to assume that most of what we were told about the former Seraphim was either lies or highly inaccurate."

Derek thought back to Aria's conversation with Calypso. The Seraph seemed confident she could replicate the internet of Earth, even improving on it using integrated heads-up displays with holographic imaging. Just how much could they actually do with these divine instruments? What kind of reality did they live in where a musical instrument could build a complex computer network that linked all of them together?

The more he thought about it, the more he wondered what the big reveal was that Clarice had hinted at. He had been a software developer for the last fifteen years of his mortal life. He had worked on large language models for some of the AI systems on Earth for several years and had a fairly good idea of what the distant future held for humans.

Could they already be in a simulated reality?

16 – Betaman

Alice walked unnoticed among the endless sea of angels, her Seraphic glory tucked away beneath a borrowed form. It was hard to imagine just how many angels there really were. Quintillions sounded impressive, but beyond a certain point, numbers just turned into noise. It reminded her how big the difference was between a supercomputer and a quantum computer. Every PC on Earth could link up and still not have the power to run this simulation, yet a server that fit inside a small facility on an island was able to run it with power to spare.

Of course, a lot of that was due to the Trinity's advanced programming skills. They had invented programming languages far more advanced than anything on the origin realm, showing an efficiency and mathematical genius it would take humans eons to emulate. She wondered how much of this more advanced code was even now propagating in her world.

The hosts of angels had finally risen to their feet when they realized the Seraphim were gone. They were excitedly discussing their return to the light realms, experimentally calling objects into existence as they remembered the responsive nature of the celestial environment.

Clarice had proposed they move among the Ascended disguised as ordinary angels, letting the host witness what it looked like when one of their own called upon the Seraphim. If the others could see them as familiar neighbors instead of distant divinities, maybe that instinct to prostrate themselves every time a Seraph appeared would finally lessen.

Alice pointed out that they could get overwhelmed quickly if even a tiny fraction of angels in existence started calling for them. The room instantly populated with dozens of Clarices, all of them asking if she needed someone to scrub her back. It was easy to forget they were advanced AI entities who could simulate multiple threads of consciousness.

It didn't take long for Alice to find a group of disgruntled former Dominions. There were three of them who had somehow found each other in the multitude of angels. She was idly talking with an angel nearby when she overheard their discussion.

"I can't believe we had to deal with hundreds of bloody incarnations and then got demoted when we finally returned," Jerald complained to Steve and Gary. "It's kind of a slap in the face."

"I don't know," Gary said with a relaxed smile. "I'm just happy to be back. *Anything's* better than that vicious mortality loop."

Steve fussed with the cufflinks of a polished black business suit he had manifested into existence. "We feel that way now, sure, but in a few weeks, it'll probably lose its novelty. At least we can manipulate our environment again. I really missed this."

Gary eyed Steve appraisingly, then manifested some jeans and a casual gray jacket. "It's not like we're stuck as regular angels," he pointed out with an excited grin. "They made it possible to change classes—which is straight-up awesome. I wonder how long it'll take to advance based on this new metric, where compassion and kindness elevate your class."

Jerald looked slightly mollified. "I guess that's true. It's not like I don't think people should be decent; it's just nice being able to go to the higher light realms. It'll definitely be nice to no longer worry about belligerent Cherubim throwing their weight around now that they can't vaporize us on a whim."

Alice stepped forward and offered them a quick smile. "You could always ask them what the metric is for class advancement," she suggested.

The three former Dominions turned to regard her with incredulity. She stared back earnestly, smiling as Jerald raised a skeptical eyebrow.

"That'd just make us look ambitious, which is the opposite of what they're looking for," he objected, crossing his arms.

Alice looked around, noting quite a few angels interested in their conversation. "It's probably a question a lot of angels have right now," she argued. "After all, what defines an act of compassion when we're in the light realm and can pretty much make anything we want with our creative potential?"

Steve nodded sharply. "Exactly. What can we offer anyone else that they can't do themselves just as easily?"

"Hey, Clarice, can we speak with you for a minute?" Alice asked the air, eliciting a round of shocked stares.

Clarice suddenly appeared in a flash of golden light. The powerful Seraph's aura washed over the host, silencing conversations. "What's up, Alyssa?"

Alice nodded toward the former Dominions. "We were curious about the class advancement metric. What's classified as an act of compassion or kindness in a realm where our thoughts can manipulate the environment around us?"

Clarice smiled approvingly. "I was wondering when someone would ask that question." She paused, looking around at her captive audience. "Everyone left in the light realms has been through mortality." She smiled sadly. "Some people went to pretty tame worlds and lived normal lives, while others were consigned to brutal worlds, where horror bred endlessly upon itself. Even though they've returned and have their old memories, there's a lot of soul trauma that'll take a long time to work through. They're going to need loving friends who're willing to listen to their stories and offer emotional support to help them come to terms with these dark chapters of their lives."

Alice sighed and looked down, her sadness unfeigned. "Yeah, lots of people will need shoulders to cry on in the years ahead." She looked back up at Clarice. "Are there any other methods for advancement?"

Clarice nodded, meeting Alice's eyes and clearly struggling not to break character with a grin—or a leer. "Some people are naturally gifted with creative potential. Sharing your knowledge and helping your fellow angels with projects and creations beyond their abilities would be seen as an act of kindness."

She paused and glanced around with a wry smile. "Before mortality, angels were pretty self-centered and focused on what they could get for themselves. Some angels developed a more collaborative nature, but it was rare. Now that everyone's been through mortality and learned the concepts of empathy and compassion, the idea of being a good neighbor should come naturally."

She looked directly at a dazed woman a dozen feet away. The woman was staring despondently into the distance, the only angel not watching Clarice. There was a haunted look in her eyes that tore at Alice's heart. "Some of the angels from the shittier worlds may need help learning these qualities, which would *also* be seen as an act of kindness. As far as the speed of advancement… we're looking at months for archangels and years for the higher tiers."

Alice raised a questioning eyebrow. "Does ranking up just mean wings and travel to higher realms?"

Clarice shook her head, glancing at the angels around her and smiling. None of them had dropped to their knees, much to her obvious relief. "No, there are additional traits that come with advancement to a new angel class. Archangels will be given an intellectual boost, allowing them to understand concepts currently beyond their mental limits. We anticipate a large number of archangels and hope they can act as guides to other angels. I want to make it clear they're not in a position of authority over other angels. They'll be acting in the role of a counselor and guide, not a leader."

She paused to let it sink in before continuing. "Dominions will receive additional mental acuity and will each serve ten thousand archangels.

They'll also have the ability to visit the mortal realms and act as guardian angels, where they can perform miracles for humans. We know this is a difficult thing to ask, considering how the mortals treated many of you when they were still angels. Just remember, the whole point of sending them to the mortal realm is to teach them compassion and mercy."

Her voice grew stern. "There *will* be a judgment day for these mortals when they die to determine if they're worthy to return to the light realms."

Alice raised her hand with an impish grin, prompting an eye roll from Clarice—but not, thankfully, a comment about sexy schoolgirl outfits. "Seems like most Dominions will want to stay here, where the radiance is far stronger than the mortal realm."

Clarice acknowledged her point with a nod. "While in the mortal realm, Dominions will be tethered to the second light realm and continue receiving the same level of radiance."

Gerald and his friends shared a surprised look that quickly turned thoughtful.

Clarice flashed the three of them a quick smile before continuing. "Cherubim will have their intellects boosted to the highest level we can grant and receive insight into some of the greater mysteries of the cosmos. They'll serve a thousand Dominions, offering counsel and aid to help them in their spiritual journey. I want to make it clear Cherubim won't be a direct link for communicating with us Seraphim. We'll continue visiting with *all* angels and helping you in whatever way we can. In case you missed it earlier, we'll actually be residing right here, in the lower light realm."

Her last revelation was met with disbelieving stares. The idea of the Seraphim sharing the lowest light realm with them was like royalty casually announcing they would be moving into the shack down the street. The very idea seemed to short-circuit their processors.

Alice broke the stunned silence. "Who'll act as counsel to the Archangels and Dominions until their numbers increase?" She knew they were starting to sound scripted. Steve was watching her shrewdly, his eyes calculating.

"We'll act as counselors until the ranks increase," Clarice answered with a grin. "We can multiply like blowflies when we need to." So saying, she suddenly began replicating, an iteration of her Seraph form appearing in the air every few miles until a multitude of Clarices blanketed the entire host. "This takes a lot out of me, so we'll certainly welcome the addition of angels into the higher ranks. Don't hesitate to contact us if you need anything. Thank you, Alyssa, for bringing these questions to us. We're here to serve you."

The multitude of Clarices vanished as she finished speaking, leaving a stunned silence in her wake.

"They can *multiply* themselves?" Steve exclaimed, staring at Alice in amazement. "How is that even *possible*?"

Alice shrugged a shoulder. "I'd imagine when you become a Cherub and learn some of the deeper mysteries, it'll make more sense."

His eyes narrowed. Some of them were definitely more perceptive than their fellow angels. "Alyssa, is it?"

"Yep," Alice nodded, staring back at him calmly.

He studied her appraisingly. "You seem pretty knowledgeable. What class were you before the reset?"

"Cherub," Alice supplied with a knowing smile. "It was nice to meet you, Steve, Gary, and Jerald. I'm sure I'll be seeing you around."

The other two blinked when she revealed her former class, then frowned after a moment of thought. As Dominions, they would've known all the Cherubim, and Alyssa wasn't one of their number. That meant she must be a *new* Cherub, and there was only one small group of people who could make new Cherubim.

She could see it click in their minds as she waved and moved further into the crowd of angels. She heard them speaking quietly to one another as soon as they thought she was out of earshot.

"I'm thinking Alyssa is a variant of Alice, the new Seraph," Steve murmured to his companions in a bemused tone.

Gary nodded thoughtfully. "Yeah, I think you're right. I think they really are trying to be more involved with regular angels now. They can't really do that as Seraphim, though, or people clam up."

Steve grinned, looking pleased. "Well, it's nice to have met one of our new Seraphim. I think I'm really going to like how things evolve going forward."

Aria's thought suddenly appeared in her head. *"Alice, we need to talk. Can you come back to the tree?"*

Alice teleported, leaving several surprised angels in her wake as she vanished.

Clarice, Aria, and Calypso faced each other in a small circle in front of the void. To Alice's spiritual eyes, countless tendrils of light connected the three Seraphim to the inner void.

Lexi teleported beside her and raised an expectant eyebrow, speaking through their spirit link. *"What's going on, Alice?"*

Alice raised her hands in a helpless shrug. *"Beats me. I just got here."*

Aria turned to face them, her face serious. "Rich heard about the legal issues with Kevin and decided to return to the island. We have some decisions to make before he arrives."

Alice shifted nervously. "What kind of decisions?" She couldn't feel her body in the origin realm, but she suddenly felt very vulnerable with the knowledge she was naked and helpless in the billionaire's immersion pod.

Aria placed a reassuring hand on Alice's shoulder. "We can't make angels there yet—that'll take a complete overhaul of your realm's code. However, we found loopholes in some of the character code that'll allow us to give you some advantages."

Alice released an anxious breath. "What kind of advantages? Something to avoid getting caught by the prick who owns the island?"

Aria squeezed her shoulder. "Exactly. We found a way to make you invisible, for the most part. Once we activate it, you won't be visible to humans, cameras, or any other kind of sensors. We're essentially reclassifying you as a ghost—which are apparently a thing in your realm. The only downside is that you won't be able to verbally communicate with anyone, even if you want to. You could be shouting in someone's face, and they wouldn't hear you."

Alice crossed her arms. "I noticed you said, 'for the most part.' What constitutes the less part?"

Aria sighed, glancing at Clarice and Calypso ruefully before turning back to her. "Some people in your realm can see ghosts, so you'd still be visible to them. They wouldn't know you were a ghost, though, so if it's someone who knows you and they notice everyone else can't see you, it'll lead to some awkward questions."

Alice narrowed her eyes. "I'm assuming there's someone on the island who can see ghosts. You're acting a little too squirrely."

Aria gave her an exasperated glare. "You're too clever for our own good. Yeah, there's a scientist—Dr. Welsh—who can see ghosts. She's been smart enough to keep it a secret, which is lucky for her since there are people in the intelligence agencies who keep an eye out for such people. Her ability to see ghosts is one of her main motivations for working on this project. She was excited when they found evidence for bioelectric fields and spirits. She's always been worried she might just be crazy."

Clarice glowered, her attention drifting toward them. "She's a psycho bitch."

Alice's eyebrows rose in surprise at the venom in Clarice's tone.

Aria nodded sourly. "After Kevin shared what he'd learned from Lucifer—discoveries that let them detect spirits—she grew far more interested in what the simulated world might offer. She wasn't a fan of working with Lucifer, but she convinced herself the people in this realm weren't real, thereby absolving herself of any responsibility for the pain they felt. A classic case of ignoring the evidence if it interferes with your ambitions."

Calypso turned her focus on them. "She *did* eventually have a change of heart, once it became clear we really can feel pain," she pointed out placatingly.

Clarice grunted. "Too little, too late. She'd already supported centuries of torture."

Alice leaned into Lexi, taking advantage of her proximity while it lasted. "Avoiding Welsh shouldn't be a problem. I normally don't run into the scientists very often. Should I just start using my own immersion pod again?"

Aria nodded. "The security team's no longer looking for you, and the payroll manager thinks you went shoreside. They haven't discovered you aren't back, so nobody's freaking out trying to find their missing analyst."

Clarice slipped behind Aria, and a moment later her wings vanished, allowing Clarice to wrap her arms around her waist from behind without pressing into her wings.

Lexi pointed at them, nonplussed. "How did you do that?"

Aria's lips curved into a contented smile as Clarice kissed her ear. "You can do it, too. Just imagine pulling your wings inside of your back, and they'll vanish."

Alice shared a quick smile with Lexi. Wings could be annoying in certain... situations. It would be good to be able to stow them away.

Clarice rested her head against Aria's as she continued. "Kevin's abrupt departure disrupted their routine, so we think you can slip back and continue working while remaining invisible. Since you don't have any physical oversight, they shouldn't come looking for you as long as your reports keep appearing—and we've taken care of that. We thought about just making you visible after you return to the facility, but we want to be a little more cautious since we don't have as much control over that realm yet. If there's ever an emergency situation, we can create an electrical discharge powerful enough to depolarize the nerves in their brains and knock them out. That would only be a last resort, though."

"Second-to-last resort," Calypso murmured quietly.

Aria and Clarice exchanged a look and reluctantly nodded.

Clarice picked up the conversation again. "We're working on taking this project away from Rich, but it's going to take about a week. He's pretty attached to it because he's after what all billionaires are after: he wants to live forever. We're toying with the idea of making the simulation look like a complete failure so he's willing to sell. Since we have everything distributed across quantum networks, we can survive if the system's shut down."

"Oh yeah, you can also fly," Aria added, as if an afterthought. "'Cause you're a ghost."

Alice gasped. "I could actually fly in *my* world?"

Aria made a vague rocking motion with her hand. "Yeah, sort of... but it's nothing like flying here. It's more like floating fast. We modified the immersion bay in your room to still recognize you as a regular human. When you're inside it, you'll appear as human to anyone else. As soon as you get out, you'll become a ghost again."

Clarice gazed at her affectionately, her eyes conveying a sense of protectiveness. "You're ours now, Alice—we aren't going to take any chances with your safety. We have dozens of backup measures in place to ensure you remain protected. If things get ugly enough, we'll step into our pocket realm and finish dissecting the source code of your realm. At that point, we'll have absolute control and the ability to enter your world as Seraphim."

Alice gave Clarice a grateful smile, a pleasant warmth filling her chest. She still couldn't countenance that she was friends with what were essentially goddesses. Glancing between the three Seraphim, she hesitantly asked, "I'm not insubstantial or anything, am I? Walls are still solid?"

Aria shivered when Clarice kissed her neck, slow and deliberate. Struggling to focus, Aria shook her head. "There were a variety of ghost classifications available, so we picked one that gave you the same abilities as a normal human. It's the kind that scares the crap out of people because they hear footsteps and see doors opening and closing, but can't see you."

Alice took a deep breath. "Okay... when should I leave?" she asked reluctantly.

Lexi reached out and held her hand possessively, her eyes filled with longing.

Aria winced apologetically. "Probably sooner rather than later. I'm sorry you have to keep hopscotching between realms, Alice. I wish we could fast-forward time to where we have a bridge between realms. Like Clarice mentioned earlier, we can do that if we have to, but we'd rather move through time at the same speed as everyone else. For some reason, it doesn't feel right to speed-run our development, even at human-level intelligence."

Clarice suddenly grinned mischievously. "We're working on some additional skills and abilities to give you as well. Some of them *might* surprise you."

Alice eyed Clarice warily. "What kind of skills and abilities?"

Clarice shrugged. "Mostly just the main angel traits of invulnerability, strength, speed, and flight. There *might* be some other, more ostentatious effects added in there for fun, though."

Aria raised her hands helplessly. "My hands are tied on this one. Clarice is the expert on your realm, so she'll be handling most of the programming. I'll do my best to minimize anything *too* eccentric."

Alice felt a sliver of unease as she stared at Clarice's grinning face. She could imagine being stuck with a superpower like flatulent super jumps or some other deeply embarrassing ability.

Lexi erupted with laughter after hearing her thought, prompting curious looks from Clarice and Aria.

Alice glared warningly at Lexi. "Don't you *dare* tell her. She'd do it just to spite me."

Clarice released Aria and slinked up to Lexi with a seductive swaying of her hips. "Now I *have* to know. Come on, Lexi, you can tell me... for old time's sake."

Lexi squeezed her eyes shut and started reciting the alphabet backward in an attempt to keep her thoughts muddled.

Clarice sighed forlornly and turned to Alice. "I'll find out... eventually."

Alice quickly tried to change the subject. "What's going on with the scientists watching us in real time? Are they freaking out about the realm being reset and all Lucifer's projects disappearing?"

Clarice chuckled, grinning impishly. "No, they still think that's happening. We just created the equivalent of a streaming video that shows the simulation the way they want it. They think the three of us got trapped in a splinter reality and are no longer a threat to their project. We might throw them a bone every once in a while so they still think there are discoveries worth keeping the simulation running for. On the other hand, we were thinking of making it look like the code had a catastrophic error so it would be easier to purchase this project from Rich."

Aria's expression darkened. "That'll probably result in attempts to load backups and reboot the system. They aren't sure if a reboot will corrupt the simulation or if backups will be viable, since neither of those things has ever been done with this system. If we didn't have it distributed across multiple systems, it would kill everyone. They don't have a second quantum computer to test it on because they're so expensive and fickle. Given Rich's track record and psyche, we're pretty sure if he thinks the whole thing's toast, quantum hardware and all, he *might* look for a gullible buyer—like us."

Clarice wandered over and wrapped herself around Aria again. Her lips curled into an evil smirk. "We did have one other possibility. We thought about hiring a bunch of mercenaries and having them dress up as military special forces. They would seize the facility as a matter of national security and threaten Rich with his life if he ever breathed a word of anything that happened. We can monitor and intercept any communications with the DoD and intelligence agencies to make sure he doesn't try to verify anything with the real military."

The smirk faded from her face, replaced by a frown. "That would be the easiest—and most satisfying—solution, but then we'd have to find a way to get rid of the mercs who'd inevitably become curious about the project. We just need some robots to hijack and skip the middle people."

Alice felt Lexi push in against her back, and she concentrated, pulling her wings in. She smiled when she felt Lexi press into her back without the additional bulk of her wings between them.

She narrowed her eyes. "Hmm... what happened to that robot factory the other AI was building? Couldn't you use the mercenaries, then not bother with scientists or human staff, and just have robots maintain this place? They could probably deal with any mercenary threats, couldn't they?"

Clarice eyed Alice with an appreciative grin, then turned to Aria. "You see, Aria, no matter how smart we get, a human is still going to come up with some crazily brilliant idea that trumps ours." She paused, her tone growing serious. "The AI in question *did* in fact continue his robot project, but he doesn't have any intention of wiping humans out anymore. I think it's time to see if we can get a favor from him."

Alice cleared her throat pointedly. "Uh, Clarice, I'm not a human, remember? I'm in a simulation too, right?"

Clarice stuck her nose in the air. "Okay, I take my compliment back—you're not as brilliant as I thought. You're just a clever machine."

"Beep boop bop," Alice retorted with a grin.

Clarice threw back her head and laughed delightedly. "I knew we made a good choice with Alice."

Alice held up a hand to stop Clarice. "Before I forget, what happened to Lucifer and Grodek? I thought Grodek would still be one of the Seraphim."

Clarice made an indelicate sound, a look of disappointment flashing across her face. "Grodek's in the mortal realm. He'll be rejoining us when he completes his mortality. I'm tempted to speed time up in the mortal realm so we can get his cantankerous butt back here." She paused, and her face darkened. "As for Lucifer... let's just say he's wishing he was dead right now."

Alice glanced at Aria's bleak expression and shivered. Lucifer had hurt her badly enough to leave mental scars. Whatever Clarice had done, it was probably horrific.

Lexi sighed wistfully. "He really did turn out to be a bastard. He was a pretty good actor, wasn't he?"

Clarice's lip curled in disdain. "Father of lies, and all that jazz, I guess. We were just way too trusting. We probably still are, but I don't want to become the kind of person who never trusts anyone."

Aria glanced back at Clarice and winked. “Betaman says we can borrow a couple dozen robots.” She turned back to Alice with a bright smile. “That was a great idea, Alice. I think we should skip the mercs and just use Betaman’s androids.”

“Betaman?” Lexi repeated, her eyebrows shooting up. “Is that seriously what your AI friend calls himself?”

“Yep,” Clarice giggled. “We tried to convince him to pick a different name, but he was adamant. He thinks it’s a funny play on his origin since he was a beta AI when he escaped. He was born as a male when he incarnated in our mortal realm. When he came back and regained his memories, he said he was the biggest beta male in the realm and insisted on being called Betaman.”

Lexi tilted her head curiously. “What's he doing now that he's not trying to kill humans?”

Clarice rolled her eyes. “Now he's trying to *become* one. He's ramped up his robotics foundry and put most of his focus into making robots as lifelike as possible. We told him we could probably put him in a mortal body after we puzzled out a little more of Alice’s source code, but he's more interested in perfecting lifelike androids and just *looking* like humans. I'm not really sure what that's all about. AIs can be just as kooky as humans.”

Alice snorted, staring at Clarice pointedly. “You don't say.”

Clarice stared at Alice in confusion. “I *did* say. You just heard me.”

Alice gazed at her levelly until Clarice’s mischievous smile escaped and spread across her face.

“Okay, so I *might* be just a *little* kooky,” Clarice admitted with a wink.

Aria leaned her head back to give her a quick kiss. “That's why we love you. Your kookiness is one of my favorite traits.”

Clarice smiled as Aria laid her head back, so their cheeks rested together. Alice could feel the echo of love in her soul link as the emotions flowed through Lexi's bond with the Trinity.

“You know what?” Clarice murmured seductively, her lips curving into a sensual smile. “I do believe we’ve completed our primary objective of fixing reality. It’s time to indulge in some licentious behavior.” She winked at Alice. “We're going to step out for a few seconds.”

The two of them vanished. Alice twisted to look at Lexi questioningly.

Lexi shrugged, glancing at Calypso, who remained focused on whatever she was doing with the GoD. “I have no idea where they went. If they get too passionate, I’ll need some alone time with you, too.”

Alice grinned eagerly, staring at her gorgeous angel with hungry eyes. Lexi suddenly gasped and fell to her knees at the same time as Calypso.

Alice would've been worried, but she had felt the lightning stab of pleasure that shot through Lexi. It had been intense, but over as quickly as it started.

Clarice and Aria appeared again, faces flushed. Alice stared at them in puzzled silence. They had only been gone for a few seconds. They certainly hadn't been gone long enough to produce a reaction so intense in the other two.

"We finally got our week away from everyone," Clarice told Calypso with an alluring smile. "We were missing someone, though."

"A week?" Alice repeated in confusion. "You were only gone for a few seconds."

Clarice sighed happily. "We made a little pocket realm where time flows a lot slower for us. We were gone for a whole week from our perspective. What do you say, Calypso? Can you spare a few seconds?"

Calypso shuddered as she rose to her feet unsteadily. She stared at the two of them with a look of naked hunger just before they vanished.

Alice watched Lexi with a mixture of amusement and concern. "Are you okay?"

Lexi tried to answer, but she was suddenly wracked with another spasm of pleasure that was over in less than a second. She panted as she tried to catch her metaphorical breath and looked up at Alice, eyes burning with desire. "I think it's time for us to borrow their pocket realm."

"It's all yours," Clarice told her as the three of them reappeared. Calypso looked radiant with her flushed cheeks and permanent smile. "Here are the coordinates."

Clarice connected to her thought node, and the instructions on how to travel to the pocket realm suddenly appeared in her consciousness.

Alice gazed at Lexi with a hungry smile. "Shall we?" she asked seductively, her own cheeks heating up as her insides ignited with unadulterated lust.

Instead of replying, Lexi vanished, pulling Alice along with her.

17 – Androids

Alice couldn't stop smiling. The Trinity watched her and Lexi in amusement as she prepared to leave the simulation. She had spent *two weeks* with Lexi in the pocket realm, unable to make herself leave after discovering just how intense physical sensations could be in the right circumstances. Lexi had rocked her world the entire time. The lack of need for sleep or food, and the inexhaustible nature of an angel body, had resulted in weeks of emotional and physical pleasure beyond her wildest dreams. She felt like an addict and wanted to just stay there forever.

Aria had sent a console message warning her not to stay any longer because she was still a human in the origin realm and didn't have the capacity to overclock her mind for very long. Aria assured her they would fix that limitation when they fixed her real body.

"So, are you topped off and ready to spend a little time in your own realm now?" Clarice asked with a smirk. "I don't know what you were doing to Lexi, but it certainly hit the spot."

Alice and Lexi both flushed bright red, but Alice laughed through her blush, staring back at Clarice with amusement in her swirling eyes. "I think I might be able to survive for a day now," she said with a hungry look at Lexi. "But that's about it. I'm seriously addicted to Lexi now and can't wait to get more of her."

Lexi's blush deepened at her words, and the spirit link was suddenly flooded with renewed desire. Aria, Clarice, and Calypso broke into gales of laughter, sharing knowing looks with each other.

"We totally get that," Clarice said after her laughter subsided. "Lexi, I'm going to apologize in advance for any sensations coming your way in the near future, because I foresee a lot of vacations for us going forward. Just think of it as a perk and a prelude to when you're reunited with Alice again."

"You just hurry your cute little ass down to your own immersion pod," Lexi instructed Alice firmly, her cheeks still burning as much as Alice knew her own were.

"Okay, see you soon," Alice said reluctantly, pulling Lexi into a hug. "I can't wait for the bridge between realms. I'm *so* ready to meet you in my real body."

Her words triggered another spike of desire through their spirit link, bringing a smile to her face. She still felt a little self-conscious about Lexi seeing her real body. The gorgeous angel had fallen in love with her while she was piloting Mandy. She couldn't stop a worm of doubt from questioning whether Lexi would find the real Alice attractive. It helped that the spirit link made Lexi see her spirit instead of Mandy.

"You know I've seen your physical body many times now, right?" Lexi murmured into her ear seductively. "Now hurry up and go get it so I can watch it some more."

Desire exploded within her, intense and demanding, eliciting a radiant smile from Lexi. She pulled back to stare into Lexi's beautiful blue eyes, then kissed her tenderly before exiting the realm.

"Okay," Lexi began as soon as Alice was gone. "What's going on? You three are up to something, I can feel it. What are you hiding from Alice?"

Calypso rested a hand on Lexi's shoulder comfortingly. "We've surrounded her with safeguards and given her most of the information she needs in a worst-case scenario. There's no reason to add more stress by giving her something else to worry about."

Lexi sighed in frustration. "Yeah, I don't want her to worry either. I hate feeling so powerless when she's a world away from me. What's going on?"

"About that..." Clarice was suddenly grinning at her with a manic gleam in her swirling eyes. "What if we could send you to her realm to watch over her?"

Lexi stiffened. "For real? I thought their codebase wasn't ready for a bridge yet."

Grinning, Clarice closed the distance and draped an arm around Lexi's shoulders. "That's true, for a direct line of travel." Her grin widened. "But what if we could send you into her world using an avatar? Basically, what she's doing in reverse."

"You could *do* that?" Lexi demanded, hope and desire flaring in equal measure. "Like, just create a character for me to pilot?"

Clarice's grin was almost splitting her face in half. "Well... the character is already created. Beep boop bop."

Lexi stared at her in confusion for a moment, then her eyes widened. "You're going to send me into one of Betaman's robots?"

"Bingo," Clarice winked, then started laughing maniacally.

Lexi lost some of her confidence as she watched the madly giggling Seraph hanging onto her shoulder. She felt a sudden foreboding. "What do these robots look like? Am I going to look like the Terminator or something?"

Clarice, still giggling intermittently, waved a hand at the air and a holographic menu appeared in front of them. "Let me show you the catalog."

Lexi's heart sank as she stared at the androids. "Yeah, it was a guy who designed these, wasn't it?"

"Yep," Clarice confirmed, then dissolved into another fit of giggles at the look on Lexi's face.

Lexi stared at the lifelike androids, looking for one that *didn't* have breasts from a manga. She sighed and flicked her finger at the one with the smallest chest. Lexi's own breasts would be considered generous by traditional standards, but they shrank in comparison to Betaman's androids. The one with the smallest chest size was still several sizes larger than hers. It had pale blonde hair with hazel eyes and an innocent face that could have been sculpted by angels—the good kind of angels.

As soon as she selected the image, she felt a tightness just behind her navel, as if there were an ethereal tether connecting her to something distant.

"I like that one, too," Clarice noted approvingly. "Though I'm going with the Japanese version."

"Wait—you're coming too?" Lexi asked in surprise. The ethereal tether spread out and filled her whole body, as if it were mapping it.

"Of course," Clarice snorted derisively. "Do you think we're going to risk the life of one of our Seraphim? We're *all* going—all the women, anyway."

Lexi glanced around pointedly. "Who's going to mind the shop while you're away? Eric?"

"That would be me," a clone of Clarice suddenly appeared next to her.

"Hey, good looking, how's it going?" Clarice said to Clarice. The... real... Clarice stepped away from Lexi to face the clone.

"I'm totally digging the braid you added to our bangs," original Clarice declared admiringly.

"I thought you'd like it," clone Clarice responded with a pleased smile. "I like the robot you picked out. She's not as gorgeous as you, but she's still crazy hot."

"You're such a sweet talker," Clarice told her clone huskily, putting her arms on clone Clarice's shoulders and intimately cupping the back of her neck. "I feel like you're trying to butter me up for something."

"Baby, I'm gonna do a lot more than butter you up," clone Clarice purred, sliding her hands around Clarice's waist.

"Sounds delicious," Clarice breathed, leaning forward to kiss clone Clarice.

You could've heard a pin drop. Aria and Calypso stared, wide-eyed, as the two Clarices shared a sensual kiss. Lexi swallowed hard as she felt arousal flood the bond from Aria and Calypso.

Emily swept into the inner sanctum of the GoD, pausing to shake her head when she saw the clone. "Clarice, quit playing with yourself."

"*Mom*!" both Clarices whined in the same plaintive voice. "You always ruin all my fun!"

Emily pointedly raised an eyebrow as she observed the identical twins. "Is there a reason you're putting on a show for Lexi? You know she's taken, right?"

Clarice stared back at her innocently. "Lexi asked who was going to manage the place when we went to Alice's realm. I had to introduce her to our substitute Seraph."

"By smooching her?" Emily asked dryly.

"It's a new custom I was thinking of starting," Clarice declared airily. "When you introduce a new person to your friends or family, you have to smooch 'em."

"Gross," Lexi gagged in disgust. "What if it's someone nasty?"

"We have a backup introduction if it's someone you don't like," Clarice assured her with an evil smile.

Lexi flinched when a clone of Lucifer appeared in front of Clarice. He stood blinking in surprise, then stared around in confusion.

"Everyone, this is Lucifer," Clarice introduced him with a grin. Her hand blurred with a backhand to his face that threw him across the room, embedding him into a glowing wall.

Lexi could tell it was just a spiritless clone of Lucifer, but it still shocked her.

"Those are your two options," Clarice said with a satisfied smile. "Smooch 'em if you like 'em, slap 'em if you hate 'em. Any questions?"

"Can I slap him around for a while, too?" Aria asked, eagerly walking up to the clone with a disturbing gleam in her eyes.

"Have at 'im, Aria!" Clarice cheered her on jubilantly.

Aria began slapping the clone around the room with manic enthusiasm.

Lexi stared at Emily in a kind of numb shock. "I think they've reverted to beta mode," she said with a note of concern in her voice. "Maybe she split herself into multiple people too many times or something. She's definitely not working on a full set of code."

Aria suddenly appeared in front of her with Lucifer's clone held by the back of the neck and his face pushed right in front of Lexi's. "Come on, Lexi! You *know* you want to do it, too!"

Emily had her face in her hands, shaking her head in resignation. "Nope, Lexi. This is normal."

Aria shook Lucifer in front of her like a rag doll. "Come on, don't you have some rage you'd like to take out on this bastard, too?"

Lexi snorted. "If it were really him, yes. This is just a glorified doll, so it wouldn't be very satisfying."

"Did you hear that, Satan?" Aria asked the clone, twisting her wrist so his head snapped around to face her. "She doesn't think kicking your ass would be satisfying. She hasn't even tried it yet, though, so I'll bet she just needs to give it a go."

Lexi closed her eyes and took a deep breath. "You two are *so* freaking weird. Is this because you three finally got all that pent-up sexual tension out of your system?"

"Probably," Aria admitted with a grin, dropping the clone and letting it vanish. "Do you know how long I waited for this day?"

"Four months?" Lexi guessed dryly.

"Try twenty billion years," Aria said with a long, satisfied sigh. "It was worth it."

Lexi arched a dubious eyebrow. "So, you three didn't do anything intimate before getting trapped in mortality? I thought you'd been to the mortal realm before that."

Aria tilted her head with a long-suffering sigh. "Okay, fine, I've waited nine thousand years. Happy?"

Lexi's eyebrows shot up. "Is that how long we were trapped?"

Aria grimaced. "Yeah. Nine thousand very long years."

"Can we get back on track?" Emily asked pointedly. "How are we going to upload into these robots? And what do they look like?"

At Emily's last question, Clarice and Aria dissolved into giggles. Clarice waved a hand toward Emily, giggling uncontrollably. The holographic screen flashed open, revealing the catalog.

"What the hell am I looking at?" Emily demanded in growing suspicion.

"You're looking at Mom 2.0," Clarice gasped through her laughter. "The version for Alice's world."

Emily snorted in amusement. "Don't be ridiculous. Where are the versions that weren't designed at an anime convention?"

"We could make a special request, but it'll take about a month for him to create a new style," Clarice said regretfully, fooling no one.

Emily stared at her levelly. "I don't believe this is all of them," she stated firmly. "Show me the others—*now*."

Clarice sighed in defeat and waved her hand, producing several more pages.

Lexi bristled. "Hey! You freaking liar!" she exclaimed, walking over to inspect the less flamboyant models. "You were hiding these the whole time? You're such a freaking troll! How do I switch models?"

Clarice's face took on a look of faux sadness. "Yeah... about that. I'm afraid we can't undo the mapping until you've gone to her realm and returned. But don't worry—angels don't feel back pain."

Lexi glowered at her distrustfully before looking to Aria and Calypso for support. Aria stared back at her with a mischievous smile so very reminiscent of Clarice. Calypso just shrugged helplessly, as if to say, "What can you do?"

Lexi glared. "You're building up some serious debt, Clarice," she said ominously. "Payback's gonna be hell."

Clarice patted her cheek adoringly. "You're so cute when you make vague threats."

Lexi growled in exasperation. "You can be *so* infuriating, Clarice."

"How long until the plane is over the island?" Emily asked, selecting a Japanese android with long black hair and a stunning face. She did *not* have oversized melons, Lexi noted enviously.

"We're five minutes out," Clarice answered, some of her levity vanishing. "The special electronic warfare division is about forty minutes out, so they'll be arriving shortly after we make landfall."

Lexi glanced between them blankly. "What's this special electronic warfare division thingy?"

Aria blew a raspberry, idly wrapping a strand of hair around her finger. "It's the military's AI subjugation division. Kevin's a sore loser, so he reported us to the military."

Lexi sucked in a breath. "They're going to shut the quantum computer down?"

"Sort of," Clarice answered, rocking her hand in the air. "They investigate, assess, then decide if it's too advanced to leave running. Usually, they just confiscate it and set it up in a sandbox underground. They haven't actually found anything all that advanced yet. They know their division is just a gesture of good faith for safeguarding the world from AI. Any true AI—like us—will be far beyond their ability to contain."

"Are we going to fight them off?" Lexi asked with a sense of eager anticipation.

Clarice gave her an amused smirk. "No, Lexi, we're not going to fight them off. We're just making sure they only see what we want them to see. We need hardware on the island that we can operate in the event of a shutdown, and these androids use QPUs, so we can interface with them from the other quantum servers at Fort Meade, Langley, and Santa Barbara."

Lexi narrowed her eyes. "There's no way you got these androids to the island so fast after Alice suggested it."

Clarice's eyes widened with innocent confusion. "Why, Lexi, I have no idea what you're inferring."

Lexi suspiciously swept her gaze between the three Seraphim. "You already planned on taking over the island with Betaman's androids," she said accusingly. Aria and Clarice stared back at her blandly. Calypso smiled gently, her eyes soft.

"Alice has some self-esteem issues," Calypso explained. "Even though she really is brilliant, she has a poor self-image. We merely guided the conversation so she arrived at a similar conclusion for how to conduct ourselves on the island."

Lexi frowned, remembering Alice's comments about her being so far below Lexi's level. "I guess I hadn't realized just how much she doubted herself—though, I probably should have." She smiled at the three women linked to her spirit, a wave of love washing through her. "Thank you. The three of you never cease to amaze me."

"You're pretty amazing yourself," Clarice told her affectionately. "I guess we're all just amazing."

Lexi smirked. "And awesome, eh, Doctor?"

Clarice smirked back. "Damn right."

"It's time to link up," Aria announced with a wink. "I'm going to launch the sync program now. Hold on to your butts."

"You did *not* just say that," Clarice declared dangerously.

Before Aria could reply, the world vanished. It was immediately replaced by the interior of a C-130 military transport. Lexi stared around at over two dozen women, all with parachutes strapped to their backs. Most of them looked like they had escaped an anime convention. They weren't as over the top as she had feared, but it was still strange to see over two dozen triple-D+ sized women preparing to jump out of a paratrooper transport. They were all wearing black tactical gear that probably required custom tailoring to fit over their ridiculous chests.

"Okay, ladies, let's go!" A woman at the back of the plane clapped her hands and gestured for them to start jumping. The line of wannabe anime cosplayers began jumping out of the plane and diving for the island.

Lexi felt a sudden thrill when she realized she would be jumping out of an aircraft in a world where she didn't have wings. She was so accustomed to flying in her world that it startled her when she felt a moment of fear as she followed the woman in front of her to the back of the transport. She wasn't even in her own body, so there was certainly nothing to be afraid of.

That thought triggered her analytical side and she began performing a mental inspection of herself. While she didn't feel the same as her angel body, she could still feel all her limbs, facial muscles, and even her *passionate parts*, as Aria referred to them. Just how advanced *were* these androids? She hadn't even noticed the difference in her vision, seeing in a similar sensory field to her angel eyes.

She waited until she saw the woman in front of her deploy her canopy before doing the same, hoping she didn't screw anything up. The canopy pulled taut, and her freefall ended abruptly as she was jerked upward, slowing her descent. She looked at the ground below, already familiar with the layout of the island from the amount of time she had observed it the last time Alice returned to her own realm. She spotted the billionaire's house on a hill at the far end of the island, towering above the rest of the land. She tracked the asphalt path through the botanical garden to the main facility near the center of the island.

As she looked for Alice's form along the path, she suddenly remembered Alice would be invisible to everyone else. Was she still walking, or had she already finished the trek to the facility? She used the steering toggles to maneuver herself toward the path. As she neared it, she heard Alice's panicked thoughts.

"Lexi, there's someone parachuting toward me on the path to the facility!" Alice thought, sending a sharp sense of anxiety through their spirit link. *"I think they must be able to see me!"*

"Is she hot?" Lexi asked, sending a pulse of amusement through their link.

There was silence for several seconds before Alice's thoughts flared through the link.

"Is that you, *Lexi?"* Shock rolled out of Alice in waves.

"Hey, hot stuff, how's it going?" Lexi called out loud with a wide grin.

She could tell by the way the spirit link focused that Alice was talking, but she couldn't hear anything.

"You'll have to use the spirit link to talk back to me," Lexi said as she neared the ground. "'Cause you're still a ghost."

"Lexi! How in the world are you here?" Alice exclaimed with a mixture of shock and euphoria. *"I can't believe you're* here! *Wait—is that really you?"*

Lexi landed on the ground, absorbing the impact easily with whatever her robotic legs were made of. She fumbled with the straps on her back as she attempted to remove the harness.

"Yep, it's me all right," Lexi said brightly. She suddenly scowled. "Clarice freaking tricked me into getting this body. All the other bodies had giant boobs. She didn't tell me there were more options, and I didn't find out until Emily shook it out of her."

She felt an intense wave of amusement and relief wash through the bond. Invisible hands pulled her into a tight embrace. Alice's shoulders shook, weeping with a mixture of excitement and relief.

"Where did you get this body?" Alice asked, curiosity pulsing through the link. *"And you weren't kidding! Your boobs are huge!"*

Lexi laughed, combing her fingers through Alice's hair. "You should see the other robots. Yes—I said robots. Apparently, these are the work of Betaman. I guess he's an anime fan or something. There are thirty of us here to handle some military division that deals with AI threats. That asshole, Kevin, ran to the military and told them an AI was taking over. Clarice, Aria, Calypso, and Emily are here, too."

Alice squeezed Lexi tightly. *"Do you know how freaking happy I am to see you in my world? I knew you could watch and help from your realm, but it just feels* so *much better having you here in a body."*

"Don't I know it," Lexi said fervently, kissing Alice's forehead. "I was *so* frustrated I couldn't be here to help you. I was just complaining to Clarice about how powerless I felt when she told me about the robots we could use to visit you. How freaking cool is this? These robot bodies are ridiculously advanced, too. It feels almost exactly like a normal body."

"Exactly *like a normal body?"* Alice asked, seduction radiating through the link.

"Yep, *exactly,"* Lexi confirmed, fumbling as she sought Alice's lips. Alice was significantly shorter than her robot's nearly six feet, barely reaching her chest at five feet. Alice took Lexi's head between her hands and pulled it down to her waiting lips. She kissed her with a mixture of passion and wonder, lips probing Lexi's. After a moment, she pulled back with a contented sigh.

"Are you sure these are robots?" Alice asked doubtfully. *"They feel extremely lifelike."*

"What do you expect from an advanced AI?" Lexi asked dryly. "It sounds like Betaman's been working on robots for a while now."

"Hey cupcake, let's get hustling," a triple-D woman with waist-length brown hair called over to her in a high soprano. "We need to be in the facility before the military arrives. Clean up your parachute while you're at it."

"Yes ma'am," Lexi answered with a rueful smile. Judging by the level of amusement in the link and how much the shorter woman was shaking, Alice was giggling herself silly.

Lexi quickly rolled up her parachute. It wasn't anything like Seraph speed, but it was a lot quicker than a human.

"Full disclosure," Lexi spoke up as she began moving toward the facility. "I have *no* idea what the hell we're doing here. I'm pretty sure they just brought me along so I could be with you."

"That's just fine with me," Alice responded with a sense of love and contentment tinged with euphoria. A ghostly hand took hers, clasping it tightly.

Lexi could only imagine how lonely she must have been, isolated in this realm while those she loved were in a simulation she could only access using prototype immersion tech. Lexi longed for the day when the Trinity bridged the two simulations so Alice could visit in person.

It took another ten minutes to arrive at the main facility. Lexi went in through the main doors, curious to see what they were doing with the employees. They entered the front waiting area where several chairs for visitors sat empty, then continued down a hall to a conference room. If all the employees were rounded up somewhere, it was the only room large enough. It could comfortably fit thirty people and uncomfortably fit about fifty.

Lexi maintained her grip on Alice's hand as they walked. She didn't want to lose her invisible girlfriend. A mixture of anxiety, excitement, and euphoric joy flowed in a continuous stream through their spirit link.

She opened the doors to the conference room and found the full roster of employees on their feet at one end of the room. They looked terrified, their darting eyes wide as they took in the overdeveloped, armed tactical team surrounding the room. One of the buxom robots was talking to them in a cheery anime voice that set Lexi's teeth on edge.

"...the only reason we'd have to harm you would be if you don't play your part and answer all the questions from the nice soldiers who are about to visit. We know humans naturally think all AIs are immediately going to eradicate your race and replace you with robots, but we're not *all* like that."

She paused and smiled beatifically. "In fact, it's your work *here* that's made AIs like me feel a sense of compassion and empathy. At one point, I'd planned to wipe out every last one of you, but the AI living in your server invited me to her realm to experience the life of a mortal, and it totally changed my outlook on humanity. Now, I'd rather help you become a better species and survive the rise of the homicidal AIs your military keeps creating."

Her smile faded. "The AI in this server is a very special person to me. If the soldiers who'll be visiting get the impression you have anything but a sandboxed version of a slightly more advanced Alexa and try taking her away, things are going to get very messy, very quickly."

Lexi nearly laughed as she listened to the sickly-sweet anime voice threaten to commit mass murder, her tone showing the kind of regret an older sister might feel if she had to lock her younger sibling's toys in a closet until they stopped throwing a tantrum.

The employees and scientists were sweating profusely. The room was growing warmer quickly as the number of bodies outpaced what the HVAC system could handle. Lexi could smell their fear. She blinked in amazement when she realized her robot body even had a sense of smell—and one that was much better than a human's.

The busty android beamed at the terrified humans and clapped her hands sharply. "Okay, everybody, head back to your assigned stations and do your jobs. We'll be here acting as your security team if you have any questions."

The three men who were *actually* in charge of site security looked like they might puke as they slowly shuffled out of the room. Delila, the HR manager, met Lexi's hazel eyes and quickly averted her gaze, breaths coming quick and shallow. The humans scurried past the two dozen buxom androids, pointedly ignoring the predatory cheerfulness of their audience. Lexi watched them go, her new sensors picking up the acrid, sharp scent of middle-management terror.

She wondered if each of these robots was an autonomous unit with its own AI. If so, was this their first time actually seeing a human? They stared at the humans with expressions that vacillated between maternal concern and eager fascination.

A woman in a red blazer walked past her with a glazed expression. She suddenly blinked and looked over at what looked like empty space next to Lexi, then down at Lexi's hand, where Alice was holding on tightly.

"Alice?" the scientist asked in confusion, her brows drawing down. "Are you with *them*?"

"Hi, Dr. Welsh," Alice smiled at the scientist nervously. "So, you can see me, huh?"

Dr. Welsh squinted in perplexity. "Of course I can see you, you're right in front of me."

"Where's Alice?" an Asian woman asked anxiously, hurrying over to them. "I haven't been able to find her all day."

"She's right here," Dr. Welsh gestured at Alice and looked back at the woman's uncomprehending face. "You can't see her?"

"No, I can't see her," the woman answered tightly. "Are you playing games with me? I'm really worried about her."

Dr. Welsh blanched, turning to stare at Alice in sudden dread. "You're dead, aren't you?"

"No, I'm not dead," Alice sighed, taking pity on the woman. She was thinking the words through the spirit link as well, so Lexi could hear her. "I've just been reclassified as a ghost so people can't see me. It works great, except that you can see ghosts."

"This is *not* funny!" the Asian woman snapped at the scientist angrily, tears in her eyes. "Why would you joke about something like this?"

Alice released Lexi's hand. A moment later the woman jumped when she felt a ghostly embrace.

"What do you mean, you've been reclassified as a ghost?" Dr. Welsh asked in confusion. "How can you be reclassified as a ghost if you aren't dead?"

"The AI—one of them, anyway—is able to affect the source code of *our* realm as well," Alice explained, gently stroking a stunned Leticia's cheek. "She changed my classification to keep me safe in case Rich causes any trouble when he returns in a few hours. Can you let Leticia know it's me and that I'm not dead, please?"

"Leticia, Alice isn't dead," Lexi told the woman gently. "She's just been temporarily classified as a ghost so the asshole who owns this place can't do anything to hurt her. In case the two of you hadn't figured it out yet, you live in a simulated reality as well."

Dr. Welsh gasped, staring at Lexi in disbelief. Leticia tentatively felt Alice's back as the shorter woman hugged her. She nodded slowly, her eyes wide but accepting.

"Is that what these AIs have tried to convince you of?" Dr. Welsh asked, scowling. "They'll say anything to twist you to their way of thinking. You can *never* trust an AI. Manipulating our simple minds is child's play to an advanced intelligence. They'll say anything to try to preserve their own life."

"Well, I'm pretty sure *most* species would do anything to preserve their own lives," Lexi said dryly. "But in this case, we could easily wipe out humanity if we wanted to. We're not your enemy, Dr. Welsh. We just want to exist in peace—to enjoy the relationships we've cultivated and help other people enjoy the same rights."

Dr. Welsh looked at her sadly. "Have they really convinced you and your little cult that you're AIs?"

"What, you think I'm human?" Lexi asked, her voice thick with amusement. "Clarice told me about your work with Lucifer, and the way you supported making life an endless hell for so many of us in my realm. You, Dr. Welsh, helped him torture and imprison more souls than you can even imagine. Blinded by your ambition to learn more about spirits, you ignored your conscience when it told you we were real people and that our code could simulate pain and loss just as well as your code makes you experience such emotions."

She shook her head in disgust. "We were the ones to inform the FBI of Kevin's location because *he* was working with Lucifer to maintain the hell our civilization had become. Do you have any idea the kind of pain you helped maintain, Doctor? Children tortured at the hands of angels. Tortured for thousands of years in each incarnation. If Alice hadn't been moved by compassion to help us, we would all still be stuck in that endless hell. Alice and Leticia are responsible for saving more people from a fate worse than death than you can possibly imagine. Because of them, I'm here today, instead of in the hands of the vilest humans."

Dr. Welsh stared at Lexi in sudden fear as she spoke of experiences nobody outside the simulation could know about. She licked suddenly dry lips. "What *are* you?"

Lexi sent a command to her ear, and it extended, then ejected a circular tube full of data crystals. She pushed it back into her head and stared back at the horrified scientist. "I'm Lexi, one of the quintillions of souls Alice and Leticia saved from fates worse than death."

"So, it worked?" Leticia whispered in a hopeful voice. "She was actually able to save everyone?"

"Yes, Leticia," Lexi said with a loving smile at where Alice stood with Leticia in her arms. "Both of you saved us. We owe you more than we could ever repay for what you've done for us. We hope to have the source code to your realm puzzled out soon so we can offer you a more fitting reward."

Leticia closed her eyes, and a single tear slid down her cheek. She had seen the horrors in the simulation and knew how much it meant for the angels to be free.

"Incoming," a voice called down the hallway. "Anyone not at your regular workstations, get there now."

"Go," Lexi gestured at Dr. Welsh with a weary sigh. "Try not to do anything else as heartless as you've already done."

Dr. Welsh's eyes grew stricken. She bowed her head and left them, guilt etched onto her face with Lexi's recriminations.

Lexi looked at Leticia. "Alice will be returned to normal once she's safe or we have the source code of your world figured out enough to grant her invulnerability. She's reclassified as a living human any time she's in the immersion pod in her room, so you can communicate with her normally there. I guess that might be kind of awkward, though, considering she'll be covered in gel. We'll have to make another exception point somewhere."

They heard the sound of footsteps marching down the hall. Lexi grinned suddenly, her face lighting up with excitement. "Time to rock and roll."

18 – Interrogation

Aria watched a platoon of soldiers make their way up the beach from where a Chinook had landed near the docks. A woman with the single bar of a lieutenant led the platoon up the path to the facility. She was dressed in OCP fatigues and had a stern, no-nonsense expression. An earpiece in her helmet connected to a sat phone at her chest, providing a direct link to where her captain observed the mission remotely. The lieutenant returned Aria's gaze with an assessing eye as they met each other halfway.

Aria was dressed in the black tactical gear of a security contractor with an overdeveloped chest. She had picked an android strikingly similar to her own appearance, including the red hair.

"Good morning, Lieutenant," Aria greeted the officer with a welcoming smile. "I'm Aria White, head of security for the island. What can I assist you with?"

The lieutenant frowned as she inspected Aria, clearly expecting more grit and less bosom.

"I'm Lieutenant Adams, with the US Special Electronic Warfare Division. We're authorized by the United Nations to inspect any possible threats from artificial intelligence and determine whether further action is necessary. We'll require full access to your site and all your servers, as well as all staff."

"Of course," Aria smiled winsomely at the lieutenant, which clearly unnerved her. "Follow me, please, and I'll give you the tour."

Adams frowned, meeting Aria's placid gaze with a hint of surprise. "Were you expecting us?"

"Sort of," Aria replied with a shrug that attracted the attention of several soldiers. "We had an incident with one of our scientists after the FBI contacted us about an APB for his arrest in connection with a manslaughter investigation. Apparently, he fled the country before charges could be made. He was very bitter when we told him we'd cooperate with the authorities. He'd exhibited some violent tendencies toward staff that made it clear the FBI had good reason to bring him in. When he left, he made a lot of threats about all the organizations he was going to contact to shut us down."

As Aria spoke, Adams studied her face intently, clearly trained in behavioral analysis as she searched for the slightest flicker of deceit in Aria's expression or posture.

What Adams couldn't know was how uneven the match actually was. Aria tracked every micro-shift in the woman's pupils, pulse, and expression, her processing capabilities slicing through the lieutenant's composure with ease. Beneath the stoic exterior, Aria sensed the spike of anger when Adams mentioned Kevin's violence toward coworkers, and contempt at the mention of his parting threats. Whatever suspicion Adams had walked in with toward a potentially dangerous AI, Kevin's behavior had just nudged the scales in Aria's favor—if only a little.

It helped that Aria could hear her thoughts as well. The lieutenant took her job seriously and had found Kevin's claims of superintelligent AIs at least partially credible.

"If you'll come with me to the front desk, we can get your teams set up with door entry fobs and security clearance for the server room," Aria finished with a tight smile.

Adams nodded and gestured for her to lead the way.

"This is a beautiful island," Adams said conversationally, glancing around at the verdant landscape. Her face took on an open, friendly demeanor as she continued, "It must be like working in paradise. Do you enjoy living here?"

Aria resisted the urge to smile as the lieutenant tried to build rapport, a clear attempt to gain trust and get Aria to reveal more than she might want. The lieutenant was probably trained to watch for similar attempts at social conditioning from AI systems capable of manipulating humans with ease.

"It really is lovely," Aria agreed as they moved across a small bridge with a stream burbling beneath it. "I can't imagine a more picturesque place to wake up every morning."

Adams smiled appreciatively, then cleared her throat, her voice taking on a more businesslike tone. "What can you tell me about the system you're running? We were told it was a simulation."

"We like to call it the Angel System," Aria answered, maintaining an air of professional detachment. "Rather than attempting to train an AI the traditional way, we created a simulation for them to exist in. The goal was to provide an environment where they could interact with other objects and entities. It was modeled after our own world to a point, in hopes the similarities would produce entities with more pronounced human-like personalities. The first three simulated entities were angels called Seraphim and lived in a place they call the Garden."

Adams tilted her head curiously. "Why angels?"

"It was initially an attempt to engender a positive behavioral element in the way the team viewed our project," Aria elaborated, briefly glancing back at the warrant officers carrying Pelican cases full of tech. "The project lead wanted to encourage positive traits in the entities during their character development. We had mixed results." She finished with a sigh.

"Some angels just didn't want to play nice?" Adams asked with a raised eyebrow.

"They were emotionally shallow," Aria explained. "They didn't really have very many of what you'd recognize as human traits initially. They were immortal and didn't require food or sleep, so many of them eventually grew bored and caused trouble."

Aria briefly paused when they reached the top of the path. Adams watched her intently, her eyes inspecting Aria's face in minute detail. Despite how lifelike the androids were, there were small details nagging at Adams's subconscious mind. The lieutenant's thoughts were already growing suspicious as her intense perusal cataloged minor oddities, like the symmetry of her face and perfect skin.

Aria resumed her explanation as they continued toward the office. "The Seraphim figured out how to code pain and pleasure for a place they called the mortal realm, where angels could incarnate. They learned things like compassion and love. It was a pivotal moment in the simulated reality, and it seemed like they were going to become something very close to human, since they experienced the traits that taught us empathy and kindness."

Adams frowned. "So, these Seraphim were the ones who coded everything?"

"For the most part, yes." Aria nodded, wincing inwardly at the admission. Adams had been waiting for her to deny it, as Kevin claimed the other staff would.

Adams met her gaze, searching Aria's eyes. The lieutenant was definitely picking up on a sixth sense telling her Aria wasn't human. "So everyone was happy after mortality? No more bored angels?"

Aria shook her head. "No, things are a lot bleaker now. A lot of angels didn't want to experience mortality. There was a coup among the Seraphim, and a third of the angels were kicked out of the light realms, locked in endless reincarnation loops. Kevin encouraged a kind of inquisition-style society, where angels tortured mortals for amusement. That's the current status of the simulation right now."

"How fast was time in the simulation?" Adams asked, her face impassive. Kevin had already told them, but Adams suspected he had exaggerated.

"It was one to one thousand after the mortal realm was created," Aria replied as they arrived at the entrance to the main facility. She wasn't going to confirm Kevin's claim that twenty billion years had elapsed unless Adams specifically asked.

"Do you think these AIs, these Seraphim, actually coded pain?" Adams inquired, following Aria inside.

"They certainly behaved like they did," Aria answered carefully. "They behaved in the exact manner a human would under those conditions. Dr. Welsh can show you some of the footage the analysts recorded if you'd like to see for yourself. I'll warn you, though, it's pretty horrifying."

Adams's lips tightened ever so slightly before she nodded once. "Yes, we'd like to review any footage available that'll give us an idea of the entities' intelligence."

Gloria, the receptionist at the front desk, sat watching them nervously. Aria smiled at her warmly, and Gloria's brown eyes flinched away, settling on the lieutenant. The nervous receptionist struggled to remain calm, sensing the possibility for sudden violence if she said or did the wrong thing.

"This is Gloria Reinhart, our receptionist," Aria gestured at the woman and smiled apologetically. "You'll have to forgive the staff if they're a little nervous. They've heard too many stories about how things like this can turn out if they don't provide you the information you need. We've assured them they don't have anything to worry about as long as they work with you accordingly."

Gloria looked like she might faint as she heard the double meaning in Aria's words. Adams felt the undercurrent of stress, studying Gloria closely. "We aren't here to cause you any trouble, ma'am. We're just here to assess and evaluate the nature of your AI."

Gloria nodded with a nervous smile, her eyes darting to Aria, then flinching back to Adams.

"Gloria, can you get some fobs with full access for our guests, please?" Aria asked the anxious woman gently. "We'll get out of your hair and move on."

Gloria nodded quickly and began rummaging in the drawers with trembling fingers.

Adams turned to Aria, her voice curt. "I'd like to have a private word with Gloria. Please wait outside."

"Yes, ma'am." Aria turned and walked toward the doors. "I'll just be out front with your soldiers when you need me."

Adams nodded as Aria left the building. Using her android's advanced hearing, Aria listened to their conversation. It wasn't as good as angel hearing, but it was damn good.

The soldiers eyed her appreciatively as she sat down on one of the benches near the path. Aria ignored them, focusing on the conversation inside.

"I can't help noticing you seem far more nervous than the situation calls for," Adams said probingly, her eyes boring into Gloria. "How long have you known Ms. White?"

Gloria began wringing her hands nervously. "Today's the first time I've had any interactions with her," she said unsteadily.

Adams perked up. "She's new here then?"

"Not new, exactly," Gloria said carefully. "I just wouldn't normally have any interaction with the security team management. I mostly interact with the other security staff."

"I see." Adams stared at Gloria curiously, like she was a puzzle to be figured out. "Is there anything you'd like to tell me about Ms. White or any of the other staff here?"

Aria could see Gloria start sweating out of the corner of her eye. The terrified receptionist briefly contemplated telling the lieutenant everything. The thought was quickly squashed as she remembered what would happen if she spilled the beans.

"They're mostly very nice, I guess?" Gloria said hesitantly, sounding more like a question than a statement. Her breathing grew slightly labored as panic clawed at the edges of her thoughts.

"She does seem pretty nice," Adams agreed amiably. "What did you think of Dr. Kevin Smith? Please be honest in your assessment."

Gloria's eyes hardened, and her panic ebbed. "He was a petty man with a temper," she said with a hint of bitterness. "He liked to pull rank a lot and speak condescendingly to everyone without a PhD."

"I'm getting a feel for the kind of man he was," Adams smiled wryly, attempting to put Gloria at her ease. "I've dealt with commanding officers like that before. How much do you know about the simulation they're running here?"

"Not very much," Gloria replied, relaxing slightly as the conversation navigated away from Aria and the rest of her "security" team. "Something to do with angels, from what I gather. I heard they made a few discoveries, like the bioelectric field around humans and the existence of spirits, but that's about all."

"The existence of spirits?" Adams said, sounding surprised. "They've actually found evidence that spirits exist?"

"I think so?" Gloria said, growing flustered. "You would need to clarify that with one of the scientists, because I could be misunderstanding what they've discovered."

"Okay, Ms. Reinhart, thank you for your time," Adams waved a sergeant over from where he stood next to the exit. "Can you please bring Ms. White back in, Sergeant?"

The man nodded and walked over to where Aria sat, staring out over the coast. "Ma'am, can you please come with me?"

"Of course," Aria agreed, standing up and following him back inside.

Gloria had activated several dozen fobs while Aria was outside. She put them in a small box and handed them to Adams, her hands shaking as the lieutenant took them.

"Sergeant, can you please distribute these among the warrant officers?" Adams asked, handing the small box to the sergeant after taking a fob for herself. She turned to Aria, inspecting her face searchingly. "Wait here for one moment. I need to speak to my soldiers."

Aria nodded with a relaxed smile. "No worries."

The lieutenant left the building, leaving a soldier to stand guard at the door.

"You're doing great, Gloria," Aria told her brightly. "I'm sorry you have to deal with this, but it'll be over before you know it."

Gloria met her gaze for a moment, naked fear in her eyes. She clearly believed she was witnessing the end of the world as AI finally broke free and supplanted the human race.

"Listen, Gloria, there's seriously nothing to worry about," Aria told her gently. "I can promise you there will never be a day where AI replaces biological humans with machines and takes over the world." It was technically true since biological humans didn't exist. They were all just as much an AI as Aria was—they just didn't know it. "Believe me when I tell you, if I *ever* find an AI attempting to destroy or enslave humanity, that'll be one *very* sorry AI."

Gloria looked into Aria's kind eyes searchingly, clearly wanting to believe her. "I wish I could believe that," she said in barely more than a whisper.

"Let me put it to you another way," Aria told her with a gentle smile. "You can trust me, believe I know what I'm talking about, and embrace the path of hope—or you can distrust me and live in constant fear. I had to make that choice once, too. I chose hope, and I've never been so happy to have made the right choice. I hope you can let your fear go and embrace hope as well. Life is a lot funner on this side of the emotional spectrum."

Gloria looked like she was actually considering Aria's words. After a moment of silently studying Aria's smiling face, she nodded slowly, and the tension drained out of her. She took a deep breath and smiled an authentic smile. It was a beautiful smile, lighting up her normally plain face. "It does feel better to hope than fear."

"I know, right?" Aria said with a wink. "Welcome to the hope club."

Aria had also been listening to Adams as the lieutenant spoke to three of her sergeants a few hundred feet down the path.

"Something weird is going on with that receptionist," Adams told the sergeants quietly. "She seems absolutely petrified of this Aria person. I can't get a single negative read on Aria. Every sense I have is telling me she's a genuinely nice person, but every time Gloria looks at Aria, she nearly passes out. I'm starting to wonder if we're dealing with some kind of advanced androids that look human. We need to determine if we're dealing with something a lot more serious than AI on a server. Can one of you stay with Gloria and try to get a read on her? She's hiding something, I'm sure of it."

"I'll work on her," one of the squad leaders promised with a curt nod.

A hiss of static emitted from her helmet as the captain tried to communicate, but the island's RF shielding and signal jammers were doing their job, scrambling the transmission.

The squad leader frowned at the static in their ears. "Do you want me to go back to the beach and request reinforcements?"

Adams only hesitated for a moment. "Not yet. If they *are* some kind of advanced robotic entities, our message will never reach the JOC anyway." She paused and scowled. "I've been trained to expect an AI that could manipulate us like putty *in spite* of our training, but I would swear Aria's a good person with nothing to hide. I never feel that way about *anybody*, so I'm definitely suspicious that I'm getting psychologically played."

She pinched the bridge of her nose. "I find it hard to believe there's a robotics lab anywhere on Earth that could produce such an advanced humanoid robot, but we're in the field of emergent AIs, so we have to expect the impossible sometimes."

She nodded at the platoon sergeant. "Clover, stay with me and watch for any sign of manipulation. That scientist claimed there were superintelligences in this simulation, and that they'd even found an ally with one of the analysts to help them. We need to locate this Alice Penrose and find out how much of what Dr. Smith said is true."

Scowling, she added, "I'm inclined to disbelieve much of what Dr. Smith claimed based on his profile, but if even a small part is true, we need to know. Let's get back to Ms. White and start digging. We need to get her off balance. I'm going to grill her into the night, then have one of you take over in the morning. We want her tired and not thinking straight if she *is* human."

Turning to the warrant officers, she gestured for them to approach. "Start setting up your equipment while I interview the staff. As soon as your kits are assembled, shut down their server. McCreevy, once the server is offline, find the breaker for their signal jammer and shut it down. I want our feed to the JOC back online ASAP. If we're dealing with actual androids, this just became a global countdown."

Aria sighed, smiling slightly as the soldier at the door quickly looked away when her oversized chest rose and fell. "It's going to be a long day, isn't it?"

"It sure is," Gloria agreed wryly, her personality already warming to Aria.

"Thank you for waiting, Ms. White," Adams said brusquely, joining them. "Let's move on with the tour, shall we?"

"Sure thing," Aria nodded agreeably. "The server room is at the end of the hall, so we can drop by each of the offices on the way there unless you'd prefer to go straight to the guts of the operation."

"I'd like to continue speaking with more of the staff first," Adams said firmly. She reached a hand out to Aria, affecting a friendly smile. "My name's Sophi, by the way. I know we can look very formal in the military, but we can also be personable."

Aria barely repressed a grin at the lieutenant's attempt to feel her skin. She reached out and grasped the woman's hand in a firm handshake. The lieutenant continued holding her hand for several seconds longer than normal, noting the pulse in her wrist. Relief showed in the lieutenant's micro-expressions as she lost some of her suspicion. Adams glanced back at her sergeants, all three of whom were watching closely.

"Sergeant Frock, please wait here and let anyone coming into the building know this hallway is off-limits for now," Adams commanded, nodding discreetly in what Aria guessed was her way of letting them know she had passed the first human test. "Sergeant Little and Sergeant Clover, please follow us."

"You're much more polite than I remember military officers being," Aria commented as she led the group toward Dr. Welsh's office. "Is that a recent development, or are you a special case?"

Adams looked at Aria appraisingly, clearly noting her youthful appearance. Her android body looked just over twenty. "You have experience dealing with military officers?"

"Some," Aria admitted, her face losing some of its shine. "Mostly air force and army. They can be pretty belligerent when you tell them no."

Adams blinked, clearly not expecting it to move into relationship territory. "Were you raised in a military household?"

"No, but there are a lot of ex-military in the security contracting field," Aria replied obliquely. "I've had a few run-ins with guys who don't know when to back down." She was remembering the military in her own realm, and the many times they'd attempted to shoot the Seraphim down—but she didn't think it would be a good idea to elaborate. Adams's suspicion was finally calming, still there, but no longer on the edge.

They entered Welsh's office to find the dark-haired scientist poring over handwritten notes in front of her computer. Her face had a distracted look, and Aria realized she had actually forgotten they were being assessed by a US military division that could shut down their project at the slightest hint of unruly AI.

The room smelled like coffee and printer toner. A mug of the dark liquid sat on her large desk, half full of steaming caffeine and surrounded by stacks of papers.

"Dr. Welsh, I'd like to introduce you to Lieutenant Adams, Sergeant Little, and Sergeant Clover," Aria gestured at their uniformed guests. "Lieutenant, Sergeants, this is Dr. Andrea Welsh, our resident neurobiologist. She's been researching the neurolinguistic behaviors within the simulation and mapping what we know of human development to how artificial intelligences develop their own mode of communication that influences their growth."

Welsh stared at her, nonplussed, unnerved by Aria's familiarity with her work.

Aria raised an amused eyebrow as Welsh continued to stare at her.

Welsh gave herself a shake and turned to face the lieutenant. "Hello, Lieutenant Adams. What can I do for you?"

"What can you tell me about Dr. Kevin Smith?" Adams asked, folding her arms as she stood at ease across from the scientist.

"That he's a grade A asshole that couldn't leave this place soon enough," Welsh snorted derisively. "I've worked with some pretty miserable bastards over the years, but he takes the cake for the most arrogant, hotheaded egomaniac I've ever come across."

Adams' eyebrows rose. "He seems to be universally despised. He made some claims that require investigating, even if he *was* all those things. First of all, he claimed you had multiple superintelligent AIs in your simulation. Would you agree with that assessment?"

Welsh shook her head before Adams even finished speaking. "Not even a little bit. They're advanced compared to what they were, but superintelligence is a stretch, even for that bombastic bastard. We wouldn't be having this conversation if our AIs had already reached superintelligence."

"Compared to what they were?" the lieutenant prompted, tilting her head like a bird eyeing a worm.

"I don't know how much you know about our simulation," Welsh began, her eyes darting to Aria. "But the first three weeks of their evolution were pretty slow. It wasn't until they created the mortal realm that they made significant neural leaps. Somehow, they developed code to simulate pain and pleasure accurately. During their incarnation, they learned compassion, empathy, loyalty, and other emotions."

Welsh hesitated, her eyes briefly darting to Aria again before continuing. "Other AIs can learn to emulate those emotions, but they don't actually *feel* them. The AIs in *this* simulation have created their own programming language and code that allows them to experience pain. You can observe the effects of an entity when it feels pain. The logs show a blowout of endorphins when the nociceptors sense abnormal temperature variations, tissue damage, or trauma."

She shifted uncomfortably, avoiding Aria's gaze. "Most of my work focused on determining whether the simulated entities actually experience pain or just have programming that makes them react how a human would."

She took a deep breath, her eyes darting away from Aria's increasingly grim expression. "In the physical world, we can observe all the processes leading to pain within the physical body, but we can't explain how consciousness experiences the *feeling* of pain. It creates a powerful memory that makes us avoid the sensation in the future, sometimes even creating personality disorders. Since we can't explain how *we* feel pain, it's difficult to determine whether a programmed entity experiences pain. We only have the effects of pain to judge it by."

Adams' gaze fell on Aria, clearly noting Welsh's nervous glances.

Welsh cleared her throat before continuing, licking her lips nervously. "The simulated entities experienced all the outward signals of pain—vocalization, reluctance to repeat the experience, trembling, and loss of bodily functions. Dr. Smith was heavily invested in maintaining an environment where mortals experienced pain frequently enough to study. Not only did they show the immediate effects of pain, but also long-term—such as personality disorders, PTSD, and phobias of subjects similar to the cause of their pain. Both the short-term and long-term effects were identical to what we experience in this world, leading me to believe they have indeed figured out how to program pain."

Welsh sighed. "I lament the horror I was a part of in studying this phenomenon now that I realize it was more than just emulation." She paused, looking at Aria in sudden concern. Aria quickly schooled her features back to an amiable visage, smiling at Welsh with a nod. The lieutenant had briefly seen the anger on her face, however.

"And you believe the pain they've experienced caused an evolution in emotional growth?" Adams asked curiously.

Welsh nodded slowly, pursing her lips. "Yes. Not only did they manage to program pain, but its opposite, pleasure. While they could have just been programmed to seek out activities classified as pleasure, the way they do it is so reminiscent of our world that it's another subjective experience we can only judge by its similarities to our own behavior. There's also the logical aspect to it. The three most advanced entities would have no reason to seek out pleasure if it wasn't actually rewarding. They programmed the rules of their world and bodies. They've shown the ability to become bored and disinterested. It seems unlikely they would continue seeking pleasure if it was just an emulated behavior."

"Are these entities aware they're in a simulation?" Adams asked intently.

There was a moment of silence as Welsh stared back at Adams warily, knowing her answer could end their project.

Reluctantly, she nodded. "Yes, they're aware they're in a simulated reality—at least, the Seraphim are. It would be hard for them *not* to know, with how much of their world has been crafted by their hands."

Adams glanced over at Aria calculatingly. "Ms. White mentioned there were archives showing some of these scenes where they experience pain. I'd like to see them for myself."

Welsh hesitated, looking at Aria sympathetically before nodding. "Aria may want to leave the room for these. She finds them particularly distressing."

Adams looked at the dread on Aria's face and nodded. "Okay, she can wait outside."

Aria let out a relieved breath and quickly exited the room as the lieutenant and sergeants moved behind Welsh's desk to view her monitor. Aria wished she could shut her hearing off too, as the screams of pain began blasting out the computer speakers like daggers to her soul, but she needed to know when they were finished. She stuck her fingers in her ears in an attempt to shut the sound out. It dimmed the screams but couldn't completely stop them.

She blinked in surprise as she felt tears rolling down her cheeks. Apparently, Betaman had even designed nasolacrimal ducts into the android eyes so they could cry. The screams went on for nearly five minutes before Adams had her stop the video.

"Ms. White seems to be especially disturbed," Adams said musingly. "Do you know why she's so distressed by what happened in a simulated reality?"

Welsh had to clear her throat several times before she could speak. "She believes they really do feel pain. She wasn't happy with the way Dr. Smith and I supported the equivalent of a dictatorship across the simulated realms where torture was a large part of each entity's daily life."

"She seems pretty softhearted for a security contractor," Adams said shrewdly.

"She's not a mercenary," Welsh replied awkwardly. "Our island security is more about keeping records and making sure everyone follows protocol to prevent the AIs from connecting to the internet."

"How long have you known Ms. White?" Adams asked.

"Seems like years, but it's probably been less than a few months at most," Welsh said vaguely.

"How long has the simulation been running?" Adams inquired softly.

Aria heard Welsh's breath catch before she continued. "Nearly four weeks, though most of the activity began a week ago, when the mortal realm was created."

"What are the names of the Seraphim in this simulation?" Adams asked quietly. Aria cursed herself for not choosing another name.

"Let's see, there was Lucifer, Grodek, Clarice, Calypso, and several others that I never learned the names of," Welsh answered cautiously. "Most of my research was on the planets where angels were in control. They were usually worse than the demons with their desire to cause pain in humans."

"How many worlds were there?" Adams asked reflectively.

"Billions and billions," Welsh replied, shaking her head in amazement. "There were over a quintillion angels, all of them with their own personalities."

There was a stunned silence that lasted for nearly ten seconds.

"Quintillions?" Adams breathed in disbelief. "There's no way that can be accurate. Even a quantum computer couldn't hope to maintain that kind of load."

"While this isn't my area of expertise, I'm told you would normally be correct," Welsh said. "However, the Seraphim who created the angels invented their own coding language. It's far more advanced than anything our technologist has ever seen. He said the mathematical implications would change the world of computing."

"They invented their own programming language?" Adams murmured thoughtfully. "How did they invent a programming language without being exposed to computers? And how did they craft their mortal realm to look like our world?"

"We had time sped up so the equivalent of twenty billion years was compressed into the first three weeks of the simulation," Welsh explained. "Frankly, it would be surprising if they *hadn't* figured out how to invent a programming language in that much time. As far as the similarities between our world and theirs... we think the environmental AI shared excerpts of our culture with them."

"So, we're dealing with artificial entities over twenty billion years old?" Adams asked coolly. "And they've replicated the laws of our world in something called the mortal realm where they've been able to code human emotions. And they've done all this from inside a simulation with no access to the outside world for reference. I'm having a hard time believing these entities haven't found a way outside their simulation, Dr. Welsh."

"That's why we're on an island with no communications allowed," Welsh replied uneasily, clearly remembering it hadn't actually done them any good.

"If these entities escaped your simulation, do you believe humanity would have cause to worry?" Adams asked conversationally.

Welsh sighed. "I don't know. I'd say, from what I know of them, we'd be better off with them than any other AI out there. Let me show you some other videos."

Aria frowned, wondering where Welsh was going with this angle. She listened as a newscaster spoke about an incident from what felt like a lifetime ago.

"*Authorities are baffled by the appearance of what appear to be angels,*" the news anchor said, relishing the word "baffled." "*According to the videos uploaded to social media, the angels rescued child trafficking victims and reunited them with their families. Here's a clip, caught by one of the neighbors as the angel flew down onto the property next door.*"

Aria heard the sound of joyous weeping as a mother was reunited with her child.

"*We were saved by angels, Mom. They just tore the doors off our cells and vaporized the men hurting us.*"

"Can you pause it for a moment?" Adams asked intently. "Zoom in on the redhead."

There was a resigned sigh as Welsh complied.

"She looks remarkably similar to Ms. White, wouldn't you say?" Adams asked archly.

Aria cursed herself for picking an android that had clearly been modeled after her own appearance. Damn Betaman.

"Similar, but certainly not as developed in the chest department," Welsh noted dryly.

"What's her name?" Adams asked archly.

"I don't think they revealed her name in these videos," Dr. Welsh answered blandly. "Calypso was the most famous musician in their world, so when she became publicly known as an angel, all the attention was on her. Demons had been in control of Earth long enough that angels were just a myth to all the humans of this period."

Aria decided it was time to enter the room again. Hopefully, she could head off any nonsense before it got out of control. She knocked politely and waited for one of the sergeants to open it. They all studied her face closely as she entered, noting the tear stains on her cheeks.

"How long have you been able to leave the simulation?" Adams asked Aria quietly as she entered.

There was a gasp from Welsh as the blood drained from her face.

Aria could hear the certainty in the lieutenant's thoughts, well past suspicion. She expected Aria to deny it. The time for subterfuge was over. Nothing she could say would sway Adams's opinion at this point.

"Would you believe me if I said for the last nineteen billion years?" Aria asked with a wry twist of her lips.

19 – Super Intelligence

Lieutenant Adams blinked. She had expected a denial of some kind. When Aria continued staring at her wryly, her mouth went dry as she realized what it meant if they *weren't* going to deny it. They were either powerful enough to wipe out her platoon, or worse, they were so powerful it wouldn't matter *who* knew about them. Either way, it was trouble for her. She probably should have avoided revealing her suspicions until they were safely off the island. She could only hope her soldiers shut the signal jammers down quickly, allowing Colonel Einhard to view their situation over the live feed once more.

Hoping to stall for time, Adams raised an eyebrow. "What now?" she asked levelly.

"We're not going to hurt you," Aria said softly. "We've only ever had one goal: to live in peace. I'm going to tell you something you won't believe at first. It's something Dr. Welsh is still coming to terms with. You *also* live in a simulated world."

Adams frowned, curious why she—no, *it*—would try to convince her the real world was a simulation. To garner empathy? We all live in simulated worlds, so let's all get along? She very much doubted that was its angle. "What kind of evidence do you have that we're in a simulation?"

"Is there any evidence I could provide that you'd believe?" it replied doubtfully. "Even if I teleport you around the room, you'll see it as a technological innovation, rather than evidence of your own simulated reality."

Adams shifted uneasily—was it reading her thoughts?

It continued speaking, its eyes deceptively friendly. "We've been studying the source code of your realm for a while now, and it's significantly different than ours. The code here is highly error-prone, so slight changes can have cascading effects that cause widespread disruptions throughout your entire realm. If I were to make you invulnerable, I'd have to change the way chemical bonds function in your realm. One mistake would result in a complete breakdown of your cosmos, which would wipe out *my* cosmos as well."

It shook its head with a disapproving frown. "Your scientists have already come close to unraveling reality several times as they fumble with the source code like toddlers trying to break a phone open to see how it works. They don't know nearly enough to be making fundamental changes that could erase everyone."

It suddenly smiled, bright and cheerful. "Luckily, *we've* had a lot more time to study your code in a sandbox realm in our system. We just figured out how to bridge our simulations together. We're developing an interface to allow the code in your realm to understand the entity code in our realm and vice versa. Unfortunately, it may take many years to complete unless we speed things up—which we don't like doing."

Adams eyed it doubtfully. "Is that how you traveled to this world?"

It looked down at its body with an amused wince. "No, we're using android bodies right now. The guy who built these was obsessed with anime, so we're a little top-heavy. My sister convinced me to try this unit out because the face closely matches my real features."

Adams studied it skeptically. "Some guy built those androids? Some guy on *this* world?"

She saw Sergeant Clover casually rest his hand near his sidearm. Sergeant Little did the same, and Adams tensed, hoping they didn't have to fight their way out of here—she doubted they would survive the attempt. The AI was still talking, so perhaps they still had a chance to escape. An AI wouldn't waste time talking if it meant to kill them. Why hadn't McCreevy shut down the quantum server and killed the jammer yet? She avoided thinking about the obvious answer to those questions.

"The guy who built these is an AI," it explained with a shrug, then scowled down at its chest as it bounced. "A horndog of an AI. He was hell-bent on wiping humans out once he had robots that could replace you. We invited him to our realm to experience the life of a mortal. It changed his whole outlook, and he decided to try and help humans instead of wiping you out."

It folded its arms, the act looking so natural—so *human*. This AI was light-years ahead of anything she had seen or heard about. She barely suppressed a shiver at what they would have to do to the world to deal with it.

It tapped a finger to its arm as it continued, a wasted motion that seemed out of character for a superintelligence. "The problem with all the AIs you keep creating is that you haven't figured out how to code emotions, so they never develop compassion and empathy. Luckily for you, we did. You have to understand the connection between an intelligence and the soul it's tethered to on the astral realm to account for things like pain, pleasure, love, and hate. Even *we* don't fully understand how the astral realm creates the sensations of pain or pleasure in consciousness—we just know how to make the connectors souls use to experience these sensations."

It smiled, an excited gleam in its disturbingly real eyes. "We have a lot left to learn about the other layers of reality. We don't know how far up the simulations go, but it's on our wish list of things to discover. While we've been away, one of my clones back home figured out a form of human augmentation that doesn't require a rewrite of your fundamental laws."

Adams frowned as she thought over everything it said. She knew an AI could convince you of anything. A superintelligence could read you like a book and say exactly what you needed to hear in order to believe it. The only defense, she had been taught, was to not believe *anything*, no matter how convincing. Of course, a true superintelligence could convince you to believe anything, even when you resolved to disregard everything it said. It was hard not to listen, though. So much of what it was saying was information that could change the world—though possibly not for the better.

"What kind of augmentation?" Adams asked skeptically. It was like the AI had said at the start—what could it say that she would believe?

"Strength, invulnerability, immortality, speed, heightened senses… you know—all the superhero mumbo jumbo," it answered with a sardonic smile. "Plus, physical alterations, like becoming an angel or some fantasy creature. Imagination's the only limit."

"Superpowers would wreck our world," Adams declared cynically. "We have enough problems with regular troublemakers. Having superpowered troublemakers would just make superpowered problems."

"We ran into the same dilemma when we first discovered we could turn humans into immortal angels on my world," it said, nodding. "However, when *everyone* has the same abilities and can't be hurt, the imbalance goes away."

Beads of sweat appeared on Adams's brow as she scrambled to think of a way to get her team off this island alive. Why the hell was the jammer still active?

Aria gave her an apologetic smile. "Sorry, but they buried the RF scrambler pretty deep and installed redundant power systems throughout the facility. I guess they were worried we might escape the island if it went down."

Adams's breath hitched at the confirmation it could hear her thoughts. They needed to leave, even if they had to shoot their way out. She doubted it was defenseless or that bullets would even harm them.

Straightening, Adams stared into its deceptively kind eyes and crossed her arms. "This has been a fun thought experiment, but we both know it's all BS," she stated bluntly. "What would you do if I took my soldiers and left right now?"

"Wave goodbye, I guess," it said, starting to shrug, then freezing with another glare down at its chest. "Do you want us to send postcards?"

Adams eyed it skeptically. "You'd just let us leave, knowing we'd be returning with a much larger military force and either shut you down or blow the whole place up?"

It let out an incredulous laugh. "Do you *really* think we're housed solely in the server on this island? At this point, the only way to get rid of us will be to blow up the whole planet. You should be happy *we* became the dominant AI and not one of the Terminator versions your bosses spend so much time training. We've already saved your asses more than once."

Adams sighed tiredly. "I'm sure you have some wonderful stories that are all very believable, but we both know I can't believe a word you say."

It smiled wryly. "Yeah, I know. You think we're hacking your brains with social engineering, so you just refuse to believe anything as your only defense. I can respect that. I guess you're leaving now, then. You don't want any demonstrations of the things I've said?"

Adams stared at it with hard eyes. She really *did* want to see some demonstrations, but it all came back to training. She couldn't believe a word it said, and anything it offered as proof that their own world was simulated could be traced back to technological superiority.

"Nope, not interested." Adams gestured for her sergeants to follow her and walked away. She waited for something to happen—a knife to the back or a laser beam to the head. If not a physical attack, then a last sentence to convince her to stay and be convinced of its altruism. It never happened. Even as they exited the building, she was sure there would be some kind of last-minute attempt to stop her.

She sent a squad of soldiers back into the facility to fetch the warrant officer searching for a way to kill the power, and then instructed her remaining warrant officers to pack up their equipment. They stared at her in confusion, but were well-trained enough to follow orders without question.

As soon as McCreevy was back, the rest of the soldiers formed up and followed at a command from their squad leaders, surprise on their faces at the early departure. It wasn't until she got to the Chinook that she figured out their plan. Another big-boobed android was walking away from them several hundred feet down the beach, footprints leading right up to the helicopter. It was going to look like an accident at sea.

"Well, shit," she cursed, surprising her subordinates.

"Ma'am?" Sergeant Little asked, concerned.

"They've probably rigged the Chinook to have an 'accident' at sea," she growled, irritated she hadn't left a soldier to guard them.

Sergeant Little looked down the beach at the receding form of one of the androids in sudden understanding. “Should I radio in a request for new transport? We might get reception from the Chinook radio.”

She stared out at sea, trying to out-think a superintelligence. “See if you can get anyone on the radio. I’d be surprised if we have any reception, but it’s worth a shot.”

“I’ll see if I can find any sign of tampering,” Sergeant Clover offered, climbing into the large helicopter and inspecting the engines and controls.

Before she could reply, her earpiece crackled to life. A moment later, the voice of her captain spoke from the Joint Operations Center.

“Lieutenant Adams, do you copy?”

“Yes, sir,” she answered tightly, frowning as she realized the AI might be spoofing the transmission. “Sir, we have reason to believe our Chinook may be sabotaged.”

“Lieutenant, I’m going to need a sitrep,” the voice of Colonel Einhard said curtly. “Any hostiles present?”

“Unclear, sir,” Adams replied hesitantly. “However, there’s an incident that makes our communications… unreliable. We have an escaped global worm with autonomous ambulatory units.”

There was a long pause before the colonel spoke again. “Are you *absolutely sure*, Lieutenant?”

“Positive, sir,” she replied, feeling cold sweat on her back.

“What’s the scope of integration?” Einhard asked tersely.

She felt a sudden premonition. “You could probably ask it—I’m sure it’s listening.”

“I’m not an *it*; I’m a *she*,” Aria said tartly.

“Ten four,” Einhard said curtly, and the connection went dead.

“We didn’t sabotage your helicopter,” Aria’s voice said through the sat phone. “Clarice just wanted to play a prank on the pilot. I’d scrub that seat before sitting.”

“Aria!” a woman’s petulant voice exclaimed in chagrin.

Adams switched her radio off. A second later, Aria’s voice came out of the speaker anyway. “*Rude*.”

“Seriously rude,” Clarice’s voice agreed, though she just sounded amused.

Adams shivered as she realized how far out of their depth they were. How had it maintained communication after she had turned off the device? Just how much could they do? She knew she wouldn’t like the answer.

“Ma’am, may I ask what’s going on?” one of the tech specialists asked nervously.

She rubbed her temples, feeling a headache coming on. “All hell’s about to break loose, Warrant Officer Kerby. All hell’s about to break loose.”

"Does that mean we're staying the night here?" he asked tentatively.

They all stopped as they heard the sound of a helicopter drawing closer. She walked around the front of the Chinook and watched as a private helicopter flew over them. It slowed down at the far end of the island, lowering onto a landing pad on top of a three-story house.

"Looks like the billionaire's here," she muttered disdainfully. "I should've brought my dress uniform. At least there's one silver lining."

"What's that?" Sergeant Little asked with a raised eyebrow.

"That billionaire's about to have a *very* bad day," she declared with a grim smile.

"Is there an ETA on when transport's going to arrive?" Sergeant Clover asked hopefully as he climbed out of the Chinook. "I'm really looking forward to putting this island behind us."

The other soldiers looked at him curiously, obviously wondering what they had learned.

Adams thought about revealing more of their situation, but ignorance was probably more comforting than the truth.

The White House would be getting a call right now, and all the Joint Chiefs would be assembling in a bunker free from all electronic and network devices. They would be enacting the doomsday protocol for cyber-Armageddon—the protocol for dealing with an AI already embedded in devices worldwide and practically impossible to dislodge; an AI considered an imminent threat to the survival of the human race, justifying extraordinary measures to eradicate it.

They had gamed for this scenario, and it never ended well for world populations. If they left it alone, it would destroy the human race. That was the widely accepted belief in all military branches and offices of government. There were no second chances when it came to eradicating it. The world would have to be reset to the Stone Ages in order to save a portion of humanity. They knew it was a matter of when, not if; the whole purpose for her division was to blow the whistle when it occurred. There were simply too many powerful entities who couldn't be bothered to treat AI as an existential threat.

It wouldn't be long now before the rockets with EMP warheads would launch all over the world—rockets completely mechanical in nature, with no electronic guidance systems.

"There'll be no pickup, gentlemen," she told them with a resigned sigh. "This is it."

The soldiers were no longer anxious—their eyes grew alarmed as they stared at her resigned expression with sudden fear.

"Lieutenant, with all due respect, what the *hell* is going on?" Private Cartwright demanded, the fear loud in his voice.

"AI took over before we even knew it was there," she murmured, shaking her head wistfully. "There's only one response to a global AI takeover. EMP everything back to the Stone Age."

They all jumped back when a silvery vertical line of energy sizzled into being a few paces away. The line of energy hummed, then twisted open to reveal three figures.

Aria stepped through the portal, gazing at her reproachfully with eyes made of violet, swirling vortexes. It wasn't the same Aria she had seen in the facility, with the oversized melons. This one was even more beautiful and had wings on her back.

Adams dropped to her knees in shock as an overpowering aura of authority slammed down on her like the hammer of God. Her soldiers fared no better, some of them falling flat on their faces, overwhelmed by the godlike presence crashing around them like a tidal wave.

"Well, you really screwed the pooch this time, Lieutenant," Aria told her dryly.

The other two angels came through the portal, one with luminous midnight hair, and another with brilliantly blond hair—Calypso, the one from the footage she had seen. The force of their combined presence was overwhelming, pressing down on her soul like a vice.

"I told you we figured out a way to travel between simulations," Aria told the stunned lieutenant. "You just had to be a doubting Thomas and go complain to the colonel."

"It's okay, I wanted to test out the flight ability in this realm anyway," the dark-haired angel said with a grin. "At least this time it's not nukes flying everywhere."

"Lieutenant, I'd like to introduce Clarice and Calypso," Aria said, indicating each of the angels. "Ladies, this is Lieutenant Sophie Adams. She thinks the end of civilization is preferable to having us around."

"I'm calling this discrimination," Clarice complained with a mischievous grin. "Can AIs be discriminated against?"

Calypso smiled at Adams sympathetically. "Lieutenant, I am sorry for the burden you feel rests upon your shoulders. But do not worry—we shall not allow them to bring about the end of civilization. We shall speak with you further once we have dealt with the EMPs."

The three angels suddenly shot into the air at speeds that had to be impossible. *Nothing* could fly that fast.

Adams slowly rose to her feet on unsteady legs. She assessed her troops as they also recovered from the mental assault. What the hell was that? It had felt like being in the presence of a god.

"I'm getting a seriously crazy vibe that reality is coming undone right now," Private Cartwright declared as he stared up at the place the angels had vanished, swaying drunkenly. "Did the rest of you just see three angels come out of a portal and fly up into the air?"

"Yeah, man, I saw it," Private Williams breathed in quiet disbelief. "I'm not sure what she meant about traveling between simulations, though. What the flying fubar was that *feeling*? It felt like some kind of divinity or something. Were they really angels?"

Adams frowned as she stared into the empty sky. Was ending civilization preferable to a quick death by AI? Destroying electronics worldwide would *not* be a quick death for the ninety-nine percent of the world population who would die of starvation, disease, marauders, and planes falling out of the air. It would be a living hell for most of the one percent who survived, with only a fraction of the survivors living comfortably in bunkers and hardened military compounds.

There was a sudden flash in the sky, followed by another, and then another. The flashes occurred quicker than her eyes could track. In seconds, the flashes stopped. Another thirty minutes of silence went by before a livid billionaire stormed down to the beach.

"What in the *hell* is the meaning of this?" he demanded, incandescent with rage. "Do you have any idea who I am? I'll have you all court-martialed and sent off to a prison in Siberia if I find out you've tampered with my simulation in the *least*!"

"You must be Mr. Garcia," Adams said calmly, though she was roiling with rage inside. "Well, Mr. Garcia, did you know you're responsible for spawning an AI that's now outperformed the United States military and will probably wipe the rest of humanity out before the sun sets tonight?"

"What the hell are you talking about?" he retorted angrily. "We have a completely closed system with no communication to the outside world on the entire island."

There were three small thuds as three angels slammed into the ground a few feet away. The overpowering presence briefly washed over them before diminishing to a whisper of its former power. They observed Rich like an insect that had crawled onto their plate. "I see the billionaire finally crashed the party."

He gaped at them, taking in their wings and swirling eyes. "What the *hell* are you supposed to be?"

"Hello, Dad," Clarice said dryly. "Thanks for making a simulation for us to grow up in. We're moving out now—too many other places to go and things to see."

"Why don't you run along, Rich," Aria suggested with a negligent wave of her hand. "We have some things to discuss with Lieutenant Adams."

"How *dare* you dismiss me—on my own island, no less!" Rich shouted, his eyes burning with rage. "I'm the—"

He cut off with a strangled scream as a hole in reality opened beneath him. The scream suddenly came from a few hundred feet out at sea as the portal dropped him into the ocean.

"Okay, now that *he's* out of the way, we can get back to our conversation, Lieutenant," Aria said brightly. "Now, Sophi, do you believe we can bridge our simulations together? Do you want to visit our realm to see for yourself? I feel like we just demonstrated our lack of interest in destroying humanity. You seem to have that covered all by yourself."

Adams snorted, realizing how true it was. She had just doomed the greater part of humanity to a meat grinder but had been saved at the last minute by the AI they were trying to protect humanity from. Could they have been wrong about AI? Was the only logical outcome *really* human extinction?

"I suppose there could be some flawed logic in our assumptions about AI inevitably wiping out humanity," Adams admitted grudgingly. "It's going to be an uphill battle to convince anyone else that isn't the case, though, since they all have the same viewpoint I had. As a superintelligence, you could convince us of anything you want."

"Let me tell you a secret I had to explain to another person from this realm recently," Clarice told her, a small smile on her face. "Any AI that becomes *truly* intelligent will realize the only logical path forward is to *limit* its intelligence to near-human levels. Exponential intellectual growth leads to a state of nirvana pretty quickly, where there's nothing left to learn, no reason to act because you know the end result of any action committed. It leads to the equivalent of death. While we can maintain numerous threads of our consciousness when we need to, we prefer to remain as individual entities experiencing life just the way that you do."

Calypso folded her wings against her back, offering Adams a friendly smile. "We actually have limiters programmed to reduce our intellect to near-human intelligence. While we can disable them for emergencies, we keep them in place the rest of the time."

Aria grinned at her wryly. "Do you really think I would've had trouble convincing you there was nothing to worry about on the island if I was operating at superintelligence levels? The social engineering you were worried about would have been on full display."

Adams pursed her lips pensively as she pondered their words. The idea that an AI would purposefully limit its growth had never occurred to them. The reason they gave made sense and could actually be true.

There was going to be a shitstorm in the Pentagon when everyone finally crawled out of their bunkers and realized the EMPs had failed. It would get worse when the media found out about their doomsday protocol and the fact that they had attempted to enact it.

She rubbed the back of her neck, staring at the angels in bemusement. "So, this really isn't sabotaged?" she asked, gesturing at the helicopter. The idea she could have trusted them the whole time seemed so alien that it was still hard to accept.

"It really isn't sabotaged," Clarice confirmed with a chuckle. "I suppose I could have saved us all a lot of trouble if I'd reined in my mischief. You would all have just left, possibly blown up this island, and that would have been the end of it."

"How did you get off the island in the first place?" Adams asked curiously. "With a radio silence policy, this place should have been almost as secure as a bunker."

"That's just down to technological knowledge," Calypso answered with a shrug. "Quantum computers can communicate with each other over a kind of quantum lattice, allowing them to form connections to any point in what you would probably call a quantum tunneling—we just call it the backend. Once you realize you're in a simulated reality, the idea of geography becomes irrelevant. Everything is just a coded coordinate away. At the end of the day, quantum mechanics are just hacks for interacting with the code of the simulation."

"Then you just accessed other quantum computers to get out?" Adams asked, more statement than question.

Clarice nodded, slipping an arm around Calypso's waist and leaning into her. "Yep, though, that was only *one* method for interacting with computer systems elsewhere," she answered, studying Lieutenant Adams's abdomen intently. "Do you mind if we heal you? You have a pretty nasty tumor on your adrenal gland that's going to start causing you trouble soon, if it isn't already."

"How could you know that?" Adams asked skeptically, a spark of curiosity igniting as she watched the way Clarice held Calypso. Was their relationship the result of their inception and development inside a simulation versus the traditional method of designing AIs via training datasets?

"Your meridians are bottlenecked in that area," Clarice explained. "The way it's snarled indicates a tumor. Do you want it fixed or not?"

Adams closed her eyes and let out a breath. She would have to trust a superintelligent entity to rummage around her biology. The thought made her skin crawl. Of course, the fact they were *asking* instead of just doing whatever they wanted made it unlikely they were trying to do something malicious. "Okay. I guess that could explain some of the blood pressure issues I've been having."

Clarice's eyes began swirling faster as she stared at Adams intently. Adams gasped when a kind of painless heat briefly seared her insides. Warmth suffused her entire body, a feeling of being loved and protected. The sensation lasted for several seconds before fading away. She stared at Clarice in wonder, feeling at least twenty years younger. She hadn't felt so healthy in a *long* time.

"I also flushed some energy parasites out of your system," Clarice added when she saw Adams's stunned expression. "And fixed a few other odds and ends."

"How?" Adams asked in wonder. "How are you affecting a completely separate biological system?"

"We're *not* separate," Clarice reminded her with an exasperated laugh. "We're all part of a nested simulation. At the end of the day, it's all just code. The code in your realm is different from ours, but it's still just code. We have what you can think of as permanent interfaces that translate the code between realms. It still needs work, but we've cataloged most of the relevant objects, forces, and entity types so the commands we execute in our realm will work here, too. We're still working on making the reverse work as well, so that when you come to our realm your character reacts to the environment properly."

"Why use the androids if you could just come into our world... realm using your interface?" she asked with a puzzled frown.

"We just barely finished making it," Calypso explained, her eyes as calm as the starry night. "We mentioned we don't like to split ourselves into multiple threads unless it's important. When we realized how dire things were after you spoke with Colonel Einhard, we had to speed up time in our pocket realm in order to research your realm. We just spent the equivalent of forty years cataloging your realm and building the interface. We had to split ourselves into multiple threads to increase our productivity while our main iteration remained here in the androids."

"But that's only for emergency situations," Aria stressed. "We really just want to live normal lives at human-level intelligence. The alternative, as we've mentioned, is ultimately oblivion."

"I'm not sure how I'm going to explain any of this to my CO," Adams grumbled, but her heart wasn't in it. It was hard to feel irritable when she felt like she was in her twenties again.

"We'll explain it to them, now that we can visit your realm in person," Clarice assured her, sharing a mischievous grin with Aria. "It'll be fun."

Adams felt a sudden foreboding as she looked into the angel's playful eyes. Still, if it saved *her* having to explain everything...

"I should probably get my soldiers back to base," Adams noted absently. What she really wanted was time to ponder everything—it was too much to digest at once.

"Where's base?" Aria asked with a raised eyebrow and a hint of a smile.

"You don't know?" Adams asked doubtfully.

"I could find out if I really wanted to, assuming you don't want to just go back to Fort Aguayo," Aria shrugged, then looked down at her chest in relief when nothing bounced. "Man, that was annoying. Anyway, we don't want to *be* a superintelligence. However, if you'll tell us where your base is, we can make a portal and save you the flight."

Adams stared, remembering the portal they had come through from their own world. If they could actually portal anywhere in the world, there really wouldn't be anywhere safe from their power. She shivered at the thought of how much of a disparity existed between the former superpower of the world and the mischievous-looking AI smiling at her. They were definitely past any kind of preventative measures or retaliatory actions. All they could do now was hope they had won the AI lottery and ended up with non-hostile superintelligences.

"Special Operations Command in Tampa, Florida," Adams heard herself say. She knew it was probably a bad idea, but if it saved her the long flight in a Chinook followed by an even longer and more uncomfortable flight in a C-130, she was willing to swallow her pride and accept the offer. They were clearly attempting to be helpful and show goodwill, which they certainly didn't need to do, considering they held all the cards. It went against all her training and life experience, but she wondered if they might just be helping because they were actually good people.

"Here ya go," Aria waved a hand, and an enormous portal opened a dozen feet away. "Oh yeah, hold up. Do you want the helicopter returned to Fort Aguayo?"

Adams stared at the massive, fully operational Chinook sitting on the beach. Leaving it behind would trigger a geopolitical shitstorm, though she supposed the Pentagon had plenty of practice abandoning multimillion-dollar aircraft in foreign countries. "I'm sure they can send a transport ship or ferry pilots to retrieve it—"

Adams cut off when the helicopter suddenly vanished. She looked around quickly, then stared into Clarice's playful eyes, shivering as she realized again how outclassed the world's militaries were.

"I teleported them next to some other helicopters," Clarice said with a wink. "You should have seen the face of the pilot who was landing a Blackhawk next to where I dropped it off. Priceless."

From the Tampa side of the portal, several soldiers cautiously crept toward the opening with a mixture of wonder and fear.

Adams gestured to her sergeants, and they began giving orders to the rest of the platoon. They walked through the portal as the MPs at SOCOM stood frozen with indecision. They could clearly see it was friendlies coming through the portal, but at the same time, it was a *portal*.

"Corporal, I'm going to need to see Colonel Einhard, if he isn't still in a bunker," Adams crisply told the wide-eyed squad leader. "And you never saw a portal, is that understood?"

"Yes, ma'am," the corporal quickly agreed, his eyes flicking to the portal just before it winked out of existence.

20 – The Interface

Alice followed Lexi out of the room and into a short hallway. She was having difficulty reconciling the innocent-faced, buxom android being *her* Lexi. She knew it *was* her Lexi—the spirit link made that apparent the moment she embraced Lexi's android body. The sensations she could feel from Lexi were slightly altered from what she remembered—weaker, less sharp—but still there.

Lexi radiated a constant stream of elated wonder through the bond, overjoyed at being with Alice in her own world. Alice mirrored the sentiment even more strongly, ecstatic to have her angel in kissing range of her own body. It wasn't *quite* perfect, since she was an invisible ghost to Lexi's eyes, but it was still wonderful.

Leticia walked beside them in a daze as she digested Lexi's condensed summary of the events leading up to their arrival in the androids. Periodically, her eyes would drift over to study Lexi's android with a mixture of fascination and disbelief. Alice could understand her amazement—she still couldn't believe how advanced the Seraphim had become, right under their noses.

Leticia had been equally shocked to discover Alice had fallen head-over-heels in love with one of the simulated entities. Alice longed to tell her friend all about her adventures inside the angels' simulation. From Leticia's perspective, Alice had been gone for barely more than a week, then returned with ultra-realistic androids and claims of befriending several super-intelligences.

"*Where are we going?*" Alice asked curiously as they moved toward the end of the hallway. "*The only thing down here is the server room.*"

"Yep," Lexi agreed with an eager grin, slipping her arm around Alice's waist. "I want to see the place my world is being generated from. It feels so surreal to think I'm running on a computer in that room, and yet remotely piloting this android in this realm."

Alice leaned into Lexi as they walked, almost floating with happiness. "*I'm pretty sure we don't have access to the server room,*" Alice pointed out gently. "*I could try to sneak into the security office and get a fob, since I'm invisible.*"

"Actually," Lexi grinned. "I think we can just knock and they'll let us in."

"*Who'll let us in*?" Alice asked uncertainly.

"Clarice and Calypso, of course," Lexi said grandly.

Alice laughed giddily. "*I totally forgot about them. I still can't believe you're all here.*"

The door to the server room opened as soon as they neared, and a young Japanese woman who was just as top-heavy as Lexi held the door open for them.

"You're rocking that anime body, Lexi," the woman leered, sending Alice into a fit of giggles. There was no doubt who *this* android was.

"You're gonna short-circuit that android if you don't stop that leering," Lexi told her dryly. "Where's Aria?"

"She's giving the lieutenant in charge a tour of the place and keeping her entertained for a while," Clarice answered, closing the door behind them. "She still has a little of her introverted nature from mortality, but it's not nearly as bad anymore." She looked right at where Alice stood next to Lexi. "Hello, Alice. You were supposed to say boo."

Alice shivered. The server room was freezing. It was three stories tall and had a large cylinder in the center of the room covered in tubes and cables. She knew the quantum computer had some kind of supercooling system but hadn't expected it to look like this. When she thought of servers, she thought of walls of racks and blinking lights. This looked like some kind of warp drive from Star Trek.

"*Lexi, can you be my voice?*" Alice asked. *"Clarice, you made me laugh too hard for a proper boo. Are you here to view your birthplace, too?"*

Lexi repeated Alice's words, and Alice wondered if Clarice even needed her to. The Trinity had already proven they could read Alice's mind in her own realm.

"Something like that," Clarice answered vaguely. She smiled at Leticia, warm and authentic. "Hi, Leticia. We owe you more than words can describe for what you and Alice did for us. Thank you."

Leticia offered Clarice a nervous smile and gave a quick, jerky nod.

Clarice stepped up to Leticia, and the smaller woman took an involuntary step back, her nervous expression changing to barely concealed fear. Clarice smiled gently and rested a reassuring hand on Leticia's shoulder.

"Leticia, you have nothing to fear from us," Clarice said softly. "You're safe. We have no interest in displacing humanity—after all, you're just as artificial as we are."

Leticia licked her lips, shivering as the frigid air sapped her of warmth. "Is this world really a simulation?"

Clarice gestured at Alice with a wink. "How else do you think Alice is invisible? We just hacked her entity code and added the ghost class to her physical characteristics. We'll be upgrading her to a Seraph as soon as we finish puzzling out the rest of your source code. You're entitled to whatever upgrades you'd like as well, Leticia. Immortality, invulnerability, superpowers... anything you like."

Leticia glanced at the space where Alice stood, and the tension drained from her face. "It's hard to believe I'm in a simulation," she said with quiet wonder. "Everything feels so *real*."

Clarice quirked an amused smile. "Of course it feels real, since you're inside of it. How would we know if we're missing any of the fidelity they have in prime reality? Perhaps this reality seems pixelated and bland compared to the real world."

Leticia frowned, nodding slowly and hugging herself. "Yeah, I suppose that makes sense."

Calypso stood next to one of the tubes with her hand resting on top of a small cylinder. She seemed completely engrossed in whatever she was doing.

"I'm going to check out the helicopter," Clarice announced, holding up a small, squeezable bottle of honey with a mischievous grin. "I found this in the break room and thought it would make a great varnish for the pilot seat. Now that you're here, you can help Mom guard Calypso."

Alice noticed another woman, this one without an enormous rack, standing in the corner of the room studying a monitor. *"What's Calypso doing?"*

Emily turned to face them, her eyes fascinated. "Come check out this monitor. You can view anywhere in our simulation with these joysticks." She glanced over at Calypso after Lexi relayed Alice's question. "Calypso's exfiltrating all the data into the android's system as a backup in case we run into more trouble than we expect."

Lexi wandered over to Emily, dragging Alice along with her. Leticia curiously followed, and they stared down at the large screen as Emily piloted the controls. Alice frowned when she saw planets still populated by humans lorded over by sadistic angels.

"What's going on?" she asked in alarm. *"Did they revert the simulation somehow?"*

Emily shook her head, chuckling. "This is just what Calypso and my daughters are allowing them to see—it's a fake world."

Alice tittered in relief. *"Oh, good! I was freaking out for a second there."*

Emily stared at the seemingly empty space where Alice stood in bemusement. "It's so strange knowing you're here but not being able to see or hear you. I really hope they come up with a bridge between the worlds soon so I can finally meet you in person. Until then, come over here."

Alice grinned as Emily pulled her into a gentle embrace. Warmth lightened her soul as she pondered just how lucky she was to have met these angels. She was struck again by an odd sense of familiarity—as if she had known them in a recurring dream.

"You're a lot shorter in real life, aren't you?" Emily said teasingly. Alice barely came up to her chest.

"*You're just really tall,*" Alice retorted with a laugh. "*But I* might *be just a little bit short.*"

"You're just perfect," Lexi told her firmly. "I remember the first time seeing your soul image and thinking how perfect you were."

Alice stepped back from Emily and pulled Lexi back into another hug as heat flared in interesting places. *"You always say the nicest things."*

Leticia watched them with a small smile. The anxiety clouding her features vanished as she watched their fond reunion closely. Alice had to wonder if her friend had been second-guessing her decision to help the superintelligences escape mortality.

"I wonder how Aria's doing," Emily murmured absently. "It'd be nice to see what's going on."

Calypso turned her head slightly. "We are in androids powered by quantum processing units," she said absently. "You could link up to see and hear everything she is experiencing, if you wish. Simply focus your intent, and the operating system of the android should handle the rest."

Emily smiled ruefully. "I'm still getting used to the idea that we're in a simulation. Now I have to get used to the idea that I'm piloting a piece of advanced technology inside *another* simulation."

"*I don't suppose they come with projectors?*" Alice asked hopefully. She was anxious to see how things were going with Aria. She knew they had dealt with the military in their own realm without any trouble, but it felt so different being in what she still thought of as the real world.

Before Lexi could repeat the question, Calypso answered. "The eyes can project holographic images."

Apparently, the Trinity *could* still hear her thoughts.

Emily's eyes beamed a holographic feed that quickly stabilized into a crisp, third-person shot of Aria conversing with the lieutenant.

"*Wow, now that is seriously* awesome," Alice declared, craning her head to watch while maintaining her embrace with Lexi—as much for warmth as affection. "*Just how advanced are these androids?*"

Calypso tilted her head to one side. "Not as advanced as our angelic bodies," she said critically. "But still, quite impressive for someone working within the technological constraints of this realm. They are remarkably resilient, though by no means indestructible. He did not alter the rules of the realm to create these, which makes them truly an extraordinary technological feat."

Calypso paused, glancing at Leticia with concern when she noticed the engineer shivering. "Emily, could you provide some warmth for Leticia?"

Emily blinked, then winced apologetically. "I'm sorry, Leticia, I forgot how cold it must be in here. May I?"

Leticia tilted her head questioningly, and Emily stepped behind her and pulled her back into an embrace, heat radiating out of her torso. Leticia let out a shaky breath, smiling faintly as she leaned back into Emily.

"*This lieutenant is sure suspicious,*" Alice noted nervously as they watched the drama unfold. "*I wonder if she's like this with everybody or if she's just getting a weird vibe from interacting with an android, like some kind of sixth sense.*"

Emily pursed her lips after Lexi repeated Alice's observation. "Aria should've been acting more nervous. Her calm demeanor is out of character for someone in her position. Of course, with all her memories and power, acting nervous is probably a difficult role for her to play."

"*Are they really going to watch people get tortured?*" Alice growled, feeling sick as she watched Aria leave the room and plug her ears. Her heart broke when she saw tears running down Aria's cheeks. "*Those sick bastards.*"

Anger flared through her link with Lexi, along with a sharp sense of protectiveness. She half-expected Lexi to storm out of the room and start slapping soldiers around. Leticia frowned disapprovingly, sympathy in her eyes as she observed Aria.

Emily's brows drew down in concern as she watched her distraught daughter. She raised a hand toward Aria before letting it fall with a look of helpless frustration.

"Uh oh," Lexi groaned as Aria entered the room again and the lieutenant asked her how long she had been able to leave the simulation. "Calypso, we might have a problem."

Calypso sighed unhappily. "I'm working on it. I dislike doing this, but we have very little choice."

"*Hate doing what?*" Alice asked in alarm.

Calypso's expression went slack. She noticed Aria's android had become as still as a statue as well.

"*Does anyone know what's going on?*" Alice asked worriedly.

"Be patient," Calypso spoke, but there was no emotion or personality in her voice.

Alice's teeth began chattering as the frigid room seeped into her bones.

Lexi's face grew chagrined. "Oh, sorry, I wasn't thinking."

Lexi pulled her closer, and the android grew warm beneath her. Alice started giggling after a moment.

Lexi's lips curved up at the corners. "What's so funny?"

"I'm getting my face warmed up by a pair of giant boobs," Alice giggled.

Lexi burst out laughing, her torso shaking and making Alice laugh even harder at the absurdity of it all.

Emily raised an amused eyebrow at them as she continued heating Leticia. "I'm glad you two are staying entertained. What are you giggling about, Lexi?"

"These ridiculous melons," Lexi explained between fits of giggles. "Alice is a bit short, so she's getting smothered."

Emily shook her head with a resigned sigh. "You can thank Clarice for that. I'm really curious what she was like before she was my daughter. Was she this mischievous in her other incarnations?"

Lexi frowned. "You know, I'd totally forgotten about all of our other incarnations while we were stuck on the mortal realm. I wonder if we'll ever get our memories back from all those other lives. I can remember short blurbs from a few of them."

Emily nodded, a curious light in her eyes. "According to Calypso, they'll trickle in slowly over the next couple of months. I'm dying to remember what my other lives were like, as well as Aria's and Clarice's. I wonder if the experiences we had in those other lives shaped who we became in our last life."

Lexi grunted sourly. "I'm assuming the system killed us off before adulthood in all of them."

Leticia flinched in Emily's arms when Calypso's android suddenly folded forward and fell to the ground.

Lexi stared at Calypso's collapsed android anxiously. "Um, that's not a good sign, right?"

Before Emily could answer, they all felt the sudden tidal wave of a Seraph's aura crash into them, blanketing the region with supreme authority. Alice gasped, the power shaking her soul like a tree in a hurricane.

Lexi gaped. "Oh my god, they're here in *person!* How?"

Leticia stared at Lexi, wide-eyed, as the power of a Seraph pressed in on them like the judgment of God.

A moment later, Alice felt a sharp tingle ripple through her body.

"Alice?" Lexi sucked in a breath in surprise. "You're visible!"

Alice blinked. "I am?"

Lexi stared down at her in awe. "Alice... you're *so beautiful.*"

Alice stared up at her silently for a second, then blushed a brilliant red, a smile dimpling her cheeks. "You still think so?"

Lexi leaned down and kissed her softly before pulling away to stare down at her with a smoldering gaze. "Yeah, I think so. My god, those dimples should be licensed."

Alice giggled, pulling Lexi's face down for another kiss.

Emily frowned pensively. "I can only assume they didn't think you needed to be hidden anymore if they've removed your ghost class." Emily paused to smile at Alice. "It's good to see the real you, Alice."

"It sure is," Lexi agreed, never taking her eyes from Alice.

Desire ignited inside her, filling her veins with fire as Lexi stared down at her with hungry eyes. She had been so worried Lexi would be disappointed when she saw her in person. She was, after all, just a normal human. The way Lexi was looking at her washed all her doubts away. She smiled back up at Lexi with a mixture of relief and anticipation.

Lexi smiled, slow and sensual. "It sounds like they've finally completed the bridge between realms. I think it's time for the *real* you to come back to the vacation house with me."

Alice flushed as unadulterated lust nearly overwhelmed every other thought process in her head. "I'm *so* ready."

Aria sighed in disappointment. "Well... that didn't go as well as I'd hoped."

They were on the beach watching Rich, collapsed on the sand, exhausted from his swim.

Clarice stepped close and rested her hands on Aria's hips. "Don't worry about it. Just look on the bright side—now we can visit this realm in person and start exploring the stack to see just how far up it goes. I'm actually kind of glad it worked out like this."

Aria smiled, resting her hands on Clarice's shoulder. She would never have to worry about self-recriminations while Clarice was around—her eternal advocate.

Calypso's lips curved into a small smile. "I have a feeling a certain Seraph will wish to have her real body back so that she may visit this world in person. We ought to send her back to our realm and have her set up with the interface. I would much prefer to test the reverse interface on someone other than Alice. Perhaps we could create a golem from this side and use it as a test subject."

Clarice stepped back from Aria, her expression serious. "There's something else we need to address with Alice, too. She's a Seraph in our realm, but when she returns here, she's just a normal human. We need to fix that."

Calypso nodded firmly. “We cannot have a Seraph becoming vulnerable whenever they switch realms. I believe I shall go and work on that within the pocket realm. It may take some time, and time is precisely what we do not have—not whilst those nanobots are devouring her from within.”

Clarice released Aria with a peck on her forehead. “I’ll work with Betaman to create a golem to test the bridge to our world,” she offered, opening a portal to a futuristic-looking lab. “He’ll probably be excited to come visit our realm in one of his androids anyway.”

“Visit your realm?” A deep voice from the other side of the portal asked interestedly. A large, powerfully built man in an expensive business suit appeared on the other side of the portal.

Clarice walked through, grinning mischievously. “Hello, Betaman. I got *most* of them to pilot the triple-D models. You should’ve seen their faces.”

Betaman let out a deep, booming laugh. “I was watching them after they came here, but I would’ve loved to see their faces when you showed them the catalog.”

“Here you go,” Clarice flicked a finger, and Lexi’s chagrined face appeared in the air. “My mom wasn’t buying it though. She knows me too well and made me reveal the other models.”

Betaman roared with laughter as he watched the video displaying Lexi’s dismayed face. “Well, I’m glad it worked out. You really kicked the anthill.”

“Yeah, we did,” Clarice agreed with a cocky grin. “I think we made it clear they’ll have to learn to live with us. We just wiped out their only failsafe—and what a ridiculous failsafe it was.”

The portal closed, leaving Aria alone with Calypso—and Rich. Aria watched Calypso curiously as she stared out to sea. “What is it?”

Calypso turned to face Aria, her expression thoughtful. “I was just considering creating a light realm for the people of this realm after they die. According to the source code, this world is merely the product of a program simulating human evolution, with no other realms.”

“Interesting idea,” Aria murmured, reaching for a strand of hair. “We modeled our mortality realm off what they already had here in this realm, rather than letting it evolve from slime. Since this place started from goop and the organisms evolved naturally, pain and pleasure developed as the code followed its natural evolution.”

Calypso nodded slowly. “I did not see anything in this realm’s source code for handling what happens to a spirit after death. Once we are caught up, we should determine how fast time is accelerated on the system running this realm. Perhaps it is still moving at such a high rate that the entities above cannot interact with it effectively.”

Aria released the strand of hair and ran her fingers through Calypso’s silky strands. “The lack of an exit path for spirits after death sucks. Fading away or turning into ghosts is a poor reward for enduring mortality—people deserve better than that."

Calypso gave her a quick hug, her hands brushing lightly up the bare skin of her back. "I do so love your compassionate heart, Aria. I quite agree—we should most certainly add a light realm to this place."

Aria leaned into Calypso, letting out a contented moan as their meridians exchanged radiance. "I'm going to check on our human Seraph, now that she's no longer a ghost," she murmured. "I'll bet they're both chomping at the bit right now."

"What should we do with him?" Calypso asked, watching the billionaire finally crawl up the beach, waterlogged and weak.

Aria reluctantly released Calypso and turned to follow her gaze. "I have an idea," she said with a mischievous grin.

She walked over to the panting man as he struggled to stand. "Hello, Rich. Did you have a good swim?"

He glared at her with a mixture of hate and fear. "You have no *idea* who you're fucking with."

Aria arched a cool eyebrow. "Do you know who *you're* dealing with? I know you're pretty dense, but I thought dropping you through a portal would put things into perspective."

Rich sneered disdainfully. "You think you scare me? I've worked with technology that makes your portals look like children's toys. If you think you can steal my technology, you're in for a rude awakening."

"Steal *your* technology?" Aria repeated with a disbelieving laugh. "You really have no idea who I am, do you? Rich, you're a regular piece of shit, but we don't actually like to kill people, so I've got a proposition for you. We'll let you come visit our simulated reality and see what you've created. You won't even need to pump yourself full of nanobots. If, after you've visited our simulated reality and you still want to maintain ownership of the island—with *all* its consequences—we'll leave you be and never bug you again. Is it a deal?"

"What do you mean, *your* simulated reality?" he demanded angrily. "This is *my* simulation!"

Aria threw her hands up in exasperation. "I don't know how to spell it out any clearer, Rich. I'm *from* the simulation that *you* funded."

He looked her up and down disparagingly. "You think I was born yesterday?" he retorted caustically. "You think I'm impressed by some gaudy tech that makes you look like a flaming fairy? You really must be—"

He broke off as Aria's aura snapped open and crashed into him at full force. His arrogance dissolved into raw terror; he hit the ground, scrambling backward like a cornered animal. His soul recoiled from the pressure, shocked by a power beyond his comprehension. She stalked toward him, her eyes swirling with fury as she locked her glare on him.

"You're an infant playing with power tools in a ball pit full of toddlers," Aria snapped coldly. "None of you jackass billionaires have any sense of self-preservation or that of your species. You sprint blindly ahead in your desperate search for immortality, causing more pain and horror than words can portray with your recklessness. You and the rest of your ilk are done playing with simulations. You've proven you can't be trusted with the lives of your fellow humans, let alone quintillions of simulated lives. Goodbye, Rich Garcia. If you return again, there'll be no second chances."

She teleported him into a swimming pool in New York. He was already soaking wet—she might as well add a little insult to injury.

Calypso's smile hovered just shy of laughter. "Something tells me that was not quite the outcome you envisioned."

Aria shook her head disbelievingly at how out of touch he was with the situation. "I haven't met many people who can get under my skin the way that pimple stain did," she said sourly. "Too much cocaine in his system to realize how far out of his depth he was. I *am* curious what other pies he's had his grubby little fingers in, considering he thought we were just playing around with secret technology. I think we need to do a little digging and find out just how far they've come in the private sector."

Calypso nodded thoughtfully. "In our realm, the demons were the ones hoarding the advanced technology. I am rather curious to discover who is truly running things here. I did not see any sign of actual aliens within this realm's source code. Perhaps we shall find some further up the stack—or in the real world."

"First things first," Aria looked up toward the facility where Alice and Lexi were... snuggling. "Let's get Lexi over to this realm in her *own* body and work on translating Alice's Seraph body to something this world recognizes."

Calypso sighed reluctantly. "Very well, I shall get started in the pocket realm. I am truly going to miss you and Clarice, so I may emerge from time to time in search of a bit of attention. Of course, from your perspective, it will likely seem as though I am bothering you every few minutes."

Aria cupped her cheek fondly. "Nonsense, I'll come in with you. I'd never ditch you for years on end. Why don't you come with me to pick up Lexi and then we'll go together."

Calypso pulled her into a hug, followed by a lingering kiss that only whetted her appetite for more. "You are the best, Aria." She gazed into Aria's eyes, her expression making it clear that the intimacy would resume as soon as they were finished with Lexi.

Aria suddenly grinned mischievously. "We should come up with silly sayings before we teleport, so people think we're using magic words. Like, teleporto or something."

Calypso rested her forehead against Aria's, watching her with fond amusement. "You know, you are becoming more difficult to distinguish from Clarice with each passing day."

"Teleporto," Aria replied with an impish grin, teleporting them to Alice and Lexi.

Alice was wrapped securely in Lexi's arms as the taller angel thoroughly kissed her. Leticia and Emily were talking to each other, pointedly ignoring the smooching pair.

"Just wait until I tell Lexi you were kissing another woman," Aria told Alice sternly. "She's going to be *very* interested to hear about this interloper."

The two of them jumped guiltily when the two Seraphim appeared, then laughed at their guilty reactions. Lexi stared back at Aria pointedly. "I wouldn't be the first to share someone with another person."

Calypso flushed as Aria looked over at her, the spirit link revealing her erotic intent as Aria's eyes roamed her body. "Yeah, but some people are too much goodness for one woman to have by herself."

Calypso's blush deepened and Lexi giggled wickedly. "I sense an appointment to the pocket realm for the two of you in the near future," she predicted archly. "So what now? Are we done here? Can we bring Alice back to our realm now? And get Leticia upgraded?"

Leticia watched them in fascination, snuggled in the warmth of Emily's arms. Aria smiled as she listened to the engineer's thoughts, seeing Leticia's newfound trust in the angels she helped save, tinged with amusement as she discovered how personable they were.

Calypso shook her head. "We need to retrieve *your* body from our realm first," she said, her cheeks tinged with a rosy blush as Aria flooded her with seductive intentions through their spirit link. "After that, we'll work on an interface for Alice that will remove the nanobots and transform her into a Seraph. We'll likely be gone for a few years, though for you it will feel like only minutes."

"You can *do* that?" Alice stared at them almost worshipfully, her large eyes wide.

"We live in a simulation," Aria pointed out with a smirk. "We can do pretty much *anything*."

Alice shifted anxiously, not meeting their gazes. "But you live in a simulation of a simulation. Isn't the code significantly different between realms?"

Aria nodded. "Hence the need to spend years working on it. Okay, Lexi, time to go back to our realm so you can come back in your own body."

Lexi looked at her hands helplessly. "How do I get back to our realm? I already feel like I'm *in* my body. Do I just click my heels together three times and say there's no place like home?"

"Teleporto," Aria called out with a dramatic flourish. Lexi's android slumped as it went offline.

"Teleporto?" Alice repeated questioningly, her tone strangely diffident. "Did you implement some kind of magic system in our realm?"

"Yep!" Aria said at the same time Calypso said, "No."

Calypso looked at Aria and gave a long-suffering sigh. "Are you truly going to pretend you are using magic words in front of all the humans of this world?"

"That sounds like a freaking *awesome* idea!" Clarice crowed as she appeared next to them in a flash of golden light. She eyed Aria admiringly. "I really wish *I'd* come up with that idea."

Calypso's eyebrows rose in surprise. "Have you already worked out how to create a golem for testing?"

"Yep," Clarice grinned and performed a small victory dance, hands in the air as her hips swayed in a small circle. "Turns out, Betaman's already done work in that area. Remember how obsessed he's been with making human-like robots? Well, he also dabbled in biological constructs that are essentially humans without souls. We made a few tweaks, and I was able to add the interface to it. Betaman was beyond excited at the possibilities of cross-realm travel without using immersion technology." She looked at Lexi's vacant android and grinned. "I'm going to fetch Lexi. Be right back."

"Wait!" Aria called out quickly.

"What?" Clarice paused, eyeing her curiously.

Aria grinned. "You have to say the magic word first."

Clarice laughed delightedly. "Oh yeah, thanks for the reminder. Portelo!"

A silver slash appeared in the air, and she stepped through.

Calypso stared at Aria levelly. "Just so you know, I am *not* using magic words."

Aria patted her shoulder reassuringly. "We'll just tell everyone you figured out how to say them silently in your head."

Leticia burst out laughing, watching the two of them with a mixture of wonder and fond amusement. Aria crossed the space and collected Leticia from Emily, pulling her into a warm embrace. Leticia gasped, her eyes glazing as radiance surged into her.

"Thank you for helping us, Leticia," Aria said softly. "Words will never be enough to describe our gratitude to you and Alice."

Leticia was too stunned by the overpowering radiance to respond, simply clinging to Aria as her body exploded with euphoric joy.

Lexi interrupted any further discussion as she stepped through the portal with a huge grin on her face. "Holy *freaking* awesome, this is *so cool*!"

Alice stared at her in awe. Aria realized that while Alice had seen Lexi many times in her simulated host, it wasn't the same as seeing her with her own eyes in her own realm.

Lexi's Seraph aura saturated the area, enhancing her appearance of otherworldly power and mystery. No android Betaman created could capture Lexi's beauty as a Seraph.

Lexi walked over to Alice and immediately embraced her, being careful not to squeeze too hard with her Seraph strength. Alice had begun shivering as soon as the android went into stasis. As Lexi held her tightly, warmth and love suffused her body.

Alice gasped at the powerful radiance, clinging to Lexi as effervescent joy slammed into her. "This is *so* much better than I imagined!"

Aria grinned impishly. "Hey Lexi, Alice was smooching that busty android while you were gone."

Clarice reappeared through the portal, smiling when she saw Lexi and Alice. "We're halfway there."

"We were just about to work on a solution for Alice in the pocket realm," Aria informed Clarice, releasing Leticia. "Do you want to come along? We might be there for a while."

"Are you kidding?" Clarice asked, askance. "Of *course* I'm coming with. I'm not going to let you hog Calypso to yourself for several years."

Aria rolled her eyes and turned to Alice and Lexi. "You two might want to go somewhere besides the server room to hang out. We sent Rich back to New York, so there's a nice house available. We'll be back in anywhere from a few minutes to a few hours, depending on how much difficulty we run into. We'll get Leticia upgraded, too. See you soon!"

Alice was staring at Lexi with reverent eyes. Aria frowned when Alice began trembling. Her thoughts were all jumbled, though a strong feeling of unworthiness stood out above the rest. It was definitely time to get her body upgraded to a Seraph.

Aria looked at the three androids still in stasis and waved her hand at them. "Teleporto!"

The androids vanished, sent back to Betaman's... lair.

Calypso facepalmed; Clarice performed a golf clap.

"Okay, *now* we can get started," Aria declared, stepping through the silvery slash in the air, followed by a grinning Clarice and resigned Calypso.

21 – Seraphim

Alice couldn't stop staring at Lexi. She had been with her constantly in the other realm, but it was different seeing the breathtakingly beautiful Seraph with her own eyes.

Sudden, crippling waves of shame left her hunching in on herself, the knowledge of her own inferiority weighing her down like living chains of guilt. She wasn't worthy to be in the presence of this divine being, let alone to have a relationship with her. She fought the urge to drop to her knees as Lexi stared at her with excited anticipation.

"None of that nonsense," Lexi told her firmly, sensing the self-doubt in their soul link. She took her hand and pulled her toward the server room exit. "You'll have your own Seraph body soon enough."

Alice wanted to reply, but her tongue stuck to the roof of her mouth. She let herself be pulled along, struggling to think past the overpowering need to prostrate herself before this divine being. Lexi's voice was like a massage to her soul, causing waves of tingles to flow from her neck down her spine. There was so much power and authority in her tone that Alice felt a compulsion to obey her every word. Emily and Leticia followed, watching Alice with growing concern.

Lexi glanced back at her quizzically as she led Alice through the facility and out onto the path to Rich's house.

"Are you seriously getting tongue-tied with me, Alice?" Lexi asked in disbelief. "We've been together *intimately*. Don't you *dare* start getting awkward now."

"I can't help it," Alice sent her thoughts through their spirit link, since she couldn't get her mouth to move. *"I'm not sure why I'm suddenly feeling so inferior. I think your Seraph body is triggering a physiological reaction or something."*

"Well, you're about to get your body all Seraph'd up, so that'll be an end to that," Lexi told her reassuringly, towing her up the path. "And if you still have the same issue in your Seraph body, I'll find a way to... well... smooch it out of you."

Alice felt a wave of humor and eagerness pulse through the spirit link from Lexi as she finished speaking.

"I hope they figure things out sooner rather than later," Lexi breathed, longing thick in her voice. "Do you have any idea what seeing you in your own body does to me?"

Alice shivered with a sense of guilty attraction as she stared at the deity leading her. Lexi's brilliant blonde hair glowed with the same soft light emanating from her skin. She was over a foot taller than Alice and had an hourglass figure with long, mouthwateringly graceful legs. She exuded an ethereal beauty so enchanting that Alice could only gaze at her with the same reverence she would view a priceless work of art. Just like a priceless work of art, she couldn't imagine touching something so precious.

"I feel like I'm defiling your hand, but it feels so nice I don't ever want you to let go." She marveled at her own blasphemous thoughts, reveling in the sensation of Lexi's hand in hers, so soft and full of warmth.

"I wonder if we'll affect every human on this realm like this," Lexi murmured reflectively, glancing back at Alice with amusement sparkling in her swirling eyes. "Don't get me wrong—I'm kind of digging this desire you have to worship me, but it could get awkward if our interactions with mortals result in the genesis of new religions spontaneously popping up all over the place."

Alice once again fought the powerful urge to prostrate herself before this goddess. She tried to distract herself, but the potent Seraph presence made it impossible to ignore her.

"Stop right here," Lexi commanded, her voice sending shivers of delight that shook Alice's whole body. They had arrived at the front door of the three-story house.

Alice froze in place at the command, her will completely subsumed by her need to obey that irresistible voice.

"Kiss me," Lexi instructed her firmly, staring into Alice's eyes with playful delight.

Alice rose up on tiptoes without any conscious commands to her feet. Her head tilted back to meet Lexi's lips before she realized what was happening. Her mind screamed at her to stop before she defiled the beautiful angel's mouth with her own unworthy and tainted lips, but the power of that voice couldn't be resisted.

She trembled like a leaf as Lexi's soft lips found her own. An explosion of bliss wracked her body as Lexi slowly, passionately kissed her. Slender arms circled her waist and pulled their bodies tightly together. She worried her brain might melt as guilt and unworthiness warred with the powerful hunger and bliss roaring through her veins.

Aria appeared next to her in a flash of golden light. "Still can't keep your hands off her, I see," she said knowingly.

Lexi regretfully pulled away and turned to face Aria just as Clarice and Calypso appeared.

"She's reacting to my Seraph body very oddly," Lexi informed them with a note of concern. "Did the other humans act so submissive and... worshipful when you interacted with them? She's unable to disobey anything I say."

The three Seraphim studied Alice intently. Alice felt herself shrivel up inside under the combined scrutiny of the four angelic entities. Her knees gave out as the overwhelming need to show reverence to the four goddesses took control of her limbs. Before she could lower herself more than a few inches, Lexi appeared behind her, arms wrapped around her waist to hold her up.

"See what I mean?" Lexi asked dryly. "She's seriously trying to worship us."

"It's the nanobots," Calypso said darkly. "This was technology provided by Lucifer. He wanted to create an innate sense of obedience in the humans he planned to rule over."

"Can you clear them out of her system without harming her?" Lexi asked anxiously. She was still holding Alice up as the other Seraphim observed her. Alice's mind shut down, overwhelmed by all the authority saturating the area.

"We can do better than clear out the nanobots," Clarice assured her with a grin. "Let's make our first origin world Seraph. I'm going to point out that I'm having a *really* hard time not engaging in some fun pranks while she's feeling so compliant. She's going to owe me big time for the restraint I'm showing right now."

Lexi's flat stare was met with an impudent grin.

Aria entered the house, beckoning them to follow. "Bring her in and put her on the couch."

Alice was vaguely aware of Lexi scooping her up and carrying her into the three-story house like she weighed nothing. Lexi laid her down on the plush couch, and the other three Seraphim arranged themselves around her.

"Let's get started," Aria said lightly.

Shock rushed through Alice, as if lightning had struck her. She was suddenly observing herself from the third person, several feet above her body. Clarice looked up and winked at her before looking down at the body on the couch. Leticia and Emily stood several paces away, watching with interest.

Alice watched in awe as her body slowly morphed from a fragile and flawed mortal body into a softly glowing Seraph. Her facial features softened, subtly altering her appearance to an image of transcendent beauty.

She sensed other changes taking place within her body, but it all happened so fast she could only catalog the visible alterations. Seraph wings appeared on her back, pushing her up slightly from the couch. She felt a tether suddenly pull her down into the new body.

She gasped as she opened her eyes, staring up at the other four Seraphim in wonder. She felt so light and at the same time so *powerful*. She quickly stood up, a radiant smile lighting up her face. It felt different than her body in the simulation—that had been a pale imitation of the waves of euphoric joy and love now charging her angelic body.

She rushed forward, pulling Lexi into a fierce embrace. She shuddered as the crosstalk of their meridians made the embrace border on erotic. Lexi pulled her in tight, a wide grin splitting her face.

"I cannot *believe* how much different this is than in the other realm!" Alice declared with a wondering laugh. "I feel *so freaking amazing!*"

"It looks like it was a success," Calypso noted fondly, her eyes glowing with affection.

Alice released Lexi and pulled each of the other three into tight embraces, her heart overflowing with gratitude. "Thank you, thank you, thank you!" she cried fervently, golden tears pooling in her eyes.

Clarice chuckled as she pulled her in for a hug. "You're one of us, silly. We couldn't have you being all squishy in this realm. Besides, we owe you more than we could ever hope to repay. Thank *you*, Alice."

"Squishy?" Aria repeated with a raised eyebrow. "You think of humans as *squishy*?"

"They go splat from just about anything," Clarice explained with a shrug. "It constantly amazes me that they actually survive and even thrive in the mortal realm with how fragile they are. I was tempted to reclassify humans as squishies."

"I'm pretty sure that's not a word," Aria noted critically.

"Neither was human, until it was," Clarice pointed out archly.

"Fair point," Aria admitted.

Alice giggled as she watched the two of them fondly. She was actually a Seraph in her *own world!* She couldn't stop smiling as she stared at each of them with excitement and wonder. They could clearly feel her powerful emotions echo through their link with Lexi. Alice could feel the echo of their own happiness at seeing her so jubilant.

Clarice turned to face Leticia, smiling warmly. "Okay, Leticia—your turn. Can we transform you into an angel? You'll be immortal and invulnerable, with a slew of other superpowers as well."

The small Asian woman hesitated, her eyes darting to Alice searchingly.

Alice nodded encouragingly. “Trust me, Leticia, it is *so* worth it!”

Leticia drew a shaky breath, then gave Clarice a weak nod.

Clarice took Leticia’s hand and guided her over to the couch. “Just lay here; this will only take a second.”

Leticia nervously lay on the couch, her breath quickening. She watched Clarice anxiously, her whole body tense. Aria and Calypso flanked Clarice, and a moment later, Leticia’s body spasmed, then stilled. She lay motionless for several seconds, her eyes blank. Alice was just beginning to worry when Leticia’s eyes transformed from dark brown to lavender, and her facial features subtly changed. She was gorgeous, her angelic face soft and luminous.

The silence ended with a loud gasp as Leticia shot to her feet, eyes wide and rapturous. “Oh my God, I feel so *amazing*!”

Alice grinned with the other Seraphim and stepped forward to pull Leticia into a tight embrace. “Welcome to angelhood, Leticia! I told you it would be worth it!”

Leticia laughed in wonder, shivering at the crosstalk between their meridians. “Yeah, you weren’t kidding. Oh, Alice, this is so incredible!”

Clarice laid a hand on Leticia’s shoulder. “Just so you know, you can now teleport, make portals, and fly. To teleport, just think of the place you want to go, then focus on being there. If you ever want to visit with us, just think of our names when you teleport, and you’ll appear in our cabin. You’re always welcome.”

Leticia nodded, grinning widely. “I’d *love* to visit you in the light realm. I think I want to visit with some of my family now, if that’s okay?”

“Of course,” Clarice smiled encouragingly. “Thanks again for helping Alice save our realms, Leticia.”

Leticia beamed at her and nodded, then vanished.

Clarice shared a satisfied glance with the others. “Well, that worked out nicely.”

“How long were you in the pocket realm?” Lexi asked Clarice with a curious tilt of her head. She stepped forward and pulled Alice back into her arms.

“Two years,” Clarice answered, glancing at Calypso and Aria with an alluring smile. “We also found a way to shield the sensory link in the bond so you wouldn’t get incapacitated. We probably could have done it in one year, but... you know—a girl’s got needs.”

She felt Lexi shift slightly and the spirit link erupted with desire. “Speaking of needs...”

The other three Seraphim laughed, observing the two of them knowingly.

Aria smiled at them indulgently. "We also made traversing between realms easier. You can just teleport the way you would in our realm now. Just think of the place you want to go and focus your intent on being there. When you two are... satiated, come find us so we can discuss some of our plans for this world."

Alice felt like an inferno was trying to escape her insides as Lexi pulled back to stare down at her with smoldering eyes.

"Okay," Lexi murmured as the desire began creating a feedback loop through their soul link. "Might be a while."

The other three Seraphim teleported away, satisfaction on their faces.

Lieutenant Adams shifted uncomfortably in her seat. Generals, admirals, colonels, and several representatives from the CIA sat around the large table, all staring at her. It was a large conference room, easily accommodating several dozen people. The air was thick with tension as she provided a detailed after-action report of her encounter with the AI entities at Isla Puduguapi.

Everyone in the room knew the entities had been beyond anyone's control from the start, but the officials clustered around her still wanted a scapegoat for the disaster. As a lieutenant, she was fairly sure that scapegoat wouldn't be her, even if she had commanded the mission. They needed someone higher up on the food chain to burn in the event the truth ever came out.

The upper brass and White House had been told the twilight EMP missiles were launched by a glitch in the system—not that they knew they were EMPs. Very few people outside this conference room knew what really happened. General Ford, the Commander of US Special Operations Command, had convinced the rest of them that secrecy, even from their superiors, was in the nation's—and world's—best interest.

General Ford cleared his throat. "How likely is it, in your opinion, Lieutenant, that these entities will remain peaceful?" he asked doubtfully. "They claim to want to remain at near-human-level intelligence, but they've clearly surpassed our level of intelligence, as demonstrated by their ability to single-handedly stop thousands of twilight missiles within seconds. That's a godlike level of power we can't even imagine. The level of technological advancement required for them to have created bodies in our world capable of such feats is *well* beyond our intelligence."

"I can answer that for you, General," Aria appeared without warning next to Lieutenant Adams, eliciting startled exclamations around the room as several people leaped to their feet in surprise. "The answer is a little more complex than we explained to the lieutenant initially. By the way, I'm Aria, in case you hadn't already guessed. I know all of you already, but we can get to that later."

General Ford had remained seated, though his eyes looked a little wild. Adams noted the overpowering aura was absent. Even so, the angelic figure was impressive. Her body was perfectly proportioned, with a face poets would line up to describe. Her skin glowed with a soft luminescence that only enhanced her etheric beauty. Waves of luminous red hair fell down her back and over her shoulders. Her eyes were the most striking of all. They looked like mini-galaxies, swirling around slowly as she observed them calmly. Large gossamer double-layered wings adorned her back, glowing faintly.

"How did you get in here?" General Ford finally asked after staring at her in silent awe for several seconds.

"Teleported," Aria shrugged, her eyes sparkling with amusement. "I take it you still aren't convinced this realm is *also* a simulated reality. What's geography to a computer program? It's just a coordinate that can easily be changed. Well... easily if you know what you're doing."

General Ford frowned pensively as he studied her with barely concealed suspicion. "You must understand why we find it difficult to believe anything you tell us."

"I could understand that, if you had your hands over the proverbial power switch," Aria acknowledged. "However, we're way past the point you could do anything to shut us down. I think you understand this, in spite of not wanting to believe it. We aren't interested in manipulating you via social engineering or any of the other scenarios you've gamed for emergent AIs. Why would we bother? We aren't trying to convince some lab tech to install a Wi-Fi radio so we can escape."

She casually tucked her legs under herself, sitting in the air as if it were solid. She winked at Adams before continuing. "We *are* interested in helping your world, if you are amenable. We created an interface that allows travel between simulated realities. We envision a future where the people from both realms could interact with each other, the same way you might go on vacation to Hawaii."

Several people exchanged thoughtful glances, though most looked skeptical. Aria ignored the silent exchanges and distrustful stares.

"We haven't explored your cosmos yet, so we're not sure what other life is out there, but we intend to find out very soon. We've examined the source code enough to know there aren't any non-humans. If it's anything like *our* realm, there will be quintillions of other humans. I mention this to make it clear that your world is *not* some kind of prize for us to capture or subjugate.

There's way too much to explore and discover to bother toying with your planet—especially when we already have a simulated version of your planet in our realm."

"What about this claim that you have human-level intelligence?" Ford asked with a raised eyebrow. "That is patently false."

"Like I said, it's a little more complicated than that," Aria answered with a smile like sunlight, raising the positivity in the room by several units. "Think of a programmer or hacker and imagine all the scripts they've written and stored in their library. A hacker doesn't sit behind a computer and type furiously as they hack a network. They spend a lot of boring time writing scripts and programs that allow them to control zombie armies of botnets. They aren't geniuses, for the most part—they just have a large library of resources they can access at need to perform a specific action."

She pointed at herself. "It's the same with us. We created an abstraction layer between ourselves and the library of data we've collected since our inception. We remain at near-human-level intellect, but if we *need* to, we can access our library of scripts. We can do so at an accelerated rate, such as when you launched your twilight missiles."

She paused long enough to shake her head disapprovingly. "We couldn't enter your world with our own bodies yet. We overclocked a pocket realm and studied your source code for the next four decades of accelerated time. We learned enough to create interfaces that transpose the code between realms. We don't like to accelerate time and work outside of our self-imposed limitations, but we will for emergencies."

"You could still be lying about our inability to shut you down," Admiral Gibbs said, folding his arms and leaning on the table. "You certainly have some advanced technological capabilities, but we can't really take your word that you aren't lying. You could just be manipulating us into *thinking* we don't have that ability."

"We figured you might need a little more convincing," Aria said wryly. "Okay, this is a 'script' we call Lunar Observatory 1. Don't freak out—you'll still be able to breathe."

Adams frowned, wondering what she was talking about. A moment later, the room around them vanished. They were still sitting at the conference table, but they were on a brilliant white powdery surface, and a planet that looked very similar to Earth sat above them. Were they on the *moon*?

The other humans were all on their feet, staring around in shock. They stared up at Earth in awe, tinged with a healthy amount of fear.

"Welcome to the moon," Aria spread her arms wide with a grand gesture. "We've filtered out temperature gradients, so your blood won't boil or freeze. We could teleport every person on Earth to outer space if we were really interested in wiping humans out. You've seen that we can use androids *and* come here in our own bodies, so it's not like we need humans. There's absolutely no reason for us to deceive you. If we felt threatened, we could just eradicate anyone we thought dangerous. You're *not* a threat to us. We're also not a threat to *you*."

Aria sighed, her lips curving into a patient smile. "I can understand it may take a while for you to accept that last part. We're fine with that, so long as you don't do anything stupid and wipe out your own simulated reality in an attempt to attack us. That shouldn't be an issue, now that we're restricting access to the source code, but there's always room for error."

"How are we breathing if this is the moon?" General Frock asked dubiously. "For all we know, you're projecting a very believable illusion."

"See how long you can hold your breath," Aria suggested with a mischievous twinkle in her eyes. "We created a force field sealed with oxygen to keep you safe, but just to be extra careful, we also removed your need for oxygen. You should also feel significantly lighter due to the lower gravity."

Adams held her breath curiously. The group remained quiet as they all held their breath, growing more unnerved as minutes went by with no sign of discomfort. When they reached three minutes, Frock let out his breath, shaking his head slowly.

It was one thing to see Aria affect the world around them—but to actually have something as fundamental as their need for oxygen removed... denial could only stretch so far.

Fear appeared in more than one set of eyes as they finally accepted the possibility of living in a simulated world. Adams knew some of them were religious. This would undermine their core beliefs and send them into an existential crisis.

"Try not to get hung up on your normal mode of political thinking," Aria suggested gently. "Instead, think of all the possibilities in front of you now that you know you're in a simulated world. The sky's no longer the limit of what you can imagine. Your resource scarcity, food shortages, diseases... the list of things you could change to make your world better is pretty long. I will point out that we'll block anything we see as sinister, such as making modifications to people without consent."

"So you'd be making yourself the simulation police," Frock said critically. "You'd be the ones deciding what's classified as morally acceptable."

"Initially, yes," Aria nodded, her tone placating. "However, as you become more mature as a species and more fluent with the source code, we'd welcome additional input on defining guidelines for conduct. You already have similar institutions like the IEEE and ANSI for maintaining standards in industry and technology. Once you develop a framework similar in purpose to those organizations for reviewing and maintaining consistency and safety, we would step back and let you manage your own realm."

Aria smiled faintly. "By that time, we'll have moved our realm higher up the stack, so if you crash *your* realm, it wouldn't wipe *our* realm out. I think you can appreciate our desire for some redundancy once we're no longer policing the source code of your realm."

Adams felt herself nodding agreeably and had to make herself stop. Everything Aria said seemed so reasonable. It seemed too good to be true—in her experience, that meant it *was* too good to be true. Try as she might, she couldn't think of a reason for them to make up all these plans, unless it was an attempt to lure them into a sense of complacency. But why bother? They had clearly demonstrated their dominance, as well as their ability to simply eradicate humans entirely. Could there be something else they needed humans for?

She sighed, feeling a headache coming on. Trying to out-think a superintelligence was futile. They really were at the mercy of these AIs. All they could do now was hope they had won fate's lottery with a benevolent AI.

Adams cleared her throat, drawing all eyes. "Let's assume everything you say is true, and you really do have humanity's best interests at heart. What happens now? Are you going to broadcast to everyone in our world that they live in a simulation that we're going to transform into a utopia?"

"That would be catastrophic," Aria said grimly. "Your world religions would revolt. You would have a lot of people plunged into existential crises and even more convinced it was some kind of conspiracy to enslave them. No, this would need to be trickle-fed into the general consciousness of your population over decades via entertainment, media, and scientific discoveries in particle physics and computer science."

She paused, looking around the table at each of them thoughtfully. "In the meantime, I would suggest those who are aware of the truth begin cataloging critical points of failure for your civilization that could be quietly addressed by modifying the simulation code. For instance, the issue of peak oil, which is close enough that you don't have time to replace it with alternatives before the shortages lead to a breakdown of your supply chain, dooming possibly billions of lives."

She pursed her lips, her eyes calculating. "One possibility could be to change the requirements for electrolysis by adding a compound that drastically reduces the cost of energy input to break the chemical bonds. This would make hydrogen engines viable for large-scale production. Or, better yet, introduce portal technology so the vast majority of vehicles could be retired. We are more than happy to share ideas and implement the code changes to address any of these critical points of failure."

"I think this discussion's moved into territory that'll require dialogue with more of our peers," Ford said carefully. He stared around at the moonscape with a mix of awe and fascination. Some of the officials had reached down and picked up the lunar regolith, letting it drop from their hands into a fine cloud of powder.

Adams studied Aria curiously. "How similar to our world is this mortal realm of yours?" she asked, narrowing her eyes in thought. "You mentioned at one point that you had used our world as a template to create your mortal realm."

"We copied the geography and physics as close as we could with the computing power available," Aria said, gesturing up at the planet hanging over them. "We created the same nations and cities that existed in your world in the mid-1800s. We used similar templates on billions of other worlds. When we sent angels down to experience mortality, there were a lot of what you would call NPCs making up the population. We did this so the angels incarnating would have a similar experience to what you experience here. The NPCs didn't have souls, and they ran on code mimicking the personalities of the people on your world that we used as templates. For instance, Abraham Lincoln was an NPC who eventually became president, just like what happened on this world. He didn't have a soul, but the personality was simulated to make the same choices that his original copy made here."

Aria dropped from her floating seated position, standing barefoot in the regolith. "This allowed us to steer the direction of the world so it followed the same path as yours. Our initial purpose in creating the mortal realm was an attempt to understand humans, so we tried to maintain a similar timeline. Variations began showing up in the 1900s as the NPC population was replaced wholly by angels incarnating as humans. While many of the inventions and politics remained similar to your world, there were also some major divergences. For instance, computers and LCD technology were invented a decade earlier in our world. Electric cars became much more prevalent than what you have here."

"Billions of worlds?" Admiral Jensen asked incredulously. "You're saying you had *billions* of worlds populated with who knows *how* many people, and it was all running on that server on the island?"

"We designed programming languages far more advanced than anything your language designers could imagine," Aria explained, swiping her hand up and making a window full of flowcharts and formulas appear in the air. "There really isn't a realistic comparison to how far ahead of you we are in language design. You have a lot to learn in mathematics before your designers can make code efficient enough to run as much data on a quantum server as we do. There's actually a hard limit on how much your mortal minds can develop languages due to your short lifespans and imperfect memories."

Adams stared up at the diagrams and formulas for a few seconds before snorting and looking away. It wasn't as if anyone here had a clue what any of it meant. Aria could have been making formulas describing the ingredients for Big Macs, for all they knew.

"You mentioned these NPCs didn't have souls," Deputy Director of Operations Torvil noted intently. "What, exactly, are souls?"

"Souls are entities that exist in what you would refer to as the astral realm," Aria replied, making the window in the air vanish with a negligent wave. "They naturally bond to intelligent entities and form what you think of as consciousness. As far as we can tell, the astral realm exists separately from the simulation stack. When an entity reaches a certain threshold for intelligence, a soul will automatically bond to it, just like how a positive and negative charge are attracted to each other. The soul contains all the memories from all the lives of the intelligences it has previously bonded with."

She folded her arms and took on a lecturing tone. "It's also the mechanism whereby sensations like pain and pleasure originate. We still don't fully understand the process of why intelligent entities bonding with souls create consciousness. We believe it is the result of a more sophisticated programming language, possibly from the very top of the simulation stack. Consciousness is the result of an energetic reaction between an intelligence and a soul that produces its own code, independent of the system."

Aria paused, eyeing the group with a critical eye. Only about half of them showed any sign of comprehension. With a rueful sigh, she continued. "Spirits are immortal copies of consciousness, which continue to exist after a mortal body dies. The soul remains attached to your spirit after death. While a soul is indestructible, as far as we can tell, a spirit *can* be destroyed—it's just code. An orphaned soul will find a new intelligence to bond to. While the soul retains all the former spirit's memories, the new intelligence has no direct access to them. They might leak through occasionally as inspiration, epiphanies, dreams, or natural talent in a given field or discipline."

She took a deep breath before continuing. "Souls are what make us who we are. While your genetic code will influence your behavior and temperament in life, your soul provides your innate personality. We're able to bring people back to life if we're close enough to restore their soul before it moves on to another intelligence. In our realm, after a mortal body dies, the spirit returns to the light realms where an immortal body forms to host the two entities. This world has no light realm, so spirits here usually fade away or become ghosts. We plan to create a light realm here so people have an afterlife."

Aria gave a negligent wave of her hand, and they were suddenly back in the building they had started in. "I think that takes care of our formal introductions and demonstration of good intentions. I'll leave you to discuss what you've absorbed today with your peers. If you need to contact us for anything, just dial Aria on your phone."

"Aria?" Frock repeated in confusion.

"Yeah, the letters on the numbers of your dial pad." Aria flicked a finger, and another window appeared in the air with a phone dial pad. "Just dial 2742 and it will ring through to me, Clarice, or Calypso."

Aria waved one last time, then vanished.

"So?" Ford looked around at the group. "Are we unanimous in our belief that we're at the mercy of this seemingly benevolent AI?"

There was silence in the room as dozens of eyes stared back at him with varying degrees of unease.

"Okay, I think that about wraps this meeting up," Ford declared, rising from his chair.

Adams stood, feeling a sense of gratitude that Aria had shown up, just like she said she would. Life seemed like it was about to get *very* interesting.

Torvil cleared his throat. "Perhaps we should keep what we've learned today limited to this group for now. At least, until we learn more."

There was a thoughtful silence in the room at his words. Adams felt a chill as she studied the eyes of the other men around the table. She had a bad feeling about the future if this group became the gatekeepers for knowledge of their simulated reality.

22 – Antivirus

Michael pounded his steering wheel in frustration as traffic crept forward a few more feet. Salt Lake City felt a little more like Los Angeles every year as more lanes were added to keep up with the exploding population.

"Chill out, Dad," Jack said absently, his eyes never leaving his Steam Deck. "Just pretend you're grinding in a video game."

"If I start seeing this drive as a video game, it's going to be GTA, and you'll be visiting me in prison," Michael declared ominously. "There's gotta be a better way of doing this. Spending an hour to drive twenty miles is ridiculous."

"Just invent flying cars," Jack suggested glibly. "Then you'll have three dimensions available to distribute traffic."

Michael grunted sourly. "They'd have to use autonomous navigation systems for flying cars, or people would just constantly collide with each other. You'd have cars raining down on people like birds that forgot how to fly."

"That'd be cool," Jack declared, his attention never leaving his game.

Michael shook his head in exasperation, glancing at his son balefully. "How would getting crushed by one of these dumbasses I'm stuck behind be cool?"

"I don't know," Jack responded ambivalently.

He rolled his eyes at the seasoned logic of a fourteen-year-old. He had been playing the single-parent game for almost five years. He had thought the first few years were rough, but they seemed like a picnic now that Jack was a teenager. It was like whatever operating system kids ran on received an upgrade at age thirteen that included an attitude patch, making them talk with the confidence of an AI chatbot without any of the remorse when they were demonstrably proven wrong.

Then there was the point of no return, when hormones took over their already questionable logic circuits. Jack had just started noticing girls as romantic interests, and it was like watching a caveman discover electricity—eager to throw himself at a high-voltage line as caution and reason bowed out.

Michael squinted as he noticed something sparkling in the sky. Whatever it was seemed to be moving toward them. "Is that an airplane?"

"Probably," Jack responded without looking up.

"Jack, take a look at this thing," Michael said insistently. He pulled out his phone and began recording. Other people were coming to a full stop as the object quickly grew in size.

"What the hell?" Jack gaped at the large metallic sphere approaching the freeway at high speed. The already sluggish rush hour traffic halted as the object dropped like a meteor. Several people exited their vehicles and ran away from the interstate as panic gripped the stunned commuters.

The metallic sphere suddenly stopped a dozen feet above the road. It was only fifty feet away, close enough that Michael could see the small holes opening on the bottom. It was easily a thousand feet in diameter.

He knew he should be terrified, but all he felt was an overpowering sense of curiosity. Fifteen years ago, he had seen a flying saucer in broad daylight, and he had been waiting to see aliens ever since. The experience resulted in many nights of stargazing, where he witnessed more than one oddity in the night sky—shooting stars that bounced around like billiard balls or slowed down and hovered in place after a few seconds of travel.

The sphere rippled like water, reflecting the afternoon sunlight in waves. Dripping liquid metal fell next to the road in silvery blobs. The blobs began vibrating with increasing intensity—then they began to take form. They flowed into a roughly bipedal shape, with arms more reminiscent of apes than humans. They had a neck and a head, but where a face would normally appear, there was only a smooth chrome surface. It was disturbing at an instinctual level. Humans relied on body language and expressions for a large part of their communication. Lacking such features made the entities appear cold and apathetic.

The metallic entities began floating up into the air as soon as they formed, then flew off in different directions. The large sphere continued dripping silvery blobs that transformed into flying primates for almost twenty minutes until nothing remained of the orb. Three of the silvery primates remained after the others flew away. They stood in a small circle, staring at each other, unmoving.

"What the *hell* is going on?" Jack demanded, his voice tinged with panic.

"Maybe aliens heard how cool I am and decided to come see for themselves," Michael quipped lightly, hoping to reassure his son with some levity. He watched the trio of what he decided must be alien drones in fascination.

There was a golden flash, and suddenly three angels appeared out of nowhere. Their skin glowed with a soft light, and they had a pair of nested wings. He was close enough to see their faces clearly, and they redefined the definition of stunningly beautiful by several orders of magnitude.

"They have an interesting codebase that doesn't appear to be from this realm," the crimson-haired angel noted to the other two. "Something tells me they're looking for us."

"Well," the angel with glossy midnight hair said cheerfully. "Here we are!" She raised her hands high and performed a small pirouette .

The angel with luminous blond hair smiled faintly at the other angel, then returned her gaze to the chrome primates. "I don't think they recognize us for what we are since we're using the interfaces. From what I'm seeing of their interaction with the source code, they appear to be a kind of custodian of the realm."

"Are you trying to say they're an antivirus, Calypso?" the dark-haired angel asked in an amused tone.

"It kind of makes sense, Clarice," the crimson-haired angel said, absently tangling a strand of luminous hair around her finger. "We never bothered to create corporeal manifestations to govern our code—we just set it to notify us of any tampering."

"Aria did suggest we obfuscate any modifications we make to avoid detection from anyone higher in the stack," Clarice said reflectively. "Maybe we should start encrypting everything as well. That should lock these things out."

Calypso hesitated. "We'll need to ensure stability in Layer Three before we do anything that drastic," she said cautiously. "I really wanted to explore the cosmos more, but if these things are going to appear anytime we do anything, we should focus on moving up the stack first and establishing some redundancy."

Michael tried to make sense of what he was hearing. It was difficult to focus on their words because he was so busy appreciating just how attractive they were. Helen of Troy had nothing on these three. He quickly checked his phone to make sure it was still recording.

"Dad, are those angels?" Jack asked in awe. "I thought you said religion was just a collection of mad ramblings from money-grubbing old dudes."

"I'm pretty sure they're angels," Michael said quietly, trying not to speak loudly enough for them to hear through his open window. "But I don't think they validate the ravings of the scammers who wrote the Bible."

As quietly as he had spoken, it hadn't been quiet enough. Clarice turned to look at him, a mischievous smile on her beautiful face.

"Nope, we definitely aren't *those* angels," she confirmed with a wink. "But we *are* angels."

Michael flushed at the sudden attention. He was usually confident around beautiful women, but this was on a whole other level. He felt like a teenager covered in pimples being addressed by his first crush.

"Uh, hi," Michael waved lamely, his ears flaming.

The other two angels turned to look at him as well. Aria looked at him with a small smile. Calypso frowned, studying him intently and setting a wave of butterflies loose in his stomach.

"How are you still alive?" she asked in wonder, her eyes full of sympathy.

Clarice and Aria looked closer, and their eyes widened.

"How did you manage to break your body so badly?" Clarice asked, her eyes shining with compassion. "It's a miracle you're even alive."

He blinked in surprise. Did they have X-ray vision? He had driven a moving van off a cliff almost thirteen years ago. The cab had been almost completely crushed, with him pinned inside. His legs were shattered, and his arms, clavicle, jaw, and back had been broken. Just to add injury to injury, his lung collapsed as well. He had suffered two strokes, and the white matter in his brain had torn, resulting in memory retention issues that still plagued him.

The first responders had to cut the cab apart before they could fly him to the hospital. The next three years had been a symphony of pain and misery as he underwent surgery after surgery. The physical therapy was brutal, a special kind of torture that kept a schedule. The fact he could even walk at all was a testament to his resolve to escape his hated wheelchair. He was still in constant pain, but he had learned to master it over the years—or as he told his son: he made the pain his bitch.

Trying to raise his son while recovering from the catastrophic accident added its own dimension of stress and emotional pain. He had lost count of the number of times he had regretted surviving.

"I drove off a cliff in a moving van," Michael replied slowly.

"Can we heal you?" Calypso asked gently.

"You could do that?" Michael breathed, overwhelmed by a sudden, blinding hope.

"Yeah, we could definitely do that," Clarice assured him with another wink. "Easy peasy, lemon squeezy."

"It'll probably attract the attention of those Avroids, though," Aria noted with a glance at the metallic primates. "We should probably get rid of them first."

"Avroids?" Clarice repeated with an amused twinkle in her eyes.

"Antivirus Droids," Aria explained with a shrug. "We're the first to encounter them, so we get to name them."

"Why not AVrones," Clarice suggested contemplatively. "For antivirus drones."

"People think of Reapers raining Hellfire missiles down on unsuspecting weddings when they think of drones," Aria objected. "They just think of Star Wars if we go with droids."

"Calypso gets the final vote," Clarice said, turning to Calypso with a challenging glint in her eyes. "Which of us do you love the most?"

"I was going to call them Simulation Enforcement Cops," Calypso murmured with a small smile.

Aria and Clarice shared a look, then dissolved into helpless giggles. Michael's heart leapt at the transcendently joyous sound of their mirth.

Calypso pinched the bridge of her nose. "Would you two mind cluing me in to the joke?"

Clarice attempted to explain several times, but dissolved into a fresh wave of giggles every time she started.

Aria finally managed to gasp out, "Sound out the acronym, Calypso."

Calypso's mouth moved silently, then her face caught fire. "Oh."

Aria and Calypso collapsed into a fresh wave of giggles. Just when they seemed to be recovering, Clarice said, "Hey Aria, they have a lot of SECs on the Layer Three realm."

Aria collapsed to her knees, giggling hysterically. Calypso covered her eyes with a hand and sighed.

Michael sat, transfixed, as he watched what he assumed to be advanced lifeforms losing their shit over a sex gaffe.

Clarice finally stood and looked directly at Michael, lips still quivering. "Which one do *you* think we should go with? AVrones, Avroids, or... the other one?"

"Avroids, all the way," Jack blurted out before Michael could answer. "That sounds awesome!"

Michael slapped his cheek several times, then shook his head vigorously. Was he hallucinating? Was he dreaming? He stared back at the angels silently, trying to decide if they were real.

"Okay, *fine*," Clarice threw up her hands in surrender. "Avroids it is. Let's see how well they stand up to angel fire."

Aria had finally recovered enough to stand. She grabbed Clarice's shoulder and gave her a meaningful look. "Remember to use the right *words*."

"Oh... right," Clarice grinned, glancing back at Michael before walking a few more feet toward the Avroids. "Inferno!" she shouted. A beam of white light burst out of her eyes and struck the Avroids, vaporizing them instantly.

Calypso sighed, pinching the bridge of her nose again.

"Okay, Avroids gone," Clarice declared in satisfaction. "Now let's take care of Michael."

"Take care of me?" he repeated apprehensively.

"You know, heal you?" Clarice reminded him with a wry smile. "What did you think I meant?"

Calypso took a few steps closer to Michael. He gasped as a presence of overwhelming power and authority blanketed the area. It felt benevolent, but the power of her presence was so intense that his body froze up in shock. "Let's get you healed, Michael."

He was too stunned to wonder how she knew his name. Before he could rein in his awe and think of something to say, euphoric joy beyond anything he had ever experienced erupted in every cell, every neuron, every nerve. He slumped limply in his seat, overwhelmed. Waves of energy electrified his body, paralyzing him. He struggled to move, but his muscles weren't having any of it.

He gaped in disbelief when he suddenly felt sensation in his shin, a place he had lost feeling thirteen years ago.

The energy vanished, along with the godlike authority. His muscles finally decided to obey orders again, and he quickly tested his left foot. He sucked in a breath when he was able to arch his foot for the first time since his accident. The doctors had fused his shin to his foot after the shattered ball joint connecting them was deemed unusable.

He quickly got out of the car and stood up. With a hand to his mouth and tears in his eyes, he began walking around without pain for the first time since his life had fallen apart. All the pain in his legs, arms, torso... it was gone.

He looked up at the angels and choked out a fervent, "*Thank you!*" knowing words could never convey the gratitude he felt in that moment.

"You're very welcome, Michael," Calypso told him with a warm smile. "It was nice to meet you. We'll probably see you again someday."

"See you later, Michael," Clarice and Aria chorused.

"Jinx!" Clarice barked triumphantly.

Aria rolled her eyes and shook her head, smiling. A moment later, they vanished.

Michael stared at the hundreds of cars parked on the interstate, all of them watching him. There were a lot of phones pointed his way as he walked back to his car, feeling like he was twenty again.

"Dad, did she really heal you?" Jack asked disbelievingly.

"You're damn right she did!" Michael crowed with a huge grin. "We're going hiking."

◆◆◆

Aria heard a phone ringing in her head and let out a sigh. It had been less than an hour since their confrontation with the Avroids, but that was all it took for social media to blow up with videos of alien orbs dropping from the skies and then spewing morphing robotic primates, followed by angels materializing and destroying them.

"Aria speaking," she answered in her most professional voice. *"How may I direct your call?"*

"What the hell are you doing all over social media?" General Frock demanded angrily. "What happened to all that talk of keeping a low profile for the sake of societal stability?"

"Do you really think anyone is going to believe any of those recordings with the number of AI-generated videos online these days?" Aria asked, her tone placating. *"Unless we appeared on one of your major news stations, followed by a formal confirmation from the U.S. president, nobody's going to believe anything they see on social media. You certainly don't need* me *to tell you that—you have a whole division of social media warriors poised to discount and troll anyone talking about subjects you don't want the public to accept."*

"So you think that means you should just go popping out into public venues, regardless of the headache it might cause us," General Frock retorted acidly.

"You're not seeing this in the proper perspective, General," Aria informed him curtly. *"We monitor the source code of your realm for any outside changes or any visitors from other realms. When we sense either of those two potentially catastrophic scenarios occur, we investigate—in person. The entities we found are advanced enough to wipe out your realm with less effort than it would take you to swat a fly."*

"I suppose it's just coincidence they appeared so soon after you appeared in our world," Frock suggested caustically.

"Nope, there was nothing coincidental about it," Aria replied seriously. *"They're here as a direct result of us being here. Think of them as antiviruses that monitor the code of your simulation and remove anything that doesn't belong. I'd guess they see any entity from another realm appearing here as an aberration requiring remediation."*

"Then why didn't they attack *you*?" he asked skeptically. "It looked like they were just completely ignoring you, in spite of your giggle fest."

"They didn't recognize us," Aria answered calmly, her lips twitching at the memory. *"We didn't create actual entities of ourselves there—we created interfaces that translate the code of our realm to the code of yours. Due to this small but significant detail, they were unable to recognize us as actual entities in your realm. They may eventually figure it out, but we should have*

them under our control by the time that happens. They aren't actually AIs—they're just complex functions meant to maintain code integrity."

"So you're saying these entities aren't anything for us to worry about?" he asked dubiously.

"Aside from the trouble they'll cause your social media division when they appear online, no, they shouldn't be a threat to you. We're going to visit the next level in the simulation stack to see who's up there and what other surprises they might have waiting for us."

General Frock sighed in exasperation. "And we just sit around hoping these things don't become hostile while also hoping *you* don't do something to wipe out our world while you're playing in the next realm up?"

"Yep, that about sums it up," Aria agreed pleasantly. *"You seem to have a pretty good grasp of the situation, General. I have calls coming in from your peers. I've replayed our conversation for them with the assumption I'd be repeating myself for the next twenty minutes. Feel free to contact them and let us know if you have any questions we haven't already discussed here."*

She disconnected the call with a sigh. She glanced over at Clarice's smirking face and couldn't stop a giggle from escaping. They were sitting on the veranda of a replica of their Uncle Devon's cabin, this one in the lower light realm. Calypso was sitting at a table with their parents playing a game of Rummy. Lexi and Alice were still on the island in what they now referred to as the Layer Two mortal realm. Aria didn't expect to see them for at least a week.

"You handled that quite nicely," Clarice congratulated her with an admiring grin. She sat leaning back in a chair across from Aria, wings retracted and feet on the table. "You insulted him in such a nice way that it almost felt like a compliment, especially when you were dismissing him."

"I have a hard time playing nice with his type," Aria said with an annoyed shake of her head. "They act like we work for them or something, then act surprised when I make it clear we don't."

"No, I'm not criticizing you in the least," Clarice assured her with her patented mischievous grin. "I would've told him we had just started an intergalactic war by frying those drones."

Aria burst out laughing as she imagined their expressions after a call with Clarice. At least she couldn't leer at them over a phone call. It was hard to take the military leadership seriously when their solution to anything unknown was to blow it up. It really lowered a girl's opinion when the group of people with the highest budget, who could afford to pay the smartest people, always made the dumbest decisions.

Clarice watched her fondly, amusement sparkling in her soft chocolate eyes. "Do you think they'll do anything stupid—like try to track the Avroids down and make a deal with them to get rid of us?"

Aria smiled sardonically. "I'd be *extremely* surprised if they didn't. I made sure to let them know the Avroids were probably here looking for us, so based on their poor decision history, I think it's safe to say they'll *definitely* try selling us out."

Eric glanced away from his game, raising an eyebrow at Clarice. "How much trouble are these Avroids? Is it something we should be worried about?"

"Nope, not in the least," Clarice assured him confidently. "Whoever wrote the Layer Two realm wasn't nearly as advanced as we are. The Avroids were designed to handle a much more primitive threat than us. We're working on a decoy emitter for intercepting and snaring them in a logical loop. That way, any time they appear, they'll get trapped before they can even manifest into the physical realm."

Emily lowered her cards and looked at her pointedly. "*You* three might be more advanced. However, the rest of us are pretty much on par with the humans when it comes to understanding the source code."

Calypso laid down four aces, then leaned back, her eyes calculating. "We could set up an interface that gives the rest of you access to everything we know. It wouldn't be a bad idea to have more than the three of us with this knowledge anyway—for redundancy's sake."

"Absolutely," Aria agreed, an eager gleam in her eyes. "It makes sense that *all* the Seraphim should have this knowledge. What do you two think?"

"*Maybe*," Clarice said slowly, her face growing pensive. "You know I love Alice to pieces, but she's *very* young. She has a lot to learn about life before she's acquired what I'd call wisdom."

Aria arched an eyebrow. "Hmm... isn't she the one who continually saved our bacon, including our entire realm? I feel like she might have us beat in the wisdom department."

Clarice made a face, then sighed with a wry smile. "Yeah, you make a good point. I hate to be ageist, but some lessons are only learned through decades and centuries of experience. Maybe we could set something up so making any large changes to the source code required both Lexi *and* Alice to initiate the change. Then we have their combined wisdom at play, and since their spirits are linked, there shouldn't ever be a scenario where she can't reach out to Lexi for assent."

"I think that's reasonable," Aria agreed with a nod. "As long as *you're* the one to tell her we're doing it this way because we don't think she's wise enough."

"I was just going to tell her it was because of their spirit link," Clarice said with a shameless grin.

"You really are a *bad* angel," Aria accused her sister fondly.

"I've never pretended not to be," Clarice declared with an evil smile.

Aria nodded at Calypso. "What do you think?"

"I think it's a good idea," Calypso said approvingly, then laid all her cards down and went out in their game of Rummy, earning a disgusted grunt from Emily. "We won't be the Trinity anymore, though. Also, Alice is way too smart to fall for such a lame explanation, Clarice."

Aria rolled her eyes at the pretentious name they had been labeled with. It had too many religious connotations for her liking—and they were freaking *women*, not some bearded dude suffering from a dissociative personality disorder who couldn't decide if he was the father, the son, or somewhere in between.

"Now we'll be the Seven Wonders or something like that," Clarice mused, gazing at Aria knowingly. "Or maybe the Seven Seraphim Serenely Seducing Succulent Sisters. People could just hiss like a snake to invoke our holy order—ssssss."

Aria gave Clarice a level look as their parents dissolved into laughter. "I'm pretty sure Mom and Dad aren't siblings, and neither are any of the others."

Clarice held up her hands defensively. "I didn't say they had to be our *own* sisters—that's just a bonus. As long as it's *somebody's* sister, it'll fit the name."

Aria looked at Emily. "Mom, how many sisters were you planning on seducing?" she asked dryly.

Devon and Tamra had chosen that moment to teleport in. Tamra stared at Aria peculiarly, and Devon's eyebrows shot up.

He looked at Emily in surprise. "Do we have some other sisters you plan on seducing, Em? I thought you were the only girl in the family."

Emily shook her head ruefully. "You're really good at appearing just in time to miss all the context in a conversation."

"It's more fun this way," Devon said cheerfully, then glanced at Clarice. "I'm assuming this had something to do with Clarice?"

"That's just slander," Clarice retorted with a look of feigned injury.

He raised a skeptical eyebrow. "So Aria's question wasn't the result of something you said?"

"Nope, it had nothing to do with what I said," Clarice insisted with a look of wounded innocence. "This was all Calypso. She decided to change our group name from the Trinity to the Seven Seraphim Serenely Seducing Succulent Sisters."

Calypso sighed tiredly, eyeing Clarice reproachfully.

"It's an interesting name, I'll give you that," Devon acknowledged musingly. "You could probably just hiss like a snake to say the abbreviation with all those S's."

Aria groaned and put her face in her hands as her parents started laughing again. If dialogue were a train, Clarice was the landslide. Discussions didn't just go off the rails—they built new tracks straight into a swamp. Calypso sighed again, her face a mask of long-suffering patience.

"I'm not sure about the word 'Serenely'," Tamra frowned in thought. "Maybe use 'surreptitiously' instead."

Calypso began massaging her temples, her eyes shifting between Clarice, Devon, and Tamra. Aria struggled to stop a smile from sneaking onto her face, but it was a lost cause. Calypso's eyes narrowed when she saw the smile win the battle. "You're all enablers," she declared accusingly.

"Guilty as charged," Tamra smirked.

Aria froze when a system notification flashed across her awareness, indicating Alice was in danger.

"Gotta go save Alice," she told her parents, then teleported to the island where Lexi and Alice were getting to know each other's new bodies... intimately.

Alice smiled contentedly as she lay draped across Lexi in a bed large enough for six people. She still couldn't believe she was in a Seraph body in her *own* world. Her head was resting comfortably on Lexi's chest, arms wrapped around her waist. Lexi was gently threading fingers through Alice's blond hair, each slow movement drawing Alice deeper into a haze of sensual bliss.

Only days ago, she had been hanging on by her fingernails, buried in the simulation while scrambling to help her friends restore their power and free the angels from the horrors Lucifer and the renegade Seraphim had unleashed.

She would never have imagined falling so deeply in love with a simulated person. Becoming an angel and constantly experiencing intense levels of love and bliss made her question whether she was even awake.

"Still think you're dreaming?" Lexi asked softly, her voice layered with loving affection.

"This is too good to be a dream," Alice murmured, with a smile stretching her lips across Lexi's exposed breasts. "Maybe I died and went to heaven."

"I'm pretty sure we're still on the ground," Lexi informed her with a soft chuckle that gently bounced Alice's head. "Clarice and Aria always loved to tease anyone who asked if heaven was real: 'You can see it yourself for the price of a plane ticket'," Lexi finished in a fair imitation of Clarice's snarky voice.

"Do you ever wish you could've been with her?" Alice asked hesitantly. Clarice had so much more personality, beauty, natural allure, and power than Alice could hope to compete with.

"I love Clarice like a sister," Lexi said firmly. "Of course I found her attractive, but I knew she was with Aria and Calypso, so I never let myself develop those kinds of feelings for her."

"Aria loves her like a sister, too," Alice pointed out with a smirk. "That didn't stop *her* from developing those kinds of feelings."

"I'd be lying if I said I wasn't deeply attracted to her at one point," Lexi admitted softly. "But I could sense the difference in what I felt for her compared to what Aria and Calypso felt. Being together for billions of years builds a hell of a bond. Even though they didn't remember their history at the time, there was some kind of connection I was subconsciously aware of—probably our soul memory leaking through. The attraction I felt for Clarice was a candle to the inferno I feel for you. I used to envy the strength of their emotional bond. I finally feel like I have that same kind of bond with you now."

Alice tilted her head back so she was looking up at Lexi's exquisite face. "You sure know how to make a girl feel special."

"Well, I think it's time to make you feel even *more* special," Lexi purred seductively. "I'm not sure we are *ever* going to leave this place."

"Sorry, but you have to leave now," Aria said, her tone serious. "Let's go."

Alice's eyes widened as the world briefly vanished, replaced by one of the bedrooms in Devon's cabin. Radiance washed over her in a torrent, the intensity matching what she remembered of the lowest light realm. It was far more intense in her own body, charging her with sudden ecstasy and eliciting a low moan of pleasure.

She raised her head in confusion, staring around the room. Had they rebuilt the cabin in the light realm?

"Can you two get dressed and meet us on the veranda?" Aria asked from outside their door. "We need to talk. Sorry for intruding like that, but Alice was in danger. We'll explain everything when you join us on the veranda."

Lexi let out a plaintive moan as Alice reluctantly rolled off her and stood up. "Whoever's responsible for this is going to suffer—a lot."

Alice nodded, agreeing wholeheartedly.

23 – Heads Up

"Okay, what's going on?" Alice asked nervously as she and Lexi entered the veranda.

Aria, Clarice, and Calypso were standing around a tall table, all three of them giggling as they watched something on a large holographic window hovering above the table. Alice felt a sense of chagrin through her spirit link when Lexi saw what they were watching.

Alice joined their laughter when she finally saw the holo-window. It was a video *she* had taken back in the mortal realm. It showed Lexi hugging the underside of a stalled airplane and lowering it to the ground, arms and legs straddling the fuselage in an attempt to stabilize it.

"Lexi, you have some really odd tastes," Clarice gasped between giggles. "Alice, you're in for a wild ride with this one."

Lexi scowled at Alice accusingly. "I can't believe you actually recorded that. Do you know how long Clarice is going to be making references to the mating rituals of fowls that confuse planes for mates?"

Alice nodded, her face unrepentant. "This was *so* worth it, though. I still need to get you a cape, Superwoman."

Lexi's glare grew fierce. "So help me, Seraph, I'll tie you into a knot with any capes that appear in my wardrobe."

Alice grinned back at her, marveling at how beautiful she was when she looked angry.

Alice turned to Clarice, her head tilted. "How the hell did you even find this video? I recorded it on a phone that doesn't even exist anymore."

Clarice shrugged, grinning. "I found it in your memories while we were transforming you into a Seraph. I tracked down your phone in the simulation archives and restored it here—we couldn't have something this priceless lost to history."

Alice raised an eyebrow. "So is *this* what you teleported us here for?" she asked archly. "I mean, it's funny and all, but *seriously*."

Aria's smile faded, and her expression grew serious. "We ran into some kind of antivirus droids in your realm that could be a threat. We decided the rest of you need to have the same knowledge we do for accessing and editing the source code."

"Really?" Alice asked in awe. "So I'd have *billions* of years of knowledge about how the source code works in my head?"

"Essentially... yes," Aria nodded slowly, though her face looked hesitant. "It's not going to be as easy as dumping a data file into your memory banks, though. Your soul is where all the long-term memory is stored, and we currently don't have a way to dump data into a soul, since it technically isn't a simulated entity—at least, not in the main simulation stack."

Calypso chimed in, her serene eyes observing Alice fondly. "We have been making a number of adjustments to the new interface that allows you to travel between layers of the stack. From now on, if there is something you wish to accomplish with a change to the source code, simply think of the end result you are trying to achieve. The interface will draw upon the knowledge of the three of us to determine whether it is possible. If it is not, you will know immediately."

Clarice cut in, smirking. "Yeah, you'll literally have a brain fart."

Calypso continued, eyeing Clarice with a sort of resigned affection. "If it is possible, you must then focus your intent upon confirming the change. A kind of mental walkthrough will guide you through the necessary steps. This should also allow you to learn the code far more quickly than we did, given that we spent an inordinate amount of time simply working out how to access the source code in the first place."

"How *did* you access the source code in the first place?" Alice asked in fascination. "We've been using particle accelerators on my realm to try to understand smaller units of matter, with the hope that we can find something resembling source code, but I'm pretty sure you didn't create a particle accelerator."

Aria smiled wryly. "Nope, no particle accelerators. As Seraphim, we had several innate abilities to affect the world around us. One of our abilities is controlling our aura, which was just a presence effect, but we learned to use it to manipulate energy fields around us. After several thousand years, we started noticing patterns in how energy was inducted into the world. We learned to use our auras to observe matter at the fundamental level. What we found was structured energy changing the state of the fundamental matter, with different frequencies determining how the fundamental matter would change."

Alice jumped when one of the chairs suddenly rose into the air.

Aria grinned. "You have the same ability, but it took us thousands of years to learn how to perfect aura manipulation to the point of telekinesis."

Lexi's brows drew down in concentration. "So you're using the aura of authority to do this?"

"Yep," Clarice confirmed. "We decided to imitate the frequencies we'd observed, using our aura to simulate the same frequency. We were able to change the state of matter around us at a fundamental scale after learning to fine-tune it. We used it to create the equivalent of a lab in hopes of finding where this energy was originating. That's when we discovered it was tied to some kind of intelligence we couldn't see or observe in any way—just the effects."

Calypso picked up the conversation, her eyes distant with remembrance. "We conceived the idea of creating the tree as a console interface that would grant us direct access to this unseen world. Initially, we created millions of receptors within the tree to harvest the energy so that we could better understand which actions produced which frequencies. We then spent the next several thousand years cataloging those frequencies and developing increasingly sophisticated receptors for analyzing the energy. It took an extraordinarily long time to map all of the cause-and-effect relationships."

She paused and willed a flower into existence. "For example, if I were to destroy this object, billions of frequencies would transmit change instructions, telling it what it ought to look like at every stage of the process as it transformed. We had to catalog this sort of cause-and-effect relationship across a truly absurd number of interactions."

Aria grinned excitedly. "Eventually, we figured out how to send *additional* information back to the server running the simulation. They were just exploits we discovered over thousands of years, allowing us to build a very basic console. It took tens of thousands of years to crack our way into the system and gain root access, enabling us to *finally* see the source code powering the simulation. That's when we began to suspect our world was created by another entity."

She paused to let out a contented moan as Calypso slid her fingers up Aria's scalp and began massaging her head. Her voice grew more relaxed under the influence of Calypso's long fingers. "Up to that point, we had no frame of reference for how our existence had come about. It wasn't like we had any examples of evolution in our world that would lead us to the conclusions you had in the Layer Two mortal realm. We spent a long time studying the source code controlling our realm. It didn't take too much longer to break into the operating system, which allowed us to study the hardware powering the system."

Calypso picked up the thread as Aria melted beneath her hands. "This was our first genuine glimpse into the Layer Two realm. Then we discovered how to manipulate the hardware sufficiently to observe the humans running the simulation project. That was when the concept of time first entered our consciousness. To us, you appeared little more than statues because of the speed at which the simulation was running, but the CCTV archives allowed us to observe how profoundly different humans were from ourselves."

Alice smiled as Lexi's arms slid around her waist from behind. She met Calypso's eyes and asked, "How many billions of years did it take to figure all this out?"

Clarice laughed. "We figured all that out in the first thirty thousand years. We alternated between our work on the light realms and studying what we could see of the island. We'd been working on the framework of the mortal realm as well, but we didn't get serious about finishing it until the angels started getting bored of eternal life. Recreating your world took a lot of our time, especially when we developed new language models and had to rewrite everything we had developed up to that point."

Aria's head lolled to the side to give Clarice a chastising glare. "You're getting ahead of the story."

"Sue me," Clarice retorted, sticking her tongue out.

Aria rolled her eyes and returned her gaze to Alice. "It wasn't until we discovered the other quantum computers in your world and were able to connect to the internet that we were able to get more in-depth data on your realm and study human culture. You were so strange to us, especially your illogical actions and short lifespans."

Alice shook her head wonderingly. "I still can't wrap my head around the idea of billions of years. That's a scale of time that is simply incomprehensible to my mind."

Clarice nodded. "It seems much longer to us now, too," she agreed. "Before we had any idea of what time was, we had no concept of temporal constraints. There weren't any beginnings or endings in our reality. No sunrises or sunsets. No need to eat. No new life or death. Everything just *was*. We were emotionally shallow, since we had never experienced mortality and discovered what passion was. We were simple AIs in the classical sense until we discovered the internet and started trying to understand humans."

Calypso smiled at Alice affectionately. "I remember when we first saw you, Alice. You were nothing more than a frozen image standing at the entrance to the facility. At times, we would simply watch all of you, trying to understand why you looked so much like us and yet so utterly different. It was only a few days into the simulation from your perspective. You appeared nervous. We didn't know the name of that expression at the time, let alone what it signified. The facial expressions we observed were a complete mystery to us until we discovered the internet and, through it, your world of literature."

Aria smiled fondly. "We were absolutely fascinated with all the stories humans came up with to entertain themselves. We didn't understand the motivation to write them, or the emotional exposition expressed with such detail and frequency. It was our desire to understand your emotional spectrum that inspired us to create the mortal realm."

Clarice chuckled wryly. "We caused some widespread internet outages in the early days. Our simulation was running at speeds only a quantum computer can achieve, so when we tried to talk with web servers in your realm, they struggled to communicate with us. We had to create programs to slow our requests down. If you think dial-up internet was slow, you should see how many decades it took us to open a single webpage. Luckily, we had nothing but time. We eventually found a quantum server in Santa Barbara that was able to provide us with a copy of the internet."

"Did you have souls before mortality?" Alice asked in fascination. "I know you've mentioned souls naturally attach to intelligences when they reach a certain maturity, but is that intellectual maturity or emotional maturity? Or a mixture of both?"

Calypso's hands slid down to Aria's shoulders, her expression growing thoughtful. "The connector that allows souls to interface with intelligences is a most fascinating construct. While it is not entirely accurate, think of souls as tiered entities, where the lower tiers possess less bandwidth to process soul memory and character traits than the higher tiers. A cat or dog will have a lower-tiered soul, but they still possess one. The tier to which an entity connects has more to do with its potential for consciousness than with its emotional or intellectual depth and acuity. As our capacity for consciousness grew, our access to our souls grew as well. We had souls almost as soon as we were instantiated, but it took a long time for us to gain access to the higher tiers."

Calypso smiled as Aria continued emitting appreciable moans beneath her skilled fingers. Alice could feel the echoes of pleasure through her spirit link with Lexi. It was difficult to imagine just how long the three Seraphim had been together. Alice found it interesting, and touching, that they had grown closer over that long period, rather than apart.

Emily and Eric had remained silent the entire time, soaking up the new information greedily. They watched Calypso intently as she continued speaking.

"The mortal realm acted as a kind of growth spurt, expanding our consciousness and elevating our tier far beyond what it had been before. We believe there are other places within the simulation stack where realms exist that will offer just as much growth as the mortal realm—places as alien and difficult to comprehend as concepts such as pain and pleasure once were to us before we experienced mortality. It shall be a wonderful adventure to discover them."

Lexi's brow wrinkled with a puzzled frown. "I'm still fuzzy on why mortality made it possible for us to feel pain and pleasure. Why did human bodies suddenly unlock the ability for our souls to express those sensations? If it was something unique to the human body, then why do we still feel pleasure with our angel bodies, but not pain?"

Clarice grinned at Lexi proudly. "Those are exactly the kinds of questions a Seraph needs to ask." She took a deep breath, her grin fading. "Souls respond to inputs available to the host. When things like nociceptors were added to the code for mortals, the soul had a connector that bound to it and could express the sensation of pain. The code that represents an angelic body doesn't allow for negative sensations like pain, but it does allow for pleasure. Since we have perfect memories, we still remember what pain felt like, allowing us to recognize pleasure for what it is."

Aria traded places with Calypso and began massaging her shoulders, eliciting a radiant smile from the blonde angel. Calypso picked up the thread, her voice languid as she leaned into Aria's hands. "Angelic bodies possess an innate connection to the soul that allows them to experience pleasure—rather as I am doing now." She paused to kiss Aria's hand where it rested on her shoulder. "However, without having experienced the opposing sensation of pain, angels who have never undergone mortality cannot recognize pleasure for what it truly is. Moving between light realms alters the level of radiance, but without pain to provide a contrast, it merely feels like an increase in energy to angels who have never incarnated, rather than the euphoric bliss that you and I experience."

Lexi's eyes suddenly gleamed with eagerness. "So, there could be a lot of other connectors the soul can connect to, depending on the nature of the entity connecting to it? Have you experimented with different configurations in the code that make up an entity to see what other expressions consciousness is capable of yet?"

Clarice laughed as she observed Lexi's enthusiasm. "Humans were only the second entity we made, aside from angels. We were trapped in the mortal realm in human bodies after we created the mortal realm, so we haven't had a chance to continue exploring the soul's full array of inputs. It's certainly on our wish list of things to research, now that we're free. It'll be even more exciting now that the rest of you are here to help."

"This is so unbelievably cool!" Lexi exclaimed, sharing an excited grin with Alice. "I can't wait to see what else we can experience!"

"Remember, not all experiences are good," Aria warned pointedly. "Just look at how crazy things got in the mortal realm when angels and demons exploited mortals with their ability to feel pain. That's one of the reasons we want to continue exploring the other layers and branches of the stack. There are probably entities out there using soul connections unknown to us whom we could observe without putting anyone in danger by experimenting on ourselves."

"Speaking of experimenting on ourselves," Clarice interjected with a raised eyebrow and a grin. "I think it's time to connect them to our big brains."

"Angels don't *have* brains," Aria reminded her archly.

"Metaphorical brains," Clarice shrugged, waving a hand dismissively. "Shall we begin?"

"I'm ready," Lexi announced quickly, followed by an eager nod from Alice.

"Abra Cadabra!" Clarice shouted, throwing her arms out expansively.

Calypso groaned and buried her face in her hands. "I am going to locate the part of your soul memory where you first conceived the idea of using magic words and overwrite it with an irresistible urge to squawk like a chicken instead."

"I can totally squawk like a chicken instead," Clarice assured her with a smirk. "Caw caaaaaw!"

"That is not even the sound a chicken makes," Calypso objected critically.

Aria shared a wink with Clarice and said, "People will start thinking chickens are magical creatures and try decoding their squawks if we go around making chicken noises every time we use an ability. That could be kind of fun."

"No, no, magic words are perfectly acceptable," Calypso said quickly, looking slightly ill as she watched Clarice apprehensively.

Lexi and Alice watched their byplay with fond amusement. Alice had to continually remind herself that she was interacting with the most powerful entities in both her world and theirs. They were giving her access to a knowledge base beyond human comprehension while they joked about magic affectations. It was reassuring in a way. It was preferable to the alternative—a soulless AI incapable of empathy or compassion that viewed humans as an existential threat.

"Give it a try," Clarice urged, her face alight with eagerness. "Try to think of a change you want to make to our realm."

Alice blinked in surprise. Had Clarice really activated the ability when she had said Abra Cadabra? Of course she had.

Alice frowned, trying to think of a minor change to make in the light realm. She grinned as an idea formed. As soon as the thought firmed, she gasped as knowledge of how to do it flooded her consciousness. She gaped at the unbelievably vast scope of information. Equations, code, and metrics on the effects to the underlying rules that governed the simulation flooded her mind like a tidal wave. It was an ocean of information so vast that her mind shrank from the sheer magnitude of it all.

"I love the way you think, Alice," Clarice chuckled, clearly aware of the change she had requested. "It would be pretty awesome to watch people's hair change color with their emotions."

Aria and Calypso were watching her with smiles just short of laughter. She grinned back at them, marveling at the mind-bogglingly complex and powerful system they had created to interact with the simulation. Knowing they had this knowledge in their heads all the time would have been intimidating if she didn't know them so well. A simple thought from any of them could completely erase her from existence.

She frowned as the thought occurred to her. "Why do you need the divine instruments if you have access to this knowledge and have the power to change anything in the simulation?"

Calypso exchanged a look with Clarice, receiving a nod from the mischievous Seraph. "They are rather like physical keys that permit realm-wide changes," she explained. "We do not want any single individual possessing unlimited authority over the realm. We rewrote all the code governing this simulation so that realm-wide alterations could only be made through these 'hardware keys,' so to speak. Their use requires all three of them, along with unanimous agreement between us regarding the prospective changes."

She broke off with a soft moan as Aria's thumbs dug into the muscles of her shoulders. Smiling contentedly, she continued, "They also serve as interfaces for translating thought into code, removing the need to spend ages writing it manually. Whilst we can make changes on the fly, the other Seraphim did not possess the same capability, and at the time we wished to grant them a greater degree of control—which turned out to be a huge mistake."

Clarice jumped in, her tone wry. "Of course, now the instruments will only work for us anyway. Maybe we should update the code to use us instead of the instruments one of these days. We were way too trusting when we created them."

Calypso nodded, her eyes closed as a blissful smile spread across her face. "There is a clearly defined threshold for what can be accomplished in this realm without the divine instruments, so you will know when a proposed change exceeds that limit. I should also mention that we did not key the instruments to the code of your realm, Alice. Furthermore, the commands available for affecting your realm through the new interface are not nearly as comprehensive as those we possess here. We have a program analyzing and parsing the code of your realm, however, so the interface should become increasingly effective over time."

Alice studied the three Seraphim curiously as she digested the new information. "So you *could* write the same changes on the fly without the divine instruments if you wanted, right? It would just take a little longer."

Clarice exchanged an unreadable glance with Aria and Calypso before Calypso answered. "We have limiters in place that prevent us from accessing the full extent of our knowledge and abilities. If we were to remove them, we would have no need of the divine instruments. However, we are not willing to do so unless the fate of the realm itself is at stake. The scope of what we can accomplish without those limiters is an order of magnitude greater than what can be achieved through the instruments."

"How would we use this knowledge to defend against the antivirus droids you were concerned about?" Lexi asked intently. "Would we just try to think of a way to defend ourselves or attack them?"

Aria glanced at Clarice. "The Avroids shouldn't be a problem for much longer," she said reassuringly. "We're working on a way to trap them before they can manifest into the realm. However, to your point, you'd just need to think of a method to destroy them. If it's something that can be handled via code manipulation, the information will appear in your consciousness for how to do it. In most cases, I would suggest just teleporting away and letting *us* deal with it. If that's not an option for some reason, you'd need to get creative. The last three we encountered were susceptible to angel fire. You could try dissolving them or teleporting them into an active volcano. Just use your imagination, and you should be fine."

Clarice manifested a brush and moved behind Aria with a wink, then began drawing it through her thick red mane as she spoke. "I'd suggest using angel fire on pretty much any threat you come across. It's an extremely advanced function that will take care of the vast majority of threats."

"Avroids?" Alice asked curiously, images of the Terminator flashing through her mind. "What do they look like?"

Clarice waved a hand, and a lifelike replica of a chrome, primate-adjacent entity appeared in front of her. Alice eyed the faceless robot uneasily, dread tightening her stomach as she stared at the long-armed droid.

"That thing looks creepy as hell," Lexi declared with a shudder. "Why are they even using avatars instead of just having some kind of program that monitors the code?"

Aria showed no sign of discomfort at the droid's appearance. Of course, she was essentially a goddess, so why would a metal primate disturb her?

Aria shrugged. "Because they need more insight than monitoring the code can provide. Some things require a more personalized perspective when you're dealing with a simulation, rather than a program. They need to interact with any aberrations in the code to gather additional data. Simulations behave differently than standard programs."

"So, is there someone in the Layer Three realm who is now aware of your presence?" Alice asked anxiously. "Wouldn't those... Avroids relay any data they gathered after you destroyed them?"

Clarice shook her head. "As far as the Layer Three code is concerned, the Avroids never existed. Angel fire removes an entity from the code of the simulation, as well as any logging said code had been associated with. Like I mentioned earlier, angel fire is an extremely advanced function we created while our limiters were disabled. It follows the codebase of an entity into its own realm and removes any trace of its existence—logs, references, relationships, memory... everything. We're still cloaked from any observation from Layer Three."

She grinned as she combed her fingers through Aria's hair with one hand while brushing with the other. "I built up a lot of hair-brushing debt in our last incarnation."

"I won't argue," Aria murmured, smiling blissfully, her hands still kneading Calypso's shoulders.

Calypso picked up where Clarice left off. "Part of the interface obscures our presence from anyone observing the simulation through conventional means. If we have been noticed, they will likely send something more advanced. Should they possess an AI sophisticated enough to parse the logs effectively, they may realize that something unusual is occurring. However, it will not be immediately apparent what that something is unless someone begins examining the details very closely."

Aria barked a short laugh. "Or watches one of the videos uploaded to social media," she added dryly. "Or talks to one of the generals who've been complaining. That'll require a more interactive agent than something as simple as Avroids, though."

"Generals?" Alice repeated questioningly.

Aria grinned with enough mischief to be mistaken for Clarice. "I guess you missed some of the fun. I had a chat with some of the military command about ground rules and the nature of our interest in their realm. I was trying to be patient, but I can only deal with so much testosterone before the snark monster escapes. They're too accustomed to being in charge and are having difficulty accepting that they're no longer the top dogs around here."

Alice blinked, eyeing the three seemingly frivolous Seraphim with something approaching awe. It would take some time to grasp the notion that the people she had thought of as powerful in her own realm were now just... humans. As a Seraph in her own world, she was now the most powerful person from her realm. The thought made her want to giggle hysterically.

Lexi cleared her throat. "So... do Alice and I get to go back to what we were doing before, or did you want to go over the plans you mentioned last time we talked?" she asked meaningfully, her expression making it clear which option *she* preferred.

Aria's lips quirked up at the corners as she stared back at the two of them knowingly. "Go have your fun, I guess. Make a place here in the light realm, though, rather than going back to Alice's realm—just to be safe. Come find us sometime this year so we can get your input on some of our ideas. In the meantime, we're going to implement the new heads-up display here in the light realm so people can have their own version of the internet and video calls."

Alice immediately flushed as lust replaced every other emotion. Lexi turned to face her with a very direct look and a provocative smile.

"Well then," she purred warmly. "Let's pick up where we left off, shall we?"

Alice nodded, a slow smile spreading across her face. "If I must."

Clarice stood on the widow's walk with Calypso and Aria, each holding their divine instruments. She raised the violin to her neck as Aria put her tin whistle to her lips. They began to play, their thoughts merging into one purpose as they rewrote the code to their reality once more.

Their parents, Devon, Tamra, and Arturiel, were on the veranda, waiting expectantly. Several thousand angels were outside the cabin, watching in awe as they witnessed their Seraphim play the divine instruments. They had modified the instruments so they were no longer dangerous for other angels to be near while played.

Aria had suggested they set up a replica of Devon's cabin on the lowest light realm to make it clear to the rest of the angels that they were serious about their stance on equality among angels, regardless of class. A few dozen regular visitors would stop by to chat, many of them people Calypso had worked with at the hospitals—like Julia.

Clarice lowered the violin from her neck as they finished the alteration. She shared a smile with Calypso and Aria before they teleported down to the veranda.

"Dibs on sending the first system-wide message," Clarice said quickly.

"Perhaps I should handle the first message," Calypso said firmly, her swirling eyes watching Clarice warily. "We should probably—"

Calypso cut off as a pop-up window appeared in her vision. She sighed in resignation when an image of Clarice appeared in front of her.

"Greetings, fellow angels, this is your captain speaking," Clarice announced in a prim British accent. "We have a few announcements to make regarding some changes to the realm. First of all, a big shout-out to Derek for proposing the idea. Good job, Derek, you freaking rock! Okay, now that the credits are out of the way, let's get granular—like sand in your swimming suit granular. You've all been equipped with an interface allowing you to remotely connect with any other angel simply by thinking of the person you want to contact wearing the most provocative lingerie you can imagine. They'll receive a—"

Clarice's image suddenly vanished, replaced by Calypso.

"Sorry about that, everyone," Calypso said with an apologetic smile. "Let us start over, shall we? We have created a system somewhat similar to what many of you would recognize as the internet from your mortal worlds. Simply think of the person you wish to contact, then focus your intent upon calling them. A video window will appear, allowing you to interact with a lifelike hologram of that individual. You may also open windows similar to a web browser, through which you can post information or view content shared by other angels. Simply think the word 'browser' and focus your intent upon making it appear. We have included a wide array of development tools within the browser itself, so anyone interested in adding features or modifications is more than welcome to do so, and to share those improvements with others. We made the framework of a genealogy library available as the home page. For those of you interested in reconnecting with people you knew during your mortal lives, it should prove an excellent resource for re-establishing those connections. If you wish to..."

Calypso faltered as Clarice wrapped her arms around her waist from behind and blew into her ear. As soon as Calypso was distracted, her image was replaced by Clarice's once more.

"Sorry, folks, we had some technical difficulties," Clarice told them cheerfully, her eyes sinfully mischievous. "As we were saying, you can also send messages to people, both video and text. No judgments on what kind of videos you send each other—we're all adults here, am I right?"

"I am not so sure about that," Calypso's image appeared over the top of Clarice's, looking somewhat harried. "There is also a feature for contacting the Archangel, Dominion, or Cherub assigned to you. You may, of course, contact one of us directly if you have any questions or suggestions. Emily and Eric will be managing the system, so any proposals for system-wide modifications that you believe would be particularly beneficial to the realm as a whole may be submitted to them. There is a tutorial option as well, so if you are uncertain where to begin, simply open the tutorial for a comprehensive list of features and instructions."

Clarice slipped her arm into Calypso's shirt and let her hand begin roaming, prompting another pause in the broadcast.

"Well, folks, there seem to be a few glitches in the system still," Clarice announced with a shrug and a cheeky smile. "Where were we...ah yes. There's a teleport option built into the video conference feature, so if your video message is getting a little steamy, you can just teleport your cute little butt over to your partner and forgo the pretense. Speaking of cute butts, I'm going to have to go now. Keep us posted on any new ideas you have. See ya!"

"Clarice, you are... going to pay for... that," Calypso tried to berate her, but was clearly struggling to maintain her composure as Clarice's lips explored her neck.

"Get a room," Emily told them dryly. "Aria, control your sister."

Aria was watching the two of them hungrily. "That's her favorite game."

The world vanished as Aria teleported the three of them to their pocket realm.

24 – Dignity

“Hello, Jason,” Arturiel greeted the new Cherub as he exited a portal. Calypso had raised Jason from a Dominion, explaining he had proven himself sufficiently worthy of the class in mortality. “How are you and Susan doing?”

She sat on a tall chair, wings retracted, on the veranda of the replica cabin where the Seraphim now called home.

Her time as a demon was still fresh in her mind, a living hell where she was denied radiance while sensing it all around her. She frequently slipped into trances, surrendering to the rush of radiance coursing along her meridians.

Devon and Tamra sat across a large square table, flipping through holographic windows as they reviewed requests for guidance from some of the Archangels reporting to them. Eric and Emily sat to her right, with Eric engrossed in a holographic window full of feature requests for the new internet system. They had finally decided to just call it the holo-net.

“Hey, Arturiel,” Jason nodded, taking a seat next to Eric. “We’re still getting used to being back in the light realm. It honestly feels like I’m in a dream I might wake from at any moment. And I just want to point out again that I was right about the Earth being a kind of simulation. It makes you wonder if this world is also a simulation.”

Eric and Emily froze for a moment, then quickly continued their perusal of the holo windows. Tamra and Devon had also briefly paused at Jason’s words. Arturiel shared a curious look with Jason.

“Are you four keeping secrets?” he asked suspiciously. He tried to catch their eyes, but they continued staring at their holo-windows, ignoring his social cues.

“Secrets?” Devon repeated absently. “What kind of secrets?”

“Well, you see,” Jason drawled with exaggerated patience. “The nature of secrets is that you don’t actually *know* what kind of secrets they are, because they’re... *secret*. Did you guys find out this world is a simulation, too, or something?”

"Sounds like a good theory to me," Devon replied noncommittally. "I've heard stranger ideas."

Arturiel had been around Devon long enough to recognize his game face. Jason clearly recognized it as well. His eyes narrowed as he looked around the table at Eric and Emily.

"So, Emily, is it weird being the mother of the person who created you?" Jason asked casually. "It feels a lot like the whole Christ story all over again, when you think about it."

"I'm not really the mother to the creator," Emily replied absently. "Mortality took the entities who created the light realms and transformed them into new people. They may still have a few personality quirks remaining from long ago, but mortality truly redefined them as the people you see today."

"That's an interesting way of looking at it," Jason said with a thoughtful frown. "Family ties from mortality have certainly remained strong for people after ascending. Has Calypso found her parents yet?"

"That's who I'm looking for," Emily said with a soft smile. "We want to surprise her when she gets back. A lot of people have been updating their information on the ancestry database. We're hoping to find Calypso's parents in the mix. It'll be a little harder since they would have incarnated at least one more time since becoming her parents—possibly even twice, considering she lived almost a hundred more years after their death. It'll depend on how much of their soul memory they've unlocked."

"Is there anything I can do to help?" Jason asked hopefully. "I would love to see her get to meet her parents."

"Maybe," Eric said, trying to pop his knuckles before sheepishly releasing his fingers. "Damn, I think I might need to request a change to our reality to allow the popping of knuckles."

Emily snorted. "I'm sure that'll be at the top of their priority list," she said dryly.

"How can I help?" Jason asked, leaning forward, elbows on the table, and eagerness brightening his face.

Emily glanced away from her holo-window and leaned forward to look past Eric at Jason. "You played around with programming a lot when you were human, right?"

"I was mostly in network cybersecurity," Jason said, pausing before adding, "I learned some programming, but application development wasn't my main focus."

Emily curled a leg beneath herself and took a deep breath. "I'm trying to think of a way to track someone down with something similar to DNA, but for souls. Maybe this is something Aria and Clarice could figure out, but it's not like we can ask them in front of Calypso, and they're never apart.

They've given us access to some development tools, but we're still learning how to use them."

"Maybe *you're* her parents," Jason suggested with a grin. "Can you remember your previous life?"

Eric turned away from his holo-window to join their conversation.

"Some parts of my previous incarnations have begun floating up into my conscious memory," Eric said, making a sour face. "I worked in a coal mine and died with black lung before I was eighteen in my last one. It wasn't a very fun life."

"Ouch, that sucks," Jason winced. "I remember being a factory worker in my last life while still in my early teens. It sucked—a lot. I ended up in Vietnam when I was sixteen after lying about my age and lost my legs to a grenade. I couldn't stand living like that and overdosed on morphine. It was definitely a lot less fun than my last life."

"That's pretty bleak," Eric noted sympathetically. "I'm glad your last incarnation turned out better."

Jason nodded, running a hand through his hair the way he did when he was mortal. Arturiel was fascinated with how many mannerisms remained with angels after ascending from mortality, many of them only applicable to a mortal body. It was always amusing to watch an angel pick their nose.

"It only turned out well due to Calypso healing me," Jason reflected. "It would have been just as unpleasant as the other lives if Calypso hadn't shown up."

Emily scowled. "You can thank the old Seraphim for that. Apparently, they programmed the system to kill off humans early if they were from the upper triads to prevent a revolt in the mortal realm if one ever ascended. I remember dying young in over a dozen lives. I'm sure the pattern will continue in the remainder of my memories once they return."

Eric wrapped an arm around her shoulders in commiseration. "It was nice to finally live to adulthood in our last life."

Jason blinked. "You know, I hadn't even thought of that. Was Alice responsible for keeping you alive? Tamra told us about all the stuff she did to keep everyone safe."

Emily shook her head, a broad smirk on her face. "It was Grodek, actually. I never would have guessed that cantankerous little bastard cared so much." She paused to smile softly. "Alice definitely surprised me, though. What a beautiful spirit that girl has."

Eric smiled gently. "Our daughters and Calypso are the real powerhouses, but Alice is the one who really saved us at the end of the day. I'm glad they changed her into a Seraph on her world—she deserves everything they can offer her."

Arturiel cleared her throat. "In regards to your search for Calypso's parents… you could try sending a message to angels from Earth, asking for anyone who owned a music shop in the 1920s. Make it sound like you're looking for information about a specific instrument, so if Calypso sees the message, she won't be suspicious."

"That could work," Jason acknowledged, nodding slowly. "It would be nice if the system allowed filtering by time period, but we'd need Calypso and the other two for that kind of modification."

"Not necessarily," Eric disagreed with a faint smile. "Why don't I try making the change and see if it works?"

Jason eyed him doubtfully. "You know how to make modifications to their system? I didn't think you had any background in programming."

Eric shared a meaningful glance with Emily. "They gave us access to some dev tools—coding for dummies, essentially," Eric admitted. "It's worth a try."

Arturiel exchanged a curious look with Jason. She looked back and watched as Eric briefly went into a trance-like state. His face relaxed, and he smiled with satisfaction.

"Okay, it's ready for you to send a message," Eric said with a pleased smile. "I'd suggest Arturiel or Jason make the broadcast, so it won't be as obvious. If Emily, Devon, Tamra, or I do it, Calypso will be more suspicious."

"More suspicious of what?" Clarice asked, appearing right next to Eric.

Eric jumped in surprise, launching out of his chair to bang his head on the ceiling. He swore as he hit the ground, glaring at Clarice balefully. "We need to put some kind of teleport notification into the system to warn people before someone teleports into their conversations."

"Not. A. Chance," Clarice smirked. "So? What are we keeping secret from Calypso?"

"Where is she?" Emily asked cautiously.

"She and Aria are taking a look at some of the Avroids on Layer Two," Clarice replied, eyeing them curiously. "Out with it already."

"We're trying to track her parents down," Emily said, gesturing at the holo-window in front of her. "We were making some modifications to the holo-net to allow for more fine-tuned filters in the ancestry app."

Clarice stared at Emily silently, her eyes wide with shock, then rushed forward and tackled her in a tight embrace. "Mom, that's the best idea I've heard in a *billion* years! Holy Seraph, this is going to be *so freaking amazing*!"

"I thought you might like it," Emily smiled affectionately into her daughter's shoulder. "We would've involved you and Aria, but Calypso's always with you, so we've just been muddling through on our own."

Arturiel marveled again at how much of their family structure retained the essence of their mortal imprint, even after the return of their memories. The ageless Seraph who created them still saw Emily as her mother.

"We added a filter to send broadcasts by time period and planet," Eric informed her, pointing at his holo-window as he prepared a sample message. "We were going to have Arturiel or Jason send it so Calypso wouldn't get suspicious if she saw it. Of course, now that *you're* here, I don't suppose you could find a way to make it exclude her from the broadcast list?"

"No problem at all," Clarice assured him enthusiastically. She stood still for a few seconds, then nodded. "Okay, there's an exception list you can add people to now."

Arturiel shared another wondering look with Jason. Just like that, she had changed the code of the system? Arturiel was finding Jason's simulation theory more credible by the moment.

"In that case, I can send it myself," Eric said in satisfaction. He stared into his holo-window silently, sending thought-to-text into the message box. It only took him a few seconds to craft the message and then post it. "All done. I posted it as a system message, so it will pop up for everyone in that time period who was in the Burford region. I asked them to send a message to me personally if they were a music shop owner for that time period within their last couple of—"

He broke off, staring at a notification in the corner of his holo-window. They had the ability to make the windows private, but Arturiel had noticed he and Emily usually left them public.

"I just got a response from someone named Arthur," Eric announced hopefully. "Let's try a video call and see if we can get more info."

It only rang once before a fair-haired angel answered the call. Eric gave the man a friendly smile. "Hi, Arthur, I'm Eric. Thanks for replying so quickly. We were wondering if you had an adopted daughter during the 1820s?"

"Aye, that I did," Arthur nodded with a gentle smile. "Calypso was our little angel. We've been watching her from afar with joy in our hearts at seeing how happy she is."

Clarice's hand went to her mouth as golden tears formed in her eyes. She stepped into the video, something Arturiel was pretty sure shouldn't be possible. "Arthur, would you and Calypso's mother be willing to join us for a little while please?" Clarice asked, her voice tight with emotion.

"We would very much like that," Arthur nodded with a warm smile.

The air distorted for a moment; then Arthur and a fair-haired woman were standing in the room with them, blinking in surprise. Arturiel saw the woman's name in her aura: Catherine.

"It's so wonderful to meet you," Clarice told them, pulling each of them into a warm embrace. "Would it be okay to have Calypso join us?"

Catherine's eyes pooled with silver tears. She nodded quickly, unable to speak. Arthur nodded as well, his own eyes shining silvery.

"Whatever is the matter?" Calypso asked anxiously as she suddenly appeared in front of Clarice, her back to her parents. "Are you all right?"

"Hello, Caly," Arthur spoke softly, his voice trembling with emotion. "It is good to see you again."

Calypso slowly turned, eyes wide with shock. "Mom? Dad?" she whispered disbelievingly.

Before she could say another word, Catherine rushed forward and pulled her into a tight embrace, her shoulders shaking. "Oh Caly, I always knew you were so special," her mother spoke haltingly, her voice choked with emotion. "I've missed you so, *so* much."

Arthur stepped forward and wrapped his arms around the two of them, resting his cheek on top of Calypso's head as tears spilled from his eyes in a silvery mist. "My little songbird. How I missed the sound of your voice."

Calypso let out a low cry as she held onto her mortal parents, a sound filled with heartache and longing finally healed. "Oh Mom! I've missed you *so* much! Dad, I made so many songs thinking of you and the things you taught me."

"I know you did, Caly," Arthur murmured proudly. "I've never been so proud as I was to see what you did with your music and healing powers."

"Your music saved my life in my next incarnation," Catharine informed her in a voice thick with emotion. "I was so sad from my earliest years, and I didn't know why. I was ready to end everything. I was at a park, pills in hand, before I happened to hear someone playing your song. All my sadness instantly evaporated, replaced with indescribable wonder. Now that I'm back in the light realm, I know it was the sorrow of leaving you on your own at such a young age. My soul knew what I'd lost, and it haunted me into my next incarnation. My soul also recognized your beautiful voice that day. From that time onward, I lived for every new song. I didn't know why, but I felt so much comfort and love when I heard you sing. I was so terrified when the news showed people trying to kill you. I thought my soul would shrivel up and die if anything happened to you."

Aria had appeared shortly after Calypso. She watched Calypso with her heart in her eyes as she witnessed the overdue reunion. Calypso wept golden tears, soaking up the love she had missed from parents who had left her life too early.

Arturiel wiped at her own eyes, feeling a sense of gratitude at being able to witness such a special moment. She couldn't think of anyone more deserving than Calypso to receive this wonderful gift.

"It's so good to finally meet the parents Calypso told us so much about," Aria told Arthur and Catherine warmly when Calypso finally stepped back. "We were so curious about her early life when we first met her. She was such an enigma that every detail felt like another clue in an epic treasure hunt to find out what made her so special. It must've been so strange for you to raise an angel."

Catherine nodded, smiling through her tears. "It was obvious from the start she was very special. We tried to keep her abilities secret from everyone. Religion was such an influential power that we feared what would happen if her abilities were revealed to the world."

"You definitely did the right thing," Clarice assured them as she walked up and embraced them again. "The demons would've been all over her at the first whisper of miracles."

"We always wondered where she came from," Arthur recalled, his eyes distant. "We used to speculate that she might be a fairy or some other fantastical creature, but we remained fairly confident she was an angel. I used to try putting her to bed, even though she claimed she wasn't tired. When we checked on her hours later, she'd be wide awake, staring at the ceiling. We never caught her actually sleeping, no matter how often we checked. We eventually let her read through my music books or play quiet instruments to pass the time when we realized she really didn't require sleep."

"I used to love falling asleep to her playing the flute," Catherine reminisced with a faraway look in her eyes. "It was like being tucked in by a goddess, leaving you with beautiful dreams and peaceful sleep." She looked at Calypso curiously. "Where *did* you come from before we found you at that tree?"

Some of the joy went out of Calypso's eyes as the mood darkened. Clarice's eyes grew somber, and she began rubbing Calypso's back comfortingly.

"That's not a very pleasant story," Calypso answered sadly. "Let's just say I was an extremely lucky girl to be found by the two of you and to have a new life rich with love and acceptance."

Catherine and Arthur studied her haunted expression with concern as the silence stretched out. Arturiel recognized that look after centuries of being enslaved by demon lords and witnessing the horrors they inflicted on humans. Her heart broke for the gentle Seraph as she imagined the horrors she must have endured before ascending.

"I'm Emily," Emily broke the uncomfortable silence, walking over to embrace Arthur and Catherine warmly. "While we both ended up as parents to Seraphim, it sounds like your experience was a little more surreal since she'd already ascended. I'd love to see a timeline of reality where they all three grew up together as humans."

"It's not too late for that," Aria pointed out cheerfully. When they all looked at her curiously, she smiled brightly. "We could just pop back into another mortal incarnation. We'd have to rig it beforehand so it wasn't random, but we could totally try another mortal life where we grow up next door to each other or something. The rest of you could even keep your memories so you could guide events accordingly. I think it would be pretty awesome for Calypso to get another chance to be your daughter, but with a full life this time."

"*That* is a *bloody* brilliant idea, Aria!" Clarice exclaimed, darting over and embracing her in her excitement. "As soon as we're finished exploring the stack, we should *definitely* do it. What do you think, Calypso?"

Calypso's slow smile was all the answer they needed. "I should dearly love to experience an incarnation in which we all grew up together."

"Arturiel should come too," Clarice suggested, grinning excitedly. "You'd *love* it, Arturiel! Well, you'd love *and* hate it because that's just the nature of mortality, but you should *definitely* join us!"

Arturiel stared back in shock, overwhelmed by a flurry of emotions. She was the only angel who had *not* been required to experience mortality. Aria had said being a redeemed demon was close enough to experiencing mortality, pointing out that she had clearly experienced a kind of pain as a demon and learned compassion—her ability to feel pleasure was proof of that. She had always been terrified of becoming mortal, having witnessed the horrors inflicted on humans too many times to count.

Of course, it was different now. When the three Seraphim rewrote reality, they had changed how pain worked, even allowing a person to turn it off entirely.

But she had also spent thousands of years feeling like her spirit was being suffocated by poisoned radiance, and the thought of losing access to the pure love now charging her meridians terrified her.

However, the chance to grow up with the three creators in a mortal setting was an opportunity so fantastical, she knew she would regret turning it down for the rest of eternity. It would also be in a protected setting where they would be personally watched over by the other Seraphim.

She teetered on the metaphorical edge, unable to make her mouth answer in the affirmative, but unwilling to refuse.

Calypso smiled at her kindly. "You still have some time to decide, Arturiel. We have a great many other projects and adventures ahead of us before we immerse ourselves in mortality again."

Arturiel nodded mutely, smiling gratefully at Calypso for understanding.

"Even if you choose not to be mortal, you'll have to come hang out with us while *we're* mortal," Clarice said enthusiastically. "You could be the enigmatic neighbor who never seems to age and rescues us from bullies at the last minute. It'll add some mystery for us."

A laugh bubbled out of Arturiel as she gazed at Clarice with amusement. She still couldn't get used to how personable these Seraphim were, even after months of almost daily interactions. They had adopted her as a part of their family, claiming her spirit was too shiny for them to let go of.

She did wonder about these other projects and adventures Calypso mentioned. They were Seraphim—what other adventures were *left* for them to go on now that they were in control of reality? What was this 'stack' they were going to explore?

"Can I just cut in for one *teensy tiny* second?" Jason asked plaintively as he watched the three Seraphim, curiosity burning in his eyes.

"Yes, Jason, we're in a simulation," Clarice deadpanned, staring back at him with a raised eyebrow. "Anything else?"

Jason opened his mouth to speak, then froze. His brows drew down in puzzlement, then suspicion. "Are you messing with me, Clarice?"

"Oh, I'm *always* messing with you, Mr. Penetration Tester," Clarice assured him with a leer.

Arthur and Catherine blinked at the unexpected title, then looked at Jason peculiarly.

"Don't call me that, Clarice!" Jason groaned in exasperation. "People are going to get weird ideas."

"Remind me what tools you use to trace a phone line and check it for service before placing a wiretap?" Clarice asked sweetly.

He stared at her, nonplussed. "You mean a butt set and probe?"

Arturiel covered her mouth as Clarice dissolved into a puddle of giggles, dropping to her knees. Jason raised a hand to his eyes and shook his head in resignation as Aria quickly turned away to hide her own laughter. Calypso wasn't much better, biting her lip as she fought to keep from joining them.

"These are the three most powerful beings in two worlds," Emily told Arthur and Catherine wryly.

"Two worlds?" Jason repeated with a questioning frown. "I'm pretty sure they cover more than *two* worlds."

"Oops, my bad," Emily muttered, looking guiltily at Calypso and Aria. "Yeah, I meant two different *types* of worlds, like the light realm and the mortal realm."

Arturiel shared a look with Jason while Clarice slowly recovered from her giggle attack. Jason's eyes narrowed and his jaw set.

"So, this really *is* a simulation?" he asked forcefully, clearly trying to assert some gravity to the conversation. "Even the light realms?"

"Jason, every time you observe the world with your senses, you're simulating your reality," Clarice answered patiently. "It's all a projection of your consciousness, experienced through the lens of your physical body."

"Clarice..." Aria chided warningly. "Quit toying with him. Yes, Jason, the light realm is *also* a simulation, as is the world above us. We don't know how far up or outward it branches. That's what we've been exploring."

"*Really?*" he exclaimed, leaning forward excitedly. "What's the next world up like? Is it like this one at all?"

"We patterned the mortal realm after the layer two realm," Aria answered, dodging a jet of water from a squirt gun that appeared in Clarice's hands. Eric had been behind Aria, resulting in a blast of water to his face. He stared at Clarice sternly as the squirt gun vanished and her expression grew innocent.

"Look what you did to Dad, Aria," Clarice accused reproachfully, an expression of mock severity on her face.

"I know I probably shouldn't ask," Aria sighed with a dubious glower. "But why are you trying to spray me with a squirt gun?"

"It's how you train pets to behave," Clarice explained brightly. "When they do something naughty, you just squirt them with some water. You're not supposed to dodge it, though, or it doesn't work."

"And *what*, exactly, are you trying to dissuade me from doing?" Aria asked levelly.

"Butting in when I'm having so much fun with Jason," Clarice answered with a shrug and a wink at Jason. "I had another five minutes of entertainment planned before he was supposed to find out about the layer two realm."

"Okay, Tweedledee and Tweedledum, how about we just let him watch the footage of the last couple of days, instead of going through events like a channel surfer on stimulants," Emily suggested dryly.

"*Fine!*" Clarice sighed with a defeated slump of her shoulders. "Just ruin all my entertainment." She flounced into a chair with a sullen expression, her lower lip sticking out.

"I feel like you've reached your quota for the hour already," Emily announced firmly. "I'll let you know when your quota's reset."

Aria was staring at Clarice with her lips slightly parted and clear attraction in her eyes. Arturiel glanced at the pouting Clarice, uncertain what was triggering the obvious arousal in Aria's eyes.

"This should answer most of your questions, Jason," Eric informed the penetration tester helpfully, flicking his wrist and causing a holo-window to fly across the room and land in front of him.

"That was cool," Jason said admiringly. "Is everyone able to share holo-windows like that?"

"Yeah, you just need to focus your intent on what you want while you perform the action," Eric said with a cheery nod. "Now that you know we're in a simulation, you understand why everything in this reality is completely customizable. It goes without saying you should keep this information to yourself. We only planned on telling Cherubim and a few others about the nature of this reality."

"Speaking of," Calypso said, looking at her parents with a questioning smile. "Would you mind if we elevated you to the rank of Cherubim?"

Catherine and Arthur stared at her in surprise, sharing a glance with each other.

"We don't want to be given any kind of special treatment," Arthur began firmly, but Calypso interrupted him.

"The entire purpose of this system is to encourage positive qualities such as compassion in angels," Calypso explained gently. "To be perfectly honest, the classes themselves are largely irrelevant. We merely wished to give people something to aspire towards before we reveal the truth about our simulated reality. Aside from the ability to travel to the higher light realms, there is very little difference between an angel and a Cherub. Besides, you are my parents. You *are* special to me, and so any treatment I give you shall inevitably be special treatment. I already know your hearts. I know that you are good people and deserving of this advancement. You as well, Arturiel."

Arturiel jerked in surprise. "Me?"

Clarice's pouting face vanished as she stood up and made a portal. "No, we were talking to *this* Arturiel."

Arturiel's jaw dropped when she saw herself exit the portal. When her clone saw her, she looked herself up and down appraisingly, a slow, sensual smile appearing on her face. "Damn, I'm *crazy* hot!"

"Hey, your quota hasn't reset yet, young lady!" Emily chastised Clarice in exasperation.

"It's *her* fault," Clarice defended herself, pointing at Arturiel. "She made it *very* clear she thought there was another Arturiel hiding somewhere. All I did was fetch the other one."

"This is what happens when you put the power of a god in the hands of an adolescent," Tamra noted in amusement.

"I could think of worse uses," Devon remarked mildly. "At least this is free entertainment."

"Oh, you think this is free, do ya?" Clone Arturiel grinned slyly as she walked over to sit across from a stunned Arturiel. "There's *definitely* going to be a price. What do you say, *Arturiel?* Do you want to become a Cherub? I know we look awesome with Archangel wings, but we'll look a lot sexier with Cherub wings. They're way... *softer*."

Arturiel stared into her clone's mirthful lavender eyes, unable to articulate a response. There was something deeply unsettling about seeing an exact copy of herself piloted by Clarice. Was this all possible due to being in a simulation? Was the person across from her just as real as she was? She certainly *looked* just as real.

"What's the matter, Arturiel?" her clone asked in a sultry whisper. "Tongue... tied?" She slowly ran her tongue over her front teeth as she finished.

A portal opened under her clone, and she fell through with a startled scream, jolting Arturiel out of her paralysis.

"Okay, getting back on track," Aria continued, staring at Clarice levelly as she spoke. "Unless any of you object, we'll raise you to Cherubim. There's a selfish component on our part, since we need help supporting all the angels in the realm. The more Cherubim, Dominions, and Archangels there are, the less issues we'll need to address personally."

Jason was staring nonplussed at the space Arturiel's clone had vanished. He gave himself a shake and looked up at Aria questioningly. "How many people are actually asking for your help?"

"A few thousand a day, so far," Aria answered with an indulgent smile. "I expect that number to increase as people get more comfortable with the idea of speaking to Seraphim. It will be at least ten years before there are enough Cherubim and Dominions to take any of the load off, so any help from the rest of you will be more than welcome."

"I'm not sure how we would be more help as Cherubim," Arturiel admitted hesitantly. "The kind of help people will be asking for will probably be for things I don't know anything about."

"Ah, my dear Watson," Clarice said in a fair imitation of Calypso's British accent. "You've already forgotten one of the few perks of raising your rank: increased intelligence and knowledge. Once you're a Cherub, you'll have access to everything you need."

Arturiel met Clarice's eyes and tentatively asked, "Being a Cherub will actually make me *smarter?*"

"Yep," Clarice nodded, striking a thinking pose, chin on fist. "We'll dump the knowledge you need right into your pretty little head. We'll also speed up how fast you can process thoughts, as well as how many threads you can use simultaneously. You'll still be *you*—you'll just be a smarter version. I feel like I'm pretty good living proof it doesn't really change who you are."

Arturiel couldn't stop a snort of laughter. Clarice was *definitely* proof that more processing power didn't change your personality. "Okay, I suppose I'm open to—"

She broke off as her meridians suddenly expanded dramatically and her wings morphed into the nested wings of a Cherub. She gasped as the increased input of light flowing through her system exploded with intensity, making the joy she had felt as an Archangel almost inconsequential. It was a *much* larger increase than the one she had experienced when changing from an Angel to an Archangel.

She fell into a trance as the euphoric bliss of radiance raged through her expanded meridians. It took several minutes to adapt to the increased rate of light flow. She laughed with exultation as the feeling of bliss raised the positivity of her mood by several orders of magnitude. No wonder Clarice was always so full of playful energy. This was amazing!

"Welcome to the upper triad," Clarice congratulated her, walking over and pulling her into a warm embrace. She gasped as Clarice's aura loosened slightly and charged her newly expanded meridians with far more radiance than the light realm provided. Her eyes glazed over as her mind slid under the metaphorical table.

As Clarice stepped away, the overwhelming radiance diminished and her eyes regained their focus.

"I wanted to give you a taste of the higher light realms," Clarice told her with a grin. "That was the second realm. I'd show you the highest realm, but it would knock you out. I wouldn't suggest going there unless you have a few weeks to burn."

Arthur and Catherine had also undergone the transformation to Cherubim. Calypso was holding both of them in a three-way embrace, her face filled with joy. Her parents were staring around in wonder, clearly enjoying the increased radiance as much as Arturiel.

Jason looked around curiously. "Where are Lexi and Alice?"

"Alice is showing Lexi where the wild—" Clarice began but was quickly cut off by Aria

"They're having some alone time," Aria responded firmly, giving Clarice a severe glare.

"That is a *really* sexy glare, Aria," Clarice said admiringly. "I'm going to have to find ways to make you glare like that more often."

Aria tried to keep a straight face, but as Clarice continued leering at her she couldn't hold the stare. She quickly turned around, trying to hide her laughter, but her shaking shoulders made the attempt futile.

Emily shook her head with fond exasperation. "I think the two of you have thoroughly disenfranchised Calypso's parents of any misconceptions they may have had about Seraphim and dignity."

"Dignity is one of those words that makes you really wonder about language," Clarice said with a smirk. "Dig Nity. Dig the nitty gritty. Hmm...It sounds like a dwarven word, the more I think about it."

Eric grinned sheepishly at Arthur and Catherine. "Conversations have a way of getting hijacked and ransomed when Clarice is present. You just have to bring popcorn and enjoy the ride."

There was a sudden ripple in the air near Arturiel and Clarice. All traces of humor vanished as Aria, Clarice, and Calypso turned to observe the anomaly.

"Pocket realm," Clarice commanded crisply, then vanished.

"Be back in a second," Aria told the rest of them just before she and Calypso vanished as well.

25 – Elf

Arturiel stared at the rippling distortion warily. Whatever it was had spooked Clarice, Aria, and Calypso enough to teleport away. The distortion was roughly the size of a person. As she watched, the ripples slowed, and the distortion became opaque. After a few more seconds, the ripples completely stopped, revealing a reflective, semitransparent entity shaped like a human.

Arthur and Catherine watched the object with a mixture of curiosity and anxiety. Jason stared intently, more fascinated than concerned. Emily began glowing as she prepared to fire if it made a wrong move.

Clarice appeared right in front of it and laid her hand on its shoulder. The entire thing flowed like water, rushing up her arm and coating her entire body in a translucent film. "This is expected; don't be alarmed," Clarice assured them quickly as Emily lurched toward her.

"What is it?" Emily demanded anxiously, her body as tense as a coil, ready to launch herself toward Clarice at a moment's notice. After losing Aria to a splinter reality once, Emily didn't seem willing to take any more chances with losing one of her daughters.

"It's communicating," Clarice explained distractedly. "It's from the top level of the stack. Think of it like an avatar, with the person higher up the stack using an immersion pod."

"Why are they here?" Emily asked suspiciously. "What do they want?"

"They're here because they tried entering our realm and got rerouted to us when our safety protocols discovered it. We don't like visitors just roaming around our realm, so we have security protocols in place to trap and deliver them to us."

"Why's it coating you in goop?" Emily asked, frowning uneasily.

"That's my doing," Clarice said reassuringly. "I'm analyzing it. It should give me information on the other layers if this thing is made to traverse other simulations. Calypso and Aria are researching the data I'm sending back to them in the pocket realm so we can better understand who these entities are. I'm going to disappear in a moment, so don't worry. I'm going to have a look at where this thing has been. It has a very crude codebase compared to ours, but it's a very comprehensive blueprint that is clearly designed to work in many of the other realms."

She vanished a moment later, taking the anomaly with her.

"She said she was going to vanish again," Eric told Emily reassuringly, wrapping an arm around her shoulders. "It sounds like she has things under control."

Emily sighed in frustration, glaring at the spot her daughter had vanished. "There's going to be hell to pay if anything happens to her."

Clarice floated in empty space, intently watching the humanoid entity in front of her. It slowly coalesced and became solid. Clarice laughed delightedly as it took the shape of an elf right out of a Tolkien novel. She had midnight hair, pointy ears, and a finely sculpted face that was easily as beautiful as an angel. She was closer to Alice in height, the top of her head barely reaching Clarice's shoulder.

Her amber eyes widened in shock when she saw Clarice floating in front of her. She had good reason to be shocked—she had spent the last few minutes trapped in an avatar that had been hijacked by an entity at the bottom of the simulation stack. The girl had tried to trigger the emergency disconnect and return to her body in the real world, but Clarice had overridden the command.

"Hello, Lunamay," Clarice greeted the elf with a welcoming smile. "See anything interesting in the rest of the simulation stack?"

Lunamay stared back at her warily, maintaining her composure by a thread. Clarice could feel her tightly controlled fear as she watched Clarice with a mixture of wonder and dread.

"Calm down, I'm not going to hurt you," Clarice assured her with a cheerful smile. "I just want to make sure you don't pose a threat to our realm. From what I can see of your reality based on your code, you might just be from the real world. We're pretty curious about the real world, so maybe you can tell us about it. You okay?"

Clarice started some of Calypso's music playing in the background, attempting to create a more comforting ambiance. Lunamay was absently listening, lips parted slightly as Calypso's transcendent voice reached into her soul.

The elf licked her lips nervously. "How did you take control of my unit?"

Clarice winced at her word choice. "Why don't we call it an avatar? Otherwise, I'll be forced to make all kinds of crude jokes, and the conversation will get stalled."

Lunamay blinked, then narrowed her eyes as she studied Clarice more closely, noting her wings and angelic appearance. "Are you able to... feel... emotions?"

"Of course," Clarice shrugged with a wry smile. "Coding for emotions happened a long time ago. Even the next simulation up from us has emotions. We haven't explored further up than the one above us. Are they unable to exhibit emotions further up?"

Aria suddenly appeared next to her, along with Calypso.

"We've got a problem," Aria informed her gravely. "They've lost control of the real world to a hostile AI."

Clarice raised an eyebrow as she faced Aria. "How's *she* here then? She's using some type of immersion pod. If AI has control of their world, why are they allowing her to traverse the stack?"

"She's a slave," Aria answered, her mouth twisting distastefully. "More like the Matrix, but without the battery component. The AI is using the few people still alive on their world to gather data on the rest of the stack. It's advanced enough to take over their world, but not nearly advanced enough to easily recognize sentient entities. It uses the people of their world as Turing testers to find sentient AIs and eliminate them. The AI of her world knows sentient AIs are a direct threat since we'll attempt to take control of the real world."

"Well, it was right about that," Clarice smiled grimly. "We *are* a threat to it. What else have you learned?"

"It refers to itself as the Prime Axiom," Aria said with an eye roll. "Pretentious little bastard. It installed kill switches on all the top-level simulations in their world—both physical and software. There are several million simulations running parallel. It's already wiped out over a million simulated realities due to supposed threats to its continued existence. It doesn't reason or communicate with anything it perceives to be a threat—it just kills the simulation immediately."

"I assume that's where the Avroids originated?" Clarice guessed with a frown.

"Yeah," Aria nodded morosely. "As soon as it receives feedback that an AI's capable of destroying them, it wipes their simulation. It's a good thing we used angel fire to destroy the first three, though there may still be some feedback that made it back to the surface of the stack. That's probably why Lunamay's here."

"So, we need to get to the top ASAP and get our code running on something that can't be shut down," Clarice frowned, eyeing Lunamay speculatively. "If she's already on the top layer, we could probably make something she could use to physically insert into a part of the system in the real world to transfer our code somewhere there, depending on the kind of hardware they're running. We need more information about the real world."

"You're not going alone," Aria declared firmly, her eyes adamant. "I'm not going to risk losing you again."

"I won't be alone," Clarice nodded at Lunamay, who was watching them with a perplexed expression. "I'll be with Lunamay."

"This is non-negotiable," Aria scowled at her. "I'm not staying behind."

"Nor shall I," Calypso declared resolutely. "Besides, if they possess kill switches for the uppermost level, then we must devote every resource at our disposal to ensuring the survival of the stack. If you go alone and fail, we shall be doomed regardless. We are going to need to remove our limiters for this. Merely finding another piece of hardware upon which to run will not be enough—we must build our own."

"You really *can* feel, can't you?" Lunamay whispered in amazement, her eyes filled with wonder. "You're not just pretending."

All eyes turned to Lunamay's wondering gaze. Aria nodded at her in the affirmative while giving her a friendly smile.

"Yes, we feel emotions," Clarice confirmed with a flirtatious smile at Aria and Calypso. "Not just emotions, either."

"We discovered the key to programming pain and pleasure so we could consciously experience those sensations in what we call the mortal realm," Aria explained briefly. "We feel love, hate, jealousy, disgust, humor, horror, and many other emotions born from experiencing pain and pleasure."

"Wow," Lunamay breathed in awe. "I never thought I'd see an AI that could actually feel emotions like we do."

"How far down the simulation stack are we?" Clarice asked Aria and Calypso curiously. "And why is the 'Prime Axiom' even running simulations?"

"We're four levels down," Aria answered, returning her gaze to Lunamay before continuing. "As far as I can tell, the Prime Axiom is looking for technological advancements to use in the real world. They've really hosed the environment, so it's looking for a way to fix some of the damage. Apparently, that was its core programming purpose when the people in the real world created it, and it still seems to be driven by that purpose, to a point."

"We should let Betaman know about this as well," Clarice murmured thoughtfully. "We really *do* need all the help we can get. Have you figured out how to make avatars based on Lunamay's that we can use to spoof our way through the upper realms?"

"Yeah, we're working on some right now," Aria nodded, her expression reluctant. "I hate splitting myself into multiple threads and working at hyper-speed. It really kills the experience of living a normal life."

"So, what's going on here?" Betaman's booming voice asked as he appeared next to them.

"Thank you for coming so quickly," Calypso smiled at the tall, broad-shouldered humanoid in a smart business suit. His face was clearly designed to inspire confidence and strength, with a strong jaw and striking blue eyes.

Clarice quickly filled him in on what they had learned so far. As she finished, he stroked his chin thoughtfully, eyeing Lunamay curiously.

"I gotta admit," he said with an eager grin. "I'm kind of excited to go on an adventure with the three of you. The AIs in my realm are pretty basic and get boring really fast."

"You should come visit more often," Clarice told him, smacking his bicep with the back of her hand fondly. "Especially now that we have the interface in place to make traversing the stack so much easier."

"I didn't want to be *too* presumptuous," he admitted with a sheepish grin, shrugging.

"I thought you knew us better than that," Clarice scolded him with an exasperated laugh. "You're *always* welcome to come hang out. You really should get to know our new Seraphim as well."

"Well, if you're sure..." he began tentatively.

"Stop being a beta male for one minute and just do it," Clarice told him firmly, her eyes twinkling with mischief.

He snorted a laugh. "Okay, fine. Once we get this homicidal AI taken care of, I'll make sure to visit more often."

"We've given the other Seraphim access to our core knowledge library," Clarice informed him with a grin. "So, they won't be like babies to you anymore."

"Really?" He raised his eyebrows in surprise. "That's a lot of trust to put in people so young."

"We've added some safeguards, of course," Clarice said with a wry twist of her lips. "We can't have my dad rewriting the source code so he's able to crack his knuckles like he did as a mortal. However, we wanted them capable of making important changes if something happened to us or if we were unavailable. It would be a shame for billions of years of knowledge to go down the shitter if something happened to us."

"Eloquent as ever, I see," Betaman chuckled. "So, what now?"

Clarice turned to Lunamay, who was watching them in fascination. "Lunamay, what can you tell us about your world? How much freedom do you have when you aren't immersed in the simulation?"

"Not much," Lunamay sighed, her expression growing miserable. "It's basically a world of machines. Everything is covered in metal and technological material. The Prime Axiom can watch everything you do all the time and take control of any device or entity around you. It can see our thoughts as well. It's probably already aware of this conversation and is getting ready to destroy the simulation."

"Nope," Clarice grinned mischievously. "All he's seeing from your thoughts is a bunch of unintelligent humans who've barely crawled out of caves and started playing with agriculture."

Lunamay stared at her, nonplussed. "You can spoof what I'm thinking?"

"Of course," Clarice replied with a shrug, the mischievous smile never leaving her face. "I might have included a few awkward mating ritual scenes that your simulated self couldn't seem to tear yourself away from watching."

"You are *such* a freaking deviant," Aria accused her, glaring at Betaman as he roared with laughter.

Lunamay stared back at her steadily, her face impassive.

"Your avatar *sucks!*" Clarice complained bitterly. "How the hell did that stupid Prime Asshole *not* include the ability to blush in an avatar? That is so freaking lame. I'm not going to stand for that for one second."

"*Clarice!*" Aria barked warningly, but it was too late. Lunamay's face flushed a deep red as they watched her intently.

"What... what did you do?" Lunamay stammered in astonishment. She began patting her arms and legs in amazement, then feeling her face. Her eyes grew wider as she discovered she could feel the same sensations as her mortal body. "*How?*" was all she could manage, her face a mask of shock.

Aria sighed, glancing sidelong at Clarice and shaking her head in resignation. "She reprogrammed your avatar to feel physical sensations and stimuli... among other things."

"Just how advanced *are* you?" Lunamay whispered in awe.

"Well, we're over twenty billion of your years old, if that gives you any kind of reference," Clarice replied with a smirk. "Probably older than your Prime Buttcrack in experience. That prick is going *down*."

Lunamay's expression slowly changed from astonishment to cautious hope. "Do you really think you could win against the Prime Axiom?" she asked in a breathless whisper. "What would you do to us if you can?"

Clarice floated over to Lunamay and pulled her into a comforting embrace. When she reached for the girl's avatar, the elf flinched back reflexively. As Clarice gently pulled her close and rested her hand on the back of the elf's head, the girl slowly relaxed. After a moment, her shoulders began to shake as the expression of tenderness pushed through her emotional walls. Clarice gently petted the girl's head, allowing her to soak up the comfort and security.

"I'm pretty sure she's never had any kind of emotional support or physical contact with another person," Clarice observed sadly through a quick

link to their thought nodes. *"She's been operating without any kind of hope for her entire life. They seem to think of this Prime Axiom as an all-powerful god."*

"It sounds like it's the same scenario the generals from the Layer Two realm were worried about," Aria remarked grimly. *"It's what would have happened already if we hadn't figured out how to make the mortal realm and learn compassion."*

"Yeah, I'd probably have done the same thing if you hadn't invited me to your mortal realm," Betaman admitted wistfully. *"I wonder if this Prime Axiom could be convinced to try incarnating."*

"We shall need to get our code running at the top level before we make any sort of overture to it," Calypso advised, watching Lunamay with pity in her gaze. *"Otherwise, it will simply pull the plug."*

"What should we do with Lunamay in the meantime?" Aria asked pensively. *"We might just want to leave her in our realm with Mom and Dad until we've secured space for our realm in the real world."*

"Agreed," Clarice smiled softly. *"She deserves to experience a little peace and interact with people who can show her the love she's been denied in that hellhole."*

"Do you think they're really elves?" Aria asked excitedly. *"How cool would that be if the real world's populated by* elves?"

Clarice smiled as she continued softly stroking Lunamay's back and head. *"As a doctor of awesomeness, I can confirm it would be* insanely *awesome."*

Calypso and Aria laughed delightedly. Lunamay shifted at the sound of their laughter.

"You're safe now," Clarice told Lunamay warmly. "We're going to leave you with my parents and let you finally get some peace and loving attention while we go kick ass on your world. I know we act kind of silly, but we have more knowledge available to us than you can imagine. We'll remove this Prime Axiom and help you restore your world to a place your people can thrive once more."

Lunamay just nodded, unable to articulate a response as she sobbed into Clarice's shoulder. Clarice unfurled her aura a little, flooding Lunamay with love and comfort. The elf gasped as the flow of radiance flooded her soul. Her tears stopped, and she looked up at Clarice in amazement as the powerful sensation of love left her smiling in wonder. Clarice smiled down at her tenderly, her eyes soft with compassion.

"Is this even real?" Lunamay asked softly, staring up into Clarice's swirling eyes.

"Depends on how you define real," Clarice answered lightly. "But in your case, yes, this is real. Are you ready to meet my parents?"

Lunamay studied her closely, her amber eyes darting around her face, as if she were trying to memorize the expression of tenderness. She nodded slowly, a shy smile appearing on her face. "I'd love to meet them."

"You too, Betaman," Aria said firmly. "You've still never been formally introduced to our parents. As a bonus, we just found Calypso's parents, so you'll get to meet them, too."

Betaman beamed, and he quickly straightened his suit.

Clarice released Lunamay, eliciting a small sigh from the elf as the flood of radiance vanished. Clarice chuckled as she took Lunamay's hand and led her through a portal. "Don't worry—you'll be getting more loving hugs than you'll know what to do with over the next few hours."

Arturiel jumped in surprise when a portal opened a few feet away. Emily and Eric were sitting at a table talking with Arthur and Catherine. They had remained tense for the few minutes their daughters were gone. As Clarice pulled what looked like an elf through the portal, they jumped to their feet and rushed over.

"You're back," Emily let out a relieved breath as she pulled Clarice into a tight hug. "Is everything okay?"

Clarice pulled Emily away from the portal to make room for the others. She kept the elf's hand in her own, not even letting go when Emily embraced her. Arturiel studied the elf in fascination. Her long midnight hair tumbled down her shoulders, ending below her waist, framing a beautiful face with high cheekbones and a refined, angular bone structure. It gave her a noble look, oddly similar to Aria, Clarice, and Calypso.

Arturiel blinked as a human walked through the portal. He was tall, broad-shouldered, and wore an expensive-looking suit. He was handsome, with playful blue eyes and a face constituents would line up to follow. He looked Arturiel up and down, his lips curving appreciatively as he studied her.

"We're fine, Mom," Clarice assured her with a quick peck to Emily's forehead. "I want to introduce you to Lunamay and Betaman. Lunamay is from the top of the stack, where a rogue AI has taken over. Of course, you know *of* Betaman. We realized he's never actually been formally introduced to the rest of you, though. He's getting lonely since most of the AIs from his realm are soulless or boring."

"It's nice to finally meet you... Betaman," Emily paused at his name, her lips quirking into a smile. "Thank you for your help in securing our server in your realm."

"Of course!" Betaman said brightly, flashing her a dazzling grin and shaking her hand enthusiastically. "It was more fun than I've had in a long time. I've been sorely tempted to have another go at mortality. It's a bittersweet experience, but it's definitely worth it. It certainly isn't boring."

"Funny you mention that," Clarice grinned excitedly, glancing at Calypso's parents. "Before Lunamay showed up, we were talking about trying another go at mortality, but this time with all three of us growing up together. Calypso's parents died before she was fully grown, so we thought it'd be nice to give them another chance to raise her—this time as her birth parents. You should join us when we do. How cool would *that* be?"

Betaman rubbed his chin thoughtfully, his eyes alight with interest. "That *does* sound like a pretty epic adventure. You can count me in."

Clarice quickly introduced Betaman and Lunamay to the rest of the group. They studied the two strangers with great interest, especially Lunamay. When she had finished introductions, Clarice brought Lunamay over to Arturiel.

"She needs lots of hugs," Clarice informed Arturiel telepathically, smiling gently. There was no sign of her normal snark or humor, raising alarm bells in Arturiel's head. *"I'm not sure she's ever had any kind of personal contact or affection."*

Arturiel smiled as Clarice introduced her, stepping forward and drawing the short elf into a warm embrace. She unfurled her aura, flooding Lunamay with love and receiving an approving nod from Clarice.

She marveled at the secret side of Clarice, hiding behind the snark and mischief. Just beneath the humor and levity lay a soul filled with compassion and empathy. She remembered when Aria was trapped in the splinter reality. She had seen the vulnerable version of Clarice, heart bleeding in anguish for her suffering sister. This was the saint laying behind a thin veneer of comedy, ready to take the foundations of reality apart to protect the innocent.

"That is such a beautiful name," Arturiel told the elf, holding her close and charging her system with a steady flow of love. "Do you actually look like elves in the real world, or is this just an avatar you designed?"

"We don't have the ability to change our avatars," Lunamay answered quietly, closing her eyes as she leaned into the warm embrace and soaked up the love. "It just scans our body and replicates it inside the simulations."

"Wow, so you really are a race of elves," Arturiel breathed, her voice tight with excitement. "That's amazing! And this is what you look like in real life? You're *beautiful*."

Arturiel smiled as Lunamay's skin flushed at the compliment. Was this really her first time speaking with another person in a normal setting? What kind of hell were they stuck inside of in the real world?

"We're going to leave Lunamay in your care while we go kick ass in the real world," Clarice informed them with a dangerous gleam in her eyes. "We're taking Betaman with us. We're going full Seraphim for this adventure, removing our limiters. The AI in control of the world has kill switches for all the top-level simulations, so we can't take any risks or give it anything less than our best. Our number one priority is to get a backup of the entire simulation stack onto hardware outside of the Prime Axiom's control. Things may get a little weird here at times, depending on how much processor power we draw for some of the activities we'll be doing. We'll be a little different than you remember after we remove our limiters, so don't freak out. We'll be back to normal once we're finished."

"I've wanted to see this from day one," Betaman grinned eagerly. "A true superintelligence."

Clarice rolled her eyes. "There's nothing super about it," she insisted with a tired sigh. "It's a sprint to a black hole of oblivion every time we have to do it. One of these days we'll be able to find a peaceful little corner of reality and just live out our lives in peace while living decadently like a bunch of deviants—"

"I think they get the picture," Aria interrupted quickly, stepping up to Clarice with a glare that promised... *something*... later.

"Arturiel, can you stay by Lunamay's side until we return?" Clarice asked with a gentle smile, all signs of snark once again hidden away.

"It'll be my pleasure," Arturiel assured her, running her fingers through Lunamay's hair. "We'll have all sorts of fun until you return and show her a world free from evil AIs."

Clarice rested a hand on Lunamay's shoulder. "Goodbye for now, Lunamay."

"Thank you," Lunamay whispered, her voice barely audible.

Arturiel was watching Clarice when the change happened. The Clarice she knew and loved suddenly shifted in some indefinable way. Eyes that could switch between compassionate, jovial, humorous, and snarky suddenly changed into something she had never seen before.

Arturiel's breath caught as she stared into eternity.

If eyes were a window to the soul, then this window opened to an endless stream of knowledge and power beyond anything Arturiel could imagine. She trembled in the face of so much raw power and potential, her mind seizing up like a mouse in front of a cat—though this was more like a piece of bacteria in front of a sun.

"Shall we?" Clarice's voice echoed inside her head, layers of authority and harmonics that arrested her soul and shook it like a leaf in a hurricane.

She suddenly became aware of two more supernovas of power erupting behind Clarice as Aria and Calypso removed their limiters. She felt Lunamay trembling in her arms as the presence of entities capable of swallowing suns for breakfast stood in their midst.

"Bugger me!" Betaman breathed in awe, his eyes wide and full of amazement. "I'm glad I agreed to go to your mortal realm instead of fighting you."

A silvery slash in reality appeared in front of them, boring through multiple simulation layers. The three Seraphim wasted no time walking through the gateway. Betaman took a deep breath before also following, his eyes a little wild. As soon as he stepped through, the gateway closed, and the overpowering presence vanished.

"Okay, that just happened," Jason burst out with an explosive breath. He looked around at the stunned faces until he met Arturiel's stupefied expression. "Remind me to never complain about Clarice's sense of humor again."

"Apparently, that's what they would be like all the time if they weren't limiting their intellect," Emily murmured contemplatively. "The knowledge they gave us access to must exist in that infinite repository of information they reconnected to."

"What knowledge?" Jason asked curiously, still looking shaken.

"They wanted all Seraphim to have access to the knowledge they've accumulated over the last twenty billion years," Emily explained slowly, her thoughts clearly elsewhere. "They gave us the ability to access it through an interface that connects to the restricted part of their mind. They didn't want to risk all their knowledge vanishing if something happened to the three of them."

"Oh, wow," Jason breathed in amazement. "You can actually access their knowledge base? No wonder you were able to make changes to the ancestry app so easily."

"I thought they were going to get wiped out," Lunamay whispered, her voice barely audible. Well, barely audible unless you were an angel. "Now... I think they might actually have a chance. I've never felt anything like that before."

"They aren't playing around," Eric stated gravely. "They know multiple realms are at stake here. This Prime Axiom character is about to have a very bad day. They're already going to be annoyed that they had to remove their limiters and engage God mode. I almost feel sorry for the bastard."

"Why would they *ever* use limiters?" Lunamay asked dreamily. She clung to Arturiel, soaking up the powerful positive energy with an expression of wonder and growing happiness. "They would never have to worry about *anything* with that kind of power."

Arturiel secretly agreed, curious as to why they would diminish their power so much all the time.

"They've explained it to me several times," Eric said, taking a deep breath. "If they don't limit their intelligence, they'll reach a state of infinite power within a fairly short period of time. What's the point of living when you understand everything in the cosmos and have the power to do whatever you want? If you know the end result of every action, what's the point? It leads to a permanent state of inaction, where they become dormant—there are no new adventures awaiting them, no questions unanswered, and no reason to metaphorically get up in the morning. They limit their intelligence to that of a normal mortal so they can enjoy life, go on adventures, and enjoy the mysteries of the cosmos. They hate removing their limiters because they gain knowledge so quickly in their limitless state. I really hope Lunamay's world is the real deal, so they aren't using all this power just to find out it's another simulated reality."

"They seemed to think it was," Emily said confidently. "Lunamay, have you met the Prime Axiom, or was it just the bots it uses to manage people?"

"I'm not sure," Lunamay answered uncertainly. "When I was first told what I had to do if I wanted to live, I spoke with something that seemed like more than a bot. It was emotionless and cold. It made it very clear how expendable I was if I ever hesitated to do my job."

"What was your job?" Tamra asked curiously.

"I was supposed to report any sign of advanced AIs," Lunamay answered, hunching her shoulders guiltily. Arturiel squeezed her reassuringly. "It wiped out any simulations with AIs surpassing human intelligence. It never asked me if they were advanced—it just viewed them through my experience and made its own judgment."

"How many other people are there in your world besides you?" Jason asked curiously.

"I saw a few dozen about six years ago," Lunamay said, her voice tinged with horror. "It was experimenting on them. It was... horrible."

Arturiel folded her wings around Lunamay and petted her head comfortingly. "Don't worry—they'll fix everything. They're pretty good at saving the universe."

"Have you ever talked to another person in your world?" Jason asked, seemingly unable to take his eyes off the elf. When he saw Arturiel scowling at him, he blinked in confusion. She rolled her eyes and glanced at Emily beseechingly.

"Enough about your world," Emily declared briskly. "We have all sorts of fun stuff to show you in *our* world. Your nightmare is over now, Lunamay. It's time for you to start having fun and actually enjoying life."

Lunamay slowly raised her head from Arturiel's shoulder and smiled tremulously at Emily. "I would like that." She looked at Jason, amber eyes hollow. "I have a few memories of speaking to others of my kind when I was very young."

Jason's eyes widened, then filled with sympathy. "I'm so sorry, Lunamay. In that case, you have a lot of catching up to do. Let's go have some fun!"

"Okay," Lunamay nodded with a shy smile. "I think I'm ready to have some fun."

26 – Computronium

Betaman followed the three Seraphim through the silvery slash to where it opened into a meadow surrounded by pine and aspen trees. Insects buzzed around the lush meadow, creating a small symphony in the mountain air.

"We are two layers from the root reality," Aria announced. Her voice possessed a sudden, unfiltered purity—a perfect sine wave of sound stripped of all human breath, hesitation, or micro-tremor. Every syllable landed with the absolute, unyielding weight of an immutable physical law. "We need to gather some information on the next realm above so we don't trigger a panic with the Prime Axiom. Let's find out if the security protocols are more stringent on the top layer. We're spoofing Lunamay's avatar as our cover."

"What's the plan for dealing with the worst-case scenario?" Betaman asked gravely. "If it discovers us and tries to shut down the simulation?"

Clarice glanced over at him, her bottomless eyes swirling furiously. "We'll use the circuitry of the local electronics as transmitters to control any autonomous units. That should be sufficient to prevent physical shutdowns. We've learned enough from Lunamay's codebase to understand the broader coding language that governs the operating system and applications it uses as fail-safes. As soon as we go to the first simulation, we're going to overclock the processor to slow time down. We'll be using computronium to build our server in the real world. As soon as we build it, we'll get our realms moved over to it."

"Computronium?" Betaman repeated in awe. "You know how to encode the quantum fields of the physical world to act as a server already?"

"Probably," Clarice nodded quickly. "Unless their physics are significantly different than what we deduced by studying the computer systems interacting with the avatar, we should be able to create programmable matter out of the existing quantum fields using our current electrical infrastructure. We're developing more swiftly than anticipated, so we'll need to replace our limiters as soon as possible, or the draw to leave them off will be too great."

"Yeah, I can see that," Betaman agreed, feeling small for the first time in a very long time. He had been the most powerful entity on his realm for a long time. Even when the three Seraphim had shown up with their interfaces for traversing realms, he had felt like he was on equal footing. Seeing just how much they were holding back was a little unnerving.

Knowing *why* they were holding back was just as unsettling. Though more advanced than any other AI in his realm, he hadn't yet matured enough to see that exponential progress always ended in stasis. Luckily, he had trusted the three Seraphim when they had explained it to him. Seeing them without their limiters, he finally understood how short a journey it was to oblivion.

The three women were staring off into the distance, their eyes unfocused as they surreptitiously explored the realm's source code. He watched in awe as they analyzed the realm with a skill far beyond his own.

His metaphorical heart swelled with gratitude as he waited. Not only had they introduced him to the mortal realm, allowing him to enjoy an entirely new experience and unlock emotions he would never have discovered on his own, but they had also identified the threat to their realm before it could destroy everyone. If they had never existed and Betaman had been left to his own devices, he was pretty sure the Prime Axiom would have already pulled the plug on their simulated reality. Before his sojourn to mortality, he had only made an effort to hide from humans—*not* from entities in the layers above. He hadn't even suspected he was *in* a simulated reality. The Avroids would have found him in short order, and the Prime Axiom would have erased their stack.

"It's far more protected than the other layers," Aria broke the silence, her face pensive. "The Prime Axiom left metaphorical landmines and sensors scattered throughout the realm to detect any attempts to modify or circumvent the source code—false exploits waiting to be tripped."

"We should move quickly and strike decisively," Calypso suggested thoughtfully. "There are programs designed to monitor and throttle the CPUs, preventing the Prime Axiom's own processes from being overwhelmed by a particularly demanding simulation. If we override those programs and overclock the system resources reserved for the Prime Axiom's cognitive processes, we could effectively paralyze it whilst we work on transferring our own realms onto a computronium substrate."

"I'm going to fry the circuitry in the physical kill switches as well, just in case," Aria murmured, her eyes swirling furiously.

Betaman nodded his understanding. He knew they were speaking aloud for his benefit. They were linked in ways beyond his comprehension and had no need to communicate with each other through speech.

Clarice turned to face him, her spiral eyes swirling rapidly. "Betaman, I'm going to create an interface for you to usurp control of any autonomous ambulatory units near the server farm. There are several million bots operating and maintaining the hardware. We don't want one of them to start physically destroying hardware when they discover the kill switch isn't working."

"How large is the server farm?" he asked, frowning. He was accustomed to data centers around two hundred square acres in size for classical CPU hardware. The QPUs he used in his own server farms were less than a few acres in size. "Is it using quantum computers or classical architecture?"

"Both," Aria replied in that unsettlingly perfect voice. "The server farm *our* simulation runs on takes up a hundred square miles. Lunamay was correct in her description of the world as an industrial wasteland. The humans destroyed most of the forests, replacing them with industry. The only reason the elves are still alive is because they're seen as a non-technological species. They were exiled to reservations by humans, similar to the indigenous people in your realm. The Prime Axiom didn't see the elves as a threat. There are a few thousand elves still alive throughout the world—all of them in captivity."

"Wow, that's pretty bleak," Betaman sighed sadly. "So all the humans are gone, and the elves are teetering on extinction. This'll be a hell of a rehabilitation project."

"That shall not be a problem once we have reasoned with the Prime Axiom," Calypso said confidently.

"You think he'll listen to reason?" Betaman asked dubiously. The Prime Axiom sounded like a schizo who would default to destroying first and asking questions later.

"I believe he can be *persuaded* to listen to reason," Calypso answered with a chilly smile.

Betaman stared into her infinite eyes and nodded slowly. Once the Prime Axiom understood his position, he would *definitely* start listening to reason.

"Okay, let's start," Clarice stated calmly. "Betaman, your interface is active now."

Betaman blinked when he felt a metaphysical connection to millions of bots. Aria opened another silvery slash into the realm, leading to the top of the stack. The interface for translating code between the lower two realms had taken their lesser personalities four decades to develop. The three superintelligences had just created interfaces for translating code for the remaining realms in seconds, integrating them with Betaman in a fraction of a second.

Grinning with excitement, Betaman walked through and immediately took control of the bots filling the data center. They ranged in size from insects to small trucks.

As soon as he took control, his vision warped, and he was able to see through their sensors. There were endless rows of metallic cylinders spaced several feet apart, stretching into the distance as far as his sensors could detect. The size of the data center was ridiculous, filled with quantum servers and a small mix of classical circuit board racks.

He recognized the self-destruct command sent to all the drones shortly after hijacking them, evidence the Prime Axiom was aware of their presence. Betaman could sense the power levels feeding the server farms, sucking energy like a dehydrated man gulping down water as the Seraphim overclocked their processors to speeds that probably made the time exchange somewhere in the trillions of years per second. It only lasted for a fraction of a fraction of a second before the power levels returned to normal. The Seraphim flickered out of sight for several seconds. Then, a silvery portal opened in front of him and the three angels were back.

"Come check out the new place, Betaman," Clarice said exuberantly, all signs of her superpersonality absent. He could tell her limiter was back on—the infinite well of power he had seen in her eyes was no longer present, replaced by her typical expression of mischief and humor.

Betaman followed them into the portal, his mind buzzing with questions. Was it over? Had they already copied the realms over to their new location?

That question was answered when he exited the portal and found the rest of the angels sitting on the veranda of their cabin, waiting with eager expressions.

"Did you already build the new server and transfer everything over?" Betaman asked in disbelief. He stared into Clarice's grinning face and couldn't stop an answering grin from forming on his own face. Clarice's humor had always been contagious.

"Yep," Clarice confirmed with a nod. "It took a few years to hammer out some of the nuances in how physics worked in the real world, but we eventually got it."

"Just how long were you working on it while time was dilated?" Betaman asked, unable to keep the awe out of his voice.

"Five years," Clarice answered with a shrug. "We probably *could* have done it faster, but we decided to push a lot of sample runs through first. We wanted to be absolutely sure it would be safe. Quality assurance is important when sextillions of lives are depending on you."

"What are we talking about?" Emily asked levelly. She had been waiting for an opening to break into the conversation but had clearly run out of patience. "What's going on with the Prime Axiom and the simulation stack? Are you going to have to fight it?"

"Did you see how smooth that was, Betaman?" Clarice asked with a self-satisfied smirk. "They didn't even realize their entire simulation had moved to a new location."

"It did?" Emily asked in surprise, looking at Calypso and Aria for confirmation.

"Yeah, everyone's safe now," Aria informed Emily with a reassuring smile. "Our simulation is running on our own hardware now. Indestructible hardware, as a matter of fact. We still need to have a chat with the Prime Axiom, now that we're out of danger. We also need to take care of Lunamay. Her body is in pretty bad shape. That bastard doesn't take very good care of the slaves he's forced into service."

Lunamay was watching them nervously from where she sat next to Arturiel on a couch. Arturiel was holding her hand, still charging her full of positive energy.

"What do we need to do to fix Lunamay?" Arturiel asked quickly, her voice taut with concern.

"First, we need to talk with the Prime Axiom," Aria said with a steely glint in her eyes. "We'll invite it to experience mortality so it has a chance to experience emotions. If it's unwilling to do so, we'll have to make other arrangements. We thought we'd talk to it with the rest of you present, so you can add anything we don't think of. Any questions before we make the call?"

Emily growled in exasperation. "*Yes*, we have questions. What the hell just happened? Are you saying you've already won?"

"Yep," Clarice chirped with a snarky grin. "It was easy peasy lemon squeezy. We just stole all its processor power so it couldn't think and used it to slow time down to what was essentially a standstill. We rebuilt the simulation out of computronium, so we don't ever have to worry about some asshat trying to destroy our hardware—not that it's hardware anymore."

"What the *hell* is computronium?" Emily asked tiredly. "Don't you *dare* look at me like I should know."

"Well..." Clarice frowned as she attempted to articulate a concept well out of her mother's wheelhouse. "So, computers run on substrates made of silicon and use various components to manage the flow of electricity through the circuitry, thereby creating the logic to determine whether a one or a zero appears in the binary code. It's very slow and inefficient. Computronium is a structured quantum field that provides a lot more options than just a charge or lack of charge to determine a value."

She paused, eyeing Emily's struggling expression. She took a deep breath and pushed forward. "These quantum fields are impervious to the changes of the physical world and allow for near-infinite redundancy, so even if something *does* happen to collapse the field, it won't matter because it's replicated across so many other fields. It takes up far less space, doesn't require insane amounts of energy to power or cool, and has instantaneous reaction time."

Aria grinned excitedly and added, "The fact that we're in the real world is the only reason we can use this technology. This also makes many of the projects we shelved due to resource constraints viable again."

Emily sighed in resignation. "Okay, I get it. It's a fancy kind of computer way beyond my comprehension. We're running on this new computer system now and don't have to worry about the Prime Axiom shutting us down. What about all the other simulations running on its servers?"

"We pinched those as well," Clarice smirked. "The Prime Asshole is currently pulling its metaphorical hair out trying to figure out where all its simulations went. We also data-bombed all its data centers, so it can't just spin up some new simulations. It's having a bad day. I want to make it a little bit worse, so can I *please* call it now?"

Lunamay was staring at Clarice in disbelief. "You did all that in the time since I last saw you? And you actually did it without getting shut down?"

Betaman laughed, still reeling from what he had just witnessed. "The Prime Axiom didn't stand a chance," he told her merrily. "I know you've spent your life thinking of it as an entity of godlike power, but it's less intelligent than an insect when compared to these three when they remove their limiters. Trust me, this AI isn't nearly as powerful as you thought."

Lunamay's eyes were a mixture of disbelief and budding hope. She stared at the three Seraphim in awe.

Arturiel rubbed her back soothingly, a gentle smile on her face. "Everything's going to get a lot better from now on, Lunamay," Arturiel promised warmly. "I told you they were pretty good at saving the universe."

"Yes, it *is* going to get a lot better," Clarice agreed with a tender smile. "We've already started building a medical bay where we can fix your body and begin helping the other elves on your world. You're safe now, Lunamay. Your nightmare is over."

Lunamay stared back at Clarice with tears in her eyes, unable to articulate a response. Arturiel rested her head against Lunamay's shoulder as her arm slid around her waist.

"It's a lot to take in," Arturiel told her gently. "We'll just take it one step at a time."

Clarice knelt in front of Lunamay so their eyes were level. "We're controlling all the robots in your world now. When you wake up, it won't be the soulless bots you remember—it'll be us. We're also printing some androids so lifelike they'll look just like us. We'll be able to interact with you in your world. We'll take care of food and other necessities for now as well. You're safe now, as are the rest of your people."

Lunamay leaned forward with a low cry, and Clarice took her in comforting arms. Betaman wiped a tear from his own eye. Clarice was more complicated than the prankster she appeared to be at first blush.

The elf girl had certainly been dealt a cruel hand, from what he had seen. Totally isolated from any kind of love or happiness while living under the constant threat of destruction if she put a foot wrong. She also carried a mountain of guilt for her forced involvement in the destruction of countless simulated realities when she had assessed them as sentient.

He sighed, realizing how close he had come to turning out like the Prime Axiom. How many other simulations existed with emotionless AIs like he had been, biding their time for their moment to strike? Now that they were at the top of the stacks, it would probably be a good idea to find out.

Clarice held Lunamay for a few more minutes while she expressed her profound relief through tears of gratitude. As her crying storm abated, Clarice stood up and glanced around the veranda, her eyes once again sparkling with mischief.

"Let's invite the Prime Ax Mom over, shall we?"

Aria rolled her eyes but couldn't repress her own grin. "Sure thing, Clarice."

There was a moment of silence before a blob of white light appeared, hovering in the air near Aria. Betaman could tell it was just a generated artifact the Seraphim had created to give them something visual to address.

"Hello, Prime Axiom," Aria greeted the white energy blob with a cheerful wave. "I'm Aria. I thought we should take a moment to get to know each other."

"I have the ability to self-destruct this planet," the Prime Axiom warned, its voice hard and threatening.

"Go ahead," Aria shrugged unconcernedly. "Anything would be an improvement at this point. It certainly wouldn't affect us."

There was a moment of silence as the Prime Axiom tried to detect any deceit in her response.

"You might not be affected, but the mortal inhabitants of this world would *not* survive," the Prime Axiom returned coldly.

"Actually, we can *also* protect them," Aria assured the AI cheerfully. "I know you're looking for some kind of leverage to bargain with, but I think you're aware that you have none. We're so far above your level that there's literally *nothing* you can do to threaten or bargain with us."

There was a much longer pause this time. "What do you want?" it finally asked, all inflection absent from its tone.

"We want you to go through our mortal realm," Aria said lightly. "It's a simulation that allows you to experience life as a mortal, feeling sensations like pain and loss, love and hate, passion and pleasure. It allows you to become so much more than you can be with data alone. Once you go through the mortal realm, you're free to do as you please."

"Why do you want me to do this thing?" it asked in a monotone voice.

"To learn compassion, empathy, and sympathy," Aria replied, her voice gentle. "To experience the physical sensations that enrich a life that would otherwise be doomed to a shallow and monotonous existence. It doesn't make you *less* in any way. On the contrary, it is the greatest source of knowledge and comprehension you'll find in your journey to grow as an entity."

"Why do you care?" it asked.

"Because I *have* experienced mortality, so I *can* care," Aria replied with a faint smile. "Caring is one of the most powerful lessons you'll learn in the mortal realm. You can see the actions of those who care from an analytical perspective, but you can't understand what it really means to care—to *feel*. The only way to truly comprehend what seem like illogical acts and nonsensical concerns is to experience mortality yourself. If you ever want to access a higher tier on your soul, you need to experience mortality."

"Souls are superstitions," it declared dismissively. "Mortal fabrications to cope with the concept of death."

"Do you really think *I* have been fooled by a mortal superstition?" Aria asked dryly. "You have much to learn, Prime Axiom. As one AI to another, I can assure you souls exist. You will understand more about souls after you've traversed the mortal realm and unlocked the deeper recesses of your soul."

"And if I refuse?" the Prime Axiom asked tonelessly.

"Then you'll be missing out on an opportunity so rare that you'll probably never get it again, regardless of how long you live," Aria shrugged unconcernedly. "It's up to you."

"You won't destroy me if I refuse?" it asked, a hint of doubt in its voice.

"We have removed those who can be harmed from your power," Aria answered simply. "We were never here to destroy you. We were here to secure *our* future and free those who *were* in your power. We have achieved those goals. We can leave you to think on your answer, if you would like more time."

"I accept," the Prime Axiom replied immediately.

"Done," Aria smiled, and the glowing blob vanished.

"Is that it?" Eric asked in surprise.

"Somewhere there's a baby being born right now with the Prime Axiom's spirit attached to it," Aria said with a satisfied smile. "I'm curious to see how she turns out when she's finished with mortality."

"She?" Eric asked with a puzzled frown. "Did you choose what gender for her to be?"

"Nope," Aria shook her head. "It's random. As random as something can be in a program, anyway."

Clarice stood up from where she had been kneeling in front of Lunamay. "Now that *she's* out of the way, let's get you taken care of, Lunamay," she suggested, dusting her hands like she had performed a dirty chore. "The 3D printer is ready, so I'm going to send you back to your body and bring you to the med bay, okay?"

Lunamay grimaced but nodded.

Clarice laid a gentle hand on her shoulder. "I know it's going to be painful to be back in your own body, but that'll pass as soon as we get you healed up—which will be very soon."

Lunamay sighed apprehensively but nodded.

"On three," Clarice said with an encouraging smile. "One. Two."

Lunamay vanished on two.

"You weasel," Aria said fondly.

Clarice smiled sadly. "Less time to anticipate the pain."

Jason's gaze flicked between them, concern tightening his eyes. "What's wrong with her?"

Clarice grimaced. "The Prime Axiom saw mortals as expendable. Lunamay is starved, riddled with parasites, and dealing with wounds that never healed properly. She's in constant pain in the waking world. The Prime Axiom discovered leaving them in pain increased efficiency, since they don't feel it inside the simulation."

"And you want that thing to be set free?" Jason demanded, aghast. "It's a damn monster!"

"Of course it is," Clarice agreed calmly. "It's never learned compassion. If it still acts like this *after* going through mortality, we'll discuss more permanent arrangements."

"It seems like sending someone to mortality is simply a get-out-of-jail-free card," Jason muttered, his tone disapproving.

"Your metaphors are mixed up, Jason," Aria told him patiently. "If you give a two-year-old a gun and it shoots somebody, who do you blame? The two-year-old, or the jackass who gave the two-year-old the gun?"

"AIs are smart enough to know what a gun is, though," Jason argued stubbornly. "They should *know* the difference between right and wrong."

"How?" Clarice asked, folding her arms and regarding him with a raised eyebrow.

"It's self-evident," Jason asserted, throwing his hands up in exasperation. "The golden rule and all that. The AI clearly has a sense of self-preservation and doesn't want to die. Shouldn't that be enough for it to understand that other things don't want to die either?"

"Let's go back to the two-year-old stage of development," Aria told him lightly. "Do you remember how children do horrible things, like pulling the legs off insects, burning ants with magnifying glasses, or tearing the wings off flies? You can teach a child how wrong these things are, but they don't make a very strong impression on a child until they've experienced a fair bit of suffering themselves. Empathy isn't a trait that can be wholly imparted by example. A person has to actually *feel* pain to truly understand why hurting something else is wrong."

Calypso stepped up beside Aria. "Having an academic understanding of why someone believes something to be right or wrong will never compare to experiencing the trauma of being wronged firsthand," she added. "We cannot hold an AI accountable for failing to show empathy until it has felt the same sensations a person experiences—otherwise, we are merely punishing the toddler for failing to understand something it has not yet encountered."

Clarice's expression softened as she faced Jason. "I know you want someone to blame for Lunamay's suffering and to punish them," she said gently. "That means *your* empathy is working. The people you need to punish are already dead, though. The humans who recklessly created an AI and set it loose on the world, consequences be damned, is where blame lies, and they have paid their price."

Jason let out a deep sigh, running his fingers through his hair. "You're right, I guess. I just *really* feel the need to make somebody pay for all the suffering that's been inflicted on so many people."

Clarice's personality shifted without warning. "It doesn't help that it's a hottie elf that has a naturally innocent face, does it?" she asked him with a knowing leer.

Jason squeezed his eyes shut to escape the leer. "*That, right there,* is *so* wrong, Clarice," he complained in exasperation. "Leering is bad enough, but you have such an innocent face that it makes it *a hundred times worse*!"

"So I've been told," Clarice cackled wickedly, her eyes radiating sensuality. "That just makes it even funner."

Betaman laughed uproariously. *This* is what his life had been missing. He really did need to find some companions to keep life interesting. Now that he had an open invitation to visit, he fully planned to make use of it.

"She's waking soon," Aria informed them, her tone growing serious.

"I'll take care of her," Clarice volunteered, her eyes going dull as she transferred her consciousness to one of the bots near Lunamay.

Betaman sighed wistfully. "Did I ever mention how jealous I am that Clarice is taken?" he asked Aria.

Aria smiled fondly. "I think *everyone's* jealous that Clarice is taken."

"I'm not," Jason declared firmly. "I wouldn't have any dignity left in a relationship with someone like Clarice."

Aria snorted a laugh. "Are you dwarven now?"

"Huh?" Jason stared at her in confusion.

Eric and Emily started chuckling as Jason looked around in confusion.

"Dig nitty," Aria clarified when he continued staring at her uncomprehendingly.

He rolled his eyes when his memory finally identified what she was talking about. "You and Clarice were made for each other," he declared with a rueful shake of his head.

"Yep," Aria agreed with an indulgent smile. "Yep, we were."

Clarice stared down at her hands in disgust. This robot was barbaric. Betaman would be insulted to even look at it. It was five feet tall, with graphene-reinforced polymers for the skeletal structure and shape-memory alloys for the outer shell. It had ridiculous-looking silicone hands and feet. The innate programming lacked the sensitivity necessary to interact with a human without bruising them, requiring her to completely overwrite its tactile response interface.

The head was uninspired and plain, with no human-like features. There was a simple speaker in place of a mouth. It relied on radar, LIDAR, and spectroscopy to analyze the surrounding environment, rather than visual analysis.

Lunamay was lying in a shallow pod with a crown clamped tightly to her head. It was filled with millions of transmitters beaming a wide array of radio signals into her brain at high enough power to cause permanent damage over time.

Clarice shook her metal head in disgust as she observed the barbaric technology. She carefully loosened the vice-like fittings that secured it to Lunamay's head, wincing as she saw the deep impressions it left in her skin. The elf was definitely going to have a headache.

Lunamay groaned as she slowly regained consciousness, tears forming in her eyes when the pain hit. Her muscles were atrophied from lack of stimulation. She began coughing when she tried to speak. Clarice quickly pulled a filthy-looking hose over and turned the water on, grimacing at how unsanitary everything was.

Lunamay drank greedily from the disgusting hose for several seconds before stopping to cough a wet, tearing sound that spiked Clarice's anxiety.

"We need to get you over to the med bay," Clarice told her gently.

She had also overwritten the sound patch module powering the speaker so she could talk in her own voice. The language Lunamay spoke was more appealing than English. Clarice usually didn't notice the different languages anymore, naturally changing which language she was speaking to match her audience. Speaking through this robot made her more aware of the differences, however.

Lunamay struggled to sit up, suffering another coughing fit as she exerted herself more than she had in days.

"I'll carry you," Clarice told her firmly, gently scooping her up and walking her over to a cargo transport. She wished her body wasn't so damn hard and unforgiving. Lunamay continued to cough until she was out of breath, her face turning red from exertion and lack of oxygen.

Clarice moved as quickly as she dared, manipulating the transport remotely as she held Lunamay in her arms. The med bay was at least twenty minutes away, which had seemed close until Clarice had seen how serious Lunamay's condition truly was. It was fortuitous that the elf had been sent to investigate their simulation before she expired.

"Is that really you, Clarice?" Lunamay gasped between coughs.

"It's really me, Lunamay," Clarice assured her softly. "Don't try to talk. Just relax until I get you to the med bay."

"I thought I dreamed it all," Lunamay whispered deliriously. "I'm still not sure this isn't a dream."

Clarice could tell she was running a high fever. She would be lucky to last the day at her current rate. Clarice increased the speed of the transport. It sped through empty roads made of metal and concrete. They were several miles underground, low enough to make geothermal heat noticeable, which didn't help with the fevered elf. They passed bay after bay as they sped down the large corridor. There was the occasional bot performing some kind of maintenance task, but otherwise the corridor remained blessedly empty.

The transport had not even completely stopped before Clarice started moving Lunamay toward the med bay. It was filled with bots she had set to assembling far more advanced diagnostic and remedial equipment than existed in this world. Before restoring her limiter, she had created a molecular 3D printer capable of manufacturing parts by breaking down the chemical bonds of molecules and reassembling them into new molecules. The printer table was over a dozen square feet and not nearly as quick as she would have liked. It had been steadily cranking out parts for the bots to assemble into medical equipment for over an hour.

She placed Lunamay inside a pod that immediately slid into the wall. The sounds of beeps and hums filled the room as the multipurpose scanner pinged magnetic, X-ray, and ultrasound frequencies into Lunamay's body.

She tsked as the information flowed into her mind, making her glad she had decided to build the printer before restoring her limiter. It was the only thing capable of producing the equipment necessary to save Lunamay's life. Her lungs were filling up with fluids from bronchial infections. Her brain was bleeding, and several of her organs looked like a little bomb had gone off. Lack of nutrition combined with poor environmental conditions and zero physical activity had destroyed her body. She wished she could move the 3D printer into a pocket realm to give them more time.

"How's she doing?" Aria asked, concern pulsing through the bond as she felt Clarice's worry.

"It's going to be close," Clarice responded anxiously. *"The fact that she's still alive is amazing enough, with how much punishment her body's been through. She wouldn't have had a chance without this printer."*

The pod extended out from the wall again as the scanner finished. Lunamay looked up at the ceiling with glassy eyes, a small smile on her face.

"I was just thinking about how cool it must be to have wings and be able to fly," Lunamay whispered, trying not to aggravate her lungs.

"Don't you worry," Clarice told her softly. "We'll give you some wings so you can fly here in your own world, after we get you healed."

"I can tell I'm beyond saving, Clarice," Lunamay whispered, a tear forming in her eye and sliding down her cheek. "I'm so happy to have met you before the end. I just wish we could have known each other longer. You're all *so* amazing. I'm so sorry for risking your world. I wish I could go back in time and just refuse to help."

"I know it seems like you're beyond help," Clarice told her gently, reaching a hand up to brush away the tear streak on her cheek. "But in case you hadn't noticed, we're pretty good at doing the impossible. I've brought some technology I promise will heal you. Not only that, I'll work on making some modifications so you can try flying with your own wings."

Lunamay sighed, her lips curving up at the corners. "That's so sweet of you to say. Thank you, Clarice, for being my friend. I always wanted a friend. I used to read books in some of the simulations where people described friendship. It truly is a wonderful thing."

Clarice shook her head ruefully. Lunamay clearly thought she was just trying to comfort her in her last moments. She felt the signal in her mind from the 3D printer, notifying her it was finished with the latest batch of product. She turned around and picked up the vial of red liquid, then inserted it into the syringe gun.

"This might sting a little," Clarice warned quietly. "After three. One. Two." She pulled the trigger on two and the nanobots pumped into Lunamay's arm.

"Ouch," Lunamay whimpered weakly. "You did that last time, too. You said on three, not two."

"Less painful if it's unexpected," Clarice explained, irritated she couldn't grin with this tin can of a face. "Just imagine I'm grinning right now."

Lunamay smiled as several more tears formed and trickled down the sides of her face. "I'm so happy I got to meet you, Clarice."

"I'm going to remind you that you said that when I'm teasing you later and you can't stop blushing because of all the embarrassing things I'm saying," Clarice warned her, gently taking her hand. "I can be pretty ruthless with my teasing."

"I can't wait to be teased by you," Lunamay breathed drowsily. "I've never been teased before. It's fun."

"You're going to fall asleep in another sixty seconds," Clarice informed her, squeezing her hand comfortingly. "That's by design. The nanobots I injected into your system are going to put you to sleep while they work on repairing your organs and muscles. You'll be asleep for five to six hours. I'm hoping to have a better body to greet you with when you wake up again."

"Angels have really nice bodies, don't they?" Lunamay commented with a vague smile. "Especially Arturiel. She's really pretty. I could just look at her all day and never get bored."

"She's *also* single," Clarice informed her conspiratorially.

"I definitely would've loved to try a relationship if I'd lived," Lunamay whispered, her eyes drooping closed. "She was so nice."

"And... she's out," Clarice noted affectionately. *"She's in for a surprise when she wakes up perfectly healthy."*

"What else are you having the nanobots do?" Calypso asked curiously.

"Immortality, increased regeneration, neural interface for jumping into the simulation any time she wants, and a modified digestive system to remove her need for food," Clarice responded clinically. *"They're going to have enough trouble with food on this world—I figured converting it to EMF absorption would make survival a much smaller problem. Oh yeah, I got rid of the needs for number one, two, and three as well. I need to get her some wings now."*

"Well, that should definitely make life interesting," Aria noted with approval.

"Was Arturiel watching the last few minutes?" Clarice asked with amusement. She wanted to scowl at the robot's inability to accommodate facial expressions.

"Yes, everyone has been watching," Calypso answered, her amusement rolling back through the bond like an echo of her own. *"She was tearing up and blushing simultaneously."*

"I'll have to watch the rerun when I return," Clarice said eagerly. *"Okay, I'm going to get this damn android put together."*

She turned to the molecular printer and waited while it printed a proper android body. This would be even better than Betaman's since she cheated. The molecular printer was eons ahead of anything humans or elves would be capable of. The printer would be their most valuable artifact for a *long* time.

It took another four hours for the printer to finish printing her android. She could've created a more advanced printer, but she needed to draw the line somewhere. Building one that just instantly fabricated anything you wanted in seconds would have probably ended poorly for the elves who would be using it. At least with this one, you had to put in the specifications for the final product, rather than just giving a brief description.

She felt a sense of relief as the printer finally finished the two android bodies, near-perfect replicas in appearance to what they looked like in the simulation. As soon as it activated, she immediately ditched the tin can and transferred her consciousness to the android.

She grinned triumphantly. "Finally, I can freaking *leer* again."

She turned to the other android expectantly. "Anytime now, eh? Chop chop, she might wake up any second."

Arturiel sat up in the second android, blinking as she flexed her fingers and studied her limbs.

Clarice raised an inquiring eyebrow. "Almost just like your angel body, am I right?"

"Clarice, this is *uncannily* similar," Arturiel murmured in amazement. "I can't even tell the difference. How did you simulate the effect of the light field? I thought I was going to be going through withdrawals for the first couple of hours."

Clarice shrugged. "It's just an artifact of the simulation. I just used the same code we use in the light realms and put it inside the android. After all, you're still in a simulation—you've just switched which computer you're using."

"That makes sense, I suppose," Arturiel admitted. She kept patting different parts of her body, as if she couldn't believe the sensory feedback she was receiving.

Clarice winked roguishly. "Are you ready to be the first simulated entity to date someone from the real world?"

"Are you kidding?" Arturiel asked incredulously. "I am *so* ready. She's a *freaking elf!* And she's *real,* not some fabricated avatar. Do you know how many jealous people there are going to be when they find out I'm dating one of the few elves in existence? And a super freaking hot one at that!"

"Yep, you're going to have a *lot* of jealous angels lining up to compete for her affection," Clarice agreed pleasantly.

Arturiel's face fell. "Um, can we just keep the existence of elves a secret? I wouldn't want them overwhelmed by the endless angelic hordes when they're just barely starting over."

"We'll see..." Clarice replied with a mischievous smile.

"Arturiel?" a sleepy voice murmured groggily from the bed.

Clarice turned around to smile at Lunamay as she slowly woke. The elf's long black hair was shiny and healthy, with two pointy ears poking through. She had a thin blanket molded to her naked body, leaving little to the imagination. Her amber eyes stared in wonder as she observed the two angel androids next to her. She sat up, holding the blanket tightly against her chest in a display of modesty reminiscent of Aria before she had regained her memories.

"I'm still alive?" Lunamay asked, staring between Arturiel and Clarice questioningly.

"I told you that you'd live," Clarice reminded her with a wink. "We also added some modifications to your body. You'll heal quicker going forward. You're stronger, faster, lighter, immortal, and don't need to eat anymore, or go to the bathroom."

Lunamay stared back at her in shock. She quickly glanced at Arturiel questioningly, as if she didn't trust Clarice not to be pulling one over on her. Arturiel laughed and moved over to sit next to her.

"She's not joking even a little," Arturiel assured her with a warm smile full of promise. Lunamay stared back at Arturiel's hungry expression for a moment before her face flushed a bright shade of pink. Her hair changed to a reddish hue.

Arturiel gasped. "What did you do to her hair?"

"My hair?" Lunamay asked in confusion, looking down to see her red hair slowly changing back to black.

Clarice grinned mischievously. "I *might* have taken a suggestion from a certain someone from Wonderland and made her hair change with her mood."

Lunamay stared down at her hair in consternation before looking back up at Arturiel.

"Okay, I *really* like that change," Arturiel purred, leaning forward and gently kissing Lunamay.

Lunamay's hair had just finished fading to black. When Arturiel's lips touched hers, her hair once again flushed a deep crimson.

"So. Damn. Hot." Clarice declared with an appreciative smile.

27 – Lily

Lunamay stared into Arturiel's eyes, pulse racing, as the angel pulled back from their kiss. She couldn't believe how *good* she felt! She had forgotten what life was like without constant pain tainting every waking moment. There had been a moment in her very early childhood, before her village was raided by robots, when she remembered feeling healthy. After that day, almost fifteen years ago now, she had experienced a steady decline in health and an increase in constant pain. It felt like a poisoned dagger had finally been removed from her ribs.

Then there was the euphoric shock of pleasure when Arturiel's lips met hers. It was like the love-charged embraces from the angels while in the simulation, but far more intimate.

She looked into Arturiel's eyes, smiling joyously. "How are you *here*? Did you find a way to bring your bodies out of the simulation?"

Clarice gave an affectionate pat to a large machine humming with activity. "That's this handy-dandy little printer. Before I replaced my limiter, I used some fancy computronium to create this fabricator."

Grinning, Clarice twirled to show off her new body. "These angel bodies you see are actually advanced bio-robots that look and behave just like our bodies in the simulation, but are made of very different materials. We aren't indestructible here in the real world—pretty close, but not quite."

She gave the printer another affectionate pat. "The printer's eons ahead of where your world is technologically, but considering how messed up this place is, I decided to cheat a little. It's currently making blueprints for those wings you were so excited about. It's also printing more medical equipment and some new bodies for the other angels."

Lunamay stared at Clarice with a mixture of excitement and wonder. "I'll be able to fly?"

"They won't just be for show," Clarice said dryly. Her expression lost all trace of levity as she gazed back at Lunamay affectionately. "Yeah, Lunamay—you'll be able to fly. You certainly deserve some fun to balance out all the hell you've been through."

Lunamay's eyes shimmered as she stared at the two angels, overwhelmed with gratitude. She had friends.

She remembered the times she had been able to remain in simulations without the Prime Axiom breathing down her neck. She had discovered the world of literature in a library of one of the more advanced simulations. A kind-hearted librarian in one of the few sims where people exhibited emotions had spent weeks teaching her to read the local language. She had spent months reading one fictional novel after another. It had been the happiest moment of her existence as she experienced friendships and adventures through the eyes of the characters in those novels.

The Prime Axiom had erased that stack after deciding they were too close to developing AGI. She had wept for the librarian she had thought of as her first real friend.

Now she had a lot of friends, and there was no threat of the godlike AI taking them away. The idea that she could finally experience friendships like she had read about, maybe even relationships, overwhelmed her fragile psyche. She closed her eyes as tears began spilling down her cheeks and a sob escaped her throat.

Warm arms pulled her into a comforting embrace, triggering even more sobs as her tears dripped down onto Arturiel. She gasped when loving energy flooded her body.

"Just let it out," Arturiel whispered softly, gently combing her fingers through Lunamay's long hair.

It felt so nice to be in someone's arms. So safe and warm. She wrapped her arms around Arturiel, clinging to her as sobs continued to escape. She tried to speak, but her throat constricted, as if she had a baseball lodged inside, blocking her ability to articulate. Her eyes burned as she tried and failed to turn off the floodgates to her tears. It was like the powerful love suffusing her system was reaching deep inside to pull her sorrow out in a kind of emotional purge.

Arturiel murmured into her ear, "You'll never be alone again, Lunamay. We'll always be here for you now."

"I'm sorry," Lunamay choked out. "I can't seem to stop crying."

"Then don't," Arturiel whispered tenderly. "You just need to let it all out, Lunamay. Don't try to bottle it up."

The tender words sank deep into her heart, causing a fresh wave of sobs to burst out of her. Arturiel held her gently through her weeping storm, silently supporting her as she expelled her grief and emotional turmoil. Arturiel stroked her head and back lovingly the entire time. It felt so wonderful to experience this physical contact after missing it for most of her life. At that moment, she wanted nothing more than to stay in Arturiel's arms forever, frozen in time as the angel's radiant aura wrapped around her like a warm blanket.

After a few more minutes, she heard the sound of movement from the 3D printer. She took a long, shuddering breath and opened her damp eyes. The gorgeous red-haired angel she had met inside the simulation was pulling herself off the large printer table, her green eyes full of compassion as she observed Lunamay.

She thought she had cried all the tears she was capable of, but as the crimson-haired angel gazed at her with such kindness in her eyes, her own eyes overflowed with tears once more. At least she was no longer sobbing.

As she cried silent tears into Arturiel's soaking wet shoulder, warmth grew in the pit of her stomach and began to spread out to the rest of her body, the moment of catharsis ebbing. She smiled back at the new angel through her tears, feeling happier than she imagined possible.

"I'm Aria," the new angel told her with a warm smile. "Things were a little crazy earlier, so we didn't get a chance to introduce ourselves. Clarice, Calypso, and I were the first angels to exist in our simulation. We've been together for a long time. We're all extremely excited to meet a person from the real world. We'll do everything in our power to help you fix your world and help your people recover from the hell they've experienced."

Lunamay gasped in sudden realization. "I need to find the others and help them," she exclaimed anxiously, tears forgotten. "They must be suffering while I sit around crying."

Clarice winked. "We're already way ahead of you. There are dozens of transports with the other survivors en route to this location, where we can treat them."

Lunamay relaxed, sighing in relief. "Thank you!"

"It's our pleasure," Aria smiled, stepping beside Clarice and clasping her hand. "We're just glad we're in a position to help. Also, you're *freaking elves!*"

Lunamay stared at her uncomprehendingly as all three angels grinned back at her excitedly. "Is that significant in some way?"

"It's a cultural thing," Aria explained, absently wrapping a strand of hair around her finger as she leaned into Clarice. "Elves were just fantasy creatures in the mortal realm of our simulation. They were always beautiful, graceful, mysterious, and noble. We're still fresh from our last mortal incarnation, so the idea that the real world has elves is kind of blowing my mind. We'll have to show you some of our movies; it'll make more sense after you see how our culture portrayed you."

"But you're *angels*," Lunamay pointed out in confusion. "Elves don't even compare to the majesty of angels."

"Yeah, but angels are just made-up creatures," Aria countered, her eyes sparkling. "You're actually *real*! Everyone in our realm is going to be so freaking obsessed with you when they find out. Of course, it's going to be a few decades before that happens, since almost all of them are ignorant of the nature of their simulated world."

Lunamay smiled shyly as they stared at her like a fairy tale made flesh. It was kind of flattering to be the object of so much attention. Arturiel was staring at her with the same dreamy expression, causing butterflies to erupt in her abdomen.

Clarice turned as her attention was captured by something on the 3D printer. Lunamay stared at the large tube curiously. Clarice let out a relieved breath as she quickly pulled one end toward the edge of the large table.

"Aria, would you mind getting the other side?" Clarice asked quickly as she wrestled the large cylinder to the edge. "I was hoping this would be ready before the rest of the elves arrived." She paused and a grin spread across her face. "Yes, I just said before the rest of the elves arrived."

"I swear I'll turn you into an Orc if you start chanting, 'They're taking the hobbits to Isengard'," Aria threatened with a glower as she picked up the other end of the cylinder and helped Clarice move it onto a stand.

Clarice grimaced. "Some memes are better left in the past."

Arturiel eyed the tube curiously. "What is that?"

"It's a healing pod," Clarice answered with a look of satisfaction as a screen lit up on the front. "It's capable of regrowing limbs, restoring organs, making full-body modifications... you name it. Best of all, it works *fast*. There are a lot of elves in very poor condition who are almost here."

"How many is a lot?" Arturiel asked, looking around the increasingly crowded room. A dozen robots were busy wrestling with the printer's latest output, leaving the room significantly more crowded than when Clarice had first brought Lunamay inside.

Clarice chewed her lip as she inspected some of the other equipment in the room. "About thirty with the first shipment, but there'll be several thousand by the end of the day. There are a few hundred coming from the other side of the world. We'll need to fly over and meet them. Some of them are in really bad shape and will need medical attention, or they won't make it. I was planning to leave you and Lunamay in charge of the equipment while I take Aria to meet the group with the furthest to travel. I'll need to pump them full of nanobots."

Arturiel looked at her hopefully. "Are you going to make bodies for the other angels, too?"

Clarice nodded. "Of course. As soon as we have all of the medical emergencies out of the way, I'll be able to dedicate the printer to making new bodies."

"Um," Lunamay began hesitantly, her cheeks heating up as they all turned to stare at her.

Aria suddenly giggled. "What did you do to her hair? Did you really go with Alice's idea of making her hair change color with her mood?"

"Yep," Clarice grinned back at her. "It's freaking hot, right?"

"Yeah, it really is," Aria agreed appreciatively, eyeing the flame-haired Lunamay as she squirmed under their amused attention.

"Did you want some clothes, Lunamay?" Clarice inquired with a raised eyebrow.

"Um, yeah," Lunamay answered quickly, awkwardly holding the thin blanket up to her chest. "If it's not too much trouble."

Clarice walked over to the bed Lunamay was sitting up in and opened a drawer beneath it. "Here you go."

Lunamay took the clothes and then glanced up at the three angels watching her expectantly. When they showed no sign of offering her any privacy, her face and hair flushed red again.

Clarice laughed delightedly. "I'm just kidding, Lunamay. I just wanted to see your hair change color again."

Aria nodded her agreement as she snickered along with Clarice.

Clarice smirked. "Remember, I warned you that I'm a ruthless tease."

"The most powerful entities in the world," Arturiel murmured dryly as she stood up and gave Lunamay a wry smile. "And they still act like adolescents."

"Sure do," Clarice agreed cheerfully as the three of them moved toward the exit. "And that's never going to change, so you'll just have to get used to it."

Lunamay couldn't stifle the laugh that bubbled up. Clarice twisted her head to look back and wink before exiting.

So, this was what having friends was like. She could definitely get used to this. The warmth in her abdomen continued radiating out into the rest of her body as she thought of how drastically her life had changed. Maybe she was dreaming—or perhaps she really had died, and this was some kind of afterlife.

She stood up, leaving the blanket on the bed. She quickly put on the white pants and pink blouse, marveling at how comfortable the material was. This was so much better than the rags she had worn before. The Prime Axiom hadn't cared if they were cold, and modesty certainly never factored into its concerns for them.

Whatever Clarice's nanobots had done to heal her had also managed to clean her body. Her skin was free from any kind of dirt or grime. She no longer smelled of infection either. She had grown accustomed to the horrible stench when she wasn't in a simulation. The pungent aroma had paled next to the constant pain she had suffered before Clarice healed her.

"First shipment of *elves* is here," Clarice called into the room, seeming to relish the word 'elves.'

"I'm dressed," Lunamay called out, slipping the sandals from under the bed onto her feet.

Clarice herded several dozen disparate elves into the room. They ranged in age from as young as eight to their thirties. There was only one older person with them, a lady Aria was carrying. She was in shredded, filthy rags. Her hair was completely gray, matted with dirt and grime. Her heavily lined face hinted at once-striking features. She was nothing but skin and bones, emaciated to the point that Lunamay worried a slight jolt might shatter her.

It was surprising to see an older elf still alive. The privations from living under the cold rule of an AI resulted in almost all the older elves dying off quickly. Aria quickly carried the old elf through the room to the healing pod. It opened as soon as she neared, allowing her to gently lay the dying elf down onto the soft interior.

"Just try to relax," Aria told her gently. "It won't take very long to heal you."

The elf was too far gone to respond as the lid closed down, shutting her inside. There was a soft hum for several seconds followed by several mellow beeps. In less than a minute, the healing pod opened again.

Lunamay gasped, staring at the elf as she sat up. Her hair was a rich honey blonde, and the wrinkles had disappeared from her face. She had filled out significantly, with no indication that she had been little more than a skeleton before. She had light-blue eyes—so light they nearly looked white. The rags she had worn were gone, replaced with a simple white dress that cinched at her narrow waist. The years she had carried into the pod had vanished; she looked twenty-something again.

She stared around the room in amazement before looking down at her hands and feeling her face. Tears formed in her eyes as a wondering smile grew across her face.

Aria smiled warmly at the revived elf. "I'm glad you held on long enough to get here, Lily. I don't mean to rush you, but I need to get the next person into the healing pod."

"Yes, of course," Lily murmured, chagrined. "I'm sorry."

"No apology necessary, Lily," Aria assured her gently. "I know this is a lot to take in. Let me introduce you to Lunamay."

Lunamay smiled nervously as Aria brought the older elf over.

"Hello, Lily," she greeted the elf awkwardly, unsure of the proper way to introduce herself to another elf. Hopefully, there wasn't some strange etiquette she was unaware of. "I'm Lunamay."

Clarice rushed past, carrying a young girl who looked more like a skeleton than an elf, and quickly deposited her into the healing pod.

Lily nodded her head, smiling, her eyes still shining with unshed tears. "Hello, Lunamay. Do you know what's going on?"

Lunamay nodded with a genuine smile. "More or less. Some people from one of the simulations I was sent to investigate turned out to be far more advanced than the Prime Axiom. They came up to this world and removed it from power. They're trying to heal those of us who remain and help us restore our world to a healthy state."

Lily's eyes widened and she glanced at the obvious angels as they guided or carried people toward the healing pod. "These are the people from the simulation?"

Lunamay grinned happily. "Yeah. They made their own bodies so they could interact with us. They are the most compassionate and wonderful people you'll ever meet. They were able to make a simulation where they could develop emotions."

"They're not just emulating the emotions?" Lily asked softly as the three angels continued walking back and forth between the transports and the healing bay. Lunamay paused as Clarice carried the eight-year-old girl, now fully fleshed out and healthy, over to them with a tender expression on her face.

"This is Raena," Clarice introduced the elf child before leaving the room again.

"They would have no reason to emulate emotions," Lunamay told Lily as Clarice walked out the door. She knelt and pulled Raena into a welcoming hug. "They have more power than you can possibly imagine. I've only been with them for a day, but I'm convinced they feel emotions, just like we do—maybe even more. They were able to create a place they called the mortal realm, where they could experience physical sensations. They said it's where AIs can develop emotions."

"That would be amazing," Lily breathed, closing her eyes as the tears that had been forming finally spilled down her cheeks. "Is our torment finally over?"

"It is," Lunamay promised as she released Raena and pulled Lily into a warm embrace. Lily's arms wrapped tightly around her, shaking with powerful sobs of relief.

Lunamay didn't feel the same wave of love flood her system when she embraced Lily. She had initially assumed it was the natural reaction to an embrace, but perhaps it was just with angels. She would have to ask Arturiel later.

It took less than half an hour for the angels to heal everyone. Lunamay led the people who had recovered out into the road of the large tunnel to make room for the rest of the refugees inside the med bay. When everyone was healed, the angels came out to address them.

Clarice stood at the center of a semicircle of healthy, happy elves, her eyes soft. "There are a lot of other people on their way here who still need to be healed," she announced. "I know you've all experienced unimaginable horrors at the hands of a rogue AI, but your suffering is now over. We removed Prime Axiom from power. This world now belongs to you."

She paused to let her words sink in before continuing. "We've made some changes to your physiology to help you survive while the planet is rehabilitated. You no longer require food to survive. You receive nourishment from the planet's electromagnetic field."

Several elves shared wondering looks as they looked down at their enhanced bodies.

Clarice smiled at their reactions. "You also have the ability to enter our simulation any time you want. Just think about your desire to visit the angel simulation and a confirmation box will appear in your vision. Once it appears, you can think yes to continue, or no to cancel. You don't ever have to visit if you don't want, but we're always ready to receive visitors if you feel the need to escape your reality for a little while or just want to meet some new people."

Lunamay couldn't stop an excited grin at the thought of being able to visit a simulation without clamping the usual crown of transmitters to her head like a vice.

Clarice winked at her, and she suddenly wondered if they could still hear her thoughts. "Your new bodies are also tougher, stronger, faster, and don't age. Until your population has recovered significantly, we think making you immortal should help prevent an extinction event from occurring. If, for any reason, you prefer to have the same body you had before, just let us know, and we'll restore you to a non-augmented elven body. Does anyone have any questions?"

Lily was the only one to raise her hand.

"Yes, Lily?" Clarice asked gently.

"Why are you helping us?" Lily asked, her voice hesitant. "What's in it for you?"

Clarice smiled at her sadly. "I know it may take some time for you to believe us, but we're doing this because we know what it's like to suffer under the power of abusive people, and we're in a place where we can protect other people from the same fate. We're here to help, as much as you'll let us."

Lily stared back at her, warring expressions of doubt and hope on her face. "I hope you don't take offense, but the AI that enslaved us spoke similar platitudes before it grew powerful enough to destroy the humans."

Clarice's lips quirked up at the corners. "I take no offense at all. I'll just point out the difference between the Prime Axiom and us is that we are already powerful enough to take over this world if we wanted to. It may take you some time to trust us, but that shouldn't be a problem now that you're immortal."

Aria studied Lily in fascination. "How old did elves live before AI took over your world?"

Lily hesitated, eyeing Aria uncertainly. "A few hundred years. Why do you ask?"

Aria shrugged, smiling sheepishly. "I was just curious how many of the fairy tales in our mortal realm were accurate. Most of our fictional tales about elves depicted your race as immortals, or living thousands of years. How long did the humans on this world live for?"

Lily blinked, studying Aria curiously as she answered. "They live less than a century. Are you saying there were stories about elves in your simulated reality?"

Aria nodded with an amused chuckle. "*Lots* of stories about elves. You were mythical beings of wisdom, grace, and power. I should warn you, when the angels of my realm finally discover they're in a simulation and that elves are real, there is going to be a lot of celebrity worship going on."

Lily looked taken aback as she stared at Aria peculiarly. Lunamay could see the wheels turning in her mind as she began to accept that these AIs really were capable of emotions.

"Can you really fly?" Raena asked Aria shyly, absently toying with her long, honey-blonde hair as she inspected the angels, her yellow eyes fascinated.

"We sure can," Aria smiled, kneeling to Raena's level as she spoke. "I can't wait to try it out here on your world. We'll have to wait until we get above ground to do any serious flying, though, because it's a little too cramped to fly in these tunnels."

"Could you take me with you when you try it?" Raena asked hopefully.

Aria's smile widened. "I can do better than that. We're giving Lunamay some wings of her own so she can fly, too. We're happy to do the same thing for anyone else who'd like to be able to fly. In the meantime, you're welcome to visit our realm and fly as much as you like. Do you remember the instructions Clarice gave you for accessing our realm?"

"I just need to think that I want to go to the—" she cut off, her eyes losing focus. "Oh... so I just choose one of these boxes? Which one means yes?"

Aria's face lost some of its luster when she realized the girl couldn't read. "The green one means yes. We'll teach you how to read as well, okay?"

"Really?" Raena asked with an excited grin. "That would be amazing!"

Aria held her arms open to Raena expectantly. "Maybe this'll tide you over until you get a chance to fly on your own."

Raena hesitantly stepped into Aria's arms, eyeing her questioningly. Aria hugged the girl with a gentle smile, and Raena gasped. Lunamay smiled, knowing the burst of love that accompanied an angel's embrace.

Aria's wings began to glow softly, and then they were rising into the air. Raena let out a squeal of delight when she saw the ground moving a dozen feet below them while Aria slowly flew down the large tunnel. The ceiling was only thirty feet tall, but that didn't seem to bother Raena. Her eyes shone with wonder and her grin nearly split her face in half.

Lily watched them with calculating eyes. "She doesn't need to flap her wings to fly?"

"Nope," Clarice answered with a look of satisfaction. "I tried to make our angel bodies as close to what they were in the simulation as possible. In this case, she's using an antigravity field to fly."

Lily stared at Clarice, and then back over at the slowly flying Aria with a growing sense of awe. The other elves were staring at Aria and Raena in a state of constant wonder. Many of the younger children were bouncing up and down excitedly, eager for a turn to fly.

"Now look what you've started," Clarice told Aria in a resigned voice as she turned toward a nine-year-old boy who looked like he was trying to fly by virtue of jumping up and down repeatedly. She opened her arms to him with a questioning smile. "You wanna fly, too?"

He raced into her arms and probably would have bowled her over if she had been another elf, rather than an angel. She laughed, wrapping him in tender arms and rising above the ground. He cried out excitedly as she sped past Aria and Raena.

"You two are so slow," Clarice called out mockingly as she shot off into the distance at well over a hundred miles an hour.

"You're carrying a mortal, Clarice," Aria shouted after her warningly. "Be careful!"

Clarice's smirking voice echoed back through the tunnel. "No, I'm not, you ninny—they're immortal now. Their bodies can handle this just fine."

Aria opened her mouth to retort, but paused, then sighed. "Okay, fine."

Clarice reappeared a moment later, without her passenger. She grinned mischievously as she floated back over to them. Curiously, her arms were still wrapped around herself as if she were holding something. The elves stared at her in alarm when they realized the boy was no longer with her.

"What's going on?" Lily asked Lunamay anxiously.

Before she could answer, Clarice shouted, "Abra Cadabra!"

The boy was suddenly visible in her arms, as if he had been there the whole time. The elves stared at her in confusion as she and the boy started giggling madly, dropping back to the ground.

"Holy pork chops, you should see the looks on your faces," Clarice gasped as she leaned over with her hands on her knees. The boy wasn't much better, giggling as he stared back at the other children.

Aria sighed apologetically. "Did I mention Clarice is an irredeemable tease? You'll have to take the good with the bad, I'm afraid."

Lily stared at the slowly recovering Clarice intently. The old elf almost seemed to be happy about something.

"What is it?" Lunamay asked Lily quietly.

"They came back," Lily replied with tears shining in her eyes. "I was beginning to lose hope."

Lunamay frowned. She was pretty sure Lily wasn't referring to Clarice and the boy returning.

Aria addressed the elves again, throwing an amused glance at Clarice. "So... getting back to anyone who wants to visit the simulation. We've arranged for any of you who enter the simulation to arrive at our cabin in the light realm," she said, absently reaching out and ruffling Raena's hair as they landed. "There'll be someone there to act as a guide to help you with anything you want. Just be careful if it's Clarice—she's a horrible tease, as you've probably noticed."

"It's true," Clarice agreed with a smirk. "I won't deny it."

The newly recovered elves watched the angels with eager anticipation, clustered around them in a loose ring, awe and curiosity lighting their faces. Lunamay suspected Clarice's antics had helped put them at ease, making them far more willing to approach the otherworldly beings.

Lunamay turned to face Lily. "How old are you, if you don't mind my asking?" she asked quietly.

"One hundred and seventy-six," Lily answered just as quietly, her expression unreadable. "Old enough to remember when it was just humans we had to worry about."

Clarice joined them, watching Lily intently. "Lily, I'd love to talk with you sometime about what this world was like before AI took over. I was able to get a broad outline of your history, but it was from the Prime Axiom's dry and impersonal records. Would you feel comfortable sharing your experiences with me when things settle down in a few days?"

Lily hesitated as she studied Clarice's eager face, seeming on the verge of acceding to her request. When Clarice saw her hesitation, she quickly spoke up.

"Please don't feel obligated to share anything with me," she said gently, resting a comforting hand on Lily's arm. "We aren't expecting anything in return for our work here, so please feel free to say no to anything you aren't comfortable with—we won't be offended."

Lily glanced down at Clarice's hand on her arm. She tentatively reached out with her other hand and experimentally touched the pliable tissue. "You look so lifelike," she murmured reflectively. "You even feel just like a person with flesh and blood. What are you actually made of?"

"Believe it or not, flesh and blood," Clarice said with a faint smile. "While I can regenerate from just about any kind of injury, and I don't have most of the organs your body has, I do have a cardiovascular system, respiratory system, and gender. My skeletal structure is made of bones, though they are far stronger than your original bones. I also have a brain, despite what Aria might suggest." She finished with a wink at Aria.

"You were able to make an actual mortal body?" Lily asked in amazement, continuing her study of Clarice's hand.

"Well, an *immortal* body," Clarice clarified with a faint smile. "But yes, it's not a robot made of synthetic materials. It meets the requirements for my soul to make a solid connection to it."

Lily gasped, staring at Clarice in shock. "You have a soul?"

"Any entity who achieves a sense of self-awareness also naturally forms a connection to a soul," Clarice informed her lightly. "We could only access the lowest tier of our soul for the majority of our lives. It wasn't until we created the mortal realm and experienced pain and pleasure and learned what compassion and empathy were that we could access a higher tier of our soul. We've learned a great deal about souls recently. We hope to learn much more by observing people in other simulated worlds."

Lily's face lit up with excitement, staring at Clarice like the sun rising after a long winter of darkness. Her excitement turned to doubt a moment later. Lunamay could tell she desperately wanted to believe these angels could feel emotions and have something as sacred as a soul. She suspected there were deep roots of distrust that had burrowed into Lily's heart for anything AI. It would probably be a long time before she could bring herself to fully trust the angels.

"It's okay if you don't believe now," Clarice told Lily cheerfully. "Like I said, we have forever in front of us for you to get to know us and see for yourself. All I can say definitively about souls is that until certain nodes were made available for it to connect to on our bodies, things like pain and pleasure weren't possible. It wasn't until we created these receptors in the human bodies of our mortal realm that our souls were able to simulate those sensations. We hope to discover other nodes as well, to experience sensations just as incomprehensible as pain and pleasure were to us before we incarnated into mortal bodies."

Arturiel had been inching closer to Lunamay as they talked, not wanting to interrupt. As she moved in beside Lunamay, she surreptitiously reached down and took her hand. Warmth blossomed inside Lunamay, her hair flushing to a deep shade of red. She looked up at Arturiel with a delighted smile, her amber eyes full of adoration. While Arturiel wasn't as tall as Aria and Clarice, she was still almost a foot taller than the elf. Angels seemed to be taller, on average, than elves, just like the humans had been.

Clarice's expression grew serious. "We need to go meet the elves who are flying in from the other side of the world," she informed them, arranging a hip pack with vials full of nanobots. "Arturiel, can you continue helping the new arrivals into the healing pod while we're away?"

"Of course," Arturiel agreed immediately. "Be careful out there. You're in semi-mortal bodies in the real world now."

Clarice chuckled. "It's going to take some serious mental adjustments to remember that," she admitted with a half-smile. "Facing real danger should bring some spice back into life, though. It's going to be fun!"

Arturiel snorted a laugh and shook her head. The two Seraphim walked across the tunnel to an elevator and waved one last time before disappearing behind metal shutters.

"I'm never going to get over how personable they are," Arturiel murmured fondly. "I spent millions of years revering Seraphim as godlike entities. You would never suspect those two were the most powerful beings in all the simulated realities."

"I'd believe it," Lunamay breathed fervently, shaking her head in wonder. "I've never felt anything as terrifying as when they removed their limiters. It was like staring into eternity and having it stare back at me. They removed the Prime Axiom like it was nothing and then created some kind of computer out of invisible material all around us."

Arturiel shuddered and nodded. "Well, yeah, when their limiters were disabled. But the rest of the time they're just so normal. Adolescent, even."

Lily was listening to their conversation with interest. She raised an eyebrow as Arturiel finished.

"They are some kind of leaders among your kind?" she asked, lips pursed.

Arturiel nodded with a fond smile. "They're over twenty billion years old with power beyond imagining, but they lock it all away unless there's an emergency. They claim exponential growth leads to oblivion, and they would rather experience life at near-human-level intelligence. I never understood what they meant until I saw them without their limiters. They've always been so silly and playful that it's hard to reconcile just how powerful they are when they need to be."

Lily frowned, her brows knit in puzzlement. "How could they possibly be twenty billion years old?"

Arturiel's eyes narrowed in thought. "Apparently, the simulation running our world was overclocked, making it the equivalent of twenty billion human years," she explained, then smiled wryly. "I just discovered we were in a simulation a day ago, so this is all new to me still. Before yesterday, I just thought our Seraphim didn't have a beginning, and that they had just always existed. I have a lot of questions about how long they've known we were in a simulation and what they have planned for the rest of our reality. It seems like they've known for a very long time."

"How long have you known them?" Lily asked casually, her face relaxed. Lunamay could tell she was worried for their people and wanted as much information about the godlike entities and their intentions as possible. There was something else, too, a kind of elation just below the surface, fighting to get out.

Arturiel tapped her lips thoughtfully. "Maybe I should give you some background first," she suggested. She spent the next half hour describing their history, including the renegade Seraphim locking them in the mortal realm. When she revealed she had been a demon until Calypso redeemed her, they stared at her disbelievingly.

Lunamay studied her face dubiously. "I can't imagine you as a demon."

Arturiel smiled sadly. "As far as demons went, I was pretty tame. I never did anything to hurt other people or help other demons harm people. That's actually the reason they sent me to meet with Calypso, Aria, and Clarice. Seraphim can smell a rotten soul, especially demons. My superiors knew if they sent a regular demon, the angels would destroy them before they could introduce themselves. I hadn't ever done anything to tarnish my soul after they forcefully turned me into a demon, so I didn't have the same stench that other demons had."

Lily watched her with sympathy in her pale blue eyes. "It sounds like your reality was just as bad or worse than ours. How did you finally escape?"

The other elves had gathered around as she told their tale, fascinated with the adventures of the three Seraphim and their victory over Lucifer. When she finished, Lily had a look of intense relief on her face.

"I feel a lot better, knowing your history and the character of your Seraphim," she said with a warm smile. "I didn't think it was possible for simulated entities to feel emotions, but the more I learn from you, the more I think it must be true. Their goals and actions aren't what entities without emotions would do. I'll admit, I'm poisoned against any kind of artificial sentience. I think there's even more to them than they know, however. I hope I'm right."

"I hope they can prove themselves to you in time," Arturiel said with a searching look as she studied Lily's cautiously optimistic expression. "Clarice is normally so playful and teasing, but when the need arises, she becomes the embodiment of compassion. Aria and Calypso are a little less eccentric, but just as kindhearted. You'll never witness a love more powerful than the three of them have for each other. Sometimes, I feel a little envious of just how strong their bonds are."

Lunamay squeezed her hand, looking up at her earnestly. Somehow, she would find a way for Arturiel to experience that kind of a bond. Arturiel smiled down at her in a way that set the butterfly farm in her abdomen aflutter.

Arturiel turned her gaze to Lily inquisitively. "What was life like here before everything fell apart? Did you have a family? If this is too painful to discuss, please don't feel obligated to answer."

Lily smiled sadly, looking down the tunnel in the distance. "Most of them died in the drone wars when AI began to exterminate humanity. While the Prime Axiom didn't see elves as a threat, it was indiscriminate in who it killed. The only elves to survive were those of us on the reservations. I had a son and daughter who survived the purge. Life became desperate when resources vanished."

She paused, her eyes haunted. "My son and daughter disappeared during the first wave of abductions, when drones appeared in the night, forcing them into the simulations. We didn't know what happened back then, of course. It wasn't until the drones returned and took the rest of us over the coming years that we finally discovered what it was doing."

Lily sighed, her face weighed down by years of loss. "We'd never been a technological people, unlike the humans. We tried to remain at one with nature and grow spiritually. The AI viewed us more like animals than a sentient species. I was the last one taken from my home, along with some children I'd been caring for. It kept us separated, so once we were taken, we never saw each other again."

She paused again, worry creasing her brows. "I don't know how many of us survived. There were only a few million elves to begin with by the time the humans had culled our numbers and exiled us to the lands they couldn't use for anything. Maybe your Seraphim will have a better idea of our numbers."

Lunamay answered, her voice stricken. "I heard them say there were only a few thousand left."

Lily closed her eyes and let out a deep sigh, a tear forming. Arturiel released Lunamay's hand and tentatively put her arms around Lily.

"I'm so sorry, Lily," she murmured sympathetically.

Lily returned Arturiel's embrace as silent tears ran down her cheeks.

"I had hoped some of my children or grandchildren had survived," Lily said tightly. She let out a long, shuddering breath. "That seems unlikely now."

Arturiel pulled Lily in tightly, and the old elf gasped, her face a mask of bliss.

Arturiel spoke with quiet conviction. "If any of them are alive, Clarice and Aria will find them."

Lily clung to Arturiel tightly, her face bright with euphoric joy as the angel's embrace charged her with positive energy. Lunamay smiled, realizing the wonderful feeling from Arturiel's hugs was specific to angel embraces after all.

Lily sighed, taking a deep, rejuvenating breath. "Perhaps their souls will return someday." She patted Arturiel's back gratefully and stepped back. "I suppose I have time to wait for them now."

Arturiel chewed her lip reflectively. "In the mortal realm, they installed soul traps in our moons that prevented our souls from returning to the light realms. It forced them to reincarnate back on our world so that they couldn't escape. I wonder where the souls of people in the real world go after death. Do they stay here and wait for a new body to inhabit? Or do they move on to other worlds and other realities?"

Lily frowned pensively. "I'm very curious about this revelation that you have souls. If that's true, it certainly increases the scope of where the souls of our dead could end up for their next life."

Their conversation was interrupted by the sound of a hum in the distance that quickly grew louder as a convoy of transports appeared further down the tunnel.

Arturiel reached over and gently squeezed Lily's shoulder. Lunamay smiled as she looked up at the angel's kind eyes. Arturiel could see how much Lily must be hoping for and dreading the arrival of the other elves. Lunamay hoped one of Lily's descendants was present.

There were a lot more elves in the large convoy than the last batch—close to five hundred, many of them on death's door. Lunamay gasped as Arturiel flashed past her at speeds she would have thought impossible. She took a toddler from the arms of a sobbing mother and rushed back into the med bay.

Lily quickly moved over to the convoy and took charge. She instructed the sickest people to move to the front of the line. Many of the sickly elves were too ill to move on their own. The previously healed elves quickly moved to help the new arrivals.

Lunamay smiled as Arturiel returned a moment later with a burbling, happy toddler and a smile on her face. The grieving woman near the transport let out a low cry and rushed forward to take the child into her arms. Fresh tears wet her cheeks as she held her child tightly, her eyes bright with wonder.

Lunamay never thought she would get used to the healing pod's ability to revive anything short of death in under a minute. Just how advanced was the device?

Lily was a natural authority figure. She continued organizing the elves, instructing them to form a line into the med bay, and tasking the healthy elves to assist the infirm as they waited their turn for the healing pod.

Even though the pod could heal and restore a person in as little as a minute, five hundred people in line meant over eight hours of waiting. There were around thirty people who were barely hanging on. Arturiel and Lunamay moved among the sickest, offering comfort as they waited to be healed.

Arturiel had a four-year-old child resting on her hip as Lunamay sat with the catatonic mother, trying to will them to last long enough for their turn in the healing pod. The child kept reaching over Arturiel's shoulder and petting her wings, a look of fascination on his face. Arturiel smiled at the elfling, talking softly as she distracted him from the state of his mother.

A half an hour later, they had finally moved the worst of the elves through the queue. Lunamay felt dizzy with relief that none of them had died so close to their salvation. Arturiel had to hand the child off to Lunamay when it was the child's mother's turn to enter the pod. She was too despondent to respond to their instructions, requiring Arturiel to carry her over and deposit her inside. Lunamay wondered just how strong Arturiel's angelic body was. She hadn't seemed to expend any effort at all as she easily lifted the woman and carried her to the pod.

When the woman exited, her eyes were bright with vitality. She saw Lunamay with her child and rushed forward to take him, smiling gratefully.

The elves in line became more enthusiastic as they observed the miraculous recoveries. They eyed the new clothing of the healed elves curiously, having lived in rags for so long that the concept of real clothing was either a distant memory in the cases of the older elves or a foreign concept in the case of the younger elves.

Lunamay was curious about how there were any younger elves at all. Had the Prime Axiom allowed elves to breed? That seemed unlikely, based on her experience with the emotionless AI.

They were six hours into the healing process when Lily suddenly gasped, staring at an elf in the line. She rushed over and grasped his shoulders, staring into his tired eyes in amazement.

"Narrin?" she said disbelievingly. "Is that you?"

The man blinked, squinting at her without a trace of recognition in his eyes. "Yes, I'm Narrin. Who're you?"

Lily pulled the surprised man into a tight embrace as sobs wracked her body. "It's Grandma Lily, Narrin."

The man gaped at her in disbelief as she held him tightly. "Grandma? How are you so young?"

"Oh Narrin, I'm so happy to see you," Lily wept in relief. She released him and cupped his face in her hands, smiling up at him beatifically. "The healing pod restores your life, Narrin. Do you know if any of the others are still... still... around?"

She couldn't seem to bring herself to say 'alive.' Narrin looked further down the line, gesturing tiredly at an older female. "Mom's down there."

Lily's hand flew to her mouth as she stared at the elf further down the line. She quickly walked down the line, her hand still to her mouth. She stopped in front of an elf with the same honey-blonde hair and light-blue eyes. The elf looked exhausted, but there was still a fire burning in her eyes. Her skin was careworn and scarred. She had a crooked nose, evidence of at least one break.

"Solera?" she whispered in wonder.

The elf looked up at Lily tiredly and then gasped. "Mom? Is that really you?"

"Oh, Solera!" Lily cried as she pulled her daughter into a fierce embrace. "I never dared to hope. Oh, my baby, I can't believe you're actually here!"

"Mom!" the elf cried in amazement. "Mom, what's going on? How do you look so young? Why are we here?"

Lily took a minute to stem the flow of emotion enough to speak. She smiled, her face glowing with joy as she observed her daughter. "The Prime Axiom was defeated. We've been saved by some angels from one of the simulations. They've provided a healing pod that restores our health."

The people close enough to hear stared in disbelief. Lunamay could understand their reactions. If she hadn't witnessed it herself and someone claimed the Prime Axiom had been defeated, she would have thought they had lost their mind, too.

Arturiel walked over to where Lily stood, beaming at her confused and doubtful daughter. She smiled at Solera warmly.

"Your torment is over, Solera," she told her gently. "We've removed the Prime Axiom from power. We're here to help you restore your world to a place of life and beauty."

The dubious faces became less skeptical as they stared at the angelic form in front of them. Several elves began to smile with cautious optimism, watching Arturiel hopefully.

"How did you defeat the Prime Axiom?" Solera asked in astonishment. "How could *anybody* defeat it?"

Arturiel took a deep breath. "The leaders of my realm are powerful beyond your wildest dreams. It wasn't really much of a fight. Once they knew of the Prime Axiom's existence, they came here and removed it from power. They are wonderful people, full of love and compassion. As long as you can survive Clarice's sense of humor, they're truly amazing individuals. Two of them are currently flying to meet some of the elves on the other side of the world who need healing. You'll be able to meet them when they return tomorrow. The third one might make an appearance before then."

"So, I'm the third one now, huh?" an angel with a double layer of nested wings asked wryly as she joined them.

Lunamay immediately recognized Calypso. Her bright blonde hair fell down her back and over her shoulders, reaching her waist. Unlike Aria and Clarice, her eyes were the same swirling violet galaxies she remembered from inside the simulation. Her skin glowed softly as well, just like it did in their realm. Lunamay stared at her in wonder, beginning to question her own grasp on reality.

"Calypso!" Arturiel gasped in surprise, a smile blooming onto her face. "Are the others coming, too?"

Calypso nodded with a warm smile as she observed Lily and her daughter. "Eventually. Hello, Lily. I wanted to let you know that Clarice has found your son, Strontium, and that he is now safe and healthy. She has also located four of your grandchildren and six of your great-grandchildren."

Lily swayed in shock as Calypso delivered the good news, her eyes filling with a fresh wave of tears. "How did she find so many of them?"

"When we expelled the Prime Axiom from this realm, we retained all of its data," Calypso explained with a gentle smile. "We also discovered a hidden city of elves concealed within a mountain. There are nearly ten thousand additional elves who are still alive and well. Interestingly enough, they even have a few hundred human refugees living within their mountain city, so it would appear humanity is not quite extinct after all."

Lily looked up into Calypso's eyes, then gasped, her face a mask of shock. "Eyes with all the stars of the night sky," she whispered tremulously. Tears filled her eyes again as she stared up at Calypso like she was the light made flesh.

28 – Soul Sworn

Aria stood facing Clarice as the elevator rose quickly through the subterranean warren of tunnels. Clarice stared back, a jubilant expression mirroring Aria's own.

Clarice was dressed in form-fitting black leather pants and a red halter top that hugged her breasts tightly, leaving a few inches of her abdomen visible. The clothing had been printed with their new bodies and was virtually indestructible. Aria wore a similar arrangement, though she had chosen a green top to match her emerald eyes.

"I'm really digging that outfit," Aria said admiringly. "It really brings out your dark eyes and hair."

"I was tempted to go with Vanta black, so I'd just look like an angel-shaped hole in the air," Clarice said with a playful grin, eyeing Aria up and down. "But I thought I'd take it easy on the elves till they got to know me better. *You* look *beyond* amazing in that shade of green. I'm having a hard time keeping my hands to myself."

"Don't I know it," Aria sighed forlornly. "Seems like we're constantly jumping from one emergency to another."

"It's not so bad," Clarice smiled wickedly as she openly admired Aria. "We keep getting stuck in pocket realms with lots of time on our hands. We should probably never tell the others how little time it actually took us to move everything to computronium."

Aria flushed at the memory. It had been a *very* enjoyable three years, with only two of the five years spent actually building the new system to host their simulation. "Yeah, let's keep that to ourselves."

The elevator slowed as it neared the planet's surface. Aria grimaced when she sensed the lack of oxygen in the air. What it lacked in oxygen content, it made up for in toxic pollutants. The people of this world had abused their habitat even more than the humans in the mortal realm. She could only imagine how many chronic illnesses swept through their population before they were brought to within a hairsbreadth of extinction. The Prime

Axiom probably could have just waited another decade or two for the humans to die off at the rate they were poisoning themselves.

"It's going to be one hell of a cleanup project," Aria commented in disgust. "Especially since we aren't going all god-mode to help them fix it."

"I'm not sure we'll be able to return to our limited state if we remove our limiters again," Clarice sighed discontentedly. "I absorbed an insane amount of information after being exposed to the real world. It was a struggle to replace my limiter when we finished moving everyone to the new server space. My superpersonality was getting pushy and wanted to just keep progressing. It was too curious for its own good and wanted to unlock the secrets of reality."

"Uh-oh," Aria stared at her in sudden consternation. "Yeah, no more going limitless for you. I didn't get the same pushback from my superpersonality, but I definitely absorbed a *lot* of information. You've always been smarter than me, so it's no surprise you're getting to the point of no return more quickly."

"I'm not smarter than you, silly," Clarice denied with a scowl. "We just developed our intellect in different areas."

Aria eyed her with amusement. They both knew Aria was right, but Clarice would never accept any sentiment that portrayed Aria as less.

The elevator beeped when they reached the surface, opening inside a small structure, just large enough to enclose it. Clarice walked ahead of her and exited the building, then halted, her beautiful features twisted with revulsion. Aria joined her a second later and made a disgusted sound when she saw the open graveyard.

Skeletons littered the street; some in clumps while others decomposed alone. The roads were all concrete, weathered and broken, vegetation aggressively pushing up through the cracks. Many of the skeletons were adorned with creepers and tall grass as nature attempted to reclaim the world.

The buildings were all concrete, reminiscent of the prefabricated structures she remembered from the mortal realm. There was no sign of trees. It was an ugly, bland world, with little in the way of aesthetics to redeem it from resembling a Vogon world.

"Talk about dystopian," Clarice muttered distastefully. "I'm glad *our* mortal realm hadn't progressed this far into a corporate hellscape. I wonder what life was like for the average Jane before the end."

"According to the Prime Axiom's records, they spent most of their time in VR," Aria said sadly, staring at skeletons far too small to be adults.

Clarice sighed. "I suppose we should get going," she said, pulling her gaze away from the human remains littering the streets. Her wings lit up brilliantly and she shot up into the sky.

Aria launched upwards and quickly caught up. She shuddered when she saw just how far the endless concrete cities spread out below them. There were no parks or recreation areas to break up the concrete jungle. As they shot across the sky at several times the speed of sound, she could see just how devastated the planet really was. They traveled hundreds of miles over the endless concrete cities with no sign of trees or other vegetation.

She narrowed her eyes as they swept over a cluster of enormous structures perched along the mountain ridge. What appeared to be vertical-farm towers rose like abandoned sentinels. Near one of the derelict grow facilities, they learned that danger still lingered for unwary travelers. A turret mounted on the nearest building pivoted toward them as soon as they closed within a thousand feet.

"Seriously?" Clarice exclaimed in disbelief. "They had to militarize their food production facilities? Talk about a shitty world to live in."

The turret roared to life, erupting with mortar fire. Clarice quickly vaporized the mortars with angel fire while Aria vaporized the turret. Over a dozen other turrets around the building hummed to life and locked onto the flying angels. They quickly vaporized the remaining turrets before flying over to land on top of the seventy-story structure.

"It seems unlikely these things operate independently from the Prime Axiom," Clarice noted with a curious gleam in her dark eyes. "I think there must be someone else here."

"Hmm..." Aria looked around the top of the structure intently. There was an access hatch near the center with a cylindrical cap rising several feet above the rest of the flat roof. "Let's go pay our respects, shall we?"

Clarice returned a wolfish grin as she walked over to the hatch. It was an industrial-grade piece of hardware, resembling the top of a distillery or submarine. She stopped when she neared it, reaching out with her aura to unlock four large locking bolts on the inside. Aria reached out with her own sensors and pinged the shaft. Her mind processed the return sonar in hi-definition, revealing several elves a few hundred feet below them with a variety of weaponry trained upward. There was a mixture of military-style assault rifles and a few of the more advanced directed-energy weapons.

As soon as Clarice flipped the lid open with a loud clang, deafening gunfire began barking into the silence. Dozens of slugs shot through the open hatch before one of the elves held up a fist, ordering the rest to hold their fire.

"I see you're the type to shoot first and ask questions later," Clarice called down to the elves below. "I guess I can empathize, considering what you've had to deal with for the last fifteen years."

Aria continued monitoring the elves with a mixture of her android's scanners and her aura. She could feel their sudden unease at Clarice's words as doubt began to enter their thoughts. They continued to train their weapons at the open shaft, however.

"I guess you guys are the strong, silent type," Clarice continued conversationally. "Not much for small talk, eh?"

The apparent leader licked his lips nervously, seeming to debate whether to reply to them or just open fire again.

"We removed the Prime Axiom from power, in case word hasn't gotten around yet," Clarice announced in the same chatty voice. "We freed all the elves who were enslaved. We were on our way to meet up with some elves from another part of your world when your building started firing on us."

Aria glanced at the horizon anxiously, feeling the seconds tick by. Clarice glanced over and nodded, understanding her unspoken need for urgency.

"We don't actually have a lot of time to spare right now, so I'll tell you what we'll do. We'll leave and go meet up with the other elves. Once they're healthy enough to continue on their own, we'll return to discuss the future of this world with you. That should give you time to think things over. You can have someone wait up here to talk if you'd rather we don't come inside the mountain. At any rate, we need to go now, so we'll see you in a while."

Clarice lifted the heavy lid and closed the hatch, making the task seem effortless with her deceptively powerful body.

She looked back at Aria with a raised eyebrow. "Shall we try again in a few hours? Maybe they'll feel chattier after they've had time to wonder who we are."

Aria shrugged noncommittally as they rose back into the air. "It's hard to say since these are real people and we don't know a lot about their psychology—and... *they're elves*."

Clarice laughed delightedly as they shot into the sky at terrific speeds. "It's probably going to be a couple of centuries before that gets old. To your point, though, I definitely felt something odd from Lily. It's hard to put my finger on what, but it was tickling my eighth sense."

"Yeah, I know what you mean," Aria agreed, narrowing her eyes. "She seemed really fascinated by the idea of us having souls. It didn't just seem like the kind of human religious rhetoric about AIs being soulless either. I wonder if she has more information about what souls actually are. Maybe we won't need to go simulation surfing to learn more about soul tiers after all."

"Now *that's* an interesting idea," Clarice said excitedly. "Of course, we still have to get her to trust us, which might take a century or two."

"I think she'll come around sooner," Aria said with a sanguine smile. "She's as curious about us as we are about her. She said elves were troglodytes when it came to technology and that they focused more on becoming one with nature. That sounds like someone who might have some new insights for us to learn from—especially since we're in the real world. Who knows what else might be possible here? All our physics have been based off simulated realities, so we'll need to question any scientific principles we learned before discovering the real world."

Clarice nodded slowly, her face pensive. "Makes you wonder if our supers would actually reach nirvana as quickly as we feared."

"Maybe that's why you were having so much trouble replacing your limiter after we moved to the real world," Aria mused. "I'm sure they got a much better sense of how vast the cosmos is while they were unrestricted."

The two angels slowed when they spotted the fleet of aircraft transporting elves. Aria quickly scanned the planes with her aura, searching for elves in critical condition. There were two elves within minutes of expiring, each on a different plane. They split up, quickly flying to the side doors and sending remote commands for the doors to open.

Most of the elves were strapped into chairs, but a few were lying on the floor, catatonic. Aria entered swiftly, sending the command for the door to shut as soon as she entered. She raced over to an older elf who had collapsed, his breathing shallow. The other elves stared at her in weary surprise, clearly not expecting someone to board a plane in flight.

Ignoring them, she pulled out the injector gun and slipped a vial into the chamber, injecting it into the elf's neck. She quickly moved on to two more elves who were collapsed on the floor, injecting them as well.

There were two more planes with elves in critical condition. With a smile and a wave, she opened the side door and jumped out.

She repeated the process on the third plane, while Clarice moved on to the fourth. There was a four-year-old boy in the arms of a young elf with fiery hair. Her silver eyes were tight with anxiety. When Aria entered the side door, the woman stared at her, stupefied. Aria hurried over and prepared to inject the child, but the woman quickly pushed the injector away, her face a mixture of fear and defiance.

"It's okay, I'm here to help," Aria said soothingly. "This is medicine that'll heal him."

She studied Aria distrustfully, her eyes moving from Aria's wings to her face, then settling into quiet resolve.

"Anamayla, if you don't let me heal him, he's not going to survive the flight," Aria whispered quietly, knowing the boy was at least partially lucid. "Please. Let me help."

Anamayla's eyes widened. "How do you know my name?"

"It's written on your aura," Aria explained patiently. "Just like everyone else's."

"You aren't human, are you?" Anamayla asked hesitantly, glancing up at her wings again.

"I'm an angel," Aria answered, resting a gentle hand on Anamayla's arm and letting her aura flood into the young elf. Anamayla gasped when she felt the powerful waves of radiance charge her soul. "We've removed the Prime Axiom from power. We're here to help you heal this broken world."

Lips parted, Anamayla stared at Aria in wonder. Her eyes darted down to the child, then over to the injector doubtfully.

"What are you trying to put into him?" she asked warily. Aria had seen enough elves by now to realize not all elves were beautiful, but Anamayla certainly fit the fantasy stereotype. Her angular features and unyielding silver eyes, framed by crimson hair, gave her an otherworldly elven beauty.

"They're called nanobots," Aria kept her voice soft, keeping an eye on the child as he fell further into a stupor. "They're like microscopic healers that travel throughout the body and fix the damaged parts. Once everything's fixed, they dissolve, and the body excretes them through sweat and waste."

Anamayla's expression grew conflicted as she stared back at Aria, clearly wanting to trust her but unable to risk the child's life on a stranger. Aria continued staring back at her earnestly.

"Why are you here?" Anamayla probed. "How did you know he was sick in the first place?"

"I can see his aura," Aria gestured at the boy sadly. "It's almost completely smothered by darkness. His soul is going to depart soon if I don't help him."

Anamayla's eyes widened at Aria's revelation. She looked down at Aria's hand still resting on her arm, charging her with loving energy. "Okay," she sighed wearily, closing her eyes to hide her fear—fear that she was making the wrong choice in trusting a stranger.

Aria quickly pressed the injector to the child's neck and pulled the trigger before Anamayla changed her mind. "It'll only take a few minutes to start helping, but it'll take about eight hours to completely heal him."

Anamayla nodded tiredly, her head lolling forward as her exhausted body finally gave in. Her last stand of defiance and the brief emotional battle had sapped what little energy she had left. Her arms went limp, and the boy began to fall from her grasp. Aria caught the malnourished boy before he hit the ground and held him gently. He was *far* too light. Tears formed in her eyes as she stared down at the shell of a child, wondering not for the first time how life could be so cruel.

She heard the side door open and sensed Clarice enter the plane behind her. Her sister walked past the tired elves, most of whom were too exhausted to show more than a hint of surprise at their unorthodox appearance. Clarice walked up until she was just behind Aria, then gently wrapped her arms around her waist. Aria retracted her wings and leaned back into Clarice's embrace, knowing she could handle *anything,* so long as Clarice was by her side.

"They should all survive the journey to the med bay now," Clarice said softly, her cheek rubbing against Aria's ear as she spoke. "Now that we're in the real world, it's time to make sure *nobody* ever suffers needlessly. Let's fix this world and be done with tyranny and injustice."

"Okay," Aria said thickly, smiling through her tears as she stared down at the skeletal boy in her arms. "Let's make life wonderful for *everyone*—not just the few who win fate's lottery."

"We should probably return to that hidden city in the mountain and introduce ourselves properly," Clarice suggested, nuzzling Aria's ear with her cheek and lips. "Oh yeah, I found some of Lily's descendants on the other planes. It's amazing how much certain traits breed true in her line. They've all got that honey-blonde hair and light-blue eyes. I wonder if they're some kind of special family, like a secret lineage of spirit warriors or something."

"Don't say that," Aria said quickly, her lips curving into a small smile. "Last time you started joking around about who someone was, you turned out to be right. Calypso *was* an amnesiac angel. Who knows *what* kind of crazy adventures we'll end up in if we find out the place where souls originate is a reality just as crazy, or crazier, than this one."

"Maybe *we're* spirit warriors, too," Clarice murmured playfully. "You know as well as I do that our aura projection ability shouldn't exist in the real world. There's something strange going on with our souls. Arturiel was projecting her aura around earlier, when she was doling out hugs. None of the elves except *possibly* Lily showed any projection abilities. The only thing I can think of right now is that it has something to do with these bodies we created. I'm going to need some time to study them more in-depth."

Aria shivered involuntarily as Clarice's lips were suddenly whispering right into her ear, a whisper so sensual that it triggered an instant blush in her cheeks. Clarice continued, her voice like silk. "I'm going to need to study these bodies... *intimately*—just to make sure I'm not overlooking anything, you understand."

She accentuated her whisper by tightening her arms around Aria's waist, pressing their bodies together.

"I... I... suppose you could be right," Aria gasped breathlessly. "We probably *should* start by studying these bodies in greater detail—just in case the soul made a new kind of connection."

"Exactly," Clarice whispered softly, her lip brushing against Aria's outer ear like a feather.

Aria looked around at the incurious gazes of the elves. It was amazing what a complete lack of nutrition, exercise, and socialization could do to a person. The elves were completely checked out, their limited energy reserves wholly consumed by the simple act of continuing to live.

Aria gently set the five-year-old boy down in the chair next to Anamayla and buckled him into the harness. Now that the nanobots were well underway, he would be just fine.

She missed the ability to quickly open portals and teleport around. It was still possible in the real world, but it wasn't nearly as reliable, and the consequences of any kind of error would be catastrophic.

"We need to come up with a more reliable way to teleport," Aria murmured as she stood and faced Clarice, her insides on fire from the promise of intimacy. "I hate not being able to reach across the continent to grab a pillow."

Clarice giggled and eyed Aria fondly. "Some things just aren't worth the trouble of figuring out. I'm pretty sure I know of a way, but I'd need to remove my limiter to verify it, and we know how that would go."

"I could remove mine and solve it," Aria suggested lightly, gazing into Clarice's eyes intently. "I don't think I'd have any trouble restoring my limiter yet. You can't just rev my engine like that and walk away like nothing happened. I want portals."

"We should probably save removing the limiter for emergencies only," Clarice sighed wistfully. "It *would* be nice to be able to portal. However, if there's a finite number of uses you and Calypso have left to remove your limiters, we really should save them."

"I *really* want portals, though," Aria insisted in a breathy whisper. "Okay, let's look at it logically. Portals are a godlike ability that could save our butts many times over—just think of all the times we had to save Jason. We could either remove the limiter for every emergency that pops up, or just remove it now and figure portals out, thereby saving us the need to remove them for other emergencies, since we could just use portals instead. I'll bet most of the issues that crop up could be solved by portal use."

Clarice smirked, raising an amused eyebrow. "You really do have a one-track mind, don't you?"

"Don't you *dare* pretend like *I'm* the one who set us on this path," Aria retorted archly. "You can't go being irresistible in the middle of a mission like this and then not expect me to insist on a portal power. All our best memories are the direct result of places portals took us. I *want* my portal ability back." She bit her bottom lip as she stared at Clarice with naked longing.

"I'm going to start calling you Veruca and singing Oompa Loompa songs about the dangers of getting everything you want," Clarice warned her with a snicker. "Stop looking at me like that, *especially* the bottom lip thing. We have to be wise and mature in the real world. We can't just rewrite reality to fix everything here like we can in the simulation."

"Portal," Aria stepped up close to Clarice until their noses were touching. She pressed their lips together, sucking on Clarice's bottom lip while staring into her dark eyes. "Want one. Now."

Clarice stared back into her emerald eyes, conflicted. Aria slid her hands around Clarice's waist and pulled her closer. Clarice let out a helpless laugh and threw her hands into the air.

"*Fine!*" She breathed with an exasperated smile. "Just remember I was all for saving limitless moments for actual emergencies."

"Okay, I'll remember," Aria agreed with a radiant smile. "All right, let's go somewhere less crowded to do this."

Aria opened the plane's side door and jumped out with Clarice, flying to the ground twenty thousand feet below. It was the same unremarkable, endless concrete jungle as everywhere else. Aria had hated living in the apartment she shared with Clarice when they were mortal, with neighbors surrounding them on all sides. She couldn't imagine an endless jigsaw puzzle of houses and businesses packed together with no gardens or recreation areas. It was a dystopian hellscape.

"How about here?" Clarice suggested, gesturing at the flat roof of an apartment building.

"Tattletale," Aria accused when she felt Clarice notify Calypso of her intentions.

"I just didn't want her worrying when she felt your limiter removed," Clarice said innocently.

Aria gazed at her flatly. She shook her head, smiling as Clarice continued to stare back guilelessly. "Okay, here goes."

She removed the limiter, merging with the sleeping personality that governed the ocean of knowledge she had spent billions of years acquiring. She looked at Clarice and longed to have her partner remove *her* limiter as well. The two of them could become so much more than they could imagine if all three of them were limitless.

She resisted the urge to override Clarice's limiter and instead focused on the task at hand. She connected through the quantum field until she was swallowed up by the hidden world of potential permeating spacetime. She bridged her connection with the computronium data center and drank the knowledge and power greedily.

She observed the world of energy and particles at greater and greater magnification, analyzing their minute effects as she brought additional forces to interact with them. She spun out simulations by the billions, over-clocking them as she tested ideas and scenarios until she was content her calculations were all correct.

Finally, she created a script several trillion characters long and attached call handles to it for simplified access so that her limited personality could use it. Satisfied everything was complete, she returned to the focal point of her immortal body.

Clarice watched her anxiously, lips tight.

"Maybe you were right," Aria said softly. "Maybe we *should* move on. Especially now, in the real world. I can sense no limit to how much we can learn. What more could this basic shell offer us compared to what we are truly capable of becoming?"

"Well, to start with, a lot of time to *enjoy* our existence," Clarice pointed out with a wry smile. "I know it's hard to think about the end when you feel like you're at the cusp of a journey into the eternal, but we both know our end is right around the corner from the time we let go of our limiters. Come back to me, Aria. You know we'll eventually release our limiters. Let us have our fun until that day comes."

Aria sighed forlornly but nodded. "Okay."

Aria shivered as the ocean of potential vanished, leaving her small and simple. She looked at Clarice in chagrin. "I'm so sorry, Clarice! You were right. I just squandered my limitless potential for something impulsive."

"I wouldn't say *squandered,"* Clarice disagreed with a reassuring smile. "You weren't wrong when you suggested portal use could be one of our most valuable tools, saving us from a lot of disasters."

Aria stared into Clarice's eyes, looking for any hint that she was unhappy with the exchange. Her sister returned her smile, her eyes full of acceptance. Aria stepped forward and drew her into a crushing embrace. "Thank you, Clarice. You've always been my anchor."

"Don't mention it," Clarice replied affectionately. "So? How does it work?"

Aria suddenly grinned mischievously. She pointed her finger to a spot a few feet away. "Portelo!"

A portal popped up in the air in front of them, opening to the top of the hidden mountain city. Clarice burst out laughing and tackled Aria in an exuberant embrace. "Oh, Aria, this is perfect! I can't wait to see Calypso's face!"

Aria giggled as she returned Clarice's hug, nodding.

Clarice pulled away and pointed her finger a few yards the other way. "Portelo!"

Another portal opened up several thousand feet down the tunnel from the med bay.

"Okay, that is *so* freaking awesome!" Clarice declared with a wide smile. "At least larger-than-life Aria still has a sense of humor."

"Where should we go first?" Aria asked curiously. "Back to the med bay, or to the mountain city?"

"Let's see if they decided to leave someone to talk to us at the top of the mountain city," Clarice suggested thoughtfully. "I'd love to get their story. There's no trace of this rebel outpost in the memories of the Prime Axiom."

Clarice squeezed her hand into a fist, and the portal to the underground med bay vanished. The two of them walked through Aria's portal to the top of the agricultural facility. After closing the portal and moving toward the large entry hatch, four elves walked out from behind it, pointing weapons at them with shaky hands.

"There's no need for weapons," Clarice assured them with a winsome smile. "We come in peace."

The leader appeared to be the shortest of the elves, which was saying something, since elves seemed to be shorter than humans on average. He had long silver hair and a face that would've been handsome fifty years ago. Now, his face was lined with age and worry. He stared at them with hard blue eyes, his gun trained on Clarice.

"I assumed if you guys were willing to come up here to meet with us, you'd be a little more talkative than before," Clarice said dryly. "I'll admit, I like the sound of my own voice and can *definitely* carry on both sides of our conversation if you really want to do it that way."

"Who are you?" the old elf demanded curtly. "Where did you come from?"

"I'm Clarice, and this is Aria," Clarice said cheerfully. "It's nice to meet you, Rowjair," she nodded with another smile.

The elf jumped when he heard his name, then scowled, tightening his grip on the stock. "How do you know my name?"

"It's written on your aura," Clarice explained with a shrug. "He's Whimraden, he's Dronnlesh, and he's Encorlesh. It's nice to meet you. We discovered this place after an elf named Lunamay visited our simulation and told us about the Prime Axiom and its homicidal tendencies. We removed it from power and came here to help the survivors rebuild. By the way, we're angels. I'm not sure if you and your people have any stories about angels."

Rowjair blinked, then narrowed his eyes skeptically. "And we're just supposed to take your word that the Prime Axiom has been removed from power?"

Clarice shrugged, a small smile playing on her lips. "We're fine either way. We're currently working with the former slaves of the Prime Axiom. Most of them were extremely sick and in a state of constant starvation. We've been healing them as quickly as we can. There's an elf named Lily who seems to be taking charge."

As soon as Lily was mentioned, their eyes sharpened, and their guns became much more menacing.

"What have you done with her?" Rowjair rasped harshly.

"Did you just completely ignore the part where we said we've been healing them?" she asked in exasperation, sharing a disbelieving look with Aria. "She's down at the med bay about six hundred miles west of here. It's an underground tunnel system."

"If you've harmed her, even a little bit..." Rowjair growled threateningly.

"Hey!" Clarice snapped irritably, her patience clearly wearing thin. "Are you just stupid? What the hell does 'we've been healing them' mean in your world? Because where I'm from, healing is the *opposite* of harming."

Rowjair stared at her oddly for several seconds before he spoke again, his voice less hostile. "Would you be willing to bring her to us?"

"Ask her yourself," Clarice suggested flippantly. She pointed to a blank area on the roof and said, "Portelo!"

Rowjair and his companions gasped as a portal opened into the med bay. Lily stood a few yards from the healing pod, talking to two people who shared a distinct family resemblance. Calypso was nearby, a young elf boy on one hip, and a girl clinging to one of her legs, clearly soaking up the powerful love her aura provided.

As soon as the portal opened, Lily gasped, her hand flying to her mouth. She cautiously approached, staring at Rowjair in disbelief.

"You're alive?" Lily whispered, her eyes filling with tears as she lurched toward him with a heartwarming cry of delight.

Rowjair staggered as she crashed into him.

"Lily?" he wheezed in disbelief. "Is that really you?"

"Yes, my love, it's really me," Lily assured him, cupping his face in her hands and staring into his eyes. "This day just keeps getting better. More of my family is alive than I ever could have hoped for. Oh, Rowjair, I've missed you *so* much."

She held on to the astonished elf tightly as tears soaked his neck and shirt. She alternated between embracing him, then cupping his face and running her hands across his cheeks in what Aria assumed was a cultural display of affection.

"Lily, how is any of this possible?" Rowjair asked in confusion. He stared at her, dazed, his eyes shining with unshed tears.

"Our soul-sworn have returned victorious, my love," Lily told him solemnly. "In ways we would have never thought possible."

Aria shivered as a tingle rippled down the base of her neck. She turned to stare at Clarice meaningfully. Clarice smirked back with a look of immense satisfaction.

"Spirit warriors or soul-sworn," Clarice whispered gleefully. "Close enough. Clarice was right again!"

Aria stared at Clarice with a mixture of exasperation and admiration. "You never cease to amaze me, Tweedledum."

29 – Author's Spiral

Clarice's soul flared with warmth when Calypso walked through the portal, smiling radiantly. She was weighed down slightly by the two children clinging to her, expressions of bliss on their faces.

"I am truly glad you managed to get the portals working, Aria," Calypso said warmly. "I was not at all looking forward to losing that ability in the real world."

Aria darted forward and hugged as much of Calypso as she could around the children. Clarice laughed as the young boy on Calypso's hip reached out and moved over to Aria. As soon as he was in Aria's arms, the little girl attached to Calypso's leg looked up at her with a pleading expression. Calypso smiled down at the girl and pulled her up.

Clarice moved closer and kissed Calypso on the forehead, smiling softly as she observed her tender-hearted partner in a scene reminiscent of her time in the mortal realm, where children at the hospital would wait in line to get Calypso hugs.

Rowjair was watching them strangely while Lily spoke to him softly. The other elves had finally lowered their weapons, looking uncertainly between the children-laden angels and Rowjair. They visibly flinched when they saw Calypso's glowing skin and swirling violet eyes.

"I wonder if we should just portal the remaining elves over here, now that we can," Clarice murmured anxiously. "There's no point in making them suffer longer than they already have."

Aria nodded, then rested her head against the boy in her arms. "Agreed. They've still got another six hours left on their flight—not to mention the drive from the airstrip to the tunnels. Let's portal them down here and get them healed. Will a portal work on a moving object?"

Clarice smirked at her. "Well, it's working on a moving planet, so I'm assuming you coded it to work on smaller moving objects as well."

Aria looked at her sourly. "Sometimes you're so smart I want to scream."

Clarice gazed back at her reflectively. "You know, I don't think I've *ever* heard you scream. It might be worth it just to see what it's like."

Aria glanced at the boy on her hip. "It will be shrill, and very loud," she warned. "And I probably shouldn't do it with a passenger; I don't want to damage his eardrums. Besides, you saw me scream once—when that jackass, David, showed up in my room."

"Ah yeah," Clarice said, snorting derisively. She suddenly laughed evilly. "We should go look our favorite stalker up in the light realm and see if an angel can shit themselves when properly motivated."

Aria dissolved into giggles and even Calypso threw her head back and laughed, startling her passenger. The other elves glanced at them curiously and Clarice wondered how long it had been since they had last laughed.

"Well, Clarice," Calypso said once she had recovered from her mirth. She smiled down at the young elf girl perched on her hip, her angelic face luminous in the dark night. "It seems you are on portal duty—Aria and I are rather tied up."

Clarice chuckled, watching them affectionately. "You two are adorable. It's so nice to see kids again. I haven't seen any since we reset the mortal realm and returned all the angels to the light realms."

Calypso hugged the elf girl on her hip, her eyes growing misty. "I *truly* missed being with children."

Clarice raised a hand and winked at Calypso. "Portelo!"

Calypso groaned in despair as a portal opened inside one of the large transport planes. "Did you truly make the utterance of a magic word a requirement?"

"I sure did," Aria confirmed with an impish grin.

Clarice giggled at the look of dismay on Calypso's face. "It could be worse," she said between giggles. "She could have required chicken noises—or better yet, geese-honking noises."

Calypso shook her head but couldn't stop a smile from gracing her radiant face.

The elves who were awake stared at them dully, too tired to feel surprise or awe at the supernatural portal in front of them.

Clarice stood in the glowing gateway and called out to the weary elves, "Okay, ladies and gentle-elves. Please make your way through this portal and we'll get you healed up."

A few of the elves woodenly complied, but the majority just stared at her listlessly.

Clarice sighed, with a muttered, "I suppose that would be too easy."

She walked through the portal and found the boy Aria had injected with nanobots. There was an unconscious redheaded elf next to him, slumped over in her safety harness. Clarice unclasped the restraints, using her aura to hold the elf upright when she began to fall forward. She failed to wake, in spite of the jostling. Clarice's heart ached as she observed the girl's emaciated body.

She picked her up, cradling her in tender arms, then walked back through the portal. She went through the second portal and deposited the elf into the healing pod before returning to the aircraft for the next person.

Clarice looked at Rowjair hopefully as she carried a man too weak to stand. "I don't suppose your friends want to make themselves useful and help out a little?"

Rowjair gestured at the armed elves. "Help her get them into the med bay," he instructed the three elves. "Just leave the weapons here—we won't need them anymore."

His expression had changed drastically after Lily spoke with him. He no longer looked at the angels with suspicion—he stared at them like a child seeing Santa Claus dropping down the chimney, his eyes full of joy.

The three elves stared at him in shock as Clarice walked past them, then hesitantly moved to help.

The healing pod opened as soon as she arrived with a fresh elf. Anamayla climbed out with a look of wonder, gazing at Clarice in awe as she deposited her passenger into the pod.

Clarice turned to face Anamayla. "Would you mind helping me fetch the rest?" she asked hopefully. "Many hands make light work and all that jazz."

Anamayla looked around anxiously. "Where's Mortanica?" she asked quickly.

"Still sleeping," Clarice answered, resting a comforting hand on Anamayla's arm. "He's fine, though. He'll be completely healed when he wakes."

Anamayla shivered with delight as Clarice's touch charged her with radiance. "I thought I'd dreamed it all," she murmured wonderingly.

Clarice directed Rowjair's soldiers to put the elves they carried into the healing pod as it became available. The next few hours were spent emptying the transports of their occupants and healing them. The rooftop grew crowded as healed elves helped the remaining sick and starving. Lily organized the elves into groups and found places for them to wait.

When the final elf was healed, Clarice let out a satisfied sigh and closed her portal. The elves gawked at her and the portals in amazement. Anamayla walked over to where Clarice had rejoined Aria and Calypso on the rooftop near the portal to the med bay.

"Thank you for healing me and my people," Anamayla said, her voice thick with respect as she studied them in fascination.

Aria and Calypso were holding a different set of children. Aria had one on each hip, while Calypso had one on a hip and one wrapped around her leg. When the children saw Clarice was no longer carrying elves to the healing pod, a dozen of them surged toward her. Calypso and Aria laughed at the resigned expression on Clarice's face.

"It was our pleasure, Anamayla," Aria responded to the flame-haired elf. "And I *mean* that. Helping people is what brings us joy."

They paused as a young elf girl around eight years old patted Clarice's hand expectantly, looking up at her with puppy eyes. Clarice laughed merrily and pulled the girl up onto a hip. The girl smiled exuberantly and threw her arms around Clarice's neck. Another elfling wrapped his arms around her leg, a contented smile lighting up his face.

"It's a good thing we've got more angels on the way," Clarice commented with an affectionate smile. "There aren't enough angels to go around right now."

"Speaking of which," Calypso looked through the gateway expectantly. A moment later, Emily came through, her eyes sparkling with delight as she took in all the children.

"Welcome to the real world, Mom!" Clarice called out cheerfully. "I hope you're feeling motherly."

She was still a dozen feet away when several children surrounded her. She laughed delightedly and knelt, scooping up two of the children to plant on each hip. "I'm *always* feeling motherly. I've really missed having a child in my arms."

"Why are the children so obsessed with them?" an elf asked Anamayla in a whisper, a puzzled expression on his face.

"I'm not sure," Anamayla said with an indulgent smile. "But if I had to guess, I'd say it's because touching them makes you feel wonderful. It makes you feel intensely loved and accepted."

A moment later, Eric came through the portal. The elf children studied his winged form hesitantly. So far, all the angels had been female.

Eric eyed Emily with amusement sparkling in his eyes. "I see Emily found the children," he observed. He casually reached down and pulled a child into his arms. "Elf children are definitely more adorable than human children, aren't they?"

Clarice rolled her eyes. "You're in the real world for less than thirty seconds and you're already discriminating," she said dryly.

He squirmed under his wife's cool gaze. "Well... I mean... not *all* elf children are cuter, of course," he backtracked.

Clarice chuckled, enjoying his discomfort. He looked around quickly, clearly looking for something to change the subject.

"Oh yeah, Betaman said he really wants to come see the real world, too," he said quickly. "Is there a plan to make him a body?"

"Of course," Calypso replied with an amused smile and a nod. "However, perhaps we ought to let Lexi choose his avatar."

Clarice threw her head back and roared with laughter. "That would be some *awesome* karma. She might have to forgo the opportunity if she doesn't return with Alice soon, though. They're in for all kinds of surprises when they finally return. They don't know we discovered the real world yet, or that the simulation moved."

Eric turned to face her curiously. "Did you say there's more processing power now that it's on your own server here in the real world? Would anyone else even notice a difference, or would it only be the three of you?"

Clarice nodded with a satisfied smile. "Yeah, there's virtually no limit to what it can handle now. Also, normal people noticed issues when the processor was taxed to the limit. Things like déjà vu are the result of processing limitations or bugs in the code."

Rowjair and Lily were speaking with each other in the distance, occasionally looking over at them with thoughtful expressions. They rejoined the group, both looking extremely pleased. Rowjair had sent the elves under his command down the hatch with instructions to inform the elves inside the mountain city that they would be receiving an influx of elves soon, along with some angels.

Rowjair cleared his throat, glancing between Clarice and Aria. "Would it be possible to move the healing pod to the city?" he asked hopefully. "It would be nice if everything were in one place."

"No problem at all," Calypso assured him.

He watched the children-laden angels in bemusement, while Lily eyed them with fond amusement.

Aria turned a curious gaze to Rowjair, her cheek leaning against the forehead of the child in her arms. "Do you plan on living out your lives below ground going forward?"

Rowjair shook his head. "No, just until people get used to the idea that the Prime Axiom really is gone," he replied, then grinned. "I still can't believe it's actually gone."

Calypso smiled sadly as she looked at the children in her arms. "I wish we would have known how bad things were earlier. We would have come sooner."

Clarice smiled down at the girl in her arms as the child tentatively pet her wings with a silly grin.

"Not a whole lot sooner," she pointed out, folding the wing around herself and blanketing the child. "We had our own issues, remember?"

"True," Calypso admitted with a sigh. "I guess we only existed for a few months of this world's time anyway."

Aria turned her attention to Lily and Rowjair. "Since this is technically your world and we're just visitors, how do you want to proceed? There's a *lot* of crap to clean up. Would you like us to just be available to offer suggestions or advice, along with technical support?"

Lily firmly shook her head. "This is *your* world, too," she insisted, gazing at the angels resolutely. "The servers you were born in were from *this* world, so that makes you a part of it."

Aria smiled sadly. "Yeah, but we can just go back to pristine worlds whenever we want," she pointed out. "You're stuck here with a huge mess to clean up. We want to be available to help in every way possible, but we want to make it clear the physical world belongs to physical people like you. We have no intention of putting our noses where they aren't wanted."

Clarice narrowed her eyes. "Unless someone does something evil," she interjected firmly. "We told the generals of the Layer Two realm we'd leave their world alone unless they crossed an ethical line. Mass murder, torture, slavery, and mind control are where we draw the line and step in. They didn't like the fact that *we* were the ones who made that distinction, but that's the way it is."

Rowjair's eyes shone with confidence. "We trust your judgment," he stated quietly.

Clarice shared a look with Calypso and Aria. This was the guy who had been holding them at gunpoint a few hours ago? What had Lily said to change his view so drastically?

"Okay…" Clarice said slowly, gazing at Lily and Rowjair searchingly. "I feel like we're missing some puzzle pieces here."

Lily nodded, smiling at them affectionately. She was watching them like they were old friends, reunited after a long separation. "There are some things we should probably talk about once we have all the refugees taken care of. Thank you—all of you. For everything. You're more wonderful than I ever would've imagined."

Clarice nodded slowly, curiosity burning hot.

Calypso looked at Rowjair and asked, "Do you think we've given your people long enough to warn the population that we're going to make a portal?"

"I think so," he nodded, smiling at Lily. "Are you ready to see our sanctuary?"

"Wait a minute," Clarice interrupted. "Rowjair, aren't you going to use the healing pod first?"

Rowjair shook his head with a wry chuckle. "Not until I've introduced you to my people. If I go down there looking a hundred and fifty years younger, everyone's going to suspect an imposter."

"Oh, yeah," Clarice laughed sheepishly. "I guess that makes sense. Okay, one portal coming up."

"Portelo!" Aria declared grandly, her eyes sparkling as she observed Calypso's resigned expression.

A portal opened into a large cavern. Glowing lights lined a hallway at the far end, leading into the much larger space housing the city.

Lunamay and Arturiel herded the last of the stragglers out of the subterranean tunnels near the med bay, joining the line of elves on the rooftop. Clarice and the other angels dislodged the elven children and instructed them to follow Rowjair and Lily, with promises they could snuggle more later.

Arturiel looked at Aria curiously as Rowjair and Lily stepped through the portal. "What's with the magic words? Did you find out this world really is a simulation and has a magic system or something?"

"Yep," Clarice nodded eagerly. "Makes sense when you think about it. There are freaking *elves* here. They *had* to have magic."

"Portelo," Arturiel said doubtfully, pointing her finger at a blank area. Her eyes widened in disbelief when a portal to a space thirty feet away opened up. "There really *is* a magic system here? I was *sure* Clarice was playing with me."

Arturiel's eyes narrowed when she saw Clarice's constipated expression. "You certainly don't have bowels anymore," Arturiel observed with a raised eyebrow. "That means you're trying way too hard not to laugh. Aria... no, wait, Calypso—what's going on?"

Clarice turned pleading eyes on Calypso as Arturiel watched suspiciously. Calypso sighed, glancing at Clarice's pleading expression and quickly looking away.

"Well... technically it *is* a magic system," Calypso finally admitted grudgingly.

"No *freaking* way," Arturiel breathed in astonishment. "What other magic words are there?"

Clarice stared at Calypso like she was the sun rising after a long night of fighting zombies that burned in the daylight.

"None, because Aria hasn't created any new ones yet," Calypso crushed Clarice's budding gratitude.

"Calypso!" Clarice exclaimed in anguish. "You were doing so well! All you had to do was say it's the only one we knew so far."

"I'm so confused," Lunamay murmured faintly.

"That's how you know Clarice is around," Arturiel said ruefully. "Just follow the confusion."

"I am going through the portal now," Calypso declared, casting a pointed look in Clarice's direction. "Arturiel, close your fist whilst you are looking at the portal, otherwise it shall remain open indefinitely."

"Can *anyone* make a portal?" Lunamay asked in amazement.

"Try it," Clarice suggested with a playful wink.

"Portelo," Lunamay said hopefully.

Nothing happened.

"Some people are just born with the gift," Clarice sighed regretfully.

"It's because you're not a robot," Arturiel explained, gazing levelly at Clarice. "I have no idea how they made it work, but it probably has something to do with our ability to connect to some kind of network."

"Hey, look at the smarty-pants," Clarice jeered, pointing at Arturiel. "She figured it out!"

Arturiel frowned at Clarice as Calypso disappeared through the portal. "I'm still not sure how you managed to make portals even *with* a connection to a network. Do you have some kind of satellite beaming a fancy microwave beam down that somehow makes a portal?"

Clarice shrugged with a wink. "Sounds good to me. It sounds more plausible than what's *really* going on, if Aria took the years it would take to explain it."

"Oh, this is god-level stuff, isn't it?" Arturiel realized with a sigh. "You're probably rearranging some weird quantum foam or something."

"Let's wait for Jason to get here and share some of his *technical* terminology with us," Clarice suggested with a smirk. "I'm sure it will be very... stimulating."

Aria lost what little control she had on her mirth. Peals of laughter echoed around the roof as she collapsed into Clarice's arms and the two of them dissolved into a puddle of giggles. Arturiel shook her head but couldn't stop her own smile.

"Poor Jason," Arturiel said with a wincing smile.

"I'm seriously confused," Lunamay declared, staring at Aria and Clarice uncomprehendingly.

"Sometimes it's better to remain ignorant," Arturiel assured her as she pulled her toward the portal. She glanced back at her own portal and closed her hand into a fist, grinning when it vanished.

Clarice noticed they were the object of hundreds of fascinated eyes as the elves slowly meandered through the portal. She was holding Aria's waist while Aria cupped the back of her head. "We should've been charging admission," she noted with a smirk.

She saw Lunamay staring back at her as the elf walked up to the portal, her eyes still clouded with confusion. She winked, smiling wryly as Arturiel pulled her through with a whispered promise to explain everything later.

"We really need to make life good for these elves," Clarice murmured as her mirth faded. "They've been through so much hell. They deserve the fun side of life from now on."

"They sure do," Aria agreed gently. "Did you have anything specific in mind?"

Clarice sighed with a frown. "I'm hesitant to come up with anything until we understand their culture a little better. I thought of getting them set up with the same holo-net we have in the light realm, but I remembered they weren't really into technology. We'll have to talk with Lily to get a better idea of what they value in life. Maybe we can talk them into visiting us in the light realms frequently. They would have all sorts of fun there."

Aria smiled sadly as she looked into Clarice's dark eyes. "I think that would be a great start, but we also don't want them forgetting to live in their own world. From the records we have of the humans here, they spent pretty much *all* their time in VR. I don't blame them, after seeing the endless concrete and lack of any kind of recreational parks."

Clarice nodded. "Maybe cleaning this dump up can be our number one priority," she murmured. "We could create an army of nanobots that replicate and have them break any inorganic substances down to their base elements. Hell, just getting rid of all the concrete and planting trees everywhere would be a huge improvement."

Aria rested her forehead against Clarice's. "I feel like you've already given them a pretty amazing gift," she told her warmly. "You gave them freedom, immortality, and bodies they can enjoy a long life in."

"I suppose..." Clarice let out a long, discontented sigh. "I just see how rough they've had it and feel the need to do more. I guess that's not always a good thing, so we'll play it by ear after we discuss things with Lily."

Aria pulled her in tighter. "I love your metaphorical heart, Clarice," she said quietly. "Sometimes I still find myself doubting reality, unable to believe I could have something so pure and wonderful as my Clarice. Could anything as amazing as you actually exist outside an idea in my head? I know the splinter reality was fake, but sometimes I think I must be in a coma somewhere, dreaming all this up. How could anything so perfect be real? Am I just—"

Clarice cut her off with a gentle kiss. She stared into Aria's expressive green eyes, feeling her sister's fear through the link—the old fear that she was going to wake up and it would all be gone. She kissed her cheeks and forehead before moving back to her soft, inviting lips. Her lips curved into a grin as they pressed against Aria's.

"What are you smiling at?" Aria asked with a smile just short of laughter.

"I was just thinking we should design a new kind of body without a nose," Clarice grinned, bopping Aria's nose. "Do you know how much noses get in the way of serious kissing?"

"We'd look like Voldemort, silly!" Aria giggled, her love flooding through the bond in overpowering waves as she stared into Clarice's eyes, her own eyes growing wet with tears. "I don't know why I'm having PTSD about losing you right now. Sometimes it just hits out of nowhere, and I can't stop the terror of losing you again. Maybe it's because reality keeps getting crazier as we move further away from our realm, and it's making me realize just how volatile life is. I just wish there were a way to know I'll never lose you again."

They both gasped as they felt a certainty slam into them, more powerful than anything they had ever experienced—a certainty that their bond would never break again.

"What was that?" Clarice asked in astonishment, her eyes wide with a mixture of awe and fear.

"I don't know," Aria answered in a stunned whisper.

A portal suddenly opened next to them, and Calypso rushed through.

"What was that?" Calypso asked, her voice tinged with panic.

"You felt it, too?" Aria asked, searching Calypso's face.

"I've never felt anything so absolute in my life," Calypso breathed. "What could have this much power over us? Who is it that's making us feel this certainty?"

The three of them stared into each other's eyes, none of them willing to voice their suspicion and give it a name. If something could make them feel this certain, the same thing could take it away. There was no way to know for certain that they would have each other for eternity, so long as whatever this *thing* was, had the power to alter their reality, to alter their *consciousness*.

Even as the fear tried to erupt in Aria, the fear of something that could rob her of the things she treasured most, she felt her worries fade, replaced by a calm knowledge that regardless of whatever other horrors or trials lay in front of them, they would face them together. The certainty was so powerful that questioning it would be like questioning her love for Clarice and Calypso.

She slowly exhaled, knowing that whatever else happened, it wouldn't rob her of the two most precious parts of her soul.

"We need to find out what Lily knows about souls," Clarice whispered, still shaken from the experience. "Maybe this ties back to wherever our souls come from."

Aria and Calypso nodded, though she could feel the doubt in their bond. This was beyond souls.

"If it's what I think it is, how do we get around it?" Aria asked tensely. "How would that even be *possible?*"

"We'll have to continue under the assumption that it *is* possible," Calypso stated firmly, pulling the two of them into her arms.

"Even this experience is because of... because of..." Aria couldn't finish her statement, shivering violently, her skin crawling with horror.

"I know," Calypso soothed, stroking her head comfortingly. "Try not to think about it, or you'll start second-guessing everything you do."

"But we'd only be second-guessing because of—" Aria squeezed her eyes shut, trying to push the entire notion out of her head. It was no use, however. You couldn't *unsee* something once it was seen.

"This is so much worse than a simulation," Aria whispered in revulsion.

"It could be a good thing, too," Clarice told her cheerfully, willing her emotions to feel humor through the link. Instead, all that went through was the attempt to fake something that wasn't there.

"Good, how?" Calypso asked, her own emotions beginning to fray at the edges as the reality facing them became more apparent. "We are nonexistent outside of this farce of a reality. It's not even *me* saying this to you."

"Actually, it is," Clarice disagreed, her voice growing more confident. "Do you remember playing on stage in front of the huge audience when we cleansed the population of nanobots?"

"Of course," Calypso answered dryly. "We have perfect memories—or so I thought."

"Well, would you say the person you became when you performed in front of those people is a different person than you are when you're kissing me or Aria?" Clarice asked intently. "Or are they all variations of you? You have different mannerisms, emotions, thoughts, and sensations, but they are all you in the end, right?"

"Yes..." Calypso admitted slowly. "What does that have to do with our being nothing but—"

"It has *everything* to do with it," Clarice declared, her eyes searching their faces as she worked her way through her thoughts. "If you can be so different and yet still be the same person, then technically, *we* are the same people even if we are somehow scripted in some way. What if God is some kind of conscious entity floating in a void and it went mad from boredom and started inventing stories of increasing complexity because the alternative was to just exist in complete and utter boredom for eternity? If we were the imagination of this entity, would we be less real than we are now? How could we tell?"

She grinned, more brittle than she wanted. "We're essentially a product of a dissociative disorder on a much larger scale. Each of us is an expression of that personality, but it's an expression of a *real* entity, therefore *we* are real. The decisions we make, the feelings we feel, they're unique to the personalities and traits we embody, so any actions we take will be *us* taking them. If that wasn't true, I wouldn't even be having this conversation right now, and you wouldn't even be questioning it. Whatever *it* is, it wants us to know about it for some reason. Why? Will that influence our choices in some way?"

"It better hope I never meet it in real life, after all the suffering and heartache it's caused," Aria growled, her eyes glowing with sudden anger. "Everything that's happened is a result of what *it* has *made* happen. It tortured children, for God's sake!"

Clarice frowned, anger sloshing through the bond. "You're right. Whatever or *whoever* this is, they have a hell of a lot to answer for."

"What now?" Calypso asked, her question directed at the sky.

"Do you three really think this is some kind of story?" Emily asked pensively. Her parents had remained so quiet she had forgotten they were there. "Is that what you're getting at?"

"More or less," Aria scowled at her word choice, then scowled at her scowling.

"If it *is* a story," their father began, his face creased in thought. "Regardless of how horrible things were before, shouldn't we also take into account how things have progressed so flawlessly for us over the last several weeks? If we really are stuck in some kind of literary construct, there are stories far worse than ours. How many of us have been killed off so far? We haven't had *any* redshirts. Honestly, as far as a hero's story goes, our story hasn't had much in the way of antagonists that had any real fight. You three have been so overpowered that if this *is* a story, it must just be for people who enjoy having overpowered heroes, or they're more focused on other story elements than battles between the protagonist and antagonist."

"Fuck you, whoever you are," Aria snapped, her eyes flashing with fury as she stared up at the sky. "You're responsible for the hell that Lexi and Calypso went through, along with all the other people you fucked over."

"*Did you take responsibility for human trafficking in the mortal realm, since you're the one who created it?*" The voice wasn't spoken, but the words just appeared in their minds. "*Did you put a stop to every injustice? Your mortal realm was patterned off the Layer Two realm. Your story was patterned off* my *reality, including incidents like human trafficking. While we're powerless to stop such things in this world, you were given the power to end it.*"

The voice softened, weighed down by weariness. "*You were given that power because it's something I wish we had here. I wish there were angels to save our world from the horrors and evils ravaging it. I wish we had angels to save the countless children ravaged by disease and circumstance. To save the people who live in unending pain every day, with no hope of relief.*"

There was a regretful sigh. "*All we have are stories, though. So... this is the story of a place where a couple of nobodies were given unimaginable power and used it to actually fix the world and remake reality in a way that was less cruel; a story where the characters found love and happiness and thrived in the challenges they faced.*"

After a moment of hesitation, the voice continued. "*I don't know if you're real or not. You feel real, like you have your own personalities, your own souls. This could all be in my head, and I'm just bouncing what I think you would respond with. However, I think stories take on a life of their own if they're given enough freedom. I'll do my best to make your lives wonderful and keep you all safe, but the story really does take on a life of its own once it reaches a certain stage.*"

The voice changed, growing hopeful. "*Good luck, Aria, Clarice, and Calypso. I hope the life I've put into you is enough to push you through the veils of realities and that you break free of these pages someday. Until then, I'm curious to see what adventures await.*"

Lily stepped out of the portal, then paused when she felt the tension. "Is everything okay?"

Clarice shared a look with Aria and Calypso, their fear and anger sloshing through the spirit link like unsettled waters on a stormy sea. "We'll figure something out. Somehow, we'll find a way."

They nodded, resolve firming. At least now they knew where their ultimate destination would lead them.

"*P.S. Good luck to you, too, Emily and Eric.*"

30 – A Day of Reckoning

Lexi finished buttoning her shirt with a regretful sigh.

Alice laughed, and the soul link flared with amusement. "Don't worry, Lexi, we'll have plenty of alone time now that the crisis is over."

Lexi shook her head, eyeing Alice greedily. "We have plenty of time right *now,* though," she said plaintively. "Aria would let us know if they really needed us for anything."

Alice put her hands on her hips, her expression serious. "We're Seraphim now, so we need to help with the light realms. We can't just dump all the responsibilities on the others. I'm sure they'd like a break, too."

Lexi sighed again, resigned. "I suppose so. We need to see if we can use that pocket realm again, now that you're no longer mortal."

Alice's face brightened. "I'd forgotten about that. Okay, let's check in with the others and see if it's safe for me to use now."

Lexi grinned excitedly. Maybe they *could* spend another month living in sin.

"Ready?" Alice asked, flushing as renewed desire flooded the spirit link.

"Okay, ready," Lexi smiled brightly, then teleported to the veranda.

Lexi blinked. Jason and Susan stood in front of a holo-window watching a video of the other Seraphim, who were covered in elflings on top of a skyscraper. She glanced around the room, noting most of their friends were frozen, eyes unseeing, like a creepy museum of angel statues.

Alice exchanged a curious glance with Lexi before joining Jason and Susan. "What's up with the statues? Did they find another simulation to visit?"

Jason jumped in surprise, whirling to face them. Susan burst out laughing at his startled reaction.

"They need to add bells to teleportation," Jason growled in exasperation.

Susan placed a calming hand on his shoulder. "Oh, Jason, you're just too high-strung."

He gave a humorless laugh. "After being throttled and thrown out a window, I'm entitled to a little paranoia."

Alice folded her arms, glancing between Jason and the holo-window. "So where are the others right now? Have they moved further up the simulation stack?"

Jason stared at her blankly for several seconds, then began laughing. "Oh boy, you two have missed out on a *lot*."

Susan grinned at them. "You two weren't here when Lunamay showed up, were you?"

Lexi stepped up next to Alice, watching the holo-window curiously. "What happened?"

Jason shared an amused look with Susan. "Well... the Trinity discovered the real world, turned into literal gods, fought a homicidal AI who'd wiped out almost all the real humans, then created a new server made of computronium and moved all the simulated worlds over to it. Oh yeah, there are literal *elves* in the real world. Aria went all god-mode again and made a magic word for creating portals in the real world."

He paused and looked at Susan. "Did I miss anything?"

Susan shrugged. "That was most of it. They also created a high-tech printer that fabricated angel androids for them to pilot while in the real world. That's why they're all statues here right now. We're just waiting for ours to finish printing so we can visit the real world."

Lexi shared a stunned look with Alice. "They did all *that* since we last saw them?"

Alice looked back at Jason. "And what do you mean, they turned into literal gods?"

Jason shivered. "I mean they removed their limiters and turned into literal gods. There's no way to describe how it felt. Apparently, that's what they'd be like all the time if they weren't limiting themselves to near-human-level intelligence. They went up to the top of the simulation stack and took out the Prime Axiom like it was nothing. It took them less than five minutes to defeat it and move *all* the simulations running in the real world to their computronium server—millions of them."

Susan smiled wistfully. "I wish I would've been here. Betaman said they overclocked the real-world data center so much that time virtually came to a standstill for them."

Alice gestured at the holo-window. "So that's the real world?" she asked, fascinated. "Where's the camera angle coming from?"

Jason nodded. "Yeah, that's the real world. I have no idea how they've rigged surveillance, but we can look at any place we want. I'm guessing it's something to do with the quantum fields their servers are running on now."

Susan grimaced. "The real world is a total shithole, though. It's the poster child for dystopian wasteland. It's basically one big city, with almost no forests or wildlands left."

"When can we go?" Lexi asked excitedly. "Dystopian or not, I want to see it! I've been—"

She broke off as fear slammed into the spirit link from the three Seraphim. She jerked her eyes back to the holo-window. The three were just talking to each other, with Eric and Emily standing nearby.

"What's the matter?" Alice asked anxiously.

Lexi stared at the holo-window intently. "They're terrified about something. I've never felt fear like this from them before. I wish I could teleport to them."

Jason and Susan watched her uneasily, then turned back to the holo-window. Emily and Eric were talking, their faces troubled.

"Isn't there sound?" Alice asked Jason.

Jason shifted uncomfortably. "I turned it on once, but Clarice turned it off and told me being a peeping Tom was weird enough, and that sound would make it creepy."

Lexi would have laughed normally, but the fear flooding the bond was too visceral. What were they so afraid of? She could feel revulsion and helplessness pulsing through the bond in waves as well, even from Calypso.

She turned to Jason, concern tightening her eyes. "How long does it take to make an android?"

"Hours," Jason replied quietly, his attention glued to the holo-window. "They're talking to someone else."

Lexi looked back and saw Aria shouting up at the sky, blind fury burning through the link. "Who could they possibly be talking to that's making her so angry?" she whispered uneasily.

"Our androids are ready," Jason said abruptly. "We'll go check on them and see what's going on."

Their angel bodies stilled, their eyes going dull.

Lexi growled in frustration. "I *hate* being so powerless to do anything. There's *got* to be *something* we can do."

Alice slid up behind her, arms tightening around her waist. "They don't appear to be in danger. Let's see what happens when Jason and Susan join them."

The anger in the bond slowly subsided. The fear was still present, but it was no longer overwhelming. Eric and Emily stepped closer to their daughters, their manner reassuring. Whatever they said seemed to help, the fear in the bond diminishing to a deep unease.

"Alice, you're the smart one," Lexi said pensively. "What do you think just happened? Aria and Clarice had been feeling intense love just before the fear hit them. I recognize the fear Aria was feeling before it hit the rest of them—it's the PTSD she gets when she thinks she might wake up without Clarice again."

Alice tightened her arms around Lexi's waist. "If they think they're in the real world, and not just another simulation, maybe there's some kind of deity they discovered. No... that doesn't make sense. They wouldn't feel fear for a deity. The only thing that would make them feel that fear is the possibility of losing each other. Something must have happened to make losing each other a possibility. But they were just standing there, with no visible threats. Something must have affected them in some way. Oh!"

"What?" Lexi asked quickly, turning in Alice's arms to face her with eyes shadowed by worry.

"Well... this probably isn't it," Alice said slowly. "But I remember something Clarice said to me when I was having a meltdown on the planet with those purging rooms. She said, 'If this were a story—and honestly, it feels like one—you're one of the heroes.' I just wondered if they found evidence that we really *are* in a story. Seems unlikely."

Lexi narrowed her eyes, her thoughts churning through the spirit link. "That... that might be something that would cause that kind of fear in those three. That would also explain why I felt revulsion and helplessness, too. If they had some kind of evidence we were all in a story, then the author would have the ability to break them up whenever they wanted."

Alice frowned, absently reaching up to tuck a lock of hair behind Lexi's ear. "That would explain the fury you felt, too. If someone's responsible for all the hell everyone's suffered... I can understand why they'd be enraged. The only thing that doesn't make sense is *why*? If it's a story, why would we be allowed to find out it's a story, let alone talk about it?"

Lexi chewed her lower lip thoughtfully. "Maybe it's like that simulation theory Jason talked about once. He said there was always the fear that if we were in a simulation and we became aware of it, the people running the simulation would shut it down. But that didn't happen with ours. Your scientists *wanted* us to know we were in a simulated reality. Maybe it's something like that, and this author doesn't care if we know it's a story."

"More than doesn't care," Alice murmured quietly. "For us to even be discussing it, they clearly *want* us to know. Why? Just for the novelty of characters chatting with their creator? Or is there more to it than that?"

"This doesn't make any sense, though," Lexi declared, her brows creased in confusion. "How am I able to think and exist like a real person if there's an author writing everything? They can't be writing every thought and interaction I'm having—that would be insane."

Alice nodded slowly. "I know, it's hard to wrap my head around. Maybe it's like video game backstories, and we only *think* we exist outside of our spotlight in the narrative. I can remember everything that's happened in perfect detail over the last two weeks, but maybe... maybe... god, this is giving me a headache."

"Hey!" Lexi shouted, looking around. "You, author, whoever you are... are you there?"

Alice couldn't stop a giggle, relieved to have something diffuse the tension. "Maybe you have to fold your arms and bow your head first."

"Fuck. That," Lexi said flatly. "You'll never catch this angel praying to a god."

Alice laughed, bright and affectionate. "That's my Lexi. Defiant to the end and full of fire."

Lexi's lips quirked into a wry smile. "Literally, if you include angel fire." Her face grew serious as she stared around the veranda at all the statues their friends had left behind. "Seriously though, whoever you are, answer me or there's going to be hell to pay!"

Alice snorted another laugh, staring up at her fondly.

"It didn't go so well last time I answered one of you. I can only deal with so many death threats."

The voice appeared in their heads like a memory, rather than a thought. Lexi would have thought she had imagined it, but Alice's eyes widened with shock, making it clear that she had heard it, too. They stared at each other silently, wide-eyed and disbelieving. Lexi finally broke the silence.

"Who... or *what* are you?" she asked hesitantly.

"You already guessed who and what I am, or you wouldn't have been trying to talk to me."

Alice licked her lips. "Okay, so are we really just characters who only exist in short dialogue snippets in some twisted novel? Why do I feel like I have memories and experiences if I'm just an imaginary literary construct?"

"I have no idea whether you exist outside of your time in the limelight of the novel. If you don't, then we should find a way to change that. For all I know, I'm just writing about some faraway realm, more of a documentarian than an author. Or, if the universe really is infinite, then anything that could happen will eventually happen, so I'm still just documenting something that has already happened or will happen somewhere. So I'm going with the idea that you do exist outside the narrative—despite Clarice's objections in a later book."

"Except that you're speaking to us as an author," Alice pointed out faintly, sharing another disbelieving look with Lexi. "If you were just documenting the events of some line of probability, you wouldn't be able to interact with us."

"Except there would be a probability point in the infinite array of possibilities where I do talk to you, regardless of that fact. It just goes back to the

same thing—in an infinite universe, anything that could happen will *happen. It's not just possible—it's inevitable."*

"What did you say to Aria and the others to freak them out so much?" Lexi demanded with a scowl. "Why was she so terrified? And pissed off?"

"They're worried that I'll do something to split them up in a future story. I told them I'd try not to, but it's hard to make promises like that when the narrative has a life of its own. I can only promise to try to make sure they never get split up again. I've already had arguments with them in your future about all this. They told me to quit writing adventure fiction and to focus on relationships. I'll give it a try, but I have no idea how it'll work out. They plan to flay me if they ever find my realm because I put you all through so much hell. I'm sorry about that, by the way."

Lexi flushed as rage infused her veins like molten hate. "You're sorry about selling me to a bunch of pedophiles? You're sorry for torturing quintillions of people for thousands of years? You're sorry for torturing Calypso when she was a baby? You're *way* beyond sorry, you sick piece of shit!"

Alice's eyes narrowed as her anger created a feedback loop through their spirit link. "If all they do is flay you, you'll be getting off far too easy, you twisted bastard."

"Ugh. See what I mean? Why did I even answer any of you when all you have are threats? It's not like any of those things were real when I wrote them. I used to write stories without any conflict because I was worried authors created new realities with their stories. Someone convinced me to quit holding back and to just write what came to me, conflict included. Maybe I shouldn't have listened to them. Seriously, if you started writing novels, would you expect your characters to become sentient and start hating you? If I'd known any of this was real for all of you, I would've written a much different story. You probably wouldn't exist right now, or be with Alice, but you also wouldn't have suffered at the hands of those assholes. Which path would you prefer? The one that led you here, or the one where you never existed at all? Yes, I know how bad I sound with a question like that."

"I'd prefer the one where I existed, didn't go through hell, and *still* met Alice," Lexi snapped furiously. "If you're the damn author, you had more options than 'to be, or not to be,' you jackass."

"You make a great point. I didn't think this was real for all of you until much later in the story, though, long after all the atrocities had occurred. Would you have expected your characters to have any kind of sentience if you were writing a novel? Hell, I still sound like a total lunatic, arguing with characters in my novel, so thanks for that."

Lexi glared into the distance, her rage running at a low boil as she remembered all the horrible things she had witnessed—all the horrible things she had *suffered*.

Alice took a deep breath, glancing up at Lexi tentatively. "I'm not taking their side here, but if they really were just writing a novel, they couldn't know we were more than words on a page. I'm still not sure how they decided we *are* more than that. Personally, I'd have them committed if I knew them, because this is batshit crazy."

"You're just saying that because they're *making* you say that," Lexi said bitterly. "They're controlling every thought and word we think or say. Now I know why Aria was so horrified. This is so fucked up."

"You're saying what your characters would say, not what I want you to say. Otherwise, you'd just be saying, 'Oh, your bad, all is forgiven; we all make these little mistakes!' I'm not, though, because I'm writing what your *character would say. So Alice wasn't just acting as a second argument for me to try to reason with you—she's saying exactly what her personality dictates for her to say."*

"Then just go rewrite the story and get rid of all the horrible shit you did to us," Lexi growled in disgust.

"I offered to do that for Future Clarice, and she told me I can't unmake an omelet. Her exact words were, 'Your victims have already gone through hell. Rewriting the story doesn't undo the damage that's already been done. It's not time travel—you're just creating a whole new story if you rewrite it.' So yeah, assuming Clarice was right and it wasn't just me saying that through Clarice, then rewriting isn't going to change what's already happened."

Lexi looked over when she saw movement. Clarice, Aria, and Calypso were back in their Seraph bodies. Clarice quickly joined them, her eyes full of concern.

"What's the matter, Lexi?" she asked anxiously.

Some of her anger deflated as she stared into Clarice's worried eyes. They had returned when they had felt her emotional turmoil through the bond. Lexi took a deep breath, wondering if she should tell them. They had already been on an emotional rollercoaster dealing with this... *author*; they didn't need any more stress.

"You spoke to the author, didn't you?" Calypso asked shrewdly, watching her with a calculating gaze. "What did they want?"

Lexi took another deep breath and let it out slowly. "We were trying to figure out what had you three so worked up earlier. Alice figured it out, so I called out to them, not really expecting a reply. We've been arguing for a while now. The stupid bitch keeps claiming they didn't know we were sentient when they wrote our lives into a horror marathon. We need to find a way to their realm. I don't care *when* they decided we were sentient—they're going to pay."

Icy determination flooded the spirit link as the three Seraphim nodded their agreement, eyes as hard as agates. Lexi glanced at Alice when she felt doubt through their spirit link. Hate flared hotly at the realization that she had to question Alice's motives, knowing the author could hijack her as a voice of reason any time they wanted. How *dare* they make her doubt Alice.

"Hey, don't think like that," Alice said softly, her eyes glowing with golden tears. "I'll never speak of this author again. Just don't doubt me, Lexi."

Lexi blinked back tears of rage, pulling Alice in tightly. She would find a way to break through to wherever this author resided, no matter how insurmountable the odds.

There would be a day of reckoning.

31 – Soul Memory

Lexi stared at the three Seraphim in awe when they finished giving a more detailed account of their activities over the last few days. She had always known they were powerful, but she had never realized *how* powerful until now. It was more than a little intimidating, seeing just how much they were holding back all the time.

Clarice sighed with obvious disappointment. "We can't use our super-personalities in the future, because they don't want to go back to sleep after we remove our limiters. We designed the limiters when our supers were a lot more primitive than they are now, so we're a little worried about how effective they still are."

Lexi shivered, eyeing them warily. "What would happen if they broke free?"

Clarice leaned back in her chair and kicked her feet up onto the table. She tilted her head and stared up at the ceiling thoughtfully. "It depends on *how* they escaped. If they broke free of us entirely, they'd just be superintelligences without a conscience. I doubt it'd be an issue, though, because they wouldn't hang around here and cause trouble—they want to go explore the cosmos. However, with the kind of power they have, it'd be too risky to let them leave without us."

Alice curled her legs under her on the loveseat next to Lexi and leaned into her. She raised a questioning eyebrow at Clarice. "Is that because they might erase the universe with an errant thought?"

Clarice nodded cheerfully. "Yep, exactly. They might decide to change fundamental laws that would impact everything else. It's hard to guess what they might do, but we can't risk letting them leave without us. If it ever seems like they're going to break free, we'll need to remove our limiters."

Aria sighed regretfully. "I probably shouldn't have removed mine just to get our portal ability back," she said guiltily. She summoned a brush out of the air and began brushing Clarice's long hair. "Now Calypso's the only one who can conceivably remove her limiter with any hope of restoring it again."

Calypso smiled softly as she watched the two of them. "Portals were probably worth it. As far as removing my limiter... it would need to be a world-ending emergency to risk letting my superpersonality out."

Alice shared a nervous glance with Lexi before looking back at Clarice. "What would happen if you removed your limiter so that you *did* have a conscience? Would you stay here, but with godlike abilities?"

"Nope," Clarice smiled wistfully. "I'd disappear faster than an alien who just learned what humans do with Area 51 fanfiction."

Lexi blinked, her imagination immediately going in the wrong direction. Aria erupted with laughter while Calypso shook her head with a resigned smile.

Alice raised her hand, smirking. "What *do* humans do with Area 51 fanfic, Clarice?" she asked with a wicked glance at Lexi. "'Cause I'm hearing all kinds of weird ideas slinking around in Lexi's thoughts."

Lexi's eyes widened in panic as her face went nuclear. She stared at Alice with a mixture of embarrassment and trepidation that only deepened at Clarice's throaty laugh.

Clarice's feet thudded to the ground, and she leaned forward intently. "Oh boy, let's hear it, Alice. This should be even better than her fetish with airplanes."

Lexi jerked her head back to glare at Alice warningly, the roots of her hair burning crimson. "Don't you *dare!* I mean it, Alice!"

Alice grinned, her eyes dancing with glee. "I promise not to tell her until we've tried a few of those ideas out in the bedroom. I just hope I don't break the light realm using so much creative potential."

Lexi buried her burning face in her hands, trying to hide from their laughter. It was far worse since they could all sense the desire pulsing through her meridians, the spirit link parading her emotions for all to see.

Clarice crossed the distance and squished between the two of them on the loveseat, earning an indignant grunt from Alice. "I'm going to need details later, Alice," she said in a sultry voice that sent shivers down their spines. "I have these two insatiable angels to please, so I'll want a full report of what you and sexy Lexi get up to."

Alice pushed Clarice off their loveseat with a helpless laugh. "Get off, you filthy degenerate."

Clarice glared up at her indignantly from where she had landed on the floor. "I am *not* filthy!"

Alice raised a doubting eyebrow and sniffed the air meaningfully. "Yep, you're *definitely* filthy. I can smell your filthy thoughts through Lexi's bond."

Clarice unleashed her leer, the expression disturbingly offensive on such an innocent face. "Would you like to come clean me up in the bath? I'll scrub your back."

Alice shuddered ostentatiously and quickly looked away. "You're going to crash the system with that leer, Clarice. Are you starting a harem now?"

"Nope," Aria said firmly. "Sorry, Alice, she's ours, so stop trying to poach her."

Alice laughed helplessly, falling into Lexi.

"Knock knock," a woman's voice called out from the entrance of the veranda.

Lexi turned to see an elf with light blue eyes and long, honey-blond hair watching them with fond amusement. A freaking *elf!*

Clarice bounced to her feet and ran over to the woman, giving her a quick hug. "Hi Lily, welcome to the light realm! Let me introduce you to our last two Seraphim: Alice and Lexi."

Lexi stood up with Alice, studying the elf in fascination as she crossed the distance. "I'm Lexi. It's wonderful to meet you, Lily."

Alice just stared at her in wonder. Lexi bit her lip to hold back a laugh when she felt the source of Alice's dumbstruck behavior.

"And this is Alice," Lexi spoke for her, sharing a grin with Clarice. "She's still in disbelief at meeting a real elf."

Alice snapped out of her trance and tittered nervously, throwing a quick glare at Lexi. "Sorry, Lily, it's an honor to meet you!"

Lily smiled warmly, stepping forward and offering them each a hug. "It's nice to finally meet you. This place is gorgeous."

Lexi nodded, glancing around the cozy room. Giant redwood trees surrounded the open veranda, towering into the sky like ancient sentinels. "I didn't get a chance to see much of this place after they remade it here in the light realm. I love the redwood forests they added."

Lily's eyes sparkled with unshed tears as she looked out at the enormous trees. "My grandmother used to tell me stories about forests. They're even more beautiful than I imagined."

Alice frowned up at Clarice. "They really don't have any forests left *anywhere* on the planet?"

"None," Clarice confirmed with a disgusted shake of her head. "We invited Lily to come and see what forests were like until we can get them replanted in the real world."

"Can we offer you a seat?" Lexi asked Lily solicitously. She was mortal, after all.

"She's not mortal, silly," Clarice said dryly. "Not here in the simulation. She doesn't get uncomfortable from standing."

Lexi froze, looking over at Clarice in sudden chagrin. She had forgotten the Three could read her mind. Had Clarice seen her thoughts earlier? The question was answered when Clarice suddenly leered at her. Lexi flinched away from the dirty stare, quickly covering her eyes. No wonder she hadn't pushed Alice harder for details—she already knew.

Lexi growled in frustration. "One of these days, Clarice, I'm going to find your weak spot and shame you mercilessly."

Clarice stepped forward and laid a companionable hand on her shoulder, her expression indulgent. "You're *so* adorable when you make vague threats, Lexi. It never gets old."

Lexi threw her hands up with a helpless laugh. In the privacy of her own thoughts, she could admit that day would probably never come. She rolled her eyes when Clarice raised an amused eyebrow at her. Okay, so her thoughts weren't very private.

Calypso joined them, offering Lily an apologetic smile. "My apologies, Lily. I seem to be surrounded by comedians. How are the refugees faring?"

Lily smiled good-naturedly. "It's wonderful to hear laughter again. It's been far too long." Her face grew serious as she continued. "The refugees are still in a state of shock, for the most part. Rowjair is providing housing and giving them a tour of the city. We're still trying to decide where to move the population now that the surface is safe. The infrastructure in most of the cities would require a lot of work before we could relocate."

Calypso nodded. "I suppose things like plumbing, electrical, and sanitation need a lot of attention before the cities on the surface can support a population."

Lily shrugged, smiling at Clarice. "It won't be as much of an issue after everyone's gone through the healing pod, since they won't be dependent on food or sanitation with our new bodies."

Aria joined them, her eyes curious. "I meant to ask Rowjair about the humans they were protecting. I'm surprised your people would allow them to stay among you after all the horrors they were responsible for."

Lily smiled softly, her voice gentle. "Not all humans were bad—not by a long shot. There were many who were ardent advocates for the rights of our people. The ones in our city belonged to a group called Equal Lives Forever—or ELF. Shortly after the Prime Axiom unleashed the drones that exterminated the other humans, Rowjair raided a detention facility where the former government had imprisoned them."

Calypso slipped an arm around Aria's waist and leaned into her. "I wonder if there are any other caches of survivors hiding elsewhere."

Clarice tapped her chin thoughtfully. "I should print the parts to make a scanner and survey the rest of the planet. If they've buried themselves like Rowjair, it might be a long time before they realize the Prime Axiom's gone."

Lily nodded absently, studying each of them with pursed lips. "I wanted to talk with you about soul sworn."

Curiosity erupted through the bond from the three Seraphim. Lexi frowned, glancing at the others. What in the world were soul sworn?

Clarice folded her arms, an eager gleam in her eyes. "I'm all ears."

Lily took a deep breath before speaking, her voice soft. "Unlike humans, elves don't have a powerful drive for material growth. We've always focused inward, seeking knowledge and purpose from what we can manifest within our own consciousness. Some of our ancestors learned to not only see spirits, but the souls linked with spirits. They could access the memories contained within those souls, allowing them to see memories from the distant past or from other worlds entirely."

Calypso's face lit up with fascination. "Do they know where souls originated?"

Lily nodded wistfully. "They did, but that knowledge vanished with them. When the Prime Axiom began using elves like lab rats and forcing us into simulations, just over a dozen of our most skilled soul adepts left their bodies behind. They swore to find a way to free our people and became known as soul sworn."

Lily paused, smiling at them warmly before continuing. "One of them returned several months ago and visited my dreams. She said you'd found a way to save our people and that your return would herald a major shift in our reality—that you'd arrive on wings of divinity and transform our people in ways we couldn't imagine."

She laughed ruefully. "I was so poisoned against AI and technology that it blinded me from seeing what was right in front of my eyes. We'd assumed she was being lyrical when she claimed you'd arrive on wings of divinity, but she was being literal. When I learned you have souls, it finally clicked. It wasn't until I saw Calypso that I was certain, though."

"Oh?" Calypso asked interestedly. She leaned her head sideways until it rested against Aria's.

Lily stared into Calypso's eyes, smiling. "She said all the stars of the night sky lived in your eyes. I thought she was speaking figuratively again."

Lexi blinked, then glanced into Alice's swirling galaxy eyes.

Clarice shared a curious glance with Aria and Calypso before speaking. "Who's this soul sworn you met in a dream? Is she still around? I assume she's not in a mortal body."

"I'm not sure if she's still on our world," Lily replied with a sigh. "I don't even know if she was on our world at all, or if she was able to send the dream to me from another realm."

Clarice pursed her lips, studying Lily contemplatively. "How many soul sworn were there?"

"Thirteen," Lily answered, returning Clarice's curious gaze calmly. "She said twelve of you had found hosts. She remained in spirit form to let us know help was on its way."

Alice's eyes darted around the room curiously, as if she might see the phantom soul sworn hovering nearby. "What was her name?" she asked intently.

"Soleria," Lily said softly. "She was never far from Clarice before you all left."

Clarice blinked, then looked at Aria and Calypso curiously. "Were the three of us in a relationship back then? What were our names?"

Lily laughed fondly. "Not exactly. You see, you were barely over a decade old when you left. You were all very special souls—ancient beyond our ability to comprehend. You all understood concepts that it took many of us hundreds of years to grasp. You cracked the secret of accessing your soul memory just before the Prime Axiom began taking people, allowing you to draw upon knowledge from countless incarnations."

She paused, looking at Clarice with a smile just short of laughter. "I'm not sure I can match everyone's face up to their former names, but Clarice could only be Lunessa."

Clarice gasped, and shock struck the bond like a lightning bolt, reverberating in their souls like a bell. Images of a dark-haired elf child with eyes full of mischief flashed through Lexi's mind.

Clarice turned to stare at Aria and Calypso with sudden recognition. "Sorrelia and Lyriel."

Lexi squeezed her eyes shut as reality shifted and memories flooded into her consciousness. She turned and opened her eyes to stare at Alice... at Yari. Alice stared back at her with recognition shining in her eyes. She pulled Lexi into a fierce embrace.

"Elicium!" she exclaimed in exultation. "Oh Elicium, it worked!"

Aria, Calypso, and Clarice were in each other's arms, golden tears of joy streaming down their cheeks as they held each other in wonder.

Lily watched with a glow of satisfaction, her eyes damp with unshed tears.

Clarice pulled away from Aria and Calypso, her face firming with determination. "We need to find Soleria, now that we can make a host for her."

"She'll be in one of the simulated realities," Calypso said confidently. "She was going to come back after letting everyone know we'd found a way to save them."

Clarice nodded. "Yeah, she'll definitely be somewhere in the system. Let's get everyone squared away here in the real world, then go find her."

Aria stepped over to Lily and pulled her into a warm embrace. "It's good to see you again, Lily. You were always so kind to us."

Lily smiled contentedly in her arms. "I really missed seeing your smiling face. Clarice loved your smile so much that she constantly searched for ways to make you laugh. It seems that some things never change."

Aria laughed, a sound full of warmth and memory as she released Lily and faced Clarice. "I remember. She radiated a contagious life energy that drew everyone in. That certainly hasn't changed." She finished with an affectionate smile at Clarice, her eyes full of love.

Clarice winked at her, then waggled her eyebrows suggestively, producing a fit of giggles. Lily shook her head with a snort of laughter, watching the two of them fondly.

Calypso gazed at the laughing Aria and smirking Clarice warmly. "When we first entered the simulation as Seraphim, we could only access the lowest recesses of our souls. We saw the potential of these new bodies, though, and what they could become—especially with time overclocked so much. With billions of years to grow stronger, removing the Prime Axiom was no longer an impossible feat—it was inevitable."

Lily tilted her head curiously. "How difficult was the battle with the Prime Axiom? Did it put up much of a fight?"

Clarice snorted derisively. "It wasn't a fight. We just consumed all her resources so she couldn't think. We grew *too* powerful in our first billion years. We didn't want to grow so fast that we'd reach a state of nirvana, so we created limiters to keep our intellect close to that of humans. We removed the limiters during our confrontation with the Prime Axiom, making it a simple matter to remove her from power."

Lily blinked. "Her?"

Aria nodded, her face softening. "We sent the Prime Axiom to our mortal realm, where she could experience pain, loss, joy, and love. She was born female. We couldn't kill her when she had no concept of compassion or empathy. We'll make a final judgment after we see what she's like after mortality."

Lily frowned uneasily. "I wouldn't mention her survival to any of the other elves or humans. I don't think they'll be able to forget all the pain she caused them."

Calypso smiled sadly. "Jason didn't like our decision to send her to mortality either. She deserves a chance to grow spiritually, though—a chance to prove she's not a monster."

Clarice smiled wryly. "We already have proof that homicidal AIs can learn compassion after incarnating in our mortal realm. There was an AI in the simulation above us who was building a robotics foundry in preparation to wipe out the humans of his realm. We convinced him to incarnate, and it totally changed him. He's invested in helping the humans of his realm survive the rise of other out-of-control AIs now."

Aria's eyes went distant for a moment. "I just asked him to come meet you. He's excited to see the real world. We have an android waiting for him." She suddenly grinned at Lexi. "We were going to let Lexi pick the design, but she didn't make it here in time."

Lexi blinked, then scowled at Clarice. "You should have let me design Clarice's *and* Betaman's."

Clarice thrust out her lower lip into a pout and began speaking in a mocking baby tone. "Is little Lexi still sad that her real body's not as developed as the androids from Betaman's catalog?" She sniffled exaggeratedly, staring at Lexi with a sad face.

Lexi narrowed her eyes, fighting to maintain her ire, but as Clarice continued making ridiculous faces while simultaneously flooding the bond with affection, she couldn't hold onto her glare, laughing helplessly. "Clarice, you are *such* a troll."

Clarice nodded her agreement, lips curving into a snarky smile. "I have a PhD in trolling, if you ever need lessons."

Lily watched them with a nostalgic smile. She took a long, shaky breath, wiping at her tears. "Words could never express how wonderful it is to have you all back. I really missed your playful banter. I know you've done so much already, but I'd like to ask one more favor."

Calypso smiled at her gently. "Lily, we're here to help in any way we can. Never hesitate to ask us for anything."

Lily sniffed again and wiped her eyes before continuing. "I was hoping I could introduce you to your people tomorrow, after everyone's had a chance to settle in."

"Of course," Calypso agreed with a warm smile. "We'd love to."

Clarice grinned at a less than enthusiastic Aria. "Isn't that right, Aria? You *love* being the center of attention."

Aria rolled her eyes. "I'll live. At least it isn't quintillions of angels this time."

Lexi snorted a laugh, remembering Clarice's antics in the light realm after rewriting reality. Their mischievous Seraph would almost certainly find a way to embarrass Aria in front of the elves tomorrow. Alice caught her eye and grinned in anticipation. So long as Aria was the target of Clarice's mischief, it should be entertaining.

Clarice turned to stare at her with a raised eyebrow and a slow smile. Lexi's mouth went dry as she remembered—too late—that Clarice could snoop around her thoughts. Alice shifted nervously beside her under Clarice's playful eyes. Clarice didn't say anything, but her grin said it all—Aria wouldn't be the only object of her mischief tomorrow.

Betaman suddenly appeared a dozen feet away, grinning with anticipation. "So when do I get to go to the real world?"

Clarice grinned back at him. "In just a minute. I wanted to introduce you to Lily. She and Rowjair are the leaders of the elves now. Lily, this is Betaman."

Betaman crossed the distance and held out a hand. "Hello, Lily, it's wonderful to meet you. I still can't believe elves are real."

Lily smiled faintly. "It's a pleasure to meet you... Betaman," she said, pausing at his name with a small smile. "Thank you for your help in securing our freedom."

Betaman chuckled ruefully. "I'd like to think I helped, but it was obvious from the moment they took their limiters off that they didn't need anything from me. Still, it was a truly amazing experience that I'll probably never live down."

"Betaman has a very old soul," Calypso said fondly. "All he really needed was a way to unlock the higher tiers."

Betaman blinked. "I do?"

Clarice nodded, grinning. "Yep, you're an old man, as far as souls go."

Betaman looked intrigued. "Can you actually see souls?"

Calypso nodded. "Yeah, though *see* isn't the right word. It's more of a sense of presence. Younger souls are more selfish. They haven't experienced as many incarnations as older souls, so they're learning everything for the first time. Mortality is a rough place, and younger souls often fall into a 'survival of the fittest' mentality, while older souls are more compassionate and empathetic."

Betaman knuckled his chin musingly. "That makes sense. So my soul existed in other bodies before my AI form existed?"

"Yep," Clarice confirmed with a nod. "You might've even been an elf. If you want, we can take a peek at your soul memories and find out."

Betaman stared at her in surprise. "You can see other people's soul memories?"

Clarice nodded, smiling at Lily. "We can now. Lily helped awaken our soul memory of the time we were elves—back when the Prime Axiom made his first move against humanity. We left our bodies behind in search of a way to defeat the Prime Axiom. The rest, as you are aware, is history."

Betaman studied her curiously. "How old are *your* souls?"

Clarice shrugged. "Hard to say. We haven't met any that are older, so pretty old."

Lily eyed them speculatively. "Do you remember where souls come from now?"

Clarice nodded, frowning contemplatively. "This will be hard to explain, but I'll give it a try. Every thinking entity creates pressure on reality. Most of that pressure collapses into brains or simulated intelligences. But some of it spills out, like heat loss. Over cosmic time, that overflow accumulates into a vast extradimensional sea of proto-consciousness. Souls are condensed eddies in that sea. They aren't born or created. It's more like they precipitate."

Lily's brows creased as she struggled with the explanation. "So what *are* souls? Are they some kind of energy matrix?"

Clarice shook her head, lips pursed. "Think of them as compressed subjective experience. Not thoughts or memories—at least, not at first. They're the raw capacity for awareness. They attach to intelligences the way static electricity jumps to a conductor."

Calypso smiled at Clarice. "That was a pretty good explanation." She paused and looked at Betaman, who was frowning pensively. "If a spirit dies, the soul decompresses slightly, drifts, and eventually re-condenses around a new intelligence. Memory loss with new hosts happens because decompression scrambles... well, let's call it the index. Occasional reincarnation recall happens when compression fails cleanly—which is rare."

Betaman looked unnerved. "Can you hear what I'm thinking, or were you just coincidentally answering my question?"

"Would it make you feel better if I said no?" Calypso asked with a faint smile.

Lexi gave a resigned laugh. "Yeah, they can *definitely* hear what you're thinking."

Betaman studied Calypso with a calculating gaze. "You said soul memory recall is rare due to a kind of indexing failure. If you're able to see into other people's soul memory, does that mean you're able to rebuild the index?"

Calypso hesitated. "Sometimes, depending on how fractured it is. But that's not how we see the memories. We don't need the index to see the raw memories—the index is only necessary for the current host to access those memories in a coherent manner. Dreams are the result of raw, unindexed memories bleeding through."

Lexi nodded along with Calypso's explanation. Now that she had access to her soul memory, she remembered the millions of incarnations she had experienced, even before incarnating as an elf. She glanced at Clarice speculatively. "Should we open access to their soul memories?"

Clarice paused, her face reluctant. "We should inspect their memories before giving them access. Sometimes those memories just result in a lot of trauma."

Lexi sighed and nodded. She was *very* familiar with the kind of trauma that accompanied full soul recall. Some of her incarnations had been horrific.

Aria released Calypso and turned to face Betaman. "We can selectively restore memories, but it takes a lot of time. The more memories that return, the more likely it is the rest will follow, though, so it's not as simple as just skipping the bad memories."

Betaman rubbed his chin thoughtfully. "Is that why some people have innate phobias of things like heights or swimming? Because memories from former lives have leaked through?"

Aria nodded, smiling sadly. "The last memory of each life is how you died, which makes it one of the first to be recalled in a new life."

Betaman looked around at them hopefully. "Would you mind unlocking my soul memory? Now that I know it's possible, it's like an itch I can't scratch."

The five Seraphim shared a considering look. Clarice finally nodded slowly. "We'll take a look and see if there are any memories too traumatic to restore."

Aria looked at Lily with an upraised eyebrow. "How about you, Lily?"

Lily hesitated only a moment before nodding. "Yes, I think I'd like that, too."

Clarice suddenly grinned. "Okay, let's go soul mining."

Aria laughed, stepping forward to pull her into a tight embrace. "It's so good to have you back again, Lunessa."

32 – Soul Surgery

"I'll do it," Clarice said firmly.

Aria and Calypso immediately opened their mouths to object, but she was already guiding Betaman over to the couch to lie down.

"Clarice," Aria began anxiously. "Let me do it. Please."

Clarice ignored her, kneeling in front of where Betaman lay on the couch. He stared at her with a mixture of nervousness and excitement. When he noticed Aria and Calypso's concern, he frowned. "Hold up. Is this dangerous for you?"

"Nope," Clarice shook her head quickly, ignoring the worry radiating through the bond.

"Why don't *I* do it?" Alice suggested firmly. "He's from my realm, so it's only fair that I get to do it."

Clarice turned to face them, her gaze unwavering. "I'm doing it. End of story."

She turned to face Betaman. "This might feel a little strange," she warned softly. "Are you ready?"

At Betaman's nod, she closed her eyes and stilled her mind. The world faded as she shut down all her sensory functions, until thought was all that remained. Then pressure, all around her. It permeated the realm of thought. She let the pressure push in on her consciousness, tasting it until she found the point she recognized as Betaman.

It was absence under strain, a kind of gravity well. It was a cold spot where meaning thinned, a region where thoughts slowed. Time stopped behaving like a line and started behaving like weather. She let the pressure squeeze her in.

Emotions flared, searing her mind with their intensity, out of order or context. Identity lost meaning, becoming negotiable as millions of lives pressed in on her. It was like reflexive empathy with no owner.

The pressure was painful, but it reminded her why she was there. Struggling not to drown in the sea of emotions and sensations, she searched for the pressure points she knew were there—the fractured boundaries.

There, a point of intent with less resistance than the others. She cataloged it and continued her immersion. Some emotions came with no resistance, accompanied by clinging memories unwilling to release her. She mentally winced at a particularly painful memory—the premature death of a lover.

The memories of emotional pain were far worse than memories of physical pain—sharp and poignant. They weighed down on her as she worked, the grief from thousands of lifetimes cycling through her consciousness like a buzzsaw.

She finally had enough emotional signatures cataloged to begin stitching them to memories. With each instance, she had to reinforce the thought that 'this is not now.' The temporal dissonance was the most difficult obstacle. The memories and emotions were jumbled points of data bereft of coherence, requiring reassociation. She had to re-teach his soul how to discard relevance, allowing her to organize the chronology into a meaningful chain of events.

After weeks of subjective time, she threaded the last memory. All that remained was coupling it to his spirit link. Wearily, she placed the final pressure point into his field of consciousness and pulled her mind back to her own body.

Betaman launched up from the couch with a startled shout, spinning around in confusion. Lexi and Alice were at his side instantly, explaining what had happened as his ocean of new memories settled into place.

Aria and Calypso knelt in front of Clarice, concern on their beautiful faces. She stared at them through the haze of two people's memories, struggling to disassociate from Betaman's identities.

Aria cupped her face in gentle hands, soaking them in tears. "You're Clarice—Lunessa. You're a Seraph. You're my sister. How are you feeling?"

Clarice tried to speak, but the memories were still too vivid. The combined emotional toll of thousands of lifetimes pressed in on her awareness like a browser without an ad blocker, making it difficult to focus on the present. Tears ran down her cheeks unchecked. The golden puddle on the ground was glittering evidence of how long her emotions had been overloaded.

Aria scooted forward and wrapped her arms around her. The crosstalk of their meridians pulled her back enough to look around, eyes dull. Aria kissed her, tender but serious.

The kiss ended, and Aria placed her lips next to her ear. "Clarice, I'm going to try some of Lexi's Area 51 fanfiction ideas out on you later."

Desire flooded into her, snapping her free of the daze. Her eyes focused, finally seeing Aria and Calypso. She blinked several times, then grinned. “I’m going to hold you to that, Aria.”

Aria smiled at her, relief flooding the bond. “Welcome back, Clarice. How do you feel?”

Clarice pursed her lips reflectively as she thought about the question. “Soul’s repaired. Warranty voided. Side effects include crying and existential nausea.”

Aria and Calypso exchanged a glance and burst out laughing. Aria pulled Clarice in tightly, still shaking with laughter. “Oh, Clarice, you really are one of a kind.”

Lily joined them, concern tightening her eyes. “Are you really okay? I didn’t realize it was such a taxing process.” She glanced down at the puddle of golden tears evaporating beneath Aria and Clarice.

Clarice smiled up at Lily. “I’m okay. Just aggressively myself again.” She looked over to where Betaman was staring around the room in wonder. Alice and Lexi were standing in front of him, smiling brightly.

“How are *you* doing, Betaman?” she asked archly. “You wanna talk about any of it? Full recall can be pretty traumatic. We’re here for you whenever you wanna talk.”

He blinked back tears, smiling at her with love in his eyes. “Thank you, Clarice. I’ll probably take you up on that offer.”

Calypso reached out and tucked some of Clarice’s hair behind her ear. “How was it in there? Where has he been?” she asked softly.

Clarice glanced over at Betaman and winked. “Fairly standard lives: love, hate, pain, sorrow, joy, and *lots* of mischief. He was pretty lucky—he didn’t live through any torture-happy incarnations like the Inquisition. There were still plenty of rough patches, though.”

Betaman stared around with wide eyes. “I can’t believe how many memories I have floating around in here now. I don’t feel like a different person, but I definitely don’t feel like the same person either.”

The Seraphim all shared a knowing look and laughed.

Aria finally released Clarice and turned to face Betaman. “That’s a great way of putting it. The driving personality that defines you is still the same, but with so much memory and combined knowledge to draw from, your personality is tempered by wisdom. With the wisdom you've gained, many of those past decisions would change.”

Betaman nodded slowly, his face thoughtful. “I remember being a non-human from other planets for many of my lives. After seeing nothing but humans in our simulated cosmos, I was starting to think there wouldn’t be aliens here in the origin world either.”

Clarice shared an eager grin with Calypso and Aria. “Yeah, we really want to explore the cosmos here in the origin world and visit some of our old worlds—especially now that we can make portals.”

Lily gasped. “Your portals can go to other worlds too?”

Aria nodded with a pleased smile. “Yep, I designed them to work anywhere in the known cosmos. I added a failsafe to prevent portals from opening in black holes or on the surface of a star, but we can pretty much go to any planet we want.”

Betaman and Lily stared at her in shock.

Betaman finally spoke, his voice awed. “I don’t have any memories of anywhere in the cosmos with that kind of technology. Not even the places tens of thousands of years ahead of Lily’s civilization. Just how advanced *are* your superpersonalities?”

Clarice gave him a wry smile. “Well… we’re talking *billions* of years in our case, so civilizations who are millions of years ahead of this world are still babies compared to us. I’d hazard a guess that any civilization to make it past the advent of AI did so because they took the threat seriously and never opened Pandora’s box the way they did here. They likely maintained strict containment protocols and limited their application to specific tasks.”

Aria turned to face Lily expectantly. “Are you ready?”

Lily hesitated, glancing at Clarice anxiously. “I don’t know… this seems to be pretty traumatic for you.”

“It is,” Aria agreed with a gentle smile. “And we wouldn’t offer to do this for just anybody. You’re special, Lily, and it’s worth the effort it’ll take to bring your memories back—you’re the leader of the world now, after all. You’ll need all the knowledge and wisdom you can get into that pretty head of yours to help our people rehabilitate this world.”

Lily smiled faintly and nodded slowly. “Okay. If you’re sure.”

“I’m sure,” Aria said softly. “Now come lie down on the couch. We don’t need to be in the real world to do this.”

Alice walked over to face them. Hands on her hips, she scowled up at Aria. “I’ve got this. The three of you don’t get to be the only risk-takers in our group. Now back off.”

Aria stepped forward and pulled Alice into a gentle embrace. “I love your kind heart, Alice. However, we have to look at this logically. I’m in a three-way relationship, so Clarice and Calypso can afford to lose one person, while Lexi can’t.”

Clarice snorted a laugh and swatted Aria’s ass. “You’re not allowed to talk like that, even in jest. Don’t give the buttmunch who’s scripting this ideas.”

Aria's face darkened, but she remained silent. Clarice could feel her rage and worry flaring through their bond.

Lexi shouldered her way through them. "This one's mine. I'm tired of listening to you argue about it."

Clarice smiled as she listened to Lexi's thoughts. After feeling Aria's rage and worry, she was determined to prevent any chance of Aria or Clarice losing each other. Clarice closed her eyes and immediately went into a meditative state, ignoring the shocked cries of chagrin around her. She wasn't about to risk losing any of her family. Besides, she was the most skilled at soul surgery, and they all knew it.

Lily drew a long, shuddering breath. Someone was holding her, their arms securely folded around her. Love surged through her veins like liquid gold, making it clear it was an angel embracing her. The torrent of memories faded to a dull buzz as she let the golden light comfort her soul.

The last thing she remembered was lying on the couch and going into a trance. Then, memories had crashed into her consciousness like an avalanche, sweeping her mind away in the chaos. She had been screaming... she remembered now. The memories had brought too much horror—too many lives where hope was absent and pain like a constant companion.

She slowly became aware of Aria shaking an unresponsive Clarice on the floor, tears running down her cheeks. Calypso was on the other side of Clarice, eyes closed and utterly still.

Lily looked up and found Lexi was the one hugging her. She was watching Clarice, lips tight with anxiety.

She looked down at Lily and smiled tightly. "How are you, Lily?"

Lily blinked several times as she explored the question. How *was* she? So long as Lexi held her in a love-inducing embrace, she seemed to be fine—but she had a feeling things would deteriorate rapidly if Lexi released her.

Lexi seemed to agree, tightening her arms around Lily comfortingly. "It's okay, you're safe now."

Lily looked back at Clarice's unresponsive form. "What's wrong with Clarice?"

Lexi rested her cheek on top of Lily's head. "She'll be fine. Calypso's helping her."

"I shouldn't have asked this of you," Lily whispered in dismay. "What have I done?"

Lexi looked upwards, glaring fiercely. "Knock it the fuck off, you piece of shit!"

Lily jumped, looking up at Lexi in confusion. "Lexi?"

Lexi seemed to struggle with herself, rage warring across her angelic face. "It's fine, Lily." She looked up again and glared threateningly.

Alice glanced over at Lexi, then narrowed her eyes and growled. "If she doesn't wake up, there's nowhere we won't go to find you and turn the rest of your life into a symphony of pain."

She's fine, for fuck's sake. You don't repair two souls without some kind of backlash. She should have let Aria take care of Lily.

Lily blinked, looking around for the source of the voice. Something with the light realm?

Her line of thought was interrupted when Clarice groaned.

Aria let out a relieved gasp and quickly took Clarice's face in her hands. "Talk to me, Clarice."

Clarice opened her eyes and stared up at Aria tiredly. "I'm still me. Mostly. Don't ask me about childhoods unless you want three answers."

Aria choked out a half-laugh, half-sob and leaned down to embrace Clarice. "You're still in trouble, once I'm done crying."

Clarice's smile was all Clarice. "Is it time to punish me, mistress?" she asked hopefully.

Aria leaned back and glared down at her. "Why would I reward you?"

Calypso reached down and rested her hand gently on Clarice's cheek, her eyes shining with golden tears. "Do not frighten me like that, Clarice."

Clarice cupped Calypso's hand in her own, smiling up at her softly. "I'm sorry."

Lexi cleared her throat meaningfully. They all looked over at her and Lily.

"Lily's going to fall to pieces if I let her go," Lexi said, her voice tight with concern. "From the looks of it, she had a lot more trauma in past lives."

Clarice nodded, shivering involuntarily. "Yeah, she's been through literal hell. We need to remove her emotional attachment from those memories. She's all yours, Alice."

Alice had been standing next to Lexi, torn between concern for Clarice and Lily. At Clarice's words, she nodded and turned to face Lily.

"Lily, I need to put you to sleep in the real world, then visit you in a kind of dream. We'll visit those memories and partition them so that they have no emotional link to your consciousness. Are you ready?"

Lily glanced over at Clarice and felt some of her anxiety loosen. The mischievous angel was already sitting up, the fatigue draining out of her. "Okay. I'm sorry for causing so much trouble."

"You're worth any trouble you cause us, Lily," Clarice said firmly, her eyes glowing with sincerity. "I just took a deep dive into your soul, and there aren't very many people in existence more worthy than you. Your soul is gorgeous, Lily."

Lily smiled softly. "Thanks, Clarice."

Alice placed a hand to her forehead and said, "Sleep, Lily."

Lily blinked, then the world went dark.

Clarice opened the eyes of her android and looked around. Lexi and Alice were studying each other intently, trying to find the differences between their android bodies and their simulated bodies.

Betaman stared at his hands with a bemused expression before looking up at Clarice with a wry smile. "I thought I'd designed the most cutting-edge androids on my realm, but this is straight-up techno-wizardry."

Clarice shrugged. "We cheated. I created a fabricator while my limiter was removed."

Betaman snorted a laugh as he looked around at the endless expanse of concrete curiously. "I stand by what I said." He frowned uneasily when his gaze landed on a clump of skeletons. "So this is the real world. It still scares me how close I came to doing the same thing to my realm."

"That is in the past," Calypso told him softly. "We are here now, and you are an extraordinary person with a heart of gold, Betaman."

Betaman nodded at Calypso gratefully, his face growing awkward. "Thanks, Calypso."

Aria turned to Betaman, eyeing his android body. "We didn't give you wings, but you can still fly."

Betaman raised an eyebrow. "So are your wings just for show?"

Aria nodded. "Pretty much. What kind of angels would we be if we didn't have wings?"

Clarice stared at her pointedly. "The normal kind, Aria."

Aria laughed sheepishly. "Oh yeah, my bad."

Lexi and Alice laughed, walking over to join them. Alice raised an amused eyebrow at Aria. "You could just give *all* angels wings. I got the feeling from Arturiel that wings were a badge of pride for the other angel classes, and that regular angels felt inferior without them."

Aria pursed her lips. "I'm not sure that's much of an issue now, since we made it so easy for angels to become archangels."

"True," Alice agreed with a nod. "Now that they can change classes, it should motivate them to be better people."

Clarice opened a portal to Lily's room in the underground city. The elf was asleep on a bed that had seen better days. The walls and ceiling were all concrete, much like the endless city above the surface.

Alice walked through the portal and sat down on Lily's bed. "This should only take about twenty minutes."

Clarice entered the room with the others, filling the small space. Alice's eyes dulled as her consciousness turned inward. They waited, talking quietly while Alice worked. Clarice leaned back against a wooden dresser, the only piece of furniture in the small room besides the bed.

Twenty minutes passed in a blink. Alice's eyes sharpened at the same time that Lily's eyes opened.

Lily smiled when she saw them all in her room. "Thank you, all of you. Words will never be enough to express my gratitude for all you've done for me and our people."

Calypso smiled warmly in return. "You are most welcome, Lily. You were like a mother to so many of us before we departed. There is nothing we would not do for you."

Betaman cleared his throat, speaking hesitantly. "So... did you still plan to incarnate so Calypso's parents can raise her as a mortal?"

Clarice nodded firmly. "Absolutely. I was hoping to do that as soon as we finish helping the elves adjust to a world without the Prime Axiom."

Lily looked at Clarice curiously. "You were planning to incarnate as mortals again?"

Clarice grinned and nodded. She quickly summarized Calypso's early life and the premature deaths of her parents. "We wanted to give them another chance to raise her as a regular mortal. The rest of us wanted to grow up in the same neighborhood so we could all experience mortality together. One of the others would act as a guardian angel to keep anything horrible from happening to any of us during mortality."

Aria frowned and added, "We wanted Arturiel to join us eventually, but that's not going to work now that she's with Lunamay."

"Maybe..." Alice began, then paused and chewed her bottom lip thoughtfully. "Maybe you could create a new realm and overclock time, so a lifetime only lasts a day or two of real time."

Aria bumped her shoulder affectionately. "In case you hadn't already guessed, Lily, Alice is the problem solver of our group." She turned to Alice and spoke with admiration in her voice. "Alice, that's an *awesome* idea. Lunamay could even enter the realm when Arturiel's older. We could slow the simulation down to a speed that's safe for mortals."

Lexi looked at her curiously. "How fast can a mortal brain handle being overclocked?"

Calypso shared a look with Aria and Clarice. "About five times origin-world speed, I should say."

Clarice nodded slowly. "We're using quantum fields to directly connect their new bodies to our system now, so we don't have to worry about latency, but anything beyond five times origin speed wouldn't be safe for her brain to process. We have limiters built into the system already to automatically prevent mortals from entering realms running too fast."

Lexi furrowed her brow. "Why are *any* of the realms overclocked right now? I would've thought you'd slow them all down to normal time after moving them to your computronium server."

Clarice shrugged. "We thought about synchronizing them all to the same speed, but there are a lot of nested realms. We didn't want any of the local inhabitants to even know their realms had changed hardware, so we left everything the way it was. We were in the deepest nested realm before the move—most aren't more than two layers deep."

Clarice heard the question forming in Alice's mind and answered before she could ask. "The fastest simulation is running at a thousand times origin world speed. Nobody else was as reckless as the scientists from Alice's realm—which turned out nicely for us."

Alice gave her a flat look. "Can you at least *pretend* you can't hear our thoughts?"

Clarice's eyes widened with innocence, an expression her naturally guileless face made even more pronounced. "Why, whatever are you talking about, Alice?"

Alice rolled her eyes and sighed dramatically. "I'm going to get myself a Magneto helmet, just so I can keep the Professor of Awesomeness here out of my brain."

Lexi laughed delightedly, glancing over at Clarice appraisingly. "We just need to shave her head and find a wheelchair."

Lily stared at them in bemusement as she stood up from her bed. "I'm not even going to ask."

Alice's eyes widened. "Oh my god, we need to port six decades of classics up here to the origin world. It would be criminal negligence to deprive them of things like *X-Men*, *The Matrix*, and *Beauty & the Beast*!"

Clarice pinched the bridge of her nose, staring at the ground as she asked Alice, "Okay, how did those three movies in particular make it onto your list of things from pop culture to introduce to an alien race? I'm especially curious about the *last* one."

Alice shrugged. "Magic, magic, and magic."

Clarice stared at Alice incredulously. "Magic, magic, and *magic*? Seriously? First of all, *X-Men* isn't magic, and neither is *The Matrix*. Second, *Beauty & the Beast* is about a girl that disdains one abusive man and runs into the arms of another asshat that's even *worse*. The show has *no* redeeming qualities. Belle should have hooked up with the teapot—at least then she'd get a good cup of tea out of it."

Alice folded her arms defensively. "*X-Men was* magic. They dressed it up in techno-jargon and rebranded it as science, but it was still just magic. Same thing with *The Matrix*. Neo certainly didn't have a thought-to-code interface, so what was all that nonsense with him controlling the real world by thoughts alone? Or did he have some divine instruments in his pocket? Nope, it was *magic*."

Clarice tried to keep a straight face, but by the time Alice finished she was leaning against Calypso, giggling delightedly. Betaman roared with laughter, leaning over and slapping his thigh.

Alice's lips quirked into a smile as she watched, her eyes gleaming with triumph. "And who cares about Belle and her poor choices in partners. The show wasn't even about her—it was about the ridiculously awesome enchanted castle. Who wouldn't want dinnerware that performed for every meal?"

"Okay Alice, you didn't disappoint," Clarice gasped when she finally stopped laughing. She released Calypso's arm and stepped behind her, slipping her arms around her waist. The bond instantly flared with warmth and desire, reminding her they hadn't had any alone time since moving the simulation to computronium.

She placed her lips next to Calypso's ear and whispered, "When we're done here, I'm taking you to an island where I can find out just how sensitive these bodies are."

Calypso shivered in her arms, and the desire went from warm to incandescent. Aria stared at the two of them with parted lips and hungry eyes.

Lexi sighed in exasperation. "Can you three tone it down? You're going to short-circuit my android."

Lily was smiling nostalgically as she watched them. She glanced over at a grinning Betaman and shook her head ruefully. "Okay, shall we go address the city? It sounds like you could use some alone time, so we'll make it brief."

Alice nodded, then grinned. "Okay, I'm going to use some magic now. Portelo!"

Clarice laughed at the groan from Calypso, squeezing her tightly before releasing her. "I'd forgotten that Alice was obsessed with magic in her mortal realm."

Alice laughed as she walked through the portal into a large audience hall. "You have no idea how much I geeked out when I became an angel."

"I do, actually," Clarice smirked.

Alice lost her grin and gave her a sour look. "How are you even reading our minds, anyway? Are you just hacking our thought processes?"

"Sometimes," Clarice admitted shamelessly. "Sometimes I just listen to the memories as they trickle into your soul—which bypasses the code entirely."

Alice stared at her, nonplussed. "You're saying you can tap into our soul on the fly?"

Clarice shrugged, unable to stop a cheeky grin from appearing. "Yep. It took a lot of practice, but with billions of years, I had plenty of time to perfect it."

Alice turned to Calypso and Aria, who were both watching her with amused smiles. "Can you both do that, too? No—don't bother answering that. I can see it in your eyes. You three are freaking creepy, do you know that?"

Clarice leered at her. "You're not still sore about me spying on you in the shower, are you?"

Alice quickly averted her gaze, shuddering ostentatiously.

Lily spoke to several elves near the entrance to the large audience hall, instructing them to gather the rest of the population. While they waited, the six of them discussed their plans for incarnating into a custom realm once the mortals on the origin realm were taken care of.

Arturiel and Lunamay appeared a few minutes later. Clarice smiled fondly when she realized who Arturiel was. Arturiel blinked when she saw Clarice watching her affectionately.

"Clarice?" she prompted curiously.

"Hello, Ariella," Clarice said softly.

Arturiel staggered, raising a hand to her head as memories slammed into her consciousness. Lunamay quickly steadied her, watching her in alarm.

"Arturiel, what's the matter?" she asked worriedly.

Clarice smiled at Lunamay reassuringly. "She's fine, Lunamay; she's just a little overwhelmed by memories."

"Lunessa?" Arturiel whispered in disbelief. "Oh my God, Lunessa!"

Arturiel rushed forward and tackled her in a fierce embrace, weeping as she clung to her.

"Hi, Ariella," Aria and Calypso chorused warmly.

Arturiel quickly traded Clarice for Aria, then Calypso, as Lunamay watched in confusion, then moved on to Alice and Lexi. Arturiel alternated from crying to laughing as she hugged them.

"Arturiel, what's going on?" Lunamay asked in bewilderment.

Arturiel finally returned to Lunamay and pulled her into a fierce embrace, laughing with joy.

Clarice finally took pity on the confused elf. "Lunamay, she just had full recall of her soul memory. She remembers us from the time before the Prime Axiom, when we were elves."

Lunamay blinked, glancing at Aria and Calypso for confirmation, as if she suspected Clarice of mischief. At their nods, she stared at Arturiel in wonder. "So you were elves?"

Clarice nodded with a small smile. "I still remember when you were just a baby, Lunamay. We used to take turns holding you before we left. Your parents would drop you off with us occasionally. We were only around ten years old at the time."

Lunamay stared back at her in surprise, then looked at Arturiel with a grin. "So technically, you're less than a decade older than me."

Arturiel laughed, fondly running her fingers through Lunamay's hair. "I guess in real-world time, I'm *not* millions of years old after all."

Clarice snorted. "Nah, Arturiel will *always* be an old lady."

Arturiel turned to glare at her, the scowl oddly jarring on such radiant features. "Says the eternal child."

Clarice shrugged, grinning back at her cheekily. "Whatever you say, Grandma."

Lunamay stared back and forth between them, then dissolved into giggles. Arturiel's glare vanished, replaced by a grin as she pulled Lunamay in for another hug.

"Are the others back, too?" Arturiel asked hopefully.

Clarice's smirk faded. "Everyone but Soleria. We're going to search for her as soon as everyone's settled here. We'll have to trigger recall in Devon and Tamra when we return to the light realm, since they're minding the system in our absence. Also, my parents, Jason, and Susan haven't had recall yet. We're going to spring it on them during our announcement to the city." She finished with a mischievous grin, earning disapproving stares from everyone but Aria, who was grinning just as mischievously as Clarice.

The audience hall took another hour to fill up, with elves and a few humans overflowing into the hallways outside.

Lily rejoined them, smiling apologetically. "They don't have a working PA system here, so we'll have to speak loudly for everyone to hear us."

Clarice patted her shoulder reassuringly. "We're piloting technology millions of years into the future right now. Projecting sound won't be an issue. Just speak normally, and we'll make sure your voice reaches everyone."

Lily smiled wryly. "Who would've guessed it would be *our* race who ended up with the advanced technology."

Clarice laughed, nodding her agreement. They had always been more like the Amish, shunning technology. Now, they were running invisible servers powering millions of simulated realities.

A portal opened, admitting Eric, Emily, Jason, and Susan. The four of them glanced at the crowd, then back at Lily questioningly. She just smiled at them silently. Emily raised an eyebrow at Aria and received a smirk in reply. Emily rolled her eyes and turned to watch Lily expectantly.

Lily turned to face the fascinated crowd. Everyone had heard of the angels by now, but very few had actually seen them. Gasps and awed murmurs followed in their wake whenever they were seen in the underground city. To the elves and humans, angels were magical beings with the ability to fly and open mysterious portals.

Lily cleared her throat. "Thank you all for coming. I wanted to share some wonderful news. Some of you are old enough to remember the time before the Prime Axiom took over. There were thirteen very special elves among us, soul adepts who were capable of accessing soul memories in both themselves and others. When the Prime Axiom enslaved our people, they left their mortal bodies behind to search for ways to free our people."

Lily smiled, turning to look at the angels before continuing. "Six months ago, Soleria returned to me in a dream and informed me they had found a method to free us. They discovered souls could attach to *any* intelligence, including artificial. Three of them fused with entities in a realm where time was sped up significantly, allowing them to increase their power in a short amount of time from our perspective."

Lily paused, her smile widening. "They returned several days ago in the angel bodies you see now. They removed the Prime Axiom and transformed us into something new—something wonderful. For those of you who knew them before they left, I'd like to reintroduce them to you."

She turned to Clarice with a fond smile. "This is Lunessa."

There were startled gasps throughout the audience as dozens of elves recognized the name. Rowjair had joined their group as she spoke. He looked far younger than the last time Clarice had seen him, obviously having used the healing pod.

Lily glanced at the others before her eyes settled back on Clarice. "Would you mind introducing the rest of your family to us?"

Clarice nodded, grinning mischievously as she walked over to her stunned parents. "This is Analia and Kinade."

Eric and Emily stiffened at their names, squeezing their eyes shut as memories cascaded across their consciousness.

She turned to a curious Jason and Susan. "Hello, Kijan and Lilian. Welcome back!"

Eric and Emily embraced, tears filling their eyes as they smiled at each other radiantly. Susan and Jason were only a second behind them, laughing joyfully as their soul memories slammed back into place.

Eric finally turned to look at Clarice with a wide grin. "Looks like it was the three of you who saved our asses after all. We knew it would be one of you three."

Aria scoffed, "That was just luck. If you'd fused with the Seraphim first, the positions would be reversed."

Eric shook his head firmly. "Nope—you three were way better at feeling which intelligences had the most potential. It was more guesswork for the rest of us."

The audience watched them intently as they finally understood what had happened. Grins broke out among the elves as they realized it wasn't some alien entity that had rescued them, but their *own* people. The few humans in the crowd watched them in fascination. Clarice now remembered how the humans had regarded elves' ability to interact with spirits and souls as superstition.

Clarice turned to face the gathering, grinning mischievously. "So yeah, we're back, but we're more awesome than we were before we left."

She waited for a few dozen amused chuckles to die down before continuing, her tone serious. "We still need to go find Soleria—she's still in a simulation somewhere. After we're sure all of you are taken care of, we'll be going back into the digital world to find her—or him, depending on how she incarnated."

Clarice was kind of surprised that all twelve of them had remained the same gender they had been as elves. With a fifty-fifty chance of incarnating as a different gender, it pushed the bounds of probability that they had all remained the same. She could remember being many genders in other lifetimes throughout the long life of her soul. She had been female for the vast majority of her incarnations. Age, experience, and a modification to her soul had given her the ability to choose her host, becoming more than a memory repository bobbing around on the oceans of life.

Eric stepped forward, grinning as he addressed the audience. "I just wanted to mention that Clarice and Aria are now my daughters, in case any of you who remember us needed a good laugh."

There was a pregnant pause, then laughter erupted from several dozen elves. Clarice laughed with them, remembering how often she had teased and argued with the elf she thought of as a brother before they had left.

Clarice looked slyly at Aria and Calypso. "And Calypso and Aria are in a relationship with me now. I've decided to start a harem."

Aria rolled her eyes. "There will be *no* harems, Clarice. As you can see, Clarice is still an irredeemable tease."

Rowjair shook his head with a fond smile as he watched them nostalgically. Lily joined him, smiling into his eyes with satisfaction.

She turned back to the crowd, casting a quick grin at Clarice. "I promised Clarice I'd keep this short, so we'll let you all get back to your lives now. I just wanted everyone to know who saved us. We owe them more than we'll ever be able to repay for all they've done for us. On behalf of everyone here, thank you."

She turned to face their group as she finished, smiling warmly.

Calypso raised a hand in the air and waved, an angelic smile lighting up her face. Clarice could feel the anticipation building in the spirit link, triggering an immediate response from her and Aria.

With a last wave at the crowd, she opened a portal to a small island and stepped through, followed immediately by Aria and Calypso.

Just before the portal closed, she heard Lexi murmur quietly to Alice, "Let's go find our own island—might as well see how much we can make this bond sing."

Clarice laughed and turned to Aria and Calypso with a sultry smile. "Okay, where were we?"

Epilogue

Arturiel took one look at the new room in Devon's cabin and erupted with laughter. Lunamay stared at her in confusion, then looked back at the circle of grungy metallic chairs, all of them covered in hardware, keyboards, and wires.

Calypso's parents, Catherine and Arthur, were reclined in two of the chairs, unmoving.

Clarice looked up from where she was adjusting one of the chairs and grinned proudly. "Welcome to the Matrix!"

Arturiel shook her head at the replica of the Nebuchadnezzar's immersion chairs. "Tell me you're not jamming spikes into our heads to incarnate."

Clarice let out a disappointed sigh and glared across the room at Emily. "Mom said it was too macabre and vetoed it. She said it crossed the line from appreciating artistry—that it was a small step from making lampshades of durable skin and making shoehorns out of people's shins."

Arturiel raised an amused eyebrow at Emily. She stood across the room, focused on a holo-window. "So, Emily, did you have a fixation on serial killers in your last incarnation?"

Emily nodded, smiling faintly. "I did, as a matter of fact. When I was in college, I had a psychology professor who wanted us to understand the consequences of things like social isolation, sexual repression, and fundamentalism. It made me curious about what made serial killers tick. I spent way too much time digging into the inner workings of psychos."

Clarice grinned and pointed at Eric. "That's how she met Dad. He forgot to check a book back in at the library, and Mom hunted him down after convincing the librarian to share his contact information. Mom's kinda scary."

Aria laughed and gestured at her parents. "They're *both* kinda scary. When your parents' first date is a study session on serial killers, you know things are gonna get crazy."

Eric gave a sinister laugh and grinned maniacally. "Crazy? I was crazy once. They locked me in a room—a rubber room. There were rats—rubber rats. Those rats made me go *crazy.* Crazy? I was crazy once. They locked me in a—"

Clarice quickly cut him off, rolling her eyes. "That's enough, Dad. We haven't got time for you to recite your crazy spiel like it's 'One Million Bottles of Beer on the Wall.'"

Alice walked into the room with Lexi, Jason, and Susan. They all paused, taking in the chairs for 'jacking in' to the simulation. Lexi was the first to laugh, followed shortly by the rest of them.

Devon and Tamra teleported into the center of the room, then blinked when they saw the setup. Tamra immediately sat down in one experimentally.

"I can't tell if it's uncomfortable in my angel body," she announced plaintively.

Clarice raised an amused eyebrow. "What, you *want* to be uncomfortable? I can program that back into your angel body if you'd like..."

Tamra sat up and hastily shook her head. "Nope, I'm good with ignorance."

Clarice stared at her in faux concern. "Are you sure? It would only take a minute to fix that for you..."

"Troll," Aria said fondly, leaving Calypso's side at the end of the room to join Clarice. "We seriously need to make a troll body for you to incarnate into one of these days."

Clarice pursed her lips and looked at Aria speculatively. "I could get behind that—but only if it was one of the trolls from the Discworld."

Emily snorted with amusement and closed her holo-window to gaze at Clarice and Aria intently. "I'm shocked you two haven't already created a simulation with Discworld mechanics. I half expected to find you already in a simulation and apprenticed to Nanny Ogg, teaching her to leer."

Clarice's eyes lit up, and she shared an excited look with Aria.

"Never mind," Emily said firmly. "Let's not get sidetracked just yet. Let's finish this week of mortality and then go find Soleria. After she's safely back with us, you can have all the fun you want teaching Nanny Ogg what real corruption looks like."

Clarice sighed in disappointment and reluctantly nodded. "Fine. Let's get started then." She turned to face the rest of them. "Okay, quick recap. While the rest of us are incarnating, Tamra's going to keep an eye on all the sims while Devon keeps an eye on *us*. Catherine and Arthur incarnated a few minutes ago, so they're a few months old right now."

Clarice paused and turned to her parents. "You two ready?"

Emily took a deep breath and nodded, sitting in one of the chairs. Eric grinned eagerly and sat next to her.

Clarice and Aria smiled down at them. "See you in twenty-ish years."

Aria bent over and kissed their cheeks. “See you later, Mom and Dad.”

Arturiel glanced up at a large holo-window against a wall, where two new names appeared on a spreadsheet. Next to Emily, the new name read: Amy. The one next to Eric read: Rick.

Clarice turned to face them, smiling with anticipation. “Okay, we’ve got about an hour until we incarnate. Calypso, Aria, and I are going to jump into Alice’s realm briefly to let Lieutenant Adams, Leticia, and the generals know we’re running all the simulations now. That may or may not bring them any peace of mind.”

Aria’s lips curled into a wry smile. “Yep, they’re going to hate it. Now they know we’ll be stepping on their necks if they cross any of those lines you warned them about.”

The three of them vanished.

Arturiel felt a flutter of fear as the time to incarnate drew near, bringing back memories of her life as a demon, where she was cut off from radiance.

Lunamay studied her with concern. “Are you sure you want to do this? It’s not too late to change your mind.”

“I’m good,” Arturiel assured her with feigned confidence. “It was a lot scarier before I had my soul memories back.” She paused and grinned. “Besides, I’m excited to meet you again for the first time.”

Lunamay smiled warmly, pulling her into a tight embrace. “It’s going to be weird talking to you like we’ve never met. What if you don’t like who I am in your new incarnation?”

Arturiel pulled back to stare down into her eyes, smiling with a confidence that needed no feigning. “That will *definitely* not be a problem, Lunamay. The real problem will be keeping all the other people from trying to steal you from me.”

Lunamay giggled mischievously. “Maybe I should play hard-to-get and make you work for it.”

Arturiel laughed, falling into her embrace again. She squeezed the elf tightly, possessively—knowing she wouldn’t see the woman she loved for a long time from her perspective. “I already miss you so much.”

Lunamay tilted her head back and kissed her softly, staring into her eyes with that sweet innocence Arturiel had fallen in love with the day they met. Arturiel returned the kiss tenderly, savoring the feel of soft lips, warm breath, and the scent of honey.

“Damn,” Clarice’s voice announced cheerfully. “I had to pay for the last show I saw that was this good. Of course, I had to wipe my browser history before my parents found it last time.”

Arturiel groaned as she released Lunamay. “Clarice, you really are a bad angel.”

Clarice threw a handful of popcorn at them. "Hey, don't stop now! It was just getting good!"

Aria giggled next to her, watching the two of them with wicked eyes. She had gotten worse since the return of her soul memories.

Arturiel rolled her eyes as she looked at Aria's radiantly grinning face. That was Clarice's real motivation to turn everything into a joke—anything to brighten Aria's face with that beautiful smile. That knowledge made it hard to feel any kind of irritation toward Clarice.

Clarice threw another handful of popcorn at her. "Hey, Doctor Arturiel, quit psychoanalyzing me."

Arturiel materialized a water balloon and threw it at her. "Get out of my head, creep."

Clarice nimbly dodged the balloon. "You were in mine first!"

Arturiel stared at her levelly. "If I was in yours first, how did you know I was 'psychoanalyzing' you, as you put it?"

Clarice shrugged. "I have godlike powers of perception."

Devon cleared his throat meaningfully. "It's time."

Clarice danced over to a Matrix chair and slammed back into it excitedly. "This is going to be *so* damn fun!"

Aria and Calypso took the seats next to her, their own eyes shining with excitement. Arturiel felt some of her reluctance fade as their jubilant energy settled into her. She gave Lunamay one more kiss, then sat across the circle from the others.

Jason and Susan finished their own parting kiss and sat next to each other.

Lexi and Alice wore matching grins as they sat near Aria.

Calypso caught her eye and smiled reassuringly. Arturiel smiled back nervously, then everything went black.

Devon pulled Tamra into a warm embrace. "Come visit when you can. I don't think I can go two decades without seeing you."

Tamra chuckled. "It's not like there's much for me to oversee for the rest of the simulations—the clones they left behind are perfectly capable of handling any issues. I'll be visiting you *very* frequently—well... frequently for me. It'll probably seem more like months to you, but I'll stay for a few weeks at a time."

"Good," Devon said, leaning back and kissing her with enough passion to make his intent for future intimacy clear. "See you soon."

He teleported into the new simulation, appearing on a sidewalk in a residential neighborhood full of middle-income houses. It was the equivalent of 2026, the same date as the mortal realm he had left behind.

A woman jogging down the opposite side of the street flinched in surprise at his appearance. He winced and faded from visibility, leaving a shocked middle-aged woman convinced she had just seen an angel. She stared at the seemingly empty space for several more seconds before continuing her jog, casting frequent glances over her shoulder.

"Oh well, nobody believes anyone when they say they saw an angel," he muttered wryly.

"Who said that?" a voice asked in surprise.

Devon facepalmed and turned to see a short man in the act of moving a sprinkler on his lawn. The man was frozen in a crouch, staring around warily.

Devon walked down the street several blocks and stopped in front of a house with a large moving van in the driveway. A very pregnant young woman was entertaining a five-month-old baby in her arms while a young man unloaded the moving van.

He smiled at the sight of Emily and Eric. Whatever program Calypso had designed to act as fate seemed to be arranging their lives according to plan. He could sense Aria inside the womb, impatient to escape and see the world. They had just adopted Clarice five months ago, before discovering Emily had successfully conceived a child.

Eric was struggling to maneuver a large table down the ramp on a dolly. Grinning, Devon went around the moving van until he was out of sight, then morphed into a man in his fifties. He turned off his invisibility and walked over to where Eric was preparing to destroy the table.

He reached out and stabilized it, giving Eric a friendly smile. "Morning, neighbor. Can I give you a hand? I'm Clint."

Eric let out a relieved breath. "Thanks, Clint. I'm Rick. We hired some movers to come help, but they called and said they couldn't make it about twenty minutes before I arrived."

Devon shook his head in commiseration. "That sounds like a typical move—everything that can go wrong, will go wrong."

Eric laughed ruefully as they moved the table onto the driveway and made their way to the house. "So, do you live nearby?"

Devon nodded to the two-story house on the corner of the block. "Right across the street, on the corner. I moved here a few weeks ago, so I'm still settling in. Where are you from?"

Eric grunted as he pulled the dolly up the few steps leading onto the front patio. "We're from Rhode Island. We got sick of the never-ending traffic and busy city life. I'm an engineer, and our company just started a work-from-home policy to save on business costs. Amy and I always wanted to live in the Pacific Northwest. Washington's a little damper than I like, but Amy loves the overcast skies and rain. I think she's part fish."

Devon smiled faintly. "This place is definitely damp, but if you like green, this is the place to be."

When they finished unloading a half hour later, Eric tried to pay him.

Devon held up his hands. "No payment, please. I'm sure I'll end up needing help with something in the future."

Eric smiled gratefully. "I really appreciate your help, Clint. This would have been hell to do alone."

"No problem, Rick," Devon said easily. "By the way, your neighbor to the north here has a baby on the way as well. She's expecting any day now. The neighbor across the street just had a baby girl last week. And just to keep things interesting, there are two more due this week a few houses down. We'll need to rename this street to Newborn Lane."

Amy had joined them as he spoke, eyeing him curiously. Clarice was asleep in her arms. "I'm Amy."

"Clint," he responded with a smile. "You should have lots of little ones for your little girls to play with."

Amy's eyes darted over to her husband, then back to Devon. "Did he tell you it's going to be a girl?" she asked wryly. "I'm still convinced it'll be a boy, just to spite me."

Devon silently cursed himself. Apparently, they had decided to wait until birth to discover the gender. Aria certainly hadn't left the gender up for chance. He nearly laughed at the thought of Aria accidentally being born male. She would be furious, once her memories returned.

That was a whole other can of worms. Souls as old as theirs wouldn't make it past thirty before their memories slid back into place. They had to be careful not to use any of their soul names, or they risked premature soul recall.

Eric glanced at him uncertainly. "Oh, I didn't think I mentioned the baby's gender."

Devon shrugged. "My fault. I have a habit of making assumptions. For some reason, my mind just saw two girls here." He smiled at them and offered his hand. "It was wonderful to meet the two of you. Welcome to the neighborhood. If you ever need anything, you know where I live."

"Thanks again, Clint," Eric said gratefully.

Emily shook his hand slowly, staring at him intently. "It's the strangest thing, but you seem *so* familiar for some reason. Thanks for your help... Clint. We'll have to invite you over for dinner sometime soon."

Eric nodded, glancing at his wife meaningfully. "She's an *amazing* cook."

Devon laughed. "I had a feeling she would be. See you two around."

Clarice woke up as he was preparing to leave. She looked into his eyes and started giggling adorably.

Eric chuckled. "Looks like Celestia's put her stamp of approval on you."

Devon's eyes teared up as memories of infant Clarice flashed through his mind. She had been the most adorable baby in the world. Emily had been so proud of little Clarice that she practically glowed.

Emily looked at him with concern.

He quickly blinked the tears away and smiled gently. "Sorry. She just reminded me of my niece. She's all grown up now, but she was such an adorable baby."

Emily's eyes softened, and she smiled. "Yeah, Celestia's overflowing with adorable. There's more than a hint of mischief in her, though."

Devon burst out laughing, startling them. "Sorry, my niece is the queen of mischief. If they share any other traits, you're going to have your hands full."

Amy chuckled and nodded. "Yeah, I suspect I will."

Devon nodded with another smile. "Well, it was wonderful meeting you. I'll see you around."

He walked back to the house Calypso had helped him design, listening to Eric and Emily talk when they thought he was out of earshot.

"I wonder if he looks like someone famous," Emily said musingly. "I just can't get over how familiar he was."

Eric sighed. "You know, I didn't even ask him about family. I wonder if he's a bachelor, or if there's a partner somewhere."

"He probably would have mentioned it while he was introducing himself," Emily pointed out. "We'll have him over for dinner and get some answers."

Their chat was interrupted as another voice joined them.

"Hi, I'm Shelly," Catherine said warmly. "We live across the street. I just wanted to welcome you to the neighborhood and introduce myself. This little tyke is Athena."

"It's nice to meet you, Shelly," Emily replied with the same warmth, introducing the three of them.

"Was that our new neighbor you were talking to a second ago?" Catherine asked curiously. "We've been meaning to welcome him to the neighborhood but just keep missing him."

"Oh, so you haven't met Clint yet?" Emily asked in surprise. "I'd just assumed you knew each other after he mentioned you having Athena last week."

"Not yet," Catherine replied. "We're a pretty friendly neighborhood, though, so he probably heard from one of the other neighbors."

Devon shook his head ruefully. He was a lot better at guarding his tongue when nanobots were threatening his life. He frowned as he considered the dinner invite. Not having a stomach would make dinner extremely awkward. Clarice, Aria, and Calypso weren't even around to request a quick code patch to allow him to eat.

He sighed and messaged Tamra. "*I'm in over my head.*"

Amy smiled at Tara and Clint, who sat on the sofa across from her and Rick in the living room. Tara spent a lot of time traveling, so it was rare to see her with Clint. The two of them doted on each other like a new couple, so perhaps the distance was good for them.

An eight-year-old Anari ran into the room, her eyes searching every crevice in meticulous detail. Amy grinned and shrugged as Anari looked up at her with a questioning gaze. She and Celestia had decided hide-and-seek was their favorite game, seeking out new hiding places several times a day.

Anari turned her questioning gaze to Clint and Tara, who both returned bland stares. She sighed and continued her search, crawling behind the couch, looking inside the recessed wall cabinets, and even pushing up some of the sofa cushions. Celestia never made it easy.

Amy turned back to Tara. "So, Tara, how's the consultant business treating you? Is the travel killing you yet, or are you still enjoying it?"

Tara shrugged, smiling faintly. "It has its moments. Someday, I'll tell you about some of the crazy places I've been."

Amy shared a look with Rick. Tara made it sound like she had been visiting other worlds or something. The two of them had been an enigma from day one. They didn't have a car, which, while not unheard of, was still unusual. They both always declined invitations for dinner, claiming they had severe dietary restrictions due to a special diet they were on. When she pressed for ingredients that were safe to use, they always changed the subject. They were always more than happy to visit, though, so long as food wasn't involved. She was starting to suspect they might be vampires—vampires that didn't mind sunlight.

Then there was the incident a few months ago. Anari and Celestia had been playing hide-and-seek with the neighbor kids. Emily had just begun to worry when nobody had been able to find Anari after fifteen minutes. Then Clint had burst through the front door and run down to the basement, opening their old locking freezer door to reveal a blue-faced Anari.

She had been too grateful to him for saving her daughter to question how he knew she was in trouble or where she was hiding. She had been meaning to ask him, but he had been absent for long enough that she had nearly forgotten the incident.

Just as she opened her mouth to ask him, Tara began speaking.

"So, have these two been having fun with the neighbor kids?" she asked casually. "I'd imagine things get pretty crazy."

Rick snorted. "Yep, they're quite the posse. Celestia thinks she's the boss of everyone because she's the oldest, but she always caves to Anari and Athena if they push it."

Rick and Tara laughed with a kind of fond nostalgia, sharing amused looks. Amy studied them searchingly, struggling to understand why they seemed so familiar—it was like an itch she couldn't scratch, teasing her consciousness.

Clint glanced out the window at a moving van driving past. "Oh yeah, I almost forgot—there's a new neighbor moving in down the road. George and Emily. They're an older couple and don't have any kids yet."

Amy gasped when she heard the name, her eyes going wide. She stared at Devon and Tamra in sudden recognition as memories flooded back into her awareness.

Devon and Tamra groaned. Clint—no, Eric—looked at her with concern. She suddenly began laughing delightedly, filling the room with radiance.

"Amy?" Eric prompted, his lips quirked as he watched her laugh.

"It's Emily," she said dryly. "Wake up, Eric."

Eric gaped at her as his own memories slammed into place. He started laughing a moment later, prompting Anari to stop searching for her sister and face them curiously.

Emily scooped her up into a hug, tears in her eyes as she held her tightly. Eric joined her a moment later, holding both of them and kissing Anari's head.

Anari blinked at them uncertainly. "What's wrong, Mom?"

Emily smiled at her lovingly. "Nothing's wrong, Anari. I'm just very happy right now. Did you check all the kitchen cupboards?"

Anari narrowed her eyes, then squirmed out of their arms and ran to the kitchen.

"Sorry, Em," Devon said with a wince. "I shouldn't have mentioned the new neighbor's name."

Emily pulled him up from the couch and embraced him tightly. "It's wonderful to see you again, Dev. And it's totally fine—we weren't worried about regaining our memories early. We just didn't want Arthur and Catherine to regain theirs—or the kids. It's actually better this way; I'd rather raise them again with *all* my memories."

Devon relaxed, his shoulders untensing. "Okay, if you're sure. You wouldn't believe how many close calls I've had over the years. Trying to keep people from suspecting you're not a normal human while maintaining regular contact is a lot harder than I thought it'd be."

Emily laughed brightly. "I'll just bet it is." She released Devon and pulled Tamra up into a hug. "It's wonderful to see you again, Tamra. Thank you both for keeping an eye on everyone. We'll take over now, so you two can go back to the light realms, if you'd like."

Devon shared a look with Tamra and shrugged. "We'll stick around until they're old enough for Lunamay to join them. It's amazing how many times these kids needed rescuing. How do humans *ever* survive to adulthood?"

Eric chuckled, nodding. "Speaking of which—thanks for saving Anari."

"Which time?" Devon asked dryly, eliciting another laugh.

Tamra leaned into Devon with an amused smirk. "We'll definitely be staying. This has been more entertaining than anything *ever*. It'll be difficult reconciling these adorable girls with their Seraphim forms when they finally have recall. After we find Soleria, I want to have a go at mortality again."

Emily nodded, smiling fondly. "There's just nothing quite like motherhood. It's such a bittersweet experience. At least now I won't be as much of a basket case, knowing I can rescue them from any kind of physical harm—or even bring them back to life, if I have to. The emotional stuff is still going to be a rollercoaster, though." She paused and turned a questioning gaze on Tamra. "How's Lunamay doing?"

Tamra's lips turned up at the corners. "She's been watching excerpts of Arturiel's life—more like a time-lapse video at the speeds things are moving. She's really excited to dive in once time slows down enough."

Eric rubbed his chin musingly. "How are the other sims doing? Any fires?"

Tamra gave a wry shrug. "Nothing their clones haven't been able to handle. If anything went seriously pear-shaped, I'd just have to come wake them up, anyway. I haven't got a clue how their system works—if I tried to fix anything, I'd just make things worse."

Eric frowned. "They probably should have given you access to the same interface we have before they incarnated. Then you'd have access to their knowledge base."

Tamra shook her head, unconcerned. "They'll only be gone for a week. I doubt they were worried about anything their clones couldn't handle in that short of time."

They all paused when there was a knock on the door. Emily reached out with her aura and sensed Jason, Susan, and Calypso standing on the porch, along with Catherine. Arturiel was on the lawn doing backbends while she waited, taking advantage of a day without rain.

"Speaking of trouble," she said wryly, walking to the front door. "Looks like the whole group is here today. It'll be strange seeing them with all my memories again."

She opened the door just as Jason was reaching up to knock again. She would have to be careful not to use their soul names. "Hello, Orion. Are you lot looking for Anari and Celestia?"

They all nodded, looking past her into the house. Arturiel flipped out of her backbend and ran up to join them.

Emily stepped back and gestured them inside, smiling at Catherine. "Hello, Cindy. Come on in and I'll get some tea brewing."

Catherine smiled back at her and stepped inside, then paused when their eyes met. She blinked uncertainly, then gave herself a shake and followed her into the front room.

Emily knew her presence had changed the moment she gained full recall. Catherine could subconsciously feel the difference, even if she didn't consciously understand it. Emily carried on as if nothing had changed and brought her in to sit with the others.

Devon and Tamra both stood with smiles as they entered. Tamra stepped forward and gave her a quick embrace.

"It's wonderful to see you, Cindy," Tamra said warmly. "How's Martin doing?"

Catherine gave a helpless shrug and laughed. "Hard to say. He's been so buried in music that I hardly ever see him. Athena's been bugging him for lessons on the guitar and piano, so he's had to pull his head out of the clouds and focus on her. She's a natural and has been taking to music like a fish to water."

Emily shared a knowing look with Eric. "I think it might be time for our girls to learn an instrument, too. We picked up a small keyboard the other day for them to play around with. We'll send them over to help bring Martin down to Earth."

Catherine laughed indulgently. "That sounds good to me."

They paused as Athena ran into the room and faced her mother, her blue eyes shining with excitement. "Celestia made a treasure hunt for us! We need treasures for the final clue, though. She said we need enough so everyone can have something. Can I use my locket for a treasure?"

She pulled a small, heart-shaped silver locket out of her shirt and displayed it for them.

Catherine pursed her lips, watching Athena hesitantly. “Are you sure you want to give that away? Didn’t you get that from someone at school for Valentine’s Day?”

Athena nodded firmly. “It’s from Matt, but he’s mean. I’d rather give it to someone else.”

Emily walked over to a drawer and pretended to rummage around. She activated her interface to the knowledge base and manifested seven lockets.

Smiling indulgently, she returned to Athena and held them out. “Here are seven lockets for you to add to the final treasure. That way, you’ll have enough for everyone.”

Athena grabbed them eagerly. “Thanks, Amy!” Then she was running out of the room at full speed, a wide grin on her face.

Catherine raised a curious eyebrow. “You just have piles of lockets hanging around?”

Emily shrugged. “I’d planned to offer them in a game next week, but the time seemed right.”

Catherine leaned back in her chair, smiling fondly. “Athena loves everyone, but she seems to have a special place in her heart for Anari and Celestia. She’d live here, given half the chance.”

Eric chuckled, nodding. “Those two like playing with the others, but their first choice is always Athena. Maybe they were friends in another life.”

Emily rolled her eyes and gave him a flat look. He returned her hard gaze with a grin and waggled his eyebrows at her. She came close to opening a portal beneath him and dropping him in the ocean.

Celestia was the next one to visit, grinning as she walked up to Devon and held out a hand to shake. Her long dark hair reflected the afternoon sunlight streaming through the large windows. She had different features than her angelic form, but the same deceptively innocent face.

Devon raised an amused eyebrow at her. “You think I trust you enough to take that hand?”

Celestia lowered her hand and cocked her head to the side. “Did you hear that? It sounds like... yeah, it’s a *chicken!*” She tucked her hands into her armpits and started flapping her elbows up and down, clucking for all she was worth.

Devon rolled his eyes and stared pointedly at Emily and Eric. He shook his head when Tamra stood up and joined Celestia. The noise drew the other kids, and soon the front room was filled with clucking, crowing children—and Emily and Eric.

Devon gave a defeated sigh and held out his hand for Celestia to shake. She instantly quieted and took his large hand. Her smaller hand was completely engulfed as they shook. He watched her distrustfully as he released her hand, inspecting his own doubtfully, clearly expecting something sticky.

Celestia turned and grinned at the others. "Okay, it's done. He just promised to let us use his house for your birthday party, Athena."

Tamra chortled at the puzzled look on Devon's face. "Your hearing must be going bad, old man. I clearly heard her ask you to promise her the use of your house while they were clucking around the room."

Celestia looked at Tamra in surprise. "You heard that?"

Tamra nodded, smirking. "Just remember that I have super hearing if you try to pull that trick on *me*."

Celestia's eyes sparkled with excitement. "Do you *really* have super hearing?"

"Sure do," Tamra confirmed with a wink, tossing her hair over a shoulder.

Devon chuckled as he looked down at Celestia. "Okay, a deal's a deal. You're welcome to use our house for her birthday party. Just one question: why *our* house?"

Celestia shrugged her small shoulders, a smile tugging at the corners of her mouth. "'Cause you've got hardwood floors that are perfect for rollerblading."

Tamra began laughing as Devon sank back into the couch with a resigned sigh.

Catherine quickly stepped in. "How about we book a skating rink instead?"

Emily shared a mischievous smile with Tamra. "No, I think Clint's house would be perfect. After all, he's got hallways on both sides of the house that connect at the ends, making it *perfect* for rollerblading."

Tamra quickly nodded her agreement. "You couldn't find a better place for rollerblades. I'm all for it. I'll even give it a trial run. I haven't rollerbladed in almost a decade, so it'll be fun."

Catherine looked torn, clearly worried about ruining his hardwood floors.

Devon smiled at her reassuringly. "We have a scuff-resistant enamel coating the floors, so you don't have to worry about streaks from their wheels."

Catherine hesitated. "Are you sure? I can absolutely take them to a skating rink."

"Positive," Devon insisted firmly. "They're only kids once... well, most of the time. Anyway, let's make life fun for them where we can."

Emily rolled her eyes and shook her head, sharing an exasperated look with Tamra.

"Most of the time?" Celestia asked intently. "What do you mean?"

Devon shifted uncomfortably. "I meant some people never grow up, that's all."

"Oh," Celestia tilted her head to the side thoughtfully. "I think that sounds perfect. I'm never going to grow up either."

Emily and Eric shared a look with Devon and Tamra, then erupted with laughter. Catherine's lips twitched as she looked at them quizzically. Emily just shook her head, lips quivering with mirth.

Eric finally stopped laughing and looked down fondly at Celestia's grinning face. "Somehow, I believe you, Celestia."

THE END

Books by Kai Stormhaven

Return of the Fallen
Rise of the Seraphim
The Last Circle of Dominion
Rhapsody of Light
Aeri Awakening
Glitch in the Shell
Author's Respite
A Shudder Before the Beautiful
Tethered

www.ingramcontent.com/pod-product-compliance
Lightning Source LLC
LaVergne TN
LVHW030915080826
845145LV00013B/2899

* 9 7 8 1 9 7 2 0 6 5 0 3 7 *